Vintage Christmas Tales

A Holiday Anthology

Vintage Christmas Tales

A Holiday Anthology

MINT EDITIONS

Vintage Christmas Tales: A Holiday Anthology features work
first published between 1823–1926.

ISBN 9781513201238 | E-ISBN 9781513127774

Mint Editions

 MINT
EDITIONS
minteditionbooks.com

Publishing Director: Jennifer Newens
Design & Production: Rachel Lopez Metzger
Project Manager: Micaela Clark
Typesetting: Mind the Margins, LLC

'Twas the Night before Christmas

'Twas the night before Christmas, when all through the house
Not a creature was stirring, not even a mouse;
The stockings were hung by the chimney with care
In hopes that St. Nicholas soon would be there;

The children were nestled all snug in their beds,
While visions of sugar plums danced in their heads;
And mamma in her kerchief, and I in my cap,
Had just settled our brains for a long winter's nap,

When out on the lawn there arose such a clatter,
I sprang from the bed to see what was the matter.
Away to the window I flew like a flash,
Tore open the shutters and threw up the sash.

The moon on the breast of the new-fallen snow
Gave the lustre of midday to objects below,
When, what to my wondering eyes should appear,
But a miniature sleigh, and eight tiny reindeer,

With a little old driver, so lively and quick,
I knew in a moment it must be St. Nick.
More rapid than eagles his coursers they came,
And he whistled, and shouted, and called them by name:

"Now, *Dasher!* Now, *Dancer!* Now, *Prancer* and *Vixen!*
On, *Comet!* On, *Cupid!* On, *Donder* and *Blitzen!*
To the top of the porch! To the top of the wall!
Now dash away! Dash away! Dash away all!"

As dry leaves that before the wild hurricane fly,
When they meet with an obstacle, mount to the sky;
So up to the housetop the coursers they flew,
With the sleigh full of Toys, and St. Nicholas too.

And then, in a twinkling, I heard on the roof
The prancing and pawing of each little hoof.
As I drew in my head, and was turning around,
Down the chimney St. Nicholas came with a bound.

He was dressed all in fur, from his head to his foot,
And his clothes were all tarnished with ashes and soot;
A bundle of toys he had flung on his back,
And he looked like a peddler just opening his pack.

His eyes—how they twinkled! His dimples how merry!
His cheeks were like roses, his nose like a cherry!
His droll little mouth was drawn up like a bow,
And the beard of his chin was as white as the snow;

The stump of a pipe he held tight in his teeth,
And the smoke it encircled his head like a wreath;
He had a broad face and a little round belly,
That shook when he laughed, like a bowlful of jelly.

He was chubby and plump, a right jolly old elf,
And I laughed when I saw him, in spite of myself;
A wink of his eye and a twist of his head,
Soon gave me to know I had nothing to dread;

He spoke not a word, but went straight to his work,
And filled all the stockings; then turned with a jerk,
And laying his finger aside of his nose,
And giving a nod, up the chimney he rose;

He sprang to his sleigh, to his team gave a whistle,
And away they all flew like the down of a thistle.
But I heard him exclaim, ere he drove out of sight,
"Happy Christmas to all, and to all a goodnight."

CONTENTS

CHRISTMAS; OR, THE GOOD FAIRY

"O DEAR! CHRISTMAS IS COMING IN a fortnight, and I have got to think up presents for everybody!" said young Ellen Stuart, as she leaned languidly back in her chair. "Dear me, it's so tedious! Everybody has got everything that can be thought of."

"O, no," said her confidential adviser, Miss Lester, in a soothing tone. "You have means of buying everything you can fancy; and when every shop and store is glittering with all manner of splendors, you cannot surely be at a loss."

"Well, now, just listen. To begin with, there's mamma. What can I get for her? I have thought of ever so many things. She has three card cases, four gold thimbles, two or three gold chains, two writing desks of different patterns; and then as to rings, brooches, boxes, and all other things, I should think she might be sick of the sight of them. I am sure I am," said she, languidly gazing on her white and jewelled fingers.

This view of the case seemed rather puzzling to the adviser, and there was silence for a few moments, when Ellen, yawning, resumed:—

"And then there's Cousins Jane and Mary; I suppose they will be coming down on me with a whole load of presents; and Mrs. B. will send me something—she did last year; and then there's Cousins William and Tom—I must get them something; and I would like to do it well enough, if I only knew what to get."

"Well," said Eleanor's aunt, who had been sitting quietly rattling her knitting needles during this speech, "it's a pity that you had not such a subject to practise on as I was when I was a girl. Presents did not fly about in those days as they do now. I remember, when I was ten years old, my father gave me a most marvellously ugly sugar dog for a Christmas gift, and I was perfectly delighted with it, the very idea of a present was so new to us."

"Dear aunt, how delighted I should be if I had any such fresh, unsophisticated body to get presents for! But to get and get for people that have more than they know what to do with now; to add pictures, books, and gilding when the centre tables are loaded with them now, and rings and jewels when they are a perfect drug! I wish myself that I were not sick, and sated, and tired with having everything in the world given me."

"Well, Eleanor," said her aunt, "if you really do want unsophisticated subjects to practise on, I can put you in the way of it. I can show you more than one family to whom you might seem to be a very good fairy, and where such gifts as you could give with all ease would seem like a magic dream."

"Why, that would really be worthwhile, aunt."

"Look over in that back alley," said her aunt. "You see those buildings?"

"That miserable row of shanties? Yes."

"Well, I have several acquaintances there who have never been tired of Christmas gifts, or gifts of any other kind. I assure you, you could make quite a sensation over there."

"Well, who is there? Let us know."

"Do you remember Owen, that used to make your shoes?"

"Yes, I remember something about him."

"Well, he has fallen into a consumption, and cannot work anymore; and he, and his wife, and three little children live in one of the rooms."

"How do they get along?"

"His wife takes in sewing sometimes, and sometimes goes out washing. Poor Owen! I was over there yesterday; he looks thin and wasted, and his wife was saying that he was parched with constant fever, and had very little appetite. She had, with great self-denial, and by restricting herself of necessary food, got him two or three oranges; and the poor fellow seemed so eager after them!"

"Poor fellow!" said Eleanor, involuntarily.

"Now," said her aunt, "suppose Owen's wife should get up on Christmas morning and find at the door a couple of dozen of oranges, and some of those nice white grapes, such as you had at your party last week; don't you think it would make a sensation?"

"Why, yes, I think very likely it might; but who else, aunt? You spoke of a great many."

"Well, on the lower floor there is a neat little room, that is always kept perfectly trim and tidy; it belongs to a young couple who have nothing beyond the husband's day wages to live on. They are, nevertheless, as cheerful and chipper as a couple of wrens; and she is up and down half a dozen times a day, to help poor Mrs. Owen. She has a baby of her own, about five months old, and of course does all the cooking, washing, and ironing for herself and husband; and yet, when Mrs. Owen goes out to wash, she takes her baby, and keeps it whole days for her."

"I'm sure she deserves that the good fairies should smile on her," said Eleanor; "one baby exhausts my stock of virtues very rapidly."

"But you ought to see her baby," said Aunt E.; "so plump, so rosy, and good-natured, and always clean as a lily. This baby is a sort of household shrine; nothing is too sacred or too good for it; and I believe the little thrifty woman feels only one temptation to be extravagant, and that is to get some ornaments to adorn this little divinity."

"Why, did she ever tell you so?"

"No; but one day, when I was coming downstairs, the door of their room was partly open, and I saw a peddler there with open box. John, the husband, was standing with a little purple cap on his hand, which he was regarding with mystified, admiring air, as if he didn't quite comprehend it, and trim little Mary gazing at it with longing eyes.

"'I think we might get it,' said John.

"'O, no,' said she, regretfully; 'yet I wish we could, it's *so pretty*!'"

"Say no more, aunt. I see the good fairy must pop a cap into the window on Christmas morning. Indeed, it shall be done. How they will wonder where it came from, and talk about it for months to come!"

"Well, then," continued her aunt, "in the next street to ours there is a miserable building, that looks as if it were just going to topple over; and away up in the third story, in a little room just under the eaves, live two poor, lonely old women. They are both nearly on to ninety. I was in there day before yesterday. One of them is constantly confined to her bed with rheumatism; the other, weak and feeble, with failing sight and trembling hands, totters about, her only helper; and they are entirely dependent on charity."

"Can't they do anything? Can't they knit?" said Eleanor.

"You are young and strong, Eleanor, and have quick eyes and nimble fingers; how long would it take you to knit a pair of stockings?"

"I?" said Eleanor. "What an idea! I never tried, but I think I could get a pair done in a week, perhaps."

"And if somebody gave you twenty-five cents for them, and out of this you had to get food, and pay room rent, and buy coal for your fire, and oil for your lamp—"

"Stop, aunt, for pity's sake!"

"Well, I will stop; but they can't: they must pay so much every month for that miserable shell they live in, or be turned into the street. The meal and flour that some kind person sends goes off for them just as it does for others, and they must get more or starve; and coal is now scarce and high priced."

"O aunt, I'm quite convinced, I'm sure; don't run me down and annihilate me with all these terrible realities. What shall I do to play good fairy to these poor old women?"

"If you will give me full power, Eleanor, I will put up a basket to be sent to them that will give them something to remember all winter."

"O, certainly I will. Let me see if I can't think of something myself."

"Well, Eleanor, suppose, then, some fifty or sixty years hence, *if* you were old, and your father, and mother, and aunts, and uncles, now so thick around you, lay cold and silent in so many graves—you have somehow got away off to a strange city, where you were never known—you live in a miserable garret, where snow blows at night through the cracks, and the fire is very apt to go out in the old cracked stove—you sit crouching over the dying embers the evening before Christmas—nobody to speak to you, nobody to care for you, except another poor old soul who lies moaning in the bed. Now, what would you like to have sent you?"

"O aunt, what a dismal picture!"

"And yet, Ella, all poor, forsaken old women are made of young girls, who expected it in their youth as little as you do, perhaps."

"Say no more, aunt. I'll buy—let me see—a comfortable warm shawl for each of these poor women; and I'll send them—let me see—O, some tea—nothing goes down with old women like tea; and I'll make John wheel some coal over to them; and, aunt, it would not be a very bad thought to send them a new stove. I remember, the other day, when mamma was pricing stoves, I saw some such nice ones for two or three dollars."

"For a new hand, Ella, you work up the idea very well," said her aunt.

"But how much ought I to give, for any one case, to these women, say?"

"How much did you give last year for any single Christmas present?"

"Why, six or seven dollars for some; those elegant souvenirs were seven dollars; that ring I gave Mrs. B. was twenty."

"And do you suppose Mrs. B. was any happier for it?"

"No, really, I don't think she cared much about it; but I had to give her something, because she had sent me something the year before, and I did not want to send a paltry present to one in her circumstances."

"Then, Ella, give the same to any poor, distressed, suffering creature who really needs it, and see in how many forms of good such a sum will appear. That one hard, cold, glittering ring, that now cheers nobody, and means nothing, that you give because you must, and she takes because she must, might, if broken up into smaller sums, send real warm and heartfelt gladness through many a cold and cheerless dwelling, through many an aching heart."

"You are getting to be an orator, aunt; but don't you approve of Christmas presents, among friends and equals?"

"Yes, indeed," said her aunt, fondly stroking her head. "I have had some Christmas presents that did me a world of good—a little bookmark, for instance, that a certain niece of mine worked for me, with wonderful secrecy, three years ago, when she was not a young lady with a purse full of money—that bookmark was a true Christmas present; and my young couple across the way are plotting a profound surprise to each other on Christmas morning. John has contrived, by an hour of extra work every night, to lay by enough to get Mary a new calico dress; and she, poor soul, has bargained away the only thing in the jewelry line she ever possessed, to be laid out on a new hat for him.

"I know, too, a washerwoman who has a poor, lame boy—a patient, gentle little fellow—who has lain quietly for weeks and months in his little crib, and his mother is going to give him a splendid Christmas present."

"What is it, pray?"

"A whole orange! Don't laugh. She will pay ten whole cents for it; for it shall be none of your common oranges, but a picked one of the very best going! She has put by the money, a cent at a time, for a whole month; and nobody knows which will be happiest in it, Willie or his mother. These are such Christmas presents as I like to think of—gifts coming from love, and tending to produce love; these are the appropriate gifts of the day."

"But don't you think that it's right for those who *have* money to give expensive presents, supposing always, as you say, they are given from real affection?"

"Sometimes, undoubtedly. The Savior did not condemn her who broke an alabaster box of ointment—*very precious*—simply as a proof of love, even although the suggestion was made, 'This might have been sold for three hundred pence, and given to the poor.' I have thought he would regard with sympathy the fond efforts which human love sometimes makes to express itself by gifts, the rarest and most costly. How I rejoiced with all my heart, when Charles Elton gave his poor mother that splendid Chinese shawl and gold watch! because I knew they came from the very fulness of his heart to a mother that he could not do too much for—a mother that has done and suffered everything for him. In some such cases, when resources are ample, a costly gift seems to have a graceful appropriateness; but I cannot approve of it if it exhausts all the means of doing for the poor; it is better, then, to give a simple offering, and to do something for those who really need it."

Eleanor looked thoughtful; her aunt laid down her knitting, and said, in a tone of gentle seriousness, "Whose birth does Christmas commemorate, Ella?"

"Our Savior's, certainly, aunt."

"Yes," said her aunt. "And when and how was he born? In a stable! Laid in a manger; thus born, that in all ages he might be known as the brother and friend of the poor. And surely, it seems but appropriate to commemorate his birthday by an especial remembrance of the lowly, the poor, the outcast, and distressed; and if Christ should come back to our city on a Christmas day, where should we think it most appropriate to his character to find him? Would he be carrying splendid gifts to splendid dwellings, or would he be gliding about in the cheerless haunts of the desolate, the poor, the forsaken, and the sorrowful?"

And here the conversation ended.

"What sort of Christmas presents is Ella buying?" said Cousin Tom, as the waiter handed in a portentous-looking package, which had been just rung in at the door.

"Let's open it," said saucy Will. "Upon my word, two great gray blanket shawls! These must be for you and me, Tom! And what's this? A great bolt of cotton flannel and gray yarn stockings!"

The doorbell rang again, and the waiter brought in another bulky parcel, and deposited it on the marble-topped centre table.

"What's here?" said Will, cutting the cord. "Whew! A perfect nest of packages! Oolong tea! Oranges! Grapes! White sugar! Bless me, Ella must be going to housekeeping!"

"Or going crazy!" said Tom; "and on my word," said he, looking out of the window, "there's a drayman ringing at our door, with a stove, with a teakettle set in the top of it!"

"Ella's cook stove, of course," said Will; and just at this moment the young lady entered, with her purse hanging gracefully over her hand.

"Now, boys, you are too bad!" she exclaimed, as each of the mischievous youngsters were gravely marching up and down, attired in a gray shawl.

"Didn't you get them for us? We thought you did," said both.

"Ella, I want some of that cotton flannel, to make me a pair of pantaloons," said Tom.

"I say, Ella," said Will, "when are you going to housekeeping? Your cooking stove is standing down in the street; 'pon my word, John is loading some coal on the dray with it."

"Ella, isn't that going to be sent to my office?" said Tom; "Do you know I do so languish for a new stove with a teakettle in the top, to heat a fellow's shaving water!"

Just then, another ring at the door, and the grinning waiter handed in a small brown paper parcel for Miss Ella. Tom made a dive at it, and staving off the brown paper, developed a jaunty little purple velvet cap, with silver tassels.

"My smoking cap, as I live!" said he; "Only I shall have to wear it on my thumb, instead of my head—too small entirely," said he, shaking his head gravely.

"Come, you saucy boys," said Aunt E., entering briskly, "what are you teasing Ella for?"

"Why, do see this lot of things, aunt! What in the world is Ella going to do with them?"

"O, I know!"

"You know! Then I can guess, aunt, it is some of your charitable works. You are going to make a juvenile Lady Bountiful of El, eh?"

Ella, who had colored to the roots of her hair at the *exposé* of her very unfashionable Christmas preparations, now took heart, and bestowed a very gentle and salutary little cuff on the saucy head that still wore the purple cap, and then hastened to gather up her various purchases.

"Laugh away," said she, gayly; "and a good many others will laugh, too, over these things. I got them to make people laugh—people that are not in the habit of laughing!"

"Well, well, I see into it," said Will; "and I tell you I think right well of the idea, too. There are worlds of money wasted, at this time of the year, in getting things that nobody wants, and nobody cares for after they are got; and I am glad, for my part, that you are going to get up a variety in this line; in fact, I should like to give you one of these stray leaves to help on," said he, dropping a ten dollar note into her paper. "I like to encourage girls to think of something besides breastpins and sugar candy."

But our story spins on too long. If anybody wants to see the results of Ella's first attempts at *good fairyism*, they can call at the doors of two or three old buildings on Christmas morning, and they shall hear all about it.

CHRISTMAS EVERY DAY

T HE LITTLE GIRL CAME INTO her papa's study, as she always did Saturday morning before breakfast, and asked for a story. He tried to beg off that morning, for he was very busy, but she would not let him. So he began:

"Well, once there was a little pig—"

She put her hand over his mouth and stopped him at the word. She said she had heard little pig-stories till she was perfectly sick of them.

"Well, what kind of story *shall* I tell, then?"

"About Christmas. It's getting to be the season. It's past Thanksgiving already."

"It seems to me," her papa argued, "that I've told as often about Christmas as I have about little pigs."

"No difference! Christmas is more interesting."

"Well!" Her papa roused himself from his writing by a great effort. "Well, then, I'll tell you about the little girl that wanted it Christmas every day in the year. How would you like that?"

"First rate!" said the little girl; and she nestled into comfortable shape in his lap, ready for listening.

"Very well, then, this little pig—Oh, what are you pounding me for?"

"Because you said little pig instead of little girl."

"I should like to know what's the difference between a little pig and a little girl that wanted it Christmas every day!"

"Papa," said the little girl, warningly, "if you don't go on, I'll *give* it to you!" And at this her papa darted off like lightning, and began to tell the story as fast as he could.

Well, once there was a little girl who liked Christmas so much that she wanted it to be Christmas every day in the year; and as soon as Thanksgiving was over she began to send postal-cards to the old Christmas Fairy to ask if she mightn't have it. But the old fairy never answered any of the postals; and after a while the little girl found out that the Fairy was pretty particular, and wouldn't notice anything but letters—not even correspondence cards in envelopes; but real letters on sheets of paper, and sealed outside with a monogram—or your initial, anyway. So, then, she began to send her letters; and in about three weeks—or just the day before Christmas, it was—she got a letter from the Fairy, saying she might have it Christmas every day for a year, and then they would see about having it longer.

The little girl was a good deal excited already, preparing for the old-fashioned, once-a-year Christmas that was coming the next day, and perhaps the Fairy's promise didn't make such an impression on her as it would have made at some other time. She just resolved to keep it to herself, and surprise everybody with it as it kept coming true; and then it slipped out of her mind altogether.

She had a splendid Christmas. She went to bed early, so as to let Santa Claus have a chance at the stockings, and in the morning she was up the first of anybody and went and felt them, and found hers all lumpy with packages of candy, and oranges and grapes, and pocket books and rubber balls, and all kinds of small presents, and her big brother's with nothing but the tongs in them, and her young lady sister's with a new silk umbrella, and her papa's and mamma's with potatoes and pieces of coal wrapped up in tissue paper, just as they always had every Christmas. Then she waited around till the rest of the family were up, and she was the first to burst into the library, when the doors were opened, and look at the large presents laid out on the library table—books, and portfolios, and boxes of stationery, and breastpins, and dolls, and little stoves, and dozens of handkerchiefs, and ink-stands, and skates, and snow shovels, and photograph frames, and little easels, and boxes of watercolors, and Turkish paste, and nougat, and candied cherries, and dolls' houses, and waterproofs—and the big Christmas tree, lighted and standing in a waste-basket in the middle.

She had a splendid Christmas all day. She ate so much candy that she did not want any breakfast; and the whole forenoon the presents kept pouring in that the expressman had not had time to deliver the night before; and she went round giving the presents she had got for other people, and came home and ate turkey and cranberry for dinner, and plum-pudding and nuts and raisins and oranges and more candy, and then went out and coasted, and came in with a stomachache, crying; and her papa said he would see if his house was turned into that sort of fool's paradise another year; and they had a light supper, and pretty early everybody went to bed cross.

Here the little girl pounded her papa in the back, again.

"Well, what now? Did I say pigs?"

"You made them *act* like pigs."

"Well, didn't they?"

"No matter; you oughtn't to put it into a story."

"Very well, then, I'll take it all out."

Her father went on:

The little girl slept very heavily, and she slept very late, but she was wakened at last by the other children dancing round her bed with their stockings full of presents in their hands.

"What is it?" said the little girl, and she rubbed her eyes and tried to rise up in bed.

"Christmas! Christmas! Christmas!" they all shouted, and waved their stockings.

"Nonsense! It was Christmas yesterday."

Her brothers and sisters just laughed. "We don't know about that. It's Christmas today, anyway. You come into the library and see."

Then all at once it flashed on the little girl that the Fairy was keeping her promise, and her year of Christmases was beginning. She was dreadfully sleepy, but she sprang up like a lark—a lark that had overeaten itself and gone to bed cross—and darted into the library.

There it was again! Books, and portfolios, and boxes of stationery, and breastpins—

"You needn't go over it all, papa; I guess I can remember just what was there," said the little girl.

Well, and there was the Christmas tree blazing away, and the family picking out their presents, but looking pretty sleepy, and her father perfectly puzzled, and her mother ready to cry. "I'm sure I don't see how I'm to dispose of all these things," said her mother, and her father said it seemed to him they had had something just like it the day before, but he supposed he must have dreamed it. This struck the little girl as the best kind of a joke; and so she ate so much candy she didn't want any breakfast, and went round carrying presents, and had turkey and cranberry for dinner, and then went out and coasted, and came in with a—

"Papa!"
"Well, what now?"
"What did you promise, you forgetful thing?"
"Oh! Oh yes!"

Well, the next day, it was just the same thing over again, but everybody getting crosser; and at the end of a week's time so many people had lost their tempers that you could pick up lost tempers anywhere; they perfectly strewed the ground. Even when people tried to recover their tempers they usually got somebody else's, and it made the most dreadful mix.

The little girl began to get frightened, keeping the secret all to herself; she wanted to tell her mother, but she didn't dare to; and she was ashamed to ask the Fairy to take back her gift, it seemed ungrateful and ill-bred, and she thought she would try to stand it, but she hardly knew how she could, for a whole year. So it went on and on, and it was Christmas on St. Valentine's Day and Washington's Birthday, just the same as any day, and it didn't skip even the First of April, though everything was counterfeit that day, and that was some *little* relief.

After a while coal and potatoes began to be awfully scarce, so many had been wrapped up in tissue paper to fool papas and mammas with. Turkeys got to be about a thousand dollars a piece—

"Papa!"
"Well, what?"
"You're beginning to fib."
"Well, *two* thousand, then."

And they got to passing off almost anything for turkeys—half-grown hummingbirds, and even rocs out of the *Arabian Nights*—the real turkeys were so scarce. And cranberries—well, they asked a diamond apiece for cranberries. All the woods and orchards were cut down for Christmas trees, and where the woods and orchards used to be it looked just like a stubble-field, with the stumps. After a while they had to make Christmas trees out of rags, and stuff them with bran, like old-fashioned dolls; but there were plenty of rags, because people got so poor, buying presents for one another, that they couldn't get any new clothes, and they just wore their old ones to tatters. They got so poor that everybody had to go to the poorhouse, except the confectioners, and the fancy storekeepers, and the picture book sellers, and the expressmen; and *they* all got so rich and proud that they would hardly wait upon a person when he came to buy. It was perfectly shameful!

Well, after it had gone on about three or four months, the little girl, whenever she came into the room in the morning and saw those great ugly, lumpy stockings dangling at the fireplace, and the disgusting presents around everywhere, used to just sit down and burst out crying. In six months she was perfectly exhausted; she couldn't even cry anymore; she just lay on the lounge and rolled her eyes and panted. About the beginning of October she took to sitting down on dolls wherever she found them—French dolls, or any kind—she hated the sight of them so; and by Thanksgiving she was crazy, and just slammed her presents across the room.

By that time people didn't carry presents around nicely anymore. They flung them over the fence, or through the window, or anything; and, instead of running their tongues out and taking great pains to write "For dear Papa," or "Mamma," or "Brother," or "Sister," or "Susie," or "Sammie," or "Billie," or "Bobbie," or "Jimmie," or "Jennie," or whoever it was, and troubling to get the spelling right, and then signing their names, and "Xmas, 18—," they used to write in the gift books, "Take it, you horrid old thing!" and then go and bang it against the front door. Nearly everybody had built barns to hold their presents, but pretty soon the barns overflowed, and then they used to let them lie out in the rain, or anywhere. Sometimes the police used to come and tell them to shovel their presents off the sidewalk, or they would arrest them.

"I thought you said everybody had gone to the poorhouse," interrupted the little girl.

"They did go, at first," said her papa; "but after a while the poorhouses got so full that they had to send the people back to their own houses.

They tried to cry, when they got back, but they couldn't make the least sound."

"Why couldn't they?"

"Because they had lost their voices, saying 'Merry Christmas' so much. Did I tell you how it was on the Fourth of July?"

"No; how was it?" And the little girl nestled closer, in expectation of something uncommon.

Well, the night before, the boys stayed up to celebrate, as they always do, and fell asleep before twelve o'clock, as usual, expecting to be wakened by the bells and cannon. But it was nearly eight o'clock before the first boy in the United States woke up, and then he found out what the trouble was. As soon as he could get his clothes on he ran out of the house and smashed a big cannon-torpedo down on the pavement; but it didn't make anymore noise than a damp wad of paper; and after he tried about twenty or thirty more, he began to pick them up and look at them. Every single torpedo was a big raisin! Then he just streaked it upstairs, and examined his firecrackers and toy pistol and two-dollar collection of fireworks, and found that they were nothing but sugar and candy painted up to look like fireworks! Before ten o'clock every boy in the United States found out that his Fourth of July things had turned into Christmas things; and then they just sat down and cried—they were so mad. There are about twenty million boys in the United States, and so you can imagine what a noise they made. Some men got together before night, with a little powder that hadn't turned into purple sugar yet, and they said they would fire off *one* cannon, anyway. But the cannon burst into a thousand pieces, for it was nothing but rock candy, and some of the men nearly got killed. The Fourth of July orations all turned into Christmas carols, and when anybody tried to read the Declaration, instead of saying, "When in the course of human events it becomes necessary," he was sure to sing, "God rest you, merry gentlemen." It was perfectly awful.

The little girl drew a deep sigh of satisfaction.

"And how was it at Thanksgiving?"

Her papa hesitated. "Well, I'm almost afraid to tell you. I'm afraid you'll think it's wicked."

"Well, tell, anyway," said the little girl.

Well, before it came Thanksgiving it had leaked out who had
caused all these Christmases. The little girl had suffered so much
that she had talked about it in her sleep; and after that hardly
anybody would play with her. People just perfectly despised
her, because if it had not been for her greediness it wouldn't
have happened; and now, when it came Thanksgiving, and she
wanted them to go to church, and have squash-pie and turkey,
and show their gratitude, they said that all the turkeys had been
eaten up for her old Christmas dinners, and if she would stop
the Christmases, they would see about the gratitude. Wasn't it
dreadful? And the very next day the little girl began to send
letters to the Christmas Fairy, and then telegrams, to stop it. But
it didn't do any good; and then she got to calling at the Fairy's
house, but the girl that came to the door always said, "Not at
home," or "Engaged," or "At dinner," or something like that; and
so it went on till it came to the old once-a-year Christmas Eve.
The little girl fell asleep, and when she woke up in the morning—

"She found it was all nothing but a dream," suggested the little girl.

"No, indeed!" said her papa. "It was all every bit true!"

"Well, what *did* she find out, then?"

"Why, that it wasn't Christmas at last, and wasn't ever going to be,
anymore. Now it's time for breakfast."

The little girl held her papa fast around the neck.

"You sha'n't go if you're going to leave it *so*!"

"How do you want it left?"

"Christmas once a year."

"All right," said her papa; and he went on again.

Well, there was the greatest rejoicing all over the country, and
it extended clear up into Canada. The people met together
everywhere, and kissed and cried for joy. The city carts went
around and gathered up all the candy and raisins and nuts, and
dumped them into the river; and it made the fish perfectly sick;
and the whole United States, as far out as Alaska, was one blaze
of bonfires, where the children were burning up their gift books
and presents of all kinds. They had the greatest *time*!

The little girl went to thank the old Fairy because she had stopped its being Christmas, and she said she hoped she would keep her promise and see that Christmas never, never came again. Then the Fairy frowned, and asked her if she was sure she knew what she meant; and the little girl asked her, Why not? And the old Fairy said that now she was behaving just as greedily as ever, and she'd better look out. This made the little girl think it all over carefully again, and she said she would be willing to have it Christmas about once in a thousand years; and then she said a hundred, and then she said ten, and at last she got down to one. Then the Fairy said that was the good old way that had pleased people ever since Christmas began, and she was agreed. Then the little girl said, "What're your shoes made of?" And the Fairy said, "Leather." And the little girl said, "Bargain's done forever," and skipped off, and hippity-hopped the whole way home, she was so glad.

"How will that do?" asked the papa.

"First rate!" said the little girl; but she hated to have the story stop, and was rather sober. However, her mamma put her head in at the door, and asked her papa:

"Are you never coming to breakfast? What have you been telling that child?"

"Oh, just a moral tale."

The little girl caught him around the neck again.

"*We* know! Don't you tell *what*, papa! Don't you tell *what*!"

Lill's Travels in Santa Claus Land

EFFIE HAD BEEN PLAYING WITH her dolls one cold December morning, and Lill had been reading, until both were tired. But it stormed too hard to go out, and, as Mrs. Pelerine had said they need not do anything for two hours, their little jaws might have been dislocated by yawning before they would as much as pick up a pin. Presently Lill said, "Effie, shall I tell you a story."

"O yes! Do!" said Effie, and she climbed up by Lill in the large rocking chair in front of the grate. She kept very still, for she knew Lill's stories were not to be interrupted by a sound, or even a motion.

The first thing Lill did was to fix her eyes on the fire, and rock backward and forward quite hard for a little while, and then she said, "Now I am going to tell you about my *thought travels*, and they are apt to be a little queerer, but O! ever so much nicer, than the other kind!"

As Lill's stories usually had a formal introduction she began: "Once upon a time, when I was taking a walk through the great field beyond the orchard, I went way on, 'round where the path turns behind the hill. And after I had walked a little way, I came to a high wall—built right up into the sky. At first I thought I had discovered the 'ends of the earth,' or perhaps I had somehow come to the great wall of China. But after walking a long way I came to a large gate, and over it was printed in beautiful gold letters, 'Santa Claus Land,' and the letters were large enough for a baby to read!"

How large that might be Lill did not stop to explain.

"But the gate was shut tight," she continued, "and though I knocked and knocked and knocked, as hard as I could, nobody came to open it. I was dreadfully disappointed, because I felt as if Santa Claus must live here all of the year except when he went out to pay Christmas visits, and it would be so lovely to see him in his own home, you know. But what was I to do? The gate was entirely too high to climb over, and there wasn't even a crack to peek through!"

Here Lill paused, and Effie drew a long breath, and looked greatly disappointed. Then Lill went on:

"But you see, as I was poking about, I pressed a bell-spring, and in a moment—jingle, jingle, jingle, the bells went ringing far and near, with such a merry sound as was never heard before. While they were still ringing the gate slowly opened and I walked in. I didn't even stop to inquire if Santa Claus was at home, for I forgot all about myself and my manners, it was so lovely. First there was a small paved square like a court; it was surrounded by rows and rows of dark green trees, with several avenues opening between them.

"In the centre of the court was a beautiful marble fountain, with streams of sugar plums and bonbons tumbling out of it. Funny looking little men were filling cornucopias at the fountain, and pretty little barefoot children, with chubby hands and dimpled shoulders, took them as soon as they were filled, and ran off with them. They were all too much occupied to speak to me, but as I came up to the fountain one of the funny little fellows gave me a cornucopia, and I marched on with the babies.

"We went down one of the avenues, which would have been very dark only it was splendidly lighted up with Christmas candles. I saw the babies were slyly eating a candy or two, so I tasted mine, and they were delicious—the real Christmas kind. After we had gone a little way, the trees were smaller and not so close together, and here there were other funny little fellows who were climbing up on ladders and tying toys and bonbons to the trees. The children stopped and delivered their packages, but I walked on, for there was something in the distance that I was curious to see. I could see that it was a large garden, that looked as if it might be well cared for, and had many things growing in it. But even in the distance it didn't look natural, and when I reached it I found it was a very uncommon kind of a garden indeed. I could scarcely believe my eyes, but there were dolls and donkeys and drays and cars and croquet coming up in long, straight rows, and ever so many other things beside. In one place the wooden dolls had only just started; their funny little heads were just above ground, and I thought they looked very much surprised at their surroundings. Farther on were china dolls, that looked quite grown up, and I suppose were ready to pull; and a gardener was hoeing a row of soldiers that didn't look in a very healthy condition, or as if they had done very well.

"The gardener looked familiar, I thought, and as I approached him he stopped work and, leaning on his hoe he said, 'How do you do, Lilian? I am very glad to see you.'

"The moment he raised his face I knew it was Santa Claus, for he looked exactly like the portrait we have of him. You can easily believe I was glad then! I ran and put both of my hands in his, fairly shouting that I was so glad to find him.

"He laughed and said:

"'Why, I am generally to be found here or hereabouts, for I work in the grounds everyday.'

"And I laughed too, because his laugh sounded so funny; like the brook going over stones, and the wind up in the trees. Two or three times, when I thought he had done he would burst out again, laughing the vowels in this way: 'Ha, ha, ha, ha! He, he, he, he, he! Hi, hi, hi, hi! Ho, ho, ho, h-o-oo!'"

Lill did it very well, and Effie laughed till the tears came to her eyes; and she could quite believe Lill when she said, "It grew to be so funny that I couldn't stand, but fell over into one of the little chairs that were growing in a bed just beyond the soldiers.

"When Santa Claus saw that he stopped suddenly, saying:

"'There, that will do. I take a hearty laugh every day, for the sake of digestion.'

"Then he added, in a whisper, 'That is the reason I live so long and don't grow old. I've been the same age ever since the chroniclers began to take notes, and those who are best able to judge think I'll continue to be this way for about one thousand eight hundred and seventy-six years longer,—they probably took a new observation at the Centennial, and they know exactly.'

"I was greatly delighted to hear this, and I told him so. He nodded and winked and said it was 'all right,' and then asked if I'd like to see the place. I said I would, so he threw down the hoe with a sigh, saying, 'I don't believe I shall have more than half a crop of soldiers this season. They came up well, but the arms and legs seem to be weak. When I get to town I'll have to send out some girls with glue pots, to stick them fast.'

"The town was at some distance, and our path took us by flowerbeds where some exquisite little toys were growing, and a hot bed where new varieties were being prop—*propagated*. Pretty soon we came to a plantation of young trees, with rattles, and rubber balls, and ivory rings growing on the branches, and as we went past they rang and bounded about in the merriest sort of a way.

"'There's a nice growth,' said Santa Claus, and it *was* a nice growth for babies; but just beyond I saw something so perfectly splendid that I didn't care about the plantation."

"Well," said Lill impressively, seeing that Effie was sufficiently expectant, "It was a lovely grove. The trees were large, with long drooping branches, and the branches were just loaded with dolls' clothes. There were elegant silk dresses, with lovely sashes of every color—"

Just here Effie couldn't help saying "O!" for she had a weakness for sashes. Lill looked stern, and put a warning hand over her mouth, and went on.

"There was everything that the most fashionable doll could want, growing in the greatest profusion. Some of the clothes had fallen, and there were funny looking girls picking them up, and packing them in trunks and boxes. 'These are all ripe,' said Santa Claus, stopping to shake a tree, and the clothes came tumbling down so fast that the workers were busier than ever. The grove was on a hill, so that we had a beautiful view of the country. First there was a park filled with reindeer, and beyond that was the town, and at one side a large farmyard filled with animals of all sorts.

"But as Santa Claus seemed in a hurry I did not stop long to look. Our path led through the park, and we stopped to call 'Prancer' and 'Dancer' and 'Donder' and 'Blitzen,' and Santa Claus fed them with lumps of sugar from his pocket. He pointed out 'Comet' and 'Cupid' in a distant part of the park; 'Dasher' and 'Vixen' were nowhere to be seen.

"Here I found most of the houses were Swiss cottages, but there were some fine churches and public buildings, all of beautifully illustrated building blocks, and we stopped for a moment at a long depot, in which a locomotive was just *smashing up*.

"Santa Claus' house stood in the middle of the town. It was an old-fashioned looking house, very broad and low, with an enormous chimney. There was wide step in front of the door, shaded by a fig tree and grapevine, and morning glories and scarlet beans clambered by the side of the latticed windows; and there were great round rose bushes, with great, round roses, on either side of the walk leading to the door."

"O! It must have smelled like a party," said Effie, and then subsided, as she remembered that she was interrupting.

"Inside, the house was just cozy and comfortable, a real grandfatherly sort of a place. A big chair was drawn up in front of the window, and a big book was open on a table in front of the chair. A great pack half made up was on the floor, and Santa Claus stopped to add a few things from his pocket. Then he went to the kitchen, and brought me a lunch of milk and strawberries and cookies, for he said I must be tired after my long walk.

"After I had rested a little while, he said if I liked I might go with him to the observatory. But just as we were starting a funny little fellow stopped at the door with a wheelbarrow full of boxes of dishes. After Santa Claus had taken the boxes out and put them in the pack he said slowly,—

"'Let me see!'

"He laid his finger beside his nose as he said it, and looked at me attentively, as if I were a sum in addition, and he was adding me up. I guess I must have come out right, for he looked satisfied, and said I'd better go to the mine first, and then join him in the observatory. Now I am afraid he was not exactly polite not to go with me himself," added Lill, gravely, "but then he apologized by saying he had some work to do. So I followed the little fellow with the wheelbarrow, and we soon came to what looked like the entrance of a cave, but I suppose it was the mine. I followed my guide to the interior without stopping to look at the boxes and piles of dishes outside. Here I found other funny little people, busily at work with picks and shovels, taking out wooden dishes from the bottom of the cave, and china and glass from the top and sides, for the dishes hung down just like stalactites in Mammoth Cave."

Here Lill opened the book she had been reading, and showed Effie a picture of the stalactites.

"It was so curious and so pretty that I should have remained longer," said Lill, "only I remembered the observatory and Santa Claus.

"When I went outside I heard his voice calling out, 'Lilian! Lilian!' It sounded a great way off, and yet somehow it seemed to fill the air just as the wind does. I only had to look for a moment, for very near by was a high tower. I wonder I did not see it before; but in these queer countries you are sure to see something new every time you look about. Santa Claus was standing up at a window near the top, and I ran to the entrance and commenced climbing the stairs. It was a long journey, and I was quite out of breath when I came to the end of it. But here there was such a cozy, luxurious little room, full of stuffed chairs and lounges, bird cages and flowers in the windows, and pictures on the wall, that it was delightful to rest. There was a lady sitting by a golden desk, writing in a large book, and Santa Claus was looking through a great telescope, and every once in a while he stopped and put his ear to a large speaking-tube. While I was resting he went on with his observations.

"Presently he said to the lady, 'Put down a good mark for Sarah Buttermilk. I see she is trying to conquer her quick temper.'

"'Two bad ones for Isaac Clappertongue; he'll drive his mother to the insane asylum yet.'

"'Bad ones all around for the Crossley children,—they quarrel too much.'

"'A good one for Harry and Alice Pleasure, they are quick to mind.'

"'And give Ruth Olive ten, for she is a peacemaker.'

"Just then he happened to look at me and saw I was rested, so he politely asked what I thought of the country. I said it was magnificent. He said he was sorry I didn't stop in the greenhouse, where he had wax dolls and other delicate things growing. I was very sorry about that, and then I said I thought he must be very happy to own so many delightful things.

"'Of course I'm happy,' said Santa Claus, and then he sighed. 'But it is an awful responsibility to reward so many children according to their deserts. For I take these observations every day, and I know who is good and who is bad.'

"I was glad he told me about this, and now, if he would only tell me what time of day he took the observations, I would have obtained really valuable information. So I stood up and made my best courtesy and said,—

"'Please, sir, would you tell me what time of day you usually look?'

"'O,' he answered, carelessly, 'any time from seven in the morning till ten at night. I am not a bit particular about time. I often go without my own meals in order to make a record of table manners. For instance: last evening I saw you turn your spoon over in your mouth, and that's very unmannerly for a girl nearly fourteen.'

"'O, I didn't know *you* were looking,' said I, very much ashamed; 'and I'll never do it again,' I promised.

"Then he said I might look through the telescope, and I looked right down into our house. There was mother very busy and very tired, and all of the children teasing. It was queer, for I was there, too, and the *baddest* of any. Pretty soon I ran to a quiet corner with a book, and in a few minutes mamma had to leave her work and call, 'Lilian, Lilian, it's time for you to practise.'

"'Yes, mamma,' I answered, 'I'll come right away.'

"As soon as I said this Santa Claus whistled for 'Comet' and 'Cupid,' and they came tearing up the tower. He put me in a tiny sleigh, and away we went, over great snowbanks of clouds, and before I had time to think I was landed in the big chair, and mamma was calling 'Lilian, Lilian, it's time for you to practise,' just as she is doing now, and I must go."

So Lill answered, "Yes, mamma," and ran to the piano.

Effie sank back in the chair to think. She wished Lill had found out how many black marks she had, and whether that lady was Mrs. Santa Claus—and had, in fact, obtained more accurate information about many things.

But when she asked about some of them afterwards, Lill said she didn't know, for the next time she had traveled in that direction she found Santa Claus Land had moved.

The Gift of the Magi

ONE DOLLAR AND EIGHTY-SEVEN CENTS. That was all. And sixty cents of it was in pennies. Pennies saved one and two at a time by bulldozing the grocer and the vegetable man and the butcher until one's cheeks burned with the silent imputation of parsimony that such close dealing implied. Three times Della counted it. One dollar and eighty-seven cents. And the next day would be Christmas.

There was clearly nothing to do but flop down on the shabby little couch and howl. So Della did it. Which instigates the moral reflection that life is made up of sobs, sniffles, and smiles, with sniffles predominating.

While the mistress of the home is gradually subsiding from the first stage to the second, take a look at the home. A furnished flat at $8 per week. It did not exactly beggar description, but it certainly had that word on the lookout for the mendicancy squad.

In the vestibule below was a letterbox into which no letter would go, and an electric button from which no mortal finger could coax a ring. Also appertaining thereunto was a card bearing the name "Mr. James Dillingham Young."

The "Dillingham" had been flung to the breeze during a former period of prosperity when its possessor was being paid $30 per week. Now, when the income was shrunk to $20, though, they were thinking seriously of contracting to a modest and unassuming D. But whenever Mr. James Dillingham Young came home and reached his flat above he was called "Jim" and greatly hugged by Mrs. James Dillingham Young, already introduced to you as Della. Which is all very good.

Della finished her cry and attended to her cheeks with the powder rag. She stood by the window and looked out dully at a gray cat walking a gray fence in a gray backyard. Tomorrow would be Christmas Day, and she had only $1.87 with which to buy Jim a present. She had been saving every penny she could for months, with this result. Twenty dollars a week doesn't go far. Expenses had been greater than she had calculated. They always are. Only $1.87 to buy a present for Jim. Her Jim. Many a happy hour she had spent planning for something nice for him. Something fine and rare and sterling—something just a little bit near to being worthy of the honor of being owned by Jim.

There was a pier glass between the windows of the room. Perhaps you have seen a pier glass in an $8 flat. A very thin and very agile person may, by observing his reflection in a rapid sequence of longitudinal strips, obtain a fairly accurate conception of his looks. Della, being slender, had mastered the art.

Suddenly she whirled from the window and stood before the glass. Her eyes were shining brilliantly, but her face had lost its color within twenty seconds. Rapidly she pulled down her hair and let it fall to its full length.

Now, there were two possessions of the James Dillingham Youngs in which they both took a mighty pride. One was Jim's gold watch that had been his father's and his grandfather's. The other was Della's hair. Had the queen of Sheba lived in the flat across the airshaft, Della would have let her hair hang out the window someday to dry just to depreciate Her Majesty's jewels and gifts. Had King Solomon been the janitor, with all his treasures piled up in the basement, Jim would have pulled out his watch every time he passed, just to see him pluck at his beard from envy.

So now Della's beautiful hair fell about her rippling and shining like a cascade of brown waters. It reached below her knee and made itself almost a garment for her. And then she did it up again nervously and quickly. Once she faltered for a minute and stood still while a tear or two splashed on the worn red carpet.

On went her old brown jacket; on went her old brown hat. With a whirl of skirts and with the brilliant sparkle still in her eyes, she fluttered out the door and down the stairs to the street.

Where she stopped the sign read: "Mme. Sofronie. Hair Goods of All Kinds." One flight up Della ran, and collected herself, panting. Madame, large, too white, chilly, hardly looked the "Sofronie."

"Will you buy my hair?" asked Della.

"I buy hair," said Madame. "Take yer hat off and let's have a sight at the looks of it."

Down rippled the brown cascade.

"Twenty dollars," said Madame, lifting the mass with a practised hand.

"Give it to me quick," said Della.

Oh, and the next two hours tripped by on rosy wings. Forget the hashed metaphor. She was ransacking the stores for Jim's present.

She found it at last. It surely had been made for Jim and no one else. There was no other like it in any of the stores, and she had turned all of them inside out. It was a platinum fob chain simple and chaste in design, properly proclaiming its value by substance alone and not by meretricious ornamentation—as all good things should do. It was even worthy of The Watch. As soon as she saw it she knew that it must be Jim's. It was like him. Quietness and value—the description applied to both. Twenty-one dollars they took from her for it, and she hurried home with the 87 cents. With that chain on his watch Jim might be properly anxious about the time in any company. Grand as the watch was, he sometimes looked at it on the sly on account of the old leather strap that he used in place of a chain.

When Della reached home her intoxication gave way a little to prudence and reason. She got out her curling irons and lighted the gas and went to work repairing the ravages made by generosity added to love. Which is always a tremendous task, dear friends—a mammoth task.

Within forty minutes her head was covered with tiny, close-lying curls that made her look wonderfully like a truant schoolboy. She looked at her reflection in the mirror long, carefully, and critically.

"If Jim doesn't kill me," she said to herself, "before he takes a second look at me, he'll say I look like a Coney Island chorus girl. But what could I do—oh! what could I do with a dollar and eighty-seven cents?"

At 7 o'clock the coffee was made and the frying pan was on the back of the stove hot and ready to cook the chops.

Jim was never late. Della doubled the fob chain in her hand and sat on the corner of the table near the door that he always entered. Then she heard his step on the stair away down on the first flight, and she turned white for just a moment. She had a habit of saying a little silent prayer about the simplest everyday things, and now she whispered: "Please God, make him think I am still pretty."

The door opened and Jim stepped in and closed it. He looked thin and very serious. Poor fellow, he was only twenty-two—and to be burdened with a family! He needed a new overcoat and he was without gloves.

Jim stopped inside the door, as immovable as a setter at the scent of quail. His eyes were fixed upon Della, and there was an expression in them that she could not read, and it terrified her. It was not anger, nor surprise, nor disapproval, nor horror, nor any of the sentiments that she had been prepared for. He simply stared at her fixedly with that peculiar expression on his face.

Della wriggled off the table and went for him.

"Jim, darling," she cried, "don't look at me that way. I had my hair cut off and sold because I couldn't have lived through Christmas without giving you a present. It'll grow out again—you won't mind, will you? I just had to do it. My hair grows awfully fast. Say 'Merry Christmas!' Jim, and let's be happy. You don't know what a nice—what a beautiful, nice gift I've got for you."

"You've cut off your hair?" asked Jim, laboriously, as if he had not arrived at that patent fact yet even after the hardest mental labor.

"Cut it off and sold it," said Della. "Don't you like me just as well, anyhow? I'm me without my hair, ain't I?"

Jim looked about the room curiously.

"You say your hair is gone?" he said, with an air almost of idiocy.

"You needn't look for it," said Della. "It's sold, I tell you—sold and gone, too. It's Christmas Eve, boy. Be good to me, for it went for you. Maybe the hairs of my head were numbered," she went on with sudden serious sweetness, "but nobody could ever count my love for you. Shall I put the chops on, Jim?"

Out of his trance Jim seemed quickly to wake. He enfolded his Della. For ten seconds let us regard with discreet scrutiny some inconsequential object in the other direction. Eight dollars a week or a million a year—what is the difference? A mathematician or a wit would give you the wrong answer. The magi brought valuable gifts, but that was not among them. This dark assertion will be illuminated later on.

Jim drew a package from his overcoat pocket and threw it upon the table.

"Don't make any mistake, Dell," he said, "about me. I don't think there's anything in the way of a haircut or a shave or a shampoo that could make me like my girl any less. But if you'll unwrap that package you may see why you had me going a while at first."

White fingers and nimble tore at the string and paper. And then an ecstatic scream of joy; and then, alas! a quick feminine change to hysterical tears and wails, necessitating the immediate employment of all the comforting powers of the lord of the flat.

For there lay The Combs—the set of combs, side and back, that Della had worshipped long in a Broadway window. Beautiful combs, pure tortoise shell, with jewelled rims—just the shade to wear in the beautiful vanished hair. They were expensive combs, she knew, and her heart had simply craved and yearned over them without the least hope of possession. And now, they were hers, but the tresses that should have adorned the coveted adornments were gone.

But she hugged them to her bosom, and at length she was able to look up with dim eyes and a smile and say: "My hair grows so fast, Jim!"

And then Della leaped up like a little singed cat and cried, "Oh, oh!"

Jim had not yet seen his beautiful present. She held it out to him eagerly upon her open palm. The dull precious metal seemed to flash with a reflection of her bright and ardent spirit.

"Isn't it a dandy, Jim? I hunted all over town to find it. You'll have to look at the time a hundred times a day now. Give me your watch. I want to see how it looks on it."

Instead of obeying, Jim tumbled down on the couch and put his hands under the back of his head and smiled.

"Dell," said he, "let's put our Christmas presents away and keep 'em a while. They're too nice to use just at present. I sold the watch to get the money to buy your combs. And now suppose you put the chops on."

The magi, as you know, were wise men—wonderfully wise men—who brought gifts to the Babe in the manger. They invented the art of giving Christmas presents. Being wise, their gifts were no doubt wise ones, possibly bearing the privilege of exchange in case of duplication. And here I have lamely related to you the uneventful chronicle of two foolish children in a flat who most unwisely sacrificed for each other the greatest treasures of their house. But in a last word to the wise of these days let it be said that of all who give gifts these two were the wisest. Of all who give and receive gifts, such as they are wisest. Everywhere they are wisest. They are the magi.

The Conversion of Hetherington

H ETHERINGTON WASN'T HALF A BAD sort of a fellow, but he had his peculiarities, most of which were the natural defects of a lack of imagination. He didn't believe in ghosts, or Santa Claus, or any of the thousands of other things that he hadn't seen with his own eyes, and as he walked home that rather chilly afternoon just before Christmas and found nearly every corner of the highway decorated with bogus Saints, wearing the shoddy regalia of Kris Kringle, the sight made him a trifle irritable. He had had a fairly good luncheon that day, one indeed that ought to have mellowed his disposition materially, but which somehow or other had not so resulted. In fact, Hetherington was in a state of raspy petulance that boded ill for his digestion, and when he had reached the corner of Forty-Second Street and Fifth Avenue, the constant iteration and reiteration of these shivering figures of the god of the Yule had got on his nerves to such an extent as to make him aggressively quarrelsome. He had controlled the asperities of his soul tolerably well on the way uptown, but the remark of a small child on the highway, made to a hurrying mother, as they passed a stalwart-looking replica of the idol of his Christmas dreams, banging away on a tambourine to attract attention to the iron pot before him, placed there to catch the pennies of the charitably inclined wayfarer—"Oh, mar, there's Sandy Claus now!"—was too much for him.

"Tush! Nonsense!" shouted Hetherington, glowering at the shivering figure in the turkey-red robe. "The idea of filling children's minds up with such balderdash! Santa Claus, indeed! There isn't a genuine Santa Claus in the whole bogus bunch."

The Saint on the corner banged his tambourine just under Hetherington's ear with just enough force to jar loose the accumulated irascibility of the well-fed gentleman.

"This is a fine job for an able-bodied man like you!" said Hetherington with a sneer. "Why don't you go to work instead of helping to perpetuate this annual fake?"

The Saint looked at him for a moment before replying.

"Speakin' to me?" he said.

"Yes. I'm speaking to you," said Hetherington. "Here's the whole country perishing for the lack of labor, and in spite of that fact this town has broken out into a veritable rash of fake Santa Clauses—"

"That'll do for you!" retorted Santa Claus. "It's easy enough for a feller with a stomach full o' victuals and plenty of warm clothes on his back to jump on a hard-workin' feller like me—"

"Hardworking?" echoed Hetherington. "I like that! You don't call loafing on a street corner this way all day long hard work, do you?"

He rather liked the man's spirit, despite his objection to his occupation.

"Suppose you try it once and find out," retorted Santa Claus, blowing on his bluish fingers in an effort to restore their clogged-up circulation. "I guess if you tried a job like this just once, standin' out in the cold from eight in the mornin' to ten at night, with nothin' but a cup o' coffee and a ham sandwich inside o' you—"

"What's that?" cried Hetherington, aghast. "Is that all you've had to eat today?"

"That's all," said the Saint, as he turned to his work with the tambourine. "Try it once, mister, and maybe you won't feel so cocksure about its not bein' work. If you're half the sport you think you are just take my place for a couple of hours."

An appeal to his sporting instinct was never lost on Hetherington.

"By George!" he cried. "I'll go you. I'll swap coats with you, and while you're filling your stomach up I'll take your place, all right."

"What'll I fill me stomach up with?" demanded the man. "I don't look like a feller with a meal ticket in his pocket, do I?"

"I'll take care of that," said Hetherington, taking out a roll of bills and peeling off a two-dollar note from the outside. "There—you take that and blow yourself, and I'll take care of the kitty here till you come back."

The exchange of externals was not long in accomplishment. The gathering of the shadows of night made it a comparatively easy matter to arrange behind a conveniently stalled and heavily laden express wagon hard by, and in a few moments the irascible but still "sporty" Hetherington, who from childhood up to the present had never been able to take a dare, found himself banging away on a tambourine and incidentally shivering in the poor red habiliments of a fraudulent Saint. For a half-hour the novelty of his position gave him a certain thrill, and no Santa Claus in town that night fulfilled his duties more vociferously than did Hetherington; but as time passed on, and the chill of a windy corner began to penetrate his bones, to say nothing of the frosty condition of his ears, which his false cotton whiskers but indifferently protected, he began to tire of his bargain.

"Gosh!" he muttered to himself, as it began to snow, and certain passing truckmen hurled the same kind of guying comments at him as had been more or less in his mind whenever he had passed a fellow Santa Claus on his way uptown, "if General Sherman were here he'd find a twin brother to War! I wish that cuss would come back."

He gazed eagerly up and down the street in the hope that the departed original would heave in sight, but in vain. A two-dollar meal evidently possessed attractions that he wished to linger over.

"Can't stand this much longer!" he muttered to himself, and then his eye caught sight of a group that filled his soul with dismay: two policemen and the struggling figure of one who appeared to have looked not wisely but too well upon the cup that cheers, the latter wearing Hetherington's overcoat and Hetherington's hat, but whose knees worked upon hinges of their own, double-back-action hinges that made his legs of no use whatsoever, either to himself or to anybody else.

"Hi there!" Hetherington cried out, as the group passed up the street on the way to the stationhouse. "That fellow's got my overcoat—"

But the only reply Hetherington got was a sturdy poke in the ribs from the nightstick of the passing officer.

"Well, I'll be jiggered!" growled Hetherington.

TEN MINUTES LATER A PASSING taxi was hailed by a shivering gentleman carrying an iron pot full of pennies and nickels and an occasional quarter in one hand, and a turkey-red coat, trimmed with white cotton cloth, thrown over his arm. Strange to say, considering the inclemency of the night, he wore neither a hat nor an overcoat.

"Where to, sir?" queried the chauffeur.

"The police station," said Hetherington. "I don't know where it is, but the one in this precinct is the one I want."

"Ye'll have to pay by the hour tonight, sir," said the chauffeur. "The station ain't a half-mile away, sir, but Heaven knows how long it'll take us to get there."

"Charge what you please," retorted Hetherington. "I'll buy your darned old machine if it's necessary, only get a move on."

The chauffeur, with some misgivings as to the mental integrity of his fare, started on their perilous journey, and three-quarters of an hour later drew up in front of the police station, where Hetherington, having been compelled in self-defense to resume the habiliments of Santa

Claus under penalty of freezing, alighted.

"Just wait, will you?" he said, as he alighted from the cab.

"I'll go in with you," said the chauffeur, acting with due caution. He had begun to fear that there was a fair chance of his having trouble getting his fare out of a very evident lunatic.

Utterly forgetful of his appearance in his festal array, Hetherington bustled into the station, and shortly found himself standing before the sergeant behind the desk.

"Well, Santa Claus," said the official, with an amused glance at the intruder, "what can I do for you tonight? There ain't many rooms with a bath left."

Hetherington flushed. He had intended to greet the sergeant with his most imposing manner, but this turkey-red abomination on his back had thrust dignity out in the cold.

"I have come, officer," he said, as impressively as he could under the circumstances, "to make some inquiries concerning a man who was brought here about an hour ago—I fear in a state of intoxication."

"We have known such things to happen here, Santa," said the officer, suavely. "In fact, this blotter here seems to indicate that one George W. Hetherington, of 561 Fifth Avenue—"

"Who?" roared Hetherington.

"George W. Hetherington is the name on the blotter," said the sergeant; "entered first as a D. D., but on investigation found to be suffering from—"

"But that's my name!" cried Hetherington. "You don't mean to tell me he claimed to be George W. Hetherington?"

"No," said the sergeant. "The poor devil didn't make any claims for himself at all. We found that name on a card in his hat, and a letter addressed to the same name in his overcoat pocket. Puttin' the two together we thought it was a good enough identification."

"Well, I'll have you to understand, sergeant—" bristled Hetherington, cockily.

"None o' that, Santa Claus—none o' that!" growled the sergeant, leaning over the desk and eying him coldly. "I don't know what game you're up to, but just one more peep in that tone and there'll be two George W. Hetheringtons in the cooler this night."

Hetherington almost tore the Santa Claus garb from his shoulders, and revealed himself as a personage of fine raiment underneath, whatever he might have appeared at a superficial glance. As he did so a crumpled piece of paper fell to the floor from the pocket of the turkey-red coat.

"I don't mean to do anything but what is right, sergeant," he said, controlling his wrath, "but what I do want is to impress it upon your mind that *I* am George W. Hetherington, and that having my name spread on the blotter of a police court isn't going to do me any good. I loaned that fellow my hat and coat to get a square meal, while I took his place—"

The officer grinned broadly, but with no assurance in his smile that he believed.

"Oh, you may not believe it," said Hetherington, "but it's true, and if this thing gets into the papers tomorrow morning—"

"Say, Larry," said the sergeant, addressing an officer off duty, "did the reporters copy that letter we found in Hetherington's pocket?"

"Reporters?" gasped Hetherington. "Good Lord, man—yuh—you don't mum—mean to say yuh—you let the reporters—"

"No, chief," replied Larry. "They ain't been in yet—I t'ink ye shoved it inter yer desk."

"So I did, so I did," grinned the sergeant. Here he opened the drawer in front of him and extracted a pretty little blue envelope which Hetherington immediately recognized as a particularly private and confidential communication from—well, somebody. This is not a *cherchez la femme* story, so we will leave the lady's name out of it altogether. It must be noted, however, that a sight of that dainty missive in the great red fist of the sergeant gave Hetherington a heart action that fifty packages of cigarettes a day could hardly inflict upon a less healthy man.

"That's the proof—" cried Hetherington, excitedly. "If that don't prove it's my overcoat nothing will."

"Right you are, Santa Claus," said the sergeant, opening the envelope and taking out the delicately scented sheet of paper within. "I'll give you two guesses at the name signed to this, and if you get it right once I'll give you the coat, and Mr. Hetherington Number One in our evening's consignment of Hetheringtons gets rechristened."

"'Anita'!" growled Hetherington.

"You win!" said the sergeant, handing over the letter.

Hetherington drew a long sigh of relief.

"I guess this is worth cigars for the house, sergeant," he said. "I'll send 'em round tomorrow—meanwhile, how about—how about the other?"

"He's gone to the hospital," said the sergeant, grimly. "The doctor says he wasn't drunk—just another case of freezing starvation."

"Starvation? And I guyed him! Great God!" muttered Hetherington to himself.

"Narrow escape, Mr. Hetherington," said the sergeant. "Ought to be a lesson to you sports. What was your game, anyhow?"

"Oh, it wasn't any game—" began Hetherington.

"Huh! Just a case of too much lunch, eh?" said the officer. "You'd had as much too much as the other feller'd had too little—that it?"

"No," said Hetherington. "Just a general lack of confidence in my fellowmen, plus a cussed habit of butting into matters that aren't any of my business; but I'm glad I butted in, just the same, if I can be of any earthly use to that poor devil of a Santa Claus. Do you suppose there's any way to find out who he is?"

"Well, we've made a good start, anyhow," said the sergeant. "We've found out who he isn't. When he comes to in the mornin', if he does, maybe he'll be able to help us identify him."

"Tomorrow!" murmured Hetherington. "And who knows but he's got a family waiting for him somewhere right now, and as badly off as he is."

"Ye dropped this, sir," said Larry, the officer off duty. "It come out of the red coat—mebbe it'll help—"

He handed Hetherington the crumpled piece of paper that had fallen to the floor when he tore Santa Claus's cloak from his back. It was sadly dirty, but on one side of it was a childish scrawl in pencil. Hetherington ran over it rapidly, and gulped.

"Read that, sergeant!" he said, huskily.

The sergeant read the following:

"DEAR SANDY CLORS:—my Popper says hell hand you this here leter when he sees you to ast you not to fergit me and jimmy like you did last yeer. you aint been to see me an jimmy since popper lost his Jobb and he says its becoz you lost our adres so ime ritin to tell you weve moved since you come the lass time and am now livin now on the Topp flor of fore 69 varrick streete noo york which youd ort not to find it hard to git down the chimbley bein on the topp flor closte to the roofe so i thort ide rite and tell you what me and jimmyd

like to hav you bring us wenn you come. I nede some noo
shues and a hatt and my lasst dol babys all wore out and sum
candy if you can work it in sumhow, not havin had much
since popper lost his jobb, and jimmies only gott one mitt left
and his shues is wore throo like mine is only a little worser,
and a baseball batt and hed like sum candy to. if there wass
anything lefft ovvur for us from lass crissmis wich you dident
kno ware to find us to giv it to us we wuddent mind havin
that two but you needent mind about that if its misslayde we
can git along all rite all rite on whot ive sed alreddy. ime leven
and jimmies nine and we hope youl hav a mery crismiss like
wede hav if youd come to see us.

"yure efexinite frend mary muligan.

"p. s dont fergit the adres topp flor 469 varrick strete noo york.
take back chimbley middel floo."

"I'm sorry to say, Mr. Hetherington," said the sergeant, clearing
his throat with vociferous unction, "that the town's full of Mary and
Jimmie Mulligans—but, anyhow, I guess this is good enough evidence
for me to scratch out your name and enter the record under James
Mulligan."

"Thank you, sergeant," said Hetherington, gratefully. "And it's good
enough evidence for me that this town needs a Santa Claus a blooming
sight more than I thought it did. What time is it?"

"Seven-thirty," replied the sergeant.

"Good!" said Hetherington. "Shops don't close till ten—I guess I've
got time. Goodnight—see you first thing in the morning. Come along,
chauffeur, I'll need you for some time yet."

"Goodnight, Mr. Hetherington," said the sergeant. "Where are you
bound in case I need you any time?"

"Me?" said Hetherington with a grin, "why, my address is 561 Fifth
Avenue, but just now I'm off to do my Christmas shopping early."

And resuming possession of his own hat and overcoat, and taking
the Santa Claus costume under his arm, Hetherington passed out, the
chauffeur following.

"These New York sports is a queer bunch!" said the sergeant as
Hetherington disappeared.

AT HALF-PAST NINE DOWNTOWN WAS pretty well deserted, which made it easy for the chauffeur of a certain red taxicab to make fairly good time down Broadway; and when at nine-forty-five the panting mechanism drew up before the grim walls of a brick tenement, numbered 469 Varick Street, the man on the box was commendably proud of his record.

"That was goin' some, sir," he said, with a broad grin on his face. "I don't believe it's ever been done quicker outside o' the fire department."

"I don't believe it has, old man," said Hetherington as he alighted.

"Now if you'll help me upstairs with these packages and that basket there, we'll bring this affair to a grand-stand finish."

The two men toiled slowly up the stairs, Hetherington puffing somewhat with the long climb; and when finally they had reached the top floor he arrayed himself in the once despised garb of Santa Claus again. Then he knocked at the door. The answer was immediate. A white-faced woman opened the door.

"Jim!" she cried. "Is it you?"

"No, madam," replied Hetherington. "It's a friend of Jim's. Fact is, Mrs. Mulligan, Jim has—"

"There's nothin' happened to Jim, has there?" she interrupted.

"Nothing at all, madam, nothing at all," said Hetherington. "The work was a little too much for him today—that's all—and he keeled over. He's safe, and comfortable in the—well, they took him to the hospital, but don't you worry—he'll be all right in a day or two, and meanwhile I'm going to look after you and the kiddies."

The chauffeur placed the basket inside the door.

"You'll find a small turkey, and some—er—some fixings in it, Mrs. Mulligan," said Hetherington. "Whatever ought to go with a turkey should be there, and—er—have the kiddies gone to bed?"

"Poor little souls, they have," said the woman.

"Well, just you tell 'em for me," said Hetherington, "that Santa Claus received little Mary's letter, will you, please? And—er—and if they don't mind a very late call like this, why I'd like to see them."

The woman looked anxiously into Hetherington's eyes for a moment, and then she tottered and sat down.

"You're sure there's nothin' the matter with Jim, sir?" she asked.

"Absolutely, Mrs. Mulligan," Hetherington answered. "It's exactly as I have told you. The cold and hunger were too much for him, but he's all right, and I'll guarantee to have him back here inside of forty-eight hours."

"I'll call the childer," said Mrs. Mulligan.

Two wide-eyed youngsters shortly stood in awed wonder before their strange visitor, never doubting for a moment that he was Santa Claus himself.

"How do you do, Miss Mulligan?" said Hetherington, with a courtly bow to the little tot of a girl. "I received your letter this afternoon, and was mighty glad to hear from you again, but I've been too busy all day to write you in return, so I thought I'd call and tell you that it's all right about those shoes, and the hat, and the new doll baby, and the things for Jimmie. Fact is, I've brought 'em with me. Reginald," he added, turning to the chauffeur, who stood grinning in the doorway, "just unfasten that bundle of shoes, will you, while I get Jimmie's new mitts and the baseball bat?"

"Yes, sir," said the chauffeur, suiting his action to the orders, and with a right good will that was pleasant to see.

"Reginald is my assistant," said Santa Claus. "Couldn't get along without Reginald these days—very busy days they are—so many new kiddies in the world, you know. There, Jimmie—there's your bat. May you score many a homerun with it. Here's a ball, too—good thing to have a ball to practise with. Someday you'll be a Giant, perhaps, and help win the pennant. Incidentally, James, old boy, there's a box of tin soldiers in this package, a bag of marbles, a select assortment of tops, and a fur coat; just try that cap on, and see if you can tell yourself from a Brownie."

The children's eyes gleamed with joy, and Jimmie let out a cheer that would have aroused the envy of a college man.

"You didn't mention it in your note, Mary, dear," continued Santa Claus, turning to the little girl, "but I thought you might like to cook a few meals for this brand new doll baby of yours, so I brought along a little stove, with a few pots and pans and kettles and things, with a small china tea set thrown in. This ought to enable you to set her up in housekeeping; and then when you go to school I have an idea you'll find this Little Red Riding Hood cloak rather nice—only it's navy blue instead of red, and it looks warm."

Hetherington placed the little cloak with its beautiful brass buttons and its warm hood over the little girl's shoulders, while she stood with her eyes popping out of her head, too delightedly entranced to be able to say a word of thanks.

"Don't forget this, sir," said the chauffeur, handing Hetherington a package tied up in blue ribbons.

"And finally," said Hetherington, after thanking Reginald for the reminder, "here is a box of candy for everybody in the place. One for Mary, one for Jimmie, one for mother, and one for popper when he comes home."

"Oh thank you, thank you, thank you!" cried the little girl, throwing herself into Hetherington's arms. "I knowed you'd come—I did, I did, I did!"

"You believed in old Santa Claus, did you, babe?" said Hetherington, huskily, as the little girl's warm cheek pressed against his own.

"Yes, I did—always," said the little girl, "though Jimmie didn't."

"I did so!" retorted Jimmie, squatting on the floor and shooting a glass agate at a bunch of miggles across the room. "I swatted Petey Halloran on the eye on'y yesterday for sayin' they wasn't no such person."

"And you did well, my son," said Hetherington. "The man or boy that says there isn't any Santa Claus is a—is a—well, never you mind, but he is one just the same."

And bidding his little friends goodnight, Hetherington, with the chauffeur close behind him, left them to the joys of the moment, with a cheerier dawn than they had known for many weary days to follow.

"Goodnight, sir," said the chauffeur, as Hetherington paid him off and added a good-sized tip into the bargain. "I didn't useter believe in Santa Claus, sir, but I do now."

"So do I," said Hetherington, as he bade the other goodnight and lightly mounted the steps to his house.

The Velveteen Rabbit

Here was once a velveteen rabbit, and in the beginning he was really splendid. He was fat and bunchy, as a rabbit should be; his coat was spotted brown and white, he had real thread whiskers, and his ears were lined with pink sateen. On Christmas morning, when he sat wedged in the top of the Boy's stocking, with a sprig of holly between his paws, the effect was charming.

There were other things in the stocking, nuts and oranges and a toy engine, and chocolate almonds and a clockwork mouse, but the Rabbit was quite the best of all. For at least two hours the Boy loved him, and then Aunts and Uncles came to dinner, and there was a great rustling of tissue paper and unwrapping of parcels, and in the excitement of looking at all the new presents the Velveteen Rabbit was forgotten.

Christmas Morning

For a long time he lived in the toy cupboard or on the nursery floor, and no one thought very much about him. He was naturally shy, and being only made of velveteen, some of the more expensive toys quite snubbed him. The mechanical toys were very superior, and looked down upon every one else; they were full of modern ideas, and pretended they were real. The model boat, who had lived through two seasons and lost most of his paint, caught the tone from them and never missed an opportunity of referring to his rigging in technical terms. The Rabbit could not claim to be a model of anything, for he didn't know that real rabbits existed; he thought they were all stuffed with sawdust like himself, and he understood that sawdust was quite out-of-date and should never be mentioned in modern circles. Even Timothy, the jointed wooden lion, who was made by the disabled soldiers, and should have had broader views, put on airs and pretended he was connected with Government. Between them all the poor little Rabbit was made to feel himself very insignificant and commonplace, and the only person who was kind to him at all was the Skin Horse.

The Skin Horse had lived longer in the nursery than any of the others. He was so old that his brown coat was bald in patches and showed the seams underneath, and most of the hairs in his tail had been pulled out to string bead necklaces. He was wise, for he had seen a long succession of mechanical toys arrive to boast and swagger, and by-and-by break their mainsprings and pass away, and he knew that they were only toys, and would never turn into anything else. For nursery magic is very strange and wonderful, and only those playthings that are old and wise and experienced like the Skin Horse understand all about it.

"What is *Real*?" asked the Rabbit one day, when they were lying side by side near the nursery fender, before Nana came to tidy the room. "Does it mean having things that buzz inside you and a stick-out handle?"

"Real isn't how you are made," said the Skin Horse. "It's a thing that happens to you. When a child loves you for a long, long time, not just to play with, but *really* loves you, then you become *Real*."

"Does it hurt?" asked the Rabbit.

"Sometimes," said the Skin Horse, for he was always truthful. "When you are Real you don't mind being hurt."

"Does it happen all at once, like being wound up," he asked, "or bit by bit?"

"It doesn't happen all at once," said the Skin Horse. "You become. It takes a long time. That's why it doesn't happen often to people who break easily, or have sharp edges, or who have to be carefully kept. Generally, by the time you are Real, most of your hair has been loved off, and your eyes drop out and you get loose in the joints and very shabby. But these things don't matter at all, because once you are Real you can't be ugly, except to people who don't understand."

"I suppose you are *real*?" said the Rabbit. And then he wished he had not said it, for he thought the Skin Horse might be sensitive. But the Skin Horse only smiled.

The Skin Horse Tells His Story

"THE BOY'S UNCLE MADE ME Real," he said. "That was a great many years ago; but once you are Real you can't become unreal again. It lasts for always."

The Rabbit sighed. He thought it would be a long time before this magic called Real happened to him. He longed to become Real, to know what it felt like; and yet the idea of growing shabby and losing his eyes and whiskers was rather sad. He wished that he could become it without these uncomfortable things happening to him.

There was a person called Nana who ruled the nursery. Sometimes she took no notice of the playthings lying about, and sometimes, for no reason whatever, she went swooping about like a great wind and hustled them away in cupboards. She called this "tidying up," and the playthings all hated it, especially the tin ones. The Rabbit didn't mind it so much, for wherever he was thrown he came down soft.

One evening, when the Boy was going to bed, he couldn't find the china dog that always slept with him. Nana was in a hurry, and it was too much trouble to hunt for china dogs at bedtime, so she simply looked about her, and seeing that the toy cupboard door stood open, she made a swoop.

"Here," she said, "take your old Bunny! He'll do to sleep with you!" And she dragged the Rabbit out by one ear, and put him into the Boy's arms.

That night, and for many nights after, the Velveteen Rabbit slept in the Boy's bed. At first he found it rather uncomfortable, for the Boy hugged him very tight, and sometimes he rolled over on him, and sometimes he pushed him so far under the pillow that the Rabbit could scarcely breathe. And he missed, too, those long moonlight hours in the nursery, when all the house was silent, and his talks with the Skin Horse. But very soon he grew to like it, for the Boy used to talk to him, and made nice tunnels for him under the bedclothes that he said were like the burrows the real rabbits lived in. And they had splendid games together, in whispers, when Nana had gone away to her supper and left the night-light burning on the mantelpiece. And when the Boy dropped off to sleep, the Rabbit would snuggle down close under his little warm chin and dream, with the Boy's hands clasped close round him all night long.

And so time went on, and the little Rabbit was very happy—so happy that he never noticed how his beautiful velveteen fur was getting shabbier and shabbier, and his tail becoming unsewn, and all the pink rubbed off his nose where the Boy had kissed him.

Spring came, and they had long days in the garden, for wherever the Boy went the Rabbit went too. He had rides in the wheelbarrow, and picnics on the grass, and lovely fairy huts built for him under the raspberry canes behind the flower border. And once, when the Boy was called away suddenly to go out to tea, the Rabbit was left out on the lawn until long after dusk, and Nana had to come and look for him with the candle because the Boy couldn't go to sleep unless he was there. He was wet through with the dew and quite earthy from diving into the burrows the Boy had made for him in the flower bed, and Nana grumbled as she rubbed him off with a corner of her apron.

Spring Time

"You must have your old Bunny!" she said. "Fancy all that fuss for a toy!"

The Boy sat up in bed and stretched out his hands.

"Give me my Bunny!" he said. "You mustn't say that. He isn't a toy. He's Real!"

When the little Rabbit heard that he was happy, for he knew that what the Skin Horse had said was true at last. The nursery magic had happened to him, and he was a toy no longer. He was Real. The Boy himself had said it.

That night he was almost too happy to sleep, and so much love stirred in his little sawdust heart that it almost burst. And into his boot-button eyes, that had long ago lost their polish, there came a look of wisdom and beauty, so that even Nana noticed it next morning when she picked him up, and said, "I declare if that old Bunny hasn't got quite a knowing expression!"

That was a wonderful Summer!

Near the house where they lived there was a wood, and in the long June evenings the Boy liked to go there after tea to play. He took the Velveteen Rabbit with him, and before he wandered off to pick flowers, or play at brigands among the trees, he always made the Rabbit a little nest somewhere among the bracken, where he would be quite cosy, for he was a kind-hearted little boy and he liked Bunny to be comfortable. One evening, while the Rabbit was lying there alone, watching the ants that ran to and fro between his velvet paws in the grass, he saw two strange beings creep out of the tall bracken near him.

They were rabbits like himself, but quite furry and brand new. They must have been very well made, for their seams didn't show at all, and they changed shape in a queer way when they moved; one minute they were long and thin and the next minute fat and bunchy, instead of always staying the same like he did. Their feet padded softly on the ground, and they crept quite close to him, twitching their noses, while the Rabbit stared hard to see which side the clockwork stuck out, for he knew that people who jump generally have something to wind them up. But he couldn't see it. They were evidently a new kind of rabbit altogether.

THEY STARED AT HIM, AND the little Rabbit stared back. And all the time their noses twitched.

"Why don't you get up and play with us?" one of them asked.

"I don't feel like it," said the Rabbit, for he didn't want to explain that he had no clockwork.

"Ho!" said the furry rabbit. "It's as easy as anything," And he gave a big hop sideways and stood on his hind legs.

"I don't believe you can!" he said.

"I can!" said the little Rabbit. "I can jump higher than anything!" He meant when the Boy threw him, but of course he didn't want to say so.

"Can you hop on your hind legs?" asked the furry rabbit.

That was a dreadful question, for the Velveteen Rabbit had no hind legs at all! The back of him was made all in one piece, like a pincushion. He sat still in the bracken, and hoped that the other rabbits wouldn't notice.

"I don't want to!" he said again.

But the wild rabbits have very sharp eyes. And this one stretched out his neck and looked.

"He hasn't got any hind legs!" he called out. "Fancy a rabbit without any hind legs!" And he began to laugh.

"I have!" cried the little Rabbit. "I have got hind legs! I am sitting on them!"

"Then stretch them out and show me, like this!" said the wild rabbit. And he began to whirl round and dance, till the little Rabbit got quite dizzy.

"I don't like dancing," he said. "I'd rather sit still!"

But all the while he was longing to dance, for a funny new tickly feeling ran through him, and he felt he would give anything in the world to be able to jump about like these rabbits did.

The strange rabbit stopped dancing, and came quite close. He came so close this time that his long whiskers brushed the Velveteen Rabbit's ear, and then he wrinkled his nose suddenly and flattened his ears and jumped backwards.

"He doesn't smell right!" he exclaimed. "He isn't a rabbit at all! He isn't real!"

"I am Real!" said the little Rabbit. "I am Real! The Boy said so!" And he nearly began to cry.

Just then there was a sound of footsteps, and the Boy ran past near them, and with a stamp of feet and a flash of white tails the two strange rabbits disappeared.

"Come back and play with me!" called the little Rabbit. "Oh, do come back! I know I am Real!"

But there was no answer, only the little ants ran to and fro, and the bracken swayed gently where the two strangers had passed. The Velveteen Rabbit was all alone.

"Oh, dear!" he thought. "Why did they run away like that? Why couldn't they stop and talk to me?"

For a long time he lay very still, watching the bracken, and hoping that they would come back. But they never returned, and presently the sun sank lower and the little white moths fluttered out, and the Boy came and carried him home.

WEEKS PASSED, AND THE LITTLE Rabbit grew very old and shabby, but the Boy loved him just as much. He loved him so hard that he loved all his whiskers off, and the pink lining to his ears turned grey, and his brown spots faded. He even began to lose his shape, and he scarcely looked like a rabbit anymore, except to the Boy. To him he was always beautiful, and that was all that the little Rabbit cared about. He didn't mind how he looked to other people, because the nursery magic had made him Real, and when you are Real shabbiness doesn't matter.

And then, one day, the Boy was ill.

His face grew very flushed, and he talked in his sleep, and his little body was so hot that it burned the Rabbit when he held him close. Strange people came and went in the nursery, and a light burned all night and through it all the little Velveteen Rabbit lay there, hidden from sight under the bedclothes, and he never stirred, for he was afraid that if they found him someone might take him away, and he knew that the Boy needed him.

It was a long weary time, for the Boy was too ill to play, and the little Rabbit found it rather dull with nothing to do all day long. But he snuggled down patiently, and looked forward to the time when the Boy should be well again, and they would go out in the garden amongst the flowers and the butterflies and play splendid games in the raspberry thicket like they used to. All sorts of delightful things he planned, and while the Boy lay half asleep he crept up close to the pillow and whispered them in his ear. And presently the fever turned, and the Boy got better. He was able to sit up in bed and look at picture books, while the little Rabbit cuddled close at his side. And one day, they let him get up and dress.

It was a bright, sunny morning, and the windows stood wide open. They had carried the Boy out on to the balcony, wrapped in a shawl, and the little Rabbit lay tangled up among the bedclothes, thinking.

The Boy was going to the seaside tomorrow. Everything was arranged, and now it only remained to carry out the doctor's orders. They talked about it all, while the little Rabbit lay under the bedclothes, with just his head peeping out, and listened. The room was to be disinfected, and all the books and toys that the Boy had played with in bed must be burnt.

"Hurrah!" thought the little Rabbit. "Tomorrow we shall go to the seaside!" For the boy had often talked of the seaside, and he wanted very much to see the big waves coming in, and the tiny crabs, and the sand castles.

Just then Nana caught sight of him.

"How about his old Bunny?" she asked.

"That?" said the doctor. "Why, it's a mass of scarlet fever germs! Burn it at once. What? Nonsense! Get him a new one. He mustn't have that anymore!"

Anxious Times

AND SO THE LITTLE RABBIT was put into a sack with the old picture books and a lot of rubbish, and carried out to the end of the garden behind the fowl-house. That was a fine place to make a bonfire, only the gardener was too busy just then to attend to it. He had the potatoes to dig and the green peas to gather, but next morning he promised to come quite early and burn the whole lot.

That night the Boy slept in a different bedroom, and he had a new bunny to sleep with him. It was a splendid bunny, all white plush with real glass eyes, but the Boy was too excited to care very much about it. For tomorrow he was going to the seaside, and that in itself was such a wonderful thing that he could think of nothing else.

And while the Boy was asleep, dreaming of the seaside, the little Rabbit lay among the old picture books in the corner behind the fowl-house, and he felt very lonely. The sack had been left untied, and so by wriggling a bit he was able to get his head through the opening and look out. He was shivering a little, for he had always been used to sleeping in a proper bed, and by this time his coat had worn so thin and threadbare from hugging that it was no longer any protection to him. Near by he could see the thicket of raspberry canes, growing tall and close like a tropical jungle, in whose shadow he had played with the Boy on bygone mornings. He thought of those long sunlit hours in the garden—how happy they were—and a great sadness came over him. He seemed to see them all pass before him, each more beautiful than the other, the fairy huts in the flowerbed, the quiet evenings in the wood when he lay in the bracken and the little ants ran over his paws; the wonderful day when he first knew that he was Real. He thought of the Skin Horse, so wise and gentle, and all that he had told him. Of what use was it to be loved and lose one's beauty and become Real if it all ended like this? And a tear, a real tear, trickled down his little shabby velvet nose and fell to the ground.

And then a strange thing happened. For where the tear had fallen a flower grew out of the ground, a mysterious flower, not at all like any that grew in the garden. It had slender green leaves the colour of emeralds, and in the centre of the leaves a blossom like a golden cup. It was so beautiful that the little Rabbit forgot to cry, and just lay there watching it. And presently the blossom opened, and out of it there stepped a fairy.

She was quite the loveliest fairy in the whole world. Her dress was of pearl and dew-drops, and there were flowers round her neck and in her hair, and her face was like the most perfect flower of all. And she came close to the little Rabbit and gathered him up in her arms and kissed him on his velveteen nose that was all damp from crying.

"Little Rabbit," she said, "don't you know who I am?"

The Rabbit looked up at her, and it seemed to him that he had seen her face before, but he couldn't think where.

"I am the nursery magic Fairy," she said. "I take care of all the playthings that the children have loved. When they are old and worn out and the children don't need them anymore, then I come and take them away with me and turn them into Real."

"Wasn't I Real before?" asked the little Rabbit.

"You were Real to the Boy," the Fairy said, "because he loved you. Now you shall be Real to every one."

The Fairy Flower

AND SHE HELD THE LITTLE Rabbit close in her arms and flew with him into the wood.

It was light now, for the moon had risen. All the forest was beautiful, and the fronds of the bracken shone like frosted silver. In the open glade between the tree trunks the wild rabbits danced with their shadows on the velvet grass, but when they saw the Fairy they all stopped dancing and stood round in a ring to stare at her.

"I've brought you a new playfellow," the Fairy said. "You must be very kind to him and teach him all he needs to know in Rabbit-land, for he is going to live with you forever and ever!"

And she kissed the little Rabbit again and put him down on the grass.

"Run and play, little Rabbit!" she said.

But the little Rabbit sat quite still for a moment and never moved. For when he saw all the wild rabbits dancing around him he suddenly remembered about his hind legs, and he didn't want them to see that he was made all in one piece. He did not know that when the Fairy kissed him that last time she had changed him altogether. And he might have sat there a long time, too shy to move, if just then something hadn't tickled his nose, and before he thought what he was doing he lifted his hind toe to scratch it.

And he found that he actually had hind legs! Instead of dingy velveteen he had brown fur, soft and shiny, his ears twitched by themselves, and his whiskers were so long that they brushed the grass. He gave one leap and the joy of using those hind legs was so great that he went springing about the turf on them, jumping sideways and whirling round as the others did, and he grew so excited that when at last he did stop to look for the Fairy she had gone.

He was a Real Rabbit at last, at home with the other rabbits.

At Last! At Last!

AUTUMN PASSED AND WINTER, AND in the Spring, when the days grew warm and sunny, the Boy went out to play in the wood behind the house. And while he was playing, two rabbits crept out from the bracken and peeped at him. One of them was brown all over, but the other had strange markings under his fur, as though long ago he had been spotted, and the spots still showed through. And about his little soft nose and his round black eyes there was something familiar, so that the Boy thought to himself:

"Why, he looks just like my old Bunny that was lost when I had scarlet fever!"

But he never knew that it really was his own Bunny, come back to look at the child who had first helped him to be Real.

A CHRISTMAS CAROL

I

MARLEY'S GHOST

MARLEY WAS DEAD, TO BEGIN with. There is no doubt whatever about that. The register of his burial was signed by the clergyman, the clerk, the undertaker, and the chief mourner. Scrooge signed it. And Scrooge's name was good upon 'Change for anything he chose to put his hand to. Old Marley was as dead as a doornail.

Mind! I don't mean to say that I know, of my own knowledge, what there is particularly dead about a doornail. I might have been inclined, myself, to regard a coffin nail as the deadest piece of ironmongery in the trade. But the wisdom of our ancestors is in the simile; and my unhallowed hands shall not disturb it, or the Country's done for. You will, therefore, permit me to repeat, emphatically, that Marley was as dead as a doornail.

Scrooge knew he was dead? Of course he did. How could it be otherwise? Scrooge and he were partners for I don't know how many years. Scrooge was his sole executor, his sole administrator, his sole assign, his sole residuary legatee, his sole friend, and sole mourner. And even Scrooge was not so dreadfully cut up by the sad event, but that he was an excellent man of business on the very day of the funeral, and solemnised it with an undoubted bargain.

The mention of Marley's funeral brings me back to the point I started from. There is no doubt that Marley was dead. This must be distinctly understood, or nothing wonderful can come of the story I am going to relate. If we were not perfectly convinced that Hamlet's Father died before the play began, there would be nothing more remarkable in his taking a stroll at night, in an easterly wind, upon his own ramparts, than there would be in any other middle-aged gentleman rashly turning out after dark in a breezy spot—say St. Paul's Churchyard, for instance— literally to astonish his son's weak mind.

Scrooge never painted out Old Marley's name. There it stood, years afterwards, above the warehouse door: Scrooge and Marley. The firm was known as Scrooge and Marley. Sometimes people new to the business called Scrooge Scrooge, and sometimes Marley, but he answered to both names. It was all the same to him.

Oh! But he was a tight-fisted hand at the grindstone, Scrooge! A squeezing, wrenching, grasping, scraping, clutching, covetous, old sinner! Hard and sharp as flint, from which no steel had ever struck out generous fire; secret, and self-contained, and solitary as an oyster. The cold within him froze his old features, nipped his pointed nose, shrivelled his cheek, stiffened his gait; made his eyes red, his thin lips blue; and spoke out shrewdly in his grating voice. A frosty rime was on his head, and on his eyebrows, and his wiry chin. He carried his own low temperature always about with him; he iced his office in the dog-days; and didn't thaw it one degree at Christmas.

External heat and cold had little influence on Scrooge. No warmth could warm, no wintry weather chill him. No wind that blew was bitterer than he, no falling snow was more intent upon its purpose, no pelting rain less open to entreaty. Foul weather didn't know where to have him. The heaviest rain, and snow, and hail, and sleet could boast of the advantage over him in only one respect. They often "came down" handsomely and Scrooge never did.

Nobody ever stopped him in the street to say, with gladsome looks, "My dear Scrooge, how are you? When will you come to see me?" No beggars implored him to bestow a trifle, no children asked him what it was o'clock, no man or woman ever once in all his life inquired the way to such and such a place, of Scrooge. Even the blind men's dogs appeared to know him; and, when they saw him coming on, would tug their owners into doorways and up courts; and then would wag their tails as though they said, "No eye at all is better than an evil eye, dark master!"

But what did Scrooge care? It was the very thing he liked. To edge his way along the crowded paths of life, warning all human sympathy to keep its distance, was what the knowing ones call "nuts" to Scrooge.

Once upon a time—of all the good days in the year, on Christmas Eve—old Scrooge sat busy in his counting house. It was cold, bleak, biting weather: foggy withal: and he could hear the people in the court outside go wheezing up and down, beating their hands upon their breasts, and stamping their feet upon the pavement stones to warm them. The City clocks had only just gone three, but it was quite dark already—it had not been light all day—and candles were flaring in the windows of the neighbouring offices, like ruddy smears upon the palpable brown air. The fog came pouring in at every chink and keyhole, and was so dense without, that, although the court was of the narrowest, the houses opposite were mere phantoms. To see the dingy cloud come drooping down, obscuring everything, one might have thought that nature lived hard by and was brewing on a large scale.

The door of Scrooge's counting house was open, that he might keep his eye upon his clerk, who in a dismal little cell beyond, a sort of tank, was copying letters. Scrooge had a very small fire, but the clerk's fire was so very much smaller that it looked like one coal. But he couldn't replenish it, for Scrooge kept the coal box in his own room; and so surely as the clerk came in with the shovel, the master predicted that it would be necessary for them to part. Wherefore the clerk put on his white comforter, and tried to warm himself at the candle; in which effort, not being a man of strong imagination, he failed.

"A merry Christmas, uncle! God save you!" cried a cheerful voice. It was the voice of Scrooge's nephew, who came upon him so quickly that this was the first intimation he had of his approach.

"Bah!" said Scrooge. "Humbug!"

He had so heated himself with rapid walking in the fog and frost, this nephew of Scrooge's, that he was all in a glow; his face was ruddy and handsome; his eyes sparkled, and his breath smoked again.

"Christmas a humbug, uncle!" said Scrooge's nephew. "You don't mean that, I am sure?"

"I do," said Scrooge. "Merry Christmas! What right have you to be merry? What reason have you to be merry? You're poor enough."

"Come, then," returned the nephew gaily. "What right have you to be dismal? What reason have you to be morose? You're rich enough."

Scrooge, having no better answer ready on the spur of the moment, said, "Bah!" again; and followed it up with "Humbug!"

"Don't be cross, uncle!" said the nephew.

"What else can I be," returned the uncle, "when I live in such a world of fools as this? Merry Christmas! Out upon merry Christmas! What's Christmastime to you but a time for paying bills without money; a time for finding yourself a year older, and not an hour richer; a time for balancing your books, and having every item in 'em through a round dozen of months presented dead against you? If I could work my will," said Scrooge indignantly, "every idiot who goes about with 'Merry Christmas' on his lips should be boiled with his own pudding, and buried with a stake of holly through his heart. He should!"

"Uncle!" pleaded the nephew.

"Nephew!" returned the uncle sternly, "keep Christmas in your own way, and let me keep it in mine."

"Keep it!" repeated Scrooge's nephew. "But you don't keep it."

"Let me leave it alone, then," said Scrooge. "Much good may it do you! Much good it has ever done you!"

"There are many things from which I might have derived good, by which I have not profited, I dare say," returned the nephew; "Christmas among the rest. But I am sure I have always thought of Christmastime, when it has come round—apart from the veneration due to its sacred name and origin, if anything belonging to it can be apart from that—as a good time; a kind, forgiving, charitable, pleasant time; the only time I know of, in the long calendar of the year, when men and women seem by one consent to open their shut-up hearts freely, and to think of people below them as if they really were fellow-passengers to the grave, and not another race of creatures bound on other journeys. And therefore, uncle, though it has never put a scrap of gold or silver in my pocket, I believe that it *has* done me good, and *will* do me good; and I say, God bless it!"

The clerk in the tank involuntarily applauded. Becoming immediately sensible of the impropriety, he poked the fire, and extinguished the last frail spark forever.

"Let me hear another sound from *you*," said Scrooge, "and you'll keep your Christmas by losing your situation! You're quite a powerful speaker, sir," he added, turning to his nephew. "I wonder you don't go into Parliament."

"Don't be angry, uncle. Come! Dine with us tomorrow."

Scrooge said that he would see him—Yes, indeed he did. He went the whole length of the expression, and said that he would see him in that extremity first.

"But why?" cried Scrooge's nephew. "Why?"

"Why did you get married?" said Scrooge.

"Because I fell in love."

"Because you fell in love!" growled Scrooge, as if that were the only one thing in the world more ridiculous than a merry Christmas. "Good afternoon!"

"Nay, uncle, but you never came to see me before that happened. Why give it as a reason for not coming now?"

"Good afternoon," said Scrooge.

"I want nothing from you; I ask nothing of you; why cannot we be friends?"

"Good afternoon!" said Scrooge.

"I am sorry, with all my heart, to find you so resolute. We have never had any quarrel to which I have been a party. But I have made the trial in homage to Christmas, and I'll keep my Christmas humour to the last. So A Merry Christmas, uncle!"

"Good afternoon," said Scrooge.

"And A Happy New Year!"

"Good afternoon!" said Scrooge.

His nephew left the room without an angry word, notwithstanding. He stopped at the outer door to bestow the greetings of the season on the clerk, who, cold as he was, was warmer than Scrooge; for he returned them cordially.

"There's another fellow," muttered Scrooge, who overheard him: "my clerk, with fifteen shillings a week, and a wife and family, talking about a merry Christmas. I'll retire to Bedlam."

This lunatic, in letting Scrooge's nephew out, had let two other people in. They were portly gentlemen, pleasant to behold, and now stood, with their hats off, in Scrooge's office. They had books and papers in their hands, and bowed to him.

"Scrooge and Marley's, I believe," said one of the gentlemen, referring to his list. "Have I the pleasure of addressing Mr. Scrooge, or Mr. Marley?"

"Mr. Marley has been dead these seven years," Scrooge replied. "He died seven years ago, this very night."

"We have no doubt his liberality is well represented by his surviving partner," said the gentleman, presenting his credentials.

It certainly was; for they had been two kindred spirits. At the ominous word "liberality" Scrooge frowned, and shook his head, and handed the credentials back.

"At this festive season of the year, Mr. Scrooge," said the gentleman, taking up a pen, "it is more than usually desirable that we should make some slight provision for the poor and destitute, who suffer greatly at the present time. Many thousands are in want of common necessaries; hundreds of thousands are in want of common comforts, sir."

"Are there no prisons?" asked Scrooge.

"Plenty of prisons," said the gentleman, laying down the pen again.

"And the Union workhouses?" demanded Scrooge. "Are they still in operation?"

"They are. Still," returned the gentleman, "I wish I could say they were not."

"The Treadmill and the Poor Law are in full vigour, then?" said Scrooge.

"Both very busy, sir."

"Oh! I was afraid, from what you said at first, that something had occurred to stop them in their useful course," said Scrooge. "I am very glad to hear it."

"Under the impression that they scarcely furnish Christian cheer of mind or body to the multitude," returned the gentleman, "a few of us are endeavouring to raise a fund to buy the Poor some meat and drink, and means of warmth. We choose this time, because it is a time, of all others, when Want is keenly felt, and Abundance rejoices. What shall I put you down for?"

"Nothing!" Scrooge replied.

"You wish to be anonymous?"

"I wish to be left alone," said Scrooge. "Since you ask me what I wish, gentlemen, that is my answer. I don't make merry myself at Christmas, and I can't afford to make idle people merry. I help to support the establishments I have mentioned—they cost enough; and those who are badly off must go there."

"Many can't go there; and many would rather die."

"If they would rather die," said Scrooge, "they had better do it, and decrease the surplus population. Besides—excuse me—I don't know that."

"But you might know it," observed the gentleman.

"It's not my business," Scrooge returned. "It's enough for a man to understand his own business, and not to interfere with other people's. Mine occupies me constantly. Good afternoon, gentlemen!"

Seeing clearly that it would be useless to pursue their point, the gentlemen withdrew. Scrooge resumed his labours with an improved opinion of himself, and in a more facetious temper than was usual with him.

Meanwhile the fog and darkness thickened so, that people ran about with flaring links, proffering their services to go before horses in carriages, and conduct them on their way. The ancient tower of a church, whose gruff old bell was always peeping slily down at Scrooge out of a Gothic window in the wall, became invisible, and struck the hours and quarters in the clouds, with tremulous vibrations afterwards, as if its teeth were chattering in its frozen head up there. The cold became intense. In the main street, at the corner of the court, some labourers were repairing the gas pipes, and had lighted a great fire in a brazier, round which a party of ragged men and boys were gathered: warming their hands and winking their eyes before the blaze in rapture. The water-plug being left in solitude, its overflowings suddenly congealed, and turned to misanthropic ice. The brightness of the shops, where holly sprigs and berries crackled in the lamp heat of the windows, made pale faces ruddy as they passed. Poulterers' and grocers' trades became a splendid joke: a glorious pageant, with which it was next to impossible to believe that such dull principles as bargain and sale had anything to do. The Lord Mayor, in the stronghold of the mighty Mansion House, gave orders to his fifty cooks and butlers to keep Christmas as a Lord Mayor's household should; and even the little tailor, whom he had fined five shillings on the previous Monday for being drunk and blood-thirsty in the streets, stirred up tomorrow's pudding in his garret, while his lean wife and the baby sallied out to buy the beef.

Foggier yet, and colder! Piercing, searching, biting cold. If the good St. Dunstan had but nipped the Evil Spirit's nose with a touch of such weather as that, instead of using his familiar weapons, then indeed he would have roared to lusty purpose. The owner of one scant young nose, gnawed and mumbled by the hungry cold as bones are gnawed by dogs, stooped down at Scrooge's keyhole to regale him with a Christmas carol; but, at the first sound of

> *"God bless you, merry gentleman,*
> *May nothing you dismay!"*

Scrooge seized the ruler with such energy of action, that the singer fled in terror, leaving the keyhole to the fog, and even more congenial frost.

At length the hour of shutting up the counting house arrived. With an ill-will Scrooge dismounted from his stool, and tacitly admitted the fact to the expectant clerk in the tank, who instantly snuffed his candle out, and put on his hat.

"You'll want all day tomorrow, I suppose?" said Scrooge.

"If quite convenient, sir."

"It's not convenient," said Scrooge, "and it's not fair. If I was to stop half a crown for it, you'd think yourself ill used, I'll be bound?"

The clerk smiled faintly.

"And yet," said Scrooge, "you don't think *me* ill used when I pay a day's wages for no work."

The clerk observed that it was only once a year.

"A poor excuse for picking a man's pocket every twenty-fifth of December!" said Scrooge, buttoning his great coat to the chin. "But

I suppose you must have the whole day. Be here all the earlier next morning."

The clerk promised that he would; and Scrooge walked out with a growl. The office was closed in a twinkling, and the clerk, with the long ends of his white comforter dangling below his waist (for he boasted no great coat), went down a slide on Cornhill, at the end of a lane of boys, twenty times, in honour of its being Christmas Eve, and then ran home to Camden Town as hard as he could pelt, to play at blindman's buff.

Scrooge took his melancholy dinner in his usual melancholy tavern; and having read all the newspapers, and beguiled the rest of the evening with his banker's book, went home to bed. He lived in chambers which had once belonged to his deceased partner. They were a gloomy suite of rooms, in a lowering pile of building up a yard, where it had so little business to be, that one could scarcely help fancying it must have run there when it was a young house, playing at hide-and-seek with other houses, and have forgotten the way out again. It was old enough now, and dreary enough; for nobody lived in it but Scrooge, the other rooms being all let out as offices. The yard was so dark that even Scrooge, who knew its every stone, was fain to grope with his hands. The fog and frost so hung about the black old gateway of the house, that it seemed as if the Genius of the Weather sat in mournful meditation on the threshold.

Now, it is a fact that there was nothing at all particular about the knocker on the door, except that it was very large. It is also a fact that Scrooge had seen it, night and morning, during his whole residence in that place; also that Scrooge had as little of what is called fancy about him as any man in the City of London, even including—which is a bold word—the corporation, aldermen, and livery. Let it also be borne in mind that Scrooge had not bestowed one thought on Marley since his last mention of his seven-years'-dead partner that afternoon. And then let any man explain to me, if he can, how it happened that Scrooge, having his key in the lock of the door, saw in the knocker, without its undergoing any intermediate process of change—not a knocker, but Marley's face.

Marley's face. It was not in impenetrable shadow, as the other objects in the yard were, but had a dismal light about it, like a bad lobster in a dark cellar. It was not angry or ferocious, but looked at Scrooge as Marley used to look: with ghostly spectacles turned up on its ghostly forehead. The hair was curiously stirred, as if by breath of hot air; and, though the eyes were wide open, they were perfectly motionless. That, and its livid colour, made it horrible; but its horror seemed to be in spite of the face, and beyond its control, rather than a part of its own expression.

As Scrooge looked fixedly at this phenomenon, it was a knocker again.

To say that he was not startled, or that his blood was not conscious of a terrible sensation to which it had been a stranger from infancy, would be untrue. But he put his hand upon the key he had relinquished, turned it sturdily, walked in, and lighted his candle.

He *did* pause, with a moment's irresolution, before he shut the door; and he *did* look cautiously behind it first, as if he half expected to be terrified with the sight of Marley's pigtail sticking out into the hall. But there was nothing on the back of the door, except the screws and nuts that held the knocker on, so he said, "Pooh, pooh!" and closed it with a bang.

The sound resounded through the house like thunder. Every room above, and every cask in the wine merchant's cellars below, appeared to have a separate peal of echoes of its own. Scrooge was not a man to be frightened by echoes. He fastened the door, and walked across the hall, and up the stairs—slowly, too—trimming his candle as he went.

You may talk vaguely about driving a coach and six up a good old flight of stairs, or through a bad young Act of Parliament; but I mean to say you might have got a hearse up that staircase, and taken it broadwise, with the splinter-bar towards the wall, and the door towards the balustrades: and done it easy. There was plenty of width for that, and room to spare; which is perhaps the reason why Scrooge thought he saw a locomotive hearse going on before him in the gloom. Half a dozen gaslamps out of the street wouldn't have lighted the entry too well, so you may suppose that it was pretty dark with Scrooge's dip.

Up Scrooge went, not caring a button for that. Darkness is cheap, and Scrooge liked it. But, before he shut his heavy door, he walked through his rooms to see that all was right. He had just enough recollection of the face to desire to do that.

Sitting room, bedroom, lumber room. All as they should be. Nobody under the table, nobody under the sofa; a small fire in the grate; spoon and basin ready; and the little saucepan of gruel (Scrooge had a cold in his head) upon the hob. Nobody under the bed; nobody in the closet; nobody in his dressing gown, which was hanging up in a suspicious attitude against the wall. Lumber room as usual. Old fireguard, old shoes, two fish baskets, washing stand on three legs, and a poker.

Quite satisfied, he closed his door, and locked himself in; double locked himself in, which was not his custom. Thus secured against surprise, he took off his cravat; put on his dressing gown and slippers, and his nightcap; and sat down before the fire to take his gruel.

It was a very low fire indeed; nothing on such a bitter night. He was obliged to sit close to it, and brood over it, before he could extract the least sensation of warmth from such a handful of fuel. The fireplace was an old one, built by some Dutch merchant long ago, and paved all round with quaint Dutch tiles, designed to illustrate the Scriptures. There were Cains and Abels, Pharaoh's daughters, Queens of Sheba, Angelic messengers descending through the air on clouds like feather beds, Abrahams, Belshazzars, Apostles putting off to sea in butter-boats, hundreds of figures to attract his thoughts; and yet that face of Marley, seven years dead, came like the ancient Prophet's rod, and swallowed up the whole. If each smooth tile had been a blank at first, with power to shape some picture on its surface from the disjointed fragments of his thoughts, there would have been a copy of old Marley's head on every one.

"Humbug!" said Scrooge; and walked across the room.

After several turns he sat down again. As he threw his head back in the chair, his glance happened to rest upon a bell, a disused bell, that hung in the room, and communicated, for some purpose now forgotten, with a chamber in the highest story of the building. It was with great astonishment, and with a strange, inexplicable dread, that, as he looked, he saw this bell begin to swing. It swung so softly in the outset that it scarcely made a sound; but soon it rang out loudly, and so did every bell in the house.

This might have lasted half a minute, or a minute, but it seemed an hour. The bells ceased, as they had begun, together. They were succeeded by a clanking noise, deep down below, as if some person were dragging a heavy chain over the casks in the wine merchant's cellar. Scrooge then remembered to have heard that ghosts in haunted houses were described as dragging chains.

The cellar door flew open with a booming sound, and then he heard the noise much louder on the floors below; then coming up the stairs; then coming straight towards his door.

"It's humbug still!" said Scrooge. "I won't believe it."

His colour changed, though, when, without a pause, it came on through the heavy door, and passed into the room before his eyes. Upon its coming in, the dying flame leaped up, as though it cried, "I know him! Marley's Ghost!" and fell again.

The same face: the very same. Marley in his pigtail, usual waistcoat, tights, and boots; the tassels on the latter bristling, like his pigtail, and his coat-skirts, and the hair upon his head. The chain he drew was clasped about his middle. It was long, and wound about him like a tail; and it was made (for Scrooge observed it closely) of cash boxes, keys, padlocks, ledgers, deeds, and heavy purses wrought in steel. His body was transparent; so that Scrooge, observing him, and looking through his waistcoat, could see the two buttons on his coat behind.

Scrooge had often heard it said that Marley had no bowels, but he had never believed it until now.

No, nor did he believe it even now. Though he looked the phantom through and through, and saw it standing before him; though he felt the chilling influence of its death-cold eyes; and marked the very texture of the folded kerchief bound about its head and chin, which wrapper he had not observed before; he was still incredulous, and fought against his senses.

"How now!" said Scrooge, caustic and cold as ever. "What do you want with me?"

"Much!"—Marley's voice, no doubt about it.

"Who are you?"

"Ask me who I *was*."

"Who *were* you, then?" said Scrooge, raising his voice. "You're particular, for a shade." He was going to say "*to* a shade," but substituted this, as more appropriate.

"In life I was your partner, Jacob Marley."

"Can you—can you sit down?" asked Scrooge, looking doubtfully at him.

"I can."

"Do it, then."

Scrooge asked the question, because he didn't know whether a ghost so transparent might find himself in a condition to take a chair; and felt that, in the event of its being impossible, it might involve the necessity of an embarrassing explanation. But the Ghost sat down on the opposite side of the fireplace, as if he were quite used to it.

"You don't believe in me," observed the Ghost.

"I don't," said Scrooge.

"What evidence would you have of my reality beyond that of your own senses?"

"I don't know," said Scrooge.

"Why do you doubt your senses?"

"Because," said Scrooge, "a little thing affects them. A slight disorder of the stomach makes them cheats. You may be an undigested bit of beef, a blot of mustard, a crumb of cheese, a fragment of an underdone potato. There's more of gravy than of grave about you, whatever you are!"

Scrooge was not much in the habit of cracking jokes, nor did he feel in his heart by any means waggish then. The truth is, that he tried to be smart, as a means of distracting his own attention, and keeping down his terror; for the spectre's voice disturbed the very marrow in his bones.

To sit staring at those fixed glazed eyes in silence, for a moment, would play, Scrooge felt, the very deuce with him. There was something very awful, too, in the spectre's being provided with an infernal atmosphere of his own. Scrooge could not feel it himself, but this was clearly the case; for though the Ghost sat perfectly motionless, its hair, and skirts, and tassels were still agitated as by the hot vapour from an oven.

"You see this toothpick?" said Scrooge, returning quickly to the charge, for the reason just assigned; and wishing, though it were only for a second, to divert the vision's stony gaze from himself.

"I do," replied the Ghost.

"You are not looking at it," said Scrooge.

"But I see it," said the Ghost, "notwithstanding."

"Well!" returned Scrooge, "I have but to swallow this, and be for the rest of my days persecuted by a legion of goblins, all of my own creation. Humbug, I tell you; humbug!"

At this the spirit raised a frightful cry, and shook its chain with such a dismal and appalling noise, that Scrooge held on tight to his chair, to save himself from falling in a swoon. But how much greater was his horror when the phantom, taking off the bandage round his head, as if it were too warm to wear indoors, its lower jaw dropped down upon its breast!

Scrooge fell upon his knees, and clasped his hands before his face.

"Mercy!" he said. "Dreadful apparition, why do you trouble me?"

"Man of the worldly mind!" replied the Ghost, "do you believe in me or not?"

"I do," said Scrooge. "I must. But why do spirits walk the earth, and why do they come to me?"

"It is required of every man," the Ghost returned, "that the spirit within him should walk abroad among his fellowmen, and travel far and wide; and, if that spirit goes not forth in life, it is condemned to do so after death. It is doomed to wander through the world—oh, woe is me!—and witness what it cannot share, but might have shared on earth, and turned to happiness!"

Again the spectre raised a cry, and shook its chain and wrung its shadowy hands.

"You are fettered," said Scrooge, trembling. "Tell me why?"

"I wear the chain I forged in life," replied the Ghost. "I made it link by link, and yard by yard; I girded it on of my own freewill, and of my own freewill I wore it. Is its pattern strange to *you?*"

Scrooge trembled more and more.

"Or would you know," pursued the Ghost, "the weight and length of the strong coil you bear yourself? It was full as heavy and as long as this, seven Christmas Eves ago. You have laboured on it since. It is a ponderous chain!"

Scrooge glanced about him on the floor, in the expectation of finding himself surrounded by some fifty or sixty fathoms of iron cable, but he could see nothing.

"Jacob!" he said imploringly. "Old Jacob Marley, tell me more! Speak comfort to me, Jacob!"

"I have none to give," the Ghost replied. "It comes from other regions, Ebenezer Scrooge, and is conveyed by other ministers, to other kinds of men. Nor can I tell you what I would. A very little more is all permitted to me. I cannot rest, I cannot stay, I cannot linger anywhere. My spirit never walked beyond our counting house—mark me;—in life my spirit never roved beyond the narrow limits of our money-changing hole; and weary journeys lie before me!"

It was a habit with Scrooge, whenever he became thoughtful, to put his hands in his breeches pockets. Pondering on what the Ghost had said, he did so now, but without lifting up his eyes, or getting off his knees.

"You must have been very slow about it, Jacob," Scrooge observed in a business-like manner, though with humility and deference.

"Slow!" the Ghost repeated.

"Seven years dead," mused Scrooge. "And travelling all the time?"

"The whole time," said the Ghost. "No rest, no peace. Incessant torture of remorse."

"You travel fast?" said Scrooge.

"On the wings of the wind," replied the Ghost.

"You might have got over a great quantity of ground in seven years," said Scrooge.

The Ghost, on hearing this, set up another cry, and clanked its chain so hideously in the dead silence of the night, that the Ward would have been justified in indicting it for a nuisance.

"Oh! Captive, bound, and double-ironed," cried the phantom, "not to know that ages of incessant labour, by immortal creatures, for this earth must pass into eternity before the good of which it is susceptible is all developed! Not to know that any Christian spirit working kindly in its little sphere, whatever it may be, will find its mortal life too short for its vast means of usefulness! Not to know that no space of regret can make amends for one life's opportunities misused! Yet such was I! Oh, such was I!"

"But you were always a good man of business, Jacob," faltered Scrooge, who now began to apply this to himself.

"Business!" cried the Ghost, wringing its hands again. "Mankind was my business. The common welfare was my business; charity, mercy, forbearance, and benevolence were, all, my business. The dealings of my trade were but a drop of water in the comprehensive ocean of my business!"

It held up its chain at arm's length, as if that were the cause of all its unavailing grief, and flung it heavily upon the ground again.

"At this time of the rolling year," the spectre said, "I suffer most. Why did I walk through crowds of fellow-beings with my eyes turned down, and never raise them to that blessed Star which led the Wise Men to a poor abode? Were there no poor homes to which its light would have conducted *me*?"

Scrooge was very much dismayed to hear the spectre going on at this rate, and began to quake exceedingly.

"Hear me!" cried the Ghost. "My time is nearly gone."

"I will," said Scrooge. "But don't be hard upon me! Don't be flowery, Jacob! Pray!"

"How it is that I appear before you in a shape that you can see, I may not tell. I have sat invisible beside you many and many a day."

It was not an agreeable idea. Scrooge shivered, and wiped the perspiration from his brow.

"That is no light part of my penance," pursued the Ghost. "I am here tonight to warn you that you have yet a chance and hope of escaping my fate. A chance and hope of my procuring, Ebenezer."

"You were always a good friend to me," said Scrooge. "Thank'ee!"

"You will be haunted," resumed the Ghost, "by Three Spirits."

Scrooge's countenance fell almost as low as the Ghost's had done.

"Is that the chance and hope you mentioned, Jacob?" he demanded in a faltering voice.

"It is."

"I—I think I'd rather not," said Scrooge.

"Without their visits," said the Ghost, "you cannot hope to shun the path I tread. Expect the first tomorrow when the bell tolls One."

"Couldn't I take 'em all at once, and have it over, Jacob?" hinted Scrooge.

"Expect the second on the next night at the same hour. The third, upon the next night when the last stroke of Twelve has ceased to vibrate. Look to see me no more; and look that, for your own sake, you remember what has passed between us!"

When it had said these words, the spectre took its wrapper from the table, and bound it round its head as before. Scrooge knew this by the smart sound its teeth made when the jaws were brought together by the bandage. He ventured to raise his eyes again, and found his supernatural visitor confronting him in an erect attitude, with its chain wound over and about its arm.

The apparition walked backward from him; and, at every step it took, the window raised itself a little, so that, when the spectre reached it, it was wide open. It beckoned Scrooge to approach, which he did. When they were within two paces of each other, Marley's Ghost held up its hand, warning him to come no nearer. Scrooge stopped.

Not so much in obedience as in surprise and fear; for, on the raising of the hand, he became sensible of confused noises in the air; incoherent sounds of lamentation and regret; wailings inexpressibly sorrowful and self-accusatory. The spectre, after listening for a moment, joined in the mournful dirge; and floated out upon the bleak, dark night.

Scrooge followed to the window: desperate in his curiosity. He looked out.

The air was filled with phantoms, wandering hither and thither in restless haste, and moaning as they went. Every one of them wore chains like Marley's Ghost; some few (they might be guilty governments) were linked together; none were free. Many had been personally known to Scrooge in their lives. He had been quite familiar with one old ghost in a white waistcoat, with a monstrous iron safe attached to its ankle, who cried piteously at being unable to assist a wretched woman with an infant, whom it saw below upon a doorstep. The misery with them all was, clearly, that they sought to interfere, for good, in human matters, and had lost the power forever.

Whether these creatures faded into mist, or mist enshrouded them, he could not tell. But they and their spirit voices faded together; and the night became as it had been when he walked home.

Scrooge closed the window, and examined the door by which the Ghost had entered. It was double locked, as he had locked it with his own hands, and the bolts were undisturbed. He tried to say "Humbug!" but stopped at the first syllable. And being, from the emotion he had undergone, or the fatigues of the day, or his glimpse of the Invisible World, or the dull conversation of the Ghost, or the lateness of the hour, much in need of repose, went straight to bed without undressing, and fell asleep upon the instant.

II

THE FIRST OF THE THREE SPIRITS

WHEN SCROOGE AWOKE IT WAS so dark, that, looking out of bed, he could scarcely distinguish the transparent window from the opaque walls of his chamber. He was endeavouring to pierce the darkness with his ferret eyes, when the chimes of a neighbouring church struck the four quarters. So he listened for the hour.

To his great astonishment, the heavy bell went on from six to seven, and from seven to eight, and regularly up to twelve; then stopped. Twelve! It was past two when he went to bed. The clock was wrong. An icicle must have got into the works. Twelve!

He touched the spring of his repeater, to correct this most preposterous clock. Its rapid little pulse beat twelve, and stopped.

"Why, it isn't possible," said Scrooge, "that I can have slept through a whole day and far into another night. It isn't possible that anything has happened to the sun, and this is twelve at noon!"

The idea being an alarming one, he scrambled out of bed, and groped his way to the window. He was obliged to rub the frost off with the sleeve of his dressing gown before he could see anything; and could see very little then. All he could make out was, that it was still very foggy and extremely cold, and that there was no noise of people running to and fro, and making a great stir, as there unquestionably would have been if night had beaten off bright day, and taken possession of the world. This was a great relief, because "Three days after sight of this First of Exchange pay to Mr. Ebenezer Scrooge or his order," and so forth, would have become a mere United States security if there were no days to count by.

Scrooge went to bed again, and thought, and thought, and thought it over and over, and could make nothing of it. The more he thought, the more perplexed he was; and, the more he endeavoured not to think, the more he thought.

Marley's Ghost bothered him exceedingly. Every time he resolved within himself, after mature inquiry, that it was all a dream, his mind flew back again, like a strong spring released, to its first position, and presented the same problem to be worked all through, "Was it a dream or not?"

Scrooge lay in this state until the chime had gone three quarters more, when he remembered, on a sudden, that the Ghost had warned him of a visitation when the bell tolled one. He resolved to lie awake until the hour was passed; and, considering that he could no more go to sleep than go to Heaven, this was, perhaps, the wisest resolution in his power.

The quarter was so long, that he was more than once convinced he must have sunk into a doze unconsciously, and missed the clock. At length it broke upon his listening ear.

"Ding, dong!"

"A quarter past," said Scrooge, counting.

"Ding, dong!"

"Half past," said Scrooge.

"Ding, dong!"

"A quarter to it," said Scrooge.

"Ding, dong!"

"The hour itself," said Scrooge triumphantly, "and nothing else!"

He spoke before the hour bell sounded, which it now did with a deep, dull, hollow, melancholy ONE. Light flashed up in the room upon the instant, and the curtains of his bed were drawn.

The curtains of his bed were drawn aside, I tell you, by a hand. Not the curtains at his feet, nor the curtains at his back, but those to which his face was addressed. The curtains of his bed were drawn aside; and Scrooge, starting up into a half-recumbent attitude, found himself face to face with the unearthly visitor who drew them: as close to it as I am now to you, and I am standing in the spirit at your elbow.

It was a strange figure—like a child: yet not so like a child as like an old man, viewed through some supernatural medium, which gave him the appearance of having receded from the view, and being diminished to a child's proportions. Its hair, which hung about its neck and down its back, was white, as if with age; and yet the face had not a wrinkle in it, and the tenderest bloom was on the skin. The arms were very long and muscular; the hands the same, as if its hold were of uncommon strength. Its legs and feet, most delicately formed, were, like those upper members, bare. It wore a tunic of the purest white; and round its waist was bound a lustrous belt, the sheen of which was beautiful. It held a branch of fresh green holly in its hand: and, in singular contradiction of that wintry emblem, had its dress trimmed with summer flowers. But the strangest thing about it was, that from the crown of its head there sprung a bright clear jet of light, by which all this was visible; and which was doubtless the occasion of its using, in its duller moments, a great extinguisher for a cap, which it now held under its arm.

Even this, though, when Scrooge looked at it with increasing steadiness, was *not* its strangest quality. For, as its belt sparkled and glittered, now in one part and now in another, and what was light one instant at another time was dark, so the figure itself fluctuated in its distinctness: being now a thing with one arm, now with one leg, now with twenty legs, now a pair of legs without a head, now a head without a body: of which dissolving parts no outline would be visible in the dense gloom wherein they melted away. And, in the very wonder of this, it would be itself again; distinct and clear as ever.

"Are you the Spirit, sir, whose coming was foretold to me?" asked Scrooge.

"I am!"

The voice was soft and gentle. Singularly low, as if, instead of being so close beside him, it were at a distance.

"Who and what are you?" Scrooge demanded.

"I am the Ghost of Christmas Past."

"Long Past?" inquired Scrooge; observant of its dwarfish stature.

"No. Your past."

Perhaps Scrooge could not have told anybody why, if anybody could have asked him; but he had a special desire to see the Spirit in his cap; and begged him to be covered.

"What!" exclaimed the Ghost, "would you so soon put out, with worldly hands, the light I give? Is it not enough that you are one of those whose passions made this cap, and force me through whole trains of years to wear it low upon my brow?"

Scrooge reverently disclaimed all intention to offend or any knowledge of having wilfully "bonneted" the Spirit at any period of his life. He then made bold to inquire what business brought him there.

"Your welfare!" said the Ghost.

Scrooge expressed himself much obliged, but could not help thinking that a night of unbroken rest would have been more conducive to that end. The Spirit must have heard him thinking, for it said immediately:

"Your reclamation, then. Take heed!"

It put out its strong hand as it spoke, and clasped him gently by the arm.

"Rise! And walk with me!"

It would have been in vain for Scrooge to plead that the weather and the hour were not adapted to pedestrian purposes; that bed was warm, and the thermometer a long way below freezing; that he was clad but lightly in his slippers, dressing gown, and nightcap; and that he had a cold upon him at that time. The grasp, though gentle as a woman's hand, was not to be resisted. He rose: but, finding that the Spirit made towards the window, clasped its robe in supplication.

"I am a mortal," Scrooge remonstrated, "and liable to fall."

"Bear but a touch of my hand *there*," said the Spirit, laying it upon his heart, "and you shall be upheld in more than this!"

As the words were spoken, they passed through the wall, and stood upon an open country road, with fields on either hand. The city had entirely vanished. Not a vestige of it was to be seen. The darkness and the mist had vanished with it, for it was a clear, cold, winter day, with the snow upon the ground.

"Good Heaven!" said Scrooge, clasping his hands together as he looked about him. "I was bred in this place. I was a boy here!"

The Spirit gazed upon him mildly. Its gentle touch, though it had been light and instantaneous, appeared still present to the old man's sense of feeling. He was conscious of a thousand odours floating in the air, each one connected with a thousand thoughts, and hopes, and joys, and cares long, long forgotten!

"Your lip is trembling," said the Ghost. "And what is that upon your cheek?"

Scrooge muttered, with an unusual catching in his voice, that it was a pimple; and begged the Ghost to lead him where he would.

"You recollect the way?" inquired the Spirit.

"Remember it!" cried Scrooge with fervour; "I could walk it blindfold."

"Strange to have forgotten it for so many years!" observed the Ghost. "Let us go on."

They walked along the road, Scrooge recognising every gate, and post, and tree, until a little market town appeared in the distance, with its bridge, its church, and winding river. Some shaggy ponies now were seen trotting towards them with boys upon their backs, who called to other boys in country gigs and carts, driven by farmers. All these boys were in great spirits, and shouted to each other, until the broad fields were so full of merry music, that the crisp air laughed to hear it.

"These are but shadows of the things that have been," said the Ghost. "They have no consciousness of us."

The jocund travellers came on; and as they came, Scrooge knew and named them every one. Why was he rejoiced beyond all bounds to see them? Why did his cold eye glisten, and his heart leap up as they went past? Why was he filled with gladness when he heard them give each other Merry Christmas, as they parted at crossroads and by-ways for their several homes? What was merry Christmas to Scrooge? Out upon merry Christmas! What good had it ever done to him?

"The school is not quite deserted," said the Ghost. "A solitary child, neglected by his friends, is left there still."

Scrooge said he knew it. And he sobbed.

They left the high road by a well-remembered lane, and soon approached a mansion of dull red brick, with a little weather-cock surmounted cupola on the roof and a bell hanging in it. It was a large house, but one of broken fortunes: for the spacious offices were little used, their walls were damp and mossy, their windows broken, and their gates decayed. Fowls clucked and strutted in the stables; and the coach-houses and sheds were overrun with grass. Nor was it more retentive of its ancient state within; for, entering the dreary hall, and glancing through the open doors of many rooms, they found them poorly furnished, cold, and vast. There was an earthly savour in the air, a chilly bareness in the place, which associated itself somehow with too much getting up by candlelight, and not too much to eat.

They went, the Ghost and Scrooge, across the hall, to a door at the back of the house. It opened before them, and disclosed a long, bare, melancholy room, made barer still by lines of plain deal forms and desks. At one of these a lonely boy was reading near a feeble fire; and Scrooge sat down upon a form, and wept to see his poor forgotten self as he had used to be.

Not a latent echo in the house, not a squeak and scuffle from the mice behind the panelling, not a drip from the half-thawed water-spout in the dull yard behind, not a sigh among the leafless boughs of one despondent poplar, not the idle swinging of an empty storehouse door, no, not a clicking in the fire, but fell upon the heart of Scrooge with softening influence, and gave a freer passage to his tears.

The Spirit touched him on the arm, and pointed to his younger self, intent upon his reading. Suddenly a man in foreign garments: wonderfully real and distinct to look at: stood outside the window, with an axe stuck in his belt, and leading by the bridle an ass laden with wood.

"Why, it's Ali Baba!" Scrooge exclaimed in ecstasy. "It's dear old honest Ali Baba! Yes, yes, I know. One Christmastime when yonder solitary child was left here all alone, he *did* come, for the first time, just like that. Poor boy! And Valentine," said Scrooge, "and his wild brother, Orson; there they go! And what's his name, who was put down in his drawers, asleep, at the gate of Damascus; don't you see him? And the Sultan's Groom turned upside down by the Genii: there he is upon his head! Serve him right! I'm glad of it. What business had *he* to be married to the Princess?"

To hear Scrooge expending all the earnestness of his nature on such subjects, in a most extraordinary voice between laughing and crying; and to see his heightened and excited face; would have been a surprise to his business friends in the City, indeed.

"There's the Parrot!" cried Scrooge. "Green body and yellow tail, with a thing like a lettuce growing out of the top of his head; there he is! Poor Robin Crusoe he called him, when he came home again after sailing round the island. 'Poor Robin Crusoe, where have you been, Robin Crusoe?' The man thought he was dreaming, but he wasn't. It was the Parrot, you know. There goes Friday, running for his life to the little creek! Halloa! Hoop! Halloo!"

Then, with a rapidity of transition very foreign to his usual character, he said, in pity for his former self, "Poor boy!" and cried again.

"I wish," Scrooge muttered, putting his hand in his pocket, and looking about him, after drying his eyes with his cuff: "but it's too late now."

"What is the matter?" asked the Spirit.

"Nothing," said Scrooge. "Nothing. There was a boy singing a Christmas Carol at my door last night. I should like to have given him something: that's all."

The Ghost smiled thoughtfully, and waved its hand: saying, as it did so, "Let us see another Christmas!"

Scrooge's former self grew larger at the words, and the room became a little darker and more dirty. The panels shrunk, the windows cracked;

fragments of plaster fell out of the ceiling, and the naked laths were shown instead; but how all this was brought about Scrooge knew no more than you do. He only knew that it was quite correct: that everything had happened so; that there he was, alone again, when all the other boys had gone home for the jolly holidays.

He was not reading now, but walking up and down despairingly. Scrooge looked at the Ghost, and, with a mournful shaking of his head, glanced anxiously towards the door.

It opened; and a little girl, much younger than the boy, came darting in, and, putting her arms about his neck, and often kissing him, addressed him as her "dear, dear brother."

"I have come to bring you home, dear brother!" said the child, clapping her tiny hands, and bending down to laugh. "To bring you home, home, home!"

"Home, little Fan?" returned the boy.

"Yes!" said the child, brimful of glee. "Home for good and all. Home forever and ever. Father is so much kinder than he used to be, that home's like Heaven! He spoke so gently to me one dear night when I was going to bed, that I was not afraid to ask him once more if you might come home; and he said yes, you should; and sent me in a coach to bring you. And you're to be a man!" said the child, opening her eyes; "and are never to come back here; but first we're to be together all the Christmas long, and have the merriest time in all the world."

"You are quite a woman, little Fan!" exclaimed the boy.

She clapped her hands and laughed, and tried to touch his head; but, being too little, laughed again, and stood on tiptoe to embrace him. Then she began to drag him, in her childish eagerness, towards the door; and he, nothing loath to go, accompanied her.

A terrible voice in the hall cried, "Bring down Master Scrooge's box, there!" and in the hall appeared the schoolmaster himself, who glared on Master Scrooge with a ferocious condescension, and threw him into a dreadful state of mind by shaking hands with him. He then conveyed him and his sister into the veriest old well of a shivering best parlour that ever was seen, where the maps upon the wall, and the celestial and terrestrial globes in the windows, were waxy with cold. Here he produced a decanter of curiously light wine, and a block of curiously heavy cake, and administered instalments of those dainties to the young people: at the same time sending out a meagre servant to offer a glass of "something" to the postboy who answered that he thanked the gentleman, but, if it was the same tap as he had tasted before, he had rather not. Master Scrooge's trunk being by this time tied on to the top of the chaise, the children bade the schoolmaster goodbye right willingly; and, getting into it, drove gaily down the garden sweep; the quick wheels dashing the hoar frost and snow from off the dark leaves of the evergreens like spray.

"Always a delicate creature, whom a breath might have withered," said the Ghost. "But she had a large heart!"

"So she had," cried Scrooge. "You're right. I will not gainsay it, Spirit. God forbid!"

"She died a woman," said the Ghost, "and had, as I think, children."

"One child," Scrooge returned.

"True," said the Ghost. "Your nephew!"

Scrooge seemed uneasy in his mind; and answered briefly, "Yes."

Although they had but that moment left the school behind them, they were now in the busy thoroughfares of a city, where shadowy passengers passed and repassed; where shadowy carts and coaches battled for the way, and all the strife and tumult of a real city were. It was made plain enough, by the dressing of the shops, that here, too, it was Christmas-time again; but it was evening, and the streets were lighted up.

The Ghost stopped at a certain warehouse door, and asked Scrooge if he knew it.

"Know it!" said Scrooge. "Was I apprenticed here?"

They went in. At sight of an old gentleman in a Welsh wig, sitting behind such a high desk, that if he had been two inches taller, he must have knocked his head against the ceiling, Scrooge cried in great excitement:

"Why, it's old Fezziwig! Bless his heart, it's Fezziwig alive again!"

Old Fezziwig laid down his pen, and looked up at the clock, which pointed to the hour of seven. He rubbed his hands; adjusted his capacious waistcoat; laughed all over himself, from his shoes to his organ of benevolence; and called out, in a comfortable, oily, rich, fat, jovial voice:

"Yo ho, there! Ebenezer! Dick!"

Scrooge's former self, now grown a young man, came briskly in, accompanied by his fellow 'prentice.

"Dick Wilkins, to be sure!" said Scrooge to the Ghost. "Bless me, yes. There he is. He was very much attached to me, was Dick. Poor Dick! Dear, dear!"

"Yo ho, my boys!" said Fezziwig. "No more work tonight. Christmas Eve, Dick. Christmas, Ebenezer! Let's have the shutters up," cried old Fezziwig with a sharp clap of his hands, "before a man can say Jack Robinson!"

You wouldn't believe how those two fellows went at it! They charged into the street with the shutters—one, two, three—had 'em up in their places—four, five, six—barred 'em and pinned 'em—seven, eight, nine—and came back before you could have got to twelve, panting like race-horses.

"Hilli-ho!" cried old Fezziwig, skipping down from the high desk with wonderful agility. "Clear away, my lads, and let's have lots of room here! Hilli-ho, Dick! Chirrup, Ebenezer!"

Clear away! There was nothing they wouldn't have cleared away, or couldn't have cleared away, with old Fezziwig looking on. It was done in a minute. Every movable was packed off, as if it were dismissed from public life for evermore; the floor was swept and watered, the lamps were trimmed, fuel was heaped upon the fire; and the warehouse was as snug, and warm, and dry, and bright a ballroom as you would desire to see upon a winter's night.

In came a fiddler with a music book, and went up to the lofty desk, and made an orchestra of it, and tuned like fifty stomachaches. In came Mrs. Fezziwig, one vast substantial smile. In came the three Miss Fezziwigs, beaming and lovable. In came the six young followers whose hearts they broke. In came all the young men and women employed in the business. In came the housemaid, with her cousin the baker. In came the cook, with her brother's particular friend the milkman. In came the boy from over the way, who was suspected of not having board enough from his master; trying to hide himself behind the girl from next door but one, who was proved to have had her ears pulled by her mistress. In they all came, one after another; some shyly, some boldly, some gracefully, some awkwardly, some pushing, some pulling; in they all came, any how and every how. Away they all went, twenty couple at once; hands half round and back again the other way; down the middle and up again; round and round in various stages of affectionate grouping; old top couple always turning up in the wrong place; new top couple starting off again as soon as they got there; all top couples at last, and not a bottom one to help them! When this result was brought about, old Fezziwig, clapping his hands to stop the dance, cried out, "Well done!" and the fiddler plunged his hot face into a pot of porter, especially provided for that purpose. But, scorning rest upon his reappearance, he instantly began again, though there were no dancers yet, as if the other fiddler had been carried home, exhausted, on a shutter, and he were a brand new man resolved to beat him out of sight, or perish.

There were more dances, and there were forfeits, and more dances, and there was cake, and there was negus, and there was a great piece of Cold Roast, and there was a great piece of Cold Boiled, and there were mince-pies, and plenty of beer. But the great effect of the evening came after the Roast and Boiled, when the fiddler (an artful dog, mind! The sort of man who knew his business better than you or I could have told it him!) struck up "Sir Roger de Coverley." Then old Fezziwig stood out to dance with Mrs. Fezziwig. Top couple, too; with a good stiff piece of work cut out for them; three or four and twenty pair of partners; people who were not to be trifled with; people who *would* dance, and had no notion of walking.

But if they had been twice as many—ah! Four times—old Fezziwig would have been a match for them, and so would Mrs. Fezziwig. As to *her*, she was worthy to be his partner in every sense of the term. If that's not high praise, tell me higher, and I'll use it. A positive light appeared to issue from Fezziwig's calves. They shone in every part of the dance like moons. You couldn't have predicted, at any given time, what would become of them next. And when old Fezziwig and Mrs. Fezziwig had gone all through the dance; advance and retire, both hands to your partner, bow and curtsy, corkscrew, thread-the-needle, and back again to your place; Fezziwig "cut"—cut so deftly, that he appeared to wink with his legs, and came upon his feet again without a stagger.

When the clock struck eleven, this domestic ball broke up. Mr. and Mrs. Fezziwig took their stations, one on either side the door, and, shaking hands with every person individually as he or she went out, wished him or her a Merry Christmas. When everybody had retired but the two 'prentices, they did the same to them; and thus the cheerful voices died away, and the lads were left to their beds; which were under a counter in the backshop.

During the whole of this time Scrooge had acted like a man out of his wits. His heart and soul were in the scene, and with his former self. He corroborated everything, remembered everything, enjoyed everything, and underwent the strangest agitation. It was not until now, when the bright faces of his former self and Dick were turned from them, that he remembered the Ghost, and became conscious that it was looking full upon him, while the light upon its head burnt very clear.

"A small matter," said the Ghost, "to make these silly folks so full of gratitude."

"Small!" echoed Scrooge.

The Spirit signed to him to listen to the two apprentices, who were pouring out their hearts in praise of Fezziwig; and, when he had done so, said:

"Why! Is it not? He has spent but a few pounds of your mortal money: three or four, perhaps. Is that so much that he deserves this praise?"

"It isn't that," said Scrooge, heated by the remark, and speaking unconsciously like his former, not his latter self. "It isn't that, Spirit. He has the power to render us happy or unhappy; to make our service light or burdensome; a pleasure or a toil. Say that his power lies in words and looks; in things so slight and insignificant that it is impossible to add and count 'em up: what then? The happiness he gives is quite as great as if it cost a fortune."

He felt the Spirit's glance, and stopped.

"What is the matter?" asked the Ghost.

"Nothing particular," said Scrooge.

"Something, I think?" the Ghost insisted.

"No," said Scrooge, "no. I should like to be able to say a word or two to my clerk just now. That's all."

His former self turned down the lamps as he gave utterance to the wish; and Scrooge and the Ghost again stood side by side in the open air.

"My time grows short," observed the Spirit. "Quick!"

This was not addressed to Scrooge, or to any one whom he could see, but it produced an immediate effect. For again Scrooge saw himself. He was older now; a man in the prime of life. His face had not the harsh and rigid lines of later years; but it had begun to wear the signs of care and avarice. There was an eager, greedy, restless motion in the eye, which showed the passion that had taken root, and where the shadow of the growing tree would fall.

He was not alone, but sat by the side of a fair young girl in a mourning dress: in whose eyes there were tears, which sparkled in the light that shone out of the Ghost of Christmas Past.

"It matters little," she said softly. "To you, very little. Another idol has displaced me; and, if it can cheer and comfort you in time to come as I would have tried to do, I have no just cause to grieve."

"What Idol has displaced you?" he rejoined.

"A golden one."

"This is the even-handed dealing of the world!" he said. "There is nothing on which it is so hard as poverty; and there is nothing it professes to condemn with such severity as the pursuit of wealth!"

"You fear the world too much," she answered gently. "All your other hopes have merged into the hope of being beyond the chance of its sordid reproach. I have seen your nobler aspirations fall off one by one, until the master passion, Gain, engrosses you. Have I not?"

"What then?" he retorted. "Even if I have grown so much wiser, what then? I am not changed towards you."

She shook her head.

"Am I?"

"Our contract is an old one. It was made when we were both poor, and content to be so, until, in good season, we could improve our worldly fortune by our patient industry. You *are* changed. When it was made you were another man."

"I was a boy," he said impatiently.

"Your own feeling tells you that you were not what you are," she returned. "I am. That which promised happiness when we were one in heart is fraught with misery now that we are two. How often and how keenly I have thought of this I will not say. It is enough that I *have* thought of it, and can release you."

"Have I ever sought release?"

"In words. No. Never."

"In what, then?"

"In a changed nature; in an altered spirit; in another atmosphere of life; another Hope as its great end. In everything that made my love of any worth or value in your sight. If this had never been between us," said the girl, looking mildly, but with steadiness, upon him, "tell me, would you seek me out and try to win me now? Ah, no!"

He seemed to yield to the justice of this supposition in spite of himself. But he said, with a struggle, "You think not."

"I would gladly think otherwise if I could," she answered. "Heaven knows! When *I* have learned a Truth like this, I know how strong and irresistible it must be. But if you were free today, tomorrow, yesterday, can even I believe that you would choose a dowerless girl—you who, in your very confidence with her, weigh everything by Gain: or, choosing her, if for a moment you were false enough to your one guiding principle to do so, do I not know that your repentance and regret would surely follow? I do; and I release you. With a full heart, for the love of him you once were."

He was about to speak; but, with her head turned from him, she resumed.

"You may—the memory of what is past half makes me hope you will—have pain in this. A very, very brief time, and you will dismiss the recollection of it gladly, as an unprofitable dream, from which it happened well that you awoke. May you be happy in the life you have chosen!"

She left him, and they parted.

"Spirit!" said Scrooge, "show me no more! Conduct me home. Why do you delight to torture me?"

"One shadow more!" exclaimed the Ghost.

"No more!" cried Scrooge. "No more! I don't wish to see it. Show me no more!"

But the relentless Ghost pinioned him in both his arms, and forced him to observe what happened next.

They were in another scene and place; a room, not very large or handsome, but full of comfort. Near to the winter fire sat a beautiful young girl, so like that last that Scrooge believed it was the same, until he saw *her*, now a comely matron, sitting opposite her daughter. The noise in this room was perfectly tumultuous, for there were more children there than Scrooge in his agitated state of mind could count; and, unlike the celebrated herd in the poem, they were not forty children conducting themselves like one, but every child was conducting itself like forty. The consequences were uproarious beyond belief; but no one seemed to care; on the contrary, the mother and daughter laughed heartily, and enjoyed it very much; and the latter, soon beginning to mingle in the sports, got pillaged by the young brigands most ruthlessly. What would I not have given to be one of them! Though I never could have been so rude, no, no! I wouldn't for the wealth of all the world have crushed that braided hair, and torn it down; and, for the precious little shoe, I wouldn't have plucked it off, God bless my soul! To save my life. As to measuring her waist in sport, as they did, bold young brood, I couldn't have done it; I should have expected my arm to have grown round it for a punishment, and never come straight again. And yet I should have dearly liked, I own, to have touched her lips; to have questioned her, that she might have opened them; to have looked upon the lashes of her downcast eyes, and never raised a blush; to have let loose waves of hair, an inch of which would be a keepsake beyond price: in short, I should have liked, I do confess, to have had the lightest licence of a child, and yet to have been man enough to know its value.

But now a knocking at the door was heard, and such a rush immediately ensued that she, with laughing face and plundered dress, was borne towards it in the centre of a flushed and boisterous group, just in time to greet the father, who came home attended by a man laden with Christmas toys and presents. Then the shouting and the struggling, and the onslaught that was made on the defenceless porter! The scaling him, with chairs for ladders, to dive into his pockets, despoil him of brown-paper parcels, hold on tight by his cravat, hug him round the neck, pummel his back, and kick his legs in irrepressible affection! The shouts of wonder and delight with which the development of every package was received! The terrible announcement that the baby had been taken in the act of putting a doll's frying pan into his mouth, and was more than suspected of having swallowed a fictitious turkey, glued on a wooden platter! The immense relief of finding this a false alarm! The joy, and gratitude, and ecstasy! They are all indescribable alike. It is enough that by degrees, the children and their emotions got out of the parlour, and, by one stair at a time, up to the top of the house, where they went to bed, and so subsided.

And now Scrooge looked on more attentively than ever, when the master of the house, having his daughter leaning fondly on him, sat down with her and her mother at his own fireside; and when he thought that such another creature, quite as graceful and as full of promise, might have called him father, and been a spring-time in the haggard winter of his life, his sight grew very dim indeed.

"Belle," said the husband, turning to his wife with a smile, "I saw an old friend of yours this afternoon."

"Who was it?"

"Guess!"

"How can I? Tut, don't I know?" she added in the same breath, laughing as he laughed. "Mr. Scrooge."

"Mr. Scrooge it was. I passed his office window; and as it was not shut up, and he had a candle inside, I could scarcely help seeing him. His partner lies upon the point of death, I hear; and there he sat alone. Quite alone in the world, I do believe."

"Spirit!" said Scrooge in a broken voice, "remove me from this place."

"I told you these were shadows of the things that have been," said the Ghost. "That they are what they are, do not blame me!"

"Remove me!" Scrooge exclaimed. "I cannot bear it!"

He turned upon the Ghost, and seeing that it looked upon him with a face in which in some strange way there were fragments of all the faces it had shown him, wrestled with it.

"Leave me! Take me back! Haunt me no longer!"

In the struggle—if that can be called a struggle in which the Ghost, with no visible resistance on its own part, was undisturbed by any effort of its adversary—Scrooge observed that its light was burning high and bright; and dimly connecting that with its influence over him, he seized the extinguisher cap, and by a sudden action pressed it down upon its head.

The Spirit dropped beneath it, so that the extinguisher covered its whole form; but, though Scrooge pressed it down with all his force, he could not hide the light, which streamed from under it in an unbroken flood upon the ground.

He was conscious of being exhausted, and overcome by an irresistible drowsiness; and, further, of being in his own bedroom. He gave the cap a parting squeeze, in which his hand relaxed; and had barely time to reel to bed before he sank into a heavy sleep.

III

THE SECOND OF THE THREE SPIRITS

AWAKING IN THE MIDDLE OF a prodigiously tough snore, and sitting up in bed to get his thoughts together, Scrooge had no occasion to be told that the bell was again upon the stroke of One. He felt that he was restored to consciousness in the right nick of time, for the especial purpose of holding a conference with the second messenger dispatched to him through Jacob Marley's intervention. But, finding that he turned uncomfortably cold when he began to wonder which of his curtains this new spectre would draw back, he put them every one aside with his own hands, and, lying down again, established a sharp look-out all round the bed. For he wished to challenge the Spirit on the moment of its appearance, and did not wish to be taken by surprise and made nervous.

Gentlemen of the free-and-easy sort, who plume themselves on being acquainted with a move or two, and being usually equal to the time of day, express the wide range of their capacity for adventure by observing that they are good for anything from pitch-and-toss to manslaughter; between which opposite extremes, no doubt, there lies a tolerably wide and comprehensive range of subjects. Without venturing for Scrooge quite as hardily as this, I don't mind calling on you to believe that he was ready for a good broad field of strange appearances, and that nothing between a baby and a rhinoceros would have astonished him very much.

Now, being prepared for almost anything, he was not by any means prepared for nothing; and consequently, when the bell struck One, and no shape appeared, he was taken with a violent fit of trembling. Five minutes, ten minutes, a quarter of an hour went by, yet nothing came. All this time he lay upon his bed, the very core and centre of a blaze of ruddy light, which streamed upon it when the clock proclaimed the hour; and which, being only light, was more alarming than a dozen ghosts, as he was powerless to make out what it meant, or would be at; and was sometimes apprehensive that he might be at that very moment an interesting case of spontaneous combustion, without having the consolation of knowing it. At last, however, he began to think—as you or I would have thought at first; for it is always the person not in the predicament who knows what ought to have been done in it, and would unquestionably have done it too—at last, I say, he began to think that the source and secret of this ghostly light might be in the adjoining room, from whence, on further tracing it, it seemed to shine. This idea taking full possession of his mind, he got up softly, and shuffled in his slippers to the door.

The moment Scrooge's hand was on the lock, a strange voice called him by his name, and bade him enter. He obeyed.

It was his own room. There was no doubt about that. But it had undergone a surprising transformation. The walls and ceiling were so hung with living green, that it looked a perfect grove; from every part of which bright gleaming berries glistened. The crisp leaves of holly, mistletoe, and ivy reflected back the light, as if so many little mirrors had been scattered there; and such a mighty blaze went roaring up the chimney as that dull petrifaction of a hearth had never known in Scrooge's time, or Marley's, or for many and many a winter season gone. Heaped up on the floor, to form a kind of throne, were turkeys, geese, game, poultry, brawn, great joints of meat, sucking-pigs, long wreaths of sausages, mince-pies, plum-puddings, barrels of oysters, red-hot chestnuts, cherry-cheeked apples, juicy oranges, luscious pears, immense twelfth-cakes, and seething bowls of punch, that made the chamber dim with their delicious steam. In easy state upon this couch there sat a jolly Giant, glorious to see; who bore a glowing torch, in shape not unlike Plenty's horn, and held it up, high up, to shed its light on Scrooge as he came peeping round the door.

"Come in!" exclaimed the Ghost. "Come in! And know me better, man!"

Scrooge entered timidly, and hung his head before this Spirit. He was not the dogged Scrooge he had been; and, though the Spirit's eyes were clear and kind, he did not like to meet them.

"I am the Ghost of Christmas Present," said the Spirit. "Look upon me!"

Scrooge reverently did so. It was clothed in one simple deep green robe, or mantle, bordered with white fur. This garment hung so loosely on the figure, that its capacious breast was bare, as if disdaining to be warded or concealed by any artifice. Its feet, observable beneath the ample folds of the garment, were also bare; and on its head it wore no other covering than a holly wreath, set here and there with shining icicles. Its dark brown curls were long and free; free as its genial face, its sparkling eye, its open hand, its cheery voice, its unconstrained demeanour, and its joyful air. Girded round its middle was an antique scabbard; but no sword was in it, and the ancient sheath was eaten up with rust.

"You have never seen the like of me before!" exclaimed the Spirit.

"Never," Scrooge made answer to it.

"Have never walked forth with the younger members of my family; meaning (for I am very young) my elder brothers born in these later years?" pursued the Phantom.

"I don't think I have," said Scrooge. "I am afraid I have not. Have you had many brothers, Spirit?"

"More than eighteen hundred," said the Ghost.

"A tremendous family to provide for," muttered Scrooge.

The Ghost of Christmas Present rose.

"Spirit," said Scrooge submissively, "conduct me where you will. I went forth last night on compulsion, and I learnt a lesson which is working now. Tonight, if you have aught to teach me, let me profit by it."

"Touch my robe!"

Scrooge did as he was told, and held it fast.

Holly, mistletoe, red berries, ivy, turkeys, geese, game, poultry, brawn, meat, pigs, sausages, oysters, pies, puddings, fruit, and punch, all vanished instantly. So did the room, the fire, the ruddy glow, the hour of night, and they stood in the city streets on Christmas morning, where (for the weather was severe) the people made a rough, but brisk and not unpleasant kind of music, in scraping the snow from the pavement in front of their dwellings, and from the tops of their houses, whence it was mad delight to the boys to see it come plumping down into the road below, and splitting into artificial little snowstorms.

The house fronts looked black enough, and the windows blacker, contrasting with the smooth white sheet of snow upon the roofs, and with the dirtier snow upon the ground; which last deposit had been ploughed up in deep furrows by the heavy wheels of carts and waggons;

furrows that crossed and recrossed each other hundreds of times where the great streets branched off; and made intricate channels, hard to trace, in the thick yellow mud and icy water. The sky was gloomy, and the shortest streets were choked up with a dingy mist, half thawed, half frozen, whose heavier particles descended in a shower of sooty atoms, as if all the chimneys in Great Britain had, by one consent, caught fire, and were blazing away to their dear hearts' content. There was nothing very cheerful in the climate or the town, and yet was there an air of cheerfulness abroad that the clearest summer air and brightest summer sun might have endeavoured to diffuse in vain.

For, the people who were shovelling away on the housetops were jovial and full of glee; calling out to one another from the parapets, and now and then exchanging a facetious snowball—better-natured missile far than many a wordy jest—laughing heartily if it went right, and not less heartily if it went wrong. The poulterers' shops were still half open, and the fruiterers' were radiant in their glory. There were great, round, pot-bellied baskets of chestnuts, shaped like the waistcoats of jolly old gentlemen, lolling at the doors, and tumbling out into the street in their apoplectic opulence. There were ruddy, brown-faced, broad-girthed Spanish onions, shining in the fatness of their growth like Spanish Friars, and winking from their shelves in wanton slyness at the girls as they went by, and glanced demurely at the hung-up mistletoe. There were pears and apples clustered high in blooming pyramids; there were bunches of grapes, made, in the shopkeepers' benevolence, to dangle from conspicuous hooks that people's mouths might water gratis as they passed; there were piles of filberts, mossy and brown, recalling, in their fragrance, ancient walks among the woods, and pleasant shufflings ankle deep through withered leaves; there were Norfolk Biffins, squab and swarthy, setting off the yellow of the oranges and lemons, and, in the great compactness of their juicy persons, urgently entreating and beseeching to be carried home in paper bags, and eaten after dinner. The very gold and silver fish, set forth among these choice fruits in a bowl, though members of a dull and stagnant-blooded race, appeared to know that there was something going on; and, to a fish, went gasping round and round their little world in slow and passionless excitement.

The Grocers'! Oh, the Grocers'! nearly closed, with perhaps two shutters down, or one; but through those gaps such glimpses! It was not alone that the scales descending on the counter made a merry sound, or that the twine and roller parted company so briskly, or that the canisters were rattled up and down like juggling tricks, or even that the blended scents of tea and coffee were so grateful to the nose, or even that the raisins were so plentiful and rare, the almonds so extremely white, the sticks of cinnamon so long and straight, the other spices so delicious, the candied fruits so caked and spotted with molten sugar as to make the coldest lookers-on feel faint, and subsequently bilious. Nor was it that the figs were moist and pulpy, or that the French plums blushed in modest tartness from their highly-decorated boxes, or that everything was good to eat and in its Christmas dress; but the customers were all so hurried and so eager in the hopeful promise of the day, that they tumbled up against each other at the door, crashing their wicker baskets wildly, and left their purchases upon the counter, and came running back to fetch them, and committed hundreds of the like mistakes, in the best humour possible; while the Grocer and his people were so frank and fresh, that the polished hearts with which they fastened their aprons behind might have been their own, worn outside for general inspection, and for Christmas daws to peck at if they chose.

But soon the steeples called good people all to church and chapel, and away they came, flocking through the streets in their best clothes, and with their gayest faces. And at the same time there emerged, from scores of by-streets, lanes, and nameless turnings, innumerable people, carrying their dinners to the bakers' shops. The sight of these poor revellers appeared to interest the Spirit very much, for he stood with Scrooge beside him in a baker's doorway, and, taking off the covers as their bearers passed, sprinkled incense on their dinners from his torch. And it was a very uncommon kind of torch, for once or twice, when there were angry words between some dinner-carriers who had jostled each other, he shed a few drops of water on them from it, and their good-humour was restored directly. For they said, it was a shame to quarrel upon Christmas Day. And so it was! God love it, so it was!

In time the bells ceased, and the bakers were shut up; and yet there was a genial shadowing forth of all these dinners, and the progress of their cooking, in the thawed blotch of wet above each baker's oven; where the pavement smoked as if its stones were cooking too.

"Is there a peculiar flavour in what you sprinkle from your torch?" asked Scrooge.

"There is. My own."

"Would it apply to any kind of dinner on this day?" asked Scrooge.

"To any kindly given. To a poor one most."

"Why to a poor one most?" asked Scrooge.

"Because it needs it most."

"Spirit!" said Scrooge after a moment's thought. "I wonder you, of all the beings in the many worlds about us, should desire to cramp these people's opportunities of innocent enjoyment."

"I!" cried the Spirit.

"You would deprive them of their means of dining every seventh day, often the only day on which they can be said to dine at all," said Scrooge; "wouldn't you?"

"I!" cried the Spirit.

"You seek to close these places on the Seventh Day," said Scrooge. "And it comes to the same thing."

"*I* seek!" exclaimed the Spirit.

"Forgive me if I am wrong. It has been done in your name, or at least in that of your family," said Scrooge.

"There are some upon this earth of yours," returned the Spirit, "who lay claim to know us, and who do their deeds of passion, pride, ill-will, hatred, envy, bigotry, and selfishness in our name, who are as strange to us, and all our kith and kin, as if they had never lived. Remember that, and charge their doings on themselves, not us."

Scrooge promised that he would; and they went on, invisible, as they had been before, into the suburbs of the town. It was a remarkable quality of the Ghost (which Scrooge had observed at the baker's), that, notwithstanding his gigantic size, he could accommodate himself to any place with ease; and that he stood beneath a low roof quite as gracefully and like a supernatural creature as it was possible he could have done in any lofty hall.

And perhaps it was the pleasure the good Spirit had in showing off this power of his, or else it was his own kind, generous, hearty nature, and his sympathy with all poor men, that led him straight to Scrooge's clerk's; for there he went, and took Scrooge with him, holding to his robe; and, on the threshold of the door, the Spirit smiled, and stopped to bless Bob Cratchit's dwelling with the sprinklings of his torch. Think of that! Bob had but fifteen "Bob" a week himself; he pocketed on Saturdays but fifteen copies of his Christian name; and yet the Ghost of Christmas Present blessed his four-roomed house!

Then up rose Mrs. Cratchit, Cratchit's wife, dressed out but poorly in a twice-turned gown, but brave in ribbons, which are cheap, and make a goodly show for sixpence; and she laid the cloth, assisted by Belinda Cratchit, second of her daughters, also brave in ribbons; while Master

Peter Cratchit plunged a fork into the saucepan of potatoes, and, getting the corners of his monstrous shirt collar (Bob's private property, conferred upon his son and heir in honour of the day) into his mouth, rejoiced to find himself so gallantly attired, and yearned to show his linen in the fashionable Parks. And now two smaller Cratchits, boy and girl, came tearing in, screaming that outside the baker's they had smelt the goose, and known it for their own; and, basking in luxurious thoughts of sage and onion, these young Cratchits danced about the table, and exalted Master Peter Cratchit to the skies, while he (not proud, although his collars nearly choked him) blew the fire, until the slow potatoes, bubbling up, knocked loudly at the saucepan lid to be let out and peeled.

"What has ever got your precious father, then?" said Mrs. Cratchit. "And your brother, Tiny Tim? And Martha warn't as late last Christmas Day by half an hour!"

"Here's Martha, mother!" said a girl, appearing as she spoke.

"Here's Martha, mother!" cried the two young Cratchits. "Hurrah! There's *such* a goose, Martha!"

"Why, bless your heart alive, my dear, how late you are!" said Mrs. Cratchit, kissing her a dozen times, and taking off her shawl and bonnet for her with officious zeal.

"We'd a deal of work to finish up last night," replied the girl, "and had to clear away this morning, mother!"

"Well! Nevermind so long as you are come," said Mrs. Cratchit. "Sit ye down before the fire, my dear, and have a warm, Lord bless ye!"

"No, no! There's father coming," cried the two young Cratchits, who were everywhere at once. "Hide, Martha, hide!"

So Martha hid herself, and in came little Bob, the father, with at least three feet of comforter, exclusive of the fringe, hanging down before him; and his threadbare clothes darned up and brushed to look seasonable; and Tiny Tim upon his shoulder. Alas for Tiny Tim, he bore a little crutch, and had his limbs supported by an iron frame!

"Why, where's our Martha?" cried Bob Cratchit, looking round.

"Not coming," said Mrs. Cratchit.

"Not coming!" said Bob with a sudden declension in his high spirits; for he had been Tim's blood horse all the way from church, and had come home rampant. "Not coming upon Christmas Day!"

Martha didn't like to see him disappointed, if it were only in joke; so she came out prematurely from behind the closet door, and ran into his arms, while the two young Cratchits hustled Tiny Tim, and bore him off into the washhouse, that he might hear the pudding singing in the copper.

"And how did little Tim behave?" asked Mrs. Cratchit when she had rallied Bob on his credulity, and Bob had hugged his daughter to his heart's content.

"As good as gold," said Bob, "and better. Somehow, he gets thoughtful, sitting by himself so much, and thinks the strangest things you ever heard. He told me, coming home, that he hoped the people saw him in the church, because he was a cripple, and it might be pleasant to them to remember upon Christmas Day who made lame beggars walk and blind men see."

Bob's voice was tremulous when he told them this, and trembled more when he said that Tiny Tim was growing strong and hearty.

His active little crutch was heard upon the floor, and back came Tiny Tim before another word was spoken, escorted by his brother and sister to his stool beside the fire; and while Bob, turning up his cuffs—as if, poor fellow, they were capable of being made more shabby—compounded some hot mixture in a jug with gin and lemons, and stirred it round and round, and put it on the hob to simmer, Master Peter and the two ubiquitous young Cratchits went to fetch the goose, with which they soon returned in high procession.

Such a bustle ensued that you might have thought a goose the rarest of all birds; a feathered phenomenon, to which a black swan was a matter of course—and, in truth, it was something very like it in that house. Mrs. Cratchit made the gravy (ready beforehand in a little saucepan) hissing hot; Master Peter mashed the potatoes with incredible vigour; Miss Belinda sweetened up the apple sauce; Martha dusted the hot plates; Bob took Tiny Tim beside him in a tiny corner at the table; the two young Cratchits set chairs for everybody, not forgetting themselves, and, mounting guard upon their posts, crammed spoons into their mouths, lest they should shriek for goose before their turn came to be helped. At last the dishes were set on, and grace was said. It was succeeded by a breathless pause, as Mrs. Cratchit, looking slowly all along the carving-knife, prepared to plunge it in the breast; but when she did, and when the long-expected gush of stuffing issued forth, one murmur of delight arose all round the board, and even Tiny Tim, excited by the two young Cratchits, beat on the table with the handle of his knife, and feebly cried Hurrah!

There never was such a goose. Bob said he didn't believe there ever was such a goose cooked. Its tenderness and flavour, size and cheapness, were the themes of universal admiration. Eked out by apple sauce and mashed potatoes, it was a sufficient dinner for the whole family; indeed, as Mrs. Cratchit said with great delight (surveying one small atom of a bone upon the dish), they hadn't ate it all at last! Yet every one had had enough, and the youngest Cratchits, in particular, were steeped in sage and onion to the eyebrows! But now, the plates being changed by Miss Belinda, Mrs. Cratchit left the room alone—too nervous to bear witnesses—to take the pudding up, and bring it in.

Suppose it should not be done enough! Suppose it should break in turning out! Suppose somebody should have got over the wall of the backyard and stolen it, while they were merry with the goose—a supposition at which the two young Cratchits became livid! All sorts of horrors were supposed.

Hallo! A great deal of steam! The pudding was out of the copper. A smell like a washing day! That was the cloth. A smell like an eating-house and a pastrycook's next door to each other, with a laundress's next door to that! That was the pudding! In half a minute Mrs. Cratchit entered—flushed, but smiling proudly—with the pudding, like a speckled cannon-ball, so hard and firm, blazing in half of half a quartern of ignited brandy, and bedight with Christmas holly stuck into the top.

Oh, a wonderful pudding! Bob Cratchit said, and calmly too, that he regarded it as the greatest success achieved by Mrs. Cratchit since their marriage. Mrs. Cratchit said that, now the weight was off her mind, she would confess she had her doubts about the quantity of flour. Everybody had something to say about it, but nobody said or thought it was at all a small pudding for a large family. It would have been flat heresy to do so. Any Cratchit would have blushed to hint at such a thing.

At last the dinner was all done, the cloth was cleared, the hearth swept, and the fire made up. The compound in the jug being tasted, and considered perfect, apples and oranges were put upon the table, and a shovel full of chestnuts on the fire. Then all the Cratchit family drew round the hearth in what Bob Cratchit called a circle, meaning half a one; and at Bob Cratchit's elbow stood the family display of glass. Two tumblers and a custard cup without a handle.

These held the hot stuff from the jug, however, as well as golden goblets would have done; and Bob served it out with beaming looks, while the chestnuts on the fire sputtered and cracked noisily. Then Bob proposed:

"A merry Christmas to us all, my dears. God bless us!"

Which all the family re-echoed.

"God bless us every one!" said Tiny Tim, the last of all.

He sat very close to his father's side, upon his little stool. Bob held his withered little hand in his, as if he loved the child, and wished to keep him by his side, and dreaded that he might be taken from him.

"Spirit," said Scrooge with an interest he had never felt before, "tell me if Tiny Tim will live."

"I see a vacant seat," replied the Ghost, "in the poor chimney-corner, and a crutch without an owner, carefully preserved. If these shadows remain unaltered by the Future, the child will die."

"No, no," said Scrooge. "Oh, no, kind Spirit! Say he will be spared."

"If these shadows remain unaltered by the Future, none other of my race," returned the Ghost, "will find him here. What then? If he be like to die, he had better do it, and decrease the surplus population."

Scrooge hung his head to hear his own words quoted by the Spirit, and was overcome with penitence and grief.

"Man," said the Ghost, "if man you be in heart, not adamant, forbear that wicked cant until you have discovered What the surplus is, and Where it is. Will you decide what men shall live, what men shall die? It may be that, in the sight of Heaven, you are more worthless and less fit to live than millions like this poor man's child. Oh God! To hear the Insect on the leaf pronouncing on the too much life among his hungry brothers in the dust!"

Scrooge bent before the Ghost's rebuke, and, trembling, cast his eyes upon the ground. But he raised them speedily on hearing his own name.

"Mr. Scrooge!" said Bob. "I'll give you Mr. Scrooge, the Founder of the Feast!"

"The Founder of the Feast, indeed!" cried Mrs. Cratchit, reddening. "I wish I had him here. I'd give him a piece of my mind to feast upon, and I hope he'd have a good appetite for it."

"My dear," said Bob, "the children! Christmas Day."

"It should be Christmas Day, I am sure," said she, "on which one drinks the health of such an odious, stingy, hard, unfeeling man as Mr. Scrooge. You know he is, Robert! Nobody knows it better than you do, poor fellow!"

"My dear!" was Bob's mild answer. "Christmas Day."

"I'll drink his health for your sake and the Day's," said Mrs. Cratchit, "not for his. Long life to him! A merry Christmas and a happy New Year! He'll be very merry and very happy, I have no doubt!"

The children drank the toast after her. It was the first of their proceedings which had no heartiness in it. Tiny Tim drank it last of all, but he didn't care twopence for it. Scrooge was the Ogre of the family. The mention of his name cast a dark shadow on the party, which was not dispelled for full five minutes.

After it had passed away they were ten times merrier than before, from the mere relief of Scrooge the Baleful being done with. Bob Cratchit told them how he had a situation in his eye for Master Peter, which would bring in, if obtained, full five-and-sixpence weekly. The two young Cratchits laughed tremendously at the idea of Peter's being a man of business; and Peter himself looked thoughtfully at the fire from between his collars, as if he were deliberating what particular investments he should favour when he came into the receipt of that bewildering income. Martha, who was a poor apprentice at a milliner's, then told them what kind of work she had to do, and how many hours she worked at a stretch, and how she meant to lie abed tomorrow morning for a good long rest; tomorrow being a holiday she passed at home. Also how she had seen a countess and a lord some days before, and how the lord "was much about as tall as Peter"; at which Peter pulled up his collars so high, that you couldn't have seen his head if you had been there. All this time the chestnuts and the jug went round and round; and by-and-by they had a song, about a lost child travelling in the snow, from Tiny Tim, who had a plaintive little voice, and sang it very well indeed.

There was nothing of high mark in this. They were not a handsome family; they were not well dressed; their shoes were far from being waterproof; their clothes were scanty; and Peter might have known, and very likely did, the inside of a pawnbroker's. But they were happy, grateful, pleased with one another, and contented with the time; and when they faded, and looked happier yet in the bright sprinklings of the Spirit's torch at parting, Scrooge had his eye upon them, and especially on Tiny Tim, until the last.

By this time it was getting dark, and snowing pretty heavily; and as Scrooge and the Spirit went along the streets, the brightness of the roaring fires in kitchens, parlours, and all sorts of rooms was wonderful. Here, the flickering of the blaze showed preparations for a cosy dinner, with hot plates baking through and through before the fire, and deep red curtains, ready to be drawn to shut out cold and darkness. There, all the children of the house were running out into the snow to meet their married sisters, brothers, cousins, uncles, aunts, and be the first to greet them. Here, again, were shadows on the window blinds of guests assembling; and there a group of handsome girls, all hooded and fur-booted, and all chattering at once, tripped lightly off to some near neighbour's house; where, woe upon the single man who saw them enter—artful witches, well they knew it—in a glow!

But, if you had judged from the numbers of people on their way to friendly gatherings, you might have thought that no one was at home to give them welcome when they got there, instead of every house expecting company, and piling up its fires half-chimney high. Blessings on it, how the Ghost exulted! How it bared its breadth of breast, and opened its capacious palm, and floated on, outpouring, with a generous hand, its bright and harmless mirth on everything within its reach! The very lamplighter, who ran on before, dotting the dusky street with specks of light, and who was dressed to spend the evening somewhere, laughed out loudly as the Spirit passed, though little kenned the lamplighter that he had any company but Christmas.

And now, without a word of warning from the Ghost, they stood upon a bleak and desert moor, where monstrous masses of rude stone were cast about, as though it were the burial place or giants; and water spread itself wheresoever it listed; or would have done so, but for the frost that held it prisoner; and nothing grew but moss and furze, and coarse, rank grass. Down in the west the setting sun had left a streak of fiery red, which glared upon the desolation for an instant, like a sullen eye, and, frowning lower, lower, lower yet, was lost in the thick gloom of darkest night.

"What place is this?" asked Scrooge.

"A place where Miners live, who labour in the bowels of the earth," returned the Spirit. "But they know me. See!"

A light shone from the window of a hut, and swiftly they advanced towards it. Passing through the wall of mud and stone, they found a cheerful company assembled round a glowing fire. An old, old man and woman, with their children and their children's children, and another generation beyond that, all decked out gaily in their holiday attire. The old man, in a voice that seldom rose above the howling of the wind upon the barren waste, was singing them a Christmas song; it had been a very old song when he was a boy; and from time to time they all joined in the chorus. So surely as they raised their voices, the old man got quite blithe and loud; and, so surely as they stopped, his vigour sank again.

The Spirit did not tarry here, but bade Scrooge hold his robe, and, passing on above the moor, sped whither? Not to sea? To sea. To Scrooge's horror, looking back, he saw the last of the land, a frightful range of rocks, behind them; and his ears were deafened by the thundering of water, as it rolled and roared, and raged among the dreadful caverns it had worn, and fiercely tried to undermine the earth.

Built upon a dismal reef of sunken rocks, some league or so from shore, on which the waters chafed and dashed, the wild year through, there stood a solitary lighthouse. Great heaps of seaweed clung to its base, and storm birds—born of the wind, one might suppose, as seaweed of the water—rose and fell about it, like the waves they skimmed.

But, even here, two men who watched the light had made a fire that through the loophole in the thick stone wall shed out a ray of brightness on the awful sea. Joining their horny hands over the rough table at which they sat, they wished each other Merry Christmas in their can of grog; and one of them, the elder too, with his face all damaged and scarred with hard weather, as the figurehead of an old ship might be, struck up a sturdy song that was like a gale in itself.

Again the Ghost sped on, above the black and heaving sea—on, on—until, being far away, as he told Scrooge, from any shore, they lighted on a ship. They stood beside the helmsman at the wheel, the look-out in the bow, the officers who had the watch; dark, ghostly figures in their several stations; but every man among them hummed a Christmas tune, or had a Christmas thought, or spoke below his breath to his companion of some bygone Christmas Day, with homeward hopes belonging to it. And every man on board, waking or sleeping, good or bad, had had a kinder word for one another on that day than on any day in the year; and had shared to some extent in its festivities; and had remembered those he cared for at a distance, and had known that they delighted to remember him.

It was a great surprise to Scrooge, while listening to the moaning of the wind, and thinking what a solemn thing it was to move on through the lonely darkness over an unknown abyss, whose depths were secrets as profound as death: it was a great surprise to Scrooge, while thus engaged, to hear a hearty laugh. It was a much greater surprise to Scrooge to recognise it as his own nephew's, and to find himself in a bright, dry, gleaming room, with the Spirit standing smiling by his side, and looking at that same nephew with approving affability!

"Ha, ha!" laughed Scrooge's nephew. "Ha, ha, ha!"

If you should happen, by any unlikely chance, to know a man more blessed in a laugh than Scrooge's nephew, all I can say is, I should like to know him too. Introduce him to me, and I'll cultivate his acquaintance.

It is a fair, even-handed, noble adjustment of things, that, while there is infection in disease and sorrow, there is nothing in the world so irresistibly contagious as laughter and good-humour. When Scrooge's nephew laughed in this way, holding his sides, rolling his head, and twisting his face into the most extravagant contortions, Scrooge's niece, by marriage, laughed as heartily as he. And their assembled friends, being not a bit behindhand, roared out lustily.

"Ha, ha! Ha, ha, ha, ha!"

"He said that Christmas was a humbug, as I live!" cried Scrooge's nephew. "He believed it, too!"

"More shame for him, Fred!" said Scrooge's niece indignantly. Bless those women! They never do anything by halves. They are always in earnest.

She was very pretty; exceedingly pretty. With a dimpled, surprised-looking, capital face; a ripe little mouth, that seemed made to be kissed—as no doubt it was; all kinds of good little dots about her chin, that melted into one another when she laughed; and the sunniest pair of eyes you ever saw in any little creature's head. Altogether she was what you would have called provoking, you know; but satisfactory, too. Oh, perfectly satisfactory!

"He's a comical old fellow," said Scrooge's nephew, "that's the truth; and not so pleasant as he might be. However, his offences carry their own punishment, and I have nothing to say against him."

"I'm sure he is very rich, Fred," hinted Scrooge's niece. "At least, you always tell *me* so."

"What of that, my dear?" said Scrooge's nephew. "His wealth is of no use to him. He don't do any good with it. He don't make himself comfortable with it. He hasn't the satisfaction of thinking—ha, ha, ha!—that he is ever going to benefit Us with it."

"I have no patience with him," observed Scrooge's niece. Scrooge's niece's sisters, and all the other ladies, expressed the same opinion.

"Oh, I have!" said Scrooge's nephew. "I am sorry for him; I couldn't be angry with him if I tried. Who suffers by his ill whims? Himself always. Here he takes it into his head to dislike us, and he won't come and dine with us. What's the consequence? He don't lose much of a dinner."

"Indeed, I think he loses a very good dinner," interrupted Scrooge's niece. Everybody else said the same, and they must be allowed to have been competent judges, because they had just had dinner; and, with the dessert upon the table, were clustered round the fire, by lamp-light.

"Well! I am very glad to hear it," said Scrooge's nephew, "because I haven't any great faith in these young housekeepers. What do *you* say, Topper?"

Topper had clearly got his eye upon one of Scrooge's niece's sisters, for he answered that a bachelor was a wretched outcast, who had no right to express an opinion on the subject. Whereat Scrooge's niece's sister—the plump one with the lace tucker, not the one with the roses—blushed.

"Do go on, Fred," said Scrooge's niece, clapping her hands. "He never finishes what he begins to say! He is such a ridiculous fellow!"

Scrooge's nephew revelled in another laugh, and, as it was impossible to keep the infection off, though the plump sister tried hard to do it with aromatic vinegar, his example was unanimously followed.

"I was only going to say," said Scrooge's nephew, "that the consequence of his taking a dislike to us, and not making merry with us, is, as I think, that he loses some pleasant moments, which could do him no harm. I am sure he loses pleasanter companions than he can find in his own thoughts, either in his mouldy old office or his dusty chambers. I mean to give him the same chance every year, whether he likes it or not, for I pity him. He may rail at Christmas till he dies, but he can't help thinking better of it—I defy him—if he finds me going there in good temper, year after year, and saying, 'Uncle Scrooge, how are you?' If it only puts him in the vein to leave his poor clerk fifty pounds, *that's* something; and I think I shook him yesterday."

It was their turn to laugh, now, at the notion of his shaking Scrooge. But, being thoroughly good-natured, and not much caring what they laughed at, so that they laughed at any rate, he encouraged them in their merriment, and passed the bottle, joyously.

After tea they had some music. For they were a musical family, and knew what they were about when they sung a Glee or Catch, I can assure you: especially Topper, who could growl away in the bass like a good one, and never swell the large veins in his forehead, or get red in the face over it. Scrooge's niece played well upon the harp; and played, among other tunes, a simple little air (a mere nothing: you might learn to whistle it in two minutes), which had been familiar to the child who fetched Scrooge from the boarding school, as he had been reminded by the Ghost of Christmas Past. When this strain of music sounded, all the things that Ghost had shown him came upon his mind; he softened more and more; and thought that if he could have listened to it often, years ago, he might have cultivated the kindnesses of life for his own happiness with his own hands, without resorting to the sexton's spade that buried Jacob Marley.

But they didn't devote the whole evening to music. After awhile they played at forfeits; for it is good to be children sometimes, and never better than at Christmas, when its mighty Founder was a child himself. Stop! There was first a game at blindman's buff. Of course there was. And I no more believe Topper was really blind than I believe he had eyes in his boots. My opinion is, that it was a done thing between him and Scrooge's nephew; and that the Ghost of Christmas Present knew it. The way he went after that plump sister in the lace tucker was an outrage on the credulity of human nature. Knocking down the fire-irons, tumbling over the chairs, bumping up against the piano, smothering himself amongst the curtains, wherever she went, there went he! He always knew where the plump sister was. He wouldn't catch anybody else. If you had fallen up against him (as some of them did) on purpose, he would have made a feint of endeavouring to seize you, which would have been an affront to your understanding, and would instantly have sidled off in the direction of the plump sister. She often cried out that it wasn't fair; and it really was not. But when, at last, he caught her; when, in spite of all her silken rustlings, and her rapid flutterings past him, he got her into a corner whence there was no escape, then his conduct was the most execrable. For his pretending not to know her; his pretending that it was necessary to touch her headdress, and further to assure himself of her identity by pressing a certain ring upon her finger, and a certain chain about her neck, was vile, monstrous! No doubt she told him her opinion of it when, another blind man being in office, they were so very confidential together behind the curtains.

Scrooge's niece was not one of the blindman's buff party, but was made comfortable with a large chair and a footstool, in a snug corner where the Ghost and Scrooge were close behind her. But she joined in the forfeits, and loved her love to admiration with all the letters of the alphabet. Likewise at the game of How, When, and Where, she was very great, and, to the secret joy of Scrooge's nephew, beat her sisters hollow: though they were sharp girls too, as Topper could have told you. There might have been twenty people there, young and old, but they all played, and so did Scrooge; for, wholly forgetting, in the interest he had in what was going on, that his voice made no sound in their ears, he sometimes came out with his guess quite loud, and very often guessed right, too, for the sharpest needle, best Whitechapel, warranted not to cut in the eye, was not sharper than Scrooge; blunt as he took it in his head to be.

The Ghost was greatly pleased to find him in this mood, and looked upon him with such favour, that he begged like a boy to be allowed to stay until the guests departed. But this the Spirit said could not be done.

"Here is a new game," said Scrooge. "One half-hour, Spirit, only one!"

It was a game called Yes and No, where Scrooge's nephew had to think of something, and the rest must find out what; he only answering to their questions yes or no, as the case was. The brisk fire of questioning to which he was exposed elicited from him that he was thinking of an animal, a live animal, rather a disagreeable animal, a savage animal, an animal that growled and grunted sometimes, and talked sometimes, and lived in London, and walked about the streets, and wasn't made a show of, and wasn't led by anybody, and didn't live in a menagerie, and was never killed in a market, and was not a horse, or an ass, or a cow, or a bull, or a tiger, or a dog, or a pig, or a cat, or a bear. At every fresh question that was put to him, this nephew burst into a fresh roar of laughter; and was so inexpressibly tickled, that he was obliged to get up off the sofa, and stamp. At last the plump sister, falling into a similar state, cried out:

"I have found it out! I know what it is, Fred! I know what it is!"

"What is it?" cried Fred.

"It's your uncle Scro-o-o-o-oge!"

Which it certainly was. Admiration was the universal sentiment, though some objected that the reply to "Is it a bear?" ought to have been "Yes": inasmuch as an answer in the negative was sufficient to have diverted their thoughts from Mr. Scrooge, supposing they had ever had any tendency that way.

"He has given us plenty of merriment, I am sure," said Fred, "and it would be ungrateful not to drink his health. Here is a glass of mulled wine ready to our hand at the moment; and I say, 'Uncle Scrooge!'"

"Well! Uncle Scrooge!" they cried.

"A merry Christmas and a happy New Year to the old man, whatever he is!" said Scrooge's nephew. "He wouldn't take it from me, but may he have it nevertheless. Uncle Scrooge!"

Uncle Scrooge had imperceptibly become so gay and light of heart, that he would have pledged the unconscious company in return, and thanked them in an inaudible speech, if the Ghost had given him time.

But the whole scene passed off in the breath of the last word spoken by his nephew; and he and the Spirit were again upon their travels.

Much they saw, and far they went, and many homes they visited, but always with a happy end. The Spirit stood beside sick-beds, and they were cheerful; on foreign lands, and they were close at home; by struggling men, and they were patient in their greater hope; by poverty, and it was rich. In almshouse, hospital, and gaol, in misery's every refuge, where vain man in his little brief authority had not made fast the door, and barred the Spirit out, he left his blessing, and taught Scrooge his precepts.

It was a long night, if it were only a night; but Scrooge had his doubts of this, because the Christmas holidays appeared to be condensed into the space of time they passed together. It was strange, too, that, while Scrooge remained unaltered in his outward form, the Ghost grew older, clearly older. Scrooge had observed this change, but never spoke of it, until they left a children's Twelfth-Night party, when, looking at the Spirit as they stood together in an open place, he noticed that its hair was grey.

"Are spirits' lives so short?" asked Scrooge.

"My life upon this globe is very brief," replied the Ghost. "It ends tonight."

"Tonight!" cried Scrooge.

"Tonight at midnight. Hark! The time is drawing near."

The chimes were ringing the three-quarters past eleven at that moment.

"Forgive me if I am not justified in what I ask," said Scrooge, looking intently at the Spirit's robe, "but I see something strange, and not belonging to yourself, protruding from your skirts. Is it a foot or a claw?"

"It might be a claw, for the flesh there is upon it," was the Spirit's sorrowful reply. "Look here."

From the foldings of its robe it brought two children; wretched, abject, frightful, hideous, miserable. They knelt down at its feet, and clung upon the outside of its garment.

"Oh, Man! Look here! Look, look, down here!" exclaimed the Ghost.

They were a boy and girl. Yellow, meagre, ragged, scowling, wolfish; but prostrate, too, in their humility. Where graceful youth should have filled their features out, and touched them with its freshest tints, a stale and shrivelled hand, like that of age, had pinched, and twisted them, and pulled them into shreds. Where angels might have sat enthroned, devils lurked, and glared out menacing. No change, no degradation, no perversion of humanity, in any grade, through all the mysteries of wonderful creation, has monsters half so horrible and dread.

Scrooge started back, appalled. Having them shown to him in this way, he tried to say they were fine children, but the words choked themselves, rather than be parties to a lie of such enormous magnitude.

"Spirit! Are they yours?" Scrooge could say no more.

"They are Man's," said the Spirit, looking down upon them. "And they cling to me, appealing from their fathers. This boy is Ignorance. This girl is Want. Beware of them both, and all of their degree, but most of all beware this boy, for on his brow I see that written which is Doom, unless the writing be erased. Deny it!" cried the Spirit, stretching out its hand towards the city. "Slander those who tell it ye! Admit it for your factious purposes, and make it worse! And bide the end!"

"Have they no refuge or resource?" cried Scrooge.

"Are there no prisons?" said the Spirit, turning on him for the last time with his own words. "Are there no workhouses?"

The bell struck Twelve.

Scrooge looked about him for the Ghost, and saw it not. As the last stroke ceased to vibrate, he remembered the prediction of old Jacob Marley, and, lifting up his eyes, beheld a solemn Phantom, draped and hooded, coming like a mist along the ground towards him.

IV

THE LAST OF THE SPIRITS

THE PHANTOM SLOWLY, GRAVELY, SILENTLY approached. When it came near him, Scrooge bent down upon his knee; for in the very air through which this Spirit moved it seemed to scatter gloom and mystery.

It was shrouded in a deep black garment, which concealed its head, its face, its form, and left nothing of it visible, save one outstretched hand. But for this, it would have been difficult to detach its figure from the night, and separate it from the darkness by which it was surrounded.

He felt that it was tall and stately when it came beside him, and that its mysterious presence filled him with a solemn dread. He knew no more, for the Spirit neither spoke nor moved.

"I am in the presence of the Ghost of Christmas Yet to Come?" said Scrooge.

The Spirit answered not, but pointed onward with its hand.

"You are about to show me shadows of the things that have not happened, but will happen in the time before us," Scrooge pursued. "Is that so, Spirit?"

The upper portion of the garment was contracted for an instant in its folds, as if the Spirit had inclined its head. That was the only answer he received.

Although well used to ghostly company by this time, Scrooge feared the silent shape so much that his legs trembled beneath him, and he found that he could hardly stand when he prepared to follow it. The Spirit paused a moment, as observing his condition, and giving him time to recover.

But Scrooge was all the worse for this. It thrilled him with a vague uncertain horror to know that, behind the dusky shroud, there were ghostly eyes intently fixed upon him, while he, though he stretched his own to the utmost, could see nothing but a spectral hand and one great heap of black.

"Ghost of the Future!" he exclaimed, "I fear you more than any spectre I have seen. But, as I know your purpose is to do me good, and as I hope to live to be another man from what I was, I am prepared to bear you company, and do it with a thankful heart. Will you not speak to me?"

It gave him no reply. The hand was pointed straight before them.

"Lead on!" said Scrooge. "Lead on! The night is waning fast, and it is precious time to me, I know. Lead on, Spirit!"

The phantom moved away as it had come towards him. Scrooge followed in the shadow of its dress, which bore him up, he thought, and carried him along.

They scarcely seemed to enter the City; for the City rather seemed to spring up about them, and encompass them of its own act. But there they were in the heart of it; on 'Change, amongst the merchants; who hurried up and down, and chinked the money in their pockets, and conversed in groups, and looked at their watches, and trifled thoughtfully with their great gold seals; and so forth, as Scrooge had seen them often.

The Spirit stopped beside one little knot of business men. Observing that the hand was pointed to them, Scrooge advanced to listen to their talk.

"No," said a great fat man with a monstrous chin, "I don't know much about it either way. I only know he's dead."

"When did he die?" inquired another.

"Last night, I believe."

"Why, what was the matter with him?" asked a third, taking a vast quantity of snuff out of a very large snuff-box. "I thought he'd never die."

"God knows," said the first with a yawn.

"What has he done with his money?" asked a red-faced gentleman with a pendulous excrescence on the end of his nose, that shook like the gills of a turkey-cock.

"I haven't heard," said the man with the large chin, yawning again. "Left it to his company, perhaps. He hasn't left it to *me*. That's all I know."

This pleasantry was received with a general laugh.

"It's likely to be a very cheap funeral," said the same speaker; "for, upon my life, I don't know of anybody to go to it. Suppose we make up a party, and volunteer?"

"I don't mind going if a lunch is provided," observed the gentleman with the excrescence on his nose. "But I must be fed if I make one."

Another laugh.

"Well, I am the most disinterested among you, after all," said the first speaker, "for I never wear black gloves, and I never eat lunch. But I'll offer to go if anybody else will. When I come to think of it, I'm not at all sure that I wasn't his most particular friend; for we used to stop and speak whenever we met. Bye, bye!"

Speakers and listeners strolled away, and mixed with other groups. Scrooge knew the men, and looked towards the Spirit for an explanation.

The Phantom glided on into a street. Its finger pointed to two persons meeting. Scrooge listened again, thinking that the explanation might lie here.

He knew these men, also, perfectly. They were men of business: very wealthy, and of great importance. He had made a point always of standing well in their esteem: in a business point of view, that is; strictly in a business point of view.

"How are you?" said one.

"How are you?" returned the other.

"Well!" said the first. "Old Scratch has got his own at last, hey?"

"So I am told," returned the second. "Cold, isn't it?"

"Seasonable for Christmastime. You are not a skater, I suppose?"

"No. No. Something else to think of. Goodmorning!"

Not another word. That was their meeting, their conversation, and their parting.

Scrooge was at first inclined to be surprised that the Spirit should attach importance to conversations apparently so trivial; but, feeling assured that they must have some hidden purpose, he set himself to consider what it was likely to be. They could scarcely be supposed to have any bearing on the death of Jacob, his old partner, for that was Past, and this Ghost's province was the Future. Nor could he think of any one immediately connected with himself, to whom he could apply them. But nothing doubting that, to whomsoever they applied, they had some latent moral for his own improvement, he resolved to treasure up every word he heard, and everything he saw; and especially to observe the shadow of himself when it appeared. For he had an expectation that the conduct of his future self would give him the clue he missed, and would render the solution of these riddles easy.

He looked about in that very place for his own image, but another man stood in his accustomed corner, and, though the clock pointed to his usual time of day for being there, he saw no likeness of himself among the multitudes that poured in through the Porch. It gave him little surprise, however; for he had been revolving in his mind a change of life, and thought and hoped he saw his newborn resolutions carried out in this.

Quiet and dark, beside him stood the Phantom, with its outstretched hand. When he roused himself from his thoughtful quest, he fancied, from the turn of the hand, and its situation in reference to himself, that the Unseen Eyes were looking at him keenly. It made him shudder, and feel very cold.

They left the busy scene, and went into an obscure part of the town, where Scrooge had never penetrated before, although he recognised its situation and its bad repute. The ways were foul and narrow; the shops and houses wretched; the people half naked, drunken, slipshod, ugly. Alleys and archways, like so many cesspools, disgorged their offences of smell, and dirt, and life upon the straggling streets; and the whole quarter reeked with crime, with filth and misery.

Far in this den of infamous resort, there was a low-browed, beetling shop, below a penthouse roof, where iron, old rags, bottles, bones, and greasy offal were bought. Upon the floor within were piled up heaps of rusty keys, nails, chains, hinges, files, scales, weights, and refuse iron of all kinds. Secrets that few would like to scrutinise were bred and hidden in mountains of unseemly rags, masses of corrupted fat, and sepulchres of bones. Sitting in among the wares he dealt in, by a charcoal stove made of old bricks, was a grey-haired rascal, nearly seventy years of age, who had screened himself from the cold air without by a frouzy curtaining of miscellaneous tatters hung upon a line, and smoked his pipe in all the luxury of calm retirement.

Scrooge and the Phantom came into the presence of this man, just as a woman with a heavy bundle slunk into the shop. But she had scarcely entered, when another woman, similarly laden, came in too, and she was closely followed by a man in faded black, who was no less startled by the sight of them than they had been upon the recognition of each other. After a short period of blank astonishment, in which the old man with the pipe had joined them, they all three burst into a laugh.

"Let the charwoman alone to be the first!" cried she who had entered first. "Let the laundress alone to be the second; and let the undertaker's man alone to be the third. Look here, old Joe, here's a chance! If we haven't all three met here without meaning it!"

"You couldn't have met in a better place," said old Joe, removing his pipe from his mouth. "Come into the parlour. You were made free of it long ago, you know; and the other two an't strangers. Stop till I shut the door of the shop. Ah! How it skreeks! There an't such a rusty bit of metal in the place as its own hinges, I believe; and I'm sure there's no such old bones here as mine. Ha! ha! We're all suitable to our calling, we're well matched. Come into the parlour. Come into the parlour."

The parlour was the space behind the screen of rags. The old man raked the fire together with an old stair-rod, and, having trimmed his smoky lamp (for it was night) with the stem of his pipe, put it into his mouth again.

While he did this, the woman who had already spoken threw her bundle on the floor, and sat down in a flaunting manner on a stool; crossing her elbows on her knees, and looking with a bold defiance at the other two.

"What odds, then? What odds, Mrs. Dilber?" said the woman. "Every person has a right to take care of themselves. *He* always did!"

"That's true, indeed!" said the laundress. "No man more so."

"Why, then, don't stand staring as if you was afraid, woman! Who's the wiser? We're not going to pick holes in each other's coats, I suppose?"

"No, indeed!" said Mrs. Dilber and the man together. "We should hope not."

"Very well, then!" cried the woman. "That's enough. Who's the worse for the loss of a few things like these? Not a dead man, I suppose?"

"No, indeed," said Mrs. Dilber, laughing.

"If he wanted to keep 'em after he was dead, a wicked old screw," pursued the woman, "why wasn't he natural in his lifetime? If he had been, he'd have had somebody to look after him when he was struck with Death, instead of lying gasping out his last there, alone by himself."

"It's the truest word that ever was spoke," said Mrs. Dilber, "It's a judgment on him."

"I wish it was a little heavier judgment," replied the woman; "and it should have been, you may depend upon it, if I could have laid my hands on anything else. Open that bundle, old Joe, and let me know the value of it. Speak out plain. I'm not afraid to be the first, nor afraid for them to see it. We knew pretty well that we were helping ourselves before we met here, I believe. It's no sin. Open the bundle, Joe."

But the gallantry of her friends would not allow of this; and the man in faded black, mounting the breach first, produced *his* plunder. It was not extensive. A seal or two, a pencil case, a pair of sleeve-buttons, and a brooch of no great value, were all. They were severally examined and appraised by old Joe, who chalked the sums he was disposed to give for each upon the wall, and added them up into a total when he found that there was nothing more to come.

"That's your account," said Joe, "and I wouldn't give another sixpence, if I was to be boiled for not doing it. Who's next?"

Mrs. Dilber was next. Sheets and towels, a little wearing apparel, two old-fashioned silver tea spoons, a pair of sugar-tongs, and a few boots. Her account was stated on the wall in the same manner.

"I always give too much to ladies. It's a weakness of mine, and that's the way I ruin myself," said old Joe. "That's your account. If you asked me for another penny, and made it an open question, I'd repent of being so liberal, and knock off half a crown."

"And now undo *my* bundle, Joe," said the first woman.

Joe went down on his knees for the greater convenience of opening it, and, having unfastened a great many knots, dragged out a large heavy roll of some dark stuff.

"What do you call this?" said Joe. "Bed curtains?"

"Ah!" returned the woman, laughing and leaning forward on her crossed arms. "Bed curtains!"

"You don't mean to say you took 'em down, rings and all, with him lying there?" said Joe.

"Yes, I do," replied the woman. "Why not?"

"You were born to make your fortune," said Joe, "and you'll certainly do it."

"I certainly shan't hold my hand, when I can get anything in it by reaching it out, for the sake of such a man as He was, I promise you, Joe," returned the woman coolly. "Don't drop that oil upon the blankets, now."

"His blankets?" asked Joe.

"Whose else's do you think?" replied the woman. "He isn't likely to take cold without 'em, I dare say."

"I hope he didn't die of anything catching? Eh?" said old Joe, stopping in his work, and looking up.

"Don't you be afraid of that," returned the woman. "I an't so fond of his company that I'd loiter about him for such things, if he did. Ah! You may look through that shirt till your eyes ache; but you won't find a hole in it, nor a threadbare place. It's the best he had, and a fine one too. They'd have wasted it, if it hadn't been for me."

"What do you call wasting of it?" asked old Joe.

"Putting it on him to be buried in, to be sure," replied the woman with a laugh. "Somebody was fool enough to do it, but I took it off again. If calico an't good enough for such a purpose, it isn't good enough for anything. It's quite as becoming to the body. He can't look uglier than he did in that one."

Scrooge listened to this dialogue in horror. As they sat grouped about their spoil, in the scanty light afforded by the old man's lamp, he viewed them with a detestation and disgust which could hardly have been greater, though they had been obscene demons, marketing the corpse itself.

"Ha, ha!" laughed the same woman when old Joe, producing a flannel bag with money in it, told out their several gains upon the ground. "This is the end of it, you see! He frightened every one away from him when he was alive, to profit us when he was dead! Ha, ha, ha!"

"Spirit!" said Scrooge, shuddering from head to foot. "I see, I see. The case of this unhappy man might be my own. My life tends that way now. Merciful Heaven, what is this?"

He recoiled in terror, for the scene had changed, and now he almost touched a bed: a bare, uncurtained bed: on which, beneath a ragged sheet, there lay a something covered up, which, though it was dumb, announced itself in awful language.

The room was very dark, too dark to be observed with any accuracy, though Scrooge glanced round it in obedience to a secret impulse, anxious to know what kind of room it was. A pale light, rising in the outer air, fell straight upon the bed: and on it, plundered and bereft, unwatched, unwept, uncared for, was the body of this man.

Scrooge glanced towards the Phantom. Its steady hand was pointed to the head. The cover was so carelessly adjusted that the slightest raising of it, the motion of a finger upon Scrooge's part, would have disclosed the face. He thought of it, felt how easy it would be to do, and longed to do it; but had no more power to withdraw the veil than to dismiss the spectre at his side.

Oh, cold, cold, rigid, dreadful Death, set up thine altar here, and dress it with such terrors as thou hast at thy command: for this is thy dominion! But of the loved, revered, and honoured head thou canst not turn one hair to thy dread purposes, or make one feature odious. It is not that the hand is heavy, and will fall down when released; it is not that the heart and pulse are still; but that the hand WAS open, generous, and true; the heart brave, warm, and tender; and the pulse a man's. Strike, Shadow, strike! And see his good deeds springing from the wound, to sow the world with life immortal!

No voice pronounced these words in Scrooge's ears, and yet he heard them when he looked upon the bed. He thought, if this man could be raised up now, what would be his foremost thoughts? Avarice, hard dealing, griping cares? They have brought him to a rich end, truly!

He lay, in the dark, empty house, with not a man, a woman, or a child to say he was kind to me in this or that, and for the memory of one kind word I will be kind to him. A cat was tearing at the door, and there was a sound of gnawing rats beneath the hearthstone. What *they* wanted in the room of death, and why they were so restless and disturbed, Scrooge did not dare to think.

"Spirit!" he said, "this is a fearful place. In leaving it, I shall not leave its lesson, trust me. Let us go!"

Still the Ghost pointed with an unmoved finger to the head.

"I understand you," Scrooge returned, "and I would do it if I could. But I have not the power, Spirit. I have not the power."

Again it seemed to look upon him.

"If there is any person in the town who feels emotion caused by this man's death," said Scrooge, quite agonised, "show that person to me, Spirit! I beseech you."

The Phantom spread its dark robe before him for a moment, like a wing; and, withdrawing it, revealed a room by daylight, where a mother and her children were.

She was expecting someone, and with anxious eagerness; for she walked up and down the room; started at every sound; looked out from the window; glanced at the clock; tried, but in vain, to work with her needle; and could hardly bear the voices of her children in their play.

At length the long-expected knock was heard. She hurried to the door, and met her husband; a man whose face was careworn and depressed, though he was young. There was a remarkable expression in it now; a kind of serious delight of which he felt ashamed, and which he struggled to repress.

He sat down to the dinner that had been hoarding for him by the fire, and, when she asked him faintly what news (which was not until after a long silence), he appeared embarrassed how to answer.

"Is it good," she said, "or bad?" to help him.

"Bad," he answered.

"We are quite ruined?"

"No. There is hope yet, Caroline."

"If *he* relents," she said, amazed, "there is! Nothing is past hope, if such a miracle has happened."

"He is past relenting," said her husband. "He is dead."

She was a mild and patient creature, if her face spoke truth; but she was thankful in her soul to hear it, and she said so with clasped hands. She prayed forgiveness the next moment, and was sorry; but the first was the emotion of her heart.

"What the half-drunken woman, whom I told you of last night, said to me when I tried to see him and obtain a week's delay, and what I thought was a mere excuse to avoid me, turns out to have been quite true. He was not only very ill, but dying, then."

"To whom will our debt be transferred?"

"I don't know. But, before that time, we shall be ready with the money; and, even though we were not, it would be bad fortune indeed to find so merciless a creditor in his successor. We may sleep tonight with light hearts, Caroline!"

Yes. Soften it as they would, their hearts were lighter. The children's faces, hushed and clustered round to hear what they so little understood, were brighter; and it was a happier house for this man's death! The only emotion that the Ghost could show him, caused by the event, was one of pleasure.

"Let me see some tenderness connected with a death," said Scrooge; "or that dark chamber, Spirit, which we left just now, will be forever present to me."

The Ghost conducted him through several streets familiar to his feet; and, as they went along, Scrooge looked here and there to find himself, but nowhere was he to be seen. They entered poor Bob Cratchit's house,—the dwelling he had visited before,—and found the mother and the children seated round the fire.

Quiet. Very quiet. The noisy little Cratchits were as still as statues in one corner, and sat looking up at Peter, who had a book before him. The mother and her daughters were engaged in sewing. But surely they were very quiet!

"'And he took a child, and set him in the midst of them.'"

Where had Scrooge heard those words? He had not dreamed them. The boy must have read them out, as he and the Spirit crossed the threshold. Why did he not go on?

The mother laid her work upon the table, and put her hand up to her face.

"The colour hurts my eyes," she said.

The colour? Ah, poor Tiny Tim!

"They're better now again," said Cratchit's wife. "It makes them weak by candlelight; and I wouldn't show weak eyes to your father, when he comes home, for the world. It must be near his time."

"Past it rather," Peter answered, shutting up his book. "But I think he has walked a little slower than he used, these few last evenings, mother."

They were very quiet again. At last she said, and in a steady, cheerful voice, that only faltered once:

"I have known him walk with—I have known him walk with Tiny Tim upon his shoulder very fast indeed."

"And so have I," cried Peter. "Often."

"And so have I," exclaimed another. So had all.

"But he was very light to carry," she resumed, intent upon her work, "and his father loved him so, that it was no trouble: no trouble. And there is your father at the door!"

She hurried out to meet him; and little Bob in his comforter—he had need of it, poor fellow—came in. His tea was ready for him on the hob, and they all tried who should help him to it most. Then the two young Cratchits got upon his knees, and laid, each child, a little cheek against his face, as if they said, "Don't mind it, father. Don't be grieved!"

Bob was very cheerful with them, and spoke pleasantly to all the family. He looked at the work upon the table, and praised the industry and speed of Mrs. Cratchit and the girls. They would be done long before Sunday, he said.

"Sunday! You went today, then, Robert?" said his wife.

"Yes, my dear," returned Bob. "I wish you could have gone. It would have done you good to see how green a place it is. But you'll see it often. I promised him that I would walk there on a Sunday. My little, little child!" cried Bob. "My little child!"

He broke down all at once. He couldn't help it. If he could have helped it, he and his child would have been farther apart, perhaps, than they were.

He left the room, and went upstairs into the room above, which was lighted cheerfully, and hung with Christmas. There was a chair set close beside the child, and there were signs of someone having been there lately. Poor Bob sat down in it, and, when he had thought a little and composed himself, he kissed the little face. He was reconciled to what had happened, and went down again quite happy.

They drew about the fire, and talked; the girls and mother working still. Bob told them of the extraordinary kindness of Mr. Scrooge's nephew, whom he had scarcely seen but once, and who, meeting him in the street that day, and seeing that he looked a little—"just a little down, you know," said Bob, inquired what had happened to distress him. "On which," said Bob, "for he is the pleasantest-spoken gentleman you ever heard, I told him. 'I am heartily sorry for it, Mr. Cratchit,' he said, 'and heartily sorry for your good wife.' By-the-bye, how he ever knew *that* I don't know."

"Knew what, my dear?"

"Why, that you were a good wife," replied Bob.

"Everybody knows that," said Peter.

"Very well observed, my boy!" cried Bob. "I hope they do. 'Heartily sorry,' he said, 'for your good wife. If I can be of service to you in any way,' he said, giving me his card, 'that's where I live. Pray come to me.' Now, it wasn't," cried Bob, "for the sake of anything he might be able to do for us, so much as for his kind way, that this was quite delightful. It really seemed as if he had known our Tiny Tim, and felt with us."

"I'm sure he's a good soul!" said Mrs. Cratchit.

"You would be sure of it, my dear," returned Bob, "if you saw and spoke to him. I shouldn't be at all surprised—mark what I say!—if he got Peter a better situation."

"Only hear that, Peter," said Mrs. Cratchit.

"And then," cried one of the girls, "Peter will be keeping company with someone, and setting up for himself."

"Get along with you!" retorted Peter, grinning.

"It's just as likely as not," said Bob, "one of these days; though there's plenty of time for that, my dear. But, however and whenever we part from one another, I am sure we shall none of us forget poor Tiny Tim—shall we—or this first parting that there was among us?"

"Never, father!" cried they all.

"And I know," said Bob, "I know, my dears, that when we recollect how patient and how mild he was, although he was a little, little child, we shall not quarrel easily among ourselves, and forget poor Tiny Tim in doing it."

"No, never, father!" they all cried again.

"I am very happy," said little Bob, "I am very happy!"

Mrs. Cratchit kissed him, his daughters kissed him, the two young Cratchits kissed him, and Peter and himself shook hands. Spirit of Tiny Tim, thy childish essence was from God!

"Spectre," said Scrooge, "something informs me that our parting moment is at hand. I know it, but I know not how. Tell me what man that was whom we saw lying dead?"

The Ghost of Christmas Yet To Come conveyed him, as before—though at a different time, he thought: indeed, there seemed no order in these latter visions, save that they were in the Future—into the resorts of business men, but showed him not himself. Indeed, the Spirit did not stay for anything, but went straight on, as to the end just now desired, until besought by Scrooge to tarry for a moment.

"This court," said Scrooge, "through which we hurry now, is where my place of occupation is, and has been for a length of time. I see the house. Let me behold what I shall be in days to come."

The Spirit stopped; the hand was pointed elsewhere.

"The house is yonder," Scrooge exclaimed. "Why do you point away?"

The inexorable finger underwent no change.

Scrooge hastened to the window of his office, and looked in. It was an office still, but not his. The furniture was not the same, and the figure in the chair was not himself. The Phantom pointed as before.

He joined it once again, and, wondering why and whither he had gone, accompanied it until they reached an iron gate. He paused to look round before entering.

A churchyard. Here, then, the wretched man, whose name he had now to learn, lay underneath the ground. It was a worthy place. Walled in by houses; overrun by grass and weeds, the growth of vegetation's death, not life; choked up with too much burying; fat with repleted appetite. A worthy place!

The Spirit stood among the graves, and pointed down to One. He advanced towards it trembling. The Phantom was exactly as it had been, but he dreaded that he saw new meaning in its solemn shape.

"Before I draw nearer to that stone to which you point," said Scrooge, "answer me one question. Are these the shadows of the things that Will be, or are they shadows of the things that May be only?"

Still the Ghost pointed downward to the grave by which it stood.

"Men's courses will foreshadow certain ends, to which, if persevered in, they must lead," said Scrooge. "But if the courses be departed from, the ends will change. Say it is thus with what you show me!"

The Spirit was immovable as ever.

Scrooge crept towards it, trembling as he went; and, following the finger, read upon the stone of the neglected grave his own name, EBENEZER SCROOGE.

"Am *I* that man who lay upon the bed?" he cried upon his knees.

The finger pointed from the grave to him, and back again.

"No, Spirit! Oh no, no!"

The finger still was there.

"Spirit!" he cried, tight clutching at its robe, "hear me! I am not the man I was. I will not be the man I must have been but for this intercourse. Why show me this, if I am past all hope?"

For the first time the hand appeared to shake.

"Good Spirit," he pursued, as down upon the ground he fell before it: "your nature intercedes for me, and pities me. Assure me that I yet may change these shadows you have shown me by an altered life?"

The kind hand trembled.

"I will honour Christmas in my heart, and try to keep it all the year. I will live in the Past, the Present, and the Future. The Spirits of all Three shall strive within me. I will not shut out the lessons that they teach. Oh, tell me I may sponge away the writing on this stone!"

In his agony, he caught the spectral hand. It sought to free itself, but he was strong in his entreaty, and detained it. The Spirit, stronger yet, repulsed him.

Holding up his hands in a last prayer to have his fate reversed, he saw an alteration in the Phantom's hood and dress. It shrunk, collapsed, and dwindled down into a bedpost.

V

The End of it

YES! AND THE BEDPOST WAS his own. The bed was his own, the room was his own. Best and happiest of all, the Time before him was his own, to make amends in!

"I will live in the Past, the Present, and the Future!" Scrooge repeated as he scrambled out of bed. "The Spirits of all Three shall strive within me. Oh, Jacob Marley! Heaven and the Christmas Time be praised for this! I say it on my knees, old Jacob; on my knees!"

He was so fluttered and so glowing with his good intentions, that his broken voice would scarcely answer to his call. He had been sobbing violently in his conflict with the Spirit, and his face was wet with tears.

"They are not torn down," cried Scrooge, folding one of his bed-curtains in his arms, "they are not torn down, rings and all. They are here—I am here—the shadows of the things that would have been may be dispelled. They will be. I know they will!"

His hands were busy with his garments all this time; turning them inside out, putting them on upside down, tearing them, mislaying them, making them parties to every kind of extravagance.

"I don't know what to do!" cried Scrooge, laughing and crying in the same breath; and making a perfect Laocoön of himself with his stockings. "I am as light as a feather, I am as happy as an angel, I am as merry as a school boy. I am as giddy as a drunken man. A merry Christmas to everybody! A happy New Year to all the world! Hallo here! Whoop! Hallo!"

He had frisked into the sitting room, and was now standing there: perfectly winded.

"There's the saucepan that the gruel was in!" cried Scrooge, starting off again, and going round the fireplace. "There's the door by which the Ghost of Jacob Marley entered! There's the corner where the Ghost of Christmas Present sat! There's the window where I saw the wandering Spirits! It's all right, it's all true, it all happened. Ha, ha, ha!"

Really, for a man who had been out of practice for so many years, it was a splendid laugh, a most illustrious laugh. The father of a long, long line of brilliant laughs!

"I don't know what day of the month it is," said Scrooge. "I don't know how long I have been among the Spirits. I don't know anything.

I'm quite a baby. Nevermind. I don't care. I'd rather be a baby. Hallo! Whoop! Hallo here!"

He was checked in his transports by the churches ringing out the lustiest peals he had ever heard. Clash, clash, hammer; ding, dong, bell! Bell, dong, ding; hammer, clang, clash! Oh, glorious, glorious!

Running to the window, he opened it, and put out his head. No fog, no mist; clear, bright, jovial, stirring, cold; cold, piping for the blood to dance to; Golden sunlight; Heavenly sky; sweet fresh air; merry bells. Oh, glorious! Glorious!

"What's today?" cried Scrooge, calling downward to a boy in Sunday clothes, who perhaps had loitered in to look about him.

"EH?" returned the boy with all his might of wonder.

"What's today, my fine fellow?" said Scrooge.

"Today!" replied the boy. "Why, CHRISTMAS DAY."

"It's Christmas Day!" said Scrooge to himself. "I haven't missed it. The Spirits have done it all in one night. They can do anything they like. Of course they can. Of course they can. Hallo, my fine fellow!"

"Hallo!" returned the boy.

"Do you know the Poulterer's in the next street but one, at the corner?" Scrooge inquired.

"I should hope I did," replied the lad.

"An intelligent boy!" said Scrooge. "A remarkable boy! Do you know whether they've sold the prize Turkey that was hanging up there?—Not the little prize Turkey: the big one?"

"What! The one as big as me?" returned the boy.

"What a delightful boy!" said Scrooge. "It's a pleasure to talk to him. Yes, my buck!"

"It's hanging there now," replied the boy.

"Is it?" said Scrooge. "Go and buy it."

"Walk-ER!" exclaimed the boy.

"No, no," said Scrooge, "I am in earnest. Go and buy it, and tell 'em to bring it here, that I may give them the directions where to take it. Come back with the man, and I'll give you a shilling. Come back with him in less than five minutes, and I'll give you half a crown!"

The boy was off like a shot. He must have had a steady hand at a trigger who could have got a shot off half so fast.

"I'll send it to Bob Cratchit's," whispered Scrooge, rubbing his hands, and splitting with a laugh. "He shan't know who sends it. It's twice the size of Tiny Tim. Joe Miller never made such a joke as sending it to Bob's will be!"

The hand in which he wrote the address was not a steady one; but write it he did, somehow, and went down-stairs to open the street-door, ready for the coming of the poulterer's man. As he stood there, waiting his arrival, the knocker caught his eye.

"I shall love it as long as I live!" cried Scrooge, patting it with his hand. "I scarcely ever looked at it before. What an honest expression it has in its face! It's a wonderful knocker!—Here's the Turkey. Hallo! Whoop! How are you? Merry Christmas!"

It *was* a Turkey! He never could have stood upon his legs, that bird. He would have snapped 'em short off in a minute, like sticks of sealing-wax.

"Why, it's impossible to carry that to Camden Town," said Scrooge. "You must have a cab."

The chuckle with which he said this, and the chuckle with which he paid for the Turkey, and the chuckle with which he paid for the cab, and the chuckle with which he recompensed the boy, were only to be exceeded by the chuckle with which he sat down breathless in his chair again, and chuckled till he cried.

Shaving was not an easy task, for his hand continued to shake very much; and shaving requires attention, even when you don't dance while you are at it. But, if he had cut the end of his nose off, he would have put a piece of sticking-plaster over it, and been quite satisfied.

He dressed himself "all in his best," and at last got out into the streets. The people were by this time pouring forth, as he had seen them with the Ghost of Christmas Present; and, walking with his hands behind him, Scrooge regarded every one with a delighted smile. He looked so irresistibly pleasant, in a word, that three or four good-humoured fellows said, "Goodmorning, sir! A merry Christmas to you!" And Scrooge said often afterwards that, of all the blithe sounds he had ever heard, those were the blithest in his ears.

He had not gone far when, coming on towards him, he beheld the portly gentleman who had walked into his counting house the day before, and said, "Scrooge and Marley's, I believe?" It sent a pang across his heart to think how this old gentleman would look upon him when they met; but he knew what path lay straight before him, and he took it.

"My dear sir," said Scrooge, quickening his pace, and taking the old gentleman by both his hands, "how do you do? I hope you succeeded yesterday. It was very kind of you. A merry Christmas to you, sir!"

"Mr. Scrooge?"

"Yes," said Scrooge. "That is my name, and I fear it may not be pleasant to you. Allow me to ask your pardon. And will you have the goodness—" Here Scrooge whispered in his ear.

"Lord bless me!" cried the gentleman, as if his breath were taken away. "My dear Mr. Scrooge, are you serious?"

"If you please," said Scrooge. "Not a farthing less. A great many back-payments are included in it, I assure you. Will you do me that favour?"

"My dear sir," said the other, shaking hands with him, "I don't know what to say to such munifi—"

"Don't say anything, please," retorted Scrooge. "Come and see me. Will you come and see me?"

"I will!" cried the old gentleman. And it was clear he meant to do it.

"Thankee," said Scrooge. "I am much obliged to you. I thank you fifty times. Bless you!"

He went to church, and walked about the streets, and watched the people hurrying to and fro, and patted the children on the head, and questioned beggars, and looked down into the kitchens of houses, and up to the windows; and found that everything could yield him pleasure. He had never dreamed that any walk—that anything—could give him so much happiness. In the afternoon he turned his steps towards his nephew's house.

He passed the door a dozen times before he had the courage to go up and knock. But he made a dash, and did it.

"Is your master at home, my dear?" said Scrooge to the girl. Nice girl! Very.

"Yes sir."

"Where is he, my love?" said Scrooge.

"He's in the dining room, sir, along with mistress. I'll show you up-stairs, if you please."

"Thank'ee. He knows me," said Scrooge, with his hand already on the dining room lock. "I'll go in here, my dear."

He turned it gently, and sidled his face in round the door. They were looking at the table (which was spread out in great array); for these young housekeepers are always nervous on such points, and like to see that everything is right.

"Fred!" said Scrooge.

Dear heart alive, how his niece by marriage started! Scrooge had forgotten, for the moment, about her sitting in the corner with the footstool, or he wouldn't have done it on any account.

"Why, bless my soul!" cried Fred, "who's that?"

"It's I. Your uncle Scrooge. I have come to dinner. Will you let me in, Fred?"

Let him in! It is a mercy he didn't shake his arm off. He was at home in five minutes. Nothing could be heartier. His niece looked just the same. So did Topper when *he* came. So did the plump sister when *she* came. So did every one when *they* came. Wonderful party, wonderful games, wonderful unanimity, won-der-ful happiness!

But he was early at the office next morning. Oh, he was early there! If he could only be there first, and catch Bob Cratchit coming late! That was the thing he had set his heart upon.

And he did it; yes, he did! The clock struck nine. No Bob. A quarter past. No Bob. He was full eighteen minutes and a half behind his time. Scrooge sat with his door wide open, that he might see him come into the tank.

His hat was off before he opened the door; his comforter too. He was on his stool in a jiffy; driving away with his pen, as if he were trying to overtake nine o'clock.

"Hallo!" growled Scrooge in his accustomed voice as near as he could feign it. "What do you mean by coming here at this time of day?"

"I am very sorry, sir," said Bob. "I *am* behind my time."

"You are!" repeated Scrooge. "Yes. I think you are. Step this way, sir, if you please."

"It's only once a year, sir," pleaded Bob, appearing from the tank. "It shall not be repeated. I was making rather merry yesterday, sir."

"Now, I'll tell you what, my friend," said Scrooge. "I am not going to stand this sort of thing any longer. And therefore," he continued, leaping from his stool, and giving Bob such a dig in the waistcoat that he staggered back into the tank again: "and therefore I am about to raise your salary!"

Bob trembled, and got a little nearer to the ruler. He had a momentary idea of knocking Scrooge down with it, holding him, and calling to the people in the court for help and a strait-waistcoat.

"A merry Christmas, Bob!" said Scrooge with an earnestness that could not be mistaken, as he clapped him on the back. "A merrier Christmas, Bob, my good fellow, than I have given you for many a year! I'll raise your salary, and endeavour to assist your struggling family, and we will discuss your affairs this very afternoon, over a Christmas bowl of smoking bishop, Bob! Make up the fires and buy another coal-scuttle before you dot another i, Bob Cratchit!"

SCROOGE WAS BETTER THAN HIS word. He did it all, and infinitely more; and to Tiny Tim, who did NOT die, he was a second father. He became as good a friend, as good a master, and as good a man as the good old City knew, or any other good old city, town, or borough in the good old world. Some people laughed to see the alteration in him, but he let them laugh, and little heeded them; for he was wise enough to know that nothing ever happened on this globe, for good, at which some people did not have their fill of laughter in the outset; and, knowing that such as these would be blind anyway, he thought it quite as well that they should wrinkle up their eyes in grins as have the malady in less attractive forms. His own heart laughed: and that was quite enough for him.

He had no further intercourse with Spirits, but lived upon the Total-Abstinence Principle ever afterwards; and it was always said of him that he knew how to keep Christmas well, if any man alive possessed the knowledge. May that be truly said of us, and all of us! And so, as Tiny Tim observed, God bless Us, Every One!

OLD CHRISTMAS

Christmas

T HERE IS NOTHING IN ENGLAND that exercises a more delightful spell over my imagination than the lingerings of the holiday customs and rural games of former times. They recall the pictures my fancy used to draw in the May morning of life, when as yet I only knew the world through books, and believed it to be all that poets had painted it; and they bring with them the flavour of those honest days of yore, in which, perhaps with equal fallacy, I am apt to think the world was more home-bred, social, and joyous than at present. I regret to say that they are daily growing more and more faint, being gradually worn away by time, but still more obliterated by modern fashion. They resemble those picturesque morsels of Gothic architecture which we see crumbling in various parts of the country, partly dilapidated by the waste of ages, and partly lost in the additions and alterations of latter days. Poetry, however, clings with cherishing fondness about the rural game and holiday revel, from which it has derived so many of its themes—as the ivy winds its rich foliage about the Gothic arch and mouldering tower, gratefully repaying their support by clasping together their tottering remains, and, as it were, embalming them in verdure.

Of all the old festivals, however, that of Christmas awakens the strongest and most heartfelt associations. There is a tone of solemn and sacred feeling that blends with our conviviality, and lifts the spirit to a state of hallowed and elevated enjoyment. The services of the church about this season are extremely tender and inspiring. They dwell on the beautiful story of the origin of our faith, and the pastoral scenes that accompanied its announcement. They gradually increase in fervour and pathos during the season of Advent, until they break forth in full jubilee on the morning that brought peace and goodwill to men. I do not know a grander effect of music on the moral feelings than to hear the full choir and the pealing organ performing a Christmas anthem in a cathedral, and filling every part of the vast pile with triumphant harmony.

It is a beautiful arrangement, also, derived from days of yore, that this festival, which commemorates the announcement of the religion of peace and love, has been made the season for gathering together of family connections, and drawing closer again those bands of kindred hearts which the cares and pleasures and sorrows of the world are continually operating to cast loose; of calling back the children of a family who have launched forth in life, and wandered widely asunder, once more to assemble about the paternal hearth, that rallying-place of the affections, there to grow young and loving again among the endearing mementoes of childhood.

There is something in the very season of the year that gives a charm to the festivity of Christmas. At other times we derive a great portion of our pleasures from the mere beauties of nature. Our feelings sally forth and dissipate themselves over the sunny landscape, and we "live abroad and everywhere." The song of the bird, the murmur of the stream, the breathing fragrance of spring, the soft voluptuousness of summer, the golden pomp of autumn; earth with its mantle of refreshing green, and heaven with its deep delicious blue and its cloudy magnificence, all fill us with mute but exquisite delight, and we revel in the luxury of mere sensation. But in the depth of winter, when nature lies despoiled of every charm, and wrapped in her shroud of sheeted snow, we turn for our gratifications to moral sources. The dreariness and desolation of the landscape, the short gloomy days and darksome nights, while they circumscribe our wanderings, shut in our feelings also from rambling abroad, and make us more keenly disposed for the pleasures of the social circle. Our thoughts are more concentrated; our friendly sympathies more aroused. We feel more sensibly the charm of each other's society, and are brought more closely together by dependence on each other for enjoyment. Heart calleth unto heart; and we draw our pleasures from the deep wells of living kindness, which lie in the quiet recesses of our bosoms; and which, when resorted to, furnish forth the pure element of domestic felicity.

The pitchy gloom without makes the heart dilate on entering the room filled with the glow and warmth of the evening fire. The ruddy blaze diffuses an artificial summer and sunshine through the room, and lights up each countenance into a kindlier welcome. Where does the honest face of hospitality expand into a broader and more cordial smile—where is the shy glance of love more sweetly eloquent—than by the winter fireside? and as the hollow blast of wintry wind rushes through the hall, claps the distant door, whistles about the casement, and rumbles down the chimney, what can be more grateful than that feeling of sober and sheltered security with which we look round upon the comfortable chamber and the scene of domestic hilarity?

The English, from the great prevalence of rural habits throughout every class of society, have always been fond of those festivals and holidays which agreeably interrupt the stillness of country life; and they were, in former days, particularly observant of the religious and social rites of Christmas. It is inspiring to read even the dry details which some antiquarians have given of the quaint humours, the burlesque pageants, the complete abandonment to mirth and good-fellowship, with which this festival was celebrated. It seemed to throw open every door, and unlock every heart. It brought the peasant and the peer together, and blended all ranks in one warm generous flow of joy and kindness. The old halls of castles and manor-houses resounded with the harp and the Christmas carol, and their ample boards groaned under the weight of hospitality. Even the poorest cottage welcomed the festive season with green decorations of bay and holly—the cheerful fire glanced its rays through the lattice, inviting the passenger to raise the latch, and join the gossip knot huddled round the hearth, beguiling the long evening with legendary jokes and oft-told Christmas tales.

One of the least pleasing effects of modern refinement is the havoc it has made among the hearty old holiday customs. It has completely taken off the sharp touchings and spirited reliefs of these embellishments of life, and has worn down society into a more smooth and polished, but certainly a less characteristic surface. Many of the games and ceremonials of Christmas have entirely disappeared, and, like the sherris sack of old Falstaff, are become matters of speculation and dispute among commentators. They flourished in times full of spirit and lustihood, when men enjoyed life roughly, but heartily and vigorously; times wild and picturesque, which have furnished poetry with its richest materials, and the drama with its most attractive variety of characters and manners. The world has become more worldly. There is more of dissipation, and less of enjoyment. Pleasure has expanded into a broader, but a shallower stream, and has forsaken many of those deep and quiet channels where it flowed sweetly through the calm bosom of domestic life. Society has acquired a more enlightened and elegant tone; but it has lost many of its strong local peculiarities, its home-bred feelings, its honest fireside delights. The traditionary customs of golden-hearted antiquity, its feudal hospitalities, and lordly wassailings, have passed away with the baronial castles and stately manor-houses in which they were celebrated. They comported with the shadowy hall, the great oaken gallery, and the tapestried parlour, but are unfitted to the light showy saloons and gay drawing rooms of the modern villa.

Shorn, however, as it is, of its ancient and festive honours, Christmas is still a period of delightful excitement in England. It is gratifying to see that home-feeling completely aroused which seems to hold so powerful a place in every English bosom. The preparations making on every side for the social board that is again to unite friends and kindred; the presents of good cheer passing and repassing, those tokens of regard, and quickeners of kind feelings; the evergreens distributed about houses and churches, emblems of peace and gladness; all these have the most pleasing effect in producing fond associations, and kindling benevolent sympathies. Even the sound of the waits, rude as may be their minstrelsy, breaks upon the mid-watches of a winter night with the effect of perfect harmony. As I have been awakened by them in that still and solemn hour, "when deep sleep falleth upon man," I have listened with a hushed delight, and connecting them with the sacred and joyous occasion, have almost fancied them into another celestial choir, announcing peace and goodwill to mankind.

How delightfully the imagination, when wrought upon by these moral influences, turns everything to melody and beauty: The very crowing of the cock, who is sometimes heard in the profound repose of the country, "telling the night watches to his feathery dames," was thought by the common people to announce the approach of this sacred festival:—

> *"Some say that ever 'gainst that season comes*
> *Wherein our Saviour's birth is celebrated,*
> *This bird of dawning singeth all night long:*
> *And then, they say, no spirit dares stir abroad;*
> *The nights are wholesome—then no planets strike,*
> *No fairy takes, no witch hath power to charm,*
> *So hallow'd and so gracious is the time."*

Amidst the general call to happiness, the bustle of the spirits, and stir of the affections, which prevail at this period, what bosom can remain insensible? It is, indeed, the season of regenerated feeling—the season for kindling, not merely the fire of hospitality in the hall, but the genial flame of charity in the heart.

The scene of early love again rises green to memory beyond the sterile waste of years; and the idea of home, fraught with the fragrance of home-dwelling joys, reanimates the drooping spirit,—as the Arabian breeze will sometimes waft the freshness of the distant fields to the weary pilgrim of the desert.

Stranger and sojourner as I am in the land—though for me no social hearth may blaze, no hospitable roof throw open its doors, nor the warm grasp of friendship welcome me at the threshold—yet I feel the influence of the season beaming into my soul from the happy looks of those around me. Surely happiness is reflective, like the light of heaven; and every countenance, bright with smiles, and glowing with innocent enjoyment, is a mirror transmitting to others the rays of a supreme and ever-shining benevolence. He who can turn churlishly away from contemplating the felicity of his fellow-beings, and sit down darkling and repining in his loneliness when all around is joyful, may have his moments of strong excitement and selfish gratification, but he wants the genial and social sympathies which constitute the charm of a merry Christmas.

The Stage Coach

IN THE PRECEDING PAPER I have made some general observations on the Christmas festivities of England, and am tempted to illustrate them by some anecdotes of a Christmas passed in the country; in perusing which I would most courteously invite my reader to lay aside the austerity of wisdom, and to put on that genuine holiday spirit which is tolerant of folly, and anxious only for amusement.

In the course of a December tour in Yorkshire, I rode for a long distance in one of the public coaches, on the day preceding Christmas. The coach was crowded, both inside and out, with passengers, who, by their talk, seemed principally bound to the mansions of relations or friends to eat the Christmas dinner. It was loaded also with hampers of game, and baskets and boxes of delicacies; and hares hung dangling their long ears about the coachman's box,—presents from distant friends for the impending feast. I had three fine rosy-cheeked schoolboys for my fellow-passengers inside, full of the buxom health and manly spirit which I have observed in the children of this country. They were returning home for the holidays in high glee, and promising themselves a world of enjoyment. It was delightful to hear the gigantic plans of pleasure of the little rogues, and the impracticable feats they were to perform during their six weeks' emancipation from the abhorred thraldom of book, birch, and pedagogue. They were full of anticipations of the meeting with the family and household, down to the very cat and dog; and of the joy they were to give their little sisters by the presents with which their pockets were crammed; but the meeting to which they seemed to look forward with the greatest impatience was with Bantam, which I found to be a pony, and, according to their talk, possessed of more virtues than any steed since the days of Bucephalus. How he could trot! how he could run! and then such leaps as he would take—there was not a hedge in the whole country that he could not clear.

They were under the particular guardianship of the coachman, to whom, whenever an opportunity presented, they addressed a host of questions, and pronounced him one of the best fellows in the whole world. Indeed, I could not but notice the more than ordinary air of bustle and importance of the coachman, who wore his hat a little on one side, and had a large bunch of Christmas greens stuck in the button-hole of his coat. He is always a personage full of mighty care and business, but he is particularly so during this season, having so many commissions to execute in consequence of the great interchange of presents. And here, perhaps, it may not be unacceptable to my untravelled readers, to have a sketch that may serve as a general representation of this very numerous and important class of functionaries, who have a dress, a manner, a language, an air, peculiar to themselves, and prevalent throughout the fraternity; so that, wherever an English stage-coachman may be seen, he cannot be mistaken for one of any other craft or mystery.

He has commonly a broad, full face, curiously mottled with red, as if the blood had been forced by hard feeding into every vessel of the skin; he is swelled into jolly dimensions by frequent potations of malt liquors, and his bulk is still further increased by a multiplicity of coats, in which he is buried like a cauliflower, the upper one reaching to his heels. He wears a broad-brimmed, low-crowned hat; a huge roll of coloured handkerchief about his neck, knowingly knotted and tucked in at the bosom; and has in summer-time a large bouquet of flowers in his button-hole; the present, most probably, of some enamoured country lass. His waistcoat is commonly of some bright colour, striped; and his small-clothes extend far below the knees, to meet a pair of jockey boots which reach about half-way up his legs.

All this costume is maintained with much precision; he has a pride in having his clothes of excellent materials; and, notwithstanding the seeming grossness of his appearance, there is still discernible that neatness and propriety of person, which is almost inherent in an Englishman. He enjoys great consequence and consideration along the road; has frequent conferences with the village housewives, who look upon him as a man of great trust and dependence; and he seems to have a good understanding with every bright-eyed country lass. The moment he arrives where the horses are to be changed, he throws down the reins with something of an air, and abandons the cattle to the care of the ostler; his duty being merely to drive from one stage to another. When off the box, his hands are thrust in the pockets of his greatcoat, and he rolls about the inn-yard with an air of the most absolute lordliness. Here he is generally surrounded by an admiring throng of ostlers, stable boys, shoe-blacks, and those nameless hangers-on that infest inns and taverns, and run errands, and do all kinds of odd jobs, for the privilege of battening on the drippings of the kitchen and the leakage of the tap room. These all look up to him as to an oracle; treasure up his cant phrases; echo his opinions about horses and other topics of jockey lore; and, above all, endeavour to imitate his air and carriage. Every ragamuffin that has a coat to his back thrusts his hands in the pockets, rolls in his gait, talks slang, and is an embryo Coachey.

Perhaps it might be owing to the pleasing serenity that reigned in my own mind, that I fancied I saw cheerfulness in every countenance throughout the journey. A stage coach, however, carries animation always with it, and puts the world in motion as it whirls along. The horn sounded at the entrance of a village, produces a general bustle. Some hasten forth to meet friends; some with bundles and bandboxes to secure places, and in the hurry of the moment can hardly take leave of the group that accompanies them. In the meantime, the coachman has a world of small commissions to execute. Sometimes he delivers a hare or pheasant; sometimes jerks a small parcel or newspaper to the door of a public-house; and sometimes, with knowing leer and words of sly import, hands to some half-blushing, half-laughing housemaid an odd-shaped billet-doux from some rustic admirer. As the coach rattles through the village, every one runs to the window, and you have glances on every side of fresh country faces, and blooming giggling girls. At the corners are assembled juntas of village idlers and wise men, who take their stations there for the important purpose of seeing company pass;

but the sagest knot is generally at the blacksmith's, to whom the passing of the coach is an event fruitful of much speculation. The smith, with the horse's heel in his lap, pauses as the vehicle whirls by; the Cyclops round the anvil suspend their ringing hammers, and suffer the iron to grow cool; and the sooty spectre in brown paper cap, labouring at the bellows, leans on the handle for a moment, and permits the asthmatic engine to heave a long-drawn sigh, while he glares through the murky smoke and sulphureous gleams of the smithy.

Perhaps the impending holiday might have given a more than usual animation to the country, for it seemed to me as if everybody was in good looks and good spirits. Game, poultry, and other luxuries of the table, were in brisk circulation in the villages; the grocers', butchers', and fruiterers' shops were thronged with customers. The housewives were stirring briskly about, putting their dwellings in order; and the glossy branches of holly, with their bright red berries, began to appear at the windows. The scene brought to mind an old writer's account of Christmas preparations:—"Now capons and hens, besides turkeys, geese, and ducks, with beef and mutton—must all die; for in twelve days a multitude of people will not be fed with a little. Now plums and spice, sugar and honey, square it among pies and broth. Now or never must music be in tune, for the youth must dance and sing to get them a heat, while the aged sit by the fire. The country maid leaves half her market, and must be sent again, if she forgets a pack of cards on Christmas Eve. Great is the contention of Holly and Ivy, whether master or dame wears the breeches. Dice and cards benefit the butler; and if the cook do not lack wit, he will sweetly lick his fingers."

I was roused from this fit of luxurious meditation by a shout from my little travelling companions. They had been looking out of the coach windows for the last few miles, recognising every tree and cottage as they approached home, and now there was a general burst of joy—"There's John! And there's old Carlo! And there's Bantam!" cried the happy little rogues, clapping their hands.

At the end of a lane there was an old sober-looking servant in livery waiting for them: he was accompanied by a superannuated pointer, and by the redoubtable Bantam, a little old rat of a pony, with a shaggy mane and long rusty tail, who stood dozing quietly by the roadside, little dreaming of the bustling times that awaited him.

I was pleased to see the fondness with which the little fellows leaped about the steady old footman, and hugged the pointer, who wriggled his whole body for joy. But Bantam was the great object of interest; all wanted to mount at once; and it was with some difficulty that John arranged that they should ride by turns, and the eldest should ride first.

Off they set at last; one on the pony, with the dog bounding and barking before him, and the others holding John's hands; both talking at once, and overpowering him by questions about home, and with school anecdotes. I looked after them with a feeling in which I do not know whether pleasure or melancholy predominated: for I was reminded of those days when, like them, I had neither known care nor sorrow, and a holiday was the summit of earthly felicity. We stopped a few moments afterwards to water the horses, and on resuming our route, a turn of the road brought us in sight of a neat country seat. I could just distinguish the forms of a lady and two young girls in the portico, and I saw my little comrades, with Bantam, Carlo, and old John, trooping along the carriage road. I leaned out of the coach window, in hopes of witnessing the happy meeting, but a grove of trees shut it from my sight.

In the evening we reached a village where I had determined to pass the night. As we drove into the great gateway of the inn, I saw on one side the light of a rousing kitchen fire, beaming through a window. I entered, and admired, for the hundredth time, that picture of convenience, neatness, and broad honest enjoyment, the kitchen of an English inn. It was of spacious dimensions, hung round with copper and tin vessels highly polished, and decorated here and there with a Christmas green. Hams, tongues, and flitches of bacon, were suspended from the ceiling; a smoke-jack made its ceaseless clanking beside the fireplace, and a clock ticked in one corner. A well-scoured deal table extended along one side of the kitchen, with a cold round of beef, and other hearty viands upon it, over which two foaming tankards of ale seemed mounting guard. Travellers of inferior order were preparing to attack this stout repast, while others sat smoking and gossiping over their ale on two high-backed oaken seats beside the fire. Trim housemaids were hurrying backwards and forwards under the directions of a fresh, bustling landlady; but still seizing an occasional moment to exchange a flippant word, and have a rallying laugh, with the group round the fire. The scene completely realised Poor Robin's humble idea of the comforts of mid-winter.

Now trees their leafy hats do bare,
To reverence Winter's silver hair;

A handsome hostess, merry host,
A pot of ale now and a toast,
Tobacco and a good coal fire,
Are things this season doth require.

I had not been long at the inn when a post-chaise drove up to the door. A young gentleman stepped out, and by the light of the lamps I caught a glimpse of a countenance which I thought I knew. I moved forward to get a nearer view, when his eye caught mine. I was not mistaken; it was Frank Bracebridge, a sprightly good-humoured young fellow, with whom I had once travelled on the Continent. Our meeting was extremely cordial; for the countenance of an old fellow-traveller always brings up the recollection of a thousand pleasant scenes, odd adventures, and excellent jokes. To discuss all these in a transient interview at an inn was impossible; and finding that I was not pressed for time, and was merely making a tour of observation, he insisted that I should give him a day or two at his father's country seat, to which he was going to pass the holidays, and which lay at a few miles' distance. "It is better than eating a solitary Christmas dinner at an inn," said he; "and I can assure you of a hearty welcome in something of the old-fashion style." His reasoning was cogent; and I must confess the preparation I had seen for universal festivity and social enjoyment had made me feel a little impatient of my loneliness. I closed, therefore, at once with his invitation: the chaise drove up to the door; and in a few moments I was on my way to the family mansion of the Bracebridges.

Christmas Eve

IT WAS A BRILLIANT MOONLIGHT night, but extremely cold; our chaise whirled rapidly over the frozen ground; the post-boy smacked his whip incessantly, and a part of the time his horses were on a gallop. "He knows where he is going," said my companion, laughing, "and is eager to arrive in time for some of the merriment and good cheer of the servants' hall. My father, you must know, is a bigoted devotee of the old school, and prides himself upon keeping up something of old English hospitality. He is a tolerable specimen of what you will rarely meet with nowadays in its purity, the old English country gentleman; for our men of fortune spend so much of their time in town, and fashion is carried so much into the country, that the strong rich peculiarities of ancient rural life are almost polished away. My father, however, from early years, took honest Peacham for his text book, instead of Chesterfield: he determined, in his own mind, that there was no condition more truly honourable and enviable than that of a country gentleman on his paternal lands, and, therefore, passes the whole of his time on his estate. He is a strenuous advocate for the revival of the old rural games and holiday observances, and is deeply read in the writers, ancient and modern, who have treated on the subject. Indeed, his favourite range of reading is among the authors who flourished at least two centuries since; who, he insists, wrote and thought more like true Englishmen than any of their successors. He even regrets sometimes that he had not been born a few centuries earlier, when England was itself, and had its peculiar manners and customs. As he lives at some distance from the main road, in rather a lonely part of the country, without any rival gentry near him, he has that most enviable of all blessings to an Englishman, an opportunity of indulging the bent of his own humour without molestation. Being representative of the oldest family in the neighbourhood, and a great part of the peasantry being his tenants, he is much looked up to, and, in general, is known simply by the appellation of 'The Squire;' a title which has been accorded to the head of the family since time immemorial. I think it best to give you these hints about my worthy old father, to prepare you for any little eccentricities that might otherwise appear absurd."

We had passed for some time along the wall of a park, and at length the chaise stopped at the gate. It was in a heavy magnificent old style, of iron bars, fancifully wrought at top into flourishes and flowers. The huge square columns that supported the gate were surmounted by the family crest. Close adjoining was the porter's lodge, sheltered under dark fir-trees, and almost buried in shrubbery.

The post-boy rang a large porter's bell, which resounded through the still frosty air, and was answered by the distant barking of dogs, with which the mansion-house seemed garrisoned. An old woman immediately appeared at the gate. As the moonlight fell strongly upon her, I had a full view of a little primitive dame, dressed very much in the antique taste, with a neat kerchief and stomacher, and her silver hair peeping from under a cap of snowy whiteness. She came curtseying forth, with many expressions of simple joy at seeing her young master. Her husband, it seems, was up at the house keeping Christmas Eve in the servants' hall; they could not do without him, as he was the best hand at a song and story in the household.

My friend proposed that we should alight and walk through the park to the hall, which was at no great distance, while the chaise should follow on. Our road wound through a noble avenue of trees, among the naked branches of which the moon glittered as she rolled through the deep vault of a cloudless sky. The lawn beyond was sheeted with a slight covering of snow, which here and there sparkled as the moonbeams caught a frosty crystal; and at a distance might be seen a thin transparent vapour, stealing up from the low grounds, and threatening gradually to shroud the landscape.

My companion looked round him with transport:—"How often," said he, "have I scampered up this avenue, on returning home on school vacations! How often have I played under these trees when a boy! I feel a degree of filial reverence for them, as we look up to those who have cherished us in childhood. My father was always scrupulous in exacting our holidays, and having us around him on family festivals. He used to direct and superintend our games with the strictness that some parents do the studies of their children. He was very particular that we should play the old English games according to their original form; and consulted old books for precedent and authority for every 'merrie disport;' yet I assure you there never was pedantry so delightful. It was the policy of the good old gentleman to make his children feel that home was the happiest place in the world; and I value this delicious home-feeling as one of the choicest gifts a parent can bestow."

We were interrupted by the clangour of a troop of dogs of all sorts and sizes, "mongrel, puppy, whelp and hound, and curs of low degree," that, disturbed by the ringing of the porter's bell, and the rattling of the chaise, came bounding, open-mouthed, across the lawn.

> —"*The little dogs and all,*
> *Tray, Blanch, and Sweetheart—see they bark at me!*"

cried Bracebridge, laughing. At the sound of his voice the bark was changed into a yelp of delight, and in a moment he was surrounded and almost overpowered by the caresses of the faithful animals.

We had now come in full view of the old family mansion, partly thrown in deep shadow, and partly lit up by the cold moonshine. It was an irregular building of some magnitude, and seemed to be of the architecture of different periods. One wing was evidently very ancient, with heavy stone-shafted bow windows jutting out and overrun with ivy, from among the foliage of which the small diamond-shaped panes of glass glittered with the moonbeams. The rest of the house was in the French taste of Charles the Second's time, having been repaired and altered, as my friend told me, by one of his ancestors, who returned with that monarch at the Restoration. The grounds about the house were laid out in the old formal manner of artificial flowerbeds, clipped shrubberies, raised terraces, and heavy stone balustrades, ornamented with urns, a leaden statue or two, and a jet of water. The old gentleman, I was told, was extremely careful to preserve this obsolete finery in all its original state. He admired this fashion in gardening; it had an air of magnificence, was courtly and noble, and befitting good old family style. The boasted imitation of nature in modern gardening had sprung up with modern republican notions, but did not suit a monarchical government; it smacked of the levelling system.—I could not help smiling at this introduction of politics into gardening, though I expressed some apprehension that I should find the old gentleman rather intolerant in his creed.—Frank assured me, however, that it was almost the only instance in which he had ever heard his father meddle with politics; and he believed that he had got this notion from a Member of Parliament who once passed a few weeks with him. The Squire was glad of any argument to defend his clipped yew-trees and formal terraces, which had been occasionally attacked by modern landscape-gardeners.

As we approached the house, we heard the sound of music, and now and then a burst of laughter from one end of the building. This, Bracebridge said, must proceed from the servants' hall, where a great deal of revelry was permitted, and even encouraged, by the Squire throughout the twelve days of Christmas, provided everything was done conformably to ancient usage. Here were kept up the old games of hoodman blind, shoe the wild mare, hot cockles, steal the white loaf, bob apple, and snapdragon: the Yule log and Christmas candle were regularly burnt, and the mistletoe, with its white berries, hung up, to the imminent peril of all the pretty housemaids.

So intent were the servants upon their sports, that we had to ring repeatedly before we could make ourselves heard. On our arrival being announced, the Squire came out to receive us, accompanied by his two other sons; one a young officer in the army, home on leave of absence; the other an Oxonian, just from the university. The Squire was a fine, healthy-looking old gentleman, with silver hair curling lightly round an open florid countenance; in which a physiognomist, with the advantage, like myself, of a previous hint or two, might discover a singular mixture of whim and benevolence.

The family meeting was warm and affectionate; as the evening was far advanced, the Squire would not permit us to change our travelling dresses, but ushered us at once to the company, which was assembled in a large old-fashioned hall. It was composed of different branches of a numerous family connection, where there were the usual proportion of old uncles and aunts, comfortably married dames, superannuated spinsters, blooming country cousins, half-fledged striplings, and bright-eyed boarding school hoydens. They were variously occupied; some at a round game of cards; others conversing around the fireplace; at one end of the hall was a group of the young folks, some nearly grown up, others of a more tender and budding age, fully engrossed by a merry game; and a profusion of wooden horses, penny trumpets, and tattered dolls, about the floor, showed traces of a troop of little fairy beings, who having frolicked through a happy day, had been carried off to slumber through a peaceful night.

While the mutual greetings were going on between Bracebridge and his relatives, I had time to scan the apartment. I have called it a hall, for so it had certainly been in old times, and the Squire had evidently endeavoured to restore it to something of its primitive state. Over the heavy projecting fireplace was suspended a picture of a warrior in armour, standing by a white horse, and on the opposite wall hung helmet, buckler, and lance. At one end an enormous pair of antlers were inserted in the wall, the branches serving as hooks on which to suspend hats, whips, and spurs; and in the corners of the apartment were fowling-pieces, fishing rods, and other sporting implements. The furniture was of the cumbrous workmanship of former days, though some articles of modern convenience had been added, and the oaken floor had been carpeted; so that the whole presented an odd mixture of parlour and hall.

The grate had been removed from the wide overwhelming fireplace, to make way for a fire of wood, in the midst of which was an enormous log glowing and blazing, and sending forth a vast volume of light and heat; this I understood was the Yule-log, which the Squire was particular in having brought in and illumined on a Christmas Eve, according to ancient custom.

It was really delightful to see the old Squire seated in his hereditary elbow-chair by the hospitable fireside of his ancestors, and looking around him like the sun of a system, beaming warmth and gladness to every heart. Even the very dog that lay stretched at his feet, as he lazily shifted his position and yawned, would look fondly up in his master's face, wag his tail against the floor, and stretch himself again to sleep, confident of kindness and protection. There is an emanation from the heart in genuine hospitality which cannot be described, but is immediately felt, and puts the stranger at once at his ease. I had not been seated many minutes by the comfortable hearth of the worthy cavalier before I found myself as much at home as if I had been one of the family.

Supper was announced shortly after our arrival. It was served up in a spacious oaken chamber, the panels of which shone with wax, and around which were several family portraits decorated with holly and ivy. Beside the accustomed lights, two great wax tapers, called Christmas candles, wreathed with greens, were placed on a highly-polished buffet among the family plate. The table was abundantly spread with substantial fare; but the Squire made his supper of frumenty, a dish made of wheat cakes boiled in milk with rich spices, being a standing dish in old times for Christmas Eve. I was happy to find my old friend, minced-pie, in the retinue of the feast; and finding him to be perfectly orthodox, and that I need not be ashamed of my predilection, I greeted him with all the warmth wherewith we usually greet an old and very genteel acquaintance.

The mirth of the company was greatly promoted by the humours of an eccentric personage whom Mr. Bracebridge always addressed with the quaint appellation of Master Simon. He was a tight, brisk little man, with the air of an arrant old bachelor. His nose was shaped like the bill of a parrot; his face slightly pitted with the smallpox, with a dry perpetual bloom on it, like a frostbitten leaf in autumn. He had an eye of great quickness and vivacity, with a drollery and lurking waggery of expression that was irresistible. He was evidently the wit of the family, dealing very much in sly jokes and innuendoes with the ladies, and making infinite merriment by harpings upon old themes; which, unfortunately, my ignorance of the family chronicles did not permit me to enjoy. It seemed to be his great delight during supper to keep a young girl next him in a continual agony of stifled laughter, in spite of her awe of the reproving looks of her mother, who sat opposite. Indeed, he was the idol of the younger part of the company, who laughed at everything he said or did, and at every turn of his countenance. I could not wonder at it; for he must have been a miracle of accomplishments in their eyes. He could imitate Punch and Judy; make an old woman of his hand, with the assistance of a burnt cork and pocket handkerchief; and cut an orange into such a ludicrous caricature, that the young folks were ready to die with laughing.

I was let briefly into his history by Frank Bracebridge. He was an old bachelor of a small independent income, which by careful management was sufficient for all his wants. He revolved through the family system like a vagrant comet in its orbit; sometimes visiting one branch, and sometimes another quite remote; as is often the case with gentlemen of extensive connections and small fortunes in England. He had a chirping, buoyant disposition, always enjoying the present moment; and his frequent change of scene and company prevented his acquiring those rusty unaccommodating habits with which old bachelors are so uncharitably charged. He was a complete family chronicle, being versed in the genealogy, history, and intermarriages of the whole house of Bracebridge, which made him a great favourite with the old folks; he was a beau of all the elder ladies and superannuated spinsters, among whom he was habitually considered rather a young fellow, and he was a master of the revels among the children; so that there was not a more popular being in the sphere in which he moved than Mr. Simon Bracebridge. Of late years he had resided almost entirely with the Squire, to whom he had become a factotum, and whom he particularly delighted by jumping with his humour in respect to old times, and by having a scrap of an old song to suit every occasion. We had presently a specimen of his last-mentioned talent; for no sooner was supper removed, and spiced wines and other beverages peculiar to the season introduced, than Master Simon was called on for a good old Christmas song. He bethought himself for a moment, and then, with a sparkle of the eye, and a voice that was by no means bad, excepting that it ran occasionally into a falsetto, like the notes of a split reed, he quavered forth a quaint old ditty,—

Now Christmas is come,
Let us beat up the drum,
And call all our neighbours together;
And when they appear,
Let us make them such cheer,
As will keep out the wind and the weather, etc.

The supper had disposed every one to gaiety, and an old harper was summoned from the servants' hall, where he had been strumming all the evening, and to all appearance comforting himself with some of the Squire's homebrewed. He was a kind of hanger-on, I was told, of the establishment, and though ostensibly a resident of the village, was oftener to be found in the Squire's kitchen than his own home, the old gentleman being fond of the sound of "harp in hall."

The dance, like most dances after supper, was a merry one; some of the older folks joined in it, and the Squire himself figured down several couples with a partner with whom he affirmed he had danced at every Christmas for nearly half a century. Master Simon, who seemed to be a kind of connecting link between the old times and the new, and to be withal a little antiquated in the taste of his accomplishments, evidently piqued himself on his dancing, and was endeavouring to gain credit by the heel and toe, rigadoon, and other graces of the ancient school; but he had unluckily assorted himself with a little romping girl from boarding school, who, by her wild vivacity, kept him continually on the stretch, and defeated all his sober attempts at elegance;—such are the ill-assorted matches to which antique gentlemen are unfortunately prone!

The young Oxonian, on the contrary, had led out one of his maiden aunts, on whom the rogue played a thousand little knaveries with impunity; he was full of practical jokes, and his delight was to tease his aunts and cousins; yet, like all madcap youngsters, he was a universal favourite among the women. The most interesting couple in the dance was the young officer and a ward of the Squire's, a beautiful blushing girl of seventeen. From several shy glances which I had noticed in the course of the evening, I suspected there was a little kindness growing up between them; and, indeed, the young soldier was just the hero to captivate a romantic girl. He was tall, slender, and handsome, and, like most young British officers of late years, had picked up various small accomplishments on the Continent—he could talk French and Italian—draw landscapes, sing very tolerably—dance divinely; but, above all, he had been wounded at Waterloo:—what girl of seventeen, well read in poetry and romance, could resist such a mirror of chivalry and perfection!

The moment the dance was over, he caught up a guitar, and lolling against the old marble fireplace, in an attitude which I am half inclined to suspect was studied, began the little French air of the Troubadour. The Squire, however, exclaimed against having anything on Christmas eve but good old English; upon which the young minstrel, casting up his eye for a moment, as if in an effort of memory, struck into another strain, and, with a charming air of gallantry, gave Herrick's "Night-Piece to Julia:"—

> Her eyes the glow-worm lend thee,
> The shooting stars attend thee,
> And the elves also,
> Whose little eyes glow
> Like the sparks of fire, befriend thee.
>
> No Will-o'-the-Wisp mislight thee;
> Nor snake or glow-worm bite thee;
> But on, on thy way,
> Not making a stay,
> Since ghost there is none to affright thee.
>
> Then let not the dark thee cumber;
> What though the moon does slumber,
> The stars of the night
> Will lend thee their light,
> Like tapers clear without number.
>
> Then, Julia, let me woo thee,
> Thus, thus to come unto me;
> And when I shall meet
> Thy silvery feet,
> My soul I'll pour into thee.

The song might have been intended in compliment to the fair Julia, for so I found his partner was called, or it might not; she, however, was certainly unconscious of any such application, for she never looked at the singer, but kept her eyes cast upon the floor. Her face was suffused, it is true, with a beautiful blush, and there was a gentle heaving of the bosom, but all that was doubtless caused by the exercise of the dance; indeed, so great was her indifference, that she was amusing herself with plucking to pieces a choice bouquet of hothouse flowers, and by the time the song was concluded, the nosegay lay in ruins on the floor.

The party now broke up for the night with the kind-hearted old custom of shaking hands. As I passed through the hall, on the way to my chamber, the dying embers of the *Yule-clog* still sent forth a dusky glow; and had it not been the season when "no spirit dares stir abroad," I should have been half tempted to steal from my room at midnight, and peep whether the fairies might not be at their revels about the hearth.

My chamber was in the old part of the mansion, the ponderous furniture of which might have been fabricated in the days of the giants. The room was panelled with cornices of heavy carved-work, in which flowers and grotesque faces were strangely intermingled; and a row of black-looking portraits stared mournfully at me from the walls. The bed was of rich though faded damask, with a lofty tester, and stood in a niche opposite a bow-window. I had scarcely got into bed when a strain of music seemed to break forth in the air just below the window. I listened, and found it proceeded from a band, which I concluded to be the waits from some neighbouring village. They went round the house, playing under the windows. I drew aside the curtains, to hear them more distinctly. The moonbeams fell through the upper part of the casement, partially lighting up the antiquated apartment. The sounds, as they receded, became more soft and aërial, and seemed to accord with quiet and moonlight. I listened and listened—they became more and more tender and remote, and, as they gradually died away, my head sank upon the pillow and I fell asleep.

> *Dark and dull night, flie hence away,*
> *And give the honour to this day*
> *That sees December turn'd to May.*
>
> * * * * *
>
> *Why does the chilling winter's morne*
> *Smile like a field beset with corn?*
> *Or smell like to a meade new-shorne,*
> *Thus on the sudden?—Come and see*
> *The cause why things thus fragrant be.*

—HERRICK

Christmas Day

WHEN I AWOKE THE NEXT morning, it seemed as if all the events of the preceding evening had been a dream, and nothing but the identity of the ancient chamber convinced me of their reality. While I lay musing on my pillow, I heard the sound of little feet pattering outside of the door, and a whispering consultation. Presently a choir of small voices chanted forth an old Christmas carol, the burden of which was,

> *Rejoice, our Saviour he was born*
> *On Christmas Day in the morning.*

I rose softly, slipped on my clothes, opened the door suddenly, and beheld one of the most beautiful little fairy groups that a painter could imagine. It consisted of a boy and two girls, the eldest not more than six, and lovely as seraphs. They were going the rounds of the house, and singing at every chamber door; but my sudden appearance frightened them into mute bashfulness. They remained for a moment playing on their lips with their fingers, and now and then stealing a shy glance, from under their eyebrows, until, as if by one impulse, they scampered away, and as they turned an angle of the gallery, I heard them laughing in triumph at their escape.

Everything conspired to produce kind and happy feelings in this stronghold of old-fashioned hospitality. The window of my chamber looked out upon what in summer would have been a beautiful landscape. There was a sloping lawn, a fine stream winding at the foot of it, and a tract of park beyond, with noble clumps of trees, and herds of deer. At a distance was a neat hamlet, with the smoke from the cottage chimneys hanging over it; and a church with its dark spire in strong relief against the clear cold sky. The house was surrounded with evergreens, according to the English custom, which would have given almost an appearance of summer; but the morning was extremely frosty; the light vapour of the preceding evening had been precipitated by the cold, and covered all the trees and every blade of grass with its fine crystallisations. The rays of a bright morning sun had a dazzling effect among the glittering foliage. A robin, perched upon the top of a mountain-ash that hung its clusters of red berries just before my window, was basking himself in the sunshine, and piping a few querulous notes; and a peacock was displaying all the glories of his train, and strutting with the pride and gravity of a Spanish grandee on the terrace-walk below.

I had scarcely dressed myself, when a servant appeared to invite me to family prayers. He showed me the way to a small chapel in the old wing of the house, where I found the principal part of the family already assembled in a kind of gallery, furnished with cushions, hassocks, and large prayer books; the servants were seated on benches below. The old gentleman read prayers from a desk in front of the gallery, and Master Simon acted as clerk, and made the responses; and I must do him the justice to say that he acquitted himself with great gravity and decorum.

The service was followed by a Christmas carol, which Mr. Bracebridge himself had constructed from a poem of his favourite author, Herrick; and it had been adapted to an old church melody by Master Simon. As there were several good voices among the household, the effect was extremely pleasing; but I was particularly gratified by the exaltation of heart, and sudden sally of grateful feeling, with which the worthy Squire delivered one stanza: his eyes glistening, and his voice rambling out of all the bounds of time and tune:

> "'Tis Thou that crown'st my glittering hearth
> With guiltlesse mirth,
> And giv'st me wassaile bowles to drink,
> Spiced to the brink:
> Lord, 'tis Thy plenty-dropping hand
> That soiles my land;
> And giv'st me for my bushell sowne,
> Twice ten for one."

I afterwards understood that early morning service was read on every Sunday and saint's day throughout the year, either by Mr. Bracebridge or by some member of the family. It was once almost universally the case at the seats of the nobility and gentry of England, and it is much to be regretted that the custom is fallen into neglect; for the dullest observer must be sensible of the order and serenity prevalent in those households, where the occasional exercise of a beautiful form of worship in the morning gives, as it were, the keynote to every temper for the day, and attunes every spirit to harmony.

Our breakfast consisted of what the Squire denominated true old English fare. He indulged in some bitter lamentations over modern breakfasts of tea-and-toast, which he censured as among the causes of modern effeminacy and weak nerves, and the decline of old English heartiness; and though he admitted them to his table to suit the palates of his guests, yet there was a brave display of cold meats, wine and ale, on the sideboard.

After breakfast I walked about the grounds with Frank Bracebridge and Master Simon, or Mr. Simon, as he was called by everybody but the Squire. We were escorted by a number of gentlemen-like dogs, that seemed loungers about the establishment; from the frisking spaniel to the steady old stag-hound; the last of which was of a race that had been in the family time out of mind: they were all obedient to a dog-whistle which hung to Master Simon's button-hole, and in the midst of their gambols would glance an eye occasionally upon a small switch he carried in his hand.

The old mansion had a still more venerable look in the yellow sunshine than by pale moonlight; and I could not but feel the force of the Squire's idea, that the formal terraces, heavily moulded balustrades, and clipped yew-trees, carried with them an air of proud aristocracy. There appeared to be an unusual number of peacocks about the place, and I was making some remarks upon what I termed a flock of them, that were basking under a sunny wall, when I was gently corrected in my phraseology by Master Simon, who told me that, according to the most ancient and approved treatise on hunting, I must say a *muster* of peacocks. "In the same way," added he, with a slight air of pedantry, "we say a flight of doves or swallows, a bevy of quails, a herd of deer, of wrens, or cranes, a skulk of foxes, or a building of rooks." He went on to inform me that, according to Sir Anthony Fitzherbert, we ought to ascribe to this bird "both understanding and glory; for being praised, he will presently set up his tail chiefly against the sun, to the intent you may the better behold the beauty thereof. But at the fall of the leaf, when his tail falleth, he will mourn and hide himself in corners, till his tail come again as it was."

I could not help smiling at this display of small erudition on so whimsical a subject; but I found that the peacocks were birds of some consequence at the hall, for Frank Bracebridge informed me that they were great favourites with his father, who was extremely careful to keep up the breed; partly because they belonged to chivalry, and were in great request at the stately banquets of the olden time; and partly because they had a pomp and magnificence about them, highly becoming an old family mansion. Nothing, he was accustomed to say, had an air of greater state and dignity than a peacock perched upon an antique stone balustrade.

Master Simon had now to hurry off, having an appointment at the parish church with the village choristers, who were to perform some music of his selection. There was something extremely agreeable in the cheerful flow of animal spirits of the little man; and I confess I had been somewhat surprised at his apt quotations from authors who certainly were not in the range of everyday reading. I mentioned this last circumstance to Frank Bracebridge, who told me with a smile that Master Simon's whole stock of erudition was confined to some half a dozen old authors, which the Squire had put into his hands, and which he read over and over, whenever he had a studious fit; as he sometimes had on a rainy day, or a long winter evening. Sir Anthony Fitzherbert's *Book of Husbandry*; Markham's *Country Contentments*; the *Tretyse of Hunting*, by Sir Thomas Cockayne, Knight; Izaak Walton's *Angler*, and two or three more such ancient worthies of the pen, were his standard authorities; and, like all men who know but a few books, he looked up to them with a kind of idolatry, and quoted them on all occasions. As to his songs, they were chiefly picked out of old books in the Squire's library, and adapted to tunes that were popular among the choice spirits of the last century. His practical application of scraps of literature, however, had caused him to be looked upon as a prodigy of book-knowledge by all the grooms, huntsmen, and small sportsmen of the neighbourhood.

While we were talking we heard the distant toll of the village bell, and I was told that the Squire was a little particular in having his household at church on a Christmas morning; considering it a day of pouring out of thanks and rejoicing; for, as old Tusser observed,

> *"At Christmas be merry, and thankful withal,*
> *And feast thy poor neighbours, the great and the small."*

"If you are disposed to go to church," said Frank Bracebridge, "I can promise you a specimen of my cousin Simon's musical achievements. As the church is destitute of an organ, he has formed a band from the village amateurs, and established a musical club for their improvement; he has also sorted a choir, as he sorted my father's pack of hounds, according to the directions of Jervaise Markham, in his Country Contentments; for the bass he has sought out all the 'deep, solemn mouths,' and for the tenor the 'loud ringing mouths,' among the country bumpkins; and for 'sweet mouths,' he has culled with curious taste among the prettiest lasses in the neighbourhood; though these last, he affirms, are the most difficult to keep in tune; your pretty female singer being exceedingly wayward and capricious, and very liable to accident."

As the morning, though frosty, was remarkably fine and clear, the most of the family walked to the church, which was a very old building of gray stone, and stood near a village, about half a mile from the park gate. Adjoining it was a low snug parsonage, which seemed coeval with the church. The front of it was perfectly matted with a yew tree that had been trained against its walls, through the dense foliage of which apertures had been formed to admit light into the small antique lattices. As we passed this sheltered nest, the parson issued forth and preceded us.

I had expected to see a sleek well-conditioned pastor, such as is often found in a snug living in the vicinity of a rich patron's table; but I was disappointed. The parson was a little, meagre, black-looking man, with a grizzled wig that was too wide, and stood off from each ear; so that his head seemed to have shrunk away within it, like a dried filbert in its shell. He wore a rusty coat, with great skirts, and pockets that would have held the church Bible and prayer book; and his small legs seemed still smaller, from being planted in large shoes, decorated with enormous buckles.

I was informed by Frank Bracebridge that the parson had been a chum of his father's at Oxford, and had received this living shortly after the latter had come to his estate. He was a complete black letter hunter, and would scarcely read a work printed in the Roman character. The editions of Caxton and Wynkin de Worde were his delight; and he was indefatigable in his researches after such old English writers as have fallen into oblivion from their worthlessness. In deference, perhaps, to the notions of Mr. Bracebridge, he had made diligent investigations into the festive rights and holiday customs of former times; and had been as zealous in the inquiry, as if he had been a boon companion; but it was merely with that plodding spirit with which men of adust temperament follow up any track of study, merely because it is denominated learning; indifferent to its intrinsic nature, whether it be the illustration of the wisdom, or of the ribaldry and obscenity of antiquity. He had poured over these old volumes so intensely, that they seemed to have been reflected into his countenance indeed; which, if the face be an index of the mind, might be compared to a title page of black letter.

On reaching the church porch, we found the parson rebuking the gray-headed sexton for having used mistletoe among the greens with which the church was decorated. It was, he observed, an unholy plant, profaned by having been used by the Druids in their mystic ceremonies; and though it might be innocently employed in the festive ornamenting of halls and kitchens, yet it had been deemed by the Fathers of the Church as unhallowed, and totally unfit for sacred purposes. So tenacious was he on this point, that the poor sexton was obliged to strip down a great part of the humble trophies of his taste, before the parson would consent to enter upon the service of the day.

The interior of the church was venerable but simple; on the walls were several mural monuments of the Bracebridges, and just beside the altar was a tomb of ancient workmanship, on which lay the effigy of a warrior in armour, with his legs crossed, a sign of his having been a crusader. I was told it was one of the family who had signalised himself in the Holy Land, and the same whose picture hung over the fireplace in the hall.

During service, Master Simon stood up in the pew, and repeated the responses very audibly; evincing that kind of ceremonious devotion punctually observed by a gentleman of the old school, and a man of old family connections. I observed, too, that he turned over the leaves of a folio prayer book with something of a flourish; possibly to show off an enormous seal-ring which enriched one of his fingers, and which had the look of a family relic. But he was evidently most solicitous about the musical part of the service, keeping his eye fixed intently on the choir, and beating time with much gesticulation and emphasis.

The orchestra was in a small gallery, and presented a most whimsical grouping of heads, piled one above the other, among which I particularly noticed that of the village tailor, a pale fellow with a retreating forehead and chin, who played on the clarionet, and seemed to have blown his face to a point; and there was another, a short pursy man, stooping and labouring at a bass viol, so as to show nothing but the top of a round bald head, like the egg of an ostrich. There were two or three pretty faces among the female singers, to which the keen air of a frosty morning had given a bright rosy tint; but the gentlemen choristers had evidently been chosen, like old Cremona fiddles, more for tone than looks; and as several had to sing from the same book, there were clusterings of odd physiognomies, not unlike those groups of cherubs we sometimes see on country tombstones.

The usual services of the choir were managed tolerably well, the vocal parts generally lagging a little behind the instrumental, and some loitering fiddler now and then making up for lost time by travelling over a passage with prodigious celerity, and clearing more bars than the keenest fox hunter, to be in at the death. But the great trial was an anthem that had been prepared and arranged by Master Simon, and on which he had founded great expectation. Unluckily there was a blunder at the very outset; the musicians became flurried; Master Simon was in a fever, everything went on lamely and irregularly until they came to a chorus beginning "Now let us sing with one accord," which seemed to be a signal for parting company: all became discord and confusion; each shifted for himself, and got to the end as well, or rather as soon, as he could, excepting one old chorister in a pair of horn spectacles bestriding and pinching a long sonorous nose; who, happening to stand a little apart, and being wrapped up in his own melody, kept on a quavering course, wriggling his head, ogling his book, and winding all up by a nasal solo of at least three bars' duration.

The parson gave us a most erudite sermon on the rites and ceremonies of Christmas, and the propriety of observing it not merely as a day of thanksgiving, but of rejoicing; supporting the correctness of his opinions by the earliest usages of the Church, and enforcing them by the authorities of Theophilus of Cesarea, St. Cyprian, St. Chrysostom, St. Augustine, and a cloud more of Saints and Fathers, from whom he made copious quotations. I was a little at a loss to perceive the necessity of such a mighty array of forces to maintain a point which no one present seemed inclined to dispute; but I soon found that the good man had a legion of ideal adversaries to contend with; having in the course of his researches on the subject of Christmas, got completely embroiled in the sectarian controversies of the Revolution, when the Puritans made such a fierce assault upon the ceremonies of the Church, and poor old Christmas was driven out of the land by proclamation of parliament. The worthy parson lived but with times past, and knew but a little of the present.

Shut up among worm-eaten tomes in the retirement of his antiquated little study, the pages of old times were to him as the gazettes of the day; while the era of the Revolution was mere modern history. He forgot that nearly two centuries had elapsed since the fiery persecution of poor mince-pie throughout the land; when plum-porridge was denounced as "mere popery," and roast beef as antichristian; and that Christmas had been brought in again triumphantly with the merry court of King Charles at the Restoration. He kindled into warmth with the ardour of his contest, and the host of imaginary foes with whom he had to combat; had a stubborn conflict with old Prynne and two or three other forgotten champions of the Roundheads, on the subject of Christmas festivity; and concluded by urging his hearers, in the most solemn and affecting manner, to stand to the traditionary customs of their fathers, and feast and make merry on this joyful anniversary of the Church.

I have seldom known a sermon attended apparently with more immediate effects; for on leaving the church the congregation seemed one and all possessed with the gaiety of spirit so earnestly enjoined by their pastor. The elder folks gathered in knots in the churchyard, greeting and shaking hands; and the children ran about crying, Ule! Ule! And repeating some uncouth rhymes, which the parson, who had joined us, informed me had been handed down from days of yore. The villagers doffed their hats to the Squire as he passed, giving him the good wishes of the season with every appearance of heartfelt sincerity, and were invited by him to the hall, to take something to keep out the cold of the weather; and I heard blessings uttered by several of the poor, which convinced me that, in the midst of his enjoyments, the worthy old cavalier had not forgotten the true Christmas virtue of charity.

On our way homeward his heart seemed overflowing with generous and happy feelings. As we passed over a rising ground which commanded something of a prospect, the sounds of rustic merriment now and then reached our ears; the Squire paused for a few moments, and looked around with an air of inexpressible benignity. The beauty of the day was of itself sufficient to inspire philanthropy. Notwithstanding the frostiness of the morning, the sun in his cloudless journey had acquired sufficient power to melt away the thin covering of snow from every southern declivity, and to bring out the living green which adorns an English landscape even in mid-winter. Large tracts of smiling verdure contrasted with the dazzling whiteness of the shaded slopes and hollows. Every sheltered bank, on which the broad rays rested, yielded its silver rill of cold and limpid water, glittering through the dripping grass; and sent up slight exhalations to contribute to the thin haze that hung just above the surface of the earth. There was something truly cheering in this triumph of warmth and verdure over the frosty thraldom of winter; it was, as the Squire observed, an emblem of Christmas hospitality, breaking through the chills of ceremony and selfishness, and thawing every heart into a flow. He pointed with pleasure to the indications of good cheer reeking from the chimneys of the comfortable farmhouses and low thatched cottages. "I love," said he, "to see this day well kept by rich and poor; it is a great thing to have one day in the year, at least, when you are sure of being welcome wherever you go, and of having, as it were, the world all thrown open to you; and I am almost disposed to join with Poor Robin, in his malediction of every churlish enemy to this honest festival:—

> *"Those who at Christmas do repine,*
> *And would fain hence despatch him,*
> *May they with old Duke Humphry dine,*
> *Or else may Squire Ketch catch 'em."*

The Squire went on to lament the deplorable decay of the games and amusements which were once prevalent at this season among the lower orders, and countenanced by the higher: when the old halls of castles and manor houses were thrown open at daylight; when the tables were covered with brawn, and beef, and humming ale; when the harp and the carol resounded all day long, and when rich and poor were alike welcome to enter and make merry. "Our old games and local customs," said he, "had a great effect in making the peasant fond of his home, and the promotion of them by the gentry made him fond of his lord. They made the times merrier, and kinder, and better; and I can truly say, with one of our old poets,—

> *"I like them well—the curious preciseness*
> *And all-pretended gravity of those*
> *That seek to banish hence these harmless sports,*
> *Have thrust away much ancient honesty.*

"The nation," continued he, "is altered; we have almost lost our simple true-hearted peasantry. They have broken asunder from the higher classes, and seem to think their interests are separate. They have become too knowing, and begin to read newspapers, listen to alehouse politicians, and talk of reform. I think one mode to keep them in good humour in these hard times would be for the nobility and gentry to pass more time on their estates, mingle more among the country people, and set the merry old English games going again."

Such was the good Squire's project for mitigating public discontent; and, indeed, he had once attempted to put his doctrine in practice, and a few years before had kept open house during the holidays in the old style. The country people, however, did not understand how to play their parts in the scene of hospitality; many uncouth circumstances occurred; the manor was overrun by all the vagrants of the country, and more beggars drawn into the neighbourhood in one week than the parish officers could get rid of in a year. Since then he had contented himself with inviting the decent part of the neighbouring peasantry to call at the hall on Christmas day, and distributing beef, and bread, and ale, among the poor, that they might make merry in their own dwellings.

We had not been long home when the sound of music was heard from a distance. A band of country lads without coats, their shirt-sleeves fancifully tied with ribands, their hats decorated with greens, and clubs in their hands, were seen advancing up the avenue, followed by a large number of villagers and peasantry. They stopped before the hall door, where the music struck up a peculiar air, and the lads performed a curious and intricate dance, advancing, retreating, and striking their clubs together, keeping exact time to the music; while one, whimsically crowned with a fox's skin, the tail of which flaunted down his back, kept capering round the skirts of the dance, and rattling a Christmas box with many antic gesticulations.

The Squire eyed this fanciful exhibition with great interest and delight, and gave me a full account of its origin, which he traced to the times when the Romans held possession of the island; plainly proving that this was a lineal descendant of the sword dance of the ancients. "It was now," he said, "nearly extinct, but he had accidentally met with traces of it in the neighbourhood, and had encouraged its revival; though, to tell the truth, it was too apt to be followed up by rough cudgel-play and broken heads in the evening."

After the dance was concluded, the whole party was entertained with brawn and beef, and stout homebrewed. The Squire himself mingled among the rustics, and was received with awkward demonstrations of deference and regard. It is true I perceived two or three of the younger peasants, as they were raising their tankards to their mouths when the Squire's back was turned, making something of a grimace, and giving each other the wink; but the moment they caught my eye they pulled grave faces, and were exceedingly demure. With Master Simon, however, they all seemed more at their ease. His varied occupations and amusements had made him well known throughout the neighbourhood. He was a visitor at every farmhouse and cottage; gossiped with the farmers and their wives; romped with their daughters; and, like that type of a vagrant bachelor, the humble bee, tolled the sweets from all the rosy lips of the country round.

The bashfulness of the guests soon gave way before good cheer and affability. There is something genuine and affectionate in the gaiety of the lower orders, when it is excited by the bounty and familiarity of those above them; the warm glow of gratitude enters into their mirth, and a kind word or a small pleasantry, frankly uttered by a patron, gladdens the heart of the dependant more than oil and wine. When the Squire had retired the merriment increased, and there was much joking and laughter, particularly between Master Simon and a hale, ruddy-faced, white-headed farmer, who appeared to be the wit of the village; for I observed all his companions to wait with open mouths for his retorts, and burst into a gratuitous laugh before they could well understand them.

The whole house indeed seemed abandoned to merriment. As I passed to my room to dress for dinner, I heard the sound of music in a small court, and, looking through a window that commanded it, I perceived a band of wandering musicians, with pandean pipes and tambourine; a pretty coquettish housemaid was dancing a jig with a smart country lad, while several of the other servants were looking on. In the midst of her sport the girl caught a glimpse of my face at the window, and, colouring up, ran off with an air of roguish affected confusion.

The Christmas Dinner

Lo, now is come the joyful'st feast!
Let every man be jolly,
Eache roome with yvie leaves is drest,
And every post with holly.
Now all our neighbours' chimneys smoke,
And Christmas blocks are burning;
Their ovens they with bak't meats choke,
And all their spits are turning.
Without the door let sorrow lie,
And if, for cold, it hap to die,
We'll bury't in a Christmas pye,
And evermore be merry.

—WITHERS's *Juvenilia*

I HAD FINISHED MY TOILET, and was loitering with Frank Bracebridge in the library, when we heard a distant thwacking sound, which he informed me was a signal for the serving up of the dinner. The Squire kept up old customs in kitchen as well as hall; and the rolling pin, struck upon the dresser by the cook, summoned the servants to carry in the meats.

Just in this nick the cook knock'd thrice,
And all the waiters in a trice
His summons did obey;
Each serving man, with dish in hand,
March'd boldly up, like our train-band,
Presented and away.

The dinner was served up in the great hall, where the Squire always held his Christmas banquet. A blazing crackling fire of logs had been heaped on to warm the spacious apartment, and the flame went sparkling and wreathing up the wide-mouthed chimney. The great picture of the crusader and his white horse had been profusely decorated with greens for the occasion; and holly and ivy had likewise been wreathed round the helmet and weapons on the opposite wall, which I understood were the arms of the same warrior. I must own, by the by, I had strong doubts about the authenticity of the painting and armour as having belonged to the crusader, they certainly having the stamp of more recent days; but I was told that the painting had been so considered time out of mind; and that as to the armour, it had been found in a lumber room, and elevated to its present situation by the Squire, who at once determined it to be the armour of the family hero; and as he was absolute authority on all such subjects in his own household, the matter had passed into current acceptation. A sideboard was set out just under this chivalric trophy, on which was a display of plate that might have vied (at least in variety) with Belshazzar's parade of the vessels of the temple; "flagons, cans, cups, beakers, goblets, basins, and ewers;" the gorgeous utensils of good companionship, that had gradually accumulated through many generations of jovial housekeepers. Before these stood the two Yule candles beaming like two stars of the first magnitude; other lights were distributed in branches, and the whole array glittered like a firmament of silver.

We were ushered into this banqueting scene with the sound of minstrelsy, the old harper being seated on a stool beside the fireplace, and twanging his instrument with a vast deal more power than melody. Never did Christmas board display a more goodly and gracious assemblage of countenances: those who were not handsome were, at least, happy; and happiness is a rare improver of your hard-favoured visage. I always consider an old English family as well worth studying as a collection of Holbein's portraits or Albert Durer's prints. There is much antiquarian lore to be acquired; much knowledge of the physiognomies of former times. Perhaps it may be from having continually before their eyes those rows of old family portraits, with which the mansions of this country are stocked; certain it is, that the quaint features of antiquity are often most faithfully perpetuated in these ancient lines; and I have traced an old family nose through a whole picture gallery, legitimately handed down from generation to generation, almost from the time of the Conquest. Something of the kind was to be observed in the worthy company around me. Many of their faces had evidently originated in a Gothic age, and been merely copied by succeeding generations; and there was one little girl, in particular, of staid demeanour, with a high Roman nose, and an antique vinegar aspect, who was a great favourite of the Squire's, being, as he said, a Bracebridge all over, and the very counterpart of one of his ancestors who figured in the court of Henry VIII.

The parson said grace, which was not a short familiar one, such as is commonly addressed to the Deity, in these unceremonious days; but a long, courtly, well-worded one of the ancient school. There was now a pause, as if something was expected; when suddenly the butler entered the hall with some degree of bustle: he was attended by a servant on each side with a large wax-light, and bore a silver dish, on which was an enormous pig's head decorated with rosemary, with a lemon in its mouth, which was placed with great formality at the head of the table. The moment this pageant made its appearance, the harper struck up a flourish; at the conclusion of which the young Oxonian, on receiving a hint from the Squire, gave, with an air of the most comic gravity, an old carol, the first verse of which was as follows:—

Caput apri defero
Reddens laudes Domino.
The boar's head in hand bring I,
With garlands gay and rosemary.
I pray you all synge merily
Qui estis in convivio.

Though prepared to witness many of these little eccentricities, from being apprised of the peculiar hobby of mine host; yet, I confess, the parade with which so odd a dish was introduced somewhat perplexed me, until I gathered from the conversation of the Squire and the parson that it was meant to represent the bringing in of the boar's head: a dish formerly served up with much ceremony, and the sound of minstrelsy and song, at great tables on Christmas day. "I like the old custom," said the Squire, "not merely because it is stately and pleasing in itself, but because it was observed at the College of Oxford, at which I was educated. When I hear the old song chanted, it brings to mind the time when I was young and gamesome—and the noble old college hall—and my fellow students loitering about in their black gowns; many of whom, poor lads, are now in their graves!"

The parson, however, whose mind was not haunted by such associations, and who was always more taken up with the text than the sentiment, objected to the Oxonian's version of the carol; which he affirmed was different from that sung at college. He went on, with the dry perseverance of a commentator, to give the college reading, accompanied by sundry annotations: addressing himself at first to the company at large; but finding their attention gradually diverted to other talk, and other objects, he lowered his tone as his number of auditors diminished, until he concluded his remarks, in an under voice, to a fat-headed old gentleman next him, who was silently engaged in the discussion of a huge plateful of turkey.

The table was literally loaded with good cheer, and presented an epitome of country abundance, in this season of overflowing larders. A distinguished post was allotted to "ancient sirloin," as mine host termed it; being, as he added, "the standard of old English hospitality, and a joint of goodly presence, and full of expectation." There were several dishes quaintly decorated, and which had evidently something traditionary in their embellishments; but about which, as I did not like to appear over-curious, I asked no questions.

I could not, however, but notice a pie, magnificently decorated with peacocks' feathers, in imitation of the tail of that bird, which overshadowed a considerable tract of the table. This the Squire confessed, with some little hesitation, was a pheasant pie, though a peacock pie was certainly the most authentical; but there had been such a mortality among the peacocks this season, that he could not prevail upon himself to have one killed.

It would be tedious, perhaps, to my wiser readers, who may not have that foolish fondness for odd and obsolete things to which I am a little given, were I to mention the other makeshifts of this worthy old humorist, by which he was endeavouring to follow up, though at humble distance, the quaint customs of antiquity. I was pleased, however, to see the respect shown to his whims by his children and relatives; who, indeed, entered readily into the full spirit of them, and seemed all well versed in their parts; having doubtless been present at many a rehearsal. I was amused, too, at the air of profound gravity with which the butler and other servants executed the duties assigned them, however eccentric. They had an old-fashioned look; having, for the most part, been brought up in the household, and grown into keeping with the antiquated mansion, and the humours of its lord; and most probably looked upon all his whimsical regulations as the established laws of honourable housekeeping.

When the cloth was removed, the butler brought in a huge silver vessel of rare and curious workmanship, which he placed before the Squire. Its appearance was hailed with acclamation; being the Wassail Bowl, so renowned in Christmas festivity. The contents had been prepared by the Squire himself; for it was a beverage in the skilful mixture of which he particularly prided himself; alleging that it was too abstruse and complex for the comprehension of an ordinary servant. It was a potation, indeed, that might well make the heart of a toper leap within him; being composed of the richest and raciest wines, highly spiced and sweetened, with roasted apples bobbing about the surface.

The old gentleman's whole countenance beamed with a serene look of indwelling delight, as he stirred this mighty bowl. Having raised it to his lips, with a hearty wish of a merry Christmas to all present, he sent it brimming round the board, for every one to follow his example, according to the primitive style; pronouncing it "the ancient fountain of good feeling, where all hearts met together."

There was much laughing and rallying as the honest emblem of Christmas joviality circulated, and was kissed rather coyly by the ladies. When it reached Master Simon he raised it in both hands, and with the air of a boon companion struck up an old Wassail chanson:

> *The browne bowle,*
> *The merry browne bowle,*
> *As it goes round about-a,*

Fill
Still,
Let the world say what it will,
And drink your fill all out-a.

The deep canne,
The merry deep canne,
As thou dost freely quaff-a,
Sing,
Fling,
Be as merry as a king,
And sound a lusty laugh-a.

Much of the conversation during dinner turned upon family topics, to which I was a stranger. There was, however, a great deal of rallying of Master Simon about some gay widow, with whom he was accused of having a flirtation. This attack was commenced by the ladies; but it was continued throughout the dinner by the fat-headed old gentleman next the parson, with the persevering assiduity of a slow-hound; being one of those long-winded jokers, who, though rather dull at starting game, are unrivalled for their talents in hunting it down. At every pause in the general conversation, he renewed his bantering in pretty much the same terms; winking hard at me with both eyes whenever he gave Master Simon what he considered a home thrust. The latter, indeed, seemed fond of being teased on the subject, as old bachelors are apt to be; and he took occasion to inform me, in an undertone, that the lady in question was a prodigiously fine woman, and drove her own curricle.

The dinner time passed away in this flow of innocent hilarity; and, though the old hall may have resounded in its time with many a scene of broader rout and revel, yet I doubt whether it ever witnessed more honest and genuine enjoyment. How easy it is for one benevolent being to diffuse pleasure around him; and how truly is a kind heart a fountain of gladness, making everything in its vicinity to freshen into smiles! The joyous disposition of the worthy Squire was perfectly contagious; he was happy himself, and disposed to make all the world happy; and the little eccentricities of his humour did but season, in a manner, the sweetness of his philanthropy.

When the ladies had retired, the conversation, as usual, became still more animated; many good things were broached which had been thought of during dinner, but which would not exactly do for a lady's ear; and though I cannot positively affirm that there was much wit uttered, yet I have certainly heard many contests of rare wit produce much less laughter. Wit, after all, is a mighty tart, pungent ingredient, and much too acid for some stomachs; but honest good humour is the oil and wine of a merry meeting, and there is no jovial companionship equal to that where the jokes are rather small, and the laughter abundant. The Squire told several long stories of early college pranks and adventures, in some of which the parson had been a sharer; though in looking at the latter, it required some effort of imagination to figure such a little dark anatomy of a man into the perpetrator of a madcap gambol. Indeed, the two college chums presented pictures of what men may be made by their different lots in life. The Squire had left the university to live lustily on his paternal domains, in the vigorous enjoyment of prosperity and sunshine, and had flourished on to a hearty and florid old age; whilst the poor parson, on the contrary, had dried and withered away, among dusty tomes, in the silence and shadows of his study. Still there seemed to be a spark of almost extinguished fire, feebly glimmering in the bottom of his soul; and as the Squire hinted at a sly story of the parson and a pretty milkmaid, whom they once met on the banks of the Isis, the old gentleman made an "alphabet of faces," which, as far as I could decipher his physiognomy, I verily believe was indicative of laughter;—indeed, I have rarely met with an old gentleman who took absolutely offence at the imputed gallantries of his youth.

I found the tide of wine and wassail fast gaining on the dry land of sober judgment. The company grew merrier and louder as their jokes grew duller. Master Simon was in as chirping a humour as a grasshopper filled with dew; his old songs grew of a warmer complexion, and he began to talk maudlin about the widow. He even gave a long song about the wooing of a widow, which he informed me he had gathered from an excellent black letter work, entitled "Cupid's Solicitor for Love," containing store of good advice for bachelors, and which he promised to lend me. The first verse was to this effect:—

> *He that will woo a widow must not dally,*
> *He must make hay while the sun doth shine;*
> *He must not stand with her, Shall I, Shall I?*
> *But boldly say, Widow, thou must be mine.*

This song inspired the fat-headed old gentleman, who made several attempts to tell a rather broad story out of Joe Miller, that was pat to the purpose; but he always stuck in the middle, everybody recollecting the latter part excepting himself. The parson, too, began to show the effects of good cheer, having gradually settled down into a doze, and his wig sitting most suspiciously on one side. Just at this juncture we were summoned to the drawing room, and, I suspect, at the private instigation of mine host, whose joviality seemed always tempered with a proper love of decorum.

After the dinner table was removed, the hall was given up to the younger members of the family, who, prompted to all kind of noisy mirth by the Oxonian and Master Simon, made its old walls ring with their merriment, as they played at romping games. I delight in witnessing the gambols of children, and particularly at this happy holiday season, and could not help stealing out of the drawing room on hearing one of their peals of laughter. I found them at the game of blind man's buff. Master Simon, who was the leader of their revels, and seemed on all occasions to fulfil the office of that ancient potentate, the Lord of Misrule, was blinded in the midst of the hall. The little beings were as busy about him as the mock fairies about Falstaff; pinching him, plucking at the skirts of his coat, and tickling him with straws. One fine blue-eyed girl of about thirteen, with her flaxen hair all in beautiful confusion, her frolic face in a glow, her frock half torn off her shoulders, a complete picture of a romp, was the chief tormentor; and from the slyness with which Master Simon avoided the smaller game, and hemmed this wild little nymph in corners, and obliged her to jump shrieking over chairs, I suspected the rogue of being not a whit more blinded than was convenient.

When I returned to the drawing room, I found the company seated round the fire, listening to the parson, who was deeply ensconced in a high-backed oaken chair, the work of some cunning artificer of yore, which had been brought from the library for his particular accommodation. From this venerable piece of furniture, with which his shadowy figure and dark weazen face so admirably accorded, he was dealing forth strange accounts of the popular superstitions and legends of the surrounding country, with which he had become acquainted in the course of his antiquarian researches. I am half inclined to think that the old gentleman was himself somewhat tinctured with superstition, as men are very apt to be who live a recluse and studious life in a sequestered part of the country, and pore over black letter tracts, so often filled with the marvellous and supernatural.

He gave us several anecdotes of the fancies of the neighbouring peasantry, concerning the effigy of the crusader which lay on the tomb by the church altar. As it was the only monument of the kind in that part of the country, it had always been regarded with feelings of superstition by the good wives of the village. It was said to get up from the tomb and walk the rounds of the churchyard in stormy nights, particularly when it thundered; and one old woman, whose cottage bordered on the churchyard, had seen it, through the windows of the church, when the moon shone, slowly pacing up and down the aisles. It was the belief that some wrong had been left unredressed by the deceased, or some treasure hidden, which kept the spirit in a state of trouble and restlessness. Some talked of gold and jewels buried in the tomb, over which the spectre kept watch; and there was a story current of a sexton in old times who endeavoured to break his way to the coffin at night; but just as he reached it, received a violent blow from the marble hand of the effigy, which stretched him senseless on the pavement. These tales were often laughed at by some of the sturdier among the rustics, yet when night came on, there were many of the stoutest unbelievers that were shy of venturing alone in the footpath that led across the churchyard.

From these and other anecdotes that followed, the crusader appeared to be the favourite hero of ghost stories throughout the vicinity. His picture, which hung up in the hall, was thought by the servants to have something supernatural about it; for they remarked that, in whatever part of the hall you went, the eyes of the warrior were still fixed on you. The old porter's wife, too, at the lodge, who had been born and brought up in the family, and was a great gossip among the maid-servants, affirmed, that in her young days she had often heard say, that on Midsummer eve, when it is well known all kinds of ghosts, goblins, and fairies become visible and walk abroad, the crusader used to mount his horse, come down from his picture, ride about the house, down the avenue, and so to the church to visit the tomb; on which occasion the church door most civilly swung open of itself: not that he needed it; for he rode through closed gates and even stone walls, and had been seen by one of the dairymaids to pass between two bars of the great park gate, making himself as thin as a sheet of paper.

All these superstitions I found had been very much countenanced by the Squire, who, though not superstitious himself, was very fond of seeing others so. He listened to every goblin tale of the neighbouring gossips with infinite gravity, and held the porter's wife in high favour on account of her talent for the marvellous. He was himself a great reader of old legends and romances, and often lamented that he could not believe in them; for a superstitious person, he thought, must live in a kind of fairyland.

Whilst we were all attention to the parson's stories, our ears were suddenly assailed by a burst of heterogeneous sounds from the hall, in which was mingled something like the clang of rude minstrelsy, with the uproar of many small voices and girlish laughter. The door suddenly flew open, and a train came trooping into the room, that might almost have been mistaken for the breaking up of the court of Fairy. That indefatigable spirit, Master Simon, in the faithful discharge of his duties as lord of misrule, had conceived the idea of a Christmas mummery, or masquing; and having called in to his assistance the Oxonian and the young officer, who were equally ripe for anything that should occasion romping and merriment, they had carried it into instant effect. The old housekeeper had been consulted; the antique clothes presses and wardrobes rummaged and made to yield up the relics of finery that had not seen the light for several generations; the younger part of the company had been privately convened from the parlour and hall, and the whole had been bedizened out, into a burlesque imitation of an antique masque.

Master Simon led the van, as "Ancient Christmas," quaintly apparelled in a ruff, a short cloak, which had very much the aspect of one of the old housekeeper's petticoats, and a hat that might have served for a village steeple, and must indubitably have figured in the days of the Covenanters. From under this his nose curved boldly forth, flushed with a frostbitten bloom, that seemed the very trophy of a December blast. He was accompanied by the blue-eyed romp, dished up as "Dame Mince-Pie," in the venerable magnificence of faded brocade, long stomacher, peaked hat, and high-heeled shoes. The young officer appeared as Robin Hood, in a sporting dress of Kendal green, and a foraging cap, with a gold tassel. The costume, to be sure, did not bear testimony to deep research, and there was an evident eye to the picturesque, natural to a young gallant in the presence of his mistress. The fair Julia hung on his arm in a pretty rustic dress, as "Maid Marian." The rest of the train had been metamorphosed in various ways; the girls trussed up in the finery of the ancient belles of the Bracebridge line, and the striplings bewhiskered with burnt cork, and gravely clad in broad skirts, hanging sleeves, and full-bottomed wigs, to represent the characters of Roast Beef, Plum Pudding, and other worthies celebrated in ancient maskings. The whole was under the control of the Oxonian, in the appropriate character of Misrule; and I observed that he exercised rather a mischievous sway with his wand over the smaller personages of the pageant.

The irruption of this motley crew, with beat of drum, according to ancient custom, was the consummation of uproar and merriment. Master Simon covered himself with glory by the stateliness with which, as Ancient Christmas, he walked a minuet with the peerless, though giggling, Dame Mince-Pie. It was followed by a dance of all the characters, which, from its medley of costumes, seemed as though the old family portraits had skipped down from their frames to join in the sport. Different centuries were figuring at cross hands and right and left; the dark ages were cutting pirouettes and rigadoons; and the days of Queen Bess jigging merrily down the middle, through a line of succeeding generations.

The worthy Squire contemplated these fantastic sports, and this resurrection of his old wardrobe, with the simple relish of childish delight. He stood chuckling and rubbing his hands, and scarcely hearing a word the parson said, notwithstanding that the latter was discoursing most authentically on the ancient and stately dance at the Paon, or Peacock, from which he conceived the minuet to be derived. For my part, I was in a continual excitement, from the varied scenes of whim and innocent gaiety passing before me. It was inspiring to see wild-eyed frolic and warmhearted hospitality breaking out from among the chills and glooms of winter, and old age throwing off his apathy, and catching once more the freshness of youthful enjoyment. I felt also an interest in the scene, from the consideration that these fleeting customs were posting fast into oblivion, and that this was, perhaps, the only family in England in which the whole of them were still punctiliously observed. There was a quaintness, too, mingled with all this revelry, that gave it a peculiar zest; it was suited to the time and place; and as the old Manor House almost reeled with mirth and wassail, it seemed echoing back the joviality of long-departed years.

But enough of Christmas and its gambols; it is time for me to pause in this garrulity. Methinks I hear the questions asked by my graver readers, "To what purpose is all this?—How is the world to be made wiser by this talk?" Alas! Is there not wisdom enough extant for the instruction of the world? And if not, are there not thousands of abler pens labouring for its improvement?—It is so much pleasanter to please than to instruct—to play the companion rather than the preceptor.

What, after all, is the mite of wisdom that I could throw into the mass of knowledge? Or how am I sure that my sagest deductions may be safe guides for the opinions of others? But in writing to amuse, if I fail, the only evil is my own disappointment. If, however, I can by any lucky chance, in these days of evil, rub out one wrinkle from the brow of care, or beguile the heavy heart of one moment of sorrow; if I can now and then penetrate through the gathering film of misanthropy, prompt a benevolent view of human nature, and make my reader more in good humour with his fellow beings and himself, surely, surely, I shall not then have written entirely in vain.

CHRISTMAS: A STORY

IT WAS IN OCTOBER THAT Mary Chavah burned over the grass of her lawn, and the flame ran free across the place where in Spring her wildflower bed was made. Two weeks later she had there a great patch of purple violets. And all Old Trail Town, which takes account of its neighbours' flowers, of the migratory birds, of eclipses, and the like, came to see the wonder.

"Mary Chavah!" said most of the village, "you're the luckiest woman alive. If a miracle was bound to happen, it'd get itself happened to you."

"I don't believe in miracles, though," Mary wrote to Jenny Wing. "These come just natural—only we don't know how."

"That *is* miracles," Jenny wrote back. "They do come natural—we don't know how."

"At this rate," said Ellen Bourne, one of Mary's neighbours, "you'll be having roses bloom in your yard about Christmas time. For a Christmas present."

"I don't believe in Christmas," Mary said. "I thought you knew that. But I'll take the roses, though, if they come in the Winter," she added, with her queer flash of smile.

When it was dusk, or early in the morning, Mary Chavah, with her long shawl over her head, stooped beside the violets and loosened the earth about them with her whole hand, and as if she reverenced violets more than fingertips. And she thought:—

"Ain't it just as if Spring was right over back of the air all the time—and it could come if we knew how to call it? But we don't know."

But whatever she thought about it, Mary kept in her heart. For it was as if not only Spring, but new life, or some other holy thing were nearer than one thought and had spoken to her, there on the edge of Winter.

And Old Trail Town asked itself:—

"Ain't Mary Chavah the funniest? Look how nice she is about everything—and yet you know she won't never keep Christmas at all. No, sir. She ain't kept a single Christmas in years. I donno why...."

II

MOVING ABOUT ON HIS LITTLE lawn in the dark, Ebenezer Rule was aware of two deeper shadows before him. They were between him and the leafless lilacs and mulberries that lined the street wall. A moment before he had been looking at that darkness and remembering how, once, as a little boy, he had slept there under the wall and had dreamed that he had a kingdom.

"Who is't?" he asked sharply.

"Hello, Ebenezer," said Simeon Buck, "it's only me and Abel. We're all."

Ebenezer Rule came toward them. It was so dark that they could barely distinguish each other. Their voices had to do it all.

"What you doing out here?" one of the deeper shadows demanded.

"Oh, nothing," said Ebenezer, irritably, "not a thing."

He did not ask them to go in the house, and the three stood there awkwardly, handling the time like a blunt instrument. Then Simeon Buck, proprietor of the Simeon Buck North American Dry Goods Exchange, plunged into what they had come to say.

"Ebenezer," he said, with those variations of intonation which mean an effort to be delicate, "is—is there any likelihood that the factory will open up this Fall?"

"No, there ain't," Ebenezer said, like something shutting.

"Nor—nor this Winter?" Simeon pursued.

"No, sir," said Ebenezer, like something opening again to shut with a bang.

"Well, if you're sure—" said Simeon.

Ebenezer cut him short. "I'm dead sure," he said. "I've turned over my orders to my brother's house in the City. He can handle 'em all and not have to pay his men a cent more wages." And this was as if something had been locked.

"Well," said Simeon, "then, Abel, I move we go ahead."

Abel Ames, proprietor of the Granger County Merchandise Emporium ("The A. T. Stewart's of the Middle West," he advertised it), sighed heavily—a vast, triple sigh, that seemed to sigh both in and out, as a schoolboy whistles.

"Well," he said, "I hate to do it. But I'll be billblowed if I want to think of paying for a third or so of this town's Christmas presents and carrying 'em right through the Winter. I done that last year, and Fourth of July I had all I could do to keep from wishing most of the crowd Merry Christmas, 'count of their still owing me. I'm a merchant and a citizen, but I ain't no patent adjustable Christmas tree."

"Me neither," Simeon said. "Last year it was *me* give a silk cloak and a Five Dollar umbrella and a fur bore and a bushel of knick-knacks to the folks in this town. My name wa'n't on the cards, but it's me that's paid for 'em—*up* to now. I'm sick of it. The storekeepers of this town may make a good thing out of Christmas, but they'd ought to get some of the credit instead of giving it all, by Josh."

"What you going to do?" inquired Ebenezer, dryly.

"Well, of course last year was an exceptional year," said Abel, "owing—"

He hesitated to say "owing to the failure of the Ebenezer Rule Factory Company," and so stammered with the utmost delicacy, and skipped a measure.

"And we thought," Simeon finished, "that if the factory wasn't going to open up this Winter, we'd work things so's to have little or no Christmas in town this year—being so much of the present giving falls on us to carry on our books."

"It ain't only the factory wages, of course," Abel interposed, "it's the folks's savings being et up in—"

"—the failure," he would have added, but skipped a mere beat instead.

"—and we want to try to give 'em a chance to pay us up for last Christmas before they come on to themselves with another celebration," he added reasonably.

Ebenezer Rule laughed—a descending scale of laughter that seemed to have no organs wherewith to function in the open, and so never got beyond the gutturals.

"How you going to fix it?" he inquired again.

"Why," said Simeon, "everybody in town's talking that they ain't going to give anybody anything for Christmas. Some means it and some don't. Some'll do it and some'll back out. But the churches has decided to omit Christmas exercises altogether this year. Some thought to have speaking pieces, but everybody concluded if they had exercises without oranges and candy the children'd go home disappointed, so they've left the whole thing slide—"

"It don't seem just right for 'em not to celebrate the birth of our Lord just because they can't afford the candy," Abel Ames observed mildly, but Simeon hurried on:—

"—slide, and my idea and Abel's is to get the town meeting to vote a petition to the same effect asking the town not to try to do anything with their Christmas this year. We heard the factory wasn't going to open, and we thought if we could tell 'em that for sure, it would settle it—and save him and me and all the rest of 'em. Would—would you be willing for us to tell the town meeting that? It's tonight—we're on the way there."

"Sure," said Ebenezer Rule, "tell 'em. And you might point out to 'em," he added, with his spasm of gutturals, "that failures is often salutary measures. Public benefactions. Fixes folks so's they can't spend their money fool."

He walked with them across the lawn, going between them and guiding them among the empty aster beds.

"They think I et up their savings in the failure," he went on, "when all I done is to bring 'em face to face with the fact that for years they've been overspending themselves. It takes Christmas to show that up. This whole Christmas business is about wore out, anyhow. Ain't it?"

"That's what," Simeon said, "it's a spendin' sham, from edge to edge."

Abel Ames was silent. The three skirted the flower beds and came out on the level sweep of turf before the house that was no house in the darkness, save that they remembered how it looked: a square, smoked thing, with a beard of dead creepers and white shades lidded over its never-lighted windows—a fit home for this man least-liked of the three hundred neighbours who made Old Trail Town. He touched the elbows of the other two men as they walked in the dark, but he rarely touched any human being. And now Abel Ames suddenly put his hand down on that of Ebenezer, where it lay in the crook of Abel's elbow.

"What you got there?" he asked.

"Nothing much," Ebenezer answered, irritably again. "It's an old glass. I was looking over some rubbish, and I found it—over back. It's a field glass."

"What you got a field glass out in the dark for?" Abel demanded.

"I used to fool with it some when I was a little shaver," Ebenezer said. He put the glass in Abel's hand. "On the sky," he added.

Abel lifted the glass and turned it on the heavens. There, above the little side lawn, the firmament had unclothed itself of branches and lay in a glorious nakedness to three horizons.

"Thunder," Abel said, "look at 'em look."

Sweeping the field with the lens, Abel spoke meanwhile.

"Seems as if I'd kind of miss all the fuss in the store around Christmas," he said,—"the extra rush and the trimming up and all."

"Abel'll miss lavishin' his store with cut paper, I guess," said Simeon; "he dotes on tassels."

"Last year," Abel went on, not lowering the glass, "I had a little kid come in the store Christmas Eve, that I'd never see before. He ask' me if he could get warm—and he set down on the edge of a chair by the stove, and he took in everything in the place. I ask' him his name, and he just smiled. I ask' him if he was glad it was Christmas, and he says, Was I. I was goin' to give him some cough drops, but when I come back from waiting on somebody he was gone. I never could find out who he was, nor see anybody that saw him. I thought mebbe this Christmas he'd come back. Lord, don't it look like a pasture of buttercups up there? Here, Simeon."

Simeon, talking, took the glass and lifted it to the stars.

"Cut paper doin's is all very well," he said, "but the worst nightmare of the year to the stores is Christmas. I always think it's come to be 'Peace on earth, good will to men and extravagance of women.' Quite a nice little till of gold pieces up there in the sky, ain't there? I'd kind o' like to stake a claim out up there—eh? Lay it out along about around that bright one down there—by Josh," he broke off, "look at that bright one."

Simeon kept looking through the glass, and he leaned a little forward to try to see the better.

"What is it?" he repeated, "what's that one? It's the biggest star I ever see—"

The other two looked where he was looking, low in the east. But they saw nothing save boughs indeterminately moving and a spatter of sparkling points not more bright than those of the upper field.

"You look," Simeon bade the vague presence that was his host; but through the glass, Ebenezer still saw nothing that challenged his sight.

"I don't know the name of a star in the sky, except the dipper," he grumbled, "but I don't see anything out of the ordinary, anyhow."

"It is," Simeon protested; "I tell you, it's the biggest star I ever saw. It's blue and purple and green and yellow—"

Abel had the glass now, and he had looked hardly sooner than he had recognized.

"Sure," he said, "I've got it. It *is* blue and purple and green and yellow, and it's as big as most stars put together. It twinkles—yes, sir, and it swings...." he broke off, laughing at the mystification of the others, and laughed so that he could not go on.

"Is it a comet, do you s'pose?" said Simeon.

"No," said Abel, "no. It's come to stay. It's our individual private star. It's the arc light in front of the Town Hall you two are looking at."

They moved to where Abel stood, and from there, up the rise of ground to the east, they could see Simeon's star, shining softly and throwing long rays, it seemed, almost to where they stood: the lamp that marked the heart of the village.

"Shucks," said Simeon.

"Sold," said Ebenezer.

"Why, I don't know," said Abel, "I kind of like to see it through the glass. It looks like it was a bigger light than we give it credit for."

"It's a big enough light," said Ebenezer, testily. It was his own plant at the factory that made possible the town's three arc lights, and these had been continued by him at the factory's closing.

"No use making fun of your friends' eyesight because you're all of twenty minutes younger than them," Simeon grumbled. "Come on, Abel. It must be gettin' round the clock."

Abel lingered.

"A man owns the hull thing with a glass o' this stamp," he said. "How much does one like that cost?" he inquired.

"I'll sell you this one—" began Ebenezer; "wait a week or two and I may sell you this one," he said. "I ain't really looked through it myself yet."

Not much after this, the two went away and left Ebenezer in the dark yard.

He stood in the middle of his little grass plot and looked through his glass again. That night there was, so to say, nothing remote about the sky, save its distance. It had none of the reticence of clouds. It made you think of a bed of golden bells, each invisible stalk trying on its own account to help forward some Spring. As he had said, he did not know one star from another, nor a planet for a planet with a name. It had been years since he had seen the heavens so near. He moved about, looking, and passed the wall of leafless lilacs and mulberries. Stars hung in his boughs like fruit for the plucking. They patterned patches of sky. He looked away and back, and it was as if the stars repeated themselves, like the chorus of everything.

"You beggars," Ebenezer said, "awful dressed up, ain't you? It must be for something up there—it ain't for anything down here, let me tell you."

He went up to his dark back door. From without there he could hear Kate Kerr, his general servant, who had sufficient personality to compel the term "housekeeper," setting sponge for bread, with a slapping, hollow sound and a force that implied a frown for every down stroke of the iron spoon. He knew how she would turn toward the door as he entered, with her way of arching eyebrows, in the manner of one about to recite the symptoms of a change for the worse—or at best to say "about the same" to everything in the universe. And when Kate Kerr spoke, she always whispered on the faintest provocation.

A sudden distaste for the entire inside of his house seized Ebenezer. He turned and wandered back down the little dark yard, looking up at the high field of the stars, with only his dim eyes.

"There must be quite a little to know about them," he thought, "if anybody was enough interested."

Then he remembered Simeon and Abel, and laughed again in his way.

"I done the town a good turn for once, didn't I?" he thought; "I've fixed folks so's they can't spend their money fool!"

Two steps from Ebenezer's front gate, Simeon and Abel overtook a woman.

She had a long shawl over her head, and she was humming some faint air of her own making.

"Coming to the meeting, Mary?" Simeon asked as they passed her.

"No," said Mary Chavah, "I started for it. But it's such a nice night I'm going to walk around."

"Things are going to go your way to that meeting, I guess," said Simeon; "ain't you always found fault with Christmas?"

"They's a lot o' nonsense about it," Mary assented; "I don't ever bother myself much with it. Why?"

"I donno but we'll all come round to your way of thinking tonight," said Simeon.

"For just this year!" Abel Ames called back, as they went on.

"You can't do much else, I guess," said Mary. "Everybody dips Christmas up out of their pocketbooks, and if there ain't nothing there, they can't dip."

The men laughed with her, and went on down the long street toward the town. Mary followed slowly, under the yellowing elms that made great golden shades for the dim post lamps. And high at the far end of the street down which they went, hung the blue arc light before the Town Hall, center to the constellation of the home lights and the shop lights and the streetlights, all near neighbours to the stream and sweep of the stars hanging a little higher and shining as by one sun.

III

IT WAS INTERESTING TO SEE how they took the proposal to drop that Christmas from the calendar there in Old Trail Town. It was so eminently a sensible thing to do, and they all knew it. Oh, every way they looked at it, it was sensible, and they admitted it. Yet, besides Mary Chavah and Ebenezer Rule, probably the only person in the town whose satisfaction in the project could be counted on to be unfeigned was little Tab Winslow. For Tab, as all the town knew, had a turkey brought up by his own hand to be the Winslows' Christmas dinner, but such had become Tab's intimacy with and fondness for the turkey that he was prepared to forego his Christmas if only that dinner were foregone, too.

"Theophilus Thistledown is such a human turkey," Tab had been heard explaining patiently; "he knows me—and he knows his name. He don't *expect* us to eat him ... why, you *can't* eat anything that knows its name."

But everyone else was just merely sensible. And they had been discussing Christmas in this sensible strain at the town meeting that night, before Simeon and Abel broached their plan for standardizing their sensible leanings.

Somebody had said that Jenny Wing, and Bruce Rule, who was Ebenezer's nephew, were expected home for Christmas, and had added that it "didn't look as if there would be much of any Christmas down to the station to meet them." On which Mis' Mortimer Bates had spoken out, philosophical to the point of brutality. Mis' Bates was little and brown and quick, and her clothes seemed always to curtain her off, so that her figure was no part of her presence.

"I ain't going to do a thing for Christmas this year," she declared, as nearly everybody in the village had intermittently declared, "not a living, breathing thing. I can't, and folks might just as well know it, flat foot. What's the use of buying tinsel and flim-flam when you're eating milk gravy to save butter and using salt sacks for handkerchiefs? I ain't educated up to see it."

Mis' Jane Moran, who had changed her chair three times to avoid a draught, sat down carefully in her fourth chair, her face twitching a little as if its muscles were connected with her joints.

"Christmas won't be no different from any other day to our house this year," she said. "We'll get up and eat our three meals and sit down and look at each other. We can't even spare a hen—she might lay if we didn't eat her."

Mis' Abby Winslow, mother of seven under fifteen, looked up from her rocking chair—Mis' Winslow always sat limp in chairs as if they were reaching out to rest her and, indeed, this occasional yielding to the force of gravity was almost her only luxury.

"You ain't thinking of the children, Mis' Bates," she said, "nor you either, Jane Moran, or you couldn't talk that way. We can't have no real Christmas, of course. But I'd planned some little things made out of what I had in the house: things that wouldn't be anything, and yet would seem a little something."

Mis' Mortimer Bates swept round at her.

"Children," she said, "ought to be showed how to do without things. Bennet and Gussie ain't expecting a sliver of nothing for Christmas—not a sliver."

Mis' Winslow unexpectedly flared up.

"Whether it shows through on the outside or not," she said, "I'll bet you they are."

"My three," Mis' Emerson Morse put in pacifically, "have been kept from popping corn and cracking nuts all Fall so's they could do both Christmas night, and it would seem like something that *was* something."

"That ain't the idea," Mis' Bates insisted; "I want them learnt to do without—" ("They'll learn that," Mis' Abby Winslow said; "they'll learn....") "Happening as it does to most every one of us not to have no Christmas, they won't be no distinctions drawn. None of the children can brag—and children is limbs of Satan for bragging," she added. (She was remembering a brief conversation overheard that day between Gussie and Pep, the minister's son:—

"I've got a doll," said Gussie.

"I've got a dollar," said Pep.

"My mamma went to a tea party," said Gussie.

"My mamma give one," said Pep.

Gussie mustered her forces. "My papa goes to work every morning," she topped it.

"My papa don't have to," said Pep, and closed the incident.)

"I can't help who's a limb of Satan," Mis' Winslow replied doggedly, "I can't seem to sense Christmas time without Christmas."

"It won't *be* Christmas time if you don't have any Christmas," Mis' Bates persisted.

"Oh, yes it will," Mis' Winslow said. "Oh, yes, it will. You can't stop that."

It was Mis' Bates, who, from the high-backed plush rocker, rapped with the blue glass paperweight on the red glass lamp and, in the absence of Mr. Bates, called the meeting to order. The Old Trail Town Society was organized on a platform of "membership unlimited, dues nothing but taking turns with the entertaining, officers to consist of:

President, the host of the evening (or wife, if any), and no minutes to bother with." And it was to a meeting so disposed on the subject of Christmas that Simeon Buck rose to present his argument.

"Mr. President," he addressed the chair.

"It's Madam President, you ninny geese," corrected Buff Miles, *sotto voce*.

"It had ought to be Madam Chairman," objected Mis' Moran; "she ain't the continuous president."

"Well, for the land sakes, call me Mis' Bates, formal, and go ahead," said the lady under discussion. "Only I bet you've forgot now what you was going to say."

"Not much I did *not*," Simeon Buck continued composedly, and, ignoring the interruptions, let his own vocative stand. Then he presented a memorandum of a sum of money. It was not a large sum. But when he quoted it, everybody looked at everybody else, stricken. For it was a sum large enough to have required, in the earning, months of work on the part of an appalling proportion of Old Trail Town.

"From the day after Thanksgiving to the night before Christmas last year," said Simeon, "that is the amount that the three hundred souls— no, I guess it must have been bodies—in our town spent in the local stores. Now, bare living expenses aside,—which ain't very much for us all, these days,—this amount may be assumed to have been spent by the lot of us for Christmas. Of course there was those," continued Mr. Buck, looking intelligently about him, "who bought most of their Christmas stuff in the City. But these—these economic traitors only make the point of what I say the more so. Without them, the town spent this truly amazing sum in keeping the holidays. Now, I ask you, frank, could the town afford that, or anything like that?"

Buff Miles spoke out of the extremity of his reflections.

"That's a funny crack," he said, "for a merchant to make. Why not leave 'em spend and leave 'em pay?"

"Oh, I'll leave 'em *pay* all right," rejoined Simeon, significantly, and stood silent and smiling until there were those in the room who uncomfortably shifted.

Then he told them the word he bore from Ebenezer Rule that as they had feared and half expected, the factory was not to open that Winter at all. Hardly a family represented in the rooms was not also representative of a factory employee, now idle these seven months, as they were periodically idle at the times of "enforced" suspension of the work.

"What I'm getting at is this," Simeon summed it up, "and Abel Ames, here, backs me up—don't you, Abel?—That hadn't we all ought to come to some joint conclusion about our Christmas this year, and roust the town up to it, like a town, and not go it blind and either get in up to our necks in debt, same as City folks, or else quit off Christmas, individual, and mebbe hurt folks's feelings? Why not move intelligent, like a town, and all agree out-and-out to leave Christmas go by this year? And have it understood, thorough?"

It was very still in the little rooms when he had finished. There seems to be no established etiquette of revolutions. But something of the unconsciousness of the enthusiast was upon Mis' Mortimer Bates, and she spoke before she knew:—

"So's we can be sure everybody else'll know it and not give something either and be disappointed too," she assented. "Well, I bet everybody'd be real relieved."

"The churches has sanctioned us doing away with Christmas this year by doing away with it themselves," observed Mis' Jane Moran. "That'd ought to be enough to go by."

"It don't seem to me Christmas is a thing for the churches to decide about," said Simeon, thoughtfully. "It seems to me the matter is up to the merchants and the grocers and the family providers. We're the ones most concerned. Us providers have got to scratch gravel to get together any Christmas at all, if any. And speaking for us merchants, I may say, we'll lay in the stock if folks'll buy it. But if they can't afford to pay for it, we don't want the stock personally."

"I guess we've all had the experience," observed Mis' Jane Moran, "of announcing we wasn't going to give any gifts *this* year, and then had somebody send something embroidered by hand, with a solid month's work on it. But if we all agree to secede from Christmas, we can lay down the law to folks so's it'll be understood: *No Christmas for nobody*."

"Not to children?" said Mis' Abby Winslow, doubtfully.

"My idea is to teach 'em to do entirely without Christmas," harped Mis' Bates. "We can't afford one. Why not let the children share in the family privation without trying to fool 'em with makeshift presents and boiled sugar?"

Over in a corner near the window plants, whose dead leaves she had been picking off, sat Ellen Bourne—Mis' Matthew Bourne she was, but nearly everybody called her Ellen Bourne. There is some law about these things: why instinctively we call some folk by the whole name, some by their first names, some by the last, some by shortening the name, some by a name not their own. Perhaps there is a name for each of us, if only we knew where to look, and folk intuitively select the one most like that. Perhaps some of us, by the sort of miracle that is growing every day, got the name that is meant for us. Perhaps some of us struggle along with consonants that spell somebody else. And how did some names get themselves so terrifically overused unless by some strange might, say, a kind of astrological irregularity.... Ellen Bourne sat by the window and suddenly looked over her shoulder at the room.

"If we've got the things made," she said, "can't we give 'em? If it's to children?"

"I think if we're going to omit, we'd ought to omit," Mis Bates held her own; "it can't matter to you, Ellen, with no children, so...." She caught herself sharply up. Ellen's little boy had died a Christmas or two ago.

"No," Ellen said, "I ain't any children, of course. But—"

"Well, I think," said Mis' Jane Moran, "that we've hit on the only way we could have hit on to chirk each other up over a hard time."

"And get off delicate ourselves same time," said Buff Miles. From the first Buff had been advocating what he called "an open Christmas," and there were those near him at the meeting to whom he had confided some plan about "church choir Christmas carol serenades," which he was loath to see set at naught.

Not much afterward Simeon Buck put the motion:—

"Mis' Chairman," he said, "I move you—and all of us—that the Old Trail Town meeting do and hereby does declare itself in favour of striking Christmas celebrations from its calendar this year. And that we circulate a petition through the town to this effect, headed by our names. And that we all own up that it's for the simple and regretful reason that not a mother's son of us can afford to buy Christmas presents this year, and what's the use of scratching to keep up appearances?"

For a breath Abel Ames hesitated; then he spoke voluntarily for the first time that evening.

"Mr. President, I second the hull of that," said he, slowly, and without looking at anybody; and then sighed his vast, triple sigh.

There was apparently nobody to vote against the motion. Mis' Winslow did not vote at all. Ellen Bourne said "No," but she said it so faintly that nobody heard save those nearest her, and they felt a bit embarrassed for her because she had spoken alone, and they tried to cover up the minute.

"Carried," said the Chair, and slipped out in the kitchen to put on the coffee.

At the meeting there was almost nobody who, in the course of the evening, did not make or reply to some form of observation on one theme. It was:—

"Well, I wish Mary Chavah'd been to the meeting. She'd have enjoyed herself."

Or, "Well, won't Mary Chavah be glad of this plan they've got? She's wanted it a good while."

Or, "We all seem to have come to Mary Chavah's way of thinking, don't we? You know, she ain't kept any Christmas for years."

Unless it was Abel Ames. He, in fact, made or replied to almost no observations that evening. He drank his coffee without cream, sugar, or spoon,—they are always overlooking somebody's essentials in this way, and such is Old Trail Town's shy courtesy that the omission is never mentioned or repaired by the victim,—and sighed his triple sigh at intervals, and went home.

"Hetty," he said to his wife, who had not gone to the meeting, "they put it through. We won't have no Christmas creditors this year. We don't have to furnish charged Christmas presents for nobody."

She looked up from the towel she was featherstitching—she was a little woman who carried her head back and had large eyes and the long, curved lashes of a child.

"I s'pose you're real relieved, ain't you, Abel?" she answered.

"My, yes," said Abel, without expression. "My, yes."

They all took the news home in different wise.

"Matthew," said Ellen Bourne, "the town meeting voted not to have any Christmas this year. That is, to ask the folks not to have any—'count of expense."

"Sensible move," said Matthew, sharpening his ax by the kitchen stove.

"It'll be a relief for most folks not to have the muss and the clutter," said Ellen's mother.

"Hey, king and country!" said Ellen's old father, whittling a stick, "I ain't done no more'n look on at a Christmas for ten years and more—with no children around so."

"I know," said Ellen Bourne, "I know...."

The announcement was greeted by Mortimer Bates with a slap of the knee.

"Goodbye, folderol!" he said. "We need a sane Christmas in the world a good sight more'n we need a sane Fourth, most places. Good work."

But Bennet and Gussie Bates burst into wails.

"Hush!" said Mis' Bates, peremptorily. "You ain't the only ones, remember. It's no Christmas for nobody!"

"I thought the rest of 'em would have one an' we could go over to theirs...." sobbed Gussie.

"I'd rather p'etend it's Christmas in other houses even if we ain't it!" mourned Bennet.

"Be my little man and woman," admonished Mis' Mortimer Bates.

At the Morans, little Emily Moran made an unexpected deduction:—

"I *won't* stay in bed all day Christmas!" she gave out.

"Stay in bed!" echoed Mis' Moran. "Why on this earth should you stay in bed?"

"Well, if we get up, then it's Christmas and you can't stop it!" little Emily triumphed.

When they told Pep, the minister's son, after a long preparation by story and other gradual approach, and a Socratic questioning cleverly winning damning admissions from Pep, he looked up in his father's face thoughtfully:—

"If they ain't no Christ's birthday this year, is it a lie that Christ was born?" he demanded.

And secretly the children took counsel with one another: Would Buff Miles, the church choir tenor, take them out after dark on Christmas Eve, to sing church choir serenades at folks' gates, or would he not? And when they thought that he might not, because this would be considered Christmas celebration and would only make the absence of present giving the more conspicuous, as in the case of the Sunday schools themselves, they faced still another theological quandary: For if it was true that Christ was born, then Christmas was his birthday; and if Christmas was his birthday, wasn't it wicked not to pay any attention?

Alone of them all, little Tab Winslow rejoiced. His brothers and sisters made the time tearful with questionings as to the effect on Santa Claus, and how would they get word to him, and would it be Christmas in the City, and why couldn't they move there, and other matters denoting the reversal of this their earth. But Tab slipped out the kitchen door, to the corner of the barn, where the great turkey gobbler who had been named held his empire trustingly.

"Oh, Theophilus Thistledown," said Tab to him, "you're the only one in this town that's goin' to have a Christmas. You ain't got to be et."

IV

THE PLACARD WAS TACKED TO the Old Trail Town post office wall, between a summons to join the Army and the Navy of the United States, and the reward offered for an escaped convict—all three manifestoes registering something of the stage of society's development.

NOTICE

> Owing to the local business depression and to the current
> private decisions to get up very few home Christmas
> celebrations this year, and also to the vote of the various
> lodges, churches, Sunday schools, etc., etc., etc., to forego the
> usual Christmas tree observances, the merchants of this town
> have one and all united with most of the folks to petition
> the rest to omit all Christmas presents, believing that the
> Christmas spirit will be kept up best by all agreeing to act
> alike. All that's willing may announce it by signing below and
> notifying others.

THE COMMITTEE.

There were only three hundred folk living in Old Trail Town. Already two thirds of their signatures were scrawled on the sheets of foolscap tacked beneath the notice.

On the day after her return home, Jenny Wing stood and stared at the notice. Her mother had written to her of the town's talk, but the placard made it seem worse.

"I'll go in on the way home and see what Mary says," she thought, and asked for the letter that lay in Mary Chavah's box, next her own. They gave her the letter without question. All Old Trail Town asks for its neighbour's mail and reads its neighbour's postmarks and gets to know the different Writings and to inquire after them, like persons. ("He ain't got so much of a curl to his M today," one will say of a superscription. "Better write right back and chirk 'im up." Or, "Here's Her that don't seal her letters good. Tell her about that, why don't you?" Or, "This Writing's a stranger to me. I'll just wait a minute to see if birth or death gets out of the envelope.")

As she closed Mary's gate and hurried up the walk, in a keen wind flowing with little pricking flakes, Jenny was startled to see both parlour windows open. The white muslin curtains were blowing idly as if June were in the air. Turning as a matter of course to the path that led to the kitchen, she was hailed by Mary, who came out the front door with a rug in her hands.

"Step right in this way," said Mary; "this door's unfastened."

"Forevermore!" Jenny said, "Mary Chavah! What you got your house all open for? You ain't moving?"

A gust of wind took Mary's answer. She tossed the rug across the icy railing of the porch and beckoned Jenny into the house, and into the parlour. And when she had greeted Jenny after the months of her absence:—

"See," Mary said exultantly, "don't it look grand and empty? Look at it first, and then come on in and I'll tell you about it."

The white-papered walls of the two rooms were bare of pictures; the floor had been sparingly laid with rugs. The walnut sofa and chairs, the table for the lamp, and the long shelves of her grandfather's books—these were all that the room held. A white arch divided the two chambers, like a benign brow whose face had long been dimmed away. It was all exquisitely clean and icy cold. A little snow drifted in through the muslin curtains. The breath of the two women showed.

"What on earth you done that for?" Jenny demanded.

Mary Chavah stood in the empty archway, the satisfaction on her face not veiling its pure austerity. She was not much past thirty-three, but she looked older, for she was gaunt. Her flesh had lost its firmness, her dressmaking had stooped her, her strong frame moved as if it habitually shouldered its way. In her broad forehead and deep eyes and somewhat in her silent mouth, you read the woman—the rest of her was obscured in her gentle reticence. She had a gray shawl, blue-bordered, folded tightly about her head and pinned under her chin, and it wrapped her to her feet.

"I feel like a thing in a new shell," she said. "Come on in where it's warm."

Instead of moving her dining room table to her kitchen, as most of Old Trail Town did in Winter, Mary had moved her cooking stove into the dining room, had improvised a calico-curtained cupboard for the utensils, and there she lived and sewed. The windows were bare.

"I'll let the parlour have curtains if it wants to," she had said, "but in the room I live in I want every strip of the sun I can get."

There were no plants, though every house in Old Trail Town had a window of green, and slips without number were offered....

"... You can have flowers all you want," she said once; "I like 'em too well to box 'em up in the house."

And there were no books.

"I don't read," she admitted; "I ain't ever read a book in my life but *Pilgrim's Progress* and the first four chapters of *Ben Hur*. What's the use of pretending, when books is such a nuisance to dust? Grandfather's books in the parlour—oh, they ain't books. They're furniture."

But she had a little bookcase whose shelves were filled with her patterns—in her dressmaking she never used a fashion plate.

"I like to make 'em up and cut 'em out," she sometimes told her friends. "I don't care nothing whatever about the dresses when they get done—more fool the women for ornamenting themselves up like lamp shades, I always think. But I just do love to fuss with the paper and make it do like I say. Land, I've got my cupboard full of more patterns than I'd ever get orders for if I lived to be born again."

She sat down before the cooking stove and drew off her woolen mittens. She folded a hand on her cheek, forcing the cheek out of drawing by her hand's pressure. There was always about her gestures a curious nakedness—indeed, about her face and hands. They were naïve, perfectly likely to reveal themselves in their current awkwardness and ugliness of momentary expression which, by its very frankness, made a new law as it broke an old one.

"Don't you tell folks I've been house cleaning," she warned Jenny. "The town would think I was crazy, with the thermometer acting up zero so. Anyway, I ain't been house cleaning. I just simply got so sick to death of all the truck piled up in this house that I had to get away from it. And this morning it looked so clean and white and smooth outdoors that I felt so cluttered up I couldn't sew. I begun on this room—and then I kept on with the parlour. I've took out the lambrequins and 'leven pictures and the whatnot and four moth-catching rugs and four sofa pillows, and I've packed the whole lot of 'em into the attic. I've done the same to my bedroom. I've emptied my house out of all the stuff the folks' and the folks' folks and their folks—clear back to Grandmother Hackett had in here—I mean the truck part. Not the good. And I guess now I've got some room to live in."

Jenny looked at her admiringly, and asked: "How did you ever do it? I can't bear to throw things away. I can't bear to move things from where they've been."

"I didn't use to want to," said Mary, "but lately—I do. The Winter's so clean, you kind of have to, to keep up. What's the news?"

"Here's a letter," Jenny said, and handed it. "I didn't look to see who it's from. I guess it's a strange Writing, anyway."

Mary glanced indifferently at it. "It's from Lily's boy, out West," she said, and laid the letter on the shelf. "I meant, what's the news about you?"

Jenny's eyes widened swiftly. "News about me?" she said. "Who said there was any news about me?"

"Nobody," Mary said evenly; "but you've been gone most a year, ain't you?"

"Oh," Jenny said, "yes...."

For really, when Old Trail Town stopped to think of it, Jenny Wing was Mrs. Bruce Rule, and had been so for a year. But no one thought of calling her that. It always takes Old Trail Town several years to adopt its marriages. They would graduate first to "Jenny Wing that was," and then to "Jenny Wing What's-name," and then to "Mis' Rule that was Jenny Wing...."

"... You tell me some news," Jenny added. "Mother don't ever write much but the necessaries."

"That's all there's been," Mary Chavah told her; "we ain't had no luxuries for news in forever."

"But there's that notice in the post office," cried Jenny. "I come home to spend Christmas, and there's that notice in the post office. Mother wrote nobody was going to do anything for Christmas, but she never wrote me that. I've brought home some little things I made—"

"Oh—Christmas!" Mary said. "Yes, they all got together and concluded best not have any. You know, since the failure—"

Mary hesitated—Ebenezer Rule was Bruce Rule's uncle.

"I know," said Jenny, "it's Uncle Ebenezer. I don't know how I'm going to tell Bruce when he comes. To think it's in our family, the reason they can't have any Christmas...."

"Nonsense," said Mary, briskly; "no Christmas presents is real sensible, my way of thinking. It's been 'leven years since I've given a Christmas present to anybody. The first Christmas after mother died, I couldn't—I just couldn't. That kind of got me out of the idea, and then I see all the nonsense of it."

"The *nonsense?*" Jenny repeated.

"If you don't like folks, you don't want to give nothing to them or take nothing from them. And if you do like 'em you don't want to have to wait to Christmas to give 'em things. Ain't that so?" Mary Chavah put it.

"*No*," said Jenny; "it ain't. Not a bit so." And when Mary laughed, questioned her, pressed her, "It seems perfectly awful to me not to have a Christmas," Jenny could say only, "I feel like the Winter didn't have no backbone to it."

"It's a dead time, Winter," Mary assented. "What's the use of tricking it up with gewgaws and pretending it's a live time? Besides, if you ain't got the money, you ain't got the money. And nobody has, this year. Unless they go ahead and buy things anyway, like the City."

Jenny shook her head. "I got seven Christmas-present relatives and ten Christmas-present friends, and I've only spent Two Dollars and Eighty cents on 'em all," she said, "for material. But I've made little things for every one of 'em. It don't seem as if that much had ought to hurt anyone."

Jenny looked past her out the window, somewhere beyond the snow.

"They's something else," she added, "it ain't all present giving...."

"Nonsense," said Mary Chavah, "take the present trading away from Christmas and see how long it'd last. I was in the City once for Christmas. I'll never forget it—never. I never see folks work like the folks worked there. The streets was Bedlam. The stores was worse. 'What'll I get him?...' 'I've just got to get something for her....' 'It don't seem as if this is nice enough after what she give me last year....' I can hear 'em yet. They spent money wicked. And I said to myself that I was glad from my head to my feet that I was done with Christmas. And I been preaching it ever since. And I'm pleased this town has had to come to it."

"It ain't the way I feel," said Jenny. She got up and wandered to the window and hardly heard while Mary went on with more of the sort. "It seems kind of like going back on the ways things are," Jenny said, as she turned. Then, as she made ready to go, she broke off and smote her hands together.

"Oh," she said, "it don't seem as if I could bear it not to have Christmas—not *this* year."

"You mean your and Bruce's first Christmas," said Mary. "Mark my words, he'll be glad to be rid of the fuss. Men always are. Come on out the front door if you're going," said Mary. "You might as well use it when it's open."

As Jenny passed the open parlour door, she looked in again at the bare room.

"Don't you *like* pictures?" she asked abruptly.

"I like 'em when I like 'em," Mary answered. "I didn't like them I had up here—I had a shot stag and a fruit piece and an eagle with a child in its claws. I've loathed 'em for years, but I ain't ever had the heart to throw 'em out till now. They're over behind the coal bin."

Jenny thought. "They's a picture over to mother's," she said, "that she ain't put up because she ain't had the money to frame it. I guess I'll bring it over after supper and see if you don't want it up here—frame or no frame." She looked at Mary and laughed. "If I bring it to you tonight," she said, "it ain't a Christmas present—legal. But if I want to call it a Christmas present inside me, the town can't help that."

"What's the picture?" Mary asked.

"I don't know who it represents," said Jenny, "but it's nice."

When Jenny had gone, Mary Chavah stood in the snow shaking the rug she had left outside, and looking at the clean, white town.

"It looks like it was waiting for something," she thought.

A door opened and shut. A child shouted. In the northeast a shining body had come sparkling above the trees—Capella of the brightness of one hundred of our suns, being born into the twilight like a little star....

Mary closed the parlour windows and stood for a moment immersed in the quiet and emptiness of the clean rooms.

"This looks like it was waiting for something, too," she thought. "But it ought to know it won't get it," she added whimsically.

Then she went back to the warm room and saw the letter on the shelf. She meant to go in a moment to the stable to make it safe there for the night; so, with the gray shawl still binding her head and falling to her feet, she sat by the stove and read the letter.

V

"... because she wasn't sick but two days and we never
thought of her dying till she was dead. Otherwise we'd have
telegraphed. She was buried yesterday, right here, and we'll
get some kind of stone. You say how you think it'd ought to
be marked. That's about all there is to tell except about *Yes*.
He's six years old now and Aunt Mary this ain't a place for

him. He's a nice little fellow and I hate for him to get rough
and he will if he stays here. I'll do the best I can and earn
money to help keep him but I want he should come and live
with you...."

"I won't have him!" said Mary Chavah, aloud.

"... he could come alone with a tag all right and I could send
his things by freight. He ain't got much. You couldn't help but
like him and I hate for him to get rough. Please answer and
oblige your loving Nephew,

"JOHN BLOOD."

Mary kept reading the letter and staring out into the snow. Her
sister Lily's boy—they wanted to send him to her. Lily's boy and Adam
Blood's—the man whose son she had thought would be her son. It was
twenty years ago that he had been coming to the house—this same
house—and she had thought that he was coming to see her, had never
thought of Lily at all till Lily had told her of her own betrothal to him.
It hurt yet. It had hurt freshly when he had died, seven years ago. Now
Lily was dead, and Adam's eldest son, John, wanted to send this little
brother to her, to have.

"I won't take him," she said a great many times, and kept reading the
letter and staring out into the snow.

For Lily she had no tears—she seldom had tears at all. But after
a little while she was conscious of a weight through her and in her,
aching in her throat, her breast, her body. She rose and went near to the
warmth of the fire, then to the freedom of the window against which
the snow lay piled, then she sat down in the place where she worked,
beside her patterns. The gray shawl still bound her head, and it was still
in her mind that she must go to the barn and lock it. But she did not
go—she sat in the darkening room with all her past crowding it....

... That first day with Adam at the Blood's picnic, given at his home-
coming. They had met with all that perilous, ready-made intimacy
which a school friendship of years before had allowed. As she had
walked beside him she had known well what he was going to mean to
her. She remembered the moment when he had contrived to ask her to
wait until the others went, so that he might walk home with her. And
when they had reached home, there on the porch—where she had just

shaken the rugs in the snow—Lily had been sitting, a stool—one of the stools now at length banished to the shed—holding the hurt ankle that had kept her from the picnic. Adam had stayed an hour, and they had sat beside Lily. He had come again and again, and they had always sat beside Lily. Mary remembered that those were the days when she was happy in *things*—in the house and the look of the rooms and of the little garden from the porch, and of the old red-cushioned rocking chairs on the tiny "stoop." She had loved her clothes and her little routines, and all these things had seemed desirable and ultimate because they two were sharing them. Then one day Mary had joined Lily and Adam there on the porch, and Lily had been looking up with new eyes, and Mary had searched her face, and then Adam's face; and they had all seemed in a sudden nakedness; and Mary had known that a great place was closed against her.

Since then house and porch and garden and routines had become like those of other places. She had always been shut outside something, and always she had borne burdens. The death of her parents, gadflys of need, worst of all a curious feeling that the place closed against her was somehow herself—that, so to say, she and herself had never once met. She used to say that to herself sometimes, "There's two of me, and we don't meet—we don't meet."

"And now he wants me to take her boy and Adam's," she kept saying; "I'll never do such a thing—never."

She thought that the news of Lily's death was what gave her the strange, bodily hurt that had seized her—the news that what she was used to was gone; that she had no sister; that the days of their being together and all the tasks of their upbringing were finished. Then she thought that the remembering of those days of her happiness and her pain, and the ache of what might have been and of what never was, had come to torture her again. But the feeling was rather the weight of some imminent thing, the ravage of something that grew with what it fed on, the grasp upon her of something that would not let her go....

She had never seen them after their marriage, and so she had never seen either of the children. Lily had once sent her a picture of John, but she had never sent one of this other little boy. Mary tried to recall what they had ever said of him. She could not even remember his baptismal name, but she knew that they had called him "Yes" because it was the first word he had learned to say, and because he had said it to everything. "The baby can say 'Yes,'" Lily had written once; "I guess it's all he'll ever

be able to say. He says it all day long. He won't try to say anything else."
And once later: "We've taken to calling the baby 'Yes,' and now he calls
himself that. 'Yes wants it,' he says, and 'Take Yes,' and 'Yes is going off
now.' His father likes it. He says yes is everything and no is nothing. I
don't think that means much, but we call him that for fun...." But Mary
could not remember what the child's real name was. What difference
did it make? As if she could have a child meddling round the house
while she was sewing. But of course this was not the real reason. The real
reason was that she could not bring up a child—did she not know that?

"... He's six years old now and Aunt Mary this ain't a place for him.
He's a nice little fellow and I hate for him to get rough and he will if
he stays here...."

She tried to think who else could take him. They had no one. Adam,
she knew, had no one. Some of the neighbours there by the ranch ... it
was absurd to send him that long journey ... so she went through it all,
denying with all the old denials. And all the while the weight in her
body grew and filled her, and she was strangely conscious of her breath.

"What ails me?" she said aloud, and got up to kindle a light. She was
amazed to see that it was seven o'clock, and long past her supper hour.
As she took from the clock shelf the key to the barn, someone rapped
at the back door and came through the cold kitchen with friendly
familiarity. It was Jenny, a shawl over her head, her face glowing with
the cold, and in her mittened hands a flat parcel.

"My hand's most froze," Jenny admitted. "I didn't want to roll this
thing, so I carried it flat out, and it blew consider'ble. It's the picture."

"Get yourself warm," Mary bade her. "I'll undo it. Who is it of?" she
added, as the papers came away.

"That's what I don't know," said Jenny, "but I've always liked it around.
I thought maybe you'd know."

It was a picture which, in those days, had not before come to Old
Trail Town. The figure was that of a youth, done by a master of the
times—the head and shoulders of a youth who seemed to be looking
passionately at something outside the picture.

"There it is, anyhow," Jenny added. "If you like it enough to hang it up,
hang it up. It's a Christmas present!" Jenny laughed elfishly.

Mary Chavah held the picture out before her.

"I do," she said; "I could take a real fancy to it. I'll have it up on the
wall. Much obliged, I'm sure. Set down a minute."

But Jenny could not do this, and Mary, the key to the barn still in her hands, followed her out. They went through the cold kitchen where the refrigerator and the ironing board and the clothes bars and all the familiar things stood in the dark. To Mary these were sunk in a great obscurity and insignificance, and even Jenny being there was unimportant beside the thing that her letter had brought to think about. They stepped out into the clear, glittering night, with its clean, white world, and its clean, dark sky on which some story was written in stars. Capella was shining almost overhead—and another star was hanging bright in the east, as if the east were always a dawning place for some new star.

"Mary!" said Jenny, there in the dark.

"Yes," Mary answered.

"You know I said I just couldn't bear not to have any Christmas—*this* Christmas?"

"Yes," Mary said.

"Did you know why?"

"I thought because it's your and Bruce's first—"

"No," Jenny said, "that isn't all why. It's something else."

She slipped her arm within Mary's and stood silent. And, Mary still not understanding,—

"It's somebody else," Jenny said faintly.

Mary stirred, turned to her in the dimness.

"Why, Jenny!" she said.

"Soon," said Jenny.

The two women stood for a moment, Jenny saying a little, Mary quiet.

"It'll be late in December," Jenny finished. "That seems so wonderful to me—so wonderful. Late in December, like—"

The cold came pricking about them, and Jenny moved to go. Mary, the shawled figure on the upper step, looked down on the shawled figure below her, and abruptly spoke.

"It's funny," Mary said, "that you should tell me that—now. I haven't told you what's in my letter."

"What was?" asked Jenny.

Mary told her. "They want I should have the little boy," she ended it.

"Oh...." Jenny said. "Mary! How wonderful for you! Why, it's almost next as wonderful as mine!"

Mary hesitated for a breath. But she was profoundly stirred by what Jenny had told her—the first time, so far as she could recall, that news like this had ever come to her directly, as a secret and a marvel. News of the village births usually came in gossip, in commiseration, in suspicion. Falling as did this confidence in a time when she was reliving her old hope, when Adam's boy stood outside her threshold, the moment quite suddenly put on its real significance.

"We can plan together," Jenny was saying. "Ain't it wonderful?"

"Ain't it?" Mary said then, simply, and kissed Jenny, when Jenny came and kissed her. Then Jenny went away.

Mary went on to the barn, and opened the door, and listened. She had brought no lantern, but the soft stillness within needed no vigilance. The hay smell from the loft and the mangers, the even breath of the cows, the quiet safety of the place, met her. She was wondering at herself, but she was struggling not at all. It was as if concerning the little boy, something had decided for her, in a soft, fierce rush of feeling not her own. She had committed herself to Jenny almost without will. But Mary felt no exultation, and the weight within her did not lift.

"I really couldn't do anything else but take him, I s'pose," she thought. "I wonder what'll come on me next?"

All the while, she was conscious of the raw smell of the clover in the hay of the mangers, as if something of Summer were there in the cold.

VI

Mary Chavah sent her letter of blunt directions concerning her sister's headstone and the few belongings which her sister had wished her to have. The last lines of the letter were about the boy.

"Send the little one along. I am not the one, but I don't know what else to tell you to do with him. Let me know when to expect him, and put his name in with his things—I can't remember his right name."

When the answer came from John Blood, a fortnight later, it said that a young fellow of those parts was starting back home shortly to spend Christmas, and would take charge of the child as far as the City, and there put him on his train for Old Trail Town. She would be notified just what day to expect him, and John knew how glad his mother would have been and his father too, and he was her grateful Nephew. P. S. He would send some money every month "toward him."

The night after she received this letter, Mary lay long awake, facing what it was going to mean to have him there: to have a child there.

She recalled what she had heard other women say about it,—stray utterances, made with the burdened look that hid a secret complacency, a kind of pleased freemasonry in a universal lot.

"The children bring so much sand into the house. You'd think it was horses."

"... the center table looks loaded and ready to start half the time ... but I can't help it, with the children's books and truck."

"... never would have another house built without a coat closet. The children's cloaks and caps and rubbers litter up everything."

"... every one of their knees out, and their underclothes outgrown, and their waists soiled, the whole time. And I do try so hard...."

Now with all these bewilderments she was to have to do. She wondered if she would know how to dress him. Once she had watched Mis' Winslow dress a child, and she remembered what unexpected places Mis' Winslow had buttoned—buttonholes that went *up and down* in the skirt bands, and so on. Armholes might be too small and garters too tight, and how was one ever to know? If it were a little girl now ... but a little boy.... What would she talk to him about while they ate together?

She lay in the dark and planned—with no pleasure, but merely because she always planned everything, her dress, her baking, what she would say to this one and that. She would put up a stove in the back parlour, and give him the room "off." She was glad that the parlour was empty and clean—"no knick-knacks for a boy to knock around," she found herself thinking. And a child would like the bedroom wallpaper, with the owl border. When Summer came he could have the room over the dining room, with the kitchen roof sloping away from it where he could dry his hazelnuts—she had thought of the pasture hazelnuts, first thing. There were a good many things a boy would like about the place: the bird house where the martins always built, the hens, the big hollow tree, the pasture ant hill.... She would have to find out the things he liked to eat. She would have to help him with his lessons—she could do that for only a little while, until he would be too old to need her. Then maybe there would come the time when he would ask her things that she would not know....

She fell asleep wondering how he would look. Already, not from any impatience to have this done, but because that was the way in which she worked, she had his room in order; and her picture of his father was by the mirror, the young face of his father. Something faded had been written below the picture, and this she had painstakingly rubbed away before she set the picture in its place. Next day, while she was working on Mis' Jane Moran's bead basque that was to be cut over and turned, she laid it aside and cut out a jacket pattern, and a plaited waist pattern—just to see if she could. These she rolled up impatiently and stuffed away in her pattern bookcase.

"I knew how to do them all the while, and I never knew I knew," she thought with annoyed surprise. "I s'pose I'll waste a lot of time pottering over him."

It was so that she spent the weeks until the letter came telling her what day the child would start. On the afternoon of the day the letter came, she went down town to the Amos Ames Emporium to buy a washbasin and pitcher for the room she meant the little boy to have. She stood looking at a basin with a row of brown dogs around the rim, when over her shoulder Mis' Abby Winslow spoke.

"You ain't buying a Christmas present for anybody, are you?" she asked warningly.

Mary started guiltily and denied it.

"Well, what in time do you want with dogs on the basin?" Mis' Winslow demanded.

Almost against her own wish, Mary told her. Mis' Winslow was one of those whose faces are invariable forerunners of the sort of thing they are going to say. With eyebrows, eyes, forehead, head, and voice she took the news.

"He is! Forever and ever more. When's he going to get here?"

"Week after next," Mary said listlessly. "It's an awful responsibility, ain't it—taking a child so?"

Mis' Winslow's face abruptly rejected its own anxious lines and let the eyes speak for it.

"I always think children is like air," she said; "you never realize how hard they're pressing down on you—but you do know you can't live without them."

Mary looked at her, her own face not lighting.

"I'd rather go along like I am," she said; "I'm used to myself the way I am."

"Mary Chavah!" said Mis' Winslow, sharply, "a vegetable sprouts. Can't you? Is these stocking caps made so's they won't ravel?" she inquired capably of Abel Ames. "These are real good value, Mary," she added kindly. "Better su'prise the little thing with one of these. A red one."

Mary counted over her money, and bought the red stocking cap and the basin with the puppies. Then she went into the street. The sense of oppression, of striving, that had seldom left her since that night in the stable, made the day a thing to be borne, to be breasted. The air was thick with snow, and in the whiteness the dreary familiarity of the drug store, the meat market, the post office, the Simeon Buck Dry Goods Exchange, smote her with a passion to escape from them all, to breed new familiars, to get free of the thing that she had said she would do.

"And I could," she thought; "I could telegraph to John not to send him. But Jenny—she can't. I don't see how she stands it...."

The thought may have been why, instead of going home, she went to see Jenny. A neighbor was in the sitting room with Mrs. Wing. Jenny met Mary at the kitchen door and stood against a background of clothes drying on lines stretched indoors.

"Don't you want to come upstairs?" Jenny said. "There ain't a fire up there—but I can show you the things."

She had put them all in the bottom drawer, as women always do; and, as women always do, had laid them so that all the lace and embroidery and pink ribbons possible showed in a flutter when the drawer was opened. Jenny took the things out, one at a time, unfolded, discussed, compared, with all the tireless zeal of a robin with a straw in its mouth or of a tree, blossoming. "Smell of them," Jenny bade her. "Honestly, wouldn't you know by the smell who they are for?" "I donno but you would," Mary admitted awkwardly, and marveled dumbly at the newness Jenny was feeling in that which, after all, was not new!

When these things were all out, a little tissue paper parcel was left lying in the drawer.

"There's one more," Mary said.

Jenny flushed, hesitated, lifted it.

"That's nothing," she said; "before I came I made some little things for its Christmas. I thought maybe it would come first, and we'd have the Christmas in my room, and I made some little things—just for fun, you know. But it won't be fair to do it now, with the whole town so set against our having any Christmas. Mary, it just seems as though I had to have a Christmas this year!"

"Oh, well," said Mary, "the baby'll be your Christmas. The town can't help that, I guess."

"I know," Jenny flashed back brightly, "you and I have got the best of them, haven't we? We've each got one present coming, anyway."

"I s'pose we have...." Mary said.

She looked at Jenny's Christmas things—a ribbon rattle, a crocheted cap, a first picture book, a cascade of colored rings—and then in grim humour at Jenny.

"It'll never miss its Christmas," she said dryly.

"Don't you think so?" said Jenny, soberly. "I donno. It seems as if it'd be kind o' lonesome to get born around Christmas and not find any going on."

She put the things away, and closed the drawer. For no appreciable reason, she kept it locked, and the key under the bureau cover.

"Do you know yet when yours is coming?" Jenny asked, as she rose.

"Week after next," Mary repeated,—"two weeks from last night," she confessed, "if he comes straight through."

"I think," said Jenny, "I think mine will be here—before then."

When they reached the foot of the stair, Mary unexpectedly refused to go in the sitting room.

"No," she said, "I must be getting home. I just come out for a minute, anyway. I'm—I'm much obliged for what you showed me," she added, and hesitated. "I've got his room fixed up real nice. There's owls on the wallpaper and puppies on the washbasin," she said. "Come in when you can and see it."

It was almost dusk when Mary reached home. While she was passing the billboard at the corner—a flare of yellow letters, as if Colour and the Alphabet had united to breed a monster—she heard children shouting. A block away, and across the street, coming home from Rolleston's hill where they had been coasting, were Bennet and Gussie Bates, little Emily, Tab Winslow, and Pep. Nearly every day of snow they passed her house. She always heard them talking, and usually she heard, across at the corner, the click of the penny-in-the-slot machine, which no child seemed able to pass without pulling. Tonight, as she heard them coming, Mary fumbled in her purse. Three, four, five pennies she found and ran across the street and dropped them in the slot machine, and gained her own door before the children came. She stood at her dark threshold, and listened. She had not reckoned in vain. One of the children pushed down on the rod, in the child's eternal hope of magic, and when magic came and three, four, five chocolates dropped obediently in their hands, Mary listened to what they said. It was not much, and it was not very coherent, but it was wholly intelligible.

"Look at!" shrieked Bennet, who had made the magic.

"*Did* it?" cried Gussie, and repeated the operation.

"It—it—it never!" said Tab Winslow, at the third.

"Make it again—make it again!" cried little Emily, and they did.

"Gorry," observed Pep, in ecstasy.

When it would give no more, they divided with the other children and ran on, their red mittens and mufflers flaming in the snow. Mary stood staring after them for a moment, then she closed her door.

"I wonder what made me do that," she thought.

In her dining room she mended the fire without taking off her hat. It was curious, she reflected; here was this room looking the way it looked, and away off there was the little fellow who had never seen the room; and in a little while he would be calling this room home, and looking for his books and his mittens, and knowing it better than any other place in the world. And there was Jenny, with that bottom drawerful, and pretty soon somebody that now was not, would be, and would be wearing the drawerful and calling Jenny "mother," and would know her better than anyone else in the world. Mary could not imagine that little boy of Lily's getting used to her—Mary—and calling her—well, what would he call her? She hadn't thought of that....

"Bother," thought Mary Chavah, "there's going to be forty nuisances about it that I s'pose I haven't even thought of yet."

She stood by the window. She had not lighted the lamp, so the world showed white, not black. Snow makes outdoors look big, she thought. But it was big—what a long journey it was to Idaho. Suppose ... something happened to the man he was to travel with. John Blood was only a boy; he would probably put the child's name and her address in the little traveler's pocket, and these would be lost. The child was hardly old enough to remember what to do. He would go astray, and none of them would ever know what had become of him ... and what would become of him? She saw him and his bundle of clothes alone in the station in the City....

She turned from the window and mechanically mended the fire again. She drew down the window shade and went to the coat closet to hang away her wraps. Then abruptly she took up her purse, counted out the money in the firelight, and went out the door and down the street in the dusk, and into the post office, which was also the telegraph office,—one which the little town owed to Ebenezer Rule, and it a rival to the other telegraph office at the station.

"How much does it cost to send a telegram?" she demanded. "Idaho," she answered the man's question, flushing at her omission.

While the man, Affer by name, laboriously looked it up,—covering incredible little dirty figures with an incredibly big dirty forefinger,—Mary stood staring at the list of names tacked below the dog-eared

Christmas Notice. She remembered that she had not yet signed it herself. She asked for a pencil—causing confusion to the little figures and delay to the big finger—and, while she waited, wrote her name. "A good, sensible move," she thought, as she signed.

When Affer gave her the rate, thrusting finger and figures jointly beneath the bars,—solicitous of his own accuracy,—Mary filed her message. It was to John Blood, and it read:—

"Be sure you tie his tag on him good."

VII

EBENEZER RULE HAD MEANT TO go to the City before cold weather came. He had there a small and decent steam-warmed flat where he boiled his own eggs and made his own coffee, read his newspapers and kept his counsel, descending nightly to the ground-floor café to dine on ambiguous dishes at tables of other bank swallows who nested in the same cliff. But as the days went by, he found himself staying on in Old Trail Town, with this excuse and that, offered by himself to himself. As, for example, that in the factory there were old account books that he must go through. And having put off this task from day to day and finding at last nothing more to dally with, he set out one morning for the ancient building down in that part of the village which was older than the rest and was where his business was conducted when it was conducted.

It had snowed in the night, and Buff Miles, who drove the village snowplow, was also driver of "the 'bus." So on the morning after a snowfall, the streets always lay buried thick until after the 8.10 Express came in; and since on the morning following a snowfall the 8.10 Express was always late, Old Trail Town lay locked in a kind of circular argument, and everybody stayed indoors or stepped high through drifts. The direct way to the factory was virtually untrodden, and Ebenezer made a detour through the business street in search of some semblance of a "track."

The light of a Winter morning is not kind, only just. It is just to the sky and discovers it to be dominant; to trees, and their lines are seen to be alive, like leaves; to folk, and no disguise avails. Summer gives complements and accessories to the good things in a human face. Winter affords nothing save disclosure. In the uncompromising cleanness of that wash of Winter light, Ebenezer Rule was himself, for anybody to see. Looking like countless other men, lean, alert, preoccupied, his tall figure stooped, his smooth, pale face like a photograph too much retouched, this commonplace man took his place in the day almost as one of its externals. With that glorious pioneer trio, mineral, vegetable and animal; and with intellect, that worthy tool, he did his day's work. His face was one that had never asked itself, say, of a Winter morning: *What else?* And the Winter light searched him pitilessly to find that question somewhere in him.

Before the Simeon Buck North American Dry Goods Exchange, Simeon Buck himself had just finished shoveling his walk, and stood wiping his snow shovel with an end of his muffler. When he saw Ebenezer, he shook the muffler at him, and then, over his left shoulder, jabbed the air with his thumb.

"Look at here," he said, his head reënforcing his gesture toward his show window, "look what I done this morning. Nice little touch—eh?"

In the show window of the Exchange—Dry Goods Exchange was just the name of it for the store carried everything—a hodgepodge of canned goods, lace curtains, kitchen utensils, wax figures, and bird cages had been ranged round a center table of golden oak. On the table stood a figure that was as familiar to Old Trail Town as was its fire engine and its sprinkling cart. Like these, appearing intermittently, the figure had seized on the imagination of the children and grown in association until it belonged to everybody, by sheer use and wont. It was a *papier-mâché* Santa Claus, three feet high, white-bearded, gray-gowned, with tall pointed cap—rather the more sober Saint Nicholas of earlier days than the rollicking, red-garbed Saint Nick of now. Only, whereas for years he had graced the window of the Exchange, bearing over his shoulder a little bough of green for a Christmas tree, this season he stood treeless, and instead bore on his shoulder a United States flag. On a placard below him Simeon had laboriously lettered:—

*High Cost of Living
and too much fuss
Makes Folks want a
Sane Christmas
Me Too. S. C.*

"Ain't that neat?" said Simeon.

Ebenezer looked. "What's the flag for?" he inquired dryly.

"Well," said Simeon, "he had to carry something. I thought of a toy gun—but that didn't seem real appropriate. A Japanese umbrella wasn't exactly in season, seems though. A flag was about the only thing I could think of to have him hold. A flag is always kind of tasty, don't you think?"

"Oh, it's harmless," Ebenezer said, "harmless."

"No hustling business," Simeon pursued, "can be contented with just *not* doing something. It ain't enough not to have no Christmas. You've got to find something that'll express nothing, and express it forcible. In business, a minus sign," said Simeon, "is as good as a plus, if you can keep it whirling round and round."

This Ebenezer mulled and chuckled over as he went on down the street. He wondered what the Emporium would do to keep up with the Exchange. But in the Emporium window there was nothing save the usual mill-end display for the winter white goods sale.

Ebenezer opened the store door and put his head in.

"Hey," he shouted at Abel, back at the desk, "can't you keep up with Simeon's window?"

Abel came down the aisle between the lengths of white stuff plaited into folds at either side. The fire had just been kindled in the stove, and the air in the store was still frosty. Abel, in his overcoat, was blowing on his fingers.

"I ain't much of any heart to," said he, "but the night before Christmas I guess'll do about right for mine."

"What'll you put up?" Ebenezer asked, closing the door behind him.

"Well, sir," said Abel, "I ain't made up my mind full yet. But I'll be billblowed if I'm going to let Christmas go by without saying something about it in the window."

"Night before Christmas'll be too late to advertise anything," said Ebenezer. "If I was in trade," he said, half closing his eyes, "I'd fill my window up with useful articles—caps and mittens and stockings and warm underwear and dishes and toothbrushes. And I'd say: 'Might as well afford these on what you saved out of Christmas.' You'd ought to get all the advertising you can out of any situation."

Abel shook his head.

"I ain't much on such," he said lightly—and then looked intently at Ebenezer. "Jenny's been buying quite a lot here for her Christmas," he said.

Ebenezer was blank. "Jenny?" he said. "Jenny Wing? I heard she was here. I ain't seen her. Is she bound to keep Christmas anyhow?"

"Just white goods, it was," said Abel, briefly.

Ebenezer frowned his lack of understanding.

"I shouldn't think her and Bruce had much of anything to buy anything with," he said. "I s'pose you know," he added, "that Bruce, the young beggar, quit working for me in the City after the—the failure? Threw up his job with me, and took God knows what to do."

Abel nodded gravely. All Old Trail Town knew that, and honoured Bruce for it.

"Headstrong couple," Ebenezer added. "So Jenny's bent on having Christmas, no matter what the town decides, is she?" he added, "it's like her, the minx."

"I don't think it was planned that way," Abel said simply; "she's only buying white goods," he repeated. And, Ebenezer still staring, "Surely you know what Jenny's come home for?" Abel said.

A moment or two later Ebenezer was out on the street again, his face turned toward the factory. He was aware that Abel caught open the door behind him and called after him, "Whenever you get ready to sell me that there star glass, you know...." Ebenezer answered something, but his responses were so often guttural and indistinguishable that his will to reply was regarded as nominal, anyway. He also knew that now, just before him, Buff Miles was proceeding with the snowplow, cutting a firm, white way, smooth and sparkling for soft treading, momentarily bordered by a feathery flux, that tumbled and heaped and then lay quiet in a glitter of crystals. But his thought went on without these things and without his will.

Bruce's baby! It would be a Rule, too.... the third generation, the third generation. And accustomed as he was to relate every experience to himself, measure it, value it by its own value to him, the effect of his reflection was at first single: The third generation of Rules. *Was he as old as that?*

It seemed only yesterday that Bruce had been a boy, in a blue necktie to match his eyes, and shoes which for some reason he always put on wrong, so that the buttons were on the inside. Bruce's baby. Good heavens! It had been a shock when Bruce graduated from the high school, a shock when he had married, but his baby ... it was incredible that he himself should be so old as that.

... This meant, then, that if Malcolm had lived, Malcolm might have had a child now....

Ebenezer had not meant to think that. It was as if the Thought came and spoke to him. He never allowed himself to think of that other life of his, when his wife, Letty, and his son Malcolm had been living. Nobody in Old Trail Town ever heard him speak of them or had ever been answered when Ebenezer had been spoken to concerning them. A high white shaft in the cemetery marked the two graves. All about them doors had been closed. But with the thought of this third generation, the doors all opened. He looked along ways that he had forgotten.

As he went he was unconscious, as he was always unconscious, of the little street. He saw the market square, not as the heart of the town, but as a place for buying and selling, and the little shops were to him not ways of providing the town with life, but ways of providing their keepers with a livelihood. Beyond these was a familiar setting, arranged that day with white background and heaped roofs and laden boughs, the houses standing side by side, like human beings. There they were, like the chorus to the thing he was thinking about. They were all thinking about it, too. Every one of them knew what he knew. Yet he never saw the bond, but he thought they were only the places where men lived who had been his factory hands and would be so yet if he had not cut them away: Ben Torrey, shoveling off his front walk with his boy sweeping behind him; August Muir, giving his little girl a ride on the snow shovel; Nettie Hatch, clearing the ice out of her mail box, while her sister—the lame one—watched from her chair by the window, interested as in a real event. Ebenezer spoke to them from some outpost of consciousness which his thought did not pass. The little street was not there, as it was never there for him, as an entity. It was merely a street. And the little town was not an entity. It was merely where he lived. He went behind Buff Miles and the snowplow—as he always went—as if space had been created for folk to live in one at a time, and as if this were his own turn.

When he reached the bend from the Old Trail to the road where the factory was, he understood at last that he had been hearing a song sung over a great many times.

> *"... One for the way it all begun,*
> *Two for the way it all has run,*
> *What three'll be for I do forget,*
> *But what's to be has not been yet....*
> *So holly and mistletoe,*
> *So holly and mistletoe,*
> *So holly and mistletoe,*
> *Over and over and over, oh."*

Buff, who was singing it, looked over his shoulder, and nodded.

"They said you can't have no Christmas on Christmas Day," he observed, grinning, "but I ain't heard nothing to prevent singing Christmas carols right up to the day that is the day."

Ebenezer halted.

"How old are you?" he abruptly demanded of Buff—whom he had known from Buff's boyhood.

"Thirty-three," said Buff, "dum it."

"You and Bruce about the same age, ain't you?" said Ebenezer.

Buff nodded.

"Well," said Ebenezer, "well...." and stood looking at him. Malcolm would have been his age, too.

"Going down to the factory, are you?" Buff said. "Wait a bit. I'll hike on down ahead of you."

He turned the snowplow down the factory road, as if he were making a triumphal progress, fashioning his snow borders with all the freedom of some sculpturing wind on summer clouds.

> *"One for the way it all begun,*
> *Two for the way it all has run...."*

He sang to the soft push and thud and clank of his going. He swept a circle in front of the little house that was the factory office, as if he had prepared the setting for a great event; and Ebenezer, following in the long, bright path, stepped into the hall of the house.

For thirty years he had been accustomed to enter the little house with his mind ready to receive its interior of desks and shelves and safes and files. Today, quite unexpectedly, as he opened the door, the thing that was in his mind was a hall stair with a red carpet, and a parlour adjoining with figured stuff at the windows and a coal fire in the stove.... And thirty-five years ago it had been that way, when he and his wife and child had lived in the little house where his business was then just starting at a machine set up in the woodshed. As his project had grown and his factory had arisen in the neighbouring lots, the family had moved farther up in the town. Remembrance had been divorced from this place for decades. Today, without warning, it waited for him on the threshold.

He had asked his bookkeeper to meet him there, but the man had not yet arrived. So Ebenezer himself kindled a fire in the rusty office stove, in the room where the figured curtains had been. The old account books that he wanted were not here on the shelves, nor in the cupboards of the cold adjoining rooms. They dated so far back that they had been filed away upstairs. He had not been upstairs in years, and his first impulse was to send his bookkeeper, when he should appear. But this, after all, was not Ebenezer's way; and he went up the stairs himself.

Each upper room was like someone unconscious in stupor or death, and still as distinct in personality as if in some ancient activity. There was the shelf he had put up in their room, the burned place on the floor where he had tipped over a lamp, tattered shreds of the paper she had hung to surprise him, the little storeroom which they had cleared out for Malcolm when he was old enough, and whose door had had to be kept closed because innumerable uncaged birds lived there....

When he had gone through the piles of account books in a closet and those he sought were not found among them, he remembered the trunkful up in the tiny loft. He let down from the passage ceiling the ladder he had once hung there, and climbed up to the little roof recess.

Light entered through four broken panes of skylight. It fell in a faint rug on the dusty floor. The roof sloped sharply, and the trunks and boxes had been pressed back to the rim of the place. Ebenezer put his hands out, groping. They touched an edge of something that swayed. He laid hold of it and drew it out and set down on the faint rug of light a small wooden hobbyhorse.

He stood staring at it, remembering it as clearly as if someone had set before him the old white gate which he bestrode in his own boyhood. It was Malcolm's hobbyhorse, dappled gray, the tail and the mane missing and the paint worn off—and tenderly licked off—his nose. When they had moved to the other house, he had bought the boy a pony, and this horse had been left behind. Something else stirred in his memory, the name by which Malcolm had used to call his hobbyhorse, some ringing name ... but he had forgotten. He thrust the thing back where it had been and went on with his search for the account books.

By the time he had found them and had got down again in the office, the bookkeeper was there, keeping up the fire and uttering, with some acumen, comments on the obvious aspects of the weather, of the climate, of the visible universe. The bookkeeper was a young man, very ready to agree with Ebenezer for the sake of future favour, but with the wistfulness of all industrial machines constructed by men from human potentialities. Also, he had a cough and thin hands and a little family and no job.

"Get to work on this book," Ebenezer bade him; "it's the one that began the business."

The man opened the book, put it to his nearsighted eyes, frowned, and glanced up at Ebenezer.

"I don't think it seems...." he began doubtfully.

"Well, don't think," said Ebenezer, sharply; "that's not needful. Read the first entries."

The bookkeeper read:—

Picking hops (4 days)	$1.00
Sewing (Mrs. Shackell) . . .	.60
Egg money (3¼ dozen) . . .	.75
Winning puzzle	2.50
	$4.86

Disbursed:

Kitchen roller	$ .10
Coffee mill	.50
Shoes for M	1.25
Water colors for M	.25
Suit for M	2.00
Gloves—me.	.50
	$4.75

Cash on hand: 11 cents.

The bookkeeper paused again. Ebenezer, frowning, reached for the book. In his wife's fine faded writing were her accounts—after the eleven cents was a funny little face with which she had been wont to illustrate her letters. Ebenezer stared, grunted, turned to the last page of the book. There, in bold figures, the other way of the leaf, was his own accounting. He remembered now—he had kept his first books in the back of the account book that she had used for the house.

Ebenezer glanced sharply at his bookkeeper. To his annoyance, the man was smiling with perfect comprehension and sympathy. Ebenezer averted his eyes, and the bookkeeper felt dimly that he had been guilty of an indelicacy toward his employer, and hastened to cover it.

"Family life does cling to a man, sir," he said.

"Do you find it so?" said Ebenezer, dryly. "Read, please."

At noon Ebenezer walked home alone through the melting snow. And the Thought that he did not think, but that spoke to him without his knowing, said:—

"Winning a puzzle—Two Dollars and a half. She never told me she tried to earn a little something that way."

VIII

"IF WE TOOK THE DAY before Christmas an' had it for Christmas," observed Tab Winslow, "would that hurt?"

"Eat your oatmeal," said Mis' Winslow, in the immemorial manner of adults.

"Would it, would it, would it?" persisted Tab, in the immemorial manner of youth.

"And have Theophilus Thistledown for dinner that day instead?" Mis' Winslow suggested with diplomacy.

On which Tab ate his oatmeal in silence.

But, like adults immemorially, Mis' Winslow bore far more the adult manner than its heart. After breakfast she stood staring out the pantry window at the sparrows on the bird box.

"It looks like Mary Chavah was going to be the only one in Trail Town to have any Christmas after all," she thought, "that little boy coming to her, so."

He was coming week after next, Mary had said, and Mis' Winslow had heard no word about it from anybody else. When "the biggest of the work" of the forenoon was finished, Mis' Winslow ran down the road to Ellen Bourne's. In Old Trail Town they always speak of it as running down, or in, or over, in the morning, with an unconscious suiting of terms to informalities.

Ellen was cleaning her silver. She had "six of each"—six knives, six forks, six spoons, all plated and seldom used, pewter with black handles serving for every day. The silver was cleaned often, though it was never on the table, save for company, and there never had been any company since Ellen had lost her little boy from fever. Having no articulateness and having no other outlet for emotion, she fed her grief by small abstentions: no guests, no diversions, no snatches of song about her work. Yet she was sane enough, and normal, only in dearth of sane and normal outlets for emotion, for energy, for personality, she had taken these strange directions for yet unharnessed forces.

"Mercy," observed Mis' Winslow, warming her hands at the cooking stove, "you got more energy."

"... than family, I guess you mean," Ellen Bourne finished. Ellen was little and fair, with slightly drooping head, and eyebrows curved to a childlike reflectiveness.

"Well, I got consider'ble more family than I got energy," said Mis' Winslow, "so I guess we even it up. Seven-under-fifteen eats up energy like so much air."

"Hey, king and country," said Ellen's old father, whittling by the fire, "you got family enough, Ellen. You got your hands full of us." He rubbed his hands through his thin upstanding silver hair on his little pink head, and his fine, pink face took on the look of father which rarely intruded, now, on his settled look of old man.

"I donno what she'd do," said Ellen's mother, "with anymore around here to pick up after. We're cluttered up enough, as it is." She was an old lady of whose outlines you took notice before your attention lay further upon her—angled waist, chin, lips, forehead, put on her a succession of zigzags. But her eyes were awake, and it was to be seen that she did not mean what she said and that she was looking anxiously at Ellen in the hope of having deceived her daughter. Ellen smiled at her brightly, and was not deceived.

"I keep pretty busy," she said.

Mis' Abby Winslow, who was not deceived either, hastened to the subject of Mary.

"I should think Mary Chavah had enough to do, too," she said, "but she's going to take Lily's little boy. Had you heard?"

"No," Ellen said, and stopped shaving silver polish.

"He's coming in two weeks," Mis' Winslow imparted; "she told me so herself. She's got his room fixed up with owls on the wallpaper. She's bought him a washbasin with a rim of puppies, and a red stocking cap. I saw her."

"How old is he?" Ellen asked, and worked again.

"I never thought to ask her," Mis' Winslow confessed; "he must be quite a little fellow. But he's coming alone from some place out West."

"Hey, king and country," Ellen's father said; "I'd hate to have a boy come here, with my head the way it is."

"And keeping the house all upset," Ellen's mother said, and asked Mis' Winslow some question about Mary; and when she turned to Ellen again,

"Why, Ellen Bourne," she said, "you've shaved up every bit of that cleaning polish and we're most done cleaning."

Ellen was looking at Mis' Winslow: "If you see her," Ellen said, "you ask her if I can't do anything to help."

Later in the day, happening in at Mis' Mortimer Bates's, Mis' Winslow found Mis' Moran there before her, and asked what they had heard "about Mary Chavah." Something in that word "about" pricks curiosity its sharpest. "Have you heard about Mary Chavah?" "It's too bad about Mary Chavah." "Isn't it queer about Mary Chavah?"—each of these is like setting flame to an edge of tissue. Omit "about" from the language, and you abate most gossip. At Mis' Winslow's phrase, both women's eyebrows curved to another arc.

Mis' Winslow told them.

"Ain't that nice?" said Mis' Moran, wholeheartedly; "I couldn't bring up another, not with my back. But I'm glad Mary's going to know what it is...."

Mis' Mortimer Bates was glad, too, but being by nature a nonconformist, she took exception.

"It's an awful undertaking for a single-handed woman," she observed.

But this sort of thing she said almost unconsciously, and the other two women regarded it with no more alarm than any other reflex.

"It's no worse starting single-handed than being left single-handed," offered Mis' Winslow somewhat ambiguously. "Lots does that's thrifty."

"Seems as if we could do a little something to help her get ready, seem's though," Mis' Moran suggested; "I donno what."

"I thought I'd slip over after supper and ask her," Mis' Winslow said; "maybe I'd best go now—and come back and tell you what she says."

Mis' Winslow found Mary Chavah sitting by her pattern bookcase, cutting out a pattern. Mary's face was flushed and her eyes were bright, and she went on with her pattern, thrilled by it as by any other creating.

"I just thought of this," Mary explained, looking vaguely at her visitor. "It come to me like a flash when I was working on Mis' Bates's basque. Will you wait just a minute, and then I'll explain it out to you."

Without invitation, Mis' Winslow laid aside her coat and waited, watching Mary curiously. She was cutting and folding and pinning her tissue paper, oblivious of any presence. Alarm, suspense, doubt, solution, triumph, came and went, and neither woman was conscious that the flame of creation burned and breathed in the room as truly as if the product were to be acknowledged.

"There!" Mary cried at last. "See it—can't you see it?—In gray wool?"

It was the pattern for a boy's topcoat, cunningly cut in new lines of seam and revers, with a pocket, a bit of braid, a line of buttons laid in as delicately as the factors in any other good composition. Mis' Winslow inevitably recognized its utility, exclaimed, and wondered.

"Mary Chavah! How did you know how to do things for children?"

"How did you know how?" Mary inquired coolly.

"Why, I've had 'em," Mis' Winslow offered simply.

"Do you honestly think that makes any difference?" Mary asked.

Mis' Winslow gasped, in the immemorial belief that the physical basis of motherhood is the guarantee of both spiritual and physical equipment.

"Could you have cut out that coat?" Mary asked.

Mis' Winslow shook her head. She was of those whose genius is for cutting over.

"Well," said Mary, "I could. It ain't having 'em that teaches you to do for 'em. You either know how, or you don't know how. That's all."

Mis' Winslow reflected that she could never make Mary understand—though any mother, she thought complacently, would know in a minute. The cutting of the coat did give her pause; but then, she summed it up, coat included, "Mary was queer"—and let it go at that.

"I didn't know," Mis' Winslow said then, "but what I could help you some about the little boy's coming. Seven-under-fifteen does teach you something, you've got to allow. Mebbe I could tell you something, now and then. Or if we could do anything to help you get ready for him...."

"Oh," said Mary, in swift penitence, "thank you, Mis' Winslow. After he comes, maybe. But these things now I don't mind doing. The real nuisance'll come afterwards, I s'pose."

Mis' Winslow smiled in soft triumph.

"*Nuisance!*" she said. "That's what I meant comes to you by having 'em. You don't think so much of the nuisance part as you did before."

"Then you don't look the thing in the face," said Mary, calmly. "That's all about that."

"Well," Mis' Winslow said pacifically, "when's he coming?"

"A week from Tuesday. A week from tomorrow," Mary told her. Mis' Winslow looked at her intently, with the light of calculation in her narrowed eyes.

"A week from Tuesday," she said. "A week from Tuesday," she repeated. "*A week from Tuesday!*" she exclaimed. "Why, Mary Chavah. That's Christmas Eve."

It was some matter of recipes that was absorbing Mis' Bates and Mis' Moran when Mis' Winslow breathlessly returned to them. They were deep in tradition, and in method, its buttonhole relation. During the weary period when nutrition has been one of the two great problems the tremendous impulse that has nourished the world was alive in the faces of the two women, a kind of creative fire, such as had burned in Mary at the cutting of her pattern. Asparagus escalloped with toast crumbs and butter was for the moment symbol of all humanity's will to keep alive.

"Ladies," said Mis' Winslow, with no other preface, "what do you think? Mary Chavah's little boy is coming from Idaho with a tag on, and when do you s'pose he's going to get here? Christmas Eve."

"Christmas Eve," repeated Mis' Bates, whose mind never lightly forsook old ways or embraced a contretemps; "what a funny time to travel."

"Likely catch the croup and be down sick on Mary's hands the first thing," said Mis' Moran. "It's a pity it ain't the Spring of the year."

Mis' Winslow looked at them searchingly to see if her thought too far outdistanced theirs.

"What struck me all of a heap," she said, "is his getting here then. *That* night. Christmas Eve."

The three woman looked at one another.

"That's so," Mis' Moran said.

"Him—that child," Mis' Winslow put it, "getting here Christmas Eve, used to Christmas all his life, ten to one knowing in his head what he hopes he'll get. And no Christmas. And him with no mother. And her only a month or so dead."

"Well," said Mis' Mortimer Bates, "it's too bad it's happened so. But it has happened so. You have to say that to your life quite often, I notice. I don't know anything to do but to say it now."

Mis' Winslow had not taken off her cloak. She sat on the edge of her chair, with her hands deep in its pockets, her black knit "fascinator" fallen back from her hair. She was looking down at her cloth overshoes, and she went on speaking as if she had hardly heard what Mis' Bates had interposed.

"He'll get in on the express," she said; "Mary said so. She don't have to go to the City to meet him. The man he travels with is going to put him on the train in the City. The little fellow'll get here after dark. After dark on Christmas Eve."

"And no time for anybody to warn him that there won't be any Christmas waiting for him," Mis' Moran observed thoughtfully.

"And like enough he'll bring a little something for Mary for a present," Mis' Winslow went on. "How'll she feel *then*?"

"Ain't it too bad it ain't last year?" Mis' Moran mourned. "Everything comes too late or too soon or not at all or else too much so, 'seems though."

Mis' Bates's impulse to nonconformity had not prevented her forehead from being drawn in their common sympathy; but it was a sympathy that saw no practical way out and existed tamely as a high window and not as a wide door.

"Well," she said, "Mary ain't exactly the one to see it so. You'll never get her to feel bad about anybody not having a Christmas. I donno, if it was any other year, as she'd be planning any different."

"No," said Mis' Winslow, thoughtfully, "Mary won't do anything. But we could."

Mis' Bates's forehead took alarm—the alarm of the sympathetic hearer who is challenged to be doer.

"*Do?*" she repeated. "You can't go back on the paper at this late day. And you can't give him a Christmas and every other of our children not have any just because we're their parents and still living. There ain't a thing to do."

Mis' Winslow's eyes were still on her overshoes. "I don't believe there's *never* 'not a thing' to do," she said, "I don't believe it."

Mis' Bates looked scandalized. "That's nonsense," she said sharply, "and it's sacrilegious besides. When God means a thing to happen, there's not a thing to do. What about earthquakes and—and cancers?"

"I don't believe he ever means earthquakes and cancers," said Mis' Winslow, to her overshoes.

"Prevent 'em, then!" challenged Mis' Bates, triumphantly.

Mis' Winslow looked up. Her eyes were shining as they had shone sometimes when one of her seven-under-fifteen had given its first sign of consciousness of more than self.

"I believe we'll do it someday," she said. "I believe there's more to us than we've got any idea of. I believe there's so much to us that one of us that found out about it and told the rest would get hounded out of town. But even now, I bet there's enough to us to do something every time— something every time, no matter what. And I believe there's something we can do about this little orphaned boy's Christmas, if we nip our brains on to it in the right place."

"Oh, dear," said Mis' Moran, "sometimes when I think about Christmas I almost wish we almost hadn't done the way we're going to do."

Mis' Bates stiffened.

"Jane Moran," she said, "do you think it's right to go head over heels in debt to celebrate the birth of our Lord?"

"No," said Mis' Moran, "I don't. But—"

"And you know nobody in Old Trail Town could afford any extravagance this year?"

"Yes," said Mis' Moran, "I do. Still—"

"And if part could and part couldn't, that makes it all the worse, don't it?"

"I know," said Mis' Moran, "I know."

"Well, then," said Mis' Bates triumphantly, "we've done the only way there is to do. Land knows, I wish there was another way. But there ain't."

Mis' Winslow looked up from her overshoes.

"I don't believe there's never 'no other way,'" she said. "There's always another way...."

"Not without money," said Mis' Bates.

"Money," Mis' Winslow said, "money. That's like setting up one day of peace on earth, good will to men, and asking admission to it."

"Mis' Winslow," said Mis' Moran, sadly, "what's the use of saying anything? You know as well as I do that Christmas is abused all up and down the land, and made a day of expense and extravagance and folks overspending themselves. And we've stopped all that in Old Trail Town. And now you're trying to make us feel bad."

"I ain't," said Mis' Winslow, "we felt bad about it already, and you know it. I'm glad we've stopped all that. But I wish't we had something to put in its place. I wish't we had."

"What in time are them children doing?" said Mis' Moran, abruptly.

The three women looked. On the side lawn, where a spreading balsam had been left untrimmed to the ground, stood little Emily Moran and Gussie and Bennet and Tab and Pep. And the four boys had their caps in their hands, and Gussie, having untied her own hood, turned to take off little Emily's. The wind, sweeping sharply round the corner of the house, blew their hair wildly and caught at muffler ends. Mis' Bates and Mis' Moran, with one impulse, ran to the side door, and Mis' Winslow followed.

"Emily," said Mis' Moran, "put on your hood this minute."

"Gussie," said Mis' Bates, "put on your cap this instant second. What you got it off for? And little Emily doing as you do—I'm su'prised at you."

The children consulted briefly, then Pep turned to the two women, by now coming down the path, Mis' Bates with her apron over her head, Mis' Moran in her shawl.

"Please," said Pep, "it's a funeral. An' we thought we'd ought to take our caps off till it gets under."

"A funeral," said Mis' Bates. "Who you burying?"

"It's just a rehearsal funeral," Pep explained; "the real one's going to be Christmas."

By now the two women were restoring hood and stocking cap to the little girls, and it was Mis' Winslow, who had followed, who spoke to Pep.

"Who's dead, Pep?" she asked.

Between the belief of "Who's dead?" and the skepticism of "Who you burying?" the child was swift to distinguish.

"Sandy Claus," he answered readily.

Mis' Winslow stood looking down at him. Pep stepped nearer.

"We're doing it for little Emily," he said confidentially. "She couldn't get it straight about where Sandy Claus would be this Christmas. The rest of us—knew. But Emily's little—so we thought we'd play bury him on her 'count."

Mis' Bates, who had not heard, turned from Gussie.

"Going to do *what* on Christmas?" she exclaimed. "You ain't to do a thing on Christmas. Or ain't you grown up, after all?"

"Well, we thought a Christmas funeral wouldn't hurt," interposed Bennet, defensively. "Can't we even have a funeral for fun on Christmas?" he ended, aggrieved.

"It's Sandy Claus's funeral," observed little Emily putting a curl from her face.

"We're goin' dress up a Sandy Claus, you know," Pep added, *sotto voce*.

"It's going to be right after breakfast, Christmas."

"Come on, come ahead, fellows," said Bennet; "I'll be corpse. Keep your lids on. I don't mind. Go ahead, sing."

Already Mis' Winslow was walking back to the house; the other two women overtook her; and from the porch they heard the children begin to sing:—

"*Go bury Saint Nicklis....*"

The rest was lost in the closing of the door.

Back in the sitting room the women stood looking at one another. Mis' Bates was frowning and all Mis' Moran's expressions were on the verge of dissolving; but in Mis' Winslow's face it was as though she had found some new way of consciousness.

"Ladies," Mis' Winslow said, "them children are out there pretending to bury Santa Claus—and so are we. And I bet we can't any of us do it."

In the room, there was a moment of silence in which familiar things seemed to join with their way of saying, "We've been keeping still all the while!" Then Mis' Winslow pushed her hair, regardless of its parting, straight back from her forehead,—a gesture with which she characterized any moment of stress.

"Ladies," she said, "I don't want we should go back on our paper, either. But mebbe there's more to Christmas than it knows about—or than we know about. Mebbe we can do something that won't interfere with the paper we've all signed, and yet that'll be something that is something. Mebbe they's things to use that ain't never been used yet.... Oh, I donno. Nor I guess you donno. But let's us find out!"

IX

Christmas Week came.

Cities by thousands made preparation. Great shops took on vast cargoes of silk and precious things and seemed ready to sail about, distributing gifts to the town, and thought better of it, and let folk come in numbers to them to pay toll for what they took. Banks opened their doors and poured out, now a little trickling stream of pay envelopes, now a torrent of green and gold. Flower stalls drew tribute from a million pots of earth where miracles had been done. Pastry counters, those mock commissariats, delicately masking as servants to necessity, made ready their pretty pretences to nutrition. The woods came moving in—acres of living green, taken in their sleep, their roots left faithful to a tryst with the sap, their tops summoned to bear an hybrid fruitage. From cathedrals rose the voices of children now singing little carols and hymns in praise of the Christ-child, now speaking little verses in praise of the saint, Nicholas, now clamouring for little new possessions. And afar from the fields that lay empty about the clustered roofs of towns came a chorus of voices of the live things, beast and fowl, being offered up in the gorgeous pagan rites of the day.

Hither and yonder in every city the grown townsfolk ran. The most had lists of names,—Grace, Margaret, Laura, Alice, Miriam, John, Philip, Father, Mother,—beautiful names and of rich portent, so that, remembering the time, one would have said that these were entered there with some import of special comradeship, of being face to face, of having realized in little what will someday be true in large. But on looking closer, the lists were found to have quite other connotations: as, Grace, bracelet; Margaret, spangled scarf; Laura, chafing-dish; Philip, smoking set; Father (Memo: Ask mother what she thinks he'd like). And every name, it seemed, stood for some bestowal of new property, mostly of luxuries, and chiefly of luxuries of decoration. And the minds of the buying adults were like lakes played upon by clouds and storm birds and lightning, and, to be sure, many stars—but all in unutterable confusion.

Also from the cargo-laden shops there came other voices in thousands, but these were mostly answers. And when one, understanding Christmas, listened to hear what part in it these behind the counter played, he heard from them no voice of sharing in the theory of peace, or even of truce, but instead:—

"Two a yard and double width. Jewelry is in the Annex. Did you want three pairs of each? Veils and neckwear three aisles over. Leather, glassware, baskets, ribbons, down the store beyond the notions. Toys and dolls are in the basement—toys and dolls are in the basement. Jewelry is in the Annex...."

So that a great part of the town seemed some strong chorus of invocation to new possessions.

But there were other voices. Whole areas of every town lay, perforce, within the days of Christmas Week—it must have been so, for there is only one calendar to embrace humanity, as there is only one way of birth and breath and death, one source of tears, one functioning for laughter. But to these reaches of the town the calendar was like another thing, for though it was upon them in name, its very presence was withdrawn. In those ill-smelling stairways and lofts there was little to divulge the imminence of anything other than themselves. And wherever some echo of Christmas Week had crept, the wistfulness or the lust was for possession also; but here one could understand its insistence. So here the voices said only, "I wish—I wish," and "I choose this—and this," at windows; or, "If I had back my nickel...." "Don't you go expecting nothink!" And over these went the whirr of machinery, beat of treadles, throb of engines, or the silence of forced idleness, or of the disease of dereliction. It was a time of many pagan observances, as when some were decked in precious stuffs and some were thrown to lions.

To all these in the towns Christmas Week came. And of them all not many stood silent and looked Christmas Week in the face. Yet it is a human experience that none is meant to die without sharing. For the season is the symbol of what happens to folk if they claim it.

Christmas is the time of withdrawal of most material life. It is the time when nature subtracts the externals, hides from man the phenomena of even her evident processes. Left alone, his thought turns inward and outward—which is to say, it lays hold upon the flowing force so slightly externalized in himself. If he finds in his own being a thousand obstructions, a thousand persons,—dogs, sorcerers, whoremongers,—he will try to escape from them all, back to the externals. But if he finds there a channel which the substance of being is using, he will be no stranger, but a familiar, with himself. Only when the channel has been long cleared, when there has left it all consciousness of striving, of self in any form, only when he finds himself empty, ready, immaculate, will he have the divine adventure. For it is then that in him the spirit of God will have its birth, then that he will first understand his own nature ... the nature of being.

Then the turn of the year comes in, the year begins to mount. Birth is in it, growth is in it, Spring is in it. Sometime, away back in beginnings, they knew this. They knew that the time of the Winter solstice is in some strange fashion the high moment of the year, as the beginning of new activity in nature and in the gods. They solemnized the return of the fiery sun wheel; they traced in those solstice days the operations on earth of Odin and Berchta. They knew in themselves a thing they could not name. And when the supreme experience took place in Christ, they made the one experience typify the other, and became conscious of the divine nature of this nativity. So, by the illuminati, the prophets, the adepts, the time that followed was yearly set aside—forty days of dwelling within the temple of self, forty days of reverence for being, of consciousness of new birth. Then the emergence, then the apotheosis of expression typifying and typified by Spring—the time when bursting, pressing life almost breaks bounds, when birth and the impulse to birth are in every form of life, without and within. These festivals are not arbitrary in date. They grow out of the universal experience.

Is it not then cause for stupefaction that this time of "divine bestowal" should have become so physical a thing? From the ancient perception, to have slipped into a sense of annual social comradeship and good will and peace was natural and fine—to live in the little what will someday be true in the large. But from this to have plunged down into a time of frantic physical bestowals, of "present trading," of lists of Grace and Margaret and Philip, of teeming shops with hunting and hunted creatures within, of sacrificial trees and beasts, of a sovereign sense of good for me and mine and a shameless show of Lord and Lady Bountiful ... how can that have come about, how can the great festival have been so dishonoured?

Not all dishonoured, for within it is its own vitality which nothing can dishonour. Through all the curious variations which it receives at our hands, something shines and sings: self-giving, joy giving, a vast, dim upflickering on humanity of what this thing really is that it seeks to observe, this thing that grips men so that no matter what they are about, they will drop it at the touch of the gong and turn to some expression, however crooked and thwarted, of the real spirit of the time. If in war, then bayonets are stacked and holly-wreathed, and candles stuck on each point! If at sea, some sailor climbs out on the bowsprit with a wreath of green. If on the western plains, a turkey wishbone for target will make the sport, at fifty paces; if at home, some great extravagance or some humble gift or some poignant wish will point the day; if at church, then mass and carol; in certain hearts, reverence,—everywhere the time takes hold of folk and receives whatever of greatness or grotesqueness they choose to give it.... So, too, the actual and vital experience which it brings to humanity is universal, is offered with cosmic regularity, cannot be escaped. Through all the tumult of the time, Christmas Week and the time that lies near to it is always waiting to claim its own, to take to itself those who will not be deceived, who see in the stupendous yearly pageant only the usual spectacle of humanity trying to say divine things in terms of things physical, because the time for the universal expression is not yet come.

When that time comes ... when the time of the worship of *things* shall be past; when the tribal sense of holiday shall have given place to the family sense, and that family shall be mankind; when shall never be seen the anomaly of celebrating in a glorification of little family tables—whose crumbs fall to those without—the birth of him who preached brotherhood; and the mockery of observing with wanton spending the birth of him who had not where to lay his head; when the rudiments of divine perception, of self-perception, of social perception, shall have grown to their next estate; when the area of consciousness shall be extended yet farther toward the outermost; when that new knowledge with which the air is charged shall let man begin to know what he is ... when that time comes, they will look back with utmost wonder at our uncouth gropings to note and honour something whose import we so obscurely discern; but perhaps, too, with wonder that so much of human love and divining should shine for us through the mists we make.

X

Two days before Christmas Ellen Bourne went through the new-fallen snow of their wood lot. Her feet left scuffled tracks clouded about by the brushing of her gown's wet hem and by a dragging corner of shawl. She came to a little evergreen tree, not four feet tall, with low-growing boughs, and she stood looking at it until her husband, who was also following the snow-filled path, overtook her.

"Matthew," she said then, "will you cut me that?"

Matthew Bourne stood with his ax on his shoulder and looked a question in slow preparation to ask one. "I just want it," she said; "I've—took a notion."

He said that she had a good many notions, it seemed to him. But he cut the little tree, with casual ease and no compunctions, and they dragged it to their home, the soft branches patterning the snow and obscuring their footprints.

"It's like real Christmas weather," Ellen said. "They can't stop that coming, anyhow."

In the kitchen Ellen's father sat before the open oven door of the cooking stove, letting the snow melt from his heavy boots.

"Hey," he said, "I was beginning to think you'd forgot about supper. What was in the trap?"

At once Ellen began talking rapidly. "Oh," she said, "we'll have some muffins tonight, father. The kind you like, with—"

"Well, what was in the trap?" the old man demanded peevishly. "Why don't you answer back? What was, Mat?"

Matthew, drying his ax blade, looked at it with one eye closed.

"Rabbit," he said.

"Where is it?" her father demanded.

"It was a young one—not as big as your fist," Ellen said. "I let it out before he got there. Where's mother?"

"Just because a thing's young, it ain't holy water," the old man complained. "Last time it was a squirrel you let go because it was young—it's like being spendthrift with manna...." he went on.

Ellen's mother appeared, gave over to Ellen the supper preparations, contented herself with auxiliary offices of china and butter getting, and talked the while, pleased that she had something to disclose.

"Ben Helders stopped in," she told. "He's going to the City tomorrow. What do you s'pose after? A boy. He's going to take him to bring up and work on the farm."

"Where's he going to get the boy?" Ellen asked.

Her mother did not know, but Mrs. Helders was going to have a new diagonal and she wanted the number of Ellen's pattern. Ben would stop for it that night.

Evenings their kitchen was a sitting room, and when the supper had been cleared away and the red cotton spread covered the table, Ellen asked her husband to bring in the little tree. She found a cracker box, handily cut a hole with a cooking knife, and set up the little tree by the kitchen window.

"What under the canopy—" said her mother, her voice cracking.

"Oh, something to do in the evening," Ellen answered. "Father's going to pop me some corn to trim it with; aren't you, father? Mother, why don't you get you a good big darning needle and string what he pops?"

"It'll make a lot of litter," said her mother, but she brought the needle, for something to do.

"Hey, king and country," said her father; "I'd ought to have somebody here to shell it for me."

"Who you trimming up a tree for?" her mother demanded; "I thought they wasn't to be any in town this year."

"It ain't Christmas yet," Ellen said only. "I guess it won't do any hurt two days before."

While the two worked, Ellen went to the cupboard drawer, and from behind her pile of kitchen towels she drew out certain things: walnuts, wrapped in shining yeast tinsel and dangling from red yarn; wishbones tied with strips of bright cloth; a tiny box, made like a house, with rudely cut doors and windows; eggshells penciled as faces; a handful of peanut owls; a glass-stoppered bottle; a long necklace of buttonhole twist spools. A certain blue paper soldier doll that she had made was upstairs, but the other things she brought and fastened to the tree.

Her husband smoked and uneasily watched her. He saw somewhat within her plan, but he was not at home there. "If the boy *had* lived and *had* been up-chamber asleep now," he thought once, "it'd be something like, to go trimming up a tree. But *this* way—"

"What you leaving the whole front of the tree bare for?" her mother asked.

"The blue paper soldier goes there. I want it should see the blue paper soldier first thing...." Ellen said, and stopped abruptly.

"You talk like you was trimming the tree for somebody," her mother observed, aggrieved.

"Maybe something might look in the window—going by," Ellen said.

"Get in there! Get your heads in there, ye beggars!" said the old man to the popcorn. "I'd ought to have somebody here to pick up them shooting kernels," he complained.

In a little while, with flat-footed stamping, Ben Helders came in. When he had the pattern number, by laborious copying against the wall under the bracket lamp, Matthew said to him:—

"Going to get a boy to work out, are you?"

Helders laughed and shifted.

"He's going to work by and by," he said. "We allow to have him to ourselves a spell first."

"Keep him around the house till Spring?"

"More," said Helders. "You see," he added, "it's like this with us ... family all gone, all married, and got their own. We figured to get hold of a little shaver and have some comfort with him before he goes to work, for life."

"Adopt him?" said Matthew, curiously.

"That's pretty near it," Helders admitted. "We've got one spoke for at the City Orphand Asylum."

Ellen Bourne turned. "How old?" she asked.

"Around five—six, we figure." Helders said it almost sheepishly.

Ellen stood facing the men, with the white festoons of popcorn in her hands.

"Matthew," she said, "let him bring us one."

Matthew stared. "You mean bring us a boy?" he asked.

"I don't care which—girl or boy. Anything young," Ellen said.

"Good Lord, Ellen," Matthew said, with high eyebrows, "ain't you got your hands full enough now?"

Ellen Bourne lifted her hands slightly and let them fall. "No," she answered.

The older woman looked at her daughter, and now first she was solicitous, as a mother.

"Ellen," she said, "you have, too, got your hands full. You're wore out all the time."

"That's it," Ellen said, "and I'm not wore out with the things I want to do."

"Hey, king and country!" the old man cried, upsetting the popper. "Don't get a child around here underfoot. I'm too old. I deserve grown folks. My head hurts me—"

"Matthew," said Ellen to her husband, "let Helders bring us one. Tomorrow—for Christmas, Mat!"

Matthew looked slowly from side to side. It seemed incredible that so large a decision should lie with a man so ineffectual.

"Seems like we'd ought to think about it a while first," he said weakly.

"Think about it!" said Ellen. "When haven't I thought about it? When have I thought about anything else but him we haven't got anymore?"

"Ellen!" the mother mourned, "you don't know what you're taking on yourself—"

"Hush, mother," Ellen said gently; "you don't know what it is. You had me."

She faced Helders. "Will you bring two when you come back tomorrow night?" she said; "and one of them for us?"

Helders looked sidewise at Matthew, who was fumbling at his pipe.

"Wouldn't you want to see it first, now?" Helders temporized. "And a girl or a boy, now?"

"No—I wouldn't want to see it first—I couldn't bear to choose. One healthy—from healthy parents—and either girl or boy," Ellen said, and stopped. "The nicest tree thing I've made is for a boy," she owned. "It's a paper soldier.... I made these things for fun," she added to Helders.

For the first time Helders observed the tree. Then he looked in the woman's face. "I'll fetch out a boy for you if you say so," he said.

"Then do," she bade.

When the four were alone again, Mat sat looking at the floor. "Every headlong thing I've ever done I've gone headlong over," he said gloomily.

Ellen took a coin from the clock shelf. "When Ben goes past tomorrow," she merely said, "you'll likely see him. Have him get some little candles for the tree."

"My head hurts me," the old man gave out; "this ain't the place for a great noisy boy."

Ellen put her hand on his shoulder almost maternally.

"See, dear," she said, "then you'd be grandfather."

"Hey?" he said; "not if it was adopted, I wouldn't."

"Why, of course. That would make it ours—and yours. See," she cried, "you've been stringing popcorn for it already, and you didn't know!"

"Be grandfather, would I?" said the old man. "Would I? Hey, king and country! Grandfather again."

Ellen was moving about the kitchen lightly, with that manner, which eager interest brings, of leaving only half footprints.

"Come on, mother," she said, "we must get the popcorn strung for sure, now!"

The mother looked up at the tree. "Seems as if," she said, wrinkling her forehead, "I used to make pink tarleton stockings for your trees and fill 'em with the corn. I donno but I've got a little piece of pink tarleton somewheres in my bottom drawer...."

... Next night they had the bracket lamp and the lamp on the shelf and the table hand lamp all burning. The little tree was gay with the white corn and the coloured trifles. The kitchen seemed to be centering in the tree, as if the room had been concerned long enough with the doings of these grown folk and now were looking ahead to see who should come next. It was the high moment of immemorial expectancy, when those who are alive turn the head to see who shall come after.

"What you been making all day, daddy?" Ellen asked, tense at every sound from without.

Her father, neat in his best clothes, blew away a last plume of shaved wood and held out something.

"I just whittled out a kind of a clothespin man," he explained. "I made one for you, once, and you liked it like everything. Mebbe a boy won't?" he added doubtfully.

"Oh, but a boy will!" Ellen cried, and tied the doll above the blue paper soldier.

"Hadn't they ought to be here pretty soon?" Matthew asked nervously. "Where's mother?"

"She's watching from the front room window," Ellen answered.

Once more Helders came stamping on the kitchen porch, but this time there was a patter of other steps, and Ellen caught open the door before he summoned. Helders stepped into the room, and with him was a little boy.

"This one?" Ellen asked, her eyes alive with her eagerness.

But Helders shook his head.

"Mis' Bourne," he said, "I'm real dead sorry. They wa'n't but the one. Just the one we'd spoke for."

"*One!*" Ellen said; "you said Orphan Asylum."

"There's only the one," Helders repeated. "The others is little bits of babies, or else spoke for like ours—long ago. It seems they do that way. But I want you should do something: I want you and Matthew should take this one. Mother and I—are older ... we ain't set store so much...."

Ellen shook her head, and made him know, with what words she could find, that it could not be so. Then she knelt and touched at the coat of the child, a small frightened thing, with cap too large for him and one mitten lost. But he looked up brightly, and his eyes stayed on the Christmas tree. Ellen said little things to him, and went to take down for him some trifle from the tree.

"I'm just as much obliged," she said quietly to Helders. "I never thought of there not being enough. We'll wait."

Helders was fumbling for something.

"Here's your candles, I thought you might want them for somethin' else," he said, and turned to Matthew: "And here's your quarter. I didn't get the toy you mentioned. I thought you wouldn't want it, without the little kid."

Matthew looked swiftly at Ellen. He had not told her that he had sent by Helders for a toy. And at that Ellen crossed abruptly to her husband, and she was standing there as they let Helders out, with the little boy.

Ellen's father pounded his knee.

"But how long'll we have to wait? How long'll we have to wait?" he demanded shrilly. "King and country, why didn't somebody ask him that?"

Matthew tore open the door.

"Helders!" he shouted, "how long did they say we'd have to wait?"

"Mebbe only a week or two—mebbe longer," Helders' voice came out of the dark. "They couldn't tell me."

Ellen's mother stood fastening up a fallen tinsel walnut.

"Let's us leave the tree right where it is," she said. "Even with it here, we won't have enough Christmas to hurt anything."

XI

ON THAT MORNING OF THE day before Christmas, Mary Chavah woke early, while it was yet dark. With closed eyes she lay, in the grip of a dream that was undissipated by her waking. In the dream she had seen a little town lying in a hollow, lighted and peopled, but without foundation.

"It isn't born yet," they told her, who looked with her, "and the people are not yet born."

"Who is the mother?" she had asked, as if everything must be born of woman.

"You," they had answered.

On which the town had swelled and rounded and swung in a hollow of cloud, globed and shining, like the world.

"You," they had kept on saying.

The sense that she must bear and mother the thing had grasped her with all the sickening force of dream fear. And when the dream slipped into the remembrance of what the day would bring her, the grotesque terror hardly lessened, and she woke to a sense of oppression and coming calamity such as not even her night of decision to take the child had brought to her, a weight as of physical faintness and sickness.

"I feel as if something was going to happen," she said, over and over.

She was wholly ignorant that in that week just passed the word had been liberated and had run round Old Trail Town in the happiest open secrecy:—

"... coming way from Idaho, with a tag on, Christmas Eve. We thought if everybody could call that night—just run into Mary's, you know, like it was any other night, and take in a little something to eat—no presents, you know ... oh, of course, no presents! Just supper, in a basket. We'd all have to eat *some*-where. It won't be any Christmas celebration, of course—oh, no, not with the paper signed and all. But just for us to kind of meet and be there, when he gets off the train from Idaho."

"Just ... like it was any other night." That was the part that abated suspicion. Indeed, that had been the very theory on which the nonobservance of Christmas had been based: the day was to be treated like any other day. And, obviously, on any other day such a simple plan as this for the welcoming of a little stranger from Idaho would have gone forward as a matter of course. Why deny him this, merely because the night of his arrival chanced to be Christmas Eve? When Christmas was to be treated *exactly* as any other day?

If, in the heart of Mis' Abby Winslow, where the plan had originated, it had originated side by side with the thought that the point of the plan was the incidence of Christmas Eve, she kept her belief secret. The open argument was unassailable, and she contented herself with that. Even Simeon Buck, confronted with it, was silent.

"Goin' back on the paper, are you?" he had at first said, "and hev a celebration?"

"Celebration of what?" Mis' Winslow demanded; "celebration of that little boy getting here all alone, 'way from Idaho. And we'd celebrate that any other night, wouldn't we? Of course we would. Our paper signing don't call for us to give everybody the cold shoulder as I know of, just because it's Christmas or Christmas Eve, either."

"No," Simeon owned, "of course it don't. Of course it don't."

As for Abel Ames, he accepted the proposal with an alacrity which he was put to it to conceal.

"So do," he said heartily, "so do. I guess we can go ahead just like it was a plain day o' the week, can't we?"

"Hetty," he said to his wife, whom that noon he went through the house to the kitchen expressly to tell, "can you bake up a basket of stuff to take over to Mary Chavah's next Tuesday night?"

She looked up from the loaf she was cutting, the habitual wonder of her childish curved lashes accented by her sudden curving of eyebrows.

"Next Tuesday?" she said, "Why, that's Christmas Eve!"

Abel explained, saying, "What of that?" and trying to speak indifferently but, in spite of himself, shining through.

"Well, that's kind of nice to do, ain't it?" she answered.

"My, yes," Abel said, emphatically, "It's a thing to do—that's the thing to do."

It was Mis' Mortimer Bates, the nonconformist by nature, in whom doubts came nearest to expression.

"I *don't* know," she said, "it kind of *does* seem like hedging."

"They ain't anybody for it to seem to," Mis' Winslow contended reasonably, "but us. And we understand."

"We was going to do entirely without a Christmas this year. Entirely without," Mis' Bates rehearsed.

"Was we going to do entirely without everyday, weekday, year-in-and-year-out milk of human kindness?" Mis' Winslow demanded. "Well, then, let's us use a little of it, same as we would on a Monday wash day."

No voice was raised in real protest. None who had signed the paper and none who had not done so could take exception to this simple way of hospitality to the little stranger with a tag on. And it was the glory of the little town being a little town that they somehow let it be known that everyone was expected to look in at Mary's that night. No one was uninvited. And this was like a part of the midwinter mystery expressing itself unbidden.

Mary alone was not told. She had consistently objected to the Christmas observances for so long that they feared the tyranny of her custom. "She might not let us do it," they said, "but if we all get there, she can't help liking it. She would on any other day...."

... So she alone in Old Trail Town woke that morning before Christmas with no knowledge of this that was afoot. And yet the day was not like any other day, because she lay there dreading it more.

She had cleared out her little sleeping room, as she had cleared the lower floor. The chamber, with its white-plastered walls, and boards nearly bare, and narrow white bed, had the look of a cell, in the first light struggling through the single snow-framed window. Here, since her childhood she had lain nightly; here she had brought her thought of Adam Blood, and had seen the thought die and had watched with it; here she had lain on the nights after her parents had died; here she had rested, body-sick with fatigue, in the years that she had toiled to keep her home. In all that time there had gone on within her many kinds of death. She had arrived somehow at a dumb feeling that these dyings were gradually uncovering her self from somewhere within; rather, uncovering some self whose existence she only dimly guessed. "They's two of me," she had thought more often of late "and we don't meet—we don't meet." She lived among her neighbors without hate, without malice; for years she had "meant nothing but love"—and this not negatively. The rebellion against Christmas was against only the falsity of its meaningless observance. The rebellion against taking the child, though somewhat grounded in her distrust of her own fitness, was really the last vestige of a self that had clung to her, in bitterness not toward Adam, but toward Lily. Ever since she had known that the child was coming she had felt a kind of spiritual exhaustion, sharpened by the strange sense of oppression that hung upon her like an illness.

"I feel as if something was going to happen," she kept saying.

In a little while she leaned toward the window at her bed's head, and looked down the hill toward Jenny's. Her heart throbbed when she saw a light there. Of late, when she had waked in the night, she had always looked, but always until now the little house had been wrapped in the darkness. Because of that light, she could not sleep again, and so presently she rose, and in the sharp chill of the room, bathed and dressed, though what had once been her savage satisfaction in braving the cold had long since become mere undramatic ability to endure it without thinking. With Mary, life and all its constructive rites had won what the sacrificial has never been able to achieve—the soul of the casual, of, so to say, second nature, which is last nature, and nature triumphant.

While she was at breakfast Mis' Abby Winslow came in.

"Mercy," Mis' Winslow said, "is it breakfast—early? I've been up hours, frosting the cakes."

"What cakes?" Mary asked idly.

Mis' Winslow flushed dully. "I ain't baked anything much in weeks before," she answered ambiguously, and hurried from the subject. "The little fellow's coming in on the Local, is he?" she said. "You ain't heard anything different?"

"Nothing different," Mary replied. "Yes, of course he's coming. They left there Saturday, or I'd have heard. The man he's with is going to get home tonight for Christmas with his folks in the City."

"Going down to meet him of course, ain't you," Mis' Winslow pursued easily.

"Why, yes," said Mary.

"Well," Mis' Winslow mounted her preparation, "I was thinking it would be kind of dark for you to bring him in here all alone. Don't you want I should come over and keep up the lights and be here when you get here?"

She watched Mary in open anxiety. If she were to refuse, it would go rather awkwardly. To her delight Mary welcomed with real relief the suggestion.

"I'd be ever so much obliged," she said; "I thought of asking somebody. I'll have a little supper set out for him before I leave."

"Yes, of course," Mis' Winslow said, eyes down. "I'll be over about seven," she added. "If the train's on time, you'll be back here around half past. The children want to go down with you—they can be at Mis' Moran's when you go by. You'll walk up from the depot, won't you? You do," she said persuasively; "the little fellow'll be glad to stretch his legs. And it'll give the children a chance to get acquainted."

"I might as well," Mary assented listlessly. "There's no need to hurry home, as I know of, except keeping you waiting."

"Oh, I don't mind," Mis' Winslow told her. "Better come around through town, too. It's some farther, but he'll like the lights. What's the little chap's name?" she asked; "I donno's I've heard you say."

Mary flushed faintly. "Do you know," she said, "I don't know his name. I can't remember that Lily ever told me. They always called him just *Yes*, because he learned to say that first."

"*Yes!*" repeated Mis' Winslow, blankly. "Why, it don't sound to me real human."

Later in the day, Mis' Mortimer Bates and Mis' Moran came in to see Mary. Both were hurried and tired, and occasionally one of them lapsed into some mental calculation. "We must remember something for the middle of the table," Mis' Bates observed to Mis' Moran, under cover of Mary's putting wood in the stove. And when Mary related the breaking of the bracket lamp, the two other women telegraphed to each other a glance of memorandum.

"Don't it seem funny to *you* to have Christmas coming on tomorrow and no flurry about it?" Mary asked.

"*No flurry!*" Mis' Bates burst out. "Oh, well," she amended, "of course this Christmas does feel a little funny to all of us. Don't you think so, Mis' Moran?"

"I donno," said Mary, thoughtfully, "but what, when folks stop chasing after Christmas and driving it before them, Christmas may turn around and come to find them."

"Mebbe so," Mis' Moran said with bright eyes, "mebbe so. Oh, Mary," she added, "ain't it nice he's coming?"

Mary looked at them, frowning a little. "It seemed like the thing had to happen," she said; "it'll fit itself in."

Before dark she took a last look about the child's room. The owl paper, the puppy washbasin, the huge calendar with its picture of a stag, the shelves for whatever things of his own he had, all pleased her newly. She had laid on his table her grandfather's Bible with pictures of Asiatic places. Below his mirror hung his father's photograph, that young face, with the unspeakable wistfulness of youth, looking somewhere outside the picture. It made her think of the passionate expectation in the face of the picture that Jenny had brought.

"Young folks in pictures always look like they was setting store by something that ain't true yet," Mary thought. "It makes you kind of feel you have to pitch in and make whatever it is come true, a little...."

It was when Mis' Winslow came back toward seven o'clock that there was news of Jenny. Mary had been twice to her door in the course of the day, and had come away feeling, in her inquiry, strangely outside the moment and alien to its incidence, as if she were somehow less alive than those in Jenny's house.

"Jenny's got a little girl," Mis' Winslow said.

Mary stood staring at her. It seemed impossible. It was like seeing the hands of time move, like becoming momentarily conscious of the swing and rush of the earth, like perceiving the sweep of the stream of stars in which our system moves.... She was startled and abashed that the news so seized upon her. Little that had ever happened to herself seemed so poignant, so warmed its place in sensation. While Mis' Winslow's mind marked time on details of time and pounds, as is the way with us immortals when another joins our ranks, Mary was receiving more consciousness. There are times when this gift is laid on swiftly, as with hands, instead of coming when none knows. Rather than with the child whom she was to meet, her thought was with Jenny as she left Mis' Winslow in the doorway and went down the street.

"Expect you back in about half an hour if the train's on time," Mis' Winslow called.

Mary nodded, and turned into the great cathedral aisle that was Old Trail Street, now arched and whitened, spectral in the dark, silver with starlight....

... Capella was in the east, high and bright, and as imperative as speech. Mary's way lay north, so that that great sun went beside her, and there was no one else abroad but these two. A coat of ice had polished the walks, so she went by the road, between the long white mounds that lined it. The road, whose curves were absorbed in the dimness, had thus lost its look of activity and lay inert as any frozen waterway. Only a little wind, the star's sparkle, and Mary's step and breath seemed living things—but from the rows of chimneys up and down the Old Trail Road, faint smoke went up, a plume, a wreath, a veil, where the village folk, invisible within quiet roof and wall, lifted common signals; and from here a window and there a window, a light shone out, a point, a ray, a glow, so that one without would almost say, "There's home."

The night before Christmas; and in not one home was there any preparation for tomorrow, Mary thought, unless one or two lawless ones had broken bounds and contrived something, from a little remembrance for somebody to a suet pudding. It was strange, she owned: no trees being trimmed, no churches lighted for practice, and the shops closed as on any other night. Only the post office had light—she went in to look in her box. Affer was there at the telegraph window, and he accosted her.

"Little boy's comin' tonight, is he?" he said, as one of the sponsors for that arrival.

"I'm on my way to the train now," Mary answered, and noted the Christmas notice with its soiled and dog-eared list still hanging on the wall. "It was a good move," she insisted to herself, as she went out into the empty street again.

"You got a merry Christmas without no odds of the paper or me either," Affer called after her; but she did not answer save with her "Thank you, Mr. Affer."

"Why do they all pretend to think it's so fine for me?" she wondered. "To cheer me up, I guess," she thought grimly.

Tonight they were all sharing the aloofness from the time, an aloofness which she herself had known for years. All save Jenny. To Jenny's house, in defiance of that dog-eared paper in the post office, Christmas had come. Not a Christmas of "present trading," not a Christmas of things at all; but *Christmas*. Unto them a child was born.

"Jenny's the only one in this town that's got a real Christmas," thought Mary, on her way to meet her own little guest.

The Simeon Buck North American Dry Goods Exchange was dark, too, and from its cave of window the gray Saint Nicholas looked out, bearing his flag—and he tonight an idle, mummy thing of no significance. The Abel Ames General Merchandise Emporium was closed, but involuntarily Mary stopped before it. In its great plate-glass window a single candle burned. She stood for a moment looking.

"Why, that's what they do, some places, to let the Christ-child in," Mary thought. "I wonder if Abel knows. How funny—for a store!"

Someone whom she did not know passed her and looked too.

"Kind o' nice," said the other.

"Real nice," Mary returned, and went on with a little glow.

Abel's candle, and the arc light shining like cold blue crystal before the dark Town Hall, and the post office light where the dog-eared list hung and the telegraph key clicked out its pretence at hand touching with all the world, these were the only lights the street showed—save Capella, that went beside her and, as she looked, seemed almost to stand above the town.

At Mis' Moran's house on the other side of the square, the children were waiting for her—Bennet and Gussie and Tab and Pep and little Emily. They ran before Mary in the road, all save little Emily, who walked clasping Mary's hand.

"Aren't you staying up late, Emily?" Mary asked her.

"Yes," assented the child, contentedly.

"Won't you be sleepy?" Mary pursued.

"I was going to stay awake anyhow," she said; "I ain't goin' sleep all night. We said so. We're goin' stay 'wake and see Santa Claus go by."

"Go by?" Mary repeated.

"Yes," the child explained; "you don't think that'll hurt, do you?" she asked anxiously. "And then," she pursued, "if we don't see him, we'll know he's dead everywheres else, too. An' then we're goin' bury him tomorrow morning, up to Gussie's house."

At the station, no one was yet about. The telegraph instrument was clicking there, too, signaling the world; a light showed in the office behind a row of sickly geraniums; the wind came down through the cut and across the tracks and swept the little platform. But the children begging to stay outside, Mary stood in a corner by the telegraph operator's bay window and looked across to the open meadows beyond the tracks and up at the great star. The meadows, sloping to an horizon hill, were even and white, as if an end of sky had been pulled down and spread upon them. Utter peace was there, not the primeval peace that is negation, but a silence that listened.

"'While shepherds watched their flocks by night, all seated on the ground,...'" Mary thought and looked along the horizon hill. The time needed an invocation from someone who watched, as many voices, through many centuries, had made invocation on Christmas Eve. For a moment, looking over the lonely white places where no one watched, as no one—save only Jenny—watched in the town, Mary forgot the children....

The shoving and grating of baggage truck wheels recalled her. Just beyond the bay window she saw little Emily lifted to the truck and the four others follow, and the ten heels dangle in air.

"Now!" said Pep. And a chant arose:

> " 'Twas the night before Christmas when all through the house
> Not a creature was stirring, not even a mouse.
> The stockings were hung by the chimney with care
> In the hope that Saint Nicholas soon would be there....."

Upborne by one, now by another, now by all three voices, the verses went on unto the end. And it was as if not only Tab and Pep and Bennet and Gussie and little Emily were chanting, but all children who had ever counted the days to Christmas and had found Christmas the one piece of magic that is looked on with kindness by a grown up world. The magic of swimming holes, for example, is largely a forbidden magic; the magic of loud noises, of fast motion, of living things in pockets, of far journeys, of going off alone, of digging caves, of building fires, of high places, of many closed doors, words, mechanisms, foods, ownerships, manners, costumes, companions, and holidays are denied them. But in Christmas their affinity for mystery is recognized, encouraged, gratified, annually provided for. The little group on the baggage truck chanted their watch over a dead body of Christmas, but its magic was there, inviolate. The singsong verses had almost the dignity of lyric expression, of the essence of familiarity with that which is unknown. As if, because humanity had always recognized that the will to Christmas was greater than it knew, these words had somehow been made to catch and reproduce, for generations, some faint spirit of the midwinter mystery.

The 'bus rattled up to the platform and Buff Miles leaped down and blanketed his horses, talking to them as was his wont.

> *"So, holly and mistletoe,*
> *So, holly and mistletoe,*
> *So, holly, and mistletoe,*
> *Over and over and over, oh...."*

He was singing as he came round the corner of the station.

"It ain't Christmas yet," he observed defensively to Mary. "It ain't forbid except for Christmas Day, is it?"

He went and bent over the children on the truck.

"Look alive as soon as you can do it," Mary heard him say to them, and wondered.

She stood looking up the track. Across the still fields, lying empty and ready for some presence, came flashing the point of flame that streamed from the headlight of the train. The light shone out like a signal flashed back to the star standing above the town.

XII

TEN MINUTES AFTER MARY CHAVAH had left her house, every window was lighted, a fire was kindled in the parlour, and neighbours came from the dark and fell to work at the baskets they had brought.

It was marvelous what homely cheer arose. The dining room table, stretched at its fullest length and white-covered, was various with the yellow and red of fruit and salads, the golden brown of cake and rolls, and the mosaic of dishes. The fire roared in the flat-topped stove on whose "wings" covered pans waited, and everywhere was that happy stir and touch and lift, that note of preparation which informs a time as sunshine or music will strike its key.

"My land, the oven—the warming oven. Mary ain't got one. However will we keep the stuff hot?" Mis' Winslow demanded. "What time is it?"

"We'd ought to had my big coffee pot. We'd ought to set two going. I donno why I didn't think of it," Mis' Moran grieved.

"Well," said Mis' Mortimer Bates, "when the men get here—if they ever *do* get here—we'll send one of 'em off somewheres for the truck we forgot. What time is it?"

"Here comes a whole cartload of folks," Mis' Moran announced. "I hope and pray they've got the oysters—they'd ought to be popped in the baking oven a minute. What time did you say it is?"

"It's twenty minutes past seven," Mis' Winslow said, pushing her hair straight back, regardless of its part, "and we ain't ready within 'leven hundred miles."

"Well, if they only all get here," Mis' Bates said, ringing golden and white stuffed eggs on Mary's blue platter; "it's their all being here when she gets here that I want. I ain't worried about the supper—much."

"The road's black with folks," Mis' Moran went on. "I'm so *deadly* afraid I didn't make enough sandwiches. Oh, I donno why it wasn't given me to make more, I'm sure."

"Who's seeing to them in the parlour? Who's getting their baskets out here? Where they finding a place for their wraps? Who's lighting the rest of the lamps? What time is it?" demanded Mis' Winslow, cutting her cakes.

"Oh," said Mis' Bates from a cloud of brown butter about the cooking stove, "I donno whether we've done right. I donno but we've broke our word to the Christmas paper. I donno whether we ain't going to get ourselves criticized for this as never folks was criticized before."

Mis' Moran changed her chair to the draughtless corner back of the cooking stove and offered to stir the savoury saucepan.

"I know it," she said, "I know it. We never planned much in the first start. It grew and it grew like it grew with its own bones. But mebbe there's some won't believe that, one secunt."

Mis' Winslow straightened up from the table and held out a hand with fingers frosting-tipped.

"Well," she said, with a great period, "if we *have* broke our word to the Christmas paper, I'd rather stand up here with my word broke this way than with it kept so good it hurt me. Is it half-past seven yet?"

"I wish Ellen Bourne was here," Mis' Bates observed. "She sent her salad dressing over and lent her silver and her Christmas rose for the table—but come she would not. I wonder if she couldn't come over now if we sent after her, last minute?"

Simeon Buck, appearing a few minutes later at the kitchen door to set a basket inside, was dispatched for Ellen Bourne, the warming oven, and the coffee pot, collectively. He took with him Abel Ames, who was waiting for him without. And it chanced that they knocked at the Bournes' door just after Ben Helders had driven away with the little boy, so that the men found the family still in the presence of the little tree.

"Hello," said Simeon, aghast, "Christmassing away all by yourselves, I'll be bound, like so many thieves. I rec'lect not seeing your names on the paper."

"No, I didn't sign," Ellen said. "I voted against it that night at the town meeting, but I guess nobody heard me."

"Well," said Simeon, "and so here you've got a Christmas of your own going forward, neat as a kitten's foot—"

"Ain't you coming over to Mary Chavah's?" Abel broke in with a kind of gentleness. "All of you?"

Ellen smote her hands together.

"I meant to go over later," she said, "and take—" She paused. "I thought we'd all go over later," she said. "I forgot about it. Why, yes, I guess we can go now, can't we? All three of us?"

Abel Ames stood looking at the tree. He half guessed that she might have dressed it for no one who would see it. He looked at Ellen and ventured what he thought.

"Ellen," he said, "if you ain't going to do anything more with that tree tonight, why not take some of the things off, and have Matthew set it on his shoulder, and bring it over to Mary's for the boy that's coming?"

Ellen hesitated. "Would they like it?" she asked. "Would folks?"

Abel smiled. "I'll take the blame," he said, "and you take the tree." And seeing Simeon hesitate, "Now let's stop by for Mis' Moran's coffee pot," he added. "Hustle up. The Local must be in."

So presently the tree, partly divested of its brightness, was carried through the streets to the other house—in more than the magic which attends the carrying in the open road of a tree, a statue, a cart filled with flowers,—for the tree was like some forbidden thing that still would be expressed.

"*He* might not come till Christmas is 'way past," Ellen thought, following. "She'll leave it standing a few days. We can go down there and look at it—if he comes."

A little way behind them, Simeon and Abel, with the coffee pot and the warming oven, were hurrying back to Mary's. They went down the deserted street where Abel's candle burned and Simeon's saint stood mute.

"When I was a little shaver," Abel said, "they used to have me stand in the open doorway Christmas Eve, and hold a candle and say a verse. I forget the verse. But I've always liked the candle in doors or windows, like tonight. Look at mine over there now—ain't it like somebody saying something?"

"Well," said Simeon, not to be outdone, "when we come by my window just now, the light hit down on it and I could of swore I see the saint smile."

"Like enough," said Abel, placidly, "like enough. You can't put Christmas out. I see that two weeks ago." He looked back at his own window. "If the little kid that come in the store last Christmas Eve tries to come in again tonight," he said, "he won't find it all pitch dark, anyway. I'd like to know who he was...."

Near the corner that turned down to the Rule Factory, they saw Ebenezer Rule coming toward them on the Old Trail Road. They called to him.

"Hello, Ebenezer," said Abel, "ain't you coming in to Mary Chavah's tonight?"

"I think not," Ebenezer answered.

"Come ahead," encouraged Simeon.

As they met, Abel spoke hesitatingly.

"Ebenezer," he said, "I was just figuring on proposing to Simeon here, that we stop in to your house—I was thinking," he broke off, "how would it be for you and him and me, that sort of stand for the merchandise end of this town, to show up at Mary's house tonight—well, it's the women have done all the work so far—and I was wondering how it would be for us three to get there with some little thing for that little kid that's coming to her—we could find something that wouldn't cost much—it hadn't *ought* to cost much, 'count of our set principles. And take it to him...." Abel ended doubtfully.

Ebenezer simply laughed his curious succession of gutturals.

"Crazy to Christmas after all, ain't you?" he said.

But Simeon wheeled and stared at Abel. For defection in their own camp he had never looked.

"I knew you'd miss it—I knew you'd miss it!" Simeon said excitedly, "cut paper and fancy tassels and—"

"No such thing," said Abel, shortly. "I was thinking of that boy getting here, that's all. And I couldn't see why we shouldn't do our share—which totin' coffee pots and warming ovens *ain't*, as I see it."

"Well, but my heavens, man!" said Simeon, "it's Christmas! You can't go giving anybody anything, can you?"

"I don't mean give it to him *for* Christmas at all," protested Abel. "I mean give it to him just like you would any other day. We'd likely take him something if it wasn't Christmas? Sort of to show our good will, like the women with the supper? Well, why not take him some little thing even if it is Christmas?"

"Oh, well," said Simeon, "that way. If you make it plain it ain't *for* Christmas—Of course, we ain't to blame for what day his train got in on."

"Sure we ain't," said Abel, confidently.

Ebenezer was moving away.

"We'll call in for you in half an hour or so," Abel's voice followed him. "We'll slip out after the boy gets there. There won't be time before ... what say, Ebenezer?"

"I think not," said Ebenezer; "you don't need me."

"Well—congratulations anyhow!" Abel called.

Ebenezer stopped on the crossing.

"What for?" he asked.

"Man alive," said Abel, "don't you know Bruce has got a little girl?"

"No," said Ebenezer, "I—didn't know. I'm obliged to you."

He turned from them, but instead of crossing the street to go to his house, he faced down the little dark street to the factory. He had walked past Jenny's once that evening, but without being able to force himself to inquire. He knew that Bruce had come a day or two before, but Bruce had sent him no word. Bruce had never sent any word since the conditions of the failure had been made plain to him, when he had resigned his position, refused the salary due him, and left Old Trail Town. Clearly, Ebenezer could make no inquiry under those circumstances, he told himself. They had cut themselves off from him, definitely.

How definitely he was cut off from them was evident as he went down the dark street to the factory. He was strangely quickened, from head to foot, with the news of the birth of Bruce's child. He went down toward the factory simply because that was the place that he knew best, and he wanted to be near it. He walked in the snow of the mid-road, facing the wind, steeped in that sense of keener being which a word may pour in the veins until the body flows with it. The third generation; the next of kin,—that which stirred in him was a satisfaction almost physical that his family was promised its future.

As he went he was unconscious, as he was always unconscious, of the little street. But, perhaps because Abel had mentioned Mary's house, he noted the folk, bound thither, whom he was meeting: Ben Torry, with a basket, and his two boys beside him; August Muir, carrying his little girl and a basket, and his wife following with a basket. Ebenezer spoke to them, and after he had passed them he thought about them for a minute.

"Quite little families," he thought. "I s'pose they get along.... I wonder how much Bruce is making a week?"

Nellie Hatch and her lame sister were watching at the lighted window, as if there were something to see.

"Must be kind of dreary work for them—living," he thought, "... I s'pose Bruce is pretty pleased ... pretty pleased."

At the corner, someone spoke to him with a note of pleasure in his voice. It was his bookkeeper, with his wife and two partly grown daughters. Ebenezer thought of his last meeting with his bookkeeper, and remembered the man's smile of perfect comprehension and sympathy, as if they two had something in common.

"Family life does cling to a man," he had said.

That was his wife on his arm, and their two daughters. On that salary of his.... Was it possible, it occurred to Ebenezer, that she was saving egg money, earning sewing money, winning prizes for puzzles—as Letty had done?

Outside the factory, the blue arc light threw a thousand shadows on the great bulk of the building, but left naked in light the little office. He stood looking at it, as he so rarely saw it, from part way across the road. Seen so, it took on another aspect, as if it had emerged from some costuming given it by the years. The office was painted brown, and discoloured. He saw it white, with lozenge panes unbroken, flowered curtains at the windows, the light of lamp and wood stove shining out. And as sharply as if it had been painted on the air, he saw some unimportant incident in his life there—a four-wheel carriage drawn up at the door with some Christmas guests just arriving, and himself and Letty and Malcolm in the open doorway. He could not remember who the guests were, or whether he had been glad to see them, and he had no wish in the world to see those guests again. But the simple, casual, homely incident became to him the sign of all that makes up everyday life, the everyday life of folk—*of folks*—from which he had so long been absent.

His eye went down the dark little street where were the houses of the men who were his factory "hands." Just for a breath he saw them as they were,—the chorus to the thing he was thinking about. They were all thinking about it, too. Every one of them knew what he knew.... Just for a breath he saw the little street as it was: an entity. Then the sight closed, but through him ran again that sense of keener being, so poignant that now, as his veins flowed with it, something deeper within him almost answered.

He wheeled impatiently from where he stood. He wanted to do something. At the end of the street he could see them crossing under the light, on their way to Mary Chavah's. Abel and Simeon might stop for him ... but how could he go there, among the folk whom he had virtually denied their Christmas? What would they have to say to him? Yet what they should say would, after all, matter nothing to him ... and perhaps he would hear them say something about Bruce and Jenny. Still, he had nothing to take there, as Abel had suggested. What had he that a boy would want to have? Unless....

He thought for a moment. Then he crossed the street to what had been his house. He went in, seeing again the hallway and stair, red-carpeted, and the door opened into the lamplit room beyond. He found and lighted an end of candle that he knew, and made his way up the stair. There he set the candle down and lowered the ladder that led to the loft.

In the loft, a gust of wind from the skylight blew out the flame of his little wick. In the darkness, the broken panes above his head looked down on him like a face, and that face the sky, thousand-eyed. He mounted a box, pushed up the frame, and put out his head. The sky lay near. The little town showed, heaped roofs and lifting smoke, and here and there a light. Sparkling in their midst was the light before the Town Hall, like an eye guarding something and answering to the light before his factory and to the other light before the station, where the world went by. High over all, climbing the east, came Capella, and seemed to be standing above the village.

As he looked, the need to express what he felt beset Ebenezer.

"Quite a little town," he thought, "quite a little town."

He closed the glass, and groped in the darkness to where the roof, sloping sharply, met the door. There he touched an edge of something that swayed, and he laid hold of and drew out that for which he had come: Malcolm's hobbyhorse.

Downstairs in the hall he set it on the floor, examined it, rocked it with one finger. The horse returned to its ancient office as if it were irrevocably ordained to service. Ebenezer, his head on one side, stood for some time regarding it. Then he slipped something in its worn saddle-pocket. Last, he lifted and settled the thing under his arm.

"I donno but I might as well walk around by Mary Chavah's house," he thought. "I needn't stay long...."

At Mary Chavah's house the two big parlours, the hall, the stairs, the dining room, even the tiny bedroom with the owl wall paper, were filled with folk come to welcome the little boy. And on the parlour table, set so that he should see it when first he entered, blazed Ellen Bourne's little tree. The coffee was hot on the stove, good things were ready on the table, and the air was electric with expectation, with the excitement of being together, with the imminent surprise to Mary, and with curiosity about the little stranger from Idaho.

"What'll we all say when he first comes in?" somebody asked.

"Might say 'Merry Christmas,'" two or three suggested.

"Mercy, no!" replied shocked voices, "not to Mary Chavah, especially."

But however they should say it, the time was quick with cheer.

At quarter to eight the gate clicked. The word passed from one to another, and by the time a step sounded on the porch the rooms were still, save for the whispers, and a voice or two that kept unconsciously on in some remote corner. But instead of the door opening to admit Mary and her little boy, a hesitating knock sounded.

Those nearest to the door questioned one another with startled looks, and one of them threw the door open. On the threshold stood Affer, the telegraph operator, who thrust in a very dirty hand and a yellow envelope.

"We don't deliver nights," he said, "but I thought she'd ought to have this one. I'm going home to wash up, and then I'll be back," he added, and left them staring at one another around the little lighted tree.

XIII

BEFORE THEY COULD GO OUT to find Mary, as a dozen would have done, she was at the threshold, alone. She seemed to understand without wonder why they were there, and with perfect naturalness she turned to them to share her trouble.

"He hasn't come," she said simply.

Her face was quite white, and because they usually saw her with a scarf or shawl over her head, she looked almost strange to them, for she wore a hat. Also she had on an unfamiliar soft-coloured wrap that had been her mother's and was kept in tissues. She had dressed carefully to go to meet the child. "I might as well dress up a little," she had thought, "and I guess he'll like colours best."

Almost before she spoke they put in her hands the telegram. They were pressing toward her, dreading, speechless, trying to hear what should be read. She stepped nearer to the light of the candles on the little tree, read, and reread in the stillness. When she looked up her face was so illumined that she was strange to them once more.

"Oh," she said, "it's his train. It was late for the Local. They've put him on the Express, and it'll drop him at the draw."

The tense air crumpled into breathings, and a soft clamour filled the rooms as they told one another, and came to tell her how glad they were. She pulled herself together and tried to slip into her natural manner.

"It did give me a turn," she confessed; "I thought he'd been—he'd got...."

She went into the dining room, still without great wonder that they were all there; but when she saw the women in white aprons, and the table arrayed, and on it Ellen Bourne's Christmas rose blooming, she broke into a little laugh.

"Oh," she said, "you done this a-purpose for *him*."

"I hope, Mary, you won't mind," Mis' Mortimer Bates said formally, "it being Christmas, so. We'd have done just the same on any other day."

"Oh," Mary said, "*mind!*"

They hardly knew her, she moved among them so flushed and laughing and conformable, praising, admiring, thanking them.

"Honestly, Mary," said Mis' Moran, finally, "we'll have you so you can't tell Christmas from any other day—it'll be so nice!"

The Express would be due at the "draw" at eight-thirty—eight-thirty-three, Affer told her when he came back, "washed up." Mary watched the clock. She had not milked or fed the cows before she went, because she had thought that *he* would like to watch the milking, and it would be something for him to do on that first evening. So, when she could, she took her shawl and slipped out to the shed for the pails and her lantern, and went alone to the stable.

Mary opened the door, and her lantern made a golden room of light within the borderless shadow. The hay smell from the loft and the mangers, the even breathing of the cows, the quiet safety of the place, met her. She hung her lantern in its accustomed place, and went about her task.

Her mind turned back to the time that had elapsed since the Local came in at the Old Trail Town station. She had stood there, with the children about her, hardly breathing while the two Trail Town men and a solitary traveling man had alighted. There had been no one else. In terror lest the child should be carried past the station, she had questioned the conductor, begged him to go in and look again, parleyed with him until he had swung his lantern. Then she had turned away with the children, utterly unable to formulate anything. There was no other train to stop at Old Trail Town that night. It must mean disaster ... indefinable disaster that had somehow engulfed him and had not pointed the way that he had gone. She recalled, now, that she had refused Buff Miles's invitation to ride, but had suffered him to take the children. Then she had set out to walk home.

On that walk home she had unlived her plans. Obscure speculations, stirring in her fear, at first tormented her, and then gave place to the conclusion that John had changed his mind, had seen perhaps that he could not after all let the child go so far, had found someone else to take him; and that the morrow would bring a letter to tell her so. In any case, she was not to have him. The conclusion swept her with the vigour of certainty. But instead of the relief for which she would have looked, that certainty gave her nothing but desolation. Until the moment when the expectation seemed to die she had not divined how it had grown into her days, as subtly as the growth of little cell and little cell. And now the weight upon her, instead of lifting, soaring in the possibility of the return of her old freedom, lay the more heavily, and her sense of oppression became abysmal.... "Something is going to happen," she had kept saying. "Something *has* happened...."

So she had got on toward her own door. There the swift relief was like an upbearing into another air, charged with more intimate largess for life. Now Mary sat in the stable in a sense of happy reality that clothed all her feeling—rather, in a sense of super reality, which she did not know how to accept.... So, slowly singing in her as she sat at her task, came that which had waited until she should open the way....

In the stable there was that fusion of shadow and light in which captive spaces reveal all their mystery. Little areas of brightness, of functioning; then dimness, then the deep. Brightness in which surfaces of worn floor, slivered wall, dusty glass, showed values more specific than those of colour. Dimness in which gray rafters with wavering edges, rough posts each with an accessory of shadow, an old harness in grotesque loops, ceased to be background and assumed roles. The background itself, modified by many an unshadowed promontory, was accented in caverns of manger and roof. The place revealed mystery and beauty in the casual business of saying what had to be said.

Mary filled her arms with hay, and turned to the manger. The raw smell of the clover smote her, and it was as sweet as Spring repromised. She stood for a moment with the hay in her arms, her breath coming swiftly....

Down on the marsh, not half an hour away, he was coming to her, to be with her, as she had grown used to imagining him. She had thought that he was not coming, and he was almost here.... She knew now that she was glad of this, no matter what it brought her; glad, as she had never known how to be glad of anything before. He was coming—there was a thrill in the words every time that she thought them. Already she was welcoming him in her heart, already he was here, already he was born into her life....

... With a soft, fierce rush of feeling not her own, it seemed to her that her point of perception was somehow drawn inward, as if she no longer saw from the old places, as if something in her that was not used to looking, looked. In the seat where her will had been was no will. But somewhere in there, beyond all conflict, she felt *herself* to be. Beyond a thousand mists, volitions, little seekings for comfort, rebellions at toil, the cryings of personality for its physical own, she stood at last, herself within herself. And that which, through the slow process of her life and of life and being immeasurably before her, had been seeking its expression, building up its own vehicle of incarnation, quite suddenly and simply flowered. It was as if the weight and the striving within her had been the pangs of some birth. She stood, as light of heart as a little child, filled with peace and tender exaltation.

These filled her on the road which she took to meet him—and took alone, for she would have no one go with her. ("What's come over Mary?" they asked one another in the kitchen. "She acts like she was somebody else and herself too.") The night lay about her as any other winter night, white and black,—a clean white world on which men set a pattern of highway and shelter, a clean dark sky on which a story is written in stars; and between—no mystery, but only growth. Out toward the drawbridge the road was not well broken. She went, stumbling in the ruts and hardly conscious of them. And Mary thought—

"Something in me is glad.

"It's as if something in me knew how to be glad more than I ever knew how alone.

"For I'm nothing but me, here in Old Trail Town, and yet it's as if Something had come, secret, on purpose to make me know why to be glad.

"It's something in the world bigger than I know about.

"It's in me, and I guess it was in folks before me, and it will be in folks always.

"It isn't just for Ebenezer Rule and the City.

"It's for everybody, here in Old Trail Town as much as anywhere.

"It's for folks that's hungry for it, and it's for folks that ain't.

"It's always been in the world and it always will be in the world, and someday we'll know what to do."

But this was hardly in her feeling, or even in her thought; it lay within her thanksgiving that the child was coming; and he only a little way down there across the marsh.

... It seemed quite credible and even fitting that the mighty, rushing, lighted Express, which seldom stopped at Old Trail Town, should that night come thundering across the marsh, and slow down at the drawbridge for her sake and the little boy's. Several coaches' length from where she stood she saw a lantern shine where they were lifting him down. She ran ankle deep through the thinly crusted snow.

"*That's* it!" said the conductor. "All the way from Idaho!" and swung his lantern from the step. "Merry Christmas!" he called back.

The little thing clasping Mary's hand suddenly leaped up and down beside her.

"Merry Christmas! Merry Christmas! Merry Christmas!" he shouted with all his might.

Mary Chavah stood silent, and as the train drew away held out her hand, still in silence, for the boy to take.

As the noise of the train lessened, he looked up.

"Are you her?" he asked soberly.

"Yes," she cried joyously, "I'm her!"

Their way led east between high banks of snow. At the end of the road was the village, looking like something lying on the great white plate of the meadows and being offered to one who needed it. At the far end of the road which was Old Trail Road, hung the blue arc light of the Town Hall, center to the constellation of the home lights and the shop lights and the street lights. There, in her house, were her neighbours, gathered to do no violence to that Christmas paper of theirs, since there was to be no "present trading," no "money spending." Nevertheless, they had drawn together by common consent, and it was Christmas Eve. She knew it now: There is no arbitrary shutting out of that for which Christmas stands. As its spirit was in the village, so its spirit is in the world—denied indeed, put upon, crowned with mockery, dragged in the dirt, bearing alien burdens, but through it all immaculate, waiting for men to cross the threshold at which it never ceases to beckon to a common heritage: Home of the world, with a thousand towers shining with uncounted lights, lying very near—above the village, at the end of the Old Trail Road, upon the earth at the end of a yet unbeaten path— where men face the sovereign fact of humanhood.

... But all this lay within Mary's dumb thanksgiving that the child was running at her side. And the vision that she saw streamed down from Capella, of the brightness of an hundred of our suns, the star that stood in the east above the village where she lived.

Lanterns glowed through the roadside shrubbery, little kindly lights, like answers; and at a bend in the road voices burst about them, and Buff Miles and the children, Gussie and Bennet and Tab and Pep and little Emily, ran, singing, and closed about Mary and the child, and went on with them, slipping into the "church choir Christmas carols," and more, that Buff had been fain to teach them. The music filled the quiet night, rose, in the children's voices, like an invocation to all time.

"One for the way it all begun,
Two for the way it all has run,
What three'll be for I do forget,
But what will be has not been yet.
So holly and mistletoe,
So holly and mistletoe,
So holly and mistletoe
Over and over and over, oh!"

Between songs the children whispered together for a minute.

"What's the new little boy's name?" asked Tab.

Nobody knew. That would be something to find out.

"Well," Tab said, "tomorrow morning, right after breakfast, I'm going to bring Theophilus Thistledown down and *lend* him to him."

"Ain't we going to bury Sandy Claus right after breakfast?" demanded Gussie.

And all the children, even little Emily, answered:

"No, let's not."

They all went on together and entered Mary's gate. Those within,—hearing the singing, had opened the door, and they brought them through that deep arch of warmth and light. Afterward, no one could remember whether or not the greeting had been "Merry Christmas," but there could have been no mistaking what everybody meant.

XIV

AT HIS GATE IN THE street wall lined with snow-bowed lilacs and mulberries, Ebenezer Rule waited in the dark for his two friends to come back. He had found Kate Kerr in his kitchen methodically making a jar of Christmas cookies. ("You've got to eat, if it is Christmas," she had defended herself in a whisper.) And to her stupefaction he had dispatched her to Mary Chavah's with her entire Christmas baking in a basket.

"I don't believe they've got near enough for all the folks I see going," he explained it.

While he went within doors he had left the hobbyhorse in the snow, close to the wall; and he came back there to wait. The street had emptied. By now everyone had gone to Mary Chavah's. Once he caught the gleam of lanterns down the road and heard children's voices singing.

For some time he heard the singing, and after it had stopped he fancied that he heard it. Startled, he looked up into the wide night lying serene above the town, and not yet become vexed by the town's shadows and interrupted by their lights. It was as if the singing came from up there. But the night kept its way of looking steadily beyond him.

... It came to Ebenezer that the night had not always been so unconscious of his presence. The one long ago, for example, when he had slept beneath this wall and dreamed that he had a kingdom; those other nights, when he had wandered abroad with his star glass. Then the night used to be something else. It had seemed to meet him, to admit him. Now he knew, and for a long time had known, that when he was abroad in the night he was there, so to say, without its permission. As for men, he could not tell when relation with them had changed, when he had begun to think of them as among the externals; but he knew that now he ran along the surface of them and let them go. He never met them as *Others*, as belonging to countless equations of which he was one term, and they playing that wonderful, near role of *Other*. Thus he had got along, as if his own individuation were the only one that had ever occurred and as if all the mass of mankind—and the Night and the Day—were undifferentiated from some substance all inimical.

Then this vast egoism had heard itself expressed in the mention of Bruce's baby—the third generation. But by the great sorcery wherewith Nature has protected herself, this mammoth sense of self, when it extends unto the next generations, becomes a keeper of the race. Ebenezer had been touched, relaxed, disintegrated. Here was an interest outside himself which was yet no external. Vast, level reaches lay about that fact, and all long unexplored. But these were peopled. He saw them peopled....

... As in the cheer and stir within the house where that night were gathered his townsfolk, his neighbours, his "hands." He had thought that their way of meeting him, if he chose to go among them, would matter nothing. Abruptly now he saw that it would matter more than he could bear. They were in there at Mary's, the rooms full of little families, getting along as best they could, taking pride in their children, looking ahead, looking ahead—*and they would not know that he understood*. He could not have defined offhand what it was that he understood. But it had, it seemed, something to do with Letty's account book and Bruce's baby....

Gradually he let himself face what it was that he was wanting to do. And when he faced that, he left the hobbyhorse where it was under the wall and went into the street.

He took his place among the externals of the Winter night, himself unconscious of them. The night, with all its content, a thing of explicable fellowships, lay waiting patiently for those of its children who knew its face. In the dark and under the snow the very elements of earth and life were obscured, as in some clear wash correcting too strong values. He moved along the village, and now his dominant consciousness was the same consciousness in which that little village lived. But he knew it only as the impulse that urged him on toward Jenny's house. If he went to Jenny's, if he signified so that he wished not to be cut off from her and Bruce and the baby, if he asked Bruce to come back to the business, these meant a lifetime of modification to the boy's ideals for that business, and modification to the lives of the "hands" back there in Mary Chavah's house—and to something else....

"What else?" he asked himself.

Mechanically he looked up and saw the heavens crowded with bright watchers. In that high field one star, brighter than the others, hung over the little town. He found himself trying to see the stars as they had looked to him years ago, when they and the night had seemed to mean something else....

"What else?" he asked himself.

The time did not seem momentous. It was only very quiet. Nothing new was there, nothing different. It had always been so. The night lay in a sovereign consciousness of being more than just itself. "Do you think that you are all just you and nothing else?" it was seen to be compassionately asking.

"What else?" Ebenezer asked himself.

He did not face this yet. But in that hour which seemed pure essence, with no attenuating sound or touch, he kept on up the hill toward Jenny's house.

Mary Chavah left ajar the door from the child's room to the room where, in the dark, the tree stood. He had wanted the door to be ajar "so the things I think about can go back and forth," he had explained.

In the dining room she wrapped herself in the gray shawl and threw up the two windows. New air swept in, cleansing, replacing, prevailing. Her guests had left her early, as is the way in Old Trail Town. Then she had had her first moments with the child alone. He had done the things that she had not thought of his doing but had inevitably recognized: Had delayed his bed-going, had magnified and repeated the offices of his journey, had shown her the contents of his pockets, had repeatedly mentioned by their first names his playmates in Idaho and shown surprise when she asked him who they were. Mary stood now by the window conscious of a wonderful thing: That it seemed as if he had been there always.

In the clean inrush of the air she was aware of a faint fragrance, coming to her once and again. She looked down at her garden, lying wrapped in white and veiled with black, like some secret being. Three elements were slowly fashioning it, while the fourth, a soft fire within her, answered them. The fragrance made it seem as if the turn of the year were very near, as if its prophecy, evident once in the October violets in her garden, were come again. But when she moved, she knew that the fragrance came from within the room, from Ellen Bourne's Christmas rose, blossoming on the table.... Above, her eye fell on the picture that Jenny had brought to her on that day when she had all but emptied the house, as if in readiness. Almost she understood now the passionate expectation in that face, not unlike the expectation of those who in her dream had kept saying "You."

There was a movement in her garden and on the walk footsteps. The three men stepped into the rectangle of lamplight—Abel, Ames and Simeon, who had left the party a little before the others and, hurrying back with the gifts that they planned, had met Ebenezer at his gate, getting home from Jenny's house. In Abel's arms was something globed, like a little world; in Simeon's, the tall, gray-gowned Saint Nicholas taken from the Exchange window, the lettered sign absent, but the little flag still in his hand; and Ebenezer was carrying the hobbyhorse. If at him the other two had wondered somewhat, they had said nothing, in that fashion of treating the essential which is as peculiar to certain simple, robust souls as to other kinds of great souls.

"Has the boy gone to bed?" Abel asked without preface.

"Yes," Mary answered, "he has. I'm sorry."

"Nevermind," Simeon whispered, "you can give him these in the morning."

Mary, her shawl half hiding her face, stooped to take what the three lifted.

"They ain't presents, you know," Abel assured her positively. "They're just—well, just to let him know."

Mary set the strange assortment on the floor of the dining room—the things that were to be nothing in themselves, only just "to let him know."

"Thank you for him," she said gently. "And thank you for me," she added.

Ebenezer fumbled for a moment at his beaver hat, and took it off. Then the other two did so to their firm-fixed caps. And with an impulse that came from no one could tell whom, the three spoke—the first time hesitatingly, the next time together and confidently.

"Merry Christmas. Merry Christmas," they said.

Mary Chavah lifted her hand.

"Merry Christmas!" she cried.

THE LIFE AND ADVENTURES
OF SANTA CLAUS

Youth

I

Burzee

H AVE YOU HEARD OF THE great Forest of Burzee? Nurse used to
sing of it when I was a child. She sang of the big tree trunks,
standing close together, with their roots intertwining below the earth
and their branches intertwining above it; of their rough coating of bark
and queer, gnarled limbs; of the bushy foliage that roofed the entire
forest, save where the sunbeams found a path through which to touch
the ground in little spots and to cast weird and curious shadows over
the mosses, the lichens and the drifts of dried leaves.

The Forest of Burzee is mighty and grand and awesome to those
who steal beneath its shade. Coming from the sunlit meadows into its
mazes it seems at first gloomy, then pleasant, and afterward filled with
neverending delights.

For hundreds of years it has flourished in all its magnificence, the
silence of its inclosure unbroken save by the chirp of busy chipmunks,
the growl of wild beasts and the songs of birds.

Yet Burzee has its inhabitants—for all this. Nature peopled it in
the beginning with Fairies, Knooks, Ryls and Nymphs. As long as the
Forest stands it will be a home, a refuge and a playground to these sweet
immortals, who revel undisturbed in its depths.

Civilization has never yet reached Burzee. Will it ever, I wonder?

II

The Child of the Forest

O NCE, SO LONG AGO OUR great-grandfathers could scarcely have
heard it mentioned, there lived within the great Forest of Burzee
a wood-nymph named Necile. She was closely related to the mighty

Queen Zurline, and her home was beneath the shade of a widespreading oak. Once every year, on Budding Day, when the trees put forth their new buds, Necile held the Golden Chalice of Ak to the lips of the Queen, who drank therefrom to the prosperity of the Forest. So you see she was a nymph of some importance, and, moreover, it is said she was highly regarded because of her beauty and grace.

When she was created she could not have told; Queen Zurline could not have told; the great Ak himself could not have told. It was long ago when the world was new and nymphs were needed to guard the forests and to minister to the wants of the young trees. Then, on some day not remembered, Necile sprang into being; radiant, lovely, straight and slim as the sapling she was created to guard.

Her hair was the color that lines a chestnut-bur; her eyes were blue in the sunlight and purple in the shade; her cheeks bloomed with the faint pink that edges the clouds at sunset; her lips were full red, pouting and sweet. For costume she adopted oak-leaf green; all the wood-nymphs dress in that color and know no other so desirable. Her dainty feet were sandal-clad, while her head remained bare of covering other than her silken tresses.

Necile's duties were few and simple. She kept hurtful weeds from growing beneath her trees and sapping the earth-food required by her charges. She frightened away the Gadgols, who took evil delight in flying against the tree trunks and wounding them so that they drooped and died from the poisonous contact. In dry seasons she carried water from the brooks and pools and moistened the roots of her thirsty dependents.

That was in the beginning. The weeds had now learned to avoid the forests where wood-nymphs dwelt; the loathsome Gadgols no longer dared come nigh; the trees had become old and sturdy and could bear the drought better than when fresh-sprouted. So Necile's duties were lessened, and time grew laggard, while succeeding years became more tiresome and uneventful than the nymph's joyous spirit loved.

Truly the forest-dwellers did not lack amusement. Each full moon they danced in the Royal Circle of the Queen. There were also the Feast of Nuts, the Jubilee of Autumn Tintings, the solemn ceremony of Leaf Shedding and the revelry of Budding Day. But these periods of enjoyment were far apart, and left many weary hours between.

That a wood-nymph should grow discontented was not thought of by Necile's sisters. It came upon her only after many years of brooding.

But when once she had settled in her mind that life was irksome she had no patience with her condition, and longed to do something of real interest and to pass her days in ways hitherto undreamed of by forest nymphs. The Law of the Forest alone restrained her from going forth in search of adventure.

While this mood lay heavy upon pretty Necile it chanced that the great Ak visited the Forest of Burzee and allowed the wood-nymphs as was their wont—to lie at his feet and listen to the words of wisdom that fell from his lips. Ak is the Master Woodsman of the world; he sees everything, and knows more than the sons of men.

That night he held the Queen's hand, for he loved the nymphs as a father loves his children; and Necile lay at his feet with many of her sisters and earnestly harkened as he spoke.

"We live so happily, my fair ones, in our forest glades," said Ak, stroking his grizzled beard thoughtfully, "that we know nothing of the sorrow and misery that fall to the lot of those poor mortals who inhabit the open spaces of the earth. They are not of our race, it is true, yet compassion well befits beings so fairly favored as ourselves. Often as I pass by the dwelling of some suffering mortal I am tempted to stop and banish the poor thing's misery. Yet suffering, in moderation, is the natural lot of mortals, and it is not our place to interfere with the laws of Nature."

"Nevertheless," said the fair Queen, nodding her golden head at the Master Woodsman, "it would not be a vain guess that Ak has often assisted these hapless mortals."

Ak smiled.

"Sometimes," he replied, "when they are very young—'children,' the mortals call them—I have stopped to rescue them from misery. The men and women I dare not interfere with; they must bear the burdens Nature has imposed upon them. But the helpless infants, the innocent children of men, have a right to be happy until they become full-grown and able to bear the trials of humanity. So I feel I am justified in assisting them. Not long ago—a year, maybe—I found four poor children huddled in a wooden hut, slowly freezing to death. Their parents had gone to a neighboring village for food, and had left a fire to warm their little ones while they were absent. But a storm arose and drifted the snow in their path, so they were long on the road. Meantime the fire went out and the frost crept into the bones of the waiting children."

"Poor things!" murmured the Queen softly. "What did you do?"

"I called Nelko, bidding him fetch wood from my forests and breathe upon it until the fire blazed again and warmed the little room where the children lay. Then they ceased shivering and fell asleep until their parents came."

"I am glad you did thus," said the good Queen, beaming upon the Master; and Necile, who had eagerly listened to every word, echoed in a whisper: "I, too, am glad!"

"And this very night," continued Ak, "as I came to the edge of Burzee I heard a feeble cry, which I judged came from a human infant. I looked about me and found, close to the forest, a helpless babe, lying quite naked upon the grasses and wailing piteously. Not far away, screened by the forest, crouched Shiegra, the lioness, intent upon devouring the infant for her evening meal."

"And what did you do, Ak?" asked the Queen, breathlessly.

"Not much, being in a hurry to greet my nymphs. But I commanded Shiegra to lie close to the babe, and to give it her milk to quiet its hunger. And I told her to send word throughout the forest, to all beasts and reptiles, that the child should not be harmed."

"I am glad you did thus," said the good Queen again, in a tone of relief; but this time Necile did not echo her words, for the nymph, filled with a strange resolve, had suddenly stolen away from the group.

Swiftly her lithe form darted through the forest paths until she reached the edge of mighty Burzee, when she paused to gaze curiously about her. Never until now had she ventured so far, for the Law of the Forest had placed the nymphs in its inmost depths.

Necile knew she was breaking the Law, but the thought did not give pause to her dainty feet. She had decided to see with her own eyes this infant Ak had told of, for she had never yet beheld a child of man. All the immortals are full-grown; there are no children among them. Peering through the trees Necile saw the child lying on the grass. But now it was sweetly sleeping, having been comforted by the milk drawn from Shiegra. It was not old enough to know what peril means; if it did not feel hunger it was content.

Softly the nymph stole to the side of the babe and knelt upon the sward, her long robe of rose leaf color spreading about her like a gossamer cloud. Her lovely countenance expressed curiosity and surprise, but, most of all, a tender, womanly pity. The babe was newborn, chubby and pink. It was entirely helpless. While the nymph gazed the infant opened its eyes, smiled upon her, and stretched out two dimpled arms. In another instant Necile had caught it to her breast and was hurrying with it through the forest paths.

III

THE ADOPTION

THE MASTER WOODSMAN SUDDENLY ROSE, with knitted brows. "There is a strange presence in the Forest," he declared. Then the Queen and her nymphs turned and saw standing before them Necile, with the sleeping infant clasped tightly in her arms and a defiant look in her deep blue eyes.

And thus for a moment they remained, the nymphs filled with surprise and consternation, but the brow of the Master Woodsman gradually clearing as he gazed intently upon the beautiful immortal who had wilfully broken the Law. Then the great Ak, to the wonder of all, laid his hand softly on Necile's flowing locks and kissed her on her fair forehead.

"For the first time within my knowledge," said he, gently, "a nymph has defied me and my laws; yet in my heart can I find no word of chiding. What is your desire, Necile?"

"Let me keep the child!" she answered, beginning to tremble and falling on her knees in supplication.

"Here, in the Forest of Burzee, where the human race has never yet penetrated?" questioned Ak.

"Here, in the Forest of Burzee," replied the nymph, boldly. "It is my home, and I am weary for lack of occupation. Let me care for the babe! See how weak and helpless it is. Surely it can not harm Burzee nor the Master Woodsman of the World!"

"But the Law, child, the Law!" cried Ak, sternly.

"The Law is made by the Master Woodsman," returned Necile; "if he bids me care for the babe he himself has saved from death, who in all the world dare oppose me?" Queen Zurline, who had listened intently to this conversation, clapped her pretty hands gleefully at the nymph's answer.

"You are fairly trapped, O Ak!" she exclaimed, laughing. "Now, I pray you, give heed to Necile's petition."

The Woodsman, as was his habit when in thought, stroked his grizzled beard slowly. Then he said:

"She shall keep the babe, and I will give it my protection. But I warn you all that as this is the first time I have relaxed the Law, so shall it be the last time. Never more, to the end of the World, shall a mortal be adopted by an immortal. Otherwise would we abandon our happy existence for one of trouble and anxiety. Goodnight, my nymphs!"

Then Ak was gone from their midst, and Necile hurried away to her bower to rejoice over her newfound treasure.

IV

CLAUS

ANOTHER DAY FOUND NECILE'S BOWER the most popular place in the Forest. The nymphs clustered around her and the child that lay asleep in her lap, with expressions of curiosity and delight. Nor were they wanting in praises for the great Ak's kindness in allowing Necile to keep the babe and to care for it. Even the Queen came to peer into the innocent childish face and to hold a helpless, chubby fist in her own fair hand.

"What shall we call him, Necile?" she asked, smiling. "He must have a name, you know."

"Let him be called Claus," answered Necile, "for that means 'a little one.'"

"Rather let him be called Neclaus,"* returned the Queen, "for that will mean 'Necile's little one.'"

The nymphs clapped their hands in delight, and Neclaus became the infant's name, although Necile loved best to call him Claus, and in afterdays many of her sisters followed her example.

Necile gathered the softest moss in all the forest for Claus to lie upon, and she made his bed in her own bower. Of food the infant had no lack. The nymphs searched the forest for bell-udders, which grow upon the goa-tree and when opened are found to be filled with sweet milk. And the soft-eyed does willingly gave a share of their milk to support the little stranger, while Shiegra, the lioness, often crept stealthily into Necile's bower and purred softly as she lay beside the babe and fed it.

So the little one flourished and grew big and sturdy day by day, while Necile taught him to speak and to walk and to play.

His thoughts and words were sweet and gentle, for the nymphs

---

* Some people have spelled this name Nicklaus and others Nicolas, which is the reason that Santa Claus is still known in some lands as St. Nicolas. But, of course, Neclaus is his right name, and Claus the nickname given him by his adopted mother, the fair nymph Necile.

knew no evil and their hearts were pure and loving. He became the pet of the forest, for Ak's decree had forbidden beast or reptile to molest him, and he walked fearlessly wherever his will guided him.

Presently the news reached the other immortals that the nymphs of Burzee had adopted a human infant, and that the act had been sanctioned by the great Ak. Therefore many of them came to visit the little stranger, looking upon him with much interest. First the Ryls, who are first cousins to the wood-nymphs, although so differently formed. For the Ryls are required to watch over the flowers and plants, as the nymphs watch over the forest trees. They search the wide world for the food required by the roots of the flowering plants, while the brilliant colors possessed by the full-blown flowers are due to the dyes placed in the soil by the Ryls, which are drawn through the little veins in the roots and the body of the plants, as they reach maturity. The Ryls are a busy people, for their flowers bloom and fade continually, but they are merry and light-hearted and are very popular with the other immortals.

Next came the Knooks, whose duty it is to watch over the beasts of the world, both gentle and wild. The Knooks have a hard time of it, since many of the beasts are ungovernable and rebel against restraint. But they know how to manage them, after all, and you will find that certain laws of the Knooks are obeyed by even the most ferocious animals. Their anxieties make the Knooks look old and worn and crooked, and their natures are a bit rough from associating with wild creatures continually; yet they are most useful to humanity and to the world in general, as their laws are the only laws the forest beasts recognize except those of the Master Woodsman.

Then there were the Fairies, the guardians of mankind, who were much interested in the adoption of Claus because their own laws forbade them to become familiar with their human charges. There are instances on record where the Fairies have shown themselves to human beings, and have even conversed with them; but they are supposed to guard the lives of mankind unseen and unknown, and if they favor some people more than others it is because these have won such distinction fairly, as the Fairies are very just and impartial. But the idea of adopting a child of men had never occurred to them because it was in every way opposed to their laws; so their curiosity was intense to behold the little stranger adopted by Necile and her sister nymphs.

Claus looked upon the immortals who thronged around him with fearless eyes and smiling lips. He rode laughingly upon the shoulders of the merry Ryls; he mischievously pulled the gray beards of the low-browed Knooks; he rested his curly head confidently upon the dainty bosom of the Fairy Queen herself. And the Ryls loved the sound of his laughter; the Knooks loved his courage; the Fairies loved his innocence.

The boy made friends of them all, and learned to know their laws intimately. No forest flower was trampled beneath his feet, lest the friendly Ryls should be grieved. He never interfered with the beasts of the forest, lest his friends the Knooks should become angry. The Fairies he loved dearly, but, knowing nothing of mankind, he could not understand that he was the only one of his race admitted to friendly intercourse with them.

Indeed, Claus came to consider that he alone, of all the forest people, had no like nor fellow. To him the forest was the world. He had no idea that millions of toiling, striving human creatures existed.

And he was happy and content.

V

The Master Woodsman

YEARS PASS SWIFTLY IN BURZEE, for the nymphs have no need to regard time in any way. Even centuries make no change in the dainty creatures; ever and ever they remain the same, immortal and unchanging.

Claus, however, being mortal, grew to manhood day by day. Necile was disturbed, presently, to find him too big to lie in her lap, and he had a desire for other food than milk. His stout legs carried him far into Burzee's heart, where he gathered supplies of nuts and berries, as well as several sweet and wholesome roots, which suited his stomach better than the belludders. He sought Necile's bower less frequently, till finally it became his custom to return thither only to sleep.

The nymph, who had come to love him dearly, was puzzled to comprehend the changed nature of her charge, and unconsciously altered her own mode of life to conform to his whims. She followed him readily through the forest paths, as did many of her sister nymphs, explaining as they walked all the mysteries of the gigantic wood and the habits and nature of the living things which dwelt beneath its shade.

The language of the beasts became clear to little Claus; but he never could understand their sulky and morose tempers. Only the squirrels, the mice and the rabbits seemed to possess cheerful and merry natures; yet would the boy laugh when the panther growled, and stroke the bear's glossy coat while the creature snarled and bared its teeth menacingly. The growls and snarls were not for Claus, he well knew, so what did they matter?

He could sing the songs of the bees, recite the poetry of the wood-flowers and relate the history of every blinking owl in Burzee. He helped the Ryls to feed their plants and the Knooks to keep order among the animals. The little immortals regarded him as a privileged person, being especially protected by Queen Zurline and her nymphs and favored by the great Ak himself.

One day the Master Woodsman came back to the forest of Burzee. He had visited, in turn, all his forests throughout the world, and they were many and broad.

Not until he entered the glade where the Queen and her nymphs were assembled to greet him did Ak remember the child he had permitted Necile to adopt. Then he found, sitting familiarly in the circle of lovely immortals, a broad-shouldered, stalwart youth, who, when erect, stood fully as high as the shoulder of the Master himself.

Ak paused, silent and frowning, to bend his piercing gaze upon Claus. The clear eyes met his own steadfastly, and the Woodsman gave a sigh of relief as he marked their placid depths and read the youth's brave and innocent heart. Nevertheless, as Ak sat beside the fair Queen, and the golden chalice, filled with rare nectar, passed from lip to lip, the Master Woodsman was strangely silent and reserved, and stroked his beard many times with a thoughtful motion.

With morning he called Claus aside, in kindly fashion, saying:

"Bid good by, for a time, to Necile and her sisters; for you shall accompany me on my journey through the world."

The venture pleased Claus, who knew well the honor of being companion of the Master Woodsman of the world. But Necile wept for the first time in her life, and clung to the boy's neck as if she could not bear to let him go. The nymph who had mothered this sturdy youth was still as dainty, as charming and beautiful as when she had dared to face Ak with the babe clasped to her breast; nor was her love less great. Ak beheld the two clinging together, seemingly as brother and sister to one another, and again he wore his thoughtful look.

VI

CLAUS DISCOVERS HUMANITY

TAKING CLAUS TO A SMALL clearing in the forest, the Master said: "Place your hand upon my girdle and hold fast while we journey through the air; for now shall we encircle the world and look upon many of the haunts of those men from whom you are descended."

These words caused Claus to marvel, for until now he had thought himself the only one of his kind upon the earth; yet in silence he grasped firmly the girdle of the great Ak, his astonishment forbidding speech.

Then the vast forest of Burzee seemed to fall away from their feet, and the youth found himself passing swiftly through the air at a great height.

Ere long there were spires beneath them, while buildings of many shapes and colors met their downward view. It was a city of men, and Ak, pausing to descend, led Claus to its inclosure. Said the Master:

"So long as you hold fast to my girdle you will remain unseen by all mankind, though seeing clearly yourself. To release your grasp will be to separate yourself forever from me and your home in Burzee."

One of the first laws of the Forest is obedience, and Claus had no thought of disobeying the Master's wish. He clung fast to the girdle and remained invisible.

Thereafter with each moment passed in the city the youth's wonder grew. He, who had supposed himself created differently from all others, now found the earth swarming with creatures of his own kind.

"Indeed," said Ak, "the immortals are few; but the mortals are many."

Claus looked earnestly upon his fellows. There were sad faces, gay and reckless faces, pleasant faces, anxious faces and kindly faces, all mingled in puzzling disorder. Some worked at tedious tasks; some strutted in impudent conceit; some were thoughtful and grave while others seemed happy and content. Men of many natures were there, as everywhere, and Claus found much to please him and much to make him sad.

But especially he noted the children—first curiously, then eagerly, then lovingly. Ragged little ones rolled in the dust of the streets, playing with scraps and pebbles. Other children, gaily dressed, were propped upon cushions and fed with sugar plums. Yet the children of the rich were not happier than those playing with the dust and pebbles, it seemed to Claus.

"Childhood is the time of man's greatest content," said Ak, following the youth's thoughts. "'Tis during these years of innocent pleasure that the little ones are most free from care."

"Tell me," said Claus, "why do not all these babies fare alike?"

"Because they are born in both cottage and palace," returned the Master. "The difference in the wealth of the parents determines the lot of the child. Some are carefully tended and clothed in silks and dainty linen; others are neglected and covered with rags."

"Yet all seem equally fair and sweet," said Claus, thoughtfully.

"While they are babes—yes;" agreed Ak. "Their joy is in being alive, and they do not stop to think. In after years the doom of mankind overtakes them, and they find they must struggle and worry, work and fret, to gain the wealth that is so dear to the hearts of men. Such things are unknown in the Forest where you were reared." Claus was silent a moment. Then he asked:

"Why was I reared in the forest, among those who are not of my race?"

Then Ak, in gentle voice, told him the story of his babyhood: how he had been abandoned at the forest's edge and left a prey to wild beasts, and how the loving nymph Necile had rescued him and brought him to manhood under the protection of the immortals.

"Yet I am not of them," said Claus, musingly.

"You are not of them," returned the Woodsman. "The nymph who cared for you as a mother seems now like a sister to you; by and by, when you grow old and gray, she will seem like a daughter. Yet another brief span and you will be but a memory, while she remains Necile."

"Then why, if man must perish, is he born?" demanded the boy.

"Everything perishes except the world itself and its keepers," answered Ak. "But while life lasts everything on earth has its use. The wise seek ways to be helpful to the world, for the helpful ones are sure to live again."

Much of this Claus failed to understand fully, but a longing seized him to become helpful to his fellows, and he remained grave and thoughtful while they resumed their journey.

They visited many dwellings of men in many parts of the world, watching farmers toil in the fields, warriors dash into cruel fray, and merchants exchange their goods for bits of white and yellow metal. And everywhere the eyes of Claus sought out the children in love and pity, for the thought of his own helpless babyhood was strong within him and he yearned to give help to the innocent little ones of his race even as he had been succored by the kindly nymph.

Day by day the Master Woodsman and his pupil traversed the earth, Ak speaking but seldom to the youth who clung steadfastly to his girdle, but guiding him into all places where he might become familiar with the lives of human beings.

And at last they returned to the grand old Forest of Burzee, where the Master set Claus down within the circle of nymphs, among whom the pretty Necile anxiously awaited him.

The brow of the great Ak was now calm and peaceful; but the brow of Claus had become lined with deep thought. Necile sighed at the change in her foster son, who until now had been ever joyous and smiling, and the thought came to her that never again would the life of the boy be the same as before this eventful journey with the Master.

VII

CLAUS LEAVES THE FOREST

WHEN GOOD QUEEN ZURLINE HAD touched the golden chalice with her fair lips and it had passed around the circle in honor of the travelers' return, the Master Woodsman of the World, who had not yet spoken, turned his gaze frankly upon Claus and said: "Well?"

The boy understood, and rose slowly to his feet beside Necile. Once only his eyes passed around the familiar circle of nymphs, every one of whom he remembered as a loving comrade; but tears came unbidden to dim his sight, so he gazed thereafter steadfastly at the Master.

"I have been ignorant," said he, simply, "until the great Ak in his kindness taught me who and what I am. You, who live so sweetly in your forest bowers, ever fair and youthful and innocent, are no fit comrades for a son of humanity. For I have looked upon man, finding him doomed to live for a brief space upon earth, to toil for the things he needs, to fade into old age, and then to pass away as the leaves in autumn. Yet every man has his mission, which is to leave the world better, in some way, than he found it. I am of the race of men, and man's lot is my lot. For your tender care of the poor, forsaken babe you adopted, as well as for your loving comradeship during my boyhood, my heart will ever overflow with gratitude. My foster-mother," here he stopped and kissed Necile's white forehead, "I shall love and cherish while life lasts. But I must leave you, to take my part in the endless struggle to which humanity is doomed, and to live my life in my own way."

"What will you do?" asked the Queen, gravely.

"I must devote myself to the care of the children of mankind, and try to make them happy," he answered. "Since your own tender care of a babe brought to me happiness and strength, it is just and right that I devote my life to the pleasure of other babes. Thus will the memory of the loving nymph Necile be planted within the hearts of thousands of my race for many years to come, and her kindly act be recounted in song and in story while the world shall last. Have I spoken well, O Master?"

"You have spoken well," returned Ak, and rising to his feet he continued: "Yet one thing must not be forgotten. Having been adopted as the child of the Forest, and the playfellow of the nymphs, you have gained a distinction which forever separates you from your kind. Therefore, when you go forth into the world of men you shall retain the protection of the Forest, and the powers you now enjoy will remain with you to assist you in your labors. In any need you may call upon the Nymphs, the Ryls, the Knooks and the Fairies, and they will serve you gladly. I, the Master Woodsman of the World, have said it, and my Word is the Law!"

Claus looked upon Ak with grateful eyes.

"This will make me mighty among men," he replied. "Protected by these kind friends I may be able to make thousands of little children happy. I will try very hard to do my duty, and I know the Forest people will give me their sympathy and help."

"We will!" said the Fairy Queen, earnestly.

"We will!" cried the merry Ryls, laughing.

"We will!" shouted the crooked Knooks, scowling.

"We will!" exclaimed the sweet nymphs, proudly. But Necile said nothing. She only folded Claus in her arms and kissed him tenderly.

"The world is big," continued the boy, turning again to his loyal friends, "but men are everywhere. I shall begin my work near my friends, so that if I meet with misfortune I can come to the Forest for counsel or help."

With that he gave them all a loving look and turned away. There was no need to say good by, by for him the sweet, wild life of the Forest was over. He went forth bravely to meet his doom—the doom of the race of man—the necessity to worry and work.

But Ak, who knew the boy's heart, was merciful and guided his steps.

Coming through Burzee to its eastern edge Claus reached the Laughing Valley of Hohaho. On each side were rolling green hills, and a brook wandered midway between them to wind afar off beyond the valley. At his back was the grim Forest; at the far end of the valley a broad plain. The eyes of the young man, which had until now reflected his grave thoughts, became brighter as he stood silent, looking out upon the Laughing Valley. Then on a sudden his eyes twinkled, as stars do on a still night, and grew merry and wide.

For at his feet the cowslips and daisies smiled on him in friendly regard; the breeze whistled gaily as it passed by and fluttered the locks on his forehead; the brook laughed joyously as it leaped over the pebbles and swept around the green curves of its banks; the bees sang sweet songs as they flew from dandelion to daffodil; the beetles chirruped happily in the long grass, and the sunbeams glinted pleasantly over all the scene.

"Here," cried Claus, stretching out his arms as if to embrace the Valley, "will I make my home!"

That was many, many years ago. It has been his home ever since. It is his home now.

Manhood

I

The Laughing Valley

WHEN CLAUS CAME THE VALLEY was empty save for the grass, the brook, the wildflowers, the bees and the butterflies. If he would make his home here and live after the fashion of men he must have a house. This puzzled him at first, but while he stood smiling in the sunshine he suddenly found beside him old Nelko, the servant of the Master Woodsman. Nelko bore an ax, strong and broad, with blade that gleamed like burnished silver. This he placed in the young man's hand, then disappeared without a word.

Claus understood, and turning to the Forest's edge he selected a number of fallen tree trunks, which he began to clear of their dead branches. He would not cut into a living tree. His life among the nymphs who guarded the Forest had taught him that a live tree is sacred, being a created thing endowed with feeling. But with the dead and fallen trees it was different. They had fulfilled their destiny, as active members of the Forest community, and now it was fitting that their remains should minister to the needs of man.

The ax bit deep into the logs at every stroke. It seemed to have a force of its own, and Claus had but to swing and guide it.

When shadows began creeping over the green hills to lie in the Valley overnight, the young man had chopped many logs into equal lengths and proper shapes for building a house such as he had seen the poorer classes of men inhabit. Then, resolving to await another day before he tried to fit the logs together, Claus ate some of the sweet roots he well knew how to find, drank deeply from the laughing brook, and lay down to sleep on the grass, first seeking a spot where no flowers grew, lest the weight of his body should crush them.

And while he slumbered and breathed in the perfume of the wondrous Valley the Spirit of Happiness crept into his heart and drove out all terror and care and misgivings. Never more would the face of Claus be clouded with anxieties; never more would the trials of life weigh him down as with a burden. The Laughing Valley had claimed him for its own.

Would that we all might live in that delightful place!—But then, maybe, it would become overcrowded. For ages it had awaited a tenant. Was it chance that led young Claus to make his home in this happy vale? Or may we guess that his thoughtful friends, the immortals, had directed his steps when he wandered away from Burzee to seek a home in the great world?

Certain it is that while the moon peered over the hilltop and flooded with its soft beams the body of the sleeping stranger, the Laughing Valley was filled with the queer, crooked shapes of the friendly Knooks. These people spoke no words, but worked with skill and swiftness. The logs Claus had trimmed with his bright ax were carried to a spot beside the brook and fitted one upon another, and during the night a strong and roomy dwelling was built.

The birds came sweeping into the Valley at daybreak, and their songs, so seldom heard in the deep wood, aroused the stranger. He rubbed the web of sleep from his eyelids and looked around. The house met his gaze.

"I must thank the Knooks for this," said he, gratefully. Then he walked to his dwelling and entered at the doorway. A large room faced him, having a fireplace at the end and a table and bench in the middle. Beside the fireplace was a cupboard. Another doorway was beyond. Claus entered here, also, and saw a smaller room with a bed against the wall and a stool set near a small stand. On the bed were many layers of dried moss brought from the Forest.

"Indeed, it is a palace!" exclaimed the smiling Claus. "I must thank the good Knooks again, for their knowledge of man's needs as well as for their labors in my behalf."

He left his new home with a glad feeling that he was not quite alone in the world, although he had chosen to abandon his Forest life. Friendships are not easily broken, and the immortals are everywhere.

Upon reaching the brook he drank of the pure water, and then sat down on the bank to laugh at the mischievous gambols of the ripples as they pushed one another against rocks or crowded desperately to see which should first reach the turn beyond. And as they raced away he listened to the song they sang:

> *"Rushing, pushing, on we go!*
> *Not a wave may gently flow—*
> *All are too excited.*
> *Ev'ry drop, delighted,*
> *Turns to spray in merry play*
> *As we tumble on our way!"*

Next Claus searched for roots to eat, while the daffodils turned their little eyes up to him laughingly and lisped their dainty song:

> *"Blooming fairly, growing rarely,*
> *Never flowerets were so gay!*
> *Perfume breathing, joy bequeathing,*
> *As our colors we display."*

It made Claus laugh to hear the little things voice their happiness as they nodded gracefully on their stems. But another strain caught his ear as the sunbeams fell gently across his face and whispered:

> *"Here is gladness, that our rays*
> *Warm the valley through the days;*
> *Here is happiness, to give*
> *Comfort unto all who live!"*

"Yes!" cried Claus in answer, "there is happiness and joy in all things here. The Laughing Valley is a valley of peace and goodwill."

He passed the day talking with the ants and beetles and exchanging jokes with the light-hearted butterflies. And at night he lay on his bed of soft moss and slept soundly.

Then came the Fairies, merry but noiseless, bringing skillets and pots and dishes and pans and all the tools necessary to prepare food and to comfort a mortal. With these they filled cupboard and fireplace, finally placing a stout suit of wool clothing on the stool by the bedside.

When Claus awoke he rubbed his eyes again, and laughed, and spoke aloud his thanks to the Fairies and the Master Woodsman who had sent them. With eager joy he examined all his new possessions, wondering what some might be used for. But, in the days when he had clung to the girdle of the great Ak and visited the cities of men, his eyes had been quick to note all the manners and customs of the race to which he belonged; so he guessed from the gifts brought by the Fairies that the Master expected him hereafter to live in the fashion of his fellow creatures.

"Which means that I must plow the earth and plant corn," he reflected; "so that when winter comes I shall have garnered food in plenty."

But, as he stood in the grassy Valley, he saw that to turn up the earth in furrows would be to destroy hundreds of pretty, helpless flowers, as well as thousands of the tender blades of grass. And this he could not bear to do.

Therefore he stretched out his arms and uttered a peculiar whistle he had learned in the Forest, afterward crying:

"Ryls of the Field Flowers—come to me!"

Instantly a dozen of the queer little Ryls were squatting upon the ground before him, and they nodded to him in cheerful greeting.

Claus gazed upon them earnestly.

"Your brothers of the Forest," he said, "I have known and loved many years. I shall love you, also, when we have become friends. To me the laws of the Ryls, whether those of the Forest or of the field, are sacred. I have never wilfully destroyed one of the flowers you tend so carefully; but I must plant grain to use for food during the cold winter, and how am I to do this without killing the little creatures that sing to me so prettily of their fragrant blossoms?"

The Yellow Ryl, he who tends the buttercups, made answer:

"Fret not, friend Claus. The great Ak has spoken to us of you. There is better work for you in life than to labor for food, and though, not being of the Forest, Ak has no command over us, nevertheless are we glad to favor one he loves. Live, therefore, to do the good work you are resolved to undertake. We, the Field Ryls, will attend to your food supplies."

After this speech the Ryls were no longer to be seen, and Claus drove from his mind the thought of tilling the earth.

When next he wandered back to his dwelling a bowl of fresh milk stood upon the table; bread was in the cupboard and sweet honey filled a dish beside it. A pretty basket of rosy apples and new-plucked grapes was also awaiting him. He called out "Thanks, my friends!" to the invisible Ryls, and straightway began to eat of the food.

Thereafter, when hungry, he had but to look into the cupboard to find goodly supplies brought by the kindly Ryls. And the Knooks cut and stacked much wood for his fireplace. And the Fairies brought him warm blankets and clothing.

So began his life in the Laughing Valley, with the favor and friendship of the immortals to minister to his every want.

II

How Claus Made the First Toy

TRULY OUR CLAUS HAD WISDOM, for his good fortune but strengthened his resolve to befriend the little ones of his own race. He knew his plan was approved by the immortals, else they would not have favored him so greatly.

So he began at once to make acquaintance with mankind. He walked through the Valley to the plain beyond, and crossed the plain in many directions to reach the abodes of men. These stood singly or in groups of dwellings called villages, and in nearly all the houses, whether big or little, Claus found children.

The youngsters soon came to know his merry, laughing face and the kind glance of his bright eyes; and the parents, while they regarded the young man with some scorn for loving children more than their elders, were content that the girls and boys had found a playfellow who seemed willing to amuse them.

So the children romped and played games with Claus, and the boys rode upon his shoulders, and the girls nestled in his strong arms, and the babies clung fondly to his knees. Wherever the young man chanced to be, the sound of childish laughter followed him; and to understand this better you must know that children were much neglected in those days and received little attention from their parents, so that it became to them a marvel that so goodly a man as Claus devoted his time to making them happy. And those who knew him were, you may be sure, very happy indeed. The sad faces of the poor and abused grew bright for once; the cripple smiled despite his misfortune; the ailing ones hushed their moans and the grieved ones their cries when their merry friend came nigh to comfort them.

Only at the beautiful palace of the Lord of Lerd and at the frowning castle of the Baron Braun was Claus refused admittance. There were children at both places; but the servants at the palace shut the door in the young stranger's face, and the fierce Baron threatened to hang him from an iron hook on the castle walls. Whereupon Claus sighed and went back to the poorer dwellings where he was welcome.

After a time the winter drew near.

The flowers lived out their lives and faded and disappeared; the beetles burrowed far into the warm earth; the butterflies deserted the meadows; and the voice of the brook grew hoarse, as if it had taken cold.

One day snowflakes filled all the air in the Laughing Valley, dancing boisterously toward the earth and clothing in pure white raiment the roof of Claus's dwelling.

At night Jack Frost rapped at the door.

"Come in!" cried Claus.

"Come out!" answered Jack, "for you have a fire inside."

So Claus came out. He had known Jack Frost in the Forest, and liked the jolly rogue, even while he mistrusted him.

"There will be rare sport for me tonight, Claus!" shouted the sprite. "Isn't this glorious weather? I shall nip scores of noses and ears and toes before daybreak."

"If you love me, Jack, spare the children," begged Claus.

"And why?" asked the other, in surprise.

"They are tender and helpless," answered Claus.

"But I love to nip the tender ones!" declared Jack. "The older ones are tough, and tire my fingers."

"The young ones are weak, and can not fight you," said Claus.

"True," agreed Jack, thoughtfully. "Well, I will not pinch a child this night—if I can resist the temptation," he promised. "Goodnight, Claus!"

"Goodnight."

The young man went in and closed the door, and Jack Frost ran on to the nearest village.

Claus threw a log on the fire, which burned up brightly. Beside the hearth sat Blinkie, a big cat give him by Peter the Knook. Her fur was soft and glossy, and she purred neverending songs of contentment.

"I shall not see the children again soon," said Claus to the cat, who kindly paused in her song to listen. "The winter is upon us, the snow will be deep for many days, and I shall be unable to play with my little friends."

The cat raised a paw and stroked her nose thoughtfully, but made no reply. So long as the fire burned and Claus sat in his easy chair by the hearth she did not mind the weather.

So passed many days and many long evenings. The cupboard was always full, but Claus became weary with having nothing to do more than to feed the fire from the big woodpile the Knooks had brought him.

One evening he picked up a stick of wood and began to cut it with his sharp knife. He had no thought, at first, except to occupy his time, and he whistled and sang to the cat as he carved away portions of the stick. Puss sat up on her haunches and watched him, listening at the same time to her master's merry whistle, which she loved to hear even more than her own purring songs.

Claus glanced at puss and then at the stick he was whittling, until presently the wood began to have a shape, and the shape was like the head of a cat, with two ears sticking upward.

Claus stopped whistling to laugh, and then both he and the cat looked at the wooden image in some surprise. Then he carved out the eyes and the nose, and rounded the lower part of the head so that it rested upon a neck.

Puss hardly knew what to make of it now, and sat up stiffly, as if watching with some suspicion what would come next.

Claus knew. The head gave him an idea. He plied his knife carefully and with skill, forming slowly the body of the cat, which he made to sit upon its haunches as the real cat did, with her tail wound around her two front legs.

The work cost him much time, but the evening was long and he had nothing better to do. Finally he gave a loud and delighted laugh at the result of his labors and placed the wooden cat, now completed, upon the hearth opposite the real one.

Puss thereupon glared at her image, raised her hair in anger, and uttered a defiant mew. The wooden cat paid no attention, and Claus, much amused, laughed again.

Then Blinkie advanced toward the wooden image to eye it closely and smell of it intelligently: Eyes and nose told her the creature was wood, in spite of its natural appearance; so puss resumed her seat and her purring, but as she neatly washed her face with her padded paw she cast more than one admiring glance at her clever master. Perhaps she felt the same satisfaction we feel when we look upon good photographs of ourselves.

The cat's master was himself pleased with his handiwork, without knowing exactly why. Indeed, he had great cause to congratulate himself that night, and all the children throughout the world should have joined him rejoicing. For Claus had made his first toy.

III

How the Ryls Colored the Toys

A HUSH LAY ON THE LAUGHING Valley now. Snow covered it like a white spread and pillows of downy flakes drifted before the dwelling where Claus sat feeding the blaze of the fire. The brook gurgled on beneath a heavy sheet of ice and all living plants and insects nestled close to Mother Earth to keep warm. The face of the moon was hid by dark clouds, and the wind, delighting in the wintry sport, pushed and whirled the snowflakes in so many directions that they could get no chance to fall to the ground.

Claus heard the wind whistling and shrieking in its play and thanked the good Knooks again for his comfortable shelter. Blinkie washed her face lazily and stared at the coals with a look of perfect content. The toy cat sat opposite the real one and gazed straight ahead, as toy cats should.

Suddenly Claus heard a noise that sounded different from the voice of the wind. It was more like a wail of suffering and despair.

He stood up and listened, but the wind, growing boisterous, shook the door and rattled the windows to distract his attention. He waited until the wind was tired and then, still listening, he heard once more the shrill cry of distress.

Quickly he drew on his coat, pulled his cap over his eyes and opened the door. The wind dashed in and scattered the embers over the hearth, at the same time blowing Blinkie's fur so furiously that she crept under the table to escape. Then the door was closed and Claus was outside, peering anxiously into the darkness.

The wind laughed and scolded and tried to push him over, but he stood firm. The helpless flakes stumbled against his eyes and dimmed his sight, but he rubbed them away and looked again. Snow was everywhere, white and glittering. It covered the earth and filled the air.

The cry was not repeated.

Claus turned to go back into the house, but the wind caught him unawares and he stumbled and fell across a snowdrift. His hand plunged into the drift and touched something that was not snow. This he seized and, pulling it gently toward him, found it to be a child. The next moment he had lifted it in his arms and carried it into the house.

The wind followed him through the door, but Claus shut it out quickly. He laid the rescued child on the hearth, and brushing away the snow he discovered it to be Weekum, a little boy who lived in a house beyond the Valley.

Claus wrapped a warm blanket around the little one and rubbed the frost from its limbs. Before long the child opened his eyes and, seeing where he was, smiled happily. Then Claus warmed milk and fed it to the boy slowly, while the cat looked on with sober curiosity. Finally the little one curled up in his friend's arms and sighed and fell asleep, and Claus, filled with gladness that he had found the wanderer, held him closely while he slumbered.

The wind, finding no more mischief to do, climbed the hill and swept on toward the north. This gave the weary snowflakes time to settle down to earth, and the Valley became still again.

The boy, having slept well in the arms of his friend, opened his eyes and sat up. Then, as a child will, he looked around the room and saw all that it contained.

"Your cat is a nice cat, Claus," he said, at last. "Let me hold it."

But puss objected and ran away.

"The other cat won't run, Claus," continued the boy. "Let me hold that one." Claus placed the toy in his arms, and the boy held it lovingly and kissed the tip of its wooden ear.

"How did you get lost in the storm, Weekum?" asked Claus.

"I started to walk to my auntie's house and lost my way," answered Weekum.

"Were you frightened?"

"It was cold," said Weekum, "and the snow got in my eyes, so I could not see. Then I kept on till I fell in the snow, without knowing where I was, and the wind blew the flakes over me and covered me up."

Claus gently stroked his head, and the boy looked up at him and smiled.

"I'm all right now," said Weekum.

"Yes," replied Claus, happily. "Now I will put you in my warm bed, and you must sleep until morning, when I will carry you back to your mother."

"May the cat sleep with me?" asked the boy.

"Yes, if you wish it to," answered Claus.

"It's a nice cat!" Weekum said, smiling, as Claus tucked the blankets around him; and presently the little one fell asleep with the wooden toy in his arms.

When morning came the sun claimed the Laughing Valley and flooded it with his rays; so Claus prepared to take the lost child back to its mother.

"May I keep the cat, Claus?" asked Weekum. "It's nicer than real cats. It doesn't run away, or scratch or bite. May I keep it?"

"Yes, indeed," answered Claus, pleased that the toy he had made could give pleasure to the child. So he wrapped the boy and the wooden cat in a warm cloak, perching the bundle upon his own broad shoulders, and then he tramped through the snow and the drifts of the Valley and across the plain beyond to the poor cottage where Weekum's mother lived.

"See, mama!" cried the boy, as soon as they entered, "I've got a cat!"

The good woman wept tears of joy over the rescue of her darling and thanked Claus many times for his kind act. So he carried a warm and happy heart back to his home in the Valley.

That night he said to puss: "I believe the children will love the wooden cats almost as well as the real ones, and they can't hurt them by pulling their tails and ears. I'll make another."

So this was the beginning of his great work.

The next cat was better made than the first. While Claus sat whittling it out the Yellow Ryl came in to make him a visit, and so pleased was he with the man's skill that he ran away and brought several of his fellows.

There sat the Red Ryl, the Black Ryl, the Green Ryl, the Blue Ryl and the Yellow Ryl in a circle on the floor, while Claus whittled and whistled and the wooden cat grew into shape.

"If it could be made the same color as the real cat, no one would know the difference," said the Yellow Ryl, thoughtfully.

"The little ones, maybe, would not know the difference," replied Claus, pleased with the idea.

"I will bring you some of the red that I color my roses and tulips with," cried the Red Ryl; "and then you can make the cat's lips and tongue red."

"I will bring some of the green that I color my grasses and leaves with," said the Green Ryl; "and then you can color the cat's eyes green."

"They will need a bit of yellow, also," remarked the Yellow Ryl; "I must fetch some of the yellow that I use to color my buttercups and goldenrods with."

"The real cat is black," said the Black Ryl; "I will bring some of the black that I use to color the eyes of my pansies with, and then you can paint your wooden cat black."

"I see you have a blue ribbon around Blinkie's neck," added the Blue Ryl. "I will get some of the color that I use to paint the bluebells and forget-me-nots with, and then you can carve a wooden ribbon on the toy cat's neck and paint it blue."

So the Ryls disappeared, and by the time Claus had finished carving out the form of the cat they were all back with the paints and brushes.

They made Blinkie sit upon the table, that Claus might paint the toy cat just the right color, and when the work was done the Ryls declared it was exactly as good as a live cat.

"That is, to all appearances," added the Red Ryl.

Blinkie seemed a little offended by the attention bestowed upon the toy, and that she might not seem to approve the imitation cat she walked to the corner of the hearth and sat down with a dignified air.

But Claus was delighted, and as soon as morning came he started out and tramped through the snow, across the Valley and the plain, until he came to a village. There, in a poor hut near the walls of the beautiful palace of the Lord of Lerd, a little girl lay upon a wretched cot, moaning with pain.

Claus approached the child and kissed her and comforted her, and then he drew the toy cat from beneath his coat, where he had hidden it, and placed it in her arms.

Ah, how well he felt himself repaid for his labor and his long walk when he saw the little one's eyes grow bright with pleasure! She hugged the kitty tight to her breast, as if it had been a precious gem, and would not let it go for a single moment. The fever was quieted, the pain grew less, and she fell into a sweet and refreshing sleep.

Claus laughed and whistled and sang all the way home. Never had he been so happy as on that day.

When he entered his house he found Shiegra, the lioness, awaiting him. Since his babyhood Shiegra had loved Claus, and while he dwelt in the Forest she had often come to visit him at Necile's bower. After Claus had gone to live in the Laughing Valley Shiegra became lonely and ill at ease, and now she had braved the snowdrifts, which all lions abhor, to see him once more. Shiegra was getting old and her teeth were beginning to fall out, while the hairs that tipped her ears and tail had changed from tawny-yellow to white.

Claus found her lying on his hearth, and he put his arms around the neck of the lioness and hugged her lovingly. The cat had retired into a far corner. She did not care to associate with Shiegra.

Claus told his old friend about the cats he had made, and how much pleasure they had given Weekum and the sick girl. Shiegra did not know much about children; indeed, if she met a child she could scarcely be trusted not to devour it. But she was interested in Claus' new labors, and said:

"These images seem to me very attractive. Yet I can not see why you should make cats, which are very unimportant animals. Suppose, now that I am here, you make the image of a lioness, the Queen of all beasts. Then, indeed, your children will be happy—and safe at the same time!"

Claus thought this was a good suggestion. So he got a piece of wood and sharpened his knife, while Shiegra crouched upon the hearth at his feet. With much care he carved the head in the likeness of the lioness, even to the two fierce teeth that curved over her lower lip and the deep, frowning lines above her wide-open eyes.

When it was finished he said:

"You have a terrible look, Shiegra."

"Then the image is like me," she answered; "for I am indeed terrible to all who are not my friends."

Claus now carved out the body, with Shiegra's long tail trailing behind it. The image of the crouching lioness was very lifelike.

"It pleases me," said Shiegra, yawning and stretching her body gracefully. "Now I will watch while you paint."

He brought the paints the Ryls had given him from the cupboard and colored the image to resemble the real Shiegra.

The lioness placed her big, padded paws upon the edge of the table and raised herself while she carefully examined the toy that was her likeness.

"You are indeed skillful!" she said, proudly. "The children will like that better than cats, I'm sure."

Then snarling at Blinkie, who arched her back in terror and whined fearfully, she walked away toward her forest home with stately strides.

IV

How Little Mayrie Became Frightened

THE WINTER WAS OVER NOW, and all the Laughing Valley was filled with joyous excitement. The brook was so happy at being free once again that it gurgled more boisterously than ever and dashed so recklessly against the rocks that it sent showers of spray high in the air. The grass thrust its sharp little blades upward through the mat of dead stalks where it had hidden from the snow, but the flowers were yet too timid to show themselves, although the Ryls were busy feeding their roots. The sun was in remarkably good humor, and sent his rays dancing merrily throughout the Valley.

Claus was eating his dinner one day when he heard a timid knock on his door.

"Come in!" he called.

No one entered, but after a pause came another rapping.

Claus jumped up and threw open the door. Before him stood a small girl holding a smaller brother fast by the hand.

"Is you Tlaus?" she asked, shyly.

"Indeed I am, my dear!" he answered, with a laugh, as he caught both children in his arms and kissed them. "You are very welcome, and you have come just in time to share my dinner."

He took them to the table and fed them with fresh milk and nut-cakes. When they had eaten enough he asked:

"Why have you made this long journey to see me?"

"I wants a tat!" replied little Mayrie; and her brother, who had not yet learned to speak many words, nodded his head and exclaimed like an echo: "Tat!"

"Oh, you want my toy cats, do you?" returned Claus, greatly pleased to discover that his creations were so popular with children.

The little visitors nodded eagerly.

"Unfortunately," he continued, "I have but one cat now ready, for I carried two to children in the town yesterday. And the one I have shall be given to your brother, Mayrie, because he is the smaller; and the next one I make shall be for you."

The boy's face was bright with smiles as he took the precious toy Claus held out to him; but little Mayrie covered her face with her arm and began to sob grievously.

"I—I—I wants a t—t—tat now!" she wailed.

Her disappointment made Claus feel miserable for a moment. Then he suddenly remembered Shiegra.

"Don't cry, darling!" he said, soothingly; "I have a toy much nicer than a cat, and you shall have that."

He went to the cupboard and drew out the image of the lioness, which he placed on the table before Mayrie.

The girl raised her arm and gave one glance at the fierce teeth and glaring eyes of the beast, and then, uttering a terrified scream, she rushed from the house. The boy followed her, also screaming lustily, and even dropping his precious cat in his fear.

For a moment Claus stood motionless, being puzzled and astonished. Then he threw Shiegra's image into the cupboard and ran after the children, calling to them not to be frightened.

Little Mayrie stopped in her flight and her brother clung to her skirt; but they both cast fearful glances at the house until Claus had assured them many times that the beast had been locked in the cupboard.

"Yet why were you frightened at seeing it?" he asked. "It is only a toy to play with!"

"It's bad!" said Mayrie, decidedly, "an'—an'—just horrid, an' not a bit nice, like tats!"

"Perhaps you are right," returned Claus, thoughtfully. "But if you will return with me to the house I will soon make you a pretty cat."

So they timidly entered the house again, having faith in their friend's words; and afterward they had the joy of watching Claus carve out a cat from a bit of wood and paint it in natural colors. It did not take him long to do this, for he had become skillful with his knife by this time, and Mayrie loved her toy the more dearly because she had seen it made.

After his little visitors had trotted away on their journey homeward Claus sat long in deep thought. And he then decided that such fierce creatures as his friend the lioness would never do as models from which to fashion his toys.

"There must be nothing to frighten the dear babies," he reflected; "and while I know Shiegra well, and am not afraid of her, it is but natural that children should look upon her image with terror. Hereafter I will choose such mild-mannered animals as squirrels and rabbits and deer and lambkins from which to carve my toys, for then the little ones will love rather than fear them."

He began his work that very day, and before bedtime had made a wooden rabbit and a lamb. They were not quite so lifelike as the cats had been, because they were formed from memory, while Blinkie had sat very still for Claus to look at while he worked.

But the new toys pleased the children nevertheless, and the fame of Claus' playthings quickly spread to every cottage on plain and in village. He always carried his gifts to the sick or crippled children, but those who were strong enough walked to the house in the Valley to ask for them, so a little path was soon worn from the plain to the door of the toymaker's cottage.

First came the children who had been playmates of Claus, before he began to make toys. These, you may be sure, were well supplied. Then children who lived farther away heard of the wonderful images and made journeys to the Valley to secure them. All little ones were welcome, and never a one went away empty-handed.

This demand for his handiwork kept Claus busily occupied, but he was quite happy in knowing the pleasure he gave to so many of the dear children. His friends the immortals were pleased with his success and supported him bravely.

The Knooks selected for him clear pieces of soft wood, that his knife might not be blunted in cutting them; the Ryls kept him supplied with paints of all colors and brushes fashioned from the tips of timothy grasses; the Fairies discovered that the workman needed saws and chisels and hammers and nails, as well as knives, and brought him a goodly array of such tools.

Claus soon turned his living room into a most wonderful workshop. He built a bench before the window, and arranged his tools and paints so that he could reach everything as he sat on his stool. And as he finished toy after toy to delight the hearts of little children he found himself growing so gay and happy that he could not refrain from singing and laughing and whistling all the day long.

"It's because I live in the Laughing Valley, where everything else laughs!" said Claus.

But that was not the reason.

V

How Bessie Blithesome Came to the Laughing Valley

ONE DAY, AS CLAUS SAT before his door to enjoy the sunshine while he busily carved the head and horns of a toy deer, he looked up and discovered a glittering cavalcade of horsemen approaching through the Valley.

When they drew nearer he saw that the band consisted of a score of men-at-arms, clad in bright armor and bearing in their hands spears and battle-axes. In front of these rode little Bessie Blithesome, the pretty daughter of that proud Lord of Lerd who had once driven Claus from his palace. Her palfrey was pure white, its bridle was covered with glittering gems, and its saddle draped with cloth of gold, richly broidered. The soldiers were sent to protect her from harm while she journeyed.

Claus was surprised, but he continued to whittle and to sing until the cavalcade drew up before him. Then the little girl leaned over the neck of her palfrey and said:

"Please, Mr. Claus, I want a toy!"

Her voice was so pleading that Claus jumped up at once and stood beside her. But he was puzzled how to answer her request.

"You are a rich lord's daughter," said he, "and have all that you desire."

"Except toys," added Bessie. "There are no toys in all the world but yours."

"And I make them for the poor children, who have nothing else to amuse them," continued Claus.

"Do poor children love to play with toys more than rich ones?" asked Bessie.

"I suppose not," said Claus, thoughtfully.

"Am I to blame because my father is a lord? Must I be denied the pretty toys I long for because other children are poorer than I?" she inquired earnestly.

"I'm afraid you must, dear," he answered; "for the poor have nothing else with which to amuse themselves. You have your pony to ride, your servants to wait on you, and every comfort that money can procure."

"But I want toys!" cried Bessie, wiping away the tears that forced themselves into her eyes. "If I can not have them, I shall be very unhappy."

Claus was troubled, for her grief recalled to him the thought that his desire was to make all children happy, without regard to their condition in life. Yet, while so many poor children were clamoring for his toys he could not bear to give one to them to Bessie Blithesome, who had so much already to make her happy.

"Listen, my child," said he, gently; "all the toys I am now making are promised to others. But the next shall be yours, since your heart so longs for it. Come to me again in two days and it shall be ready for you."

Bessie gave a cry of delight, and leaning over her pony's neck she kissed Claus prettily upon his forehead. Then, calling to her men-at-arms, she rode gaily away, leaving Claus to resume his work.

"If I am to supply the rich children as well as the poor ones," he thought, "I shall not have a spare moment in the whole year! But is it right I should give to the rich? Surely I must go to Necile and talk with her about this matter."

So when he had finished the toy deer, which was very like a deer he had known in the Forest glades, he walked into Burzee and made his way to the bower of the beautiful Nymph Necile, who had been his foster mother.

She greeted him tenderly and lovingly, listening with interest to his story of the visit of Bessie Blithesome.

"And now tell me," said he, "shall I give toys to rich children?"

"We of the Forest know nothing of riches," she replied. "It seems to me that one child is like another child, since they are all made of the same clay, and that riches are like a gown, which may be put on or taken away, leaving the child unchanged. But the Fairies are guardians of mankind, and know mortal children better than I. Let us call the Fairy Queen."

This was done, and the Queen of the Fairies sat beside them and heard Claus relate his reasons for thinking the rich children could get along without his toys, and also what the Nymph had said.

"Necile is right," declared the Queen; "for, whether it be rich or poor, a child's longings for pretty playthings are but natural. Rich Bessie's heart may suffer as much grief as poor Mayrie's; she can be just as lonely and discontented, and just as gay and happy. I think, friend Claus, it is your duty to make all little ones glad, whether they chance to live in palaces or in cottages."

"Your words are wise, fair Queen," replied Claus, "and my heart tells me they are as just as they are wise. Hereafter all children may claim my services."

Then he bowed before the gracious Fairy and, kissing Necile's red lips, went back into his Valley.

At the brook he stopped to drink, and afterward he sat on the bank and took a piece of moist clay in his hands while he thought what sort of toy he should make for Bessie Blithesome. He did not notice that his fingers were working the clay into shape until, glancing downward, he found he had unconsciously formed a head that bore a slight resemblance to the Nymph Necile!

At once he became interested. Gathering more of the clay from the bank he carried it to his house. Then, with the aid of his knife and a bit of wood he succeeded in working the clay into the image of a toy nymph. With skillful strokes he formed long, waving hair on the head and covered the body with a gown of oakleaves, while the two feet sticking out at the bottom of the gown were clad in sandals.

But the clay was soft, and Claus found he must handle it gently to avoid ruining his pretty work.

"Perhaps the rays of the sun will draw out the moisture and cause the clay to become hard," he thought. So he laid the image on a flat board and placed it in the glare of the sun.

This done, he went to his bench and began painting the toy deer, and soon he became so interested in the work that he forgot all about the clay nymph. But next morning, happening to notice it as it lay on the board, he found the sun had baked it to the hardness of stone, and it was strong enough to be safely handled.

Claus now painted the nymph with great care in the likeness of Necile, giving it deep-blue eyes, white teeth, rosy lips and ruddy-brown hair. The gown he colored oak-leaf green, and when the paint was dry Claus himself was charmed with the new toy. Of course it was not nearly so lovely as the real Necile; but, considering the material of which it was made, Claus thought it was very beautiful.

When Bessie, riding upon her white palfrey, came to his dwelling next day, Claus presented her with the new toy. The little girl's eyes were brighter than ever as she examined the pretty image, and she loved it at once, and held it close to her breast, as a mother does to her child.

"What is it called, Claus?" she asked.

Now Claus knew that Nymphs do not like to be spoken of by mortals, so he could not tell Bessie it was an image of Necile he had given her. But as it was a new toy he searched his mind for a new name to call it by, and the first word he thought of he decided would do very well.

"It is called a dolly, my dear," he said to Bessie.

"I shall call the dolly my baby," returned Bessie, kissing it fondly; "and I shall tend it and care for it just as Nurse cares for me. Thank you very much, Claus; your gift has made me happier than I have ever been before!"

Then she rode away, hugging the toy in her arms, and Claus, seeing her delight, thought he would make another dolly, better and more natural than the first.

He brought more clay from the brook, and remembering that Bessie had called the dolly her baby he resolved to form this one into a baby's image. That was no difficult task to the clever workman, and soon the baby dolly was lying on the board and placed in the sun to dry. Then, with the clay that was left, he began to make an image of Bessie Blithesome herself.

This was not so easy, for he found he could not make the silken robe of the lord's daughter out of the common clay. So he called the Fairies to his aid, and asked them to bring him colored silks with which to make a real dress for the clay image. The Fairies set off at once on their errand, and before nightfall they returned with a generous supply of silks and laces and golden threads.

Claus now became impatient to complete his new dolly, and instead of waiting for the next day's sun he placed the clay image upon his hearth and covered it over with glowing coals. By morning, when he drew the dolly from the ashes, it had baked as hard as if it had lain a full day in the hot sun.

Now our Claus became a dressmaker as well as a toymaker. He cut the lavender silk, and nearly sewed it into a beautiful gown that just fitted the new dolly. And he put a lace collar around its neck and pink silk shoes on its feet. The natural color of baked clay is a light gray, but Claus painted the face to resemble the color of flesh, and he gave the dolly Bessie's brown eyes and golden hair and rosy cheeks.

It was really a beautiful thing to look upon, and sure to bring joy to some childish heart. While Claus was admiring it he heard a knock at his door, and little Mayrie entered. Her face was sad and her eyes red with continued weeping.

"Why, what has grieved you, my dear?" asked Claus, taking the child in his arms.

"I've—I've—bwoke my tat!" sobbed Mayrie.

"How?" he inquired, his eyes twinkling.

"I—I dwopped him, an' bwoke off him's tail; an'—an'—then I dwopped him an' bwoke off him's ear! An'—an' now him's all spoilt!"

Claus laughed.

"Nevermind, Mayrie dear," he said. "How would you like this new dolly, instead of a cat?"

Mayrie looked at the silk-robed dolly and her eyes grew big with astonishment.

"Oh, Tlaus!" she cried, clapping her small hands together with rapture; "tan I have 'at boo'ful lady?"

"Do you like it?" he asked.

"I love it!" said she. "It's better 'an tats!"

"Then take it, dear, and be careful not to break it."

Mayrie took the dolly with a joy that was almost reverent, and her face dimpled with smiles as she started along the path toward home.

VI

THE WICKEDNESS OF THE AWGWAS

I MUST NOW TELL YOU SOMETHING about the Awgwas, that terrible race of creatures which caused our good Claus so much trouble and nearly succeeded in robbing the children of the world of their earliest and best friend.

I do not like to mention the Awgwas, but they are a part of this history, and can not be ignored. They were neither mortals nor immortals, but stood midway between those classes of beings. The Awgwas were invisible to ordinary people, but not to immortals. They could pass swiftly through the air from one part of the world to another, and had the power of influencing the minds of human beings to do their wicked will.

They were of gigantic stature and had coarse, scowling countenances which showed plainly their hatred of all mankind. They possessed no consciences whatever and delighted only in evil deeds.

Their homes were in rocky, mountainous places, from whence they sallied forth to accomplish their wicked purposes.

The one of their number that could think of the most horrible deed for them to do was always elected the King Awgwa, and all the race obeyed his orders. Sometimes these creatures lived to become a hundred years old, but usually they fought so fiercely among themselves that many were destroyed in combat, and when they died that was the end of them. Mortals were powerless to harm them and the immortals shuddered when the Awgwas were mentioned, and always avoided them. So they flourished for many years unopposed and accomplished much evil.

I am glad to assure you that these vile creatures have long since perished and passed from earth; but in the days when Claus was making his first toys they were a numerous and powerful tribe.

One of the principal sports of the Awgwas was to inspire angry passions in the hearts of little children, so that they quarreled and fought with one another. They would tempt boys to eat of unripe fruit, and then delight in the pain they suffered; they urged little girls to disobey their parents, and then would laugh when the children were punished. I do not know what causes a child to be naughty in these days, but when the Awgwas were on earth naughty children were usually under their influence.

Now, when Claus began to make children happy he kept them out of the power of the Awgwas; for children possessing such lovely playthings as he gave them had no wish to obey the evil thoughts the Awgwas tried to thrust into their minds.

Therefore, one year when the wicked tribe was to elect a new King, they chose an Awgwa who proposed to destroy Claus and take him away from the children.

"There are, as you know, fewer naughty children in the world since Claus came to the Laughing Valley and began to make his toys," said the new King, as he squatted upon a rock and looked around at the scowling faces of his people. "Why, Bessie Blithesome has not stamped her foot once this month, nor has Mayrie's brother slapped his sister's face or thrown the puppy into the rain barrel. Little Weekum took his bath last night without screaming or struggling, because his mother had promised he should take his toy cat to bed with him! Such a condition of affairs is awful for any Awgwa to think of, and the only way we can direct the naughty actions of children is to take this person Claus away from them."

"Good! Good!" cried the big Awgwas, in a chorus, and they clapped their hands to applaud the speech of the King.

"But what shall we do with him?" asked one of the creatures.

"I have a plan," replied the wicked King; and what his plan was you will soon discover.

That night Claus went to bed feeling very happy, for he had completed no less than four pretty toys during the day, and they were sure, he thought, to make four little children happy. But while he slept the band of invisible Awgwas surrounded his bed, bound him with stout cords, and then flew away with him to the middle of a dark forest in far off Ethop, where they laid him down and left him.

When morning came Claus found himself thousands of miles from any human being, a prisoner in the wild jungle of an unknown land.

From the limb of a tree above his head swayed a huge python, one of those reptiles that are able to crush a man's bones in their coils. A few yards away crouched a savage panther, its glaring red eyes fixed full on the helpless Claus. One of those monstrous spotted spiders whose sting is death crept stealthily toward him over the matted leaves, which shriveled and turned black at its very touch.

But Claus had been reared in Burzee, and was not afraid.

"Come to me, ye Knooks of the Forest!" he cried, and gave the low, peculiar whistle that the Knooks know.

The panther, which was about to spring upon its victim, turned and slunk away. The python swung itself into the tree and disappeared among the leaves. The spider stopped short in its advance and hid beneath a rotting log.

Claus had no time to notice them, for he was surrounded by a band of harsh-featured Knooks, more crooked and deformed in appearance than any he had ever seen.

"Who are you that call on us?" demanded one, in a gruff voice.

"The friend of your brothers in Burzee," answered Claus. "I have been brought here by my enemies, the Awgwas, and left to perish miserably. Yet now I implore your help to release me and to send me home again."

"Have you the sign?" asked another.

"Yes," said Claus.

They cut his bonds, and with his free arms he made the secret sign of the Knooks.

Instantly they assisted him to stand upon his feet, and they brought him food and drink to strengthen him.

"Our brothers of Burzee make queer friends," grumbled an ancient Knook whose flowing beard was pure white. "But he who knows our secret sign and signal is entitled to our help, whoever he may be. Close your eyes, stranger, and we will conduct you to your home. Where shall we seek it?"

"'Tis in the Laughing Valley," answered Claus, shutting his eyes.

"There is but one Laughing Valley in the known world, so we can not go astray," remarked the Knook.

As he spoke the sound of his voice seemed to die away, so Claus opened his eyes to see what caused the change. To his astonishment he found himself seated on the bench by his own door, with the Laughing Valley spread out before him. That day he visited the Wood-Nymphs and related his adventure to Queen Zurline and Necile.

"The Awgwas have become your enemies," said the lovely Queen, thoughtfully; "so we must do all we can to protect you from their power."

"It was cowardly to bind him while he slept," remarked Necile, with indignation.

"The evil ones are ever cowardly," answered Zurline, "but our friend's slumber shall not be disturbed again."

The Queen herself came to the dwelling of Claus that evening and placed her Seal on every door and window, to keep out the Awgwas. And under the Seal of Queen Zurline was placed the Seal of the Fairies and the Seal of the Ryls and the Seals of the Knooks, that the charm might become more powerful.

And Claus carried his toys to the children again, and made many more of the little ones happy.

You may guess how angry the King Awgwa and his fierce band were when it was known to them that Claus had escaped from the Forest of Ethop.

They raged madly for a whole week, and then held another meeting among the rocks.

"It is useless to carry him where the Knooks reign," said the King, "for he has their protection. So let us cast him into a cave of our own mountains, where he will surely perish."

This was promptly agreed to, and the wicked band set out that night to seize Claus. But they found his dwelling guarded by the Seals of the Immortals and were obliged to go away baffled and disappointed.

"Nevermind," said the King; "he does not sleep always!"

Next day, as Claus traveled to the village across the plain, where he intended to present a toy squirrel to a lame boy, he was suddenly set upon by the Awgwas, who seized him and carried him away to the mountains.

There they thrust him within a deep cavern and rolled many huge rocks against the entrance to prevent his escape.

Deprived thus of light and food, and with little air to breathe, our Claus was, indeed, in a pitiful plight. But he spoke the mystic words of the Fairies, which always command their friendly aid, and they came to his rescue and transported him to the Laughing Valley in the twinkling of an eye.

Thus the Awgwas discovered they might not destroy one who had earned the friendship of the immortals; so the evil band sought other means of keeping Claus from bringing happiness to children and so making them obedient.

Whenever Claus set out to carry his toys to the little ones an Awgwa, who had been set to watch his movements, sprang upon him and snatched the toys from his grasp. And the children were no more disappointed than was Claus when he was obliged to return home disconsolate. Still he persevered, and made many toys for his little friends and started with them for the villages. And always the Awgwas robbed him as soon as he had left the Valley.

They threw the stolen playthings into one of their lonely caverns, and quite a heap of toys accumulated before Claus became discouraged and gave up all attempts to leave the Valley. Then children began coming to him, since they found he did not go to them; but the wicked Awgwas flew around them and caused their steps to stray and the paths to become crooked, so never a little one could find a way into the Laughing Valley.

Lonely days now fell upon Claus, for he was denied the pleasure of bringing happiness to the children whom he had learned to love. Yet he bore up bravely, for he thought surely the time would come when the Awgwas would abandon their evil designs to injure him.

He devoted all his hours to toymaking, and when one plaything had been completed he stood it on a shelf he had built for that purpose. When the shelf became filled with rows of toys he made another one, and filled that also. So that in time he had many shelves filled with gay and beautiful toys representing horses, dogs, cats, elephants, lambs, rabbits and deer, as well as pretty dolls of all sizes and balls and marbles of baked clay painted in gay colors.

Often, as he glanced at this array of childish treasures, the heart of good old Claus became sad, so greatly did he long to carry the toys to his children. And at last, because he could bear it no longer, he ventured to go to the great Ak, to whom he told the story of his persecution by the Awgwas, and begged the Master Woodsman to assist him.

VII

The Great Battle Between Good and Evil

Ak listened gravely to the recital of Claus, stroking his beard the while with the slow, graceful motion that betokened deep thought. He nodded approvingly when Claus told how the Knooks and Fairies had saved him from death, and frowned when he heard how the Awgwas had stolen the children's toys. At last he said:

"From the beginning I have approved the work you are doing among the children of men, and it annoys me that your good deeds should be thwarted by the Awgwas. We immortals have no connection whatever with the evil creatures who have attacked you. Always have we avoided them, and they, in turn, have hitherto taken care not to cross our pathway. But in this matter I find they have interfered with one of our friends, and I will ask them to abandon their persecutions, as you are under our protection."

Claus thanked the Master Woodsman most gratefully and returned to his Valley, while Ak, who never delayed carrying out his promises, at once traveled to the mountains of the Awgwas.

There, standing on the bare rocks, he called on the King and his people to appear.

Instantly the place was filled with throngs of the scowling Awgwas, and their King, perching himself on a point of rock, demanded fiercely:

"Who dares call on us?"

"It is I, the Master Woodsman of the World," responded Ak.

"Here are no forests for you to claim," cried the King, angrily. "We owe no allegiance to you, nor to any immortal!"

"That is true," replied Ak, calmly. "Yet you have ventured to interfere with the actions of Claus, who dwells in the Laughing Valley, and is under our protection."

Many of the Awgwas began muttering at this speech, and their King turned threateningly on the Master Woodsman.

"You are set to rule the forests, but the plains and the valleys are ours!" he shouted. "Keep to your own dark woods! We will do as we please with Claus."

"You shall not harm our friend in any way!" replied Ak.

"Shall we not?" asked the King, impudently. "You will see! Our powers are vastly superior to those of mortals, and fully as great as those of immortals."

"It is your conceit that misleads you!" said Ak, sternly. "You are a transient race, passing from life into nothingness. We, who live forever, pity but despise you. On earth you are scorned by all, and in Heaven you have no place! Even the mortals, after their earth life, enter another existence for all time, and so are your superiors. How then dare you, who are neither mortal nor immortal, refuse to obey my wish?"

The Awgwas sprang to their feet with menacing gestures, but their King motioned them back.

"Never before," he cried to Ak, while his voice trembled with rage, "has an immortal declared himself the master of the Awgwas! Never shall an immortal venture to interfere with our actions again! For we will avenge your scornful words by killing your friend Claus within three days. Nor you, nor all the immortals can save him from our wrath. We defy your powers! Begone, Master Woodsman of the World! In the country of the Awgwas you have no place."

"It is war!" declared Ak, with flashing eyes.

"It is war!" returned the King, savagely. "In three days your friend will be dead."

The Master turned away and came to his Forest of Burzee, where he called a meeting of the immortals and told them of the defiance of the Awgwas and their purpose to kill Claus within three days.

The little folk listened to him quietly.

"What shall we do?" asked Ak.

"These creatures are of no benefit to the world," said the Prince of the Knooks; "we must destroy them."

"Their lives are devoted only to evil deeds," said the Prince of the Ryls. "We must destroy them."

"They have no conscience, and endeavor to make all mortals as bad as themselves," said the Queen of the Fairies. "We must destroy them."

"They have defied the great Ak, and threaten the life of our adopted son," said beautiful Queen Zurline. "We must destroy them."

The Master Woodsman smiled.

"You speak well," said he. "These Awgwas we know to be a powerful race, and they will fight desperately; yet the outcome is certain. For we who live can never die, even though conquered by our enemies, while every Awgwa who is struck down is one foe the less to oppose us. Prepare, then, for battle, and let us resolve to show no mercy to the wicked!"

Thus arose that terrible war between the immortals and the spirits of evil which is sung of in Fairyland to this very day.

The King Awgwa and his band determined to carry out the threat to destroy Claus. They now hated him for two reasons: he made children happy and was a friend of the Master Woodsman. But since Ak's visit they had reason to fear the opposition of the immortals, and they dreaded defeat. So the King sent swift messengers to all parts of the world to summon every evil creature to his aid.

And on the third day after the declaration of war a mighty army was at the command of the King Awgwa. There were three hundred Asiatic Dragons, breathing fire that consumed everything it touched. These hated mankind and all good spirits. And there were the three-eyed Giants of Tatary, a host in themselves, who liked nothing better than to fight. And next came the Black Demons from Patalonia, with great spreading wings like those of a bat, which swept terror and misery through the world as they beat upon the air. And joined to these were the Goozzle-Goblins, with long talons as sharp as swords, with which they clawed the flesh from their foes. Finally, every mountain Awgwa in the world had come to participate in the great battle with the immortals.

The King Awgwa looked around upon this vast army and his heart beat high with wicked pride, for he believed he would surely triumph over his gentle enemies, who had never before been known to fight. But the Master Woodsman had not been idle. None of his people was used to warfare, yet now that they were called upon to face the hosts of evil they willingly prepared for the fray.

Ak had commanded them to assemble in the Laughing Valley, where Claus, ignorant of the terrible battle that was to be waged on his account, was quietly making his toys.

Soon the entire Valley, from hill to hill, was filled with the little immortals. The Master Woodsman stood first, bearing a gleaming ax that shone like burnished silver. Next came the Ryls, armed with sharp thorns from bramblebushes. Then the Knooks, bearing the spears they used when they were forced to prod their savage beasts into submission. The Fairies, dressed in white gauze with rainbow-hued wings, bore golden wands, and the Wood-nymphs, in their uniforms of oak-leaf green, carried switches from ash trees as weapons.

Loud laughed the Awgwa King when he beheld the size and the arms of his foes. To be sure the mighty ax of the Woodsman was to be dreaded, but the sweet-faced Nymphs and pretty Fairies, the gentle

Ryls and crooked Knooks were such harmless folk that he almost felt shame at having called such a terrible host to oppose them.

"Since these fools dare fight," he said to the leader of the Tatary Giants, "I will overwhelm them with our evil powers!"

To begin the battle he poised a great stone in his left hand and cast it full against the sturdy form of the Master Woodsman, who turned it aside with his ax. Then rushed the three-eyed Giants of Tatary upon the Knooks, and the Goozzle-Goblins upon the Ryls, and the firebreathing Dragons upon the sweet Fairies. Because the Nymphs were Ak's own people the band of Awgwas sought them out, thinking to overcome them with ease.

But it is the Law that while Evil, unopposed, may accomplish terrible deeds, the powers of Good can never be overthrown when opposed to Evil. Well had it been for the King Awgwa had he known the Law!

His ignorance cost him his existence, for one flash of the ax borne by the Master Woodsman of the World cleft the wicked King in twain and rid the earth of the vilest creature it contained.

Greatly marveled the Tatary Giants when the spears of the little Knooks pierced their thick walls of flesh and sent them reeling to the ground with howls of agony.

Woe came upon the sharp-taloned Goblins when the thorns of the Ryls reached their savage hearts and let their life-blood sprinkle all the plain. And afterward from every drop a thistle grew.

The Dragons paused astonished before the Fairy wands, from whence rushed a power that caused their fiery breaths to flow back on themselves so that they shriveled away and died.

As for the Awgwas, they had scant time to realize how they were destroyed, for the ash switches of the Nymphs bore a charm unknown to any Awgwa, and turned their foes into clods of earth at the slightest touch!

When Ak leaned upon his gleaming ax and turned to look over the field of battle he saw the few Giants who were able to run disappearing over the distant hills on their return to Tatary. The Goblins had perished every one, as had the terrible Dragons, while all that remained of the wicked Awgwas was a great number of earthen hillocks dotting the plain.

And now the immortals melted from the Valley like dew at sunrise, to resume their duties in the Forest, while Ak walked slowly and thoughtfully to the house of Claus and entered.

"You have many toys ready for the children," said the Woodsman, "and now you may carry them across the plain to the dwellings and the villages without fear."

"Will not the Awgwas harm me?" asked Claus, eagerly.

"The Awgwas," said Ak, "have perished!"

Now I will gladly have done with wicked spirits and with fighting and bloodshed. It was not from choice that I told of the Awgwas and their allies, and of their great battle with the immortals. They were part of this history, and could not be avoided.

VIII

The First Journey with the Reindeer

Those were happy days for Claus when he carried his accumulation of toys to the children who had awaited them so long. During his imprisonment in the Valley he had been so industrious that all his shelves were filled with playthings, and after quickly supplying the little ones living near by he saw he must now extend his travels to wider fields.

Remembering the time when he had journeyed with Ak through all the world, he know children were everywhere, and he longed to make as many as possible happy with his gifts.

So he loaded a great sack with all kinds of toys, slung it upon his back that he might carry it more easily, and started off on a longer trip than he had yet undertaken.

Wherever he showed his merry face, in hamlet or in farmhouse, he received a cordial welcome, for his fame had spread into far lands. At each village the children swarmed about him, following his footsteps wherever he went; and the women thanked him gratefully for the joy he brought their little ones; and the men looked upon him curiously that he should devote his time to such a queer occupation as toymaking. But every one smiled on him and gave him kindly words, and Claus felt amply repaid for his long journey.

When the sack was empty he went back again to the Laughing Valley and once more filled it to the brim. This time he followed another road, into a different part of the country, and carried happiness to many children who never before had owned a toy or guessed that such a delightful plaything existed.

After a third journey, so far away that Claus was many days walking the distance, the store of toys became exhausted and without delay he set about making a fresh supply.

From seeing so many children and studying their tastes he had acquired several new ideas about toys.

The dollies were, he had found, the most delightful of all playthings for babies and little girls, and often those who could not say "dolly" would call for a "doll" in their sweet baby talk. So Claus resolved to make many dolls, of all sizes, and to dress them in bright-colored clothing. The older boys—and even some of the girls—loved the images of animals, so he still made cats and elephants and horses. And many of the little fellows had musical natures, and longed for drums and cymbals and whistles and horns. So he made a number of toy drums, with tiny sticks to beat them with; and he made whistles from the willow trees, and horns from the bog-reeds, and cymbals from bits of beaten metal.

All this kept him busily at work, and before he realized it the winter season came, with deeper snows than usual, and he knew he could not leave the Valley with his heavy pack. Moreover, the next trip would take him farther from home than every before, and Jack Frost was mischievous enough to nip his nose and ears if he undertook the long journey while the Frost King reigned. The Frost King was Jack's father and never reproved him for his pranks.

So Claus remained at his work bench; but he whistled and sang as merrily as ever, for he would allow no disappointment to sour his temper or make him unhappy.

One bright morning he looked from his window and saw two of the deer he had known in the Forest walking toward his house.

Claus was surprised; not that the friendly deer should visit him, but that they walked on the surface of the snow as easily as if it were solid ground, notwithstanding the fact that throughout the Valley the snow lay many feet deep. He had walked out of his house a day or two before and had sunk to his armpits in a drift.

So when the deer came near he opened the door and called to them:

"Goodmorning, Flossie! Tell me how you are able to walk on the snow so easily."

"It is frozen hard," answered Flossie.

"The Frost King has breathed on it," said Glossie, coming up, "and the surface is now as solid as ice."

"Perhaps," remarked Claus, thoughtfully, "I might now carry my pack of toys to the children."

"Is it a long journey?" asked Flossie.

"Yes; it will take me many days, for the pack is heavy," answered Claus.

"Then the snow would melt before you could get back," said the deer. "You must wait until spring, Claus."

Claus sighed. "Had I your fleet feet," said he, "I could make the journey in a day."

"But you have not," returned Glossie, looking at his own slender legs with pride.

"Perhaps I could ride upon your back," Claus ventured to remark, after a pause.

"Oh no; our backs are not strong enough to bear your weight," said Flossie, decidedly. "But if you had a sledge, and could harness us to it, we might draw you easily, and your pack as well."

"I'll make a sledge!" exclaimed Claus. "Will you agree to draw me if I do?"

"Well," replied Flossie, "we must first go and ask the Knooks, who are our guardians, for permission; but if they consent, and you can make a sledge and harness, we will gladly assist you."

"Then go at once!" cried Claus, eagerly. "I am sure the friendly Knooks will give their consent, and by the time you are back I shall be ready to harness you to my sledge."

Flossie and Glossie, being deer of much intelligence, had long wished to see the great world, so they gladly ran over the frozen snow to ask the Knooks if they might carry Claus on his journey.

Meantime the toymaker hurriedly began the construction of a sledge, using material from his woodpile. He made two long runners that turned upward at the front ends, and across these nailed short boards, to make a platform. It was soon completed, but was as rude in appearance as it is possible for a sledge to be.

The harness was more difficult to prepare, but Claus twisted strong cords together and knotted them so they would fit around the necks of the deer, in the shape of a collar. From these ran other cords to fasten the deer to the front of the sledge.

Before the work was completed Glossie and Flossie were back from the Forest, having been granted permission by Will Knook to make the journey with Claus provided they would to Burzee by daybreak the next morning.

"That is not a very long time," said Flossie; "but we are swift and strong, and if we get started by this evening we can travel many miles during the night."

Claus decided to make the attempt, so he hurried on his preparations as fast as possible. After a time he fastened the collars around the necks of his steeds and harnessed them to his rude sledge. Then he placed a stool on the little platform, to serve as a seat, and filled a sack with his prettiest toys.

"How do you intend to guide us?" asked Glossie. "We have never been out of the Forest before, except to visit your house, so we shall not know the way."

Claus thought about that for a moment. Then he brought more cords and fastened two of them to the spreading antlers of each deer, one on the right and the other on the left.

"Those will be my reins," said Claus, "and when I pull them to the right or to the left you must go in that direction. If I do not pull the reins at all you may go straight ahead."

"Very well," answered Glossie and Flossie; and then they asked: "Are you ready?"

Claus seated himself upon the stool, placed the sack of toys at his feet, and then gathered up the reins.

"All ready!" he shouted; "away we go!"

The deer leaned forward, lifted their slender limbs, and the next moment away flew the sledge over the frozen snow. The swiftness of the motion surprised Claus, for in a few strides they were across the Valley and gliding over the broad plain beyond.

The day had melted into evening by the time they started; for, swiftly as Claus had worked, many hours had been consumed in making his preparations. But the moon shone brightly to light their way, and Claus soon decided it was just as pleasant to travel by night as by day.

The deer liked it better; for, although they wished to see something of the world, they were timid about meeting men, and now all the dwellers in the towns and farmhouses were sound asleep and could not see them.

Away and away they sped, on and on over the hills and through the valleys and across the plains until they reached a village where Claus had never been before.

Here he called on them to stop, and they immediately obeyed. But a new difficulty now presented itself, for the people had locked their doors when they went to bed, and Claus found he could not enter the houses to leave his toys.

"I am afraid, my friends, we have made our journey for nothing," said he, "for I shall be obliged to carry my playthings back home again without giving them to the children of this village."

"What's the matter?" asked Flossie.

"The doors are locked," answered Claus, "and I can not get in."

Glossie looked around at the houses. The snow was quite deep in that village, and just before them was a roof only a few feet above the sledge. A broad chimney, which seemed to Glossie big enough to admit Claus, was at the peak of the roof.

"Why don't you climb down that chimney?" asked Glossie.

Claus looked at it.

"That would be easy enough if I were on top of the roof," he answered.

"Then hold fast and we will take you there," said the deer, and they gave one bound to the roof and landed beside the big chimney.

"Good!" cried Claus, well pleased, and he slung the pack of toys over his shoulder and got into the chimney.

There was plenty of soot on the bricks, but he did not mind that, and by placing his hands and knees against the sides he crept downward until he had reached the fireplace. Leaping lightly over the smoldering coals he found himself in a large sitting room, where a dim light was burning.

From this room two doorways led into smaller chambers. In one a woman lay asleep, with a baby beside her in a crib.

Claus laughed, but he did not laugh aloud for fear of waking the baby. Then he slipped a big doll from his pack and laid it in the crib. The little one smiled, as if it dreamed of the pretty plaything it was to find on the morrow, and Claus crept softly from the room and entered at the other doorway.

Here were two boys, fast asleep with their arms around each other's neck. Claus gazed at them lovingly a moment and then placed upon the bed a drum, two horns and a wooden elephant.

He did not linger, now that his work in this house was done, but climbed the chimney again and seated himself on his sledge.

"Can you find another chimney?" he asked the reindeer.

"Easily enough," replied Glossie and Flossie.

Down to the edge of the roof they raced, and then, without pausing, leaped through the air to the top of the next building, where a huge, old-fashioned chimney stood.

"Don't be so long, this time," called Flossie, "or we shall never get back to the Forest by daybreak."

Claus made a trip down this chimney also and found five children sleeping in the house, all of whom were quickly supplied with toys.

When he returned the deer sprang to the next roof, but on descending the chimney Claus found no children there at all. That was not often the case in this village, however, so he lost less time than you might suppose in visiting the dreary homes where there were no little ones.

When he had climbed down the chimneys of all the houses in that village, and had left a toy for every sleeping child, Claus found that his great sack was not yet half emptied.

"Onward, friends!" he called to the deer; "we must seek another village."

So away they dashed, although it was long past midnight, and in a surprisingly short time they came to a large city, the largest Claus had ever visited since he began to make toys. But, nothing daunted by the throng of houses, he set to work at once and his beautiful steeds carried him rapidly from one roof to another, only the highest being beyond the leaps of the agile deer.

At last the supply of toys was exhausted and Claus seated himself in the sledge, with the empty sack at his feet, and turned the heads of Glossie and Flossie toward home.

Presently Flossie asked:

"What is that gray streak in the sky?"

"It is the coming dawn of day," answered Claus, surprised to find that it was so late.

"Good gracious!" exclaimed Glossie; "then we shall not be home by daybreak, and the Knooks will punish us and never let us come again."

"We must race for the Laughing Valley and make our best speed," returned Flossie; "so hold fast, friend Claus!"

Claus held fast and the next moment was flying so swiftly over the snow that he could not see the trees as they whirled past. Up hill and down dale, swift as an arrow shot from a bow they dashed, and Claus shut his eyes to keep the wind out of them and left the deer to find their own way.

It seemed to him they were plunging through space, but he was not at all afraid. The Knooks were severe masters, and must be obeyed at all hazards, and the gray streak in the sky was growing brighter every moment.

Finally the sledge came to a sudden stop and Claus, who was taken unawares, tumbled from his seat into a snowdrift. As he picked himself up he heard the deer crying:

"Quick, friend, quick! Cut away our harness!"

He drew his knife and rapidly severed the cords, and then he wiped the moisture from his eyes and looked around him.

The sledge had come to a stop in the Laughing Valley, only a few feet, he found, from his own door. In the East the day was breaking, and turning to the edge of Burzee he saw Glossie and Flossie just disappearing in the Forest.

IX

"Santa Claus!"

Claus thought that none of the children would ever know where the toys came from which they found by their bedsides when they wakened the following morning. But kindly deeds are sure to bring fame, and fame has many wings to carry its tidings into far lands; so for miles and miles in every direction people were talking of Claus and his wonderful gifts to children. The sweet generousness of his work caused a few selfish folk to sneer, but even these were forced to admit their respect for a man so gentle-natured that he loved to devote his life to pleasing the helpless little ones of his race.

Therefore the inhabitants of every city and village had been eagerly watching the coming of Claus, and remarkable stories of his beautiful playthings were told the children to keep them patient and contented.

When, on the morning following the first trip of Claus with his deer, the little ones came running to their parents with the pretty toys they had found, and asked from whence they came, they was but one reply to the question.

"The good Claus must have been here, my darlings; for his are the only toys in all the world!"

"But how did he get in?" asked the children.

At this the fathers shook their heads, being themselves unable to understand how Claus had gained admittance to their homes; but the mothers, watching the glad faces of their dear ones, whispered that the good Claus was no mortal man but assuredly a Saint, and they piously blessed his name for the happiness he had bestowed upon their children.

"A Saint," said one, with bowed head, "has no need to unlock doors if it pleases him to enter our homes."

And, afterward, when a child was naughty or disobedient, its mother would say:

"You must pray to the good Santa Claus for forgiveness. He does not like naughty children, and, unless you repent, he will bring you no more pretty toys."

But Santa Claus himself would not have approved this speech. He brought toys to the children because they were little and helpless, and because he loved them. He knew that the best of children were sometimes naughty, and that the naughty ones were often good. It is the way with children, the world over, and he would not have changed their natures had he possessed the power to do so.

And that is how our Claus became Santa Claus. It is possible for any man, by good deeds, to enshrine himself as a Saint in the hearts of the people.

X

CHRISTMAS EVE

THE DAY THAT BROKE AS Claus returned from his night ride with Glossie and Flossie brought to him a new trouble. Will Knook, the chief guardian of the deer, came to him, surly and ill-tempered, to complain that he had kept Glossie and Flossie beyond daybreak, in opposition to his orders.

"Yet it could not have been very long after daybreak," said Claus.

"It was one minute after," answered Will Knook, "and that is as bad as one hour. I shall set the stinging gnats on Glossie and Flossie, and they will thus suffer terribly for their disobedience."

"Don't do that!" begged Claus. "It was my fault."

But Will Knook would listen to no excuses, and went away grumbling and growling in his ill-natured way.

For this reason Claus entered the Forest to consult Necile about rescuing the good deer from punishment. To his delight he found his old friend, the Master Woodsman, seated in the circle of Nymphs.

Ak listened to the story of the night journey to the children and of the great assistance the deer had been to Claus by drawing his sledge over the frozen snow.

"I do not wish my friends to be punished if I can save them," said the toymaker, when he had finished the relation. "They were only one minute late, and they ran swifter than a bird flies to get home before daybreak."

Ak stroked his beard thoughtfully a moment, and then sent for the Prince of the Knooks, who rules all his people in Burzee, and also for the Queen of the Fairies and the Prince of the Ryls.

When all had assembled Claus told his story again, at Ak's command, and then the Master addressed the Prince of the Knooks, saying:

"The good work that Claus is doing among mankind deserves the support of every honest immortal. Already he is called a Saint in some of the towns, and before long the name of Santa Claus will be lovingly known in every home that is blessed with children. Moreover, he is a son of our Forest, so we owe him our encouragement. You, Ruler of the Knooks, have known him these many years; am I not right in saying he deserves our friendship?"

The Prince, crooked and sour of visage as all Knooks are, looked only upon the dead leaves at his feet and muttered: "You are the Master Woodsman of the World!"

Ak smiled, but continued, in soft tones: "It seems that the deer which are guarded by your people can be of great assistance to Claus, and as they seem willing to draw his sledge I beg that you will permit him to use their services whenever he pleases."

The Prince did not reply, but tapped the curled point of his sandal with the tip of his spear, as if in thought.

Then the Fairy Queen spoke to him in this way: "If you consent to Ak's request I will see that no harm comes to your deer while they are away from the Forest."

And the Prince of the Ryls added: "For my part I will allow to every deer that assists Claus the privilege of eating my casa plants, which give strength, and my grawle plants, which give fleetness of foot, and my marbon plants, which give long life."

And the Queen of the Nymphs said: "The deer which draw the sledge of Claus will be permitted to bathe in the Forest pool of Nares, which will give them sleek coats and wonderful beauty."

The Prince of the Knooks, hearing these promises, shifted uneasily on his seat, for in his heart he hated to refuse a request of his fellow immortals, although they were asking an unusual favor at his hands, and the Knooks are unaccustomed to granting favors of any kind. Finally he turned to his servants and said:

"Call Will Knook."

When surly Will came and heard the demands of the immortals he protested loudly against granting them.

"Deer are deer," said he, "and nothing but deer. Were they horses it would be right to harness them like horses. But no one harnesses deer because they are free, wild creatures, owing no service of any sort to mankind. It would degrade my deer to labor for Claus, who is only a man in spite of the friendship lavished on him by the immortals."

"You have heard," said the Prince to Ak. "There is truth in what Will says."

"Call Glossie and Flossie," returned the Master.

The deer were brought to the conference and Ak asked them if they objected to drawing the sledge for Claus.

"No, indeed!" replied Glossie; "we enjoyed the trip very much."

"And we tried to get home by daybreak," added Flossie, "but were unfortunately a minute too late."

"A minute lost at daybreak doesn't matter," said Ak. "You are forgiven for that delay."

"Provided it does not happen again," said the Prince of the Knooks, sternly.

"And will you permit them to make another journey with me?" asked Claus, eagerly.

The Prince reflected while he gazed at Will, who was scowling, and at the Master Woodsman, who was smiling.

Then he stood up and addressed the company as follows:

"Since you all urge me to grant the favor I will permit the deer to go with Claus once every year, on Christmas Eve, provided they always return to the Forest by daybreak. He may select any number he pleases, up to ten, to draw his sledge, and those shall be known among us as Reindeer, to distinguish them from the others. And they shall bathe in the Pool of Nares, and eat the casa and grawle and marbon plants and shall be under the especial protection of the Fairy Queen. And now cease scowling, Will Knook, for my words shall be obeyed!"

He hobbled quickly away through the trees, to avoid the thanks of Claus and the approval of the other immortals, and Will, looking as cross as ever, followed him.

But Ak was satisfied, knowing that he could rely on the promise of the Prince, however grudgingly given; and Glossie and Flossie ran home, kicking up their heels delightedly at every step.

"When is Christmas Eve?" Claus asked the Master.

"In about ten days," he replied.

"Then I can not use the deer this year," said Claus, thoughtfully, "for I shall not have time enough to make my sackful of toys."

"The shrewd Prince foresaw that," responded Ak, "and therefore named Christmas Eve as the day you might use the deer, knowing it would cause you to lose an entire year."

"If I only had the toys the Awgwas stole from me," said Claus, sadly, "I could easily fill my sack for the children."

"Where are they?" asked the Master.

"I do not know," replied Claus, "but the wicked Awgwas probably hid them in the mountains."

Ak turned to the Fairy Queen.

"Can you find them?" he asked.

"I will try," she replied, brightly.

Then Claus went back to the Laughing Valley, to work as hard as he could, and a band of Fairies immediately flew to the mountain that had been haunted by the Awgwas and began a search for the stolen toys.

The Fairies, as we well know, possess wonderful powers; but the cunning Awgwas had hidden the toys in a deep cave and covered the opening with rocks, so no one could look in. Therefore all search for the missing playthings proved in vain for several days, and Claus, who sat at home waiting for news from the Fairies, almost despaired of getting the toys before Christmas Eve.

He worked hard every moment, but it took considerable time to carve out and to shape each toy and to paint it properly, so that on the morning before Christmas Eve only half of one small shelf above the window was filled with playthings ready for the children.

But on this morning the Fairies who were searching in the mountains had a new thought. They joined hands and moved in a straight line through the rocks that formed the mountain, beginning at the topmost peak and working downward, so that no spot could be missed by their bright eyes. And at last they discovered the cave where the toys had been heaped up by the wicked Awgwas.

It did not take them long to burst open the mouth of the cave, and then each one seized as many toys as he could carry and they all flew to Claus and laid the treasure before him.

The good man was rejoiced to receive, just in the nick of time, such a store of playthings with which to load his sledge, and he sent word to Glossie and Flossie to be ready for the journey at nightfall.

With all his other labors he had managed to find time, since the last trip, to repair the harness and to strengthen his sledge, so that when the deer came to him at twilight he had no difficulty in harnessing them.

"We must go in another direction tonight," he told them, "where we shall find children I have never yet visited. And we must travel fast and work quickly, for my sack is full of toys and running over the brim!"

So, just as the moon arose, they dashed out of the Laughing Valley and across the plain and over the hills to the south. The air was sharp and frosty and the starlight touched the snowflakes and made them glitter like countless diamonds. The reindeer leaped onward with strong, steady bounds, and Claus' heart was so light and merry that he laughed and sang while the wind whistled past his ears:

> *"With a ho, ho, ho!*
> *And a ha, ha, ha!*
> *And a ho, ho! ha, ha, hee!*
> *Now away we go*
> *O'er the frozen snow,*
> *As merry as we can be!"*

Jack Frost heard him and came racing up with his nippers, but when he saw it was Claus he laughed and turned away again.

The mother owls heard him as he passed near a wood and stuck their heads out of the hollow places in the tree trunks; but when they saw who it was they whispered to the owlets nestling near them that it was only Santa Claus carrying toys to the children. It is strange how much those mother owls know.

Claus stopped at some of the scattered farmhouses and climbed down the chimneys to leave presents for the babies. Soon after he reached a village and worked merrily for an hour distributing playthings among the sleeping little ones. Then away again he went, signing his joyous carol:

> *"Now away we go*
> *O'er the gleaming snow,*
> *While the deer run swift and free!*
> *For to girls and boys*
> *We carry the toys*
> *That will fill their hearts with glee!"*

The deer liked the sound of his deep bass voice and kept time to the song with their hoofbeats on the hard snow; but soon they stopped at another chimney and Santa Claus, with sparkling eyes and face brushed red by the wind, climbed down its smoky sides and left a present for every child the house contained.

It was a merry, happy night. Swiftly the deer ran, and busily their driver worked to scatter his gifts among the sleeping children.

But the sack was empty at last, and the sledge headed homeward; and now again the race with daybreak began. Glossie and Flossie had no mind to be rebuked a second time for tardiness, so they fled with a swiftness that enabled them to pass the gale on which the Frost King rode, and soon brought them to the Laughing Valley.

It is true when Claus released his steeds from their harness the eastern sky was streaked with gray, but Glossie and Flossie were deep in the Forest before day fairly broke.

Claus was so wearied with his night's work that he threw himself upon his bed and fell into a deep slumber, and while he slept the Christmas sun appeared in the sky and shone upon hundreds of happy homes where the sound of childish laughter proclaimed that Santa Claus had made them a visit.

God bless him! It was his first Christmas Eve, and for hundreds of years since then he has nobly fulfilled his mission to bring happiness to the hearts of little children.

XI

How the First Stockings were Hung by the Chimneys

WHEN YOU REMEMBER THAT NO child, until Santa Claus began his travels, had ever known the pleasure of possessing a toy, you will understand how joy crept into the homes of those who had been favored with a visit from the good man, and how they talked of him day by day in loving tones and were honestly grateful for his kindly deeds. It is true that great warriors and mighty kings and clever scholars of that day were often spoken of by the people; but no one of them was so greatly beloved as Santa Claus, because none other was so unselfish as to devote himself to making others happy. For a generous deed lives longer than a great battle or a king's decree of a scholar's essay, because it spreads and leaves its mark on all nature and endures through many generations.

The bargain made with the Knook Prince changed the plans of Claus for all future time; for, being able to use the reindeer on but one night of each year, he decided to devote all the other days to the manufacture of playthings, and on Christmas Eve to carry them to the children of the world.

But a year's work would, he knew, result in a vast accumulation of toys, so he resolved to build a new sledge that would be larger and stronger and better-fitted for swift travel than the old and clumsy one.

His first act was to visit the Gnome King, with whom he made a bargain to exchange three drums, a trumpet and two dolls for a pair of fine steel runners, curled beautifully at the ends. For the Gnome King had children of his own, who, living in the hollows under the earth, in mines and caverns, needed something to amuse them.

In three days the steel runners were ready, and when Claus brought the playthings to the Gnome King, his Majesty was so greatly pleased with them that he presented Claus with a string of sweet-toned sleigh-bells, in addition to the runners.

"These will please Glossie and Flossie," said Claus, as he jingled the bells and listened to their merry sound. "But I should have two strings of bells, one for each deer."

"Bring me another trumpet and a toy cat," replied the King, "and you shall have a second string of bells like the first."

"It is a bargain!" cried Claus, and he went home again for the toys.

The new sledge was carefully built, the Knooks bringing plenty of strong but thin boards to use in its construction. Claus made a high, rounding dashboard to keep off the snow cast behind by the fleet hoofs of the deer; and he made high sides to the platform so that many toys could be carried, and finally he mounted the sledge upon the slender steel runners made by the Gnome King.

It was certainly a handsome sledge, and big and roomy. Claus painted it in bright colors, although no one was likely to see it during his midnight journeys, and when all was finished he sent for Glossie and Flossie to come and look at it.

The deer admired the sledge, but gravely declared it was too big and heavy for them to draw.

"We might pull it over the snow, to be sure," said Glossie; "but we would not pull it fast enough to enable us to visit the faraway cities and villages and return to the Forest by daybreak."

"Then I must add two more deer to my team," declared Claus, after a moment's thought.

"The Knook Prince allowed you as many as ten. Why not use them all?" asked Flossie. "Then we could speed like the lightning and leap to the highest roofs with ease."

"A team of ten reindeer!" cried Claus, delightedly. "That will be splendid. Please return to the Forest at once and select eight other deer as like yourselves as possible. And you must all eat of the casa plant, to become strong, and of the grawle plant, to become fleet of foot, and of the marbon plant, that you may live long to accompany me on my journeys. Likewise it will be well for you to bathe in the Pool of Nares, which the lovely Queen Zurline declares will render you rarely beautiful. Should you perform these duties faithfully there is no doubt that on next Christmas Eve my ten reindeer will be the most powerful and beautiful steeds the world has ever seen!"

So Glossie and Flossie went to the Forest to choose their mates, and Claus began to consider the question of a harness for them all.

In the end he called upon Peter Knook for assistance, for Peter's heart is as kind as his body is crooked, and he is remarkably shrewd, as well. And Peter agreed to furnish strips of tough leather for the harness.

This leather was cut from the skins of lions that had reached such an advanced age that they died naturally, and on one side was tawny hair while the other side was cured to the softness of velvet by the deft Knooks. When Claus received these strips of leather he sewed them neatly into a harness for the ten reindeer, and it proved strong and serviceable and lasted him for many years.

The harness and sledge were prepared at odd times, for Claus devoted most of his days to the making of toys. These were now much better than the first ones had been, for the immortals often came to his house to watch him work and to offer suggestions. It was Necile's idea to make some of the dolls say "papa" and "mama." It was a thought of the Knooks to put a squeak inside the lambs, so that when a child squeezed them they would say "baa-a-a-a!" And the Fairy Queen advised Claus to put whistles in the birds, so they could be made to sing, and wheels on the horses, so children could draw them around. Many animals perished in the Forest, from one cause or another, and their fur was brought to Claus that he might cover with it the small images of beasts he made for playthings. A merry Ryl suggested that Claus make a donkey with a nodding head, which he did, and afterward found that it amused the little ones immensely. And so the toys grew in beauty and attractiveness every day, until they were the wonder of even the immortals.

When another Christmas Eve drew near there was a monster load of beautiful gifts for the children ready to be loaded upon the big sledge.

Claus filled three sacks to the brim, and tucked every corner of the sledge-box full of toys besides.

Then, at twilight, the ten reindeer appeared and Flossie introduced them all to Claus. They were Racer and Pacer, Reckless and Speckless, Fearless and Peerless, and Ready and Steady, who, with Glossie and Flossie, made up the ten who have traversed the world these hundreds of years with their generous master. They were all exceedingly beautiful, with slender limbs, spreading antlers, velvety dark eyes and smooth coats of fawn color spotted with white.

Claus loved them at once, and has loved them ever since, for they are loyal friends and have rendered him priceless service.

The new harness fitted them nicely and soon they were all fastened to the sledge by twos, with Glossie and Flossie in the lead. These wore the strings of sleigh-bells, and were so delighted with the music they made that they kept prancing up and down to make the bells ring.

Claus now seated himself in the sledge, drew a warm robe over his knees and his fur cap over his ears, and cracked his long whip as a signal to start.

Instantly the ten leaped forward and were away like the wind, while jolly Claus laughed gleefully to see them run and shouted a song in his big, hearty voice:

> *"With a ho, ho, ho!*
> *And a ha, ha, ha!*
> *And a ho, ho, ha, ha, hee!*
> *Now away we go*
> *O'er the frozen snow,*
> *As merry as we can be!*
>
> *There are many joys*
> *In our load of toys,*
> *As many a child will know;*
> *We'll scatter them wide*
> *On our wild night ride*
> *O'er the crisp and sparkling snow!"*

Now it was on this same Christmas Eve that little Margot and her brother Dick and her cousins Ned and Sara, who were visiting at Margot's house, came in from making a snow man, with their clothes damp, their mittens dripping and their shoes and stockings wet through and through. They were not scolded, for Margot's mother knew the snow was melting, but they were sent early to bed that their clothes might be hung over chairs to dry. The shoes were placed on the red tiles of the hearth, where the heat from the hot embers would strike them, and the stockings were carefully hung in a row by the chimney, directly over the fireplace. That was the reason Santa Claus noticed them when he came down the chimney that night and all the household were fast asleep. He was in a tremendous hurry and seeing the stockings all belonged to children he quickly stuffed his toys into them and dashed up the chimney again, appearing on the roof so suddenly that the reindeer were astonished at his agility.

"I wish they would all hang up their stockings," he thought, as he drove to the next chimney. "It would save me a lot of time and I could then visit more children before daybreak."

When Margot and Dick and Ned and Sara jumped out of bed next morning and ran downstairs to get their stockings from the fireplace they were filled with delight to find the toys from Santa Claus inside them. In face, I think they found more presents in their stockings than any other children of that city had received, for Santa Claus was in a hurry and did not stop to count the toys.

Of course they told all their little friends about it, and of course every one of them decided to hang his own stockings by the fireplace the next Christmas Eve. Even Bessie Blithesome, who made a visit to that city with her father, the great Lord of Lerd, heard the story from the children and hung her own pretty stockings by the chimney when she returned home at Christmas time.

On his next trip Santa Claus found so many stockings hung up in anticipation of his visit that he could fill them in a jiffy and be away again in half the time required to hunt the children up and place the toys by their bedsides.

The custom grew year after year, and has always been a great help to Santa Claus. And, with so many children to visit, he surely needs all the help we are able to give him.

XII

The First Christmas Tree

C LAUS HAD ALWAYS KEPT HIS promise to the Knooks by returning to the Laughing Valley by daybreak, but only the swiftness of his reindeer has enabled him to do this, for he travels over all the world.

He loved his work and he loved the brisk night ride on his sledge and the gay tinkle of the sleigh bells. On that first trip with the ten reindeer only Glossie and Flossie wore bells; but each year thereafter for eight years Claus carried presents to the children of the Gnome King, and that good-natured monarch gave him in return a string of bells at each visit, so that finally every one of the ten deer was supplied, and you may imagine what a merry tune the bells played as the sledge sped over the snow.

The children's stockings were so long that it required a great many toys to fill them, and soon Claus found there were other things besides toys that children love. So he sent some of the Fairies, who were always his good friends, into the Tropics, from whence they returned with great bags full of oranges and bananas which they had plucked from the trees. And other Fairies flew to the wonderful Valley of Phunnyland, where delicious candies and bonbons grow thickly on the bushes, and returned laden with many boxes of sweetmeats for the little ones. These things Santa Claus, on each Christmas Eve, placed in the long stockings, together with his toys, and the children were glad to get them, you may be sure.

There are also warm countries where there is no snow in winter, but Claus and his reindeer visited them as well as the colder climes, for there were little wheels inside the runners of his sledge which permitted it to run as smoothly over bare ground as on the snow. And the children who lived in the warm countries learned to know the name of Santa Claus as well as those who lived nearer to the Laughing Valley.

Once, just as the reindeer were ready to start on their yearly trip, a Fairy came to Claus and told him of three little children who lived beneath a rude tent of skins on a broad plain where there were no trees whatever. These poor babies were miserable and unhappy, for their parents were ignorant people who neglected them sadly. Claus resolved to visit these children before he returned home, and during his ride he picked up the bushy top of a pine tree which the wind had broken off and placed it in his sledge.

It was nearly morning when the deer stopped before the lonely tent of skins where the poor children lay asleep. Claus at once planted the bit of pine tree in the sand and stuck many candles on the branches. Then he hung some of his prettiest toys on the tree, as well as several bags of candies. It did not take long to do all this, for Santa Claus works quickly, and when all was ready he lighted the candles and, thrusting his head in at the opening of the tent, he shouted:

"Merry Christmas, little ones!"

With that he leaped into his sledge and was out of sight before the children, rubbing the sleep from their eyes, could come out to see who had called them.

You can imagine the wonder and joy of those little ones, who had never in their lives known a real pleasure before, when they saw the tree, sparkling with lights that shone brilliant in the gray dawn and hung with toys enough to make them happy for years to come! They joined hands and danced around the tree, shouting and laughing, until they were obliged to pause for breath. And their parents, also, came out to look and wonder, and thereafter had more respect and consideration for their children, since Santa Claus had honored them with such beautiful gifts.

The idea of the Christmas tree pleased Claus, and so the following year he carried many of them in his sledge and set them up in the homes of poor people who seldom saw trees, and placed candles and toys on the branches. Of course he could not carry enough trees in one load of all who wanted them, but in some homes the fathers were able to get trees and have them all ready for Santa Claus when he arrived; and these the good Claus always decorated as prettily as possible and hung with toys enough for all the children who came to see the tree lighted.

These novel ideas and the generous manner in which they were carried out made the children long for that one night in the year when their friend Santa Claus should visit them, and as such anticipation is very pleasant and comforting the little ones gleaned much happiness by wondering what would happen when Santa Claus next arrived.

Perhaps you remember that stern Baron Braun who once drove Claus from his castle and forbade him to visit his children? Well, many years afterward, when the old Baron was dead and his son ruled in his place, the new Baron Braun came to the house of Claus with his train of knights and pages and henchmen and, dismounting from his charger, bared his head humbly before the friend of children.

"My father did not know your goodness and worth," he said, "and therefore threatened to hang you from the castle walls. But I have children of my own, who long for a visit from Santa Claus, and I have come to beg that you will favor them hereafter as you do other children."

Claus was pleased with this speech, for Castle Braun was the only place he had never visited, and he gladly promised to bring presents to the Baron's children the next Christmas Eve.

The Baron went away contented, and Claus kept his promise faithfully.

Thus did this man, through very goodness, conquer the hearts of all; and it is no wonder he was ever merry and gay, for there was no home in the wide world where he was not welcomed more royally than any king.

OLD AGE

I

THE MANTLE OF IMMORTALITY

AND NOW WE COME TO a turning-point in the career of Santa Claus, and it is my duty to relate the most remarkable that has happened since the world began or mankind was created.

We have followed the life of Claus from the time he was found a helpless infant by the Wood-Nymph Necile and reared to manhood in the great Forest of Burzee. And we know how he began to make toys for children and how, with the assistance and goodwill of the immortals, he was able to distribute them to the little ones throughout the world.

For many years he carried on this noble work; for the simple, hard-working life he led gave him perfect health and strength. And doubtless a man can live longer in the beautiful Laughing Valley, where there are no cares and everything is peaceful and merry, than in any other part of the world.

But when many years had rolled away Santa Claus grew old. The long beard of golden brown that once covered his cheeks and chin gradually became gray, and finally turned to pure white. His hair was white, too, and there were wrinkles at the corners of his eyes, which showed plainly when he laughed. He had never been a very tall man, and now he became fat, and waddled very much like a duck when he walked. But in spite of these things he remained as lively as ever, and was just as jolly and gay, and his kind eyes sparkled as brightly as they did that first day when he came to the Laughing Valley.

Yet a time is sure to come when every mortal who has grown old and lived his life is required to leave this world for another; so it is no wonder that, after Santa Claus had driven his reindeer on many and many a Christmas Eve, those stanch friends finally whispered among themselves that they had probably drawn his sledge for the last time.

Then all the Forest of Burzee became sad and all the Laughing Valley was hushed; for every living thing that had known Claus had used to love him and to brighten at the sound of his footsteps or the notes of his merry whistle.

No doubt the old man's strength was at last exhausted, for he made no more toys, but lay on his bed as in a dream.

The Nymph Necile, she who had reared him and been his foster-mother, was still youthful and strong and beautiful, and it seemed to her but a short time since this aged, gray-bearded man had lain in her arms and smiled on her with his innocent, baby lips.

In this is shown the difference between mortals and immortals.

It was fortunate that the great Ak came to the Forest at this time. Necile sought him with troubled eyes and told him of the fate that threatened their friend Claus.

At once the Master became grave, and he leaned upon his ax and stroked his grizzled beard thoughtfully for many minutes. Then suddenly he stood up straight, and poised his powerful head with firm resolve, and stretched out his great right arm as if determined on doing some mighty deed. For a thought had come to him so grand in its conception that all the world might well bow before the Master Woodsman and honor his name forever!

It is well known that when the great Ak once undertakes to do a thing he never hesitates an instant. Now he summoned his fleetest messengers, and sent them in a flash to many parts of the earth. And when they were gone he turned to the anxious Necile and comforted her, saying:

"Be of good heart, my child; our friend still lives. And now run to your Queen and tell her that I have summoned a council of all the immortals of the world to meet with me here in Burzee this night. If they obey, and harken unto my words, Claus will drive his reindeer for countless ages yet to come."

At midnight there was a wondrous scene in the ancient Forest of Burzee, where for the first time in many centuries the rulers of the immortals who inhabit the earth were gathered together.

There was the Queen of the Water Sprites, whose beautiful form was as clear as crystal but continually dripped water on the bank of moss where she sat. And beside her was the King of the Sleep Fays, who carried a wand from the end of which a fine dust fell all around, so that no mortal could keep awake long enough to see him, as mortal eyes were sure to close in sleep as soon as the dust filled them. And next to him sat the Gnome King, whose people inhabit all that region under the earth's surface, where they guard the precious metals and the jewel stones that lie buried in rock and ore. At his right hand stood the King of the Sound Imps, who had wings on his feet, for his people are swift to carry all sounds that are made. When they are busy they carry the sounds but short distances, for there are many of them; but sometimes they speed with the sounds to places miles and miles away from where they are made. The King of the Sound Imps had an anxious and careworn face, for most people have no consideration for his Imps and, especially the boys and girls, make a great many unnecessary sounds which the Imps are obliged to carry when they might be better employed.

The next in the circle of immortals was the King of the Wind Demons, slender of frame, restless and uneasy at being confined to one place for even an hour. Once in a while he would leave his place and circle around the glade, and each time he did this the Fairy Queen was obliged to untangle the flowing locks of her golden hair and tuck them back of her pink ears. But she did not complain, for it was not often that the King of the Wind Demons came into the heart of the Forest. After the Fairy Queen, whose home you know was in old Burzee, came the King of the Light Elves, with his two Princes, Flash and Twilight, at his back. He never went anywhere without his Princes, for they were so mischievous that he dared not let them wander alone.

Prince Flash bore a lightning-bolt in his right hand and a horn of gunpowder in his left, and his bright eyes roved constantly around, as if he longed to use his blinding flashes. Prince Twilight held a great snuffer in one hand and a big black cloak in the other, and it is well known that unless Twilight is carefully watched the snuffers or the cloak will throw everything into darkness, and Darkness is the greatest enemy the King of the Light Elves has.

In addition to the immortals I have named were the King of the Knooks, who had come from his home in the jungles of India; and the King of the Ryls, who lived among the gay flowers and luscious fruits of Valencia. Sweet Queen Zurline of the Wood-Nymphs completed the circle of immortals.

But in the center of the circle sat three others who possessed powers so great that all the Kings and Queens showed them reverence.

These were Ak, the Master Woodsman of the World, who rules the forests and the orchards and the groves; and Kern, the Master Husbandman of the World, who rules the grain fields and the meadows and the gardens; and Bo, the Master Mariner of the World, who rules the seas and all the craft that float thereon. And all other immortals are more or less subject to these three.

When all had assembled the Master Woodsman of the World stood up to address them, since he himself had summoned them to the council.

Very clearly he told them the story of Claus, beginning at the time when as a babe he had been adopted a child of the Forest, and telling of his noble and generous nature and his life-long labors to make children happy.

"And now," said Ak, "when he had won the love of all the world, the Spirit of Death is hovering over him. Of all men who have inhabited the earth none other so well deserves immortality, for such a life can not be spared so long as there are children of mankind to miss him and to grieve over his loss. We immortals are the servants of the world, and to serve the world we were permitted in the Beginning to exist. But what one of us is more worthy of immortality than this man Claus, who so sweetly ministers to the little children?"

He paused and glanced around the circle, to find every immortal listening to him eagerly and nodding approval. Finally the King of the Wind Demons, who had been whistling softly to himself, cried out:

"What is your desire, O Ak?"

"To bestow upon Claus the Mantle of Immortality!" said Ak, boldly.

That this demand was wholly unexpected was proved by the immortals springing to their feet and looking into each other's face with dismay and then upon Ak with wonder. For it was a grave matter, this parting with the Mantle of Immortality.

The Queen of the Water Sprites spoke in her low, clear voice, and the words sounded like raindrops splashing upon a window-pane.

"In all the world there is but one Mantle of Immortality," she said.

The King of the Sound Fays added:

"It has existed since the Beginning, and no mortal has ever dared to claim it."

And the Master Mariner of the World arose and stretched his limbs, saying:

"Only by the vote of every immortal can it be bestowed upon a mortal."

"I know all this," answered Ak, quietly. "But the Mantle exists, and if it was created, as you say, in the Beginning, it was because the Supreme Master knew that some day it would be required. Until now no mortal has deserved it, but who among you dares deny that the good Claus deserves it? Will you not all vote to bestow it upon him?"

They were silent, still looking upon one another questioningly.

"Of what use is the Mantle of Immortality unless it is worn?" demanded Ak. "What will it profit any one of us to allow it to remain in its lonely shrine for all time to come?"

"Enough!" cried the Gnome King, abruptly. "We will vote on the matter, yes or no. For my part, I say yes!"

"And I!" said the Fairy Queen, promptly, and Ak rewarded her with a smile.

"My people in Burzee tell me they have learned to love him; therefore I vote to give Claus the Mantle," said the King of the Ryls.

"He is already a comrade of the Knooks," announced the ancient King of that band. "Let him have immortality!"

"Let him have it—let him have it!" sighed the King of the Wind Demons.

"Why not?" asked the King of the Sleep Fays. "He never disturbs the slumbers my people allow humanity. Let the good Claus be immortal!"

"I do not object," said the King of the Sound Imps.

"Nor I," murmured the Queen of the Water Sprites.

"If Claus does not receive the Mantle it is clear none other can ever claim it," remarked the King of the Light Elves, "so let us have done with the thing for all time."

"The Wood-Nymphs were first to adopt him," said Queen Zurline. "Of course I shall vote to make him immortal."

Ak now turned to the Master Husbandman of the World, who held up his right arm and said "Yes!"

And the Master Mariner of the World did likewise, after which Ak, with sparkling eyes and smiling face, cried out:

"I thank you, fellow immortals! For all have voted 'yes,' and so to our dear Claus shall fall the one Mantle of Immortality that it is in our power to bestow!"

"Let us fetch it at once," said the Fay King; "I'm in a hurry."

They bowed assent, and instantly the Forest glade was deserted. But in a place midway between the earth and the sky was suspended a gleaming crypt of gold and platinum, aglow with soft lights shed from the facets of countless gems. Within a high dome hung the precious Mantle of Immortality, and each immortal placed a hand on the hem of the splendid Robe and said, as with one voice:

"We bestow this Mantle upon Claus, who is called the Patron Saint of Children!"

At this the Mantle came away from its lofty crypt, and they carried it to the house in the Laughing Valley.

The Spirit of Death was crouching very near to the bedside of Claus, and as the immortals approached she sprang up and motioned them back with an angry gesture. But when her eyes fell upon the Mantle they bore she shrank away with a low moan of disappointment and quitted that house forever.

Softly and silently the immortal Band dropped upon Claus the precious Mantle, and it closed about him and sank into the outlines of his body and disappeared from view. It became a part of his being, and neither mortal nor immortal might ever take it from him.

Then the Kings and Queens who had wrought this great deed dispersed to their various homes, and all were well contented that they had added another immortal to their Band.

And Claus slept on, the red blood of everlasting life coursing swiftly through his veins; and on his brow was a tiny drop of water that had fallen from the ever-melting gown of the Queen of the Water Sprites, and over his lips hovered a tender kiss that had been left by the sweet Nymph Necile. For she had stolen in when the others were gone to gaze with rapture upon the immortal form of her foster son.

II

WHEN THE WORLD GREW OLD

THE NEXT MORNING, WHEN SANTA Claus opened his eyes and gazed around the familiar room, which he had feared he might never see again, he was astonished to find his old strength renewed and to feel the red blood of perfect health coursing through his veins. He sprang from his bed and stood where the bright sunshine came in through his window and flooded him with its merry, dancing rays. He did not then understand what had happened to restore to him the vigor of youth, but in spite of the fact that his beard remained the color of snow and that wrinkles still lingered in the corners of his bright eyes, old Santa Claus felt as brisk and merry as a boy of sixteen, and was soon whistling contentedly as he busied himself fashioning new toys.

Then Ak came to him and told of the Mantle of Immortality and how Claus had won it through his love for little children.

It made old Santa look grave for a moment to think he had been so favored; but it also made him glad to realize that now he need never fear being parted from his dear ones. At once he began preparations for making a remarkable assortment of pretty and amusing playthings, and in larger quantities than ever before; for now that he might always devote himself to this work he decided that no child in the world, poor or rich, should hereafter go without a Christmas gift if he could manage to supply it.

The world was new in the days when dear old Santa Claus first began toymaking and won, by his loving deeds, the Mantle of Immortality. And the task of supplying cheering words, sympathy and pretty playthings to all the young of his race did not seem a difficult undertaking at all. But every year more and more children were born into the world, and these, when they grew up, began spreading slowly over all the face of the earth, seeking new homes; so that Santa Claus found each year that his journeys must extend farther and farther from the Laughing Valley, and that the packs of toys must be made larger and ever larger.

So at length he took counsel with his fellow immortals how his work might keep pace with the increasing number of children that none might be neglected. And the immortals were so greatly interested in his labors that they gladly rendered him their assistance. Ak gave him his man Kilter, "the silent and swift." And the Knook Prince gave him Peter, who was more crooked and less surly than any of his brothers. And the Ryl Prince gave him Nuter, the sweetest tempered Ryl ever known. And the Fairy Queen gave him Wisk, that tiny, mischievous but lovable Fairy who knows today almost as many children as does Santa Claus himself.

With these people to help make the toys and to keep his house in order and to look after the sledge and the harness, Santa Claus found it much easier to prepare his yearly load of gifts, and his days began to follow one another smoothly and pleasantly.

Yet after a few generations his worries were renewed, for it was remarkable how the number of people continued to grow, and how many more children there were every year to be served. When the people filled all the cities and lands of one country they wandered into another part of the world; and the men cut down the trees in many of the great forests that had been ruled by Ak, and with the wood they built new cities, and where the forests had been were fields of grain and herds of browsing cattle.

You might think the Master Woodsman would rebel at the loss of his forests; but not so. The wisdom of Ak was mighty and farseeing.

"The world was made for men," said he to Santa Claus, "and I have but guarded the forests until men needed them for their use. I am glad my strong trees can furnish shelter for men's weak bodies, and warm them through the cold winters. But I hope they will not cut down all the trees, for mankind needs the shelter of the woods in summer as much as the warmth of blazing logs in winter. And, however crowded the world may grow, I do not think men will ever come to Burzee, nor to the Great Black Forest, nor to the wooded wilderness of Braz; unless they seek their shades for pleasure and not to destroy their giant trees."

By and by people made ships from the tree trunks and crossed over oceans and built cities in far lands; but the oceans made little difference to the journeys of Santa Claus. His reindeer sped over the waters as swiftly as over land, and his sledge headed from east to west and followed in the wake of the sun. So that as the earth rolled slowly over Santa Claus had all of twenty-four hours to encircle it each Christmas Eve, and the speedy reindeer enjoyed these wonderful journeys more and more.

So year after year, and generation after generation, and century after century, the world grew older and the people became more numerous and the labors of Santa Claus steadily increased. The fame of his good deeds spread to every household where children dwelt. And all the little ones loved him dearly; and the fathers and mothers honored him for the happiness he had given them when they too were young; and the aged grandsires and granddames remembered him with tender gratitude and blessed his name.

III

THE DEPUTIES OF SANTA CLAUS

HOWEVER, THERE WAS ONE EVIL following in the path of civilization that caused Santa Claus a vast amount of trouble before he discovered a way to overcome it. But, fortunately, it was the last trial he was forced to undergo.

One Christmas Eve, when his reindeer had leaped to the top of a new building, Santa Claus was surprised to find that the chimney had been built much smaller than usual. But he had no time to think about it just then, so he drew in his breath and made himself as small as possible and slid down the chimney.

"I ought to be at the bottom by this time," he thought, as he continued to slip downward; but no fireplace of any sort met his view, and by and by he reached the very end of the chimney, which was in the cellar.

"This is odd!" he reflected, much puzzled by this experience. "If there is no fireplace, what on earth is the chimney good for?"

Then he began to climb out again, and found it hard work—the space being so small. And on his way up he noticed a thin, round pipe sticking through the side of the chimney, but could not guess what it was for.

Finally he reached the roof and said to the reindeer:

"There was no need of my going down that chimney, for I could find no fireplace through which to enter the house. I fear the children who live there must go without playthings this Christmas."

Then he drove on, but soon came to another new house with a small chimney. This caused Santa Claus to shake his head doubtfully, but he tried the chimney, nevertheless, and found it exactly like the other. Moreover, he nearly stuck fast in the narrow flue and tore his jacket trying to get out again; so, although he came to several such chimneys that night, he did not venture to descend any more of them.

"What in the world are people thinking of, to build such useless chimneys?" he exclaimed. "In all the years I have traveled with my reindeer I have never seen the like before."

True enough; but Santa Claus had not then discovered that stoves had been invented and were fast coming into use. When he did find it out he wondered how the builders of those houses could have so little consideration for him, when they knew very well it was his custom to climb down chimneys and enter houses by way of the fireplaces. Perhaps the men who built those houses had outgrown their own love for toys, and were indifferent whether Santa Claus called on their children or not. Whatever the explanation might be, the poor children were forced to bear the burden of grief and disappointment.

The following year Santa Claus found more and more of the new-fashioned chimneys that had no fireplaces, and the next year still more. The third year, so numerous had the narrow chimneys become, he even had a few toys left in his sledge that he was unable to give away, because he could not get to the children.

The matter had now become so serious that it worried the good man greatly, and he decided to talk it over with Kilter and Peter and Nuter and Wisk.

Kilter already knew something about it, for it had been his duty to run around to all the houses, just before Christmas, and gather up the notes and letters to Santa Claus that the children had written, telling what they wished put in their stockings or hung on their Christmas trees. But Kilter was a silent fellow, and seldom spoke of what he saw in the cities and villages. The others were very indignant.

"Those people act as if they do not wish their children to be made happy!" said sensible Peter, in a vexed tone. "The idea of shutting out such a generous friend to their little ones!"

"But it is my intention to make children happy whether their parents wish it or not," returned Santa Claus. "Years ago, when I first began making toys, children were even more neglected by their parents than they are now; so I have learned to pay no attention to thoughtless or selfish parents, but to consider only the longings of childhood."

"You are right, my master," said Nuter, the Ryl; "many children would lack a friend if you did not consider them, and try to make them happy."

"Then," declared the laughing Wisk, "we must abandon any thought of using these new-fashioned chimneys, but become burglars, and break into the houses some other way."

"What way?" asked Santa Claus.

"Why, walls of brick and wood and plaster are nothing to Fairies. I can easily pass through them whenever I wish, and so can Peter and Nuter and Kilter. Is it not so, comrades?"

"I often pass through the walls when I gather up the letters," said Kilter, and that was a long speech for him, and so surprised Peter and Nuter that their big round eyes nearly popped out of their heads.

"Therefore," continued the Fairy, "you may as well take us with you on your next journey, and when we come to one of those houses with stoves instead of fireplaces we will distribute the toys to the children without the need of using a chimney."

"That seems to me a good plan," replied Santa Claus, well pleased at having solved the problem. "We will try it next year."

That was how the Fairy, the Pixie, the Knook and the Ryl all rode in the sledge with their master the following Christmas Eve; and they had no trouble at all in entering the new-fashioned houses and leaving toys for the children that lived in them.

And their deft services not only relieved Santa Claus of much labor, but enabled him to complete his own work more quickly than usual, so that the merry party found themselves at home with an empty sledge a full hour before daybreak.

The only drawback to the journey was that the mischievous Wisk persisted in tickling the reindeer with a long feather, to see them jump; and Santa Claus found it necessary to watch him every minute and to tweak his long ears once or twice to make him behave himself.

But, taken all together, the trip was a great success, and to this day the four little folk always accompany Santa Claus on his yearly ride and help him in the distribution of his gifts.

But the indifference of parents, which had so annoyed the good Saint, did not continue very long, and Santa Claus soon found they were really anxious he should visit their homes on Christmas Eve and leave presents for their children.

So, to lighten his task, which was fast becoming very difficult indeed, old Santa decided to ask the parents to assist him.

"Get your Christmas trees all ready for my coming," he said to them; "and then I shall be able to leave the presents without loss of time, and you can put them on the trees when I am gone."

And to others he said: "See that the children's stockings are hung up in readiness for my coming, and then I can fill them as quick as a wink."

And often, when parents were kind and good-natured, Santa Claus would simply fling down his package of gifts and leave the fathers and mothers to fill the stockings after he had darted away in his sledge.

"I will make all loving parents my deputies!" cried the jolly old fellow, "and they shall help me do my work. For in this way I shall save many precious minutes and few children need be neglected for lack of time to visit them."

Besides carrying around the big packs in his swift-flying sledge old Santa began to send great heaps of toys to the toy shops, so that if parents wanted larger supplies for their children they could easily get them; and if any children were, by chance, missed by Santa Claus on his yearly rounds, they could go to the toy shops and get enough to make them happy and contented. For the loving friend of the little ones decided that no child, if he could help it, should long for toys in vain.

And the toy-shops also proved convenient whenever a child fell ill, and needed a new toy to amuse it; and sometimes, on birthdays, the fathers and mothers go to the toy shops and get pretty gifts for their children in honor of the happy event.

Perhaps you will now understand how, in spite of the bigness of the world, Santa Claus is able to supply all the children with beautiful gifts. To be sure, the old gentleman is rarely seen in these days; but it is not because he tries to keep out of sight, I assure you. Santa Claus is the same loving friend of children that in the old days used to play and romp with them by the hour; and I know he would love to do the same now, if he had the time. But, you see, he is so busy all the year making toys, and so hurried on that one night when he visits our homes with his packs, that he comes and goes among us like a flash; and it is almost impossible to catch a glimpse of him.

And, although there are millions and millions more children in the world than there used to be, Santa Claus has never been known to complain of their increasing numbers.

"The more the merrier!" he cries, with his jolly laugh; and the only difference to him is the fact that his little workmen have to make their busy fingers fly faster every year to satisfy the demands of so many little ones.

"In all this world there is nothing so beautiful as a happy child," says good old Santa Claus; and if he had his way the children would all be beautiful, for all would be happy.

A KIDNAPPED SANTA CLAUS

S ANTA CLAUS LIVES IN THE Laughing Valley, where stands the big, rambling castle in which his toys are manufactured. His workmen, selected from the ryls, knooks, pixies and fairies, live with him, and every one is as busy as can be from one year's end to another.

It is called the Laughing Valley because everything there is happy and gay. The brook chuckles to itself as it leaps rollicking between its green banks; the wind whistles merrily in the trees; the sunbeams dance lightly over the soft grass, and the violets and wild flowers look smilingly up from their green nests. To laugh one needs to be happy; to be happy one needs to be content. And throughout the Laughing Valley of Santa Claus contentment reigns supreme.

On one side is the mighty Forest of Burzee. At the other side stands the huge mountain that contains the Caves of the Daemons. And between them the Valley lies smiling and peaceful.

One would thing that our good old Santa Claus, who devotes his days to making children happy, would have no enemies on all the earth; and, as a matter of fact, for a long period of time he encountered nothing but love wherever he might go.

But the Daemons who live in the mountain caves grew to hate Santa Claus very much, and all for the simple reason that he made children happy.

The Caves of the Daemons are five in number. A broad pathway leads up to the first cave, which is a finely arched cavern at the foot of the mountain, the entrance being beautifully carved and decorated. In it resides the Daemon of Selfishness. Back of this is another cavern inhabited by the Daemon of Envy. The cave of the Daemon of Hatred is next in order, and through this one passes to the home of the Daemon of Malice—situated in a dark and fearful cave in the very heart of the mountain. I do not know what lies beyond this. Some say there are terrible pitfalls leading to death and destruction, and this may very well be true. However, from each one of the four caves mentioned there is a small, narrow tunnel leading to the fifth cave—a cozy little room occupied by the Daemon of Repentance. And as the rocky floors of these passages are well worn by the track of passing feet, I judge that many wanderers in the Caves of the Daemons have escaped through the tunnels to the abode of the Daemon of Repentance, who is said to be a pleasant sort of fellow who gladly opens for one a little door admitting you into fresh air and sunshine again.

Well, these Daemons of the Caves, thinking they had great cause to dislike old Santa Claus, held a meeting one day to discuss the matter.

"I'm really getting lonesome," said the Daemon of Selfishness. "For Santa Claus distributes so many pretty Christmas gifts to all the children that they become happy and generous, through his example, and keep away from my cave."

"I'm having the same trouble," rejoined the Daemon of Envy. "The little ones seem quite content with Santa Claus, and there are few, indeed, that I can coax to become envious."

"And that makes it bad for me!" declared the Daemon of Hatred. "For if no children pass through the Caves of Selfishness and Envy, none can get to MY cavern."

"Or to mine," added the Daemon of Malice.

"For my part," said the Daemon of Repentance, "it is easily seen that if children do not visit your caves they have no need to visit mine; so that I am quite as neglected as you are."

"And all because of this person they call Santa Claus!" exclaimed the Daemon of Envy. "He is simply ruining our business, and something must be done at once."

To this they readily agreed; but what to do was another and more difficult matter to settle. They knew that Santa Claus worked all through the year at his castle in the Laughing Valley, preparing the gifts he was to distribute on Christmas Eve; and at first they resolved to try to tempt him into their caves, that they might lead him on to the terrible pitfalls that ended in destruction.

So the very next day, while Santa Claus was busily at work, surrounded by his little band of assistants, the Daemon of Selfishness came to him and said:

"These toys are wonderfully bright and pretty. Why do you not keep them for yourself? It's a pity to give them to those noisy boys and fretful girls, who break and destroy them so quickly."

"Nonsense!" cried the old graybeard, his bright eyes twinkling merrily as he turned toward the tempting Daemon. "The boys and girls are never so noisy and fretful after receiving my presents, and if I can make them happy for one day in the year I am quite content."

So the Daemon went back to the others, who awaited him in their caves, and said:

"I have failed, for Santa Claus is not at all selfish."

The following day the Daemon of Envy visited Santa Claus. Said he: "The toy shops are full of playthings quite as pretty as those you are making. What a shame it is that they should interfere with your business! They make toys by machinery much quicker than you can make them by hand; and they sell them for money, while you get nothing at all for your work."

But Santa Claus refused to be envious of the toy shops.

"I can supply the little ones but once a year—on Christmas Eve," he answered; "for the children are many, and I am but one. And as my work is one of love and kindness I would be ashamed to receive money for my little gifts. But throughout all the year the children must be amused in some way, and so the toy shops are able to bring much happiness to my little friends. I like the toy shops, and am glad to see them prosper."

In spite of the second rebuff, the Daemon of Hatred thought he would try to influence Santa Claus. So the next day he entered the busy workshop and said:

"Goodmorning, Santa! I have bad news for you."

"Then run away, like a good fellow," answered Santa Claus. "Bad news is something that should be kept secret and never told."

"You cannot escape this, however," declared the Daemon; "for in the world are a good many who do not believe in Santa Claus, and these you are bound to hate bitterly, since they have so wronged you."

"Stuff and rubbish!" cried Santa.

"And there are others who resent your making children happy and who sneer at you and call you a foolish old rattlepate! You are quite right to hate such base slanderers, and you ought to be revenged upon them for their evil words."

"But I don't hate 'em!" exclaimed Santa Claus positively. "Such people do me no real harm, but merely render themselves and their children unhappy. Poor things! I'd much rather help them any day than injure them."

Indeed, the Daemons could not tempt old Santa Claus in any way. On the contrary, he was shrewd enough to see that their object in visiting him was to make mischief and trouble, and his cheery laughter disconcerted the evil ones and showed to them the folly of such an undertaking. So they abandoned honeyed words and determined to use force.

It was well known that no harm can come to Santa Claus while he is in the Laughing Valley, for the fairies, and ryls, and knooks all protect him. But on Christmas Eve he drives his reindeer out into the big world, carrying a sleighload of toys and pretty gifts to the children; and this was the time and the occasion when his enemies had the best chance to injure him. So the Daemons laid their plans and awaited the arrival of Christmas Eve.

The moon shone big and white in the sky, and the snow lay crisp and sparkling on the ground as Santa Claus cracked his whip and sped away out of the Valley into the great world beyond. The roomy sleigh was packed full with huge sacks of toys, and as the reindeer dashed onward our jolly old Santa laughed and whistled and sang for very joy. For in all his merry life this was the one day in the year when he was happiest—the day he lovingly bestowed the treasures of his workshop upon the little children.

It would be a busy night for him, he well knew. As he whistled and shouted and cracked his whip again, he reviewed in mind all the towns and cities and farmhouses where he was expected, and figured that he had just enough presents to go around and make every child happy. The reindeer knew exactly what was expected of them, and dashed along so swiftly that their feet scarcely seemed to touch the snow-covered ground.

Suddenly a strange thing happened: a rope shot through the moonlight and a big noose that was in the end of it settled over the arms and body of Santa Claus and drew tight. Before he could resist or even cry out he was jerked from the seat of the sleigh and tumbled head foremost into a snowbank, while the reindeer rushed onward with the load of toys and carried it quickly out of sight and sound.

Such a surprising experience confused old Santa for a moment, and when he had collected his senses he found that the wicked Daemons had pulled him from the snowdrift and bound him tightly with many coils of the stout rope. And then they carried the kidnapped Santa Claus away to their mountain, where they thrust the prisoner into a secret cave and chained him to the rocky wall so that he could not escape.

"Ha, ha!" laughed the Daemons, rubbing their hands together with cruel glee. "What will the children do now? How they will cry and scold and storm when they find there are no toys in their stockings and no gifts on their Christmas trees! And what a lot of punishment they will receive from their parents, and how they will flock to our Caves of Selfishness, and Envy, and Hatred, and Malice! We have done a mighty clever thing, we Daemons of the Caves!"

Now it so chanced that on this Christmas Eve the good Santa Claus had taken with him in his sleigh Nuter the Ryl, Peter the Knook, Kilter the Pixie, and a small fairy named Wisk—his four favorite assistants. These little people he had often found very useful in helping him to distribute his gifts to the children, and when their master was so suddenly dragged from the sleigh they were all snugly tucked underneath the seat, where the sharp wind could not reach them.

The tiny immortals knew nothing of the capture of Santa Claus until some time after he had disappeared. But finally they missed his cheery voice, and as their master always sang or whistled on his journeys, the silence warned them that something was wrong.

Little Wisk stuck out his head from underneath the seat and found Santa Claus gone and no one to direct the flight of the reindeer.

"Whoa!" he called out, and the deer obediently slackened speed and came to a halt.

Peter and Nuter and Kilter all jumped upon the seat and looked back over the track made by the sleigh. But Santa Claus had been left miles and miles behind.

"What shall we do?" asked Wisk anxiously, all the mirth and mischief banished from his wee face by this great calamity.

"We must go back at once and find our master," said Nuter the Ryl, who thought and spoke with much deliberation.

"No, no!" exclaimed Peter the Knook, who, cross and crabbed though he was, might always be depended upon in an emergency. "If we delay, or go back, there will not be time to get the toys to the children before morning; and that would grieve Santa Claus more than anything else."

"It is certain that some wicked creatures have captured him," added Kilter thoughtfully, "and their object must be to make the children unhappy. So our first duty is to get the toys distributed as carefully as if Santa Claus were himself present. Afterward we can search for our master and easily secure his freedom."

This seemed such good and sensible advice that the others at once resolved to adopt it. So Peter the Knook called to the reindeer, and the faithful animals again sprang forward and dashed over hill and valley, through forest and plain, until they came to the houses wherein children lay sleeping and dreaming of the pretty gifts they would find on Christmas morning.

The little immortals had set themselves a difficult task; for although they had assisted Santa Claus on many of his journeys, their master had always directed and guided them and told them exactly what he wished them to do. But now they had to distribute the toys according to their own judgment, and they did not understand children as well as did old Santa. So it is no wonder they made some laughable errors.

Mamie Brown, who wanted a doll, got a drum instead; and a drum is of no use to a girl who loves dolls. And Charlie Smith, who delights to romp and play out of doors, and who wanted some new rubber boots to keep his feet dry, received a sewing box filled with colored worsteds and threads and needles, which made him so provoked that he thoughtlessly called our dear Santa Claus a fraud.

Had there been many such mistakes the Daemons would have accomplished their evil purpose and made the children unhappy. But the little friends of the absent Santa Claus labored faithfully and intelligently to carry out their master's ideas, and they made fewer errors than might be expected under such unusual circumstances.

And, although they worked as swiftly as possible, day had begun to break before the toys and other presents were all distributed; so for the first time in many years the reindeer trotted into the Laughing Valley, on their return, in broad daylight, with the brilliant sun peeping over the edge of the forest to prove they were far behind their accustomed hours.

Having put the deer in the stable, the little folk began to wonder how they might rescue their master; and they realized they must discover, first of all, what had happened to him and where he was.

So Wisk the Fairy transported himself to the bower of the Fairy Queen, which was located deep in the heart of the Forest of Burzee; and once there, it did not take him long to find out all about the naughty Daemons and how they had kidnapped the good Santa Claus to prevent his making children happy. The Fairy Queen also promised her assistance, and then, fortified by this powerful support, Wisk flew back to where Nuter and Peter and Kilter awaited him, and the four counseled together and laid plans to rescue their master from his enemies.

It is possible that Santa Claus was not as merry as usual during the night that succeeded his capture. For although he had faith in the judgment of his little friends he could not avoid a certain amount of worry, and an anxious look would creep at times into his kind old eyes as he thought of the disappointment that might await his dear little children. And the Daemons, who guarded him by turns, one after another, did not neglect to taunt him with contemptuous words in his helpless condition.

When Christmas Day dawned the Daemon of Malice was guarding the prisoner, and his tongue was sharper than that of any of the others.

"The children are waking up, Santa!" he cried. "They are waking up to find their stockings empty! Ho, ho! How they will quarrel, and wail, and stamp their feet in anger! Our caves will be full today, old Santa! Our caves are sure to be full!"

But to this, as to other like taunts, Santa Claus answered nothing. He was much grieved by his capture, it is true; but his courage did not forsake him. And, finding that the prisoner would not reply to his jeers, the Daemon of Malice presently went away, and sent the Daemon of Repentance to take his place.

This last personage was not so disagreeable as the others. He had gentle and refined features, and his voice was soft and pleasant in tone.

"My brother Daemons do not trust me overmuch," said he, as he entered the cavern; "but it is morning, now, and the mischief is done. You cannot visit the children again for another year."

"That is true," answered Santa Claus, almost cheerfully; "Christmas Eve is past, and for the first time in centuries I have not visited my children."

"The little ones will be greatly disappointed," murmured the Daemon of Repentance, almost regretfully; "but that cannot be helped now. Their grief is likely to make the children selfish and envious and hateful, and if they come to the Caves of the Daemons today I shall get a chance to lead some of them to my Cave of Repentance."

"Do you never repent, yourself?" asked Santa Claus, curiously.

"Oh, yes, indeed," answered the Daemon. "I am even now repenting that I assisted in your capture. Of course it is too late to remedy the evil that has been done; but repentance, you know, can come only after an evil thought or deed, for in the beginning there is nothing to repent of."

"So I understand," said Santa Claus. "Those who avoid evil need never visit your cave."

"As a rule, that is true," replied the Daemon; "yet you, who have done no evil, are about to visit my cave at once; for to prove that I sincerely regret my share in your capture I am going to permit you to escape."

This speech greatly surprised the prisoner, until he reflected that it was just what might be expected of the Daemon of Repentance. The fellow at once busied himself untying the knots that bound Santa Claus and unlocking the chains that fastened him to the wall. Then he led the way through a long tunnel until they both emerged in the Cave of Repentance.

"I hope you will forgive me," said the Daemon pleadingly. "I am not really a bad person, you know; and I believe I accomplish a great deal of good in the world."

With this he opened a back door that let in a flood of sunshine, and Santa Claus sniffed the fresh air gratefully.

"I bear no malice," said he to the Daemon, in a gentle voice; "and I am sure the world would be a dreary place without you. So, goodmorning, and a Merry Christmas to you!"

With these words he stepped out to greet the bright morning, and a moment later he was trudging along, whistling softly to himself, on his way to his home in the Laughing Valley.

Marching over the snow toward the mountain was a vast army, made up of the most curious creatures imaginable. There were numberless knooks from the forest, as rough and crooked in appearance as the gnarled branches of the trees they ministered to. And there were dainty ryls from the fields, each one bearing the emblem of the flower or plant it guarded. Behind these were many ranks of pixies, gnomes and nymphs, and in the rear a thousand beautiful fairies floated along in gorgeous array.

This wonderful army was led by Wisk, Peter, Nuter, and Kilter, who had assembled it to rescue Santa Claus from captivity and to punish the Daemons who had dared to take him away from his beloved children.

And, although they looked so bright and peaceful, the little immortals were armed with powers that would be very terrible to those who had incurred their anger. Woe to the Daemons of the Caves if this mighty army of vengeance ever met them!

But lo! coming to meet his loyal friends appeared the imposing form of Santa Claus, his white beard floating in the breeze and his bright eyes sparkling with pleasure at this proof of the love and veneration he had inspired in the hearts of the most powerful creatures in existence.

And while they clustered around him and danced with glee at his safe return, he gave them earnest thanks for their support. But Wisk, and Nuter, and Peter, and Kilter, he embraced affectionately.

"It is useless to pursue the Daemons," said Santa Claus to the army. "They have their place in the world, and can never be destroyed. But that is a great pity, nevertheless," he continued musingly.

So the fairies, and knooks, and pixies, and ryls all escorted the good man to his castle, and there left him to talk over the events of the night with his little assistants.

Wisk had already rendered himself invisible and flown through the big world to see how the children were getting along on this bright

Christmas morning; and by the time he returned, Peter had finished telling Santa Claus of how they had distributed the toys.

"We really did very well," cried the fairy, in a pleased voice; "for I found little unhappiness among the children this morning. Still, you must not get captured again, my dear master; for we might not be so fortunate another time in carrying out your ideas."

He then related the mistakes that had been made, and which he had not discovered until his tour of inspection. And Santa Claus at once sent him with rubber boots for Charlie Smith, and a doll for Mamie Brown; so that even those two disappointed ones became happy.

As for the wicked Daemons of the Caves, they were filled with anger and chagrin when they found that their clever capture of Santa Claus had come to naught. Indeed, no one on that Christmas Day appeared to be at all selfish, or envious, or hateful. And, realizing that while the children's saint had so many powerful friends it was folly to oppose him, the Daemons never again attempted to interfere with his journeys on Christmas Eve.

A REVERSIBLE SANTA CLAUS

I

Mr. William B. Aikins, *alias* "Softy" Hubbard, *alias* Billy The Hopper, paused for breath behind a hedge that bordered a quiet lane and peered out into the highway at a roadster whose tail light advertised its presence to his felonious gaze. It was Christmas Eve, and after a day of unseasonable warmth a slow, drizzling rain was whimsically changing to snow.

The Hopper was blowing from two hours' hard travel over rough country. He had stumbled through woodlands, flattened himself in fence corners to avoid the eyes of curious motorists speeding homeward or flying about distributing Christmas gifts, and he was now bent upon committing himself to an inter-urban trolley line that would afford comfortable transportation for the remainder of his journey. Twenty miles, he estimated, still lay between him and his domicile.

The rain had penetrated his clothing and vigorous exercise had not greatly diminished the chill in his blood. His heart knocked violently against his ribs and he was dismayed by his shortness of wind. The Hopper was not so young as in the days when his agility and genius for effecting a quick "getaway" had earned for him his sobriquet. The last time his Bertillon measurements were checked (he was subjected to this humiliating experience in Omaha during the Ak-Sar-Ben carnival three years earlier) official note was taken of the fact that The Hopper's hair, long carried in the records as black, was rapidly whitening.

At forty-eight a crook—even so resourceful and versatile a member of the fraternity as The Hopper—begins to mistrust himself. For the greater part of his life, when not in durance vile, The Hopper had been in hiding, and the state or condition of being a fugitive, hunted by keen-eyed agents of justice, is not, from all accounts, an enviable one. His latest experience of involuntary servitude had been under the auspices of the State of Oregon, for a trifling indiscretion in the way of safeblowing. Having served his sentence, he skillfully effaced himself by a year's siesta on a pineapple plantation in Hawaii. The island climate was not wholly pleasing to The Hopper, and when pineapples palled he took passage from Honolulu as a stoker, reached San Francisco (not greatly chastened in spirit), and by a series of characteristic hops, skips, and jumps across the continent landed in Maine by way of the Canadian provinces. The Hopper needed money. He was not without a certain crude philosophy, and it had been his dream to acquire by some brilliant *coup* a sufficient fortune upon which to retire and live as a decent, law-abiding citizen for the remainder of his days. This ambition, or at least the means to its fulfillment, can hardly be defended as praiseworthy, but The Hopper was a singular character and we must take him as we find him. Many prison chaplains and jail visitors bearing tracts had striven with little success to implant moral ideals in the mind and soul of The Hopper, but he was still to be catalogued among the impenitent; and as he moved southward through the Commonwealth of Maine he was so oppressed by his poverty, as contrasted with the world's abundance, that he lifted forty thousand dollars in a neat bundle from an express car which Providence had sidetracked, apparently for his personal enrichment, on the upper waters of the Penobscot. Whereupon he began perforce playing his old game of artful dodging, exercising his best powers as a hopper and skipper. Forty thousand dollars is no inconsiderable sum of money, and the success of this master stroke of his career was not to be jeopardized by careless moves. By craftily hiding in the big woods and making himself agreeable to isolated lumberjacks who rarely saw newspapers, he arrived in due course on Manhattan Island, where with shrewd judgment he avoided the haunts of his kind while planning a future commensurate with his new dignity as a capitalist.

He spent a year as a diligent and faithful employee of a garage which served a fashionable quarter of the metropolis; then, animated by a worthy desire to continue to lead an honest life, he purchased a chicken farm fifteen miles as the crow flies from Center Church, New Haven, and boldly opened a bank account in that academic center in his newly adopted name of Charles S. Stevens, of Happy Hill Farm. Feeling the need of companionship, he married a lady somewhat his junior, a shoplifter of the second class, whom he had known before the vigilance of the metropolitan police necessitated his removal to the Far West. Mrs. Stevens's inferior talents as a petty larcenist had led her into many difficulties, and she gratefully availed herself of The Hopper's offer of his heart and hand.

They had added to their establishment a retired yegg who had lost an eye by the premature popping of the "soup" (i.e., nitro-glycerin) poured

A REVERSIBLE SANTA CLAUS

into the crevices of a country post office in Missouri. In offering shelter to Mr. James Whitesides, *alias* "Humpy" Thompson, The Hopper's motives had not been wholly unselfish, as Humpy had been entrusted with the herding of poultry in several penitentiaries and was familiar with the most advanced scientific thought on chicken culture.

The roadster was headed toward his home and The Hopper contemplated it in the deepening dusk with greedy eyes. His labors in the New York garage had familiarized him with automobiles, and while he was not ignorant of the pains and penalties inflicted upon lawless persons who appropriate motors illegally, he was the victim of an irresistible temptation to jump into the machine thus left in the highway, drive as near home as he dared, and then abandon it. The owner of the roadster was presumably eating his evening meal in peace in the snug little cottage behind the shrubbery, and The Hopper was aware of no sound reason why he should not seize the vehicle and further widen the distance between himself and a suspicious-looking gentleman he had observed on the New Haven local.

The Hopper's conscience was not altogether at ease, as he had, that afternoon, possessed himself of a bill book that was protruding from the breast pocket of a dignified citizen whose strap he had shared in a crowded subway train. Having foresworn crime as a means of livelihood, The Hopper was chagrined that he had suffered himself to be beguiled into stealing by the mere propinquity of a piece of red leather. He was angry at the world as well as himself. People should not go about with bill books sticking out of their pockets; it was unfair and unjust to those weak members of the human race who yield readily to temptation.

He had agreed with Mary when she married him and the chicken farm that they would respect the Ten Commandments and all statutory laws, State and Federal, and he was painfully conscious that when he confessed his sin she would deal severely with him. Even Humpy, now enjoying a peace that he had rarely known outside the walls of prison, even Humpy would be bitter. The thought that he was again among the hunted would depress Mary and Humpy, and he knew that their harshness would be intensified because of his violation of the unwritten law of the underworld in resorting to purse-lifting, an infringement upon a branch of felony despicable and greatly inferior in dignity to safe-blowing.

These reflections spurred The Hopper to action, for the sooner he reached home the more quickly he could explain his protracted stay in

New York (to which metropolis he had repaired in the hope of making a better price for eggs with the commission merchants who handled his products), submit himself to Mary's chastisement, and promise to sin no more. By returning on Christmas Eve, of all times, again a fugitive, he knew that he would merit the unsparing condemnation that Mary and Humpy would visit upon him. It was possible, it was even quite likely, that the short, stocky gentleman he had seen on the New Haven local was not a "bull"—not really a detective who had observed the little transaction in the subway; but the very uncertainty annoyed The Hopper. In his happy and profitable year at Happy Hill Farm he had learned to prize his personal comfort, and he was humiliated to find that he had been frightened into leaving the train at Bansford to continue his journey afoot, and merely because a man had looked at him a little queerly.

Any Christmas spirit that had taken root in The Hopper's soul had been disturbed, not to say seriously threatened with extinction, by the untoward occurrences of the afternoon.

II

THE HOPPER WAITED FOR A limousine to pass and then crawled out of his hiding place, jumped into the roadster, and was at once in motion. He glanced back, fearing that the owner might have heard his departure, and then, satisfied of his immediate security, negotiated a difficult turn in the road and settled himself with a feeling of relief to careful but expeditious flight. It was at this moment, when he had urged the car to its highest speed, that a noise startled him—an amazing little chirrupy sound which corresponded to none of the familiar forewarnings of engine trouble. With his eyes to the front he listened for a repetition of the sound. It rose again—it was like a perplexing cheep and chirrup, changing to a chortle of glee.

"Goo-goo! Goo-goo-goo!"

The car was skimming a dark stretch of road and a superstitious awe fell upon The Hopper. Murder, he gratefully remembered, had never been among his crimes, though he had once winged a too-inquisitive policeman in Kansas City. He glanced over his shoulder, but saw no pursuing ghost in the snowy highway; then, looking down apprehensively, he detected on the seat beside him what appeared to be an animate bundle, and, prompted by a louder "goo-goo," he put out his hand. His fingers touched something warm and soft and were promptly seized and held by Something.

The Hopper snatched his hand free of the tentacles of the unknown and shook it violently. The nature of the Something troubled him. He renewed his experiments, steering with his left hand and exposing the right to what now seemed to be the grasp of two very small mittened hands.

"Goo-goo! Goody; teep wunnin'!"

"A kid!" The Hopper gasped.

That he had eloped with a child was the blackest of the day's calamities. He experienced a strange sinking feeling in the stomach. In moments of apprehension a crook's thoughts run naturally into periods of penal servitude, and the punishment for kidnaping, The Hopper recalled, was severe. He stopped the car and inspected his unwelcome fellow passenger by the light of matches. Two big blue eyes stared at him from a hood and two mittens were poked into his face. Two small feet, wrapped tightly in a blanket, kicked at him energetically.

"Detup! Mate um skedaddle!"

Obedient to this command The Hopper made the car skedaddle, but superstitious dread settled upon him more heavily. He was satisfied now that from the moment he transferred the strap-hanger's bill book to his own pocket he had been hoodooed. Only a jinx of the most malevolent type could have prompted his hurried exit from a train to dodge an imaginary "bull." Only the blackest of evil spirits could be responsible for this involuntary kidnaping!

"Mate um wun! Mate um 'ippity stip!"

The mittened hands reached for the wheel at this juncture and an unlooked-for "jippity skip" precipitated the young passenger into The Hopper's lap.

This mishap was attended with the jolliest baby laughter. Gently but with much firmness The Hopper restored the youngster to an upright position and supported him until sure he was able to sustain himself.

"Ye better set still, little feller," he admonished.

The little feller seemed in no wise astonished to find himself abroad with a perfect stranger and his courage and good cheer were not lost upon The Hopper. He wanted to be severe, to vent his rage for the day's calamities upon the only human being within range, but in spite of himself he felt no animosity toward the friendly little bundle of humanity beside him. Still, he had stolen a baby and it was incumbent upon him to free himself at once of the appalling burden; but a baby is not so easily disposed of. He could not, without seriously imperiling his liberty, return to the cottage. It was the rule of housebreakers, he recalled, to avoid babies. He had heard it said by burglars of wide experience and unquestioned wisdom that babies were the most dangerous of all burglar alarms. All things considered, kidnaping and automobile theft were not a happy combination with which to appear before a criminal court. The Hopper was vexed because the child did not cry; if he had shown a bad disposition The Hopper might have abandoned him; but the youngster was the cheeriest and most agreeable of traveling companions. Indeed, The Hopper's spirits rose under his continued "goo-gooing" and chirruping.

"Nice little Shaver!" he said, patting the child's knees.

Little Shaver was so pleased by this friendly demonstration that he threw up his arms in an effort to embrace The Hopper.

"Bil-lee," he gurgled delightedly.

The Hopper was so astonished at being addressed in his own lawful name by a strange baby that he barely averted a collision with a passing motor truck. It was unbelievable that the baby really knew his name, but perhaps it was a good omen that he had hit upon it. The Hopper's resentment against the dark fate that seemed to pursue him vanished. Even though he had stolen a baby, it was a merry, brave little baby who didn't mind at all being run away with! He dismissed the thought of planting the little shaver at a door, ringing the bell and running away; this was no way to treat a friendly child that had done him no injury, and The Hopper highly resolved to do the square thing by the youngster even at personal inconvenience and risk.

The snow was now falling in generous Christmasy flakes, and the high speed the car had again attained was evidently deeply gratifying to the young person, whose reckless tumbling about made it necessary for The Hopper to keep a hand on him.

"Steady, little un; steady!" The Hopper kept mumbling.

His wits were busy trying to devise some means of getting rid of the youngster without exposing himself to the danger of arrest. By this time someone was undoubtedly busily engaged in searching for both baby and car; the police far and near would be notified, and would be on the lookout for a smart roadster containing a stolen child.

"Merry Christmas!" a boy shouted from a farm gate.

"M'y Kwismus!" piped Shaver.

The Hopper decided to run the machine home and there ponder the disposition of his blithe companion with the care the unusual circumstances demanded.

"'Urry up; me's goin' 'ome to me's gwanpa's kwismus t'ee!"

"Right ye be, little un; right ye be!" affirmed The Hopper.

The youngster was evidently blessed with a sanguine and confiding nature. His reference to his grandfather's Christmas tree impinged sharply upon The Hopper's conscience. Christmas had never figured very prominently in his scheme of life. About the only Christmases that he recalled with any pleasure were those that he had spent in prison, and those were marked only by Christmas dinners varying with the generosity of a series of wardens.

But Shaver was entitled to all the joys of Christmas, and The Hopper had no desire to deprive him of them.

"Keep a-larfin', Shaver, keep a-larfin'," said the Hopper. "Ole Hop ain't a-goin' to hurt ye!"

The Hopper, feeling his way cautiously round the fringes of New Haven, arrived presently at Happy Hill Farm, where he ran the car in among the chicken sheds behind the cottage and carefully extinguished the lights.

"Now, Shaver, out ye come!"

Whereupon Shaver obediently jumped into his arms.

III

THE HOPPER KNOCKED TWICE AT the back door, waited an instant, and knocked again. As he completed the signal the door was opened guardedly. A man and woman surveyed him in hostile silence as he pushed past them, kicked the door shut, and deposited the blinking child on the kitchen table. Humpy, the one-eyed, jumped to the windows and jammed the green shades close into the frames. The woman scowlingly waited for the head of the house to explain himself, and this, with the perversity of one who knows the dramatic value of suspense, he was in no haste to do.

"Well," Mary questioned sharply. "What ye got there, Bill?"

The Hopper was regarding Shaver with a grin of benevolent satisfaction. The youngster had seized a bottle of catsup and was making heroic efforts to raise it to his mouth, and the Hopper was intensely tickled by Shaver's efforts to swallow the bottle. Mrs. Stevens, *alias*

Weeping Mary, was not amused, and her husband's enjoyment of the child's antics irritated her.

"Come out with ut, Bill!" she commanded, seizing the bottle. "What ye been doin'?"

Shaver's big blue eyes expressed surprise and displeasure at being deprived of his plaything, but he recovered quickly and reached for a plate with which he began thumping the table.

"Out with ut, Hop!" snapped Humpy nervously. "Nothin' wuz said about kidnapin', an' I don't stand for ut!"

"When I heard the machine comin' in the yard I knowed somethin' was wrong an' I guess it couldn't be no worse," added Mary, beginning to cry. "You hadn't no right to do ut, Bill. Hookin' a buzz-buzz an' a kid an' when we wuz playin' the white card! You ought t' 'a' told me, Bill, what ye went to town fer, an' it bein' Christmas, an' all."

That he should have chosen for his fall the Christmas season of all times was reprehensible, a fact which Mary and Humpy impressed upon him in the strongest terms. The Hopper was fully aware of the inopportuneness of his transgressions, but not to the point of encouraging his wife to abuse him.

As he clumsily tried to unfasten Shaver's hood, Mary pushed him aside and with shaking fingers removed the child's wraps. Shaver's cheeks were rosy from his drive through the cold; he was a plump, healthy little shaver and The Hopper viewed him with intense pride. Mary held the hood and coat to the light and inspected them with a sophisticated eye. They were of excellent quality and workmanship, and she shook her head and sighed deeply as she placed them carefully on a chair.

"It ain't on the square, Hop," protested Humpy, whose lone eye expressed the most poignant sorrow at The Hopper's derelictions. Humpy was tall and lean, with a thin, many-lined face. He was an ill-favored person at best, and his habit of turning his head constantly as though to compel his single eye to perform double service gave one an impression of restless watchfulness.

"Cute little Shaver, ain't 'e? Give Shaver somethin' to eat, Mary. I guess milk'll be the right ticket considerin' th' size of 'im. How ole you make 'im? Not more'n three, I reckon?"

"Two. He ain't more'n two, that kid."

"A nice little feller; you're a cute un, ain't ye, Shaver?"

Shaver nodded his head solemnly. Having wearied of playing with the plate he gravely inspected the trio; found something amusing in

Humpy's bizarre countenance and laughed merrily. Finding no response to his friendly overtures he appealed to Mary.

"Me wants me's paw-widge," he announced.

"Porridge," interpreted Humpy with the air of one whose superior breeding makes him the proper arbiter of the speech of children of high social station. Whereupon Shaver appreciatively poked his forefinger into Humpy's surviving optic.

"I'll see what I got," muttered Mary. "What ye used t' eatin' for supper, honey?"

The "honey" was a concession, and The Hopper, who was giving Shaver his watch to play with, bent a commendatory glance upon his spouse.

"Go on an' tell us what ye done," said Mary, doggedly busying herself about the stove.

The Hopper drew a chair to the table to be within reach of Shaver and related succinctly his day's adventures.

"A dip!" moaned Mary as he described the seizure of the purse in the subway.

"You hadn't no right to do ut, Hop!" bleated Humpy, who had tipped his chair against the wall and was sucking a cold pipe. And then, professional curiosity overmastering his shocked conscience, he added: "What'd she measure, Hop?"

The Hopper grinned.

"Flubbed! Nothin' but papers," he confessed ruefully.

Mary and Humpy expressed their indignation and contempt in unequivocal terms, which they repeated after he told of the suspected "bull" whose presence on the local had so alarmed him. A frank description of his flight and of his seizure of the roadster only added to their bitterness.

Humpy rose and paced the floor with the quick, short stride of men habituated to narrow spaces. The Hopper watched the telltale step so disagreeably reminiscent of evil times and shrugged his shoulders impatiently.

"Set down, Hump; ye make me nervous. I got thinkin' to do."

"Ye'd better be quick about doin' ut!" Humpy snorted with an oath.

"Cut the cussin'!" The Hopper admonished sharply. Since his retirement to private life he had sought diligently to free his speech of profanity and thieves' slang, as not only unbecoming in a respectable chicken farmer, but likely to arouse suspicions as to his origin and previous condition of servitude. "Can't ye see Shaver ain't use to ut? Shaver's a little gent; he's a reg'ler little juke; that's wot Shaver is."

"The more 'way up he is the worse fer us," whimpered Humpy. "It's kidnapin', that's wot ut is!"

"That's wot it *ain't*," declared The Hopper, averting a calamity to his watch, which Shaver was swinging by its chain. "He was took by accident I tell ye! I'm goin' to take Shaver back to his ma—ain't I, Shaver?"

"Take 'im back!" echoed Mary.

Humpy crumpled up in his chair at this new evidence of The Hopper's insanity.

"I'm goin' to make a Chris'mas present o' Shaver to his ma," reaffirmed The Hopper, pinching the nearer ruddy cheek of the merry, contented guest.

Shaver kicked The Hopper in the stomach and emitted a chortle expressive of unshakable confidence in The Hopper's ability to restore him to his lawful owners. This confidence was not, however, manifested toward Mary, who had prepared with care the only cereal her pantry afforded, and now approached Shaver, bowl and spoon in hand. Shaver, taken by surprise, inspected his supper with disdain and spurned it with a vigor that sent the spoon rattling across the floor.

"Me wants me's paw-widge bowl! Me wants me's *own* paw-widge bowl!" he screamed.

Mary expostulated; Humpy offered advice as to the best manner of dealing with the refractory Shaver, who gave further expression to his resentment by throwing The Hopper's watch with violence against the wall. That the table service of The Hopper's establishment was not to Shaver's liking was manifested in repeated rejections of the plain white bowl in which Mary offered the porridge. He demanded his very own porridge bowl with the increasing vehemence of one who is willing to starve rather than accept so palpable a substitute. He threw himself back on the table and lay there kicking and crying. Other needs now occurred to Shaver: he wanted his papa; he wanted his mamma; he wanted to go to his gwan'pa's. He clamored for Santa Claus and numerous Christmas trees which, it seemed, had been promised him at the houses of his kinsfolk. It was amazing and bewildering that the heart of one so young could desire so many things that were not immediately attainable. He had begun to suspect that he was among strangers who were not of his way of life, and this was fraught with the gravest danger.

"They'll hear 'im hollerin' in China," wailed the pessimistic Humpy, running about the room and examining the fastenings of doors and windows. "Folks goin' along the road'll hear 'im, an' it's terms fer the whole bunch!"

The Hopper began pacing the floor with Shaver, while Humpy and Mary denounced the child for unreasonableness and lack of discipline, not overlooking the stupidity and criminal carelessness of The Hopper in projecting so lawless a youngster into their domestic circle.

"Twenty years, that's wot ut is!" mourned Humpy.

"Ye kin get the chair fer kidnapin'," Mary added dolefully. "Ye gotta get 'im out o' here, Bill."

Pleasant predictions of a long prison term with capital punishment as the happy alternative failed to disturb The Hopper. To their surprise and somewhat to their shame he won the Shaver to a tractable humor. There was nothing in The Hopper's known past to justify any expectation that he could quiet a crying baby, and yet Shaver with a child's unerring instinct realized that The Hopper meant to be kind. He patted The Hopper's face with one fat little paw, chokingly declaring that he was hungry.

"'Course Shaver's hungry; an' Shaver's goin' to eat nice porridge Aunt Mary made fer 'im. Shaver's goin' to have 'is own porridge bowl to-morry—yes, sir-ee, oo is, little Shaver!"

Restored to the table, Shaver opened his mouth in obedience to The Hopper's patient pleading and swallowed a spoonful of the mush, Humpy holding the bowl out of sight in tactful deference to the child's delicate æsthetic sensibilities. A tumbler of milk was sipped with grateful gasps.

The Hopper grinned, proud of his success, while Mary and Humpy viewed his efforts with somewhat grudging admiration, and waited patiently until The Hopper took the wholly surfeited Shaver in his arms and began pacing the floor, humming softly. In normal circumstances The Hopper was not musical, and Humpy and Mary exchanged looks which, when interpreted, pointed to nothing less than a belief that the owner of Happy Hill Farm was bereft of his senses. There was some question as to whether Shaver should be undressed. Mary discouraged the idea and Humpy took a like view.

"Ye gotta chuck 'im quick; that's what ye gotta do," said Mary hoarsely. "We don't want 'im sleepin' here."

Whereupon The Hopper demonstrated his entire independence by carrying the Shaver to Humpy's bed and partially undressing him. While this was in progress, Shaver suddenly opened his eyes wide and raising one foot until it approximated the perpendicular, reached for it with his chubby hands.

"Sant' Claus comin'; m'y Kwismus!"

"Jes' listen to Shaver!" chuckled The Hopper. "'Course Santy is comin,' an' we're goin' to hang up Shaver's stockin', ain't we, Shaver?"

He pinned both stockings to the footboard of Humpy's bed. By the time this was accomplished under the hostile eyes of Mary and Humpy, Shaver slept the sleep of the innocent.

IV

THEY WATCHED THE CHILD IN silence for a few minutes and then Mary detached a gold locket from his neck and bore it to the kitchen for examination.

"Ye gotta move quick, Hop," Humpy urged. "The white card's what we wuz all goin' to play. We wuz fixed nice here, an' things goin' easy; an' the yard full o' br'ilers. I don't want to do no more time. I'm an ole man, Hop."

"Cut ut!" ordered The Hopper, taking the locket from Mary and weighing it critically in his hand. They bent over him as he scrutinized the face on which was inscribed:—

Roger Livingston Talbot
June 13, 1913

"Lemme see; he's two an' a harf. Ye purty nigh guessed 'im right, Mary."

The sight of the gold trinket, the probability that the Shaver belonged to a family of wealth, proved disturbing to Humpy's late protestations of virtue.

"They'd be a heap o' kale in ut, Hop. His folks is rich, I reckon. Ef we wuzn't playin' the white card—"

Ignoring this shocking evidence of Humpy's moral instability, The Hopper became lost in reverie, meditatively drawing at his pipe.

"We ain't never goin' to quit playin' ut square," he announced, to Mary's manifest relief. "I hadn't ought t' 'a' done th' dippin'. It were a mistake. My ole head wuzn't workin' right er I wouldn't 'a' slipped. But ye needn't jump on me no more."

"Wot ye goin' to do with that kid? Ye tell me that!" demanded Mary, unwilling too readily to accept The Hopper's repentance at face value.

"I'm goin' to take 'im to 'is folks, that's wot I'm goin' to do with 'im," announced The Hopper.

"Yer crazy—yer plum' crazy!" cried Humpy, slapping his knees excitedly. "Ye kin take 'im to an orphant asylum an' tell um ye found 'im in that machine ye lifted. And mebbe ye'll git by with ut an' mebbe ye won't, but ye gotta keep me out of ut!"

"I found the machine in th' road, right here by th' house; an' th' kid was in ut all by hisself. An' bein' humin an' respectible I brought 'im in to keep 'im from freezin' t' death," said The Hopper, as though repeating lines he was committing to memory. "They ain't nobody can say as I didn't. Ef I git pinched, that's my spiel to th' cops. It ain't kidnapin'; it's life-savin', that's wot ut is! I'm a-goin' back an' have a look at that place where I got 'im. Kind o' queer they left the kid out there in the buzz-wagon; *mighty* queer, now's I think of ut. Little house back from the road; lots o' trees an' bushes in front. Didn't seem to be no lights. He keeps talkin' about Chris'mas at his grandpa's. Folks must 'a' been goin' to take th' kid somewheres fer Chris'mas. I guess it'll throw a skeer into 'em to find him up an' gone."

"They's rich, an' all the big bulls'll be lookin' fer 'im; ye'd better 'phone the New Haven cops ye've picked 'im up. Then they'll come out, an' yer spiel about findin' 'im'll sound easy an' sensible like."

The Hopper, puffing his pipe philosophically, paid no heed to Humpy's suggestion even when supported warmly by Mary.

"I gotta find some way o' puttin' th' kid back without seein' no cops. I'll jes' take a sneak back an' have a look at th' place," said The Hopper. "I ain't goin' to turn Shaver over to no cops. Ye can't take no chances with 'em. They don't know nothin' about us bein' here, but they ain't fools, an' I ain't goin' to give none o' 'em a squint at me!"

He defended his plan against a joint attack by Mary and Humpy, who saw in it only further proof of his tottering reason. He was obliged to tell them in harsh terms to be quiet, and he added to their rage by the deliberation with which he made his preparations to leave.

He opened the door of a clock and drew out a revolver which he examined carefully and thrust into his pocket. Mary groaned; Humpy beat the air in impotent despair. The Hopper possessed himself also of a jimmy and an electric lamp. The latter he flashed upon the face of the sleeping Shaver, who turned restlessly for a moment and then lay still again. He smoothed the coverlet over the tiny form, while Mary and Humpy huddled in the doorway. Mary wept; Humpy was awed into silence by his old friend's perversity. For years he had admired The Hopper's cleverness, his genius for extricating himself from difficulties; he was deeply shaken to think that one who had stood so high in one of the most exacting of professions should have fallen so low. As The Hopper imperturbably buttoned his coat and walked toward the door, Humpy set his back against it in a last attempt to save his friend from his own foolhardiness.

"Ef anybody turns up here an' asks for th' kid, ye kin tell 'em wot I said. We finds 'im in th' road right here by the farm when we're doin' th' night chores an' takes 'im in t' keep 'im from freezin'. Ye'll have th' machine an' kid here to show 'em. An' as fer me, I'm off lookin' fer his folks."

Mary buried her face in her apron and wept despairingly. The Hopper, noting for the first time that Humpy was guarding the door, roughly pushed him aside and stood for a moment with his hand on the knob.

"They's things wot is," he remarked with a last attempt to justify his course, "an' things wot ain't. I reckon I'll take a peek at that place an' see wot's th' best way t' shake th' kid. Ye can't jes' run up to a house in a machine with his folks all settin' round cryin' an' cops askin' questions. Ye got to do some plannin' an' thinkin'. I'm goin' t' clean ut all up before daylight, an' ye needn't worry none about ut. Hop ain't worryin'; jes' leave ut t' Hop!"

There was no alternative but to leave it to Hop, and they stood mute as he went out and softly closed the door.

V

THE SNOW HAD CEASED AND the stars shone brightly on a white world as The Hopper made his way by various trolley lines to the house from which he had snatched Shaver. On a New Haven car he debated the prospects of more snow with a policeman who seemed oblivious to the fact that a child had been stolen—shamelessly carried off by a man with a long police record. Merry Christmas passed from lip to lip as if all creation were attuned to the note of love and peace, and crime were an undreamed of thing.

For two years The Hopper had led an exemplary life and he was keenly alive now to the joy of adventure. His lapses of the day were unfortunate; he thought of them with regret and misgivings, but he was zestful for whatever the unknown held in store for him. Abroad again with a pistol in his pocket, he was a lawless being, but with the difference that he was intent now upon making restitution, though in such manner as would give him something akin to the old thrill that he experienced when he enjoyed the reputation of being one of the most skillful yeggs in the country. The successful thief is of necessity an imaginative person; he must be able to visualize the unseen and to deal with a thousand hidden contingencies. At best the chances are against him; with all his ingenuity the broad, heavy hand of the law is likely at any moment to close upon him from some unexpected quarter. The Hopper knew this, and knew, too, that in yielding to the exhilaration of the hour he was likely to come to grief. Justice has a long memory, and if he again made himself the object of police scrutiny that little forty-thousand dollar affair in Maine might still be fixed upon him.

When he reached the house from whose gate he had removed the roadster with Shaver attached, he studied it with the eye of an experienced strategist. No gleam anywhere published the presence of frantic parents bewailing the loss of a baby. The cottage lay snugly behind its barrier of elms and shrubbery as though its young heir had not vanished into the void. The Hopper was a deliberating being and he gave careful weight to these circumstances as he crept round the walk, in which the snow lay undisturbed, and investigated the rear of the premises. The lattice door of the summer kitchen opened readily, and, after satisfying himself that no one was stirring in the lower part of the house, he pried up the sash of a window and stepped in. The larder was well stocked, as though in preparation for a Christmas feast, and he passed on to the dining room, whose appointments spoke for good taste and a degree of prosperity in the householder.

Cautious flashes of his lamp disclosed on the table a hamper, in which were packed a silver cup, plate, and bowl which at once awoke the Hopper's interest. Here indubitably was proof that this was the home of Shaver, now sleeping sweetly in Humpy's bed, and this was the porridge bowl for which Shaver's soul had yearned. If Shaver did not belong to the house, he had at least been a visitor there, and it struck The Hopper as a reasonable assumption that Shaver had been deposited in the roadster while his lawful guardians returned to the cottage for the hamper preparatory to an excursion of some sort. But The Hopper groped in the dark for an explanation of the calmness with which the householders accepted the loss of the child. It was not in human nature for the parents of a youngster so handsome and in every way so delightful as Shaver to permit him to be stolen from under their very noses without making an outcry. The Hopper examined the silver pieces and found them engraved with the name borne by the locket. He crept through a living room and came to a Christmas tree—the smallest of Christmas trees. Beside it lay a number of packages designed clearly for none other than young Roger Livingston Talbot.

Housebreaking is a very different business from the forcible entry of country post offices, and The Hopper was nervous. This particular house seemed utterly deserted. He stole upstairs and found doors open and a disorder indicative of the occupants' hasty departure. His attention was arrested by a small room finished in white, with a white enameled bed, and other furniture to match. A generous litter of toys was the last proof needed to establish the house as Shaver's true domicile. Indeed, there was every indication that Shaver was the central figure of this home of whose charm and atmosphere The Hopper was vaguely sensible. A frieze of dancing children and watercolor sketches of Shaver's head, dabbed here and there in the most unlooked-for places, hinted at an artistic household. This impression was strengthened when The Hopper, bewildered and baffled, returned to the lower floor and found a studio opening off the living room. The Hopper had never visited a studio before, and satisfied now that he was the sole occupant of the house, he passed passed about shooting his light upon unfinished canvases, pausing finally before an easel supporting a portrait of Shaver—newly finished, he discovered, by poking his finger into the wet paint. Something fell to the floor and he picked up a large sheet of drawing paper on which this message was written in charcoal:—

Six-thirty.

Dear Sweetheart:—

This is a fine trick you have played on me, you dear girl! I've been expecting you back all afternoon. At six I decided that you were going to spend the night with your infuriated parent and thought I'd try my luck with mine! I put Billie into the roadster and, leaving him there, ran over to the Flemings's to say Merry Christmas and tell 'em we were off for the night. They kept me just a minute to look at those new Jap prints Jim's so crazy about, and while I was gone you came along and skipped with Billie and the car! I suppose this means that you've been making headway with your dad and want to try the effect of Billie's blandishments. Good luck! But you might have stopped long enough to tell me about it! How fine it would be if everything could be straightened out for Christmas! Do you remember the first time I kissed you—it was on Christmas Eve four years ago at the Billings's dance! I'm just trolleying out to father's to see what an evening session will do. I'll be back early in the morning.

Love always,
ROGER.

Billie was undoubtedly Shaver's nickname. This delighted The Hopper. That they should possess the same name appeared to create a strong bond of comradeship. The writer of the note was presumably the child's father and the "Dear Sweetheart" the youngster's mother. The Hopper was not reassured by these disclosures. The return of Shaver to his parents was far from being the pleasant little Christmas Eve adventure he had imagined. He had only the lowest opinion of a father who would, on a winter evening, carelessly leave his baby in a motor car while he looked at pictures, and who, finding both motor and baby gone, would take it for granted that the baby's mother had run off with them. But these people were artists, and artists, The Hopper had heard, were a queer breed, sadly lacking in common sense. He tore the note into strips which he stuffed into his pocket.

Depressed by the impenetrable wall of mystery along which he was groping, he returned to the living room, raised one of the windows and unbolted the front door to make sure of an exit in case these strange, foolish Talbots should unexpectedly return. The shades were up and he shielded his light carefully with his cap as he passed rapidly about the room. It began to look very much as though Shaver would spend Christmas at Happy Hill Farm—a possibility that had not figured in The Hopper's calculations.

Flashing his lamp for a last survey a letter propped against a lamp on the table arrested his eye. He dropped to the floor and crawled into a corner where he turned his light upon the note and read, not without difficulty, the following:—

Dear Roger:—

I've just got back from father's where I spent the last three hours talking over our troubles. I didn't tell you I was going, knowing you would think it foolish, but it seemed best, dear, and I hope you'll forgive me. And now I find that you've gone off with Billie, and I'm guessing that you've gone to *your* father's to see what you can do. I'm taking the trolley into New Haven to ask Mamie Palmer about that cook she thought we might get, and if possible I'll bring the girl home with me. Don't trouble about me, as I'll be perfectly safe, and, as you know, I rather enjoy prowling around at night. You'll certainly get back before I do, but if I'm not here don't be alarmed.

We are so happy in each other, dear, and if only we could get our foolish fathers to stop hating each other, how beautiful everything would be! And we could all have such a merry, merry Christmas!

MURIEL.

The Hopper's acquaintance with the epistolary art was the slightest, but even to a mind unfamiliar with this branch of literature it was plain that Shaver's parents were involved in some difficulty that was attributable, not to any lessening of affection between them, but to a row of some sort between their respective fathers. Muriel, running into the house to write her note, had failed to see Roger's letter in the studio, and this was very fortunate for The Hopper; but Muriel might return at any moment, and it would add nothing to the plausibility of the story he meant to tell if he were found in the house.

VI

ANXIOUS AND DEJECTED AT THE increasing difficulties that confronted him, he was moving toward the door when a light, buoyant step sounded on the veranda. In a moment the living room lights were switched on from the entry and a woman called out sharply:—

"Stop right where you are or I'll shoot!"

The authoritative voice of the speaker, the quickness with which she had grasped the situation and leveled her revolver, brought The Hopper to an abrupt halt in the middle of the room, where he fell with a discordant crash across the keyboard of a grand piano. He turned, cowering, to confront a tall, young woman in a long ulster who advanced toward him slowly, but with every mark of determination upon her face. The Hopper stared beyond the gun, held in a very steady hand, into a pair of fearless dark eyes. In all his experiences he had never been cornered by a woman, and he stood gaping at his captor in astonishment. She was a very pretty young woman, with cheeks that still had the curve of youth, but with a chin that spoke for much firmness of character. A fur toque perched a little to one side gave her a boyish air.

This undoubtedly was Shaver's mother who had caught him prowling in her house, and all The Hopper's plans for explaining her son's disappearance and returning him in a manner to win praise and gratitude went glimmering. There was nothing in the appearance of this Muriel to encourage a hope that she was either embarrassed or alarmed by his presence. He had been captured many times, but the trick had never been turned by anyone so cool as this young woman. She seemed to be pondering with the greatest calmness what disposition she should make of him. In the intentness of her thought the revolver wavered for an instant, and The Hopper, without taking his eyes from her, made a cat-like spring that brought him to the window he had raised against just such an emergency.

"None of that!" she cried, walking slowly toward him without lowering the pistol. "If you attempt to jump from that window I'll shoot! But it's cold in here and you may lower it."

The Hopper, weighing the chances, decided that the odds were heavily against escape, and lowered the window.

"Now," said Muriel, "step into that corner and keep your hands up where I can watch them."

The Hopper obeyed her instructions strictly. There was a telephone on the table near her and he expected her to summon help; but to his surprise she calmly seated herself, resting her right elbow on the arm of the chair, her head slightly tilted to one side, as she inspected him with greater attention along the blueblack barrel of her automatic. Unless he made a dash for liberty this extraordinary woman would, at her leisure, turn him over to the police as a housebreaker and his peaceful life as a chicken farmer would be at an end. Her prolonged silence troubled The

Hopper. He had not been more nervous when waiting for the report of the juries which at times had passed upon his conduct, or for judges to fix his term of imprisonment.

"Yes'm," he muttered, with a view to ending a silence that had become intolerable.

Her eyes danced to the accompaniment of her thoughts, but in no way did she betray the slightest perturbation.

"I ain't done nothin'; hones' to God, I ain't!" he protested brokenly.

"I saw you through the window when you entered this room and I was watching while you read that note," said his captor. "I thought it funny that you should do that instead of packing up the silver. Do you mind telling me just why you read that note?"

"Well, miss, I jes' thought it kind o' funny there wuzn't nobody round an' the letter was layin' there all open, an' I didn't see no harm in lookin'.'"

"It was awfully clever of you to crawl into the corner so nobody could see your light from the windows," she said with a tinge of admiration. "I suppose you thought you might find out how long the people of the house were likely to be gone and how much time you could spend here. Was that it?"

"I reckon ut wuz some thin' like that," he agreed.

This was received with the noncommittal "Um" of a person whose thoughts are elsewhere. Then, as though she were eliciting from an artist or man of letters a frank opinion as to his own ideas of his attainments and professional standing, she asked, with a meditative air that puzzled him as much as her question:—

"Just how good a burglar are you? Can you do a job neatly and safely?"

The Hopper, staggered by her inquiry and overcome by modesty, shrugged his shoulders and twisted about uncomfortably.

"I reckon as how you've pinched me I ain't much good," he replied, and was rewarded with a smile followed by a light little laugh. He was beginning to feel pleased that she manifested no fear of him. In fact, he had decided that Shaver's mother was the most remarkable woman he had ever encountered, and by all odds the handsomest. He began to take heart. Perhaps after all he might hit upon some way of restoring Shaver to his proper place in the house of Talbot without making himself liable to a long term for kidnaping.

"If you're really a successful burglar—one who doesn't just poke abound in empty houses as you were doing here, but clever and brave enough to break into houses where people are living and steal things without making a mess of it; and if you can play fair about it—then I think—I think—maybe—we can come to terms!"

"Yes'm!" faltered The Hopper, beginning to wonder if Mary and Humpy had been right in saying that he had lost his mind. He was so astonished that his arms wavered, but she was instantly on her feet and the little automatic was again on a level with his eyes.

"Excuse me, miss, I didn't mean to drop 'em. I weren't goin' to do nothin'. Hones' I wuzn't!" he pleaded with real contrition. "It jes' seemed kind o' funny what ye said."

He grinned sheepishly. If she knew that her Billie, *alias* Shaver, was not with her husband at his father's house, she would not be dallying in this fashion. And if the young father, who painted pictures, and left notes in his studio in a blind faith that his wife would find them,—if that trusting soul knew that Billie was asleep in a house all of whose inmates had done penance behind prison bars, he would very quickly become a man of action. The Hopper had never heard of such careless parenthood! These people were children! His heart warmed to them in pity and admiration, as it had to little Billie.

"I forgot to ask you whether you are armed," she remarked, with just as much composure as though she were asking him whether he took two lumps of sugar in his tea; and then she added, "I suppose I ought to have asked you that in the first place."

"I gotta gun in my coat—right side," he confessed. "An' that's all I got," he added, batting his eyes under the spell of her bewildering smile.

With her left hand she cautiously extracted his revolver and backed away with it to the table.

"If you'd lied to me I should have killed you; do you understand?"

"Yes'm," murmured The Hopper meekly.

She had spoken as though homicide were a common incident of her life, but a gleam of humor in the eyes she was watching vigilantly abated her severity.

"You may sit down—there, please!"

She pointed to a much bepillowed davenport and The Hopper sank down on it, still with his hands up. To his deepening mystification she backed to the windows and lowered the shades, and this done she sat down with the table between them, remarking,—

"You may put your hands down now, Mr. —?"

He hesitated, decided that it was unwise to give any of his names; and respecting his scruples she said with great magnanimity:—

"Of course you wouldn't want to tell me your name, so don't trouble about that."

She sat, wholly tranquil, her arms upon the table, both hands caressing the small automatic, while his own revolver, of different pattern and larger caliber, lay close by. His status was now established as that of a gentleman making a social call upon a lady who, in the pleasantest manner imaginable and yet with undeniable resoluteness, kept a deadly weapon pointed in the general direction of his person.

A clock on the mantel struck eleven with a low, silvery note. Muriel waited for the last stroke and then spoke crisply and directly.

"We were speaking of that letter I left lying here on the table. You didn't understand it, of course; you couldn't—not really. So I will explain it to you. My husband and I married against our fathers' wishes; both of them were opposed to it."

She waited for this to sink into his perturbed consciousness. The Hopper frowned and leaned forward to express his sympathetic interest in this confidential disclosure.

"My father," she resumed, "is just as stupid as my father-in-law and they have both continued to make us just as uncomfortable as possible. The cause of the trouble is ridiculous. There's nothing against my husband or me, you understand; it's simply a bitter jealousy between the two men due to the fact that they are rival collectors."

The Hopper stared blankly. The only collectors with whom he had enjoyed any acquaintance were persons who presented bills for payment.

"They are collectors," Muriel hastened to explain, "of ceramics— precious porcelains and that sort of thing."

"Yes'm," assented The Hopper, who hadn't the faintest notion of what she meant.

"For years, whenever there have been important sales of these things, which men fight for and are willing to die for—whenever there has been something specially fine in the market, my father-in-law—he's Mr. Talbot—and Mr. Wilton—he's my father—have bid for them. There are auctions, you know, and people come from all over the world looking for a chance to buy the rarest pieces. They've explored China and Japan hunting for prizes and they are experts—men of rare taste and judgment—what you call connoisseurs."

The Hopper nodded gravely at the unfamiliar word, convinced that not only were Muriel and her husband quite insane, but that they had inherited the infirmity.

"The trouble has been," Muriel continued, "that Mr. Talbot and my father both like the same kind of thing; and when one has got something the other wanted, of course it has added to the ill-feeling. This has been going on for years and recently they have grown more bitter. When Roger and I ran off and got married, that didn't help matters any; but just within a few days something has happened to make things much worse than ever."

The Hopper's complete absorption in this novel recital was so manifest that she put down the revolver with which she had been idling and folded her hands.

"Thank ye, miss," mumbled The Hopper.

"Only last week," Muriel continued, "my father-in-law bought one of those pottery treasures—a plum blossom vase made in China hundreds of years ago and very, very valuable. It belonged to a Philadelphia collector who died not long ago and Mr. Talbot bought it from the executor of the estate, who happened to be an old friend of his. Father was very angry, for he had been led to believe that this vase was going to be offered at auction and he'd have a chance to bid on it. And just before that father had got hold of a jar—a perfectly wonderful piece of red Lang-Yao—that collectors everywhere have coveted for years. This made Mr. Talbot furious at father. My husband is at his father's now trying to make him see the folly of all this, and I visited *my* father today to try to persuade him to stop being so foolish. You see I wanted us all to be happy for Christmas! Of course, Christmas ought to be a time of gladness for everybody. Even people in your—er—profession must feel that Christmas is one day in the year when all hard feelings should be forgotten and everybody should try to make others happy."

"I guess yer right, miss. Ut sure seems foolish fer folks t' git mad about jugs like you says. Wuz they empty, miss?"

"Empty!" repeated Muriel wonderingly, not understanding at once that her visitor was unaware that the "jugs" men fought over were valued as art treasures and not for their possible contents. Then she laughed merrily, as only the mother of Shaver could laugh.

"Oh! Of course they're *empty!* That does seem to make it sillier, doesn't it? But they're like famous pictures, you know, or any beautiful work of art that only happens occasionally. Perhaps it seems odd to you that men can be so crazy about such things, but I suppose sometimes you have wanted things very, very much, and—oh!"

She paused, plainly confused by her tactlessness in suggesting to a member of his profession the extremities to which one may be led by covetousness.

"Yes, miss," he remarked hastily; and he rubbed his nose with the back of his hand, and grinned indulgently as he realized the cause of her embarrassment. It crossed his mind that she might be playing a trick of some kind; that her story, which seemed to him wholly fantastic and not at all like a chronicle of the acts of veritable human beings, was merely a device for detaining him until help arrived. But he dismissed this immediately as unworthy of one so pleasing, so beautiful, so perfectly qualified to be the mother of Shaver!

"Well, just before luncheon, without telling my husband where I was going, I ran away to papa's, hoping to persuade him to end this silly feud. I spent the afternoon there and he was very unreasonable. He feels that Mr. Talbot wasn't fair about that Philadelphia purchase, and I gave it up and came home. I got here a little after dark and found my husband had taken Billie—that's our little boy—and gone. I knew, of course, that he had gone to *his* father's hoping to bring him round, for both our fathers are simply crazy about Billie. But you see I never go to Mr. Talbot's and my husband never goes—Dear me!" she broke off suddenly. "I suppose I ought to telephone and see if Billie is all right."

The Hopper, greatly alarmed, thrust his head forward as she pondered this. If she telephoned to her father-in-law's to ask about Billie, the jig would be up! He drew his hand across his face and fell back with relief as she went on, a little absently:—

"Mr. Talbot hates telephoning, and it might be that my husband is just getting him to the point of making concessions, and I shouldn't want to interrupt. It's so late now that of course Roger and Billie will spend the night there. And Billie and Christmas ought to be a combination that would soften the hardest heart! You ought to see—you just ought to see Billie! He's the cunningest, dearest baby in the world!"

The Hopper sat pigeon-toed, beset by countless conflicting emotions. His ingenuity was taxed to its utmost by the demands of this complex situation. But for his returning suspicion that Muriel was leading up to something; that she was detaining him for some purpose not yet apparent, he would have told her of her husband's note and confessed that the adored Billie was at that moment enjoying the reluctant hospitality of Happy Hill Farm. He resolved to continue his policy of silence as to the young heir's whereabouts until Muriel had shown her hand. She had not wholly abandoned the thought of telephoning to her father-in-law's, he found, from her next remark.

"You think it's all right, don't you? It's strange Roger didn't leave me a note of some kind. Our cook left a week ago and there was no one here when he left."

"I reckon as how yer kid's all right, miss," he answered consolingly.

Her voluble confidences had enthralled him, and her reference of this matter to his judgment was enormously flattering. On the rough edges of society where he had spent most of his life, fellow craftsmen had frequently solicited his advice, chiefly as to the disposition of their ill-gotten gains or regarding safe harbors of refuge, but to be taken into counsel by the only gentlewoman he had ever met roused his self-respect, touched a chivalry that never before had been wakened in The Hopper's soul. She was so like a child in her guilelessness, and so brave amid her perplexities!

"Oh, I know Roger will take beautiful care of Billie. And now," she smiled radiantly, "you're probably wondering what I've been driving at all this time. Maybe"—she added softly—"maybe it's providential, your turning up here in this way!"

She uttered this happily, with a little note of triumph and another of her smiles that seemed to illuminate the universe. The Hopper had been called many names in his varied career, but never before had he been invested with the attributes of an agent of Providence.

"They's things wot is an' they's things wot ain't, miss; I reckon I ain't as bad as some. I mean to be on the square, miss."

"I believe that," she said. "I've always heard there's honor among thieves, and"—she lowered her voice to a whisper—"it's possible I might become one myself!"

The Hopper's eyes opened wide and he crossed and uncrossed his legs nervously in his agitation.

"If—if"—she began slowly, bending forward with a grave, earnest look in her eyes and clasping her fingers tightly—"if we could only get hold of father's Lang-Yao jar and that plum blossom vase Mr. Talbot has—if we could only do that!"

The Hopper swallowed hard. This fearless, pretty young woman was calmly suggesting that he commit two felonies, little knowing that his score for the day already aggregated three—purse-snatching, the theft of an automobile from her own door, and what might very readily be construed as the kidnaping of her own child!

"I don't know, miss," he said feebly, calculating that the sum total of even minimum penalties for the five crimes would outrun his natural life and consume an eternity of reincarnations.

"Of course it wouldn't be stealing in the ordinary sense," she explained. "What I want you to do is to play the part of what we will call a reversible Santa Claus, who takes things away from stupid people who don't enjoy them anyhow. And maybe if they lost these things they'd behave themselves. I could explain afterward that it was all my fault, and of course I wouldn't let any harm come to *you*. I'd be responsible, and of course I'd see you safely out of it; you would have to rely on me for that. I'm trusting *you* and you'd have to trust *me!*"

"Oh, I'd trust ye, miss! An' ef I was to get pinched I wouldn't never squeal on ye. We don't never blab on a pal, miss!"

He was afraid she might resent being called a "pal," but his use of the term apparently pleased her.

"We understand each other, then. It really won't be very difficult, for papa's place is over on the Sound and Mr. Talbot's is right next to it, so you wouldn't have far to go."

Her utter failure to comprehend the enormity of the thing she was proposing affected him queerly. Even among hardened criminals in the underworld such undertakings are suggested cautiously; but Muriel was ordering a burglary as though it were a pound of butter or a dozen eggs!

"Father keeps his most valuable glazes in a safe in the pantry," she resumed after a moment's reflection, "but I can give you the combination. That will make it a lot easier."

The Hopper assented, with a pontifical nod, to this sanguine view of the matter.

"Mr. Talbot keeps his finest pieces in a cabinet built into the bookshelves in his library. It's on the left side as you stand in the drawing room door, and you look for the works of Thomas Carlyle. There's a dozen or so volumes of Carlyle, only they're not books,—not really,—but just the backs of books painted on the steel of a safe. And if you press a spring in the upper right hand corner of the shelf just over these books the whole section swings out. I suppose you've seen that sort of hiding place for valuables?"

"Well, not exactly, miss. But havin' a tip helps, an' ef there ain't no soup to pour—"

"Soup?" inquired Muriel, wrinkling her pretty brows.

"That's the juice we pour into the cracks of a safe to blow out the lid with," The Hopper elucidated. "Ut's a lot handier ef you've got the combination. Ut usually ain't jes' layin' around."

"I should hope not!" exclaimed Muriel.

She took a sheet of paper from the leathern stationery rack and fell to scribbling, while he furtively eyed the window and again put from him the thought of flight.

"There! That's the combination of papa's safe." She turned her wrist and glanced at her watch. "It's half-past eleven and you can catch a trolley in ten minutes that will take you right past papa's house. The butler's an old man who forgets to lock the windows half the time, and there's one in the conservatory with a broken catch. I noticed it today when I was thinking about stealing the jar myself!"

They were established on so firm a basis of mutual confidence that when he rose and walked to the table she didn't lift her eyes from the paper on which she was drawing a diagram of her father's house. He stood watching her nimble fingers, fascinated by the boldness of her plan for restoring amity between Shaver's grandfathers, and filled with admiration for her resourcefulness.

He asked a few questions as to exits and entrances and fixed in his mind a very accurate picture of the home of her father. She then proceeded to enlighten him as to the ways and means of entering the home of her father-in-law, which she sketched with equal facility.

"There's a French window—a narrow glass door—on the veranda. I think you might get in *there!*" She made a jab with the pencil. "Of course I should hate awfully to have you get caught! But you must have had a lot of experience, and with all the help I'm giving you—!"

A sudden lifting of her head gave him the full benefit of her eyes and he averted his gaze reverently.

"There's always a chance o' bein' nabbed, miss," he suggested with feeling.

Shaver's mother wielded the same hypnotic power, highly intensified, that he had felt in Shaver. He knew that he was going to attempt what she asked; that he was committed to the project of robbing two houses merely to please a pretty young woman who invited his cooperation at the point of a revolver!

"Papa's always a sound sleeper," she was saying. "When I was a little girl a burglar went all through our house and carried off his clothes and he never knew it until the next morning. But you'll have to be careful at Mr. Talbot's, for he suffers horribly from insomnia."

"They got any o' them fancy burglar alarms?" asked The Hopper as he concluded his examination of her sketches.

"Oh, I forgot to tell you about that!" she cried contritely. "There's nothing of the kind at Mr. Talbot's, but at papa's there's a switch in the living room, right back of a bust—a white marble thing on a pedestal. You turn it off *there*. Half the time papa forgets to switch it on before he goes to bed. And another thing—be careful about stumbling over that bearskin rug in the hall. People are always sticking their feet into its jaws."

"I'll look out for ut, miss."

Burglar alarms and the jaws of wild beasts were not inviting hazards. The programme she outlined so light-heartedly was full of complexities. It was almost pathetic that any one could so cheerfully and irresponsibly suggest the perpetration of a crime. The terms she used in describing the loot he was to filch were much stranger to him than Chinese, but it was fairly clear that at the Talbot house he was to steal a blue-and-white thing and at the Wilton's a red one. The form and size of these articles she illustrated with graceful gestures.

"If I thought you were likely to make a mistake I'd—I'd go with you!" she declared.

"Oh, no, miss; ye couldn't do that! I guess I can do ut fer ye. Ut's jes' a *leetle* ticklish. I reckon ef yer pa wuz to nab me ut'd go hard with me."

"I wouldn't let him be hard on you," she replied earnestly. "And now I haven't said anything about a—a—about what we will call a *reward* for bringing me these porcelains. I shall expect to pay you; I couldn't think of taking up your time, you know, for nothing!"

"Lor', miss, I couldn't take nothin' at all fer doin' ut! Ye see ut wuz sort of accidental our meetin', and besides, I ain't no housebreaker—not, as ye may say, reg'ler. I'll be glad to do ut fer ye, miss, an' ye can rely on me doin' my best fer ye. Ye've treated me right, miss, an' I ain't a-goin' t' fergit ut!"

The Hopper spoke with feeling. Shaver's mother had, albeit at the pistol point, confided her most intimate domestic affairs to him. He realized, without finding just these words for it, that she had in effect decorated him with the symbol of her order of knighthood and he had every honorable—or dishonorable!—intention of proving himself worthy of her confidence.

"If ye please, miss," he said, pointing toward his confiscated revolver.

"Certainly; you may take it. But of course you won't kill anybody?"

"No, miss; only I'm sort o' lonesome without ut when I'm on a job."

"And you do understand," she said, following him to the door and noting in the distance the headlight of an approaching trolley, "that I'm only doing this in the hope that good may come of it. It isn't really criminal, you know; if you succeed, it may mean the happiest Christmas of my life!"

"Yes, miss. I won't come back till mornin', but don't you worry none. We gotta play safe, miss, an' ef I land th' jugs I'll find cover till I kin deliver 'em safe."

"Thank you; oh, thank you ever so much! And good luck!"

She put out her hand; he held it gingerly for a moment in his rough fingers and ran for the car.

VII

THE HOPPER, IN HIS ROLE of the Reversible Santa Claus, dropped off the car at the crossing Muriel had carefully described, waited for the car to vanish, and warily entered the Wilton estate through a gate set in the stone wall. The clouds of the early evening had passed and the stars marched through the heavens resplendently, proclaiming peace on earth and goodwill toward men. They were almost oppressively brilliant, seen through the clear, cold atmosphere, and as The Hopper slipped from one big tree to another on his tangential course to the house, he fortified his courage by muttering, "They's things wot is an' things wot ain't!"—Finding much comfort and stimulus in the phrase.

Arriving at the conservatory in due course, he found that Muriel's averments as to the vulnerability of that corner of her father's house were correct in every particular. He entered with ease, sniffed the warm, moist air, and, leaving the door slightly ajar, sought the pantry, lowered the shades, and, helping himself to a candle from a silver candelabrum, readily found the safe hidden away in one of the cupboards. He was surprised to find himself more nervous with the combination in his hand than on memorable occasions in the old days when he had broken into country post offices and assaulted safes by force. In his haste he twice failed to give the proper turns, but the third time the knob caught, and in a moment the door swung open disclosing shelves filled with vases, bottles, bowls, and plates in bewildering variety. A chest of silver appealed to him distractingly as a much more tangible asset than the pottery, and he dizzily contemplated a jewel case containing a diamond necklace with a pearl pendant. The moment was a critical one in The Hopper's eventful career. This dazzling prize was his for the taking, and he knew the operator of a fence in Chicago who would dispose of the necklace and make him a fair return. But visions of Muriel, the beautiful, the confiding, and of her little Shaver asleep on Humpy's bed, rose before him. He steeled his heart against temptation, drew his candle along the shelf and scrutinized the glazes. There could be no mistaking the red Lang-Yao whose brilliant tints kindled in the candle glow. He lifted it tenderly, verifying the various points of Muriel's description, set it down on the floor and locked the safe.

He was retracing his steps toward the conservatory and had reached the main hall when the creaking of the stairsteps brought him up with a start. Someone was descending, slowly and cautiously. For a second time and with grateful appreciation of Muriel's forethought, he carefully avoided the ferocious jaws of the bear, noiselessly continued on to the conservatory, crept through the door, closed it, and then, crouching on the steps, awaited developments. The caution exercised by the person descending the stairway was not that of a householder who has been roused from slumber by a disquieting noise. The Hopper was keenly interested in this fact.

With his face against the glass he watched the actions of a tall, elderly man with a short, grayish beard, who wore a golf cap pulled low on his head—points noted by The Hopper in the flashes of an electric lamp with which the gentleman was guiding himself. His face was clearly the original of a photograph The Hopper had seen on the table at Muriel's cottage—Mr. Wilton, Muriel's father, The Hopper surmised; but just why the owner of the establishment should be prowling about in this fashion taxed his speculative powers to the utmost. Warned by steps on the cement floor of the conservatory, he left the door in haste and flattened himself against the wall of the house some distance away and again awaited developments.

Wilton's figure was a blur in the starlight as he stepped out into the walk and started furtively across the grounds. His conduct greatly displeased The Hopper, as likely to interfere with the further carrying out of Muriel's instructions. The Lang-Yao jar was much too large to go into his pocket and not big enough to fit snugly under his arm, and as the walk was slippery he was beset by the fear that he might fall and smash this absurd thing that had caused so bitter an enmity between Shaver's grandfathers. The soft snow on the lawn gave him a surer footing and he crept after Wilton, who was carefully pursuing his way toward a house whose gables were faintly limned against the sky. This, according to Muriel's diagram, was the Talbot place. The Hopper greatly mistrusted conditions he didn't understand, and he was at a loss to account for Wilton's strange actions.

He lost sight of him for several minutes, then the faint click of a latch marked the prowler's proximity to a hedge that separated the two estates. The Hopper crept forward, found a gate through which Wilton had entered his neighbor's property, and stole after him. Wilton had been swallowed up by the deep shadow of the house, but The Hopper was aware, from an occasional scraping of feet, that he was still moving forward. He crawled over the snow until he reached a large tree whose boughs, sharply limned against the stars, brushed the eaves of the house.

The Hopper was aroused, tremendously aroused, by the unaccountable actions of Muriel's father. It flashed upon him that Wilton, in his deep hatred of his rival collector, was about to set fire to Talbot's house, and incendiarism was a crime which The Hopper, with all his moral obliquity, greatly abhorred.

Several minutes passed, a period of anxious waiting, and then a sound reached him which, to his keen professional sense, seemed singularly like the forcing of a window. The Hopper knew just how much pressure is necessary to the successful snapping back of a window catch, and Wilton had done the trick neatly and with a minimum amount of noise. The window thus assaulted was not, he now determined, the French window suggested by Muriel, but one opening on a terrace which ran along the front of the house. The Hopper heard the sash moving slowly in the frame. He reached the steps, deposited the jar in a pile of snow, and was soon peering into a room where Wilton's presence was advertised by the fitful flashing of his lamp in a far corner.

"He's beat me to ut!" muttered The Hopper, realizing that Muriel's father was indeed on burglary bent, his obvious purpose being to purloin, extract, and remove from its secret hiding place the coveted plum blossom vase. Muriel, in her longing for a Christmas of peace and happiness, had not reckoned with her father's passionate desire to possess the porcelain treasure—a desire which could hardly fail to cause scandal, if it did not land him behind prison bars.

This had not been in the programme, and The Hopper weighed judicially his further duty in the matter. Often as he had been the chief actor in daring robberies, he had never before enjoyed the high privilege of watching a rival's labors with complete detachment. Wilton must have known of the concealed cupboard whose panel fraudulently represented the works of Thomas Carlyle, the intent spectator reflected, just as Muriel had known, for though he used his lamp sparingly Wilton had found his way to it without difficulty.

The Hopper had no intention of permitting this monstrous larceny to be committed in contravention of his own rights in the premises, and he was considering the best method of wresting the vase from the hands of the insolent Wilton when events began to multiply with startling rapidity. The panel swung open and the thief's lamp flashed upon shelves of pottery.

At that moment a shout rose from somewhere in the house, and the library lights were thrown on, revealing Wilton before the shelves and their precious contents. A short, stout gentleman with a gleaming bald pate, clad in pajamas, dashed across the room, and with a yell of rage flung himself upon the intruder with a violence that bore them both to the floor.

"Roger! Roger!" bawled the smaller man, as he struggled with his adversary, who wriggled from under and rolled over upon Talbot, whose arms were clasped tightly about his neck. This embrace seemed likely to continue for some time, so tenaciously had the little man gripped his neighbor. The fat legs of the infuriated householder pawed the air as he hugged Wilton, who was now trying to free his head and gain a position of greater dignity. Occasionally, as opportunity offered, the little man yelled vociferously, and from remote recesses of the house came answering cries demanding information as to the nature and whereabouts of the disturbance.

The contestants addressed themselves vigorously to a spirited rough-and-tumble fight. Talbot, who was the more easily observed by reason of his shining pate and the pink stripes of his pajamas, appeared to be revolving about the person of his neighbor. Wilton, though taller, lacked the rotund Talbot's liveliness of attack.

An authoritative voice, which The Hopper attributed to Shaver's father, anxiously demanding what was the matter, terminated The Hopper's enjoyment of the struggle. Enough was the matter to satisfy The Hopper that a prolonged stay in the neighborhood might be highly detrimental to his future liberty. The combatants had rolled a considerable distance away from the shelves and were near a door leading into a room beyond. A young man in a bath wrapper dashed upon the scene, and in his precipitate arrival upon the battlefield fell sprawling across the prone figures. The Hopper, suddenly inspired to deeds of prowess, crawled through the window, sprang past the three men, seized the blue-and-white vase which Wilton had separated from the rest of Talbot's treasures, and then with one hop gained the window. As he turned for a last look, a pistol cracked and he landed upon the terrace amid a shower of glass from a shattered pane.

A woman of unmistakable Celtic origin screamed murder from a third-story window. The thought of murder was disagreeable to The Hopper. Shaver's father had missed him by only the matter of a foot or two, and as he had no intention of offering himself again as a target he stood not upon the order of his going.

He effected a running pickup of the Lang-Yao, and with this art treasure under one arm and the plum blossom vase under the other, he sprinted for the highway, stumbling over shrubbery, bumping into a stone bench that all but caused disaster, and finally reached the road on which he continued his flight toward New Haven, followed by cries in many keys and a fusillade of pistol shots.

Arriving presently at a hamlet, where he paused for breath in the rear of a country store, he found a basket and a quantity of paper in which he carefully packed his loot. Over the top he spread some faded lettuce leaves and discarded carnations which communicated something of a blithe holiday air to his encumbrance. Elsewhere he found a bicycle under a shed, and while cycling over a snowy road in the dark, hampered by a basket containing pottery representative of the highest genius of the Orient, was not without its difficulties and dangers, The Hopper made rapid progress.

Halfway through New Haven he approached two policemen and slowed down to allay suspicion.

"Merry Chris'mas!" he called as he passed them and increased his weight upon the pedals.

The officers of the law, cheered as by a greeting from Santa Claus himself, responded with an equally hearty Merry Christmas.

VIII

AT THREE O'CLOCK THE HOPPER reached Happy Hill Farm, knocked as before at the kitchen door, and was admitted by Humpy.

"Wot ye got now?" snarled the reformed yeggman.

"He's gone and done ut ag'in!" wailed Mary, as she spied the basket.

"I sure done ut, all right," admitted The Hopper good-naturedly, as he set the basket on the table where a few hours earlier he had deposited Shaver. "How's the kid?"

Grudging assurances that Shaver was asleep and hostile glances directed at the mysterious basket did not disturb his equanimity.

Humpy was thwarted in an attempt to pry into the contents of the basket by a tart reprimand from The Hopper, who with maddening deliberation drew forth the two glazes, found that they had come through the night's vicissitudes unscathed, and held them at arm's length, turning them about in leisurely fashion as though lost in admiration of their loveliness. Then he lighted his pipe, seated himself in Mary's rocker, and told his story.

It was no easy matter to communicate to his irritable and contumelious auditors the sense of Muriel's charm, or the reasonableness of her request that he commit burglary merely to assist her in settling a family row. Mary could not understand it; Humpy paced the room nervously, shaking his head and muttering. It was their judgment, stated with much frankness, that if he had been a fool in the first place to steal the child, his character was now blackened beyond any hope by his later crimes. Mary wept copiously; Humpy most annoyingly kept counting upon his fingers as he reckoned the "time" that was in store for all of them.

"I guess I got into ut an' I guess I'll git out," remarked The Hopper serenely. He was disposed to treat them with high condescension, as incapable of appreciating the lofty philosophy of life by which he was sustained. Meanwhile, he gloated over the loot of the night.

"Them things is wurt' mints; they's more valible than di'mon's, them things is! Only eddicated folks knows about 'em. They's fer emp'rors and kings t' set up in their palaces, an' men goes nutty jes' hankerin' fer 'em. The pigtails made 'em thousand o' years back, an' th' secret died with 'em. They ain't never goin' to be no more jugs like them settin' right there. An' them two ole sports give up their business jes' t' chase things like them. They's some folks goes loony about chickens, an' hosses, an' fancy dogs, but this here kind o' collectin' 's only fer millionaires. They's more difficult t' pick than a lucky race-hoss. They's barrels o' that stuff in them houses, that looked jes' as good as them there, but nowheres as valible."

An informal lecture on Chinese ceramics before daylight on Christmas morning was not to the liking of the anxious and nerve-torn Mary and Humpy. They brought The Hopper down from his lofty heights to practical questions touching his plans, for the disposal of Shaver in the first instance, and the ceramics in the second. The Hopper was singularly unmoved by their forebodings.

"I guess th' lady got me to do ut!" he retorted finally. "Ef I do time fer ut I reckon's how she's in fer ut, too! An' I seen her pap breakin' into a house an' I guess I'd be a state's witness fer that! I reckon they ain't goin' t' put nothin' over on Hop! I guess they won't peep much about kidnapin' with th' kid safe an' us pickin' 'im up out o' th' road an' shelterin' 'im. Them folks is goin' to be awful nice to Hop fer all he done fer 'em." And then, finding that they were impressed by his defense, thus elaborated, he magnanimously referred to the bill book which had started him on his downward course.

"That were a mistake; I grant ye ut were a mistake o' jedgment. I'm goin' to keep to th' white card. But ut's kind o' funny about that poke— queerest thing that ever happened."

He drew out the book and eyed the name on the flap. Humpy tried to grab it, but The Hopper, frustrating the attempt, read his colleague a sharp lesson in good manners. He restored it to his pocket and glanced at the clock.

"We gotta do somethin' about Shaver's stockin's. Ut ain't fair fer a kid to wake up an' think Santy missed 'im. Ye got some candy, Mary; we kin put candy into 'em; that's reg'ler."

Humpy brought in Shaver's stockings and they were stuffed with the candy and popcorn Mary had provided to adorn their Christmas feast. Humpy inventoried his belongings, but could think of nothing but a revolver that seemed a suitable gift for Shaver. This Mary scornfully rejected as improper for one so young. Whereupon Humpy produced a Mexican silver dollar, a treasured pocket piece preserved through many tribulations, and dropped it reverently into one of the stockings. Two brass buttons of unknown history, a mouth-organ Mary had bought for a neighbor boy who assisted at times in the poultry yard, and a silver spectacle case of uncertain antecedents were added.

"We ought t' 'a' colored eggs fer 'im!" said The Hopper with sudden inspiration, after the stockings had been restored to Shaver's bed. "Some yaller an' pink eggs would 'a' been the right ticket."

Mary scoffed at the idea. Eggs wasn't proper fer Christmas; eggs was fer Easter. Humpy added the weight of his personal experience of Christian holidays to this statement. While a trusty in the Missouri penitentiary with the chicken yard in his keeping, he remembered distinctly that eggs were in demand for purposes of decoration by the warden's children sometime in the spring; mebbe it was Easter, mebbe it was Decoration Day; Humpy was not sure of anything except that it wasn't Christmas.

The Hopper was meek under correction. It having been settled that colored eggs would not be appropriate for Christmas he yielded to their demand that he show some enthusiasm for disposing of his ill-gotten treasures before the police arrived to take the matter out of his hands.

"I guess that Muriel'll be glad to see me," he remarked. "I guess me and her understands each other. They's things wot is an' things wot ain't; an' I guess Hop ain't goin' to spend no Chris'mas in jail. It's the white card an' poultry an' eggs fer us; an' we're goin' t' put in a couple more incubators right away. I'm thinkin' some o' rentin' that acre across th' brook back yonder an' raisin' turkeys. They's mints in turks, ef ye kin keep 'em from gettin' their feet wet an' dyin' o' pneumonia, which wipes out thousands o' them birds. I reckon ye might make some coffee, Mary."

The Christmas dawn found them at the table, where they were renewing a pledge to play "the white card" when a cry from Shaver brought them to their feet.

Shaver was highly pleased with his Christmas stockings, but his pleasure was nothing to that of The Hopper, Mary, and Humpy, as they stood about the bed and watched him. Mary and Humpy were so relieved by The Hopper's promises to lead a better life that they were now disposed to treat their guest with the most distinguished consideration. Humpy, absenting himself to perform his morning tasks in the poultry-houses, returned bringing a basket containing six newly hatched chicks. These cheeped and ran over Shaver's fat legs and performed exactly as though they knew they were a part of his Christmas entertainment. Humpy, proud of having thought of the chicks, demanded the privilege of serving Shaver's breakfast. Shaver ate his porridge without a murmur, so happy was he over his new playthings.

Mary bathed and dressed him with care. As the candy had stuck to the stockings in spots, it was decided after a family conference that Shaver would have to wear them wrong side out as there was no time to be wasted in washing them. By eight o'clock The Hopper announced that it was time for Shaver to go home. Shaver expressed alarm at the thought of leaving his chicks; whereupon Humpy conferred two of them upon him in the best imitation of baby talk that he could muster.

"Me's tate um to me's gwanpas," said Shaver; "chickee for me's two gwanpas,"—a remark which caused The Hopper to shake for a moment with mirth as he recalled his last view of Shaver's "gwanpas" in a death grip upon the floor of "Gwanpa" Talbot's house.

IX

WHEN THE HOPPER ROLLED AWAY from Happy Hill Farm in the stolen machine, accompanied by one stolen child and forty thousand dollars' worth of stolen pottery, Mary wept, whether because of the parting with Shaver, or because she feared that The Hopper would never return, was not clear.

Humpy, too, showed signs of tears, but concealed his weakness by performing a grotesque dance, dancing grotesquely by the side of the car, much to Shaver's joy—a joy enhanced just as the car reached the gate, where, as a farewell attention, Humpy fell down and rolled over and over in the snow.

The Hopper's wits were alert as he bore Shaver homeward. By this time it was likely that the confiding young Talbots had conferred over the telephone and knew that their offspring had disappeared. Doubtless the New Haven police had been notified, and he chose his route with discretion to avoid unpleasant encounters. Shaver, his spirits keyed to holiday pitch, babbled ceaselessly, and The Hopper, highly elated, babbled back at him.

They arrived presently at the rear of the young Talbots' premises, and The Hopper, with Shaver trotting at his side, advanced cautiously upon the house bearing the two baskets, one containing Shaver's chicks, the other the precious porcelains. In his survey of the landscape he noted with trepidation the presence of two big limousines in the highway in front of the cottage and decided that if possible he must see Muriel alone and make his report to her.

The moment he entered the kitchen he heard the clash of voices in angry dispute in the living room. Even Shaver was startled by the violence of the conversation in progress within, and clutched tightly a fold of The Hopper's trousers.

"I tell you it's John Wilton who has stolen Billie!" a man cried tempestuously. "Anybody who would enter a neighbor's house in the dead of night and try to rob him—rob him, yes, and *murder* him in the most brutal fashion—would not scruple to steal his own grandchild!"

"Me's gwanpa," whispered Shaver, gripping The Hopper's hand, "an' 'im's mad."

That Mr. Talbot was very angry indeed was established beyond cavil. However, Mr. Wilton was apparently quite capable of taking care of himself in the dispute.

"You talk about my stealing when you robbed me of my Lang-Yao—bribed my servants to plunder my safe! I want you to understand once for all, Roger Talbot, that if that jar isn't returned within one hour,—within one hour, sir,—I shall turn you over to the police!"

"Liar!" bellowed Talbot, who possessed a voice of great resonance. "You can't mitigate your foul crime by charging me with another! I never saw your jar; I never wanted it! I wouldn't have the thing on my place!"

Muriel's voice, full of tears, was lifted in expostulation.

"How can you talk of your silly vases when Billie's lost! Billie's been stolen—and you two men can think of nothing but pot-ter-ree!"

Shaver lifted a startled face to The Hopper.

"Mamma's cwyin'; gwanpa's hurted mamma!"

The strategic moment had arrived when Shaver must be thrust forward as an interruption to the exchange of disagreeable epithets by his grandfathers.

"You trot right in there t' yer ma, Shaver. Ole Hop ain't goin' t' let 'em hurt ye!"

He led the child through the dining room to the living room door and pushed him gently on the scene of strife. Talbot, senior, was pacing the floor with angry strides, declaiming upon his wrongs,—indeed, his theme might have been the misery of the whole human race from the vigor of his lamentations. His son was keeping step with him, vainly attempting to persuade him to sit down. Wilton, with a patch over his right eye, was trying to disengage himself from his daughter's arms with the obvious intention of doing violence to his neighbor.

"I'm sure papa never meant to hurt you; it was all a dreadful mistake," she moaned.

"He had an accomplice," Talbot thundered, "and while he was trying to kill me there in my own house the plum blossom vase was carried off; and if Roger hadn't pushed him out of the window after his hireling—I'd—I'd—"

A shriek from Muriel happily prevented the completion of a sentence that gave every promise of intensifying the prevailing hard feeling.

"Look!" Muriel cried. "It's Billie come back! Oh, Billie!"

She sprang toward the door and clasped the frightened child to her heart. The three men gathered round them, staring dully. The Hopper from behind the door waited for Muriel's joy over Billie's return to communicate itself to his father and the two grandfathers.

"Me's dot two chick-ees for Kwismus," announced Billie, wriggling in his mother's arms.

Muriel, having satisfied herself that Billie was intact,—that he even bore the marks of maternal care,—was in the act of transferring him to his bewildered father, when, turning a tear-stained face toward the door, she saw The Hopper awkwardly twisting the derby which he had donned as proper for a morning call of ceremony. She walked toward him with quick, eager step.

"You—you came back!" she faltered, stifling a sob.

"Yes'm," responded The Hopper, rubbing his hand across his nose. His appearance roused Billie's father to a sense of his parental responsibility.

"You brought the boy back! You are the kidnaper!"

"Roger," cried Muriel protestingly, "don't speak like that! I'm sure this gentleman can explain how he came to bring Billie."

The quickness with which she regained her composure, the ease with which she adjusted herself to the unforeseen situation, pleased The Hopper greatly. He had not misjudged Muriel; she was an admirable ally, an ideal confederate. She gave him a quick little nod, as much as to say, "Go on, sir; we understand each other perfectly,"—though, of course, she did not understand, nor was she enlightened until sometime later, as to just how The Hopper became possessed of Billie.

Billie's father declared his purpose to invoke the law upon his son's kidnapers no matter where they might be found.

"I reckon as mebbe ut wuz a kidnapin' an' I reckon as mebbe ut wuzn't," The Hopper began unhurriedly. "I live over Shell Road way; poultry and eggs is my line; Happy Hill Farm. Stevens's the name—Charles S. Stevens. An' I found Shaver—'scuse me, but ut seemed sort o' nat'ral name fer 'im?—I found 'im a settin' up in th' machine over there by my place, chipper's ye please. I takes 'im into my house an' Mary'—that's th' missus—she gives 'im supper and puts 'im t' sleep. An' we thinks mebbe somebody'd come along askin' fer 'im. An' then this mornin' I calls th' New Haven police, an' they tole me about you folks, an' me and Shaver comes right over."

This was entirely plausible and his hearers, The Hopper noted with relief, accepted it at face value.

"How dear of you!" cried Muriel. "Won't you have this chair, Mr. Stevens!"

"Most remarkable!" exclaimed Wilton. "Some scoundrelly tramp picked up the car and finding there was a baby inside left it at the roadside like the brute he was!"

Billie had addressed himself promptly to the Christmas tree, to his very own Christmas tree that was laden with gifts that had been assembled by the family for his delectation. Efforts of Grandfather Wilton to extract from the child some account of the man who had run away with him were unavailing. Billie was busy, very busy, indeed. After much patient effort he stopped sorting the animals in a bright new Noah's Ark to point his finger at The Hopper and remark:—

"'Ims nice mans; 'ims let Bil-lee play wif 'ims watch!"

As Billie had broken the watch his acknowledgment of The Hopper's courtesy in letting him play with it brought a grin to The Hopper's face.

Now that Billie had been returned and his absence satisfactorily accounted for, the two connoisseurs showed signs of renewing their quarrel. Responsive to a demand from Billie, The Hopper got down on the floor to assist in the proper mating of Noah's animals. Billie's father was scrutinizing him fixedly and The Hopper wondered whether Muriel's handsome young husband had recognized him as the person who had vanished through the window of the Talbot home bearing the plum blossom vase. The thought was disquieting; but feigning deep interest in the Ark he listened attentively to a violent tirade upon which the senior Talbot was launched.

"My God!" he cried bitterly, planting himself before Wilton in a belligerent attitude, "every infernal thing that can happen to a man happened to me yesterday. It wasn't enough that you robbed me and tried to murder me—yes, you did, sir!—But when I was in the city I was robbed in the subway by a pickpocket. A thief took my bill book containing invaluable data I had just received from my agent in China giving me a clue to porcelains, sir, such as you never dreamed of! Some more of your work—Don't you contradict me! You don't contradict me! Roger, he doesn't contradict me!"

Wilton, choking with indignation at this new onslaught, was unable to contradict him.

Pained by the situation, The Hopper rose from the floor and coughed timidly.

"Shaver, go fetch yer chickies. Bring yer chickies in an' put 'em on th' boat."

Billie obediently trotted off toward the kitchen and The Hopper turned his back upon the Christmas tree, drew out the pocket book and faced the company.

"I beg yer pardon, gents, but mebbe this is th' book yer fightin' about. Kind o' funny like! I picked ut up on th' local yistiddy afternoon. I wuz goin' t' turn ut int' th' agint, but I clean fergot ut. I guess them papers may be valible. I never touched none of 'em."

Talbot snatched the bill book and hastily examined the contents. His brow relaxed and he was grumbling something about a reward when Billie reappeared, laboriously dragging two baskets.

"Bil-lee's dot chick-*ees*! Bil-lee's dot pitty dishes. Bil-lee make dishes go 'ippity!"

Before he could make the two jars go 'ippity, The Hopper leaped across the room and seized the basket. He tore off the towel with which he had carefully covered the stolen pottery and disclosed the contents for inspection.

"'Scuse me, gents; no crowdin'," he warned as the connoisseurs sprang toward him. He placed the porcelains carefully on the floor under the Christmas tree. "Now ye kin listen t' me, gents. I reckon I'm goin' t' have somethin' t' say about this here crockery. I stole 'em—I stole 'em fer th' lady there, she thinkin' ef ye didn't have 'em no more ye'd stop rowin' about 'em. Ye kin call th' bulls an' turn me over ef ye likes; but I ain't goin' t' have ye fussin' an' causin' th' lady trouble no more. I ain't goin' to stand fer ut!"

"Robber!" shouted Talbot. "You entered my house at the instance of this man; it was you—"

"I never saw the gent before," declared The Hopper hotly. "I ain't never had no thin' to do with neither o' ye."

"He's telling the truth!" protested Muriel, laughing hysterically. "I did it—I got him to take them!"

The two collectors were not interested in explanations; they were hungrily eyeing their property. Wilton attempted to pass The Hopper and reach the Christmas tree under whose protecting boughs the two vases were looking their loveliest.

"Stand back," commanded The Hopper, "an' stop callin' names! I guess ef I'm yanked fer this I ain't th' only one that's goin' t' do time fer house breakin'."

This statement, made with considerable vigor, had a sobering effect upon Wilton, but Talbot began dancing round the tree looking for a chance to pounce upon the porcelains.

"Ef ye don't set down—the whole caboodle o' ye—I'll smash 'em—I'll smash 'em both! I'll bust 'em—sure as shootin'!" shouted The Hopper.

They cowered before him; Muriel wept softly; Billie played with his chickies, disdainful of the world's woe. The Hopper, holding the two angry men at bay, was enjoying his command of the situation.

"You gents ain't got no business to be fussin' an' causin' yer childern trouble. An' ye ain't goin' to have these pretty jugs to fuss about no more. I'm goin' t' give 'em away; I'm goin' to make a Chris'mas present of 'em to Shaver. They're goin' to be little Shaver's right here, all orderly an' peace'ble, or I'll tromp on 'em! Looky here, Shaver, wot Santy Claus brought ye!"

"Nice dood Sant' Claus!" cried Billie, diving under the davenport in quest of the wandering chicks.

Silence held the grown ups. The Hopper stood patiently by the Christmas tree, awaiting the result of his diplomacy.

Then suddenly Wilton laughed—a loud laugh expressive of relief. He turned to Talbot and put out his hand.

"It looks as though Muriel and her friend here had cornered us! The idea of pooling our trophies and giving them as a Christmas present to Billie appeals to me strongly. And, besides we've got to prepare somebody to love these things after we're gone. We can work together and train Billie to be the greatest collector in America!"

"Please, father," urged Roger as Talbot frowned and shook his head impatiently.

Billie, struck with the happy thought of hanging one of his chickies on the Christmas tree, caused them all to laugh at this moment. It was difficult to refuse to be generous on Christmas morning in the presence of the happy child!

"Well," said Talbot, a reluctant smile crossing his face, "I guess it's all in the family anyway."

The Hopper, feeling that his work as the Reversible Santa Claus was finished, was rapidly retreating through the dining room when Muriel and Roger ran after him.

"We're going to take you home," cried Muriel, beaming.

"Yer car's at the back gate, all right-side-up," said The Hopper, "but I kin go on the trolley."

"Indeed you won't! Roger will take you home. Oh, don't be alarmed! My husband knows everything about our conspiracy. And we want you to come back this afternoon. You know I owe you an apology for thinking—for thinking you were—you were—a—"

"They's things wot is an' things wot ain't, miss. Circumstantial evidence sends lots o' men to th' chair. Ut's a heap more happy like," The

Hopper continued in his best philosophical vein, "t' play th' white card, helpin' widders an' orfants an' settlin' fusses. When ye ast me t' steal them jugs I hadn't th' heart t' refuse ye, miss. I wuz scared to tell ye I had yer baby an' ye seemed so sort o' trustin' like. An' ut bein' Chris'mus an' all."

When he steadfastly refused to promise to return, Muriel announced that they would visit The Hopper late in the afternoon and bring Billie along to express their thanks more formally.

"I'll be glad to see ye," replied The Hopper, though a little doubtfully and shame-facedly. "But ye mustn't git me into no more house-breakin' scrapes," he added with a grin. "It's mighty dangerous, miss, fer amachures, like me an' yer pa!"

X

MARY WAS NOT WHOLLY PLEASED at the prospect of visitors, but she fell to work with Humpy to put the house in order. At five o'clock not one, but three automobiles drove into the yard, filling Humpy with alarm lest at last The Hopper's sins had overtaken him, and they were all about to be hauled away to spend the rest of their lives in prison. It was not the police, but the young Talbots, with Billie and his grandfathers, on their way to a family celebration at the house of an aunt of Muriel's.

The grandfathers were restored to perfect amity, and were deeply curious now about The Hopper, whom the peace-loving Muriel had cajoled into robbing their houses.

"And you're only an honest chicken farmer, after all!" exclaimed Talbot, senior, when they were all sitting in a semicircle about the fireplace in Mary's parlor. "I hoped you were really a burglar; I always wanted to know a burglar."

Humpy had chopped down a small fir that had adorned the front yard and had set it up as a Christmas tree—an attention that was not lost upon Billie. The Hopper had brought some mechanical toys from town, and Humpy essayed the agreeable task of teaching the youngster how to operate them. Mary produced coffee and pound cake for the guests; The Hopper assumed the role of lord of the manor with a benevolent air that was intended as much to impress Mary and Humpy as the guests.

"Of course," said Mr. Wilton, whose appearance was the least bit comical by reason of his bandaged head,—"of course it was very foolish for a man of your sterling character to allow a young woman like my daughter to bully you into robbing houses for her. Why, when Roger fired at you as you were jumping out of the window, he didn't miss you more than a foot! It would have been ghastly for all of us if he had killed you!"

"Well, o' course it all begun from my goin' into th' little house lookin' fer Shaver's folks," replied The Hopper.

"But you haven't told us how you came to find our house," said Roger, suggesting a perfectly natural line of inquiries that caused Humpy to become deeply preoccupied with a pump he was operating in a basin of water for Billie's benefit.

"Well, ut jes' looked like a house that Shaver would belong to, cute an' comfortable like," said The Hopper; "I jes' suspicioned it wuz th' place as I wuz passin' along."

"I don't think we'd better begin trying to establish alibis," remarked Muriel, very gently, "for we might get into terrible scrapes. Why, if Mr. Stevens hadn't been so splendid about *everything* and wasn't just the kindest man in the world, he could make it very ugly for me."

"I shudder to think of what he might do to me," said Wilton, glancing guardedly at his neighbor.

"The main thing," said Talbot,—"the main thing is that Mr. Stevens has done for us all what nobody else could ever have done. He's made us see how foolish it is to quarrel about mere baubles. He's settled all our troubles for us, and for my part I'll say his solution is entirely satisfactory."

"Quite right," exclaimed Wilton. "If I ever have any delicate business negotiations that are beyond my powers I'm going to engage Mr. Stevens to handle them."

"My business's hens an' eggs," said The Hopper modestly; "an' we're doin' purty well."

When they rose to go (a move that evoked strident protests from Billie, who was enjoying himself hugely with Humpy) they were all in the jolliest humor.

"We must be neighborly," said Muriel, shaking hands with Mary, who was at the point of tears so great was her emotion at the success of The Hopper's party. "And we're going to buy all our chickens and eggs from you. We never have any luck raising our own."

Whereupon The Hopper imperturbably pressed upon each of the visitors a neat card stating his name (his latest and let us hope his last!) with the proper rural route designation of Happy Hill Farm.

The Hopper carried Billie out to his Grandfather Wilton's car, while Humpy walked beside him bearing the gifts from the Happy Hill

Farm Christmas tree. From the door Mary watched them depart amid a chorus of merry Christmases, out of which Billie's little pipe rang cheerily.

When The Hopper and Humpy returned to the house, they abandoned the parlor for the greater coziness of the kitchen and there took account of the events of the momentous twenty-four hours.

"Them's what I call nice folks," said Humpy. "They jes' put us on an' wore us like we wuz a pair o' ole slippers."

"They wuzn't uppish—not to speak of," Mary agreed. "I guess that girl's got more gumption than any of 'em. She's got 'em straightened up now and I guess she'll take care they don't cut up no more monkey-shines about that Chinese stuff. Her husban' seemed sort o' gentle like."

"Artists is that way," volunteered The Hopper, as though from deep experience of art and life. "I jes' been thinkin' that knowin' folks like that an' findin' 'em humin, makin' mistakes like th' rest of us, kind o' makes ut seem easier fer us all t' play th' game straight. Ut's goin' to be th' white card fer me—jes' chickens an' eggs, an' here's hopin' the bulls don't ever find out we're settled here."

Humpy, having gone into the parlor to tend the fire, returned with two envelopes he had found on the mantel. There was a check for a thousand dollars in each, one from Wilton, the other from Talbot, with "Merry Christmas" written across the visiting cards of those gentlemen. The Hopper permitted Mary and Humpy to examine them and then laid them on the kitchen table, while he deliberated. His meditations were so prolonged that they grew nervous.

"I reckon they could spare ut, after all ye done fer 'em, Hop," remarked Humpy.

"They's millionaires, an' money ain't nothin' to 'em," said The Hopper.

"We can buy a motor truck," suggested Mary, "to haul our stuff to town; an' mebbe we can build a new shed to keep ut in."

The Hopper set the catsup bottle on the checks and rubbed his cheek, squinting at the ceiling in the manner of one who means to be careful of his speech.

"They's things wot is an' things wot ain't," he began. "We ain't none o' us ever got nowheres bein' crooked. I been figurin' that I still got about twenty thousan' o' that bunch o' green I pulled out o' that express car, planted in places where 'taint doin' nobody no good. I guess ef I do ut careful I kin send ut back to the company, a little at a time, an' they'd never know where ut come from."

Mary wept; Humpy stared, his mouth open, his one eye rolling queerly.

"I guess we kin put a little chunk away every year," The Hopper went on. "We'd be comfortabler doin' ut. We could square up ef we lived long enough, which we don't need t' worry about, that bein' the Lord's business. You an' me's cracked a good many safes, Hump, but we never made no money at ut, takin' out th' time we done."

"He's got religion; that's wot he's got!" moaned Humpy, as though this marked the ultimate tragedy of The Hopper's life.

"Mebbe ut's religion an' mebbe ut's jes' sense," pursued The Hopper, unshaken by Humpy's charge. "They wuz a chaplin in th' Minnesoty pen as used t' say ef we're all square with our own selves ut's goin' to be all right with God. I guess I got a good deal o' squarin' t' do, but I'm goin' t' begin ut. An' all these things happenin' along o' Chris'mus, an' little Shaver an' his ma bein' so friendly like, an' her gittin' me t' help straighten out them ole gents, an' doin' all I done an' not gettin' pinched seems more 'n jes' luck; it's providential's wot ut is!"

This, uttered in a challenging tone, evoked a sob from Humpy, who announced that he "felt like" he was going to die.

"It's th' Chris'mus time, I reckon," said Mary, watching The Hopper deposit the two checks in the clock. "It's the only decent Chris'mus I ever knowed!"

THE END

TOMMY TROT'S VISIT TO SANTA CLAUS

I

THE LITTLE BOY WHOSE STORY is told here lived in the beautiful country of "Once upon a Time." His name, as I heard it, was Tommy Trot; but I think that, maybe, this was only a nickname. When he was about your age, he had, on Christmas Eve, the wonderful adventure of seeing Santa Claus in his own country, where he lives and makes all the beautiful things that boys and girls get at Christmas. In fact, he not only went to see him in his own wonderful city away up toward the North Pole, where the snow never melts and the Aurora lightens up the sky; but he and his friend, Johnny Stout, went with dogs and guns to hunt the great polar bear whose skin afterwards always lay in front of the big library fireplace in Tommy's home.

This is the way it all happened.

Tommy lived in a big house on top of quite a high hill, not far from a town which could be seen clearly from the front portico and windows. Around the house was a large lawn with trees and shrubbery in it, and at the back was a big lot, in one corner of which stood the stables and barns, while on the other side sloped down a long steep hill to a little stream bordered with willows and maples and with a tract of woodland beyond. This lot was known as the "cow pasture," and the woodland was known as the "wood-lot," while yet beyond was a field which Peake, the farmer, always spoke of as the "big field." On the other side of the cow-lot, where the stables stood, was a road which ran down the hill and across the stream and beyond the woods, and on the other side of this road near the bottom of the hill was the little house in which lived Johnny Stout and his mother. They had no fields or lots, but only a backyard in which there were chickens and pigeons and, in the Fall, just before Tommy's visit to Santa Claus, two white goats, named "Billy" and "Carry," which Johnny had broken and used to drive to a little rough wagon which he had made himself out of a box set on four wheels.

Tommy had no brothers or sisters, and the only cousins he had in town were little girls younger than himself, to whom he had to "give up" when anyone was around, so he was not as fond of them as he should have been; and Sate, his dog, a terrier of temper and humours, was about his only real playmate. He used to play by himself and he was often very lonely, though he had more toys than any other boy he knew. In fact, he had so many toys that he was unable to enjoy any one of them very long, and after having them a little while he usually broke them up. He used to enjoy the stories which his father read to him out of Mother Goose and the fairy books and the tales he told him of travellers and hunters who had shot lions and bears and Bengal tigers; but when he grew tired of this, he often wished he could go out in the street and play all the time like Johnny Stout and some of the other boys. Several times he slipped out into the road beyond the cow-lot to try to get a chance to play with Johnny who was only about a year older than he, but could do so many things which Tommy could not do that he quite envied him. It was one of the proudest days of his life when Johnny let him come over and drive his goats, and when he went home that evening, although he was quite cold, he was so full of having driven them that he could not think or talk of anything else, and when Christmas drew near, one of the first things he wrote to ask Santa Claus for, when he put the letter in the library fire, was a wagon and a pair of goats. Even his father's statement that he feared he was too small yet for Santa Claus to bring him such things, did not wholly dampen his hope.

He even began to dream of being able to go out sometime and join the bigger boys in coasting down the long hill on the other side from Johnny Stout's, for though his father and mother thought he was still rather small to do this, his father had promised that he might do it sometime, and Tommy thought "sometime" would be after his next birthday. When the heavy snow fell just before Christmas he began to be sorry that he had broken up the sled Santa Claus had given him the Christmas before. In fact, Tommy had never wanted a sled so much as he did the afternoon two days before Christmas, when he persuaded his father to take him out again to the coasting hill to see the boys coasting. There were all sorts of sleds: short sleds and long sleds, bob sleds and flexible fliers. They held one, two, three, and sometimes even half a dozen boys and girls—for there were girls, too—all shouting and laughing as they went flying down the hill, some sitting and some lying down, but all flying and shouting, and none taking the least notice of Tommy. Sate made them take notice of him; for he would rush out after the sleds, barking just as if they had been cats, and several times he got bowled over—once, indeed, he got tangled up in the string of a sled and was dragged squealing with fright down the hill. Suddenly, however, Tommy gave a jump. Among the sleds flying by, most of them painted red, and very fine looking, was a plain, unpainted one, and lying full length upon it, on his stomach, with his heels high in the air, was Johnny Stout, with a red comforter around his neck, and a big cap pulled down over his ears. Tommy knew him at once.

"Look, father, look!" he cried, pointing; but Johnny's sled was far down the hill before his father could see him. A few minutes later he came trudging up the hill again and, seeing Tommy, ran across and asked him if he would like to have a ride. Tommy's heart bounded, but sank within him again when his father said, "I am afraid he is rather little."

"Oh! I'll take care of him, sir," said Johnny, whose cheeks were glowing. Tommy began to jump up and down.

"Please, father, please," he urged. His father only smiled.

"Why, you are not so very big yourself," he said to Johnny.

"Big enough to take care of him," said Johnny.

"Why, father, he's awful big," chimed in Tommy.

"Do you think so?" laughed his father. He turned to Johnny. "What is your name?"

"Johnny, sir. I live down below your house." He pointed across toward his own home.

"I know him," said Tommy proudly. "He has got goats and he let me drive them."

"Yes, he can drive," said Johnny, condescendingly, with a nod, and Tommy was proud of his praise. His father looked at him.

"Is your sled strong?" he asked.

"Yes, sir. I made it myself," said Johnny, and he gave the sled a good kick to show how strong it was.

"All right," said Tommy's father. They followed Johnny to the top of the slide, and Tommy got on in front and his father tucked his coat in.

"Hold on and don't be afraid," he said.

"Afraid!" said Tommy contemptuously. Just then Johnny, with a whoop and a push which almost upset Tommy, flung himself on behind and away they went down the hill, as Johnny said, "just ski-uting."

Tommy had had sledding in his own yard; but he had never before had any real coasting like this, and he had never dreamed before of anything like the thrill of dashing down that long hill, flying like the wind, with Johnny on behind, yelling "Look out!" to everyone, and guiding so that the sled tore in and out among the others, and at the foot of the hill actually turned around the curve and went far on down the road.

"You're all right," said Johnny, and Tommy had never felt prouder. His only regret was that the hill did not tilt up the other way so that they could coast back instead of having to trudge back on foot.

When they got back again to the top of the hill, Tommy's father wanted to know if they had had enough, but Tommy told him he never could have enough. So they coasted down again and again, until at length his father thought they had better be going home, and Johnny said he had to go home, too, "to help his mother."

"How do you help?" asked Tommy's father, as they started off.

"Oh, just little ways," said Johnny. "I get wood—and split it up—and go to Mr. Bucket's and get her things for her—draw water and feed the cow, when we had a cow—we ain't got a cow now since our cow died—and—oh—just a few little things like that."

Tommy's father made no reply, and Tommy, himself, was divided between wonder that Johnny could call all that work "just a few little things," and shame that he should say, "ain't got," which he, himself, had been told he must never say.

His father, however, presently asked, "Who is Mr. Bucket?"

"Don't you know Mr. Bucket?" said Johnny. "He keeps that grocery on Hill Street. He gave me the box I made this old thing out of."

"Oh," said Tommy's father, and turned and looked the sled over again.

"What was the matter with your cow?" asked Tommy.

"Broke her leg—right here," and Johnny pulled up his trousers and showed just where the leg was broken below the knee. "The doctor said she must be killed, and so she was; but Mr. Bucket said he could have saved her if the 'Siety would've let him. He'd 'a just swung her up until she got well."

"How?" asked Tommy, much interested.

"What Society?" asked his father.

Johnny answered the last question first. "'Pervention of Cruelty,'" he said, shortly.

"Oh," said Tommy's father.

"I know how she broke her leg," said Johnny.

"How did she break her leg?" inquired Tommy.

"A boy done it. I know him and I know he done it, and someday I'm going to catch him when he ain't looking for me."

"You have not had a cow since?" inquired Tommy's father. "Then you do not have to go and drive her up and milk her when the weather is cold?"

"Oh, I would not mind that," said Johnny cheerily. "I'd drive her up if the weather was as cold as Greenland, and milk her, too, so I had her. I used to love to feed her and I didn't mind carryin' milk around; for I used to get money for it for my mother to buy things with; but now, since that boy broke her leg and the 'Siety killed her——"

He did not say what there was since; he just stopped talking and presently Tommy's father said: "You do not have so much money since?"

"No, sir!" said Johnny, "and my mother has to work a heap harder, you see."

"And you work too?"

"Some," said Johnny. "I sell papers and clean off the sidewalk when there is snow to clean off, and run errands for Mr. Bucket and do a few things. Well, I've got to go along," he added, "I've got some things to do now. I was just trying this old sled over on the hill to see how she would go. I've got some work to do now"; and he trotted off, whistling and dragging his sled behind him.

As Tommy and his father turned into their grounds, his father asked, "Where did he say he lived?"

"Wait, I'll show you," said Tommy, proud of his knowledge. "Down there," (pointing). "See that little house down in the bottom, away over beyond the cow pasture?"

"How do you know he lives there?"

"Because I've been there. He's got goats," said Tommy, "and he let me drive them. I wish I had some goats. I wish Santa Claus would bring me two goats like Johnny's."

"Which would you rather have? Goats or a cow?" asked his father.

"Goats," said Tommy, promptly.

"I wonder if Johnny would!" laughed his father.

"Father, where is Greenland?" said Tommy, presently.

"A country away up at the North—away up in that direction." His father pointed far across the cow pasture, which lay shining in the evening light. "I must show it to you on the map."

"Is it very cold there?" asked Tommy.

"Very cold in winter."

"Colder than this?"

"Oh, yes, because it is so far north that the sun never gets up in winter to warm it, and away up there the winter is just one long night and the summer one long day."

"Why, that's where Santa Claus comes from," said Tommy. "Do people live up there?"

"People called Eskimos," said his father, "who live by fishing and hunting."

"Tell me about them," said Tommy. "What do they hunt?"

"Bears," said his father, "polar bears—and walrus—and seals—and——"

"Oh, tell me about them," said Tommy, eagerly.

So, as they walked along, his father told him of the strange little, flat-faced people, who live all winter in houses made of ice and snow and hunted on the ice-floes for polar bears and seals and walrus, and in the summer got in their little kiaks and paddled around, hunting for seals and walrus with their arrows and harpoons, on the "pans" or smooth ice, where every family of "harps" or seals have their own private door, gnawed down through the ice with their teeth.

"I wish I could go there," said Tommy, his eyes gazing across the long, white glistening fields with the dark border of the woodland beyond and the rich saffron of the winter sky above the tree-tops stretching across in a border below the steelly white of the upper heavens.

"What would you do?" asked his father.

"Hunt polar bears," said Tommy promptly. "I'd get one most as big as the library, so mother could give you the skin; because I heard her say she would like to have one in front of the library fire, and the only way she could get one would be to give it to you for Christmas."

His father laughed. "All right, get a big one."

"You will have to give me a gun. A real gun that will shoot. A big one—so big." Tommy measured with his arms out straight. "Bigger than that. And I tell you what I would do. I would get Johnny and we would hitch his goats to the sled and drive all the way up there and hunt polar bears, and I'd hunt for sealskins, too, so you could give mother a coat. I heard her say she wanted you to give her one. Wouldn't it be fine if I could get a great big bearskin and a sealskin, too! I wish I had Johnny's goats!"

"You must have dogs up there to draw your sled," said his father.

"All right! After I got there I would get Santa Claus to give me some," said Tommy. "But you give me the gun."

His father laughed again. "Well, maybe—someday," said he.

"'Someday' is too far away," said Tommy. "I want to go now."

"Not so far away when you are my age," said his father smiling. "Ah, there is where the North Star is," he said, pointing. "You cannot see it yet. I will show it to you later, so you can steer by it."

"That is the way Santa Claus comes," said Tommy, his eyes on the Northern sky. "I am going to wait for him tomorrow night."

"You know he does not bring things to boys who keep awake!"

"I know; but I won't let him see me."

As they trudged along Tommy suddenly asked, "Don't you wish, Father, Santa Claus would bring Johnny a cow for his mother?"

"Why, yes," said his father.

"Like Cowslip or Rose or even old Crumpled Horn?"

"Like our cows!" echoed his father, absently. "Why, yes."

"Because they are all fine cows, you know. Peake says so, and Peake knows a good cow," said Tommy, proud of his intimacy with the farmer. "I tell you what I am going to do when I get home," he declared. "I am going to write another letter to Santa Claus and put it in the chimney and ask him to send Johnny a whole lot of things: a cow and a gun and all sorts of things. Do you think it's too late for him to get it now?"

"I don't know. It is pretty late," said his father. "Why didn't you ask him to send these things to Johnny when you wrote your other letter?"

"I did not think of it," said Tommy, frankly. "I forgot him."

"Do you ask only for yourself?"

"No. For little Sis and Mother and Peake and one other, but I'm not going to tell you who he is."

His father smiled. "Not Johnny?"

"No," said Tommy. "I forgot him."

"I am afraid I did, too," said his father slowly. "Well, write another and try. You can never tell. Trying is better than crying."

This was two days before Christmas. And the next afternoon Tommy went again with his father to the coasting-hill to see the boys and once more take a coast with Johnny. But no Johnny was there and no other boy asked Tommy if he wanted a ride. So, they returned home much disappointed, his father telling him more about the Eskimos and the polar bears. But, just as they were turning the corner before reaching the gate which led into their grounds, they came on Johnny struggling along through the snow, under the weight of a big basket full of bundles. At sight of them he swung the basket down in the snow with a loud, "Whew, that's heavy! I tell you." Tommy ran forward to meet him.

"We have been looking for you," he said.

"I could not go today," explained Johnny. "I had to work. I am working for Mr. Bucket today to make some money to buy Christmas things."

"How much do you make?" asked Tommy's father.

"Half a dollar today, if I work late. I generally make ten cents, sometimes fifteen."

"That is a pretty heavy load—in the snow," said Tommy's father, as Johnny stooped and swung his basket up on his hip.

"Oh, I can manage it," said the boy, cheerfully. "A boy stole my sled last night, or I would carry it on that."

"Stole your sled!" cried Tommy.

"Yes, I left it outside the door when I was getting my load to put on, and when I came out it was gone. I wish I could catch him."

"I am going to watch for him, too," said Tommy.

"If I had a box I could make another one," said Johnny. "Maybe, Mr. Bucket will give me one after Christmas. He said maybe he would. Then I will give you another ride." He called over his shoulder to them, as he trudged off, "Well, goodbye. I hope you will have a merry Christmas, and that Santa Claus will bring you lots of things," and away he trudged. They wished him a merry Christmas, too, and then turned into their grounds.

"Father," said Tommy, suddenly, "let's give Johnny a sled."

"Yes," said his father, "you might give him yours—the one you got last Christmas."

"I haven't got it now. It's gone," said Tommy.

"Did someone take it—like Johnny's?"

"No, I broke it," said Tommy, crestfallen.

"You might mend it?" suggested his father.

"I broke it all up," said Tommy, sadly.

"Ah, that is a pity," said his father.

Tommy was still thinking.

"Father, why can't I give him a box?" he said. "The basement and the woodshed are full of big boxes."

"Why not give him the one I gave you a few days ago?"

"I broke it up, too," said Tommy shamefacedly.

"Oh," said his father. "That's a pity. Johnny could have made a sled out of it." Tommy felt very troubled, and he began to think what he might do.

"If you will give me another, I will give it to Johnny," he said presently.

"Why, I'll tell you what I will do," said his father. "I will furnish the box if you will carry it over to Johnny's home."

"All right. I will do it," said Tommy promptly. So as soon as they reached home Tommy dived down into the basement and soon came out, puffing and blowing, dragging along with him a big box as high as his head.

"I am afraid that is too big for you to carry," suggested his father.

"Oh, I will make Richard carry it."

"Richard is my servant, not yours," said his father. "Besides, you were to carry it yourself."

"It is too big for me. The snow is too deep."

"Now, if you had not broken up your sled you might carry it on that," said his father.

"Yes," said Tommy sadly. "I wish I had not broken it up. I'll be bound that I don't break up the next one I get."

"That's a good beginning," said his father. "But wishing alone will never do anything, not even if you had the magical wishing-cap I read you about. You must not only wish; you must help yourself. Now, Johnny would make a sled out of that box."

"I wish I could," said Tommy. "I would try if I had some tools. I wish I had some tools."

"What tools would you need?"

Tommy thought a minute. "Why, a hammer and some nails."

"A hammer and nails would hardly make a sled by themselves."

"Why, no. I wish I had a saw, too."

"I thought Santa Claus brought you all these tools last Christmas?" suggested his father.

"He did; but I lost them," said Tommy.

"Did you ever hunt for them?"

"Some. I have hunted for the hammer."

"Well, suppose you hunt again. Look everywhere. If you find any I might lend you the others. You might look in my lumber room." Tommy ran off and soon returned with a hammer and some nails which he had found, and a few minutes later his father brought a saw and a hatchet, and they selected a good box, which Tommy could drag out, and put it in the back hall.

"Now," said Tommy, "what shall we do next?"

"That is for you to say," said his father. "Johnny does not ask that question. He thinks for himself."

"Well, we must knock this box to pieces," said Tommy.

"I think so, too," assented his father. "Very carefully, so as not to split the boards."

"Yes, very carefully," said Tommy, and he began to hammer. The nails, however, were in very tight and there was a strip of iron along each of the edges, through which they were driven, so it was hard work; but when Tommy really tried and could not get the boards off, his father helped him, and soon the strips were off and the boards quickly followed.

"Now what shall we do?" asked his father.

"Why, we must make the sled."

"Yes—but how?"

"Why, we must have runners and then the top to sit on. That's all."

"Very well. Go ahead," said his father. So Tommy picked up two boards and looked at them. But they were square at the ends.

"We must make the runners," he said sadly.

"That's so," said his father.

"Will you saw them for me?" asked Tommy.

"Yes, if you will show me where to saw." Tommy pondered.

"Wait," he said, and he ran off, and in a moment came back with a picture of a sled in a magazine. "Now make it this way," he said, showing his father how he should saw the edges.

He was surprised to see how well his father could do this, and his admiration for him increased as he found that he could handle the tools quite as well as Peake, the farmer; and soon the sled began to look like a real sled with runners, sawed true, and with cross pieces for the feet to rest on, and even with a strip of iron, taken from the edges of the boxes, carefully nailed on the bottom of the runners.

Suddenly Tommy cried, "Father, why not give Johnny this sled?"

"The very thing!" exclaimed his father with a smile. And Tommy felt quite proud of having suggested it.

"I wish it had a place to hitch on the goats," said Tommy, thoughtfully.

"Let's make one," said his father; and in a few minutes two holes were bored in the front of the runners.

It was now about dusk, and Tommy said he would like to take the sled down to Johnny's house and leave it at his door where he could find it when he came home from work, and, maybe, he might think Santa Claus had brought it. So he and his father went together, Tommy dragging the sled and, while his father waited at the gate, Tommy took the sled and put it in the yard at the little side door of Johnny's home. As they were going along, he said, pointing to a small shed-like out-building at the end of the little yard, "That's the cow house. He keeps his goats there, too. Don't you wish Santa Claus would bring his mother a cow? I don't see how he could get down that small chimney!" he said, gazing at the little flue which came out of the roof. "I wonder if he does?"

"I wonder if he does?" said his father to himself.

When Tommy slipped back again and found his father waiting for him at the gate, he thought he had never had so fine a time in all his life. He determined to make a sled for somebody every Christmas.

II

When they reached home Tommy, after warming his hands and telling his mother about the sled, set to work to write a letter to Santa Claus on behalf of Johnny, and as he wrote, a number of things came to him that he thought Johnny would like to have. He remembered that he had no gloves and that his hands were very red; that his cap was very old and too small for him; that a real flexible flier would be a fine thing for him. Then, as he had asked for a gun for himself to hunt polar bears with and a fur coat to go out with in the snow, he added these in Johnny's letter also; in fact, he asked for Johnny just the things he had asked for himself, except the goats, and, as Johnny had two goats, it was not necessary to ask for them for him. Instead of goats, however, he asked that Santa Claus might give Johnny's mother a cow, as good as one of their cows. As he was not a very rapid writer it took him some time to write this letter, especially, as he did not know how to spell a good many words, and had to ask his mother how to spell them, for his father had gone out soon after their return from taking the sled to Johnny, and immediately after showing him the picture of the polar bear and the map of the North Pole region. Then when the letter was all done, signed and sealed, Tommy carefully dropped it in the fire in the library, and watched it as it first twisted up, then burst into a blaze, and finally disappeared in flame and smoke up the big chimney, hoping that it would blow away like the wind to Santa Claus to catch him before he started out that night on his round of visits.

By this time his supper was ready and he found that he was very hungry. He had no sooner finished it than he drew up in a big chair by the warm fire, and began to wonder whether Santa Claus would get his letter in time, and, if so, what he would bring Johnny. The fire was warm and his eyes soon began "to draw straws," but he did not wish to go to bed quite yet and, indeed, had a lingering hope that when his father returned he might coax him into letting him go out again and slide with Johnny and then, perhaps, stand a chance of seeing Santa Claus come up the long hill, with his reindeer flying like the wind over the snow and taking the roofs of the houses with a single bound. So he moved over to the sofa where he could see better, and where it would not be likely his sleepiness would be observed.

The last thing he recalled in the sitting room was when he parted the heavy curtains at the foot of the sofa and looked out at the snow stretching away down the hill toward the woods, and shining in the light of the great round moon which had just come up over the side of the yard to the eastward. Then he curled up in the corner of the sofa as wide awake as a boy could be who had made up his mind to keep awake until midnight. The next thing he remembered was Sate jumping up and snuggling by him, and the next was his father coming in and telling him Johnny was waiting outside with his sled and the two goats hitched to it to take a long ride, and his wrapping him up carefully in his heavy overcoat. In a second he was out in the yard and made a dash for the cow-lot, and there, sure enough, was Johnny waiting for him at the gate in the cow pasture with a curious little peaked cap on his head and his coat collar turned up around his chin and tied with a great red comforter, so that only his eyes and nose peeped over it. As Tommy had never seen Johnny with that cap on before, he asked him where he had got it, and he said he had swapped caps with a little old man he had met driving a cow in the road as he came home. He could not keep this cap on his head, so Johnny had given him his in place of it, as it fitted him very well. And there were the two goats hitched to the very sled Tommy had made. In a minute they were on the sled, Tommy in front with the reins and Johnny sitting behind. Just as they were about to start, to Tommy's horror, out came Sate, and do as they might, Sate would not go back; but jumped up on the sled and settled down at Tommy's feet, and as Johnny said he did not mind and that Sate would keep Tommy's feet warm, they let him stay, which proved in the end to be a very fortunate thing. Just after they had fixed themselves comfortably, Johnny said, "Are you ready?" "Ready!" said Tommy, and gathered up the reins, and the next moment the goats started off, at first at a walk and then at a little trot, while Tommy was telling Johnny what his father had told him about the night in Santa Claus's country being so long that sometimes the sun did not rise above the horizon for several months.

"If it's as long as that," said Johnny, "we might go and see the old fellow and get back before midnight? I wish we could go."

"So do I," said Tommy, "but I'm afraid we might not find our way." He remembered just then that all one had to do was to steer by the

North Star, and at that moment he caught sight of the star right over the goats' heads.

The coast was clear and the snow was up to the top of the fences. The moon made it as light as day and never again would there be such a chance. It came to him, too, that on the map all the lines ran together at the North Pole, so that one could hardly miss his way, and if he should, there were Eskimos to guide him. So when Johnny said, "Let's go and try," he agreed, for if they once got there, Santa Claus, himself, might bring them back with him.

For a moment they went along as though they were coasting down a hill, with the little North Star shining directly in front of them as they glided along.

Just then Tommy said, "I wish the goats were reindeer. Let's pretend they are."

"So do I," said Johnny.

At this instant something happened; the goats gave a jump which sent a cloud of fine snow up into the boys' faces; the sled gave a great leap and on a sudden they began to tear along like the wind. The snow fields flew by them, and the trees, standing up to their knees in snow, simply tore along to the rear.

"They are running away!" said Tommy, as soon as he could catch his breath.

"All right. Let them run," said Johnny. "But steer by the North Star." And so they did.

When the cloud of snow in their faces cleared away, Tommy could scarcely believe his eyes.

"Look, Johnny!" he cried. "They are real reindeer. Real live ones. Look at their antlers."

"I know," said Johnny. "That little man said he wanted to swap with me."

So they flew on, up hill and down dale, over fields of white snow where the fences and rocks were buried and the cuts were filled up level; down frozen streams, winding through great forests where the pines were mantled with white; in between great walls of black rock towering above them, with the stars shining down like fires; out again across the vast stretches of snow with the Pole Star ever twisting and turning and coming before them again, until the sky seemed lit up with wonderful colours, and great bands of light were shooting up and sinking down only to shoot up again with a crackling like packs of pop-crackers in the distance.

The wind sang in their ears, nipped their noses, and made Tommy drowsy, and presently he must have fallen asleep; for just as he was conscious that Johnny had taken the reins, and, with one arm on either side of him was holding him on his shoulder, there was a great jolt and a sort of crash as of breaking through. He would have fallen off the sled if Johnny had not held him tight.

When he opened his eyes they seemed to be passing through a sort of silvery haze, as though the moonlight were shining through a fine mist of silvery drops which shed the softest radiance over everything. And suddenly through this enchanting light they came to a beautiful city, with walls around it of crystal, all rimmed with gold, like the clouds at sunset. Before them was a great gate through which shone a wonderful light, and inside they saw a wide street all lit up. As they reached the gate there was a sort of peal, as of bells, and out poured a guard of little men in uniform with little swords at their sides and guns in their hands, who saluted, while their officer, who had a letter in his hand, halted them with a challenge.

"Who goes there?"

"Friends," said Tommy, standing up and saluting, as he had seen soldiers do at the fort.

"Advance, friends, and give the countersign." Tommy thought they were lost and his heart sank.

But Johnny said, "Goodwill."

"All right," said the captain and stepped back.

"Who gave you that sled?" he asked.

"Tommy," said Johnny. "This little boy here made it and gave it to me."

"This is the one," said the captain to a guard, looking at a letter in his hand. "Let them by."

They drove in at the gate and found themselves in a broad street filled with enchanting things more beautiful than Tommy had ever dreamed of. The trees which lined it were Christmas trees, and the lights on them made the street as bright as noonday.

Here the reindeer slackened their pace, and as they turned down the great street they could see through the windows rooms brilliantly lighted, in which were hosts of people bustling about as busy as bees, working at Christmas things of all sorts and descriptions. They suddenly came to the gate of a great palace-like place, which the reindeer appeared to know, for they turned in at the gate just as Tommy's father's horses always turned in at their gate at home, and as they drove up to the door, with a shout of, "Here they are!" out poured a number of the same little people—like those they had already seen at the gate. Some helped them out, some stood like a guard, and some took their reindeer to drive them to the stable.

"You are just in time," said the captain of this party, as he stepped forward and saluted them. "The old Gentleman has been waiting for you, sending out to the gate to watch for you all evening."

Tommy was about to ask, "How did he know we were coming?" but before he could get the words out, the little man said, "Oh, he knows all that boys do, especially about Christmas time. That's his business."

"My!" thought Tommy, "I shall have to mind what I even think up here. He answers just as if I had said it. I hope he knows what I want for Christmas."

"Wait and see," said the little man; and Tommy, though he was glad to hear it, determined not to think anymore just then, but he was sorry he had not thought to wish for more things while he was wishing.

"Oh, don't worry about that," said the guard. "Santa Claus doesn't care much what you ask for for yourself. Even if he gives those things, you soon get tired of them or lose them or break them up. It is the things one asks for for others that he gives pleasure with. That's the reason he has such a good time himself, because he gives all the things to others."

Tommy tried to think what he had ever given to anyone. He had given pieces of candy and cake when he had plenty, but the sled was the only thing he had ever really given. He was about to mention this when the guard mentioned it for him.

"Oh, that sled was all right," he said, with a little nod. "Come in," and the great ice doors opened before them, and in they walked.

They passed through a great hall, all ice, as transparent as glass, though curiously it was warm and dry and filled with every kind of Christmas "things:"—everything that Tommy had ever seen, and a myriad more that he had never dreamed of. They were packed and stacked on either side, and a lot of little people, like those he had already seen, were working among them, tossing them about and shouting to each other with glee to "Look out," just as the boys did when coasting on the hill.

"I tell you," said one, "the Governor will have a busy time tonight. It beats last Christmas." And he made a run and a jump, and lit on a big pile of bundles which suddenly toppled over with him and nearly buried him as he sprawled on the slippery floor. This seemed a huge joke to all the others and they screamed with laughter at "Old Smartie," as they called him, and poured more bundles down on him, just as though they were having a pillow fight. Then when Old Smartie had at last gotten on his feet, they had a great game of tag among the piles and over them, and the first thing Tommy knew he and Johnny were at it as hard as anybody. He was very proud because Johnny could jump over piles as high as the best of them. Tommy, himself, however, could not jump; for they led him to a pile so high that he could not see over it; and on top were the fragments of all the things he had ever had and had broken up. He could not help crying a little; but just then in dashed a number of little men and gathering them up, rushed out with them. Tommy was wondering what they were going to do with them, when his friend, the guard, said: "We mend some of them; and some we keep to remind you with. Now try again." Tommy tried and did very well, only his left foot had gone to sleep in the sled and had not quite waked up.

"That was because Sate went to sleep on it," said his friend, the guard, and Tommy wondered how he knew Sate's name.

"Why," said the guard, "we have to know dogs' names to keep them from barking at us and waking everybody up. Let me lend you these boots," and with that he kicked off his boots. "Now, jump," and Tommy gave a jump and lit in them, as he sometimes did in his father's shoes. No sooner had Tommy put them on than he found that he could jump over the highest pile in the room.

"Look, look!" cried several of the others. "The captain has lent that little boy his 'Seven Leaguers.'"

"I know where he is going," said one; "to jump over the North Pole."

"No," laughed another. "He is going to catch the cow that 'jumped over the moon,' for Johnny Stout's mother."

Just then a message came that "Old Santa," as they called him, was waiting to see the two boys who had come in the new box sled, as he wanted to know how their mothers were and what they wished for Christmas. So there was a great scurrying to get their heads brushed before the bell rang again, and Tommy got soap in his eyes wetting the brush to make his hair lie smooth, while Johnny's left shoe came off and dropped in a hole in the floor. Smartie, however, told him that that was for the "Old Woman who lived in a shoe" to feed her cow in, and this was considered a great joke.

The next minute the door opened and they entered a great apartment, filled with the softest light from a blazing fire, and Tommy was sure it was his father's back before him at the fireplace; but when the man turned it was Santa Claus, only he did not have on his whiskers, and looked ever so much younger than in his pictures. At first he did not even look at them, he was so busy receiving mail that came fluttering down the chimney in a perfect snowstorm. As the letters came he gathered them up and handed them to a lady who was seated on the floor, saying, "Put that in," to which the lady always answered, "Just the thing," in a voice so like his mother's that Tommy felt quite at home. He was just wondering when "Sometime" would come, when Santa Claus picked up a letter, which had been thrown on the floor, and tossed it to the lady, saying, "Here's that letter from that little boy, Tommy Trot. Put some of those things in so he can break them up. He asked only for himself and much joy he will get out of them." Tommy shrank back behind Johnny. He wanted to say that he had written another letter to ask for things for others, but he had lost his tongue. Just then, however, Santa Claus put up his hand and pulled out another letter.

"Now," he said, as he glanced at it, "this is more like it. He is improving. I see he has asked for a lot of things for a friend of his named Johnny. Johnny Stout—who is he? It seems to me I hardly remember him or where he lives."

"Yes," said Johnny, stepping up. "That's me. He gave me a sled, too, and he made it himself."

Santa Claus turned and looked at him and his expression turned to a smile; in fact, Tommy thought he really winked at Johnny.

"Oh, I know that sled. It was a pretty good sled, too," he said.

This gave Tommy courage, and he stepped forward and said, "He lives in a little bit of a house near our place—just that way—" He turned and pointed. "I'll show it to you when you come."

"Good," said Santa Claus. "I'll show it to you and you show it to me. We are apt to overlook those little houses. So you are Tommy Trot?" he said. "Glad to see you," and he turned and held out his hand to Tommy. "I sent my reindeer to fetch you and I am glad you made that sled, for it is only a sled made for others that can get up here. You see, everything here, except the North Pole, is made for someone else, and that's the reason we have such a good time up here. If you like, I'll take you around and show you and Johnny our shops." This was exactly what Tommy wanted, so he thanked him politely.

"I'll be back in a little while," said Santa Claus to the lady, "for as soon as the boys are all asleep I must set out. I have a great many stockings to fill this year. See that everything is ready. Come along, boys," and next minute they were going through room after room and shop after shop, filled with so many things that Tommy could not keep them straight in his mind. He wondered how anyone could have thought of so many things, except his mother, of course; she always thought of everything for everyone. Some of them he wished for, but every time he thought of wanting a thing for himself the lights got dim, so that he stopped thinking about himself at all, and turned to speak to Johnny, but he was gone.

Presently Santa Claus said: "These are just my stores. Now we will go and see where some of these things are made." He gave a whistle, and the next second up dashed a sled with a team of reindeer in it, and who was there holding the reins but Johnny, with his little cap perched on the top of his head! At Tommy's surprise Santa Claus gave a laugh that made him shake all over like a bowl full of jelly, quite as Tommy had read he did in a poem he had learned the Christmas before, called "The Night Before Christmas, when all through the house."

"That comes of knowing how to drive goats," said Santa Claus. "Johnny knows a lot and I am going to give him a job, because he works so hard," and with that Tommy's boots suddenly jumped him into the sled, and Santa Claus stepped in behind him and pulled up a big robe over them.

"Here goes," he said, and at the word they turned the corner, and there was a gate of ice that looked like the mirrored doors in Tommy's mother's room, which opened before them, and they dashed along between great piles of things, throwing them on both sides like snow from a sled runner, and before Tommy knew it they were gliding along a road, which Tommy felt he had seen somewhere before, though he could not remember where. The houses on the roadside did not seem to have any front walls at all, and everywhere the people within were working like beavers; some sewing, some cutting out, some sawing and hammering, all making something, all laughing or smiling. They were mostly dressed like grown up people, but when they turned their faces they all looked young. Tommy was wondering why this was, when Santa Claus said that was because they were "Working for others. They grow young every Christmas. This is Christmas Land and Kindness Town." They turned another corner and were whisking by a little house, inside of which was someone sewing for dear life on a jacket. Tommy knew the place by the little backyard.

"Stop, stop!" he cried, pointing. "That's Johnny's home and that's Johnny's mother sewing. She's laughing. I expect she's making that for Johnny."

"Where?" asked Santa Claus, turning. Tommy pointed back, "There, there!" but they had whisked around a corner.

"I was so busy looking at that big house that I did not see it," said Santa Claus.

"That's our house," said Tommy. "I tell you what," he said presently, "if I get anything—I'll give him some." Santa Claus smiled.

So they dashed along, making all sorts of turns and curves, through streets lined with shops full of Christmas things and thronged with people hurrying along with their arms full of bundles; out again into the open; by little houses half buried in snow, with a light shining dimly through their upper windows; on through forests of Christmas trees, hung with toys and not yet lighted, and presently in a wink were again at Santa Claus's home, in a great hall. All along the sides were cases filled with all sorts of toys, guns, uniforms, sleds, skates, snow shoes, fur gloves, fur coats, books, toy dogs, ponies, goats, cows, everything.

III

TOMMY WAS JUST THINKING HOW he would love to carry his mother a polar bearskin for his father, and his father a sealskin coat for his mother, when Santa Claus came up behind him and tweaked his ear.

"Ah!" he said, "so you want something—something you can't get?"

"Not for myself," said Tommy, shamefacedly.

"So," said Santa Claus, with a look much like Tommy's father when he was pleased. "I know that. They don't have them exactly about here. The teddy bears drove them out. You have to go away off to find them." He waved his hand to show how far off it was.

"I should like to hunt them, if I only had a gun!" said Tommy;—"and one for Johnny, too," he added quickly.

Santa Claus winked again. "Well," he said slowly, just as Tommy's father always did when Tommy asked for something and he was considering—"well, I'll think about it." He walked up and touched a spring, and the glass door flew open. "Try these guns," he said; and Tommy tipped up and took one out. It, however, seemed a little light to shoot polar bears with and he put it back and took another. That, however, was rather heavy.

"Try this," said Santa Claus, handing him one, and it was the very thing. "Load right; aim right; and shoot right," said he, "and you'll get your prize every time. And, above all, stand your ground."

"Now, if I only had some dogs!" thought Tommy, looking around at a case full of all sorts of animals; ponies and cows; and dogs and cats; some big, some little, and some middle-sized. "I wish those were real dogs."

"Where's Sate?" asked Santa Claus.

"Sate can't pull a sled," said Tommy. "He's too little. Besides, he ain't an Eskimo dog—I mean he isn't," he corrected quickly, seeing Santa Claus look at him. "But he's awful bad after cats." Just then, to his horror, he saw Sate in the showcase with his eye on a big, white cat. He could hardly keep from crying out; but he called to him very quietly, "Come here, come here, Sate. Don't you hear me, sir? Come here."

He was just about to go up and seize him when Santa Claus said: "He's all right. He's just getting acquainted."

"My! How much he talks like Peake," thought Tommy. "I wonder if he is his uncle."

Just then Sate began to nose among some little brownish-gray dogs, and so, Tommy called, "Here—come here—come along," and out walked not only Sate, but six other dogs, and stood in a line just as though they were hitched to a sled, the six finest Eskimo dogs Tommy had ever seen.

"Aren't they beauties!" said Santa Claus. "I never saw a finer lot; big-boned, broad-backed, husky fellows. They'll scale an ice mountain like my reindeer. And if they ever get in sight of a bear!" He made a gesture as much as to say, "Let him look out."

"What are their names?" said Tommy, who always wanted to know everyone's name.

"Buster and Muster and Fluster, and Joe and Rob and Mac."

"Ain't one of them named Towser?" asked Tommy. "I thought one was always named Towser."

"No, that's a book name," said Santa Claus so scornfully that Tommy was sorry he had asked him, especially as he added, "Isn't, not ain't."

"But they haint any harness," said Tommy, using the word Peake always used,—"I mean, hisn't any—no, I mean haven't any harness. I wish I had some harness for them."

"Pooh! Wishing doesn't do anything by itself," said Santa Claus.

"Oh! I tell you. I've a lot of string that came off some Christmas things my mother got for some poor people. I put it in my pocket to give it to Johnny to mend his goat harness with, and I never thought of it when I saw him last night."

"So," said Santa Claus. "That's better. Let's see it."

Tommy felt in his pocket, and at first he could not find it. "I've lost it," he said sorrowfully.

"Try again," said Santa Claus.

Tommy felt again in a careless sort of way.

"No, I've lost it," he said. "It must have dropped out."

"You're always losing something," said Santa Claus. "Now, Johnny would have used that. You are sure you had it?"

Tommy nodded. "Sure; I put it right in this pocket."

"Then you've got it now. Feel in your other pockets."

"I've felt there two times," said Tommy.

"Then feel again," said Santa Claus. And Tommy felt again, and sure enough, there it was. He pulled it out, and as it came it turned to harness—six sets of wonderful dog harness, made of curious leather thongs, and on every breast-strap was the name of the dog.

As Tommy made a dive for it and began to put the harness on the dogs, Santa Claus said, "String on bundles bought for others sometimes comes in quite handy."

Even then Tommy did not know how to put the harness on the dogs. As fast as he got it on one, Sate would begin to play with him and he would get all tangled up in it. Tommy could have cried with shame, but he remembered what his father had told him about, "Trying instead of crying"; so he kept on, and the first thing he knew they were all harnessed. Just then he heard a noise behind him and there was Johnny with another team of dogs just like his, hitched to his box sled, on which they had come, and on it a great pile of things tied, and in his hand a list of what he had—food of all kinds in little cans; bread and butter, and even cake, like that he had given away; dried beef; pemmican; coffee and tea, all put up in little cases; cooking utensils; a frying pan and a coffee pot and a few other things—tin cups and so forth; knives and everything that he had read that boys had when they went camping, matches and a flint stone in a box with tinder, in case the matches gave out or got wet; hatchets and saws and tools to make ice houses or to mend their sleds with, in fact, everything that Tommy's father had ever told him men used when they went into the woods. And on top of all, in cases, was the ammunition they would need.

"Now, if we had a tent," said Johnny. But Santa Claus said, "You don't need tents up there."

"I know," said Tommy. "You sleep in bags made of skin or in houses made of snow."

Santa Claus gave Johnny a wink. "That boy is improving," he said. "He knows some things;" and with that he took out of the case and gave both Tommy and Johnny big heavy coats of whitish fur and two bags made of skin. "And now," he said, "you will have to be off if you want to get back here before I leave, for though the night is very long, I must be getting away soon," and all of a sudden the door opened and there was the North Star straight ahead, and at a whistle from Santa Claus away went the dogs, one sled right behind the other, and Sate, galloping for life and barking with joy, alongside.

The last thing Tommy heard Santa Claus say was, "Load right, aim right, and shoot right; and stand your ground."

In a short time they were out of the light of the buildings and on a great treeless waste of snow and ice, much rougher than anything Tommy had ever seen; where it was almost dark and the ice seemed to turn up on edge. They had to work their way along slowly between jagged ice peaks, and sometimes they came to places which it seemed they could never get over, but by dint of pushing and hauling and pulling, they always got over in the end. The first meal they took was only a bite, because they did not want to waste time, and they were soon on their sleds again, dashing along, and Tommy was glad, when, after some hours of hard work, Johnny said he thought they had better turn in, as in a few hours they ought to be where Santa Claus had told them they could find polar bears, and they ought to be fresh when they struck their tracks. They set to work, unhitched the dogs, untied the packs and got out their camp-outfit, and having dug a great hole in the snow behind an ice peak, where the wind did not blow so hard, and having gathered some dry wood, which seemed to have been caught in the ice as if on purpose for them, they lit a fire, and getting out their frying pan they stuck two chops on sticks and toasted them, and had the best supper Tommy had ever eaten. The bones they gave to the dogs. Johnny suggested tying up the dogs, but Tommy was so sleepy, he said: "Oh, no, they won't go away. Besides, suppose a bear should come while we are asleep." They took their guns so as to be ready in case a polar bear should come nosing around, and each one crawled into his bag and was soon fast asleep, Sate having crawled into Tommy's bag with him and snuggled up close to keep him warm.

It seemed to Tommy only a minute before he heard Johnny calling, and he crawled out to find him looking around in dismay. Every dog had disappeared except Sate.

"We are lost!" said Johnny. "We must try to get back or we shall freeze to death." He climbed up on top of an ice peak and looked around in every direction; but not a dog was in sight. "We must hurry up," he said, "and go back after them. Why didn't we tie them last night! We must take something to eat with us." So they set to work and got out of the bag all they could carry, and with their guns and ammunition were about to start back.

"We must hide the rest of the things in a cache," said Tommy, "so that if we ever come back we may find them."

"What's a cache?" said Johnny.

Tommy was proud that he knew something Johnny did not know. He explained that a "cache" was a hiding place.

So they put the things back in the bag and covered them up with snow, and Tommy, taking up his gun and pack, gave a whistle to Sate, who was nosing around. Suddenly the snow around began to move, and out from under the snow appeared first the head of one dog and then of another, until everyone—Buster and Muster and Fluster and the rest—had come up and stood shaking himself to get the snow out of his coat. Then Tommy remembered that his father had told him that that was the way the Eskimo dogs often kept themselves warm when they slept, by boring down deep in the snow. Never were two boys more delighted. In a jiffy they had uncovered the sled, eaten breakfast, fed the dogs and hitched them up again, and were once more on their way. They had not gone far, though it seemed to Tommy a long, long way, when the ice in the distance seemed to Tommy to turn to great mountain-like icebergs. "That's where they are," said Tommy. "They are always on icebergs in the pictures." Feeling sure that they must be near them, they tied their dogs to the biggest blocks of ice they could find, and even tied Sate, and taking each his gun and a bag of extra ammunition, they started forward on foot. As Tommy's ammunition was very heavy, he was glad when Johnny offered to carry it for him. Even so, they had not gone very far, though it seemed far enough to Tommy, when he proposed turning back and getting something to eat. As they turned they lost the North Star, and when they looked for it again they could not tell which it was. Johnny thought it was one, Tommy was sure it was another. So they tried first one and then the other, and finally gave themselves up as lost. They went supperless to bed that night or rather that time, and Tommy never wished himself in bed at home so much, or said his prayers harder, or prayed for the poor more earnestly. They were soon up again and were working along through the ice peaks, growing hungrier and hungrier, when, going over a rise of ice, they saw not far off a little black dot on the snow which they thought might be bear or seal. With gun in hand they crept along slowly and watchfully, and soon they got close enough to see that there was a little man, an Eskimo, armed with a spear and bow and arrows and with four or five dogs and a rough little sled, something like Johnny's sled, but with runners made of frozen salmon. At first he appeared rather afraid of them, but they soon made signs to him that they were friends and were lost and very hungry. With a grin which showed his white teeth he pointed to his runners, and borrowing Tommy's knife, he clipped a piece off of them for each of them and handed it back with the knife; Tommy knew that he ought not to eat with his knife, but he was so hungry that he thought it would be overlooked. Having breakfasted on frozen runner, they were fortunate enough to make the Eskimo understand that they wanted to find a polar bear. He made signs to them to follow him and he would guide them where they would find one. "Can you shoot?" he asked, making a sign with his bow and arrow.

"Can we shoot!" laughed both Tommy and Johnny. "Watch us. See that big green piece of ice there?" They pointed at an ice peak near by. "Well, watch us!" And first Johnny and then Tommy blazed away at it, and the way the icicles came clattering down satisfied them. They wished all that trip that the ice peak had been a bear. So they followed him, and a great guide he was. He showed them how to avoid the rough places in the ice fields, and, in fact, seemed quite as much at home in that waste of ice and snow as Johnny was back in town.

He always kept near the coast, he said, as he could find both bear and seal there. They had reached a very rough place, when, as they were going along, he stopped suddenly and pointed far off across the ice. Neither Tommy nor Johnny could see anything except ice and snow, try as they might. But they understood from his excitement that somewhere in the distance was a seal or possibly even a polar bear and, gun in hand, with beating hearts, they followed him as he stole carefully through the ice peaks, working his way along, and every now and then cautioning them to stoop so as not to be seen.

So they crept along until they reached the foot of a high ridge of ice piled up below a long ledge of black rock which seemed to rise out of the frozen sea. Up this they worked their way, stooping low, the guide in front, clutching his bow and arrow, Johnny next, clutching his gun, and Tommy behind, clutching his, each treading in the other's tracks. Suddenly, as he neared the top, the guide dropped flat on the snow. Johnny followed his example and Tommy did the same. They knew that they must be close to the bear and they held their breath; for the guide, having examined his bow and arrows carefully, began to wriggle along on his stomach. Johnny and Tommy wriggled along behind him, clutching their guns. Just at the top of the ledge the guide quietly slipped an arrow out of his quiver and held it in his hand, as he slowly raised his head and peeped over. Johnny and Tommy, guns in hand, crept up beside him to peep also. At that instant, however, before Tommy could see anything, the guide sprang to his feet. "Whiz," by Tommy's ear went an arrow at a great white object towering above them at the entrance of what seemed a sort of cave, and two more arrows followed it, whizzing by his ear so quickly that they were all three sticking in deep before Tommy took in that the object was a great white polar bear, with his head turned from them, in the act of going in the cave. As the arrows struck him, he twisted himself and bit savagely at them, breaking off all but one, which was lodged back of his shoulder. As he reared up on his hind legs and tried to get at this arrow, he seemed to Tommy as high as the great wardrobe at home. Tommy, however, had no time to do much thinking, for in twisting around the bear caught sight of them. As he turned toward them, the guide with a yell that sounded like "Look out!" dodged behind, but both Tommy and Johnny threw up their guns and pulled the trigger. What was their horror to find that they both had forgotten to load their guns after showing the guide how they could shoot. The next second, with jaws wide open, the bear made a dash for them. Tommy's heart leapt into his throat. He glanced around to see if he could run and climb a tree, for he knew that grizzlies could not climb, and he hoped that polar bears could not climb either, while Tommy prided himself on climbing and had often climbed the apple tree in the pasture at home; but there was not a tree or a shrub in sight, and all he saw was the little guide running for life and disappearing behind an ice peak.

"Run, Johnny!" cried Tommy, and, "Run, Tommy!" cried Johnny at the same moment. But they had no time to run, for the next second the bear was upon them, his eyes glaring, his great teeth gleaming, his huge jaws wide open, from which came a growl that shook the ice under their feet. As the bear sprang for them Johnny was more directly in his way, but, happily, his foot slipped from under him and he fell flat on his back just as the bear lit, or he would have been crushed instantly. Even as it was, he was stunned and lay quite still under the bear, which for the moment seemed to be dazed. Either he could not tell what had become of Johnny, or else he could not make up his mind whether to eat Johnny up at once or to leave him and catch Tommy first and then eat them both together. He seemed to decide on the latter, for, standing up, he fixed his eyes on Tommy and took a step across Johnny's prostrate body, with his mouth open wider than before, his eyes glaring more fiercely, and with a roar and a growl that made the ice peaks shed a shower of icicles. Then it was that Tommy seemed to have become a different boy. In fact, no sooner had Johnny gone down than Tommy forgot all about himself and his own safety, and thought only of Johnny and how he could save him. And, oh, how sorry he was that he had let Johnny carry all the ammunition, even though it was heavy! For his gun was empty and Johnny had every cartridge. Tommy was never so scared in all his life. He tried to cry out, but his throat was parched, so he began to say his prayers, and remembering what Santa Claus had said about boys who asked only for themselves, he tried to pray for Johnny.

At this moment happened what appeared almost a miracle. By Tommy dashed a little hairy ball and flew at the bear like a tiger; and there was Sate, a part of his rope still about his neck, clinging to the bear for life. The bear deliberately stopped and looked around as if he were too surprised to move; but Sate's teeth were in him, and then the efforts of the bear to catch him were really funny. He snapped and snarled and snarled and snapped; but Sate was artful enough to dodge him, and the bear's huge paws simply beat the air and knocked up the snow. Do what he might, he could not touch Sate. Finally the bear did what bears always do when bees settle on them when they are robbing their hives—he began to roll over and over, and the more he rolled the more he tied himself up in the rope around Sate. As he rolled away from Johnny, Tommy dashed forward and picked up Johnny's gun, coolly loaded it, loading it right, too, and, springing forward, raised the gun to his shoulder. The bear, however, rolled so rapidly that Tommy was afraid he might shoot Sate, and before he could fire, the bear, with Sate still clinging to him, rolled inside the mouth of the cave. Tommy was in despair. At this moment, however, he heard a sound, and there was Johnny just getting on his feet. He had never been so glad to see anyone.

"Where is the bear?" asked Johnny, looking around, still a little dazed. Tommy pointed to the cave.

"In there, with Sate tied to him."

"We must save him," said Johnny.

Carefully dividing the ammunition now, both boys loaded their guns, and hurrying down the icy slope, carefully approached the mouth of the cave, guns in hand, in case the bear should appear.

Inside it was so dark that they could at first see nothing, but they could hear the sound of the struggle going on between Sate and the bear. Suddenly Sate changed his note and gave a little cry as of pain. At the sound of his distress Tommy forgot himself.

"Follow me!" he cried. "He is choking!" And not waiting even to look behind to see whether Johnny was with him, he dashed forward into the cave, gun in hand, thinking only to save Sate. Stumbling and slipping, he kept on, and turning a corner there right in front of him were the two eyes of the bear, glaring in the darkness like coals of fire. Pushing boldly up and aiming straight between the two eyes, Tommy pulled the trigger. With a growl which mingled with the sound of the gun, the bear made a spring for him and fell right at his feet, rolled up in a great ball. Happily for Sate, he lit just on top of the ball. Tommy whipped out his knife and cut the cord from about Sate's throat, and had him in his arms when Johnny came up.

The next thing was to skin the bear, and this the boys expected to find as hard work as ever even Johnny had done; but, fortunately, the bear had been so surprised at Tommy's courage and skill in aiming that when the bullet hit him he had almost jumped out of his skin. So, after they had worked a little while, the skin came off quite easily. What surprised Johnny was that it was all tanned, but Tommy had always rather thought that bears wore their skin tanned on the inside and lined, too. The next thing was to have a dinner of bear meat, for, as Tommy well remembered, all bear hunters ate bear steaks. They were about to go down to the shore to hunt along for driftwood, when, their eyes becoming accustomed to the darkness, they found a pile of wood in the corner of the cave, which satisfied them that at sometime in the past this cave had been used by robbers or pirates, who probably had been driven away by this great bear, or possibly might even have been eaten up by him.

At first they had some little difficulty in making a fire, as their matches, warranted waterproof, had all got damp when Tommy fell into the water—an incident I forgot to mention; but after trying and trying, the tinder caught from the flint and they quickly had a fine fire crackling in a corner of the cave, and here they cooked bear steak and had the finest dinner they had had since they came into the Arctic Regions. They were just thinking of going after the dogs and the sleds, when up came the dogs dragging the sleds behind them, and without a word, pitched in to make a hearty meal of bear meat themselves. It seemed as if they had got a whiff of the fresh steak and pulled the sleds loose from the ice points to which they were fastened. They were not, however, allowed to eat in any peace until they had all recognized that Sate was the hero of this bear fight, for he gave himself as many airs as though he had not only got the bear, but had shot and skinned it.

It was at this moment that the Eskimo guide came back, jabbering with delight, and with his white teeth shining, just as if he had been as brave as Sate. At first, Tommy and Johnny were inclined to be very cold to him and pointed their fingers at him as a coward, but when he said he had only one arrow left and had wanted that to get a sealskin coat for Tommy's mother, and, as he had the sealskin coat, they could not contradict him, but graciously gave him, in exchange for the coat, the bear meat which the dogs had not eaten.

Having packed everything on the sled carefully, with the sealskin coat on top of the pack and the bear's fur on top of that, and having bid their Eskimo friend goodbye, they turned their backs on the North Pole and struck out for home.

They had hardly started, however, when the sound of sleigh bells reached them, coming from far over the snow, and before they could tell where it was, who should appear, sailing along over the ice peaks, but Santa Claus himself, in his own sleigh, all packed with Christmas things, his eight reindeer shining in the moonlight and his bells jingling merrily. Such a shout as he gave when he found that they had actually got the bear and had the robe to show for it! It did them good; and both Tommy and Johnny vied with each other in telling what the other had done. Santa Claus was so pleased that he made them both get in his sleigh to tell him about it. He let Sate get in too, and snuggle down right at their feet. Johnny's box sled he hitched on behind. The dogs were turned loose. At first Tommy feared they might get lost, but Santa Claus said they would soon find their way home.

"In fact," he said with a wink, "you have not been so far away as you think. Now tell me all about it," he said. So Tommy began to tell him, beginning at the very beginning when Johnny took him on his sled. But he had only got as far as the sofa, when he fell asleep, and he never knew how he got back home. When he waked up he was in bed.

He never could recall exactly what happened. Afterward he recalled Santa Claus saying to him, "You must show me where Johnny lives, for I'm afraid I forgot him last Christmas." Then he remembered that once he heard Santa Claus calling to him in a whisper, "Tommy Trot, Tommy Trot," and though he was very sleepy he raised himself up to find Santa Claus standing up in the sled in Johnny's backyard, with Johnny fast asleep in his arms; and that Santa Claus said to him, "I want to put Johnny in bed without waking him up, and I want you to follow me, and put these things which I have piled up here on the sled you made for him, in his stocking by the fire." He remembered that at a whistle to the deer they sprang with a bound to the roof, the sled sailing behind them; but how he got down he never could recall, and he never knew how he got back home.

When he waked next morning there was the polar bearskin which he and Johnny had brought back with them, not to mention the sealskin coat, and though Johnny, when he next saw him, was too much excited at first by his new sled and the fine fresh cow which his mother had found in her cow-house that morning, to talk about anything else, yet, when he and his mother came over after breakfast to see Tommy's father and thank him for something, they said that Santa Claus had paid them a visit such as he never had paid before, and they brought with them Johnny's goats, which they insisted on giving Tommy as a Christmas present. So Tommy Trot knew that Santa Claus had got his letter.

THE HISTORY OF A NUTCRACKER

I

GODFATHER DROSSELMAYER

IN THE CITY OF NUREMBERG lived a much-respected Chief Justice called Judge Silberhaus, which means, "house of silver." He had two children, a nine-year-old boy, Fritz, and a daughter Mary who was seven and a half years old. They were both very attractive children but so different in appearance and nature that one would have never have taken them for brother and sister. Fritz was a fine big boy, chubby, blustering and frolicsome, stamping his foot at the least opposition, convinced that all things in the world were created for his pleasure and whims. He would continue in this conviction until his father, irritated by the shouting and stamping, would emerge from his study and lifting the index finger of his right hand to the level of his frowning eyebrow, would remark, "Monsieur *Fritz*!"

Then Fritz would want to sink under the floor.

As to his mother, it goes without saying that no matter how high she raised her finger or even her hand, Fritz paid not the slightest attention.

Mary, on the other hand, was a delicate pale child, with long curling ringlets falling over her little shoulders like a moving sheaf of gold. She was modest, sweet, affable, sympathetic to all troubles, even those of her dolls, obedient to the slightest sign from her mother and never gave trouble to Miss Trudchen, the governess. Consequently, everyone loved Mary.

Now, in the year 17— came the twenty-fourth day of December. You may not know, my dear children, that the twenty-fourth of December is the day before Christmas, being the day when the Infant Jesus was born in a manager between a donkey and a cow. I must now explain one thing to you.

The most ill-informed ones among you have heard it said that each country has its customs; the best informed ones doubtless know already that Nuremberg is a German city is renowned for its toys, dolls, and polichinelles, which are sent in well-filled cases to all the countries of the world. The children of Nuremberg therefore should be the happiest children on earth. At least they are not like the inhabitants of Ostend who have an abundance of oysters only to see them wasted. Thus Germany, quite a different country than France, has likewise different customs. In France, the first day of the New Year is the day for exchanging presents. In Germany the gift day is the twenty-fourth of December, that is to say, the night before Christmas. Across the Rhine gifts are given in this way: a large tree is installed on a low table in the living room and its branches are hung with toys. Those too large for the branches are put on the table; them the children are reminded that the good little angel had given them some of the presents which he received from the three wise kings. This is not wholly untrue because you know it is from the Infant Jesus that all good things of this world come.

I do not need to tell you that among the fortunate children of Nuremberg, I mean those who at Christmas receive many toys of all kinds, were the little boy and girl of Judge Silberhaus. Besides their parents who adored them, they had a godfather called Godfather Drosselmayer who adored them also. I must describe briefly this illustrious personage who occupied in the City of Nuremberg a position almost as distinguished as that of Judge Silberhaus. Godfather Drosselmayer, Medical Commissioner, was not at all a good-looking fellow; far from it. He was a tall, spare man, about five feet, eight inches high. He was so round-shouldered and stooped that in spite of his long limbs he could pick up a handkerchief without seeming to bend over. His face was like a wrinkled apple touched by April frost. In the place of his right eye was a large black plaster; he was perfectly bald, a drawback which was offset by a luxuriant and curly wig, an ingenious work of his own, made of spun glass. On account of this remarkable head-covering he always carried his hat under his arm. The one remaining eye, however, was alive and brilliant, seeming to perform the functions of its missing comrade as well as its own, so rapidly did it make the rounds of a room wherein Godfather Drosselmayer wished to take in all details at one glance, or focus itself steadily upon people whose inmost thoughts he desired to know.

Godfather Drosselmayer, through the study of men and animals, had become familiar with all the resources of machinery so that he made men who walked, saluted, presented arms; women who danced, played the harpsichord and the violin; dogs which fetched, carried and barked; birds which flew, hopped and sang; fish which swam and ate. He had finally succeeded in making dolls and polichinelles pronounce in a harsh and monotonous voice a few words, simple ones it is true, like papa and mamma. Nevertheless, in spite of all these dubious attempts, Godfather Drosselmayer did not despair but insisted that someday he would succeed in making real men, women, dogs, birds and fish. It goes without saying that his two godchildren, to whom he had promised his first experiments in this field, were always full of pleasant anticipations.

You can clearly see that Godfather Drosselmayer's mechanical skills made him a very useful friend. When a clock got out of order in the house of Judge Silberhaus and in spite of attempts on the part of ordinary clockmakers its hands ceased indicating the hour, its *tick tock* subsided, its movement stopped, they sent for the godfather. He would arrive on a run, having, like all true artists, a real affection for his hobby. Taken to the lifeless timepiece he would lift out the movement and place it between his knees. Ten, tongue sticking out, his one eye glowing like a carbuncle, his glass wig on the floor beside him, he would draw form his pocket a collection of miscellaneous small instruments made by himself for purposes known only to himself, choose the sharpest ones and plunge them into the clock. This operation, while it worried Mary who could not believe that the clock did not suffer, nevertheless restored the patient so that, once replaced in its case, it would begin to stir and strike more beautifully than ever. Then the room appeared to live once more.

On one occasion, touched by the coaxing of Mary, who was sadly watching their dog as he laboriously turned the kitchen spit, Godfather Drosselmayer had condescended, from the heights of his scientific knowledge, to make an automatic dog. Thereafter, Turk, sensitive to the cold, after three years of working so near the fire, warmed his nose and paws before the blaze like a veritable gentleman with nothing to do but watch his successor who, once started, would keep at his task indefinitely. After the Judge, his wife, Fritz and Mary, Turk was certainly the member of the household who most loved and venerated Godfather Drosselmayer. He made a great fuss every time he saw him arrive, announcing by joyous barks and the wagging of his tail that the quaint old man was near even before he touched the knocker.

On this Christmas Eve just as dusk was falling Fritz and Mary, who had not been allowed in the drawing room, were sitting in one corner of the dining room. While Miss Trudchen, their governess, was knitting near the window to catch the last rays of the sun, the children were seized with a sort of vague uneasiness because the lights had not yet been brought in. They were speaking in low voices to each other as people do when a little frightened.

"Fritz," said Mary, "surely mother and father are busy with the Christmas tree for ever since morning I have been hearing things being moved about in the drawing room."

"Yes," said Fritz, "and about ten minutes ago I realized from the way Turk was barking that Godfather was coming."

"Oh gracious!" cried Mary, clapping her hands, "what do you suppose that the good godfather will bring us? I think it will be a beautiful garden all planted with trees, along which will run a lovely river, its grassy banks bordered with flowers. On this river, maybe there will be silver swans with golden collars and a young girl feeding them marzipan which they will eat out of her apron."

"In the first place," said Fritz in the superior tone peculiar to him, which his parents regarded as one of his gravest faults, "you should know, Miss Mary, that swans do not eat marzipan."

"I believe you," said Mary, "but as you are a year and a half older than I you ought to know more about such things."

Fritz swaggered a bit and resumed: "I think I can say that if Godfather Drosselmayer brings anything it will be a fortress with soldiers to guard, cannons to defend, and enemies to attack it. There will be splendid battles."

"I do not like battles," said Mary. "If he brings a fortress, as you think, it will be for you; except that I want to nurse the wounded ones."

"Whatever he brings," said Fritz, "you know that it will be neither for you nor for me, because, with the excuse that his presents are true works of art, they will be taken away as soon as we get them and put on the top shelf of the big glass cupboard which even father can reach only by standing on a chair. That is why I like our other toys better than those that Godfather Drosselmayer brings. We can have them to play with at least until they are broken."

"Yes, I do too," replied Mary, "only it is not necessary to repeat this to Godfather."

"Why?"

"Because it would hurt his feelings to know that we do not like his toys as well as the others. He thinks they make us happy. We must not let him know that he is mistaken."

"Oh, bah!" said Fritz.

"Miss Mary is right, Master Fritz," said Miss Trudchen, who ordinarily kept silent, only speaking when she felt the occasion demanded it.

"See here," said Mary in an animated tone to prevent Fritz from replying rudely to the governess, "let us try to guess what we will get. I have confided to mother that Miss Rose, my doll, is getting more and more awkward in spite of my constant scoldings, and keeping falling on her nose. As this never happens without leaving disagreeable traces, it is impossible to take her out anymore; her face goes badly with her pretty clothes."

"I have reminded father," said Fritz, "that a big chestnut horse would be fine in my stable. I told him, too, that there can be no well-organized army without light cavalry and that I need a squadron of hussars to complete my division."

At this point Miss Trudchen considered it time to speak again. "Monsieur Fritz and Miss Mary," she said, "you know every well that it is the good angel who gives and blesses all these beautiful toys. Do not choose in advance what you want. He knows much better than you what will please you."

"Oh!" cried Fritz; "and yet last year he sent me foot soldiers, although, as I have just said, I should have been better satisfied with a squadron of hussars."

"For my part I have only to thank my good angel," said Mary; "for I did but ask for a doll last yar, and I not only had the doll, but also a beautiful white dove, with red feet and beak."

In the meantime the night had altogether drawn in, and the children, who by degrees spoke lower and lower and grew closer and closer together, fancied that they heard the wings of their guardian angels fluttering near them, and a sweet music in the distance, like that of an organ accompanying the Hymn of Nativity, beneath the gloomy arches of a cathedral. Presently a sudden light shone upon the wall for a moment, and Fritz and Mary believed that it was their guardian angel, who, after depositing the toys in the drawing room, flew away in the midst of a golden lustre to visit other children who were expecting him with the same impatience as themselves.

Immediately afterwards a bell rang—the door was thrown violently open—and so strong a light burst into the apartment that the children were dazzled, and uttered cries of surprise and alarm.

The judge and his wife then appeared at the door, and took the hands of their children, saying, "Come, little dears, and see what the guardian angels have sent you."

The children hastened to the drawing room; and Miss Trudchen, having placed her work upon a chair, followed them.

II

The Christmas Tree

M Y DEAR CHILDREN, YOU ALL know the beautiful toy stalls in the Soho Bazaar, the Pantheon, and the Lowther Arcade; and your parents have often taken you there, to permit you to choose whatever you liked best. Then you have stopped short, with longing eyes and open mouth; and you have experienced a pleasure which you will never again know in your lives—no, not even when you become men and acquire titles or fortunes. Well, that same joy was felt by Fritz and Mary when they entered the drawing room and saw the great tree growing as it were from the middle of the table, and covered with blossoms made of sugar, and sugar plums instead of fruit—the whole glittering by the light of a hundred Christmas candles concealed amidst the leaves. At that beautiful sight Fritz leapt for joy, and danced about in a manner which showed how well he had attended to the lessons of his dancing master. On her side, Mary could not restrain two large tears of joy which, like liquid pearls, rolled down her countenance, that was open and smiling as a rose in June.

But the children's joy knew no bounds when they came to examine all the pretty things which covered the table. There was a beautiful doll, twice as large as Miss Rose; and there was also a charming silk frock, hung on a stand in such a manner that Mary could walk round it. Fritz was also well pleased; for he found upon the table a squadron of hussars, with red jackets and gold lace, and mounted on white horses; while on the carpet, near the table, stood the famous horse which he so much longed to see in his stables. In a moment did this modern Alexander leap upon the back of that brilliant Bucephalus, which was already saddled and bridled; and, having ridden two or three times round the table, he got off again, declaring that though the animal was very spirited and restive, he should soon be able to tame him in such a manner that ere a month passed the horse would be as quiet as a lamb.

But at the moment when Fritz set his foot upon the ground, and when Mary was baptising her new doll by the name of Clara, the bell rang a second time; and the children turned towards that corner of the room whence the sound came.

They then beheld something which had hitherto escaped their attention, so intent had they been upon the beautiful Christmas tree. In fact, the corner of the room of which I have just spoken, was concealed, or cutoff as it were, by a large Chinese screen, behind a which there was a certain noise accompanied by a certain sweet music, which proved something unusual was going on in that quarter. The children then recollected that they had not yet seen the doctor; and they both exclaimed at the same moment, "Oh! Godpapa Drosselmayer!"

At these words—and as if it had only waited for that exclamation to put itself in motion—the screen opened inwards, and showed not only Godfather Drosselmayer, but something more!

In the midst of a green meadow, decorated with flowers, stood a magnificent country seat, with numerous windows, all made of real glass, in front, and two gilt towers on the wings. At the same moment the jingling of bells was heard from within—the doors and windows opened—and the rooms inside were discovered lighted up by wax-tapers half an inch high. In those rooms were several little gentlemen and ladies, all walking about: the gentlemen splendidly dressed in laced coats, and silk waistcoats and breeches, each with a sword by his side, and a hat under his arm; the ladies gorgeously attired in brocades, their hair dressed in the style of the eighteenth century, and each one holding a fan in her hand, wherewith they all fanned themselves as if overcome by the heat.

In the central drawing room, which actually seemed to be on fire, so splendid was the lustre of the crystal chandelier, filled with wax candles, a number of children were dancing to the jingling music; the boys all in round jackets, and the girls all in short frocks. At the same time a gentleman, clad in a furred cloak, appeared at the window of an adjoining chamber, made signs, and then disappeared again; while Godfather Drosselmayer himself, with his drab frock coat, the patch on his eye, and the glass wig—so like the original, although only three inches high, that the puppet might be taken for the doctor, as if seen at a great distance—went out and in the front door of the mansion with the air of a gentleman, inviting those who were walking outside to enter his abode.

The first moment was one of surprise and delight for the two children; but, having watched the building for a few minutes with his elbows resting on the table, Fritz rose and exclaimed, "But, Godpapa Drosselmayer, why do you keep going in and coming out by the same door? You must be tired of going backwards and forwards like that. Come, enter by that door there, and come out by this one here."

And Fritz pointed with his finger to the doors of the two towers.

"No, that cannot be done," answered Godfather Drosselmayer.

"Well, then," said Fritz, "do me the pleasure of going up those stairs, and taking the place of that gentleman at the window: then tell him to go down to the door."

"It is impossible, my dear Fritz," again said the doctor.

"At all events the children have danced enough: let them go and walk, while the gentlemen and ladies who are now walking, dance in their turn."

"But you are not reasonable, you little rogue," cried the godpapa, who began to grow angry: "the mechanism must move in a certain way."

"Then let me go into the house," said Fritz.

"Now you are silly, my dear boy," observed the judge: "you see that it is impossible for you to enter the house, since the vanes on the top of the towers scarcely come up to your shoulders."

Fritz yielded to this reasoning and held his tongue; but in a few moments, seeing that the ladies and gentlemen kept on walking, that the children would not leave off dancing, that the gentleman with the furred cloak appeared and disappeared at regular intervals, and that Godfather Drosselmayer did not leave the door, he again broke silence.

"My dear godpapa," said he, "if all these little figures can do nothing more than what again, you may take them away they are doing over and over tomorrow, for I do not care about them; and I like my horse much better, because it runs when I choose—and my hussars, because they maneuvre at my command, and wheel to the right or left, or march forward or backward, and are not shut up in any house like your poor little people who can only move over and over in the same way."

With these words he turned his back upon Godfather Drosselmayer and the house, hastened to the table, and drew up his hussars in battle array.

As for Mary, she had slipped away very gently, because the motions of the little figures in the house seemed to her to be very tiresome: but, as she was a charming child, she said nothing, for fear of wounding the feelings of Godpapa Drosselmayer. Indeed, the moment Fritz had turned his back, the doctor said to the judge and his wife, in a tone of vexation, "This masterpiece is not fit for children; and I will put my house back again into the box, and take it away."

But the judge's wife approached him, and, in order to atone for her son's rudeness, begged Godfather Drosselmayer to explain to her all the secrets of the beautiful house, and praised the ingenuity of the mechanism to such an extent, that she not only made the doctor forget his vexation, but put him into such a good humour, that he drew from the pockets of his drab coat a number of little men and women, with horn complexions, white eyes, and gilt hands and feet. Besides the beauty of their appearance, these little men and women sent forth a delicious perfume, because they were made of cinnamon.

At this moment Miss Trudchen called Mary, and offered to help her to put on the pretty little silk frock which she had so much admired on first entering the drawing room; but Mary, in spite of her usual politeness, did not answer the governess, so much was she occupied with a new person age whom she had discovered amongst the toys, and to whom, my dear children, I must briefly direct your attention, since he is actually the hero of my tale, in which Miss Trudchen, Mary, Fritz, the judge, the judge's lady, and even Godfather Drosselmayer, are only secondary characters.

III

The Little Man With The Wooden Cloak

I TOLD YOU THAT MARY DID not reply to the invitation of Miss Trudchen, because she had just discovered a new toy which she had not before perceived.

Indeed, by dint of making his hussars march and counter march about the table, Fritz had brought to light a charming little gentleman, who, leaning in a melancholy mood against the trunk of the Christmas tree, awaited, in silence and polite reserve, the moment when his turn to be inspected should arrive. We must pause to notice the appearance of this little man, to whom I gave the epithet "charming" somewhat hastily; for, in addition to his body being too long and large for the miserable little thin legs which supported it, his head was of a size so enormous that it was quite at variance with the proportions indicated not only by nature, but also by those drawing-masters who know much better than even Nature herself.

But if there were any fault in his person, that defect was atoned for by the excellence of his toilette, which denoted at once a man of education and taste. He wore a braided frock coat of violet-coloured velvet, all frogged and covered with buttons; trousers of the same material; and the most charming little Wellington boots ever seen on the feet of a student or an officer. But there were two circumstances which seemed strange in respect to a man who preserved such elegant taste: the one was an ugly narrow cloak made of wood, and which hung down like a pig's tail from the nape of his neck to the middle of his back; and the other was a wretched cap, such as peasants sometimes wear in Switzerland, upon his head. But Mary, when she perceived those two objects which seemed so unsuitable to the rest of his costume, remembered that Godfather Drosselmayer himself wore above his drab coat a little collar of no better appearance than the wooden cloak belonging to the little gentleman in the military frock; and that the doctor often covered his own bald head with an ugly—an absolutely frightful cap, unlike all other ugly caps in the world—although this circumstance did not prevent the doctor from being an excellent godpapa. She even thought to herself that were Godpapa Drosselmayer to imitate altogether the dress of the little gentleman with the wooden cloak, he could not possibly become so genteel and interesting as the puppet.

You can very well believe that all these reflections on the part of Mary were not made without a close inspection of the little man, whom she liked from the very first moment that she saw him. Then, the more she looked at him, the more she was struck by the sweetness and amiability which were expressed by his countenance. His clear green eyes, which were certainly rather goggle, beamed with serenity and kindness. The frizzled beard of white cotton, extending beneath his chin, seemed to become him amazingly, because it set off the charming smile of his mouth, which was rather wide perhaps; but then, the lips were as red as vermilion!

Thus was it that, after examining the little man for upwards of ten minutes, without daring to touch it, Mary exclaimed, "Oh! Dear papa, whose is that funny figure leaning against the Christmas tree?"

"It belongs to no one in particular," answered the judge; "but to both of you together."

"How do you mean, dear papa? I do not understand you."

"This little man," continued the judge, "will help you both; for it is he who in future will crack all your nuts for you; and he belongs as much to Fritz as to you, and as much to you as to Fritz."

Thus speaking, the judge took up the little man very carefully, and raising his wooden cloak, made him open his mouth by a very simple motion, and display two rows of sharp white teeth. Mary then placed a nut in the little man's mouth; and crack—crack—the shell was broken into a dozen pieces, and the kernel fell whole and sound into Mary's hand. The little girl then learnt that the dandified gentleman belonged to that ancient and respectable race of Nutcrackers whose origin is as ancient as that of the town of Nuremberg, and that he continued to exercise the honourable calling, of his forefathers. Mary, delighted to have made this discovery, leapt for joy; whereupon the Judge said, "Well, my dear little Mary, since the Nutcracker pleases you so much, although it belongs equally to Fritz and yourself, it is to you that I especially trust it. I place it in your care."

With these words the judge handed the little fellow to Mary, who took the puppet in her arms, and began to practise it in its vocation, choosing, however—so good washer heart—the smallest nuts, that it might not be compelled to open its mouth too wide, because by so doing its face assumed a most ridiculous expression. Then Miss Trudchen drew near to behold the little puppet in her turn; and for her also did it perform its duty in the most unassuming and obliging manner in the world, although she was but a dependent.

While he was employed in training his horse and parading his hussars, Master Fritz heard the crack-crack so often repeated, that he felt sure something new was going on. He accordingly looked up and turned his large inquiring eyes upon the group composed of the judge, Mary, and Miss Trudchen; and, when he observed the little man with the wooden cloak in his sister's arms, he leapt from his horse, and, without waiting to put the animal in its stable, hastened towards Mary. Then what a joyous shout of laughter burst from his lips as he espied the funny appearance of the little man opening his large mouth, Fritz also demanded his share of the nuts which the puppet cracked; and this was of course granted. Next he wanted to hold the little man while he cracked the nuts; and this wish was also gratified. Only, in spite of the remonstrances of his sister, Fritz chose the largest and hardest nuts to cram into his mouth; so that at the fifth or sixth c-r-r-ack! And out fell three of the poor little fellow's teeth. At the same time his chin fell and became tremulous like that of an old man.

"Oh! My poor Nutcracker!" cried Mary, snatching the little man from the hands of Fritz.

"What a stupid fellow he is!" cried the boy: "he pretends to be a nutcracker, and his jaws are as brittle as glass. He is a false nutcracker, and does not understand his duty. Give him to me, Mary; I will make him go on cracking my nuts, even if he loses all his teeth in doing so, and his chin is dislocated entirely. But how you seem to feel for the lazy fellow!"

"No—no—no!" cried Mary, clasping the little man in her arms: "no—you shall not have my Nutcracker! See how he looks at me, as much as to tell me that his poor jaw is hurt. Fie, Fritz! you are very ill-natured—you beat your horses; and the other day you shot one of your soldiers."

"I beat my horses when they are restive," said Fritz, with an air of importance; "and as for the soldier whom I shot the other day, he was a wretched scoundrel that I never have been able to do anything with for the last year, and who deserted one fine morning with his arms and baggage—a crime that is punished by death in all countries. Besides, all these things are matters of discipline which do not regard women. I do not prevent you from boxing your doll's ears; so don't try to hinder me from whipping my horses or shooting my soldiers. But I want the Nutcracker."

"Papa—papa! Help—help!" cried Mary, wrapping the little man in her pocket handkerchief: "Help! Fritz is going to take the Nutcracker from me!"

At Mary's cries, not only the judge drew near the children; but his wife and Godfather Drosselmayer also ran towards them. The two children told their stories in their own way—Mary wishing to keep the Nutcracker, and Fritz anxious to have it again. But to the astonishment of Mary, Godfather Drosselmayer a smile that seemed perfectly frightful to the little girl, decided in favour of Fritz. Happily for the poor Nutcracker, the judge and his wife took Little Mary's part.

"My dear Fritz," said the judge, "I trusted the Nutcracker to the care of your sister; and as far as my knowledge of surgery goes, I see that the poor creature is very unwell, and requires attention. I therefore give him over solely to the care of Mary, until he is quite well; and no one must say a word against my decision. And you, Fritz, who stand up so firmly in behalf of military discipline, when did you ever hear of making a wounded soldier return to his duty? The wounded always go to the hospital until they are cured; and if they be disabled by their wounds, they are entitled to pensions."

Fritz was about to reply; but the judge raised his forefinger to a level with his right eye, and said, "Master Fritz!"

You have already seen what influence those two words had upon the little boy:—thus, ashamed at having drawn upon himself the reprimand conveyed in those words, he slipped quietly off, without giving any answer, to the table where his hussars were posted: then, having placed the sentinels in their stations, he marched off the rest to their quarters for the night.

In the meantime, Mary picked up the three little teeth which had fallen from the Nutcracker's mouth, and kept the Nutcracker himself well wrapped up in the pocket handkerchief; she had also bound up his chin with a pretty white ribbon which she cut from the frock. On his side, the little man, who was at first very pale and much frightened, seemed quite contented in the care of his protectress, and gradually acquired confidence, when he felt himself gently rocked in her arms.

Then Mary perceived that Godfather Drosselmayer watched with mocking smiles the care which she bestowed upon the little man with the wooden cloak; and it struck her that the single eye of the doctor had acquired an expression of spite and malignity which she had never before seen. She therefore tried to get away from him; but Godfather Drosselmayer burst out laughing, saying, "Well my dear god daughter, I am really astonished that a pretty little girl like you can be so devoted to an ugly little urchin like that."

Mary turned round; and, much as she loved her godfather, even the compliment which he paid her did not make amends for the unjust attack he made upon the person of her Nutcracker. She even felt—contrary to her usual disposition—very angry; and that vague comparison which she had before formed between the little man with the wooden cloak and her godfather, returned to her memory.

"Godpapa Drosselmayer," she said, "you are unkind towards my little Nutcracker, whom you call an ugly urchin. Who knows whether you would even look so well as he, even if you had his pretty little military coat, his pretty little breeches, and his pretty little boots!"

At these words Mary's parents burst out laughing; and the doctor's nose grew prodigiously longer. Why did the doctor's nose grow so much longer? Mary, surprised by the effect of her remark, could not guess the reason.

But as there are never any effects without causes, that reason no doubt belonged to some strange and unknown cause, which we must explain.

IV

Wonderful Events

I DO NOT KNOW, MY DEAR little friends, whether you remember that I spoke of a certain large cupboard, with glass windows, in which the children's toys were locked up. This cupboard was on the right of the door of the judge's own room. Mary was still a baby in the cradle, and Fritz had only just began to walk, when the judge had that cupboard made by a very skilful carpenter, who put such brilliant glass in the frames, that the toys appeared a thousand times finer when ranged on the shelves than when they were held in the hand. Upon the top shelf of all, which neither Fritz nor Mary could reach, the beautiful pieces of workmanship of Godfather Drosselmayer were placed. Immediately beneath was the shelf containing the picture books; and the two lower shelves were given to Fritz and Mary, who filled them in the way they liked best. It seemed, however, to have been tacitly agreed upon between the two children, that Fritz should hold possession of the higher shelf of the two, for the marshalling of his troops, and that Mary should keep the lower shelf for her dolls and their households. This arrangement was entered into on the eve of Christmas Day. Fritz placed his soldiers upon his own shelf; and Mary, having thrust Miss Rose into a corner, gave the bedroom, formed by the lowest shelf, to Miss Clara, with whom she invited herself to pass the evening and enjoy a supper of sugar plums. Miss Clara, on casting her eyes around, saw that everything was in proper order; her table well spread with sugar plums and conserved fruits, and her nice white bed with its white counterpane, all so neat and comfortable. She therefore felt very well satisfied with her new apartment.

While all these arrangements were being made, the evening wore away: midnight was approaching—Godfather Drosselmayer had been gone a long time—and yet the children could not be persuaded to quit the cupboard.

Contrary to custom, it was Fritz that yielded first to the persuasion of his parents, who told him that it was time to go to bed.

"Well," said he, "after all the exercise which my poor hussars have had today, they must be fatigued; and as those excellent soldiers all know their duty towards me—and as, so long as I remain here, they will not close their eyes—I must retire."

With these words—and having given them the watchword, to prevent them from being surprised by a patrol of the enemy—Fritz went off to bed.

But this was not the case with Mary; and as her mamma, who was about to follow her husband to their bed-chamber, desired her to tear herself away from the dearly beloved cupboard, little Mary said, "Only one moment, dear mamma—a single moment: do let me finish all I have to do here. There are a hundred or more important things to put to rights; and the moment I have settled them, I promise to go to bed."

Mary requested this favour in so touching and plaintive a tone,— she was, moreover, so glad and obedient a child—that her mother did not hesitate to grant her request. Nevertheless, as Miss Trudchen had already gone up stairs to get Mary's bed ready, the judge's wife, thinking that her daughter might forget to put out the candles, performed that duty herself, leaving only a light in the lamp hanging from the ceiling.

"Do not be long before you go to your room, dear little Mary," said the judge's wife; "for if you remain up too long, you will not be able to rise at your usual hour tomorrow morning."

With these words the lady quitted the room and closed the door behind her.

The moment Mary found herself alone, she bethought herself, above all things, of her poor little Nutcracker; for she had contrived to keep it in her arms, wrapped up in her pocket handkerchief. She placed him upon the table very gently, unrolled her handkerchief, and examined his chin. The Nutcracker still seemed to suffer much pain, and appeared very cross.

"Ah! My dear little fellow," she said in a low tone, "do not be angry, I pray, because my brother Fritz hurt you so much. He had no evil intention, rest well assured; only his manners have become rough, and his heart is a little hardened by his soldier's life. Otherwise he is a very good boy, I can assure you; and I know that when you are better acquainted with him, you will forgive him. Besides, to atone for the injury which he has done you, I will take care of you; which I will do so attentively that in a few days you will be quite well. As for putting in the teeth again and fastening your chin properly, that is the business of Godpapa Drosselmayer, who perfectly understands those kind of things."

Mary could say no more; for the moment she pronounced the name of her Godfather Drosselmayer, the Nutcracker, to whom this discourse was addressed, made so dreadful a grimace, and his eyes suddenly flashed so brightly, that the little girl stopped short in affright, and stepped a pace back. But as the Nutcracker immediately afterwards resumed its amiable expression and its melancholy smile, she fancied that she must have been the sport of an illusion, and that the flame of the lamp, agitated by a current of air, had thus disfigured the little man. She even laughed at herself, saying, "I am indeed very foolish to think that this wooden puppet could make faces to me. Come, let me draw near the poor fellow, and take that care of him which he requires."

Having thus mused within herself, Mary took the puppet once more in her arms, drew near the cupboard, knocked at the glass door, which Fritz had closed, and said to the new doll, "I beg of you, Miss Clara, to give up your bed to my poor Nutcracker, who is unwell, and to shift for yourself on the sofa tonight. Remember that you are in excellent health yourself, as your round and rosy cheeks sufficiently prove. Moreover, a night is soon passed; the sofa is very comfortable; and there will not be many dolls in Nuremberg as well lodged as yourself."

Miss Clara, as you may very well suppose, did not utter a word; but it struck Mary that she seemed very sulky and discontented; but Mary whose conscience, told her that she had treated Miss Clara in the most considerate manner, used no farther ceremony with her, but, drawing the bed towards her, placed the Nutcracker in it, covering him with the clothes up to the very chin: she then thought that she knew nothing, as yet of the real disposition of Miss Clara, whom she had only seen for a few hours; but that as Miss Clara had appeared to be in a very bad humour at losing her bed, some evil might happen to the poor invalid if he were left with so insolent a person.

She therefore placed the bed, with the Nutcracker in it, upon the second shelf, close by the ridge where Fritz's cavalry were quartered: then, having laid Miss Clara upon the sofa, she closed the cupboard, and was about to rejoin Miss Trudchen in the bed chamber, when all round the room the poor little girl heard a variety of low scratching sounds, coming from behind the chairs, the store, and the cupboard. The large clock which hung against the wall, and which was surmounted by a large gilt owl, instead of a cuckoo, as is usual with old German clocks, began that usual whirring sound which gives warning of striking; and yet it did not strike. Mary glanced towards it, and saw that the immense gilt owl had drooped its wings in such a way that they covered the entire clock, and that the bird thrust forward as far as it could its hideous cat-like head, with the round eyes and the crooked beak. Then the whirring sound of the clock became louder and louder, and gradually changed into the resemblance of a human voice, until it appeared as if these words issued from the beak of the owl: "Clocks, clocks, clocks! Whir, whir, whirl in a low tone! The king of the mice has a sharp ear! Sing him his old song! Strike, strike, strike, clocks all: sound his last hour—for his fate is nigh at hand!"

And then, dong-dong-dong—the clock struck twelve in a hollow and gloomy tone.

Mary was very much frightened. She began to shudder from head to foot; and she was about to run away from the room, when she beheld Godfather Drosselmayer seated upon the clock instead of the owl, the two skirts of his coat having taken the place of the drooping wings of the bird. At that spectacle, Mary remained nailed as it were to the spot with astonishment; and she began to cry, saying, "What are you doing up there, Godpapa Drosselmayer? Come down here, and don't frighten me like that, naughty Godpapa Drosselmayer."

But at these words there began a sharp whistling and furious kind of tittering all around: then in a few moments Mary heard thousands of little feet treading behind the walls; and next she saw thousands of little lights through the joints in the wainscot. When I say little lights, I am wrong—I mean thousands of little shining eyes. Mary full well perceived that there was an entire population of mice about to enter the room. And, in fact, in the course of five minutes, thousands and thousands of mice made their appearance by the creases of the door and the joints of the floor, and began to gallop hither and thither, until at length they ranged themselves in order of battle, as Fritz was wont to draw up his wooden soldiers. All this seemed very amusing to Mary; and as she did not feel towards mice that absurd alarm which so many foolish children experience, she thought she should divert herself with the sight, when there suddenly rang through the room a whistling so sharp, so terrible, and so long, that a cold shudder passed over her.

At the same time, a plank was raised up by some power underneath, and the king of the mice, with seven heads all wearing gold crowns, appeared at her very feet, in the midst of the mortar and plaster that was broken up; and each of his seven mouths began to whistle and scream horribly, while the body to which those seven heads belonged forced its way through the opening. The entire army advanced towards the king, speaking with their little mouths three times in chorus. Then the various regiments marched across the room, directing their course towards the cupboard, and surrounding Mary on all sides, so that she began to beat a retreat.

I have already told you that Mary was not a timid child; but when she thus saw herself surrounded by the crowds of mice, commanded by that monster with seven heads, fear seized upon her, and her heart began to beat so violently, that it seemed as if it would burst from her chest. Her blood appeared to freeze in her veins, her breath failed her; and, half fainting, she retreated with trembling steps. At length pir-r-r-r-r! and the pieces of one of the panes in the cupboard, broken by her elbow which knocked against it, fell upon the floor. She felt at the moment an acute pain in the left arm; but at the same time her heart grew lighter, for she no longer heard that squeaking which had so much frightened her.

Indeed, everything had again become quiet around her; the mice had disappeared; and she thought that, terrified by the noise of the glass which was broken, they had sought refuge in their holes.

But almost immediately afterwards, a strange noise commenced in the cupboard; and numerous little sharp voices exclaimed, "To arms! To arms! To arms!" At the same time the music of Godfather Drosselmayer's country house, which had been placed upon the top shelf of the cupboard, began to play; and on all sides she heard the words, "Quick! Rise to arms! To arms!"

Mary turned round. The cupboard was lighted up in a wondrous manner, and all was bustle within. All the harlequins, the clowns, the punches, and the other puppets scampered about; while the dolls set to work to make lint and prepare bandages for the wounded. At length the Nutcracker himself threw off—all the clothes, and jumped off the bed, crying, "Foolish troop of mice! Return to your holes, or you must encounter me!"

But at that menace a loud whistling echoed through the room; and Mary perceived that the mice had not returned to their holes; but that, frightened by the noise of the broken glass, they had sought refuge beneath the chairs and tables, whence they were now beginning to issue again.

On his side, Nutcracker, far from being terrified by the whistling, seemed to gather fresh courage.

"Despicable king of the mice," he exclaimed; "it is thou, then! Thou acceptest the death which I have so long offered you? Come on, and let this night decide between us. And you, my, good friends—my companions, my brethren, if it be indeed true that we are united in bonds of affection, support me in this perilous contest! On! On!—Let those who love me, follow!"

Never did a proclamation produce such an effect.

Two harlequins, a clown, two punches, and three other puppets, cried out in a loud tone, "Yes, my lord, we are your's in life and death! We will conquer under your command, or die with you!"

At these words, which proved that there was an echo to his speech in the heart of his friends, Nutcracker felt himself so excited, that he drew his sword, and without calculating the dreadful height on which he stood, leapt from the second shelf. Mary, upon perceiving that dangerous leap, gave a piercing cry; for Nutcracker seemed on the point of being dashed to pieces; when Miss Clara, who was on the lower shelf, darted from the sofa and received him in her arms.

"Ah! My dear little Clara," said Mary, clasping her hands together with emotion: "how have I mistaken your disposition!"

But Miss Clara, thinking only of the present events, said to the Nutcracker, "What! My lord—wounded and suffering as you are, you are plunging head long into new dangers! Content yourself with commanding the army, and let the others fight! Your courage is known; and you can do no good by giving fresh proof of it!"

And as she spoke, Clara endeavoured to restrain the gallant Nutcracker by holding him tight in her arms; but he began to struggle and kick in such a manner that Miss Clara was obliged to let him glide down. He slipped from her arms, and fell on his knees at her feet in a most graceful manner, saying, "Princess, believe me, that although at a certain period you were unjust towards me, I shall always remember you, even in the midst of battle!"

Miss Clara stooped as low down as possible, and, taking him by his little arm, compelled him to rise: then taking off her waistband all glittering with spangles, she made a scarf of it, and sought to pass it over the shoulder of the young hero; but he, stepping back a few paces, and bowing at the time in acknowledgment great a favour, untied the same of so little white ribbon with which Mary had bound up his chin, and tied it round his waist, after pressing it to his lips. Then, light as a bird, he leapt from the shelf on the floor, brandishing his sabre all the time.

Immediately did the squeakings and creakings of the mice begin over again; and the king of the mice, as if to reply to the challenge of the Nutcracker, issued from beneath the great table in the middle of the room, followed by the main body of his army. At the same time, the wings, on the right and left, began to appear from beneath the armchair, under which they had taken refuge.

V

The Battle

"TRUMPETS, SOUND THE CHARGE! DRUMS, beat the alarm!" exclaimed the valiant Nutcracker.

And at the same moment the trumpets of Fritz's hussars began to sound, while the drums of his infantry began to beat, and the rumbling of cannon was also heard. At the same time a band of musicians was formed of fat Figaros with their guitars, Swiss peasants with their horns, and Negroes with their triangles. And all these persons, though not called upon by the Nutcracker, did not the less begin to descend from shelf to shelf, playing the beautiful march of the "British Grenadiers."

The music no doubt excited the most peaceably inclined puppets; for, at the same moment, a kind of militia, commanded by the beadle of the parish, was formed, consisting of harlequins, punches, clowns, and pantaloons. Arming themselves with anything that fell in their way, they were soon ready for battle.

All was bustle, even to a man-cook, who, quitting his fire, came down with his spit, on which was a half-roasted turkey, and went and took his place in the ranks. The Nutcracker placed himself at the head of this valiant battalion, which, to the shame of the regular troops, was ready first.

I must tell you everything, or else you might think that I am inclined to be too favourable to that glorious militia; and therefore I must say that if the infantry and cavalry of Master Fritz were not ready so soon as the others, it was because they were all shut up in four boxes. The poor prisoners might therefore well hear the trumpet and drum which called them to battle: they were shut up, and could not get out. Mary heard them stirring in their boxes, like crayfish in a basket; but, in spite of their efforts, they could not free themselves. At length the grenadiers, less tightly fastened in than the others, succeeded in raising the lid of their box, and then helped to liberate the light infantry. In another instant, these were free; and, well knowing how useful cavalry is in a battle, they hastened to release the hussars, who began to canter gaily about, and range themselves four deep upon the flanks.

But if the regular troops were thus somewhat behind hand, in consequence of the excellent discipline in which Fritz maintained them, they speedily, repaired the lost time: for infantry, cavalry, and artillery began to descend with the fury of an avalanche, amidst the plaudits of Miss Rose and Miss Clara, who clapped their hands as they passed, and encouraged them with their voices, as the ladies from whom they were descended most likely were wont to do in the days of ancient chivalry.

Meantime the king of the mice perceived that he had to encounter an entire army.

In fact, the Nutcracker was in the centre with his gallant band of militia; on the left was the regiment of hussars, waiting only the moment to charge; on the right was stationed a formidable battalion of infantry; while, upon a footstool which commanded the entire scene of battle, was a park of ten cannon. In addition to these forces, a powerful reserve, composed of gingerbread men, and warriors made of sugar of different colours, had remained in the cupboard, and already began to bustle about. The king of the mice had, however, gone too far to retreat; and he gave the signal by a squeak, which was repeated by all the forces under his command.

At the same moment the battery on the foot stool replied with a volley of shot amongst the masses of mice.

The regiment of hussars rushed onward to the charge, so that on one side the dust raised by their horses' feet, and on the other the smoke of the cannon, concealed the plain of battle from the eyes of Mary, but in the midst of the roar of the cannon, the shouts of the combatants, and the groans of the dying, she heard the voice of the Nutcracker ever rising above the din.

"Serjeant Harlequin," he cried, "take twenty men, and fall upon the flank of the enemy. Lieutenant Punch, form into a square. Captain Puppet, fire in platoons. Colonel of Hussars, charge in masses, and not four deep, as you are doing. Bravo, good leaden soldiers—bravo! If all my troops behave as well as you, the day is ours!"

But, by these encouraging words even, Mary was at no loss to perceive that the battle was deadly, and that the victory remained doubtful. The mice, thrown back by the hussars—decimated by the fire of the platoons—and shattered by the park of artillery, returned again and again to the charge, biting and tearing all who came in their way. It was like the combats in the days of chivalry—a furious struggle foot to foot and hand to hand, each one bent upon attack or defence, without waiting to think of his neighbour Nutcracker vainly endeavoured to direct the evolutions in a disciplined manner, and form his troops into dense columns. The hussars, assailed by a numerous corps of mice, were scattered, and failed to rally round their colonel; a vast bat talion of the enemy had cut them off from the main body of their army, and had actually advanced up to the militia, which performed prodigies of valour. The beadle of the parish used his battle-axe most gallantly; the man-cook ran whole ranks of mice through with his spit; the leaden soldiers remained firm as a wall; but Harlequin and his twenty men had been driven back, and were forced to retreat under cover of the battery; and Lieutenant Punch's square had been broken up. The remains of his troops fled and threw the militia into disorder; and Captain Puppet, doubtless for want of cartridges, had ceased to fire, and was in full retreat. In consequence of this backward movement throughout the line, the park of cannon was exposed.

The king of the mice, perceiving that the success of the fight depended upon the capture of that battery, ordered his bravest troops to attack it. The foot stool was accordingly stormed in a moment, and the artillery men were cut to pieces by the side of their cannon.

One of them set fire to his powder wagon, and met a heroic death with twenty of his comrades. But all this display was useless against numbers; and in a short time a volley of shot, fired upon them from their own cannon, and which swept the forces commanded by the Nutcracker, convinced him that the battery of the footstool had fallen into the hands of the enemy.

From that moment the battle was lost, and the Nutcracker now thought only of beating an honourable retreat: but, in order to give breathing time to his troops, he summoned the reserve to his aid.

Thereupon the gingerbread men and the corps of sugar warriors descended from the cupboard and took part in the battle. They were certainly fresh, but very inexperienced, troops: the gingerbread men especially were very awkward, and, hitting right and left, did as much injury to friends as to enemies. The sugar warriors stood firm; but they were of such different natures—emperors, knights, Tyrolese peasants, gardeners, cupids, monkeys, lions, and crocodiles—that they could not combine their movements, and were strong only as a mass.

Their arrival, however, produced some good; for scarcely had the mice tasted the gingerbread men and the sugar warriors, when they left the leaden soldiers, whom they found very hard to bite, and turned also from the punches, harlequins, beadles, and cooks, who were only stuffed with bran, to fall upon the unfortunate reserve, which in a moment was surrounded by thousands of mice, and, after an heroic defence, devoured arms and baggage.

Nutcracker attempted to profit by that moment to rally his army; but the terrible spectacle of the destruction of the reserve had struck terror to the bravest hearts. Captain Puppet was as pale as death; Harlequin's clothes were in rags; a mouse had penetrated into Punch's hump, and, like the youthful Spartan's fox, began to devour his entrails; and not only was the colonel of the hussars a prisoner with a large portion of his troops, but the mice had even formed a squadron of cavalry, by means of the horses thus taken.

The unfortunate Nutcracker had no chance of victory left: he could not even retreat with honour; and therefore he determined to die.

He placed himself at the head of a small body of men, resolved like himself to sell their lives dearly.

In the meantime terror reigned among the dolls: Miss Clara and Miss Rose wrung their hands, and gave vent to loud cries.

"Alas!" exclaimed Miss Clara; "Must I die in the flower of my youth—I, the daughter of a king, and born to such brilliant destinies?"

"Alas!" said Miss Rose; "Am I doomed to fall into the hands of the enemy, and be devoured by the filthy mice?"

The other dolls ran about in tears; their cries mingling with those of Miss Clara and Miss Rose.

Meanwhile matters went worse and worse with Nutcracker: he was abandoned by the few friends who had remained faithful to him. The remains of the squadron of hussars took refuge in the cupboard; the leaden soldiers had all fallen into the power of the enemy; the cannoneers had long previously been dispersed; and the militia was cut to pieces, like the three hundred Spartans of Leonidas, without yielding a step. Nutcracker had planted himself against the lower part of the cupboard, which he vainly sought to climb up: he could not do so without the aid of Miss Rose or Miss Clara; and they had found nothing better to do than to faint. Nutcracker made a last effort, collected all his courage, and cried in an agony of despair, "A horse! A horse! My kingdom for a horse!" But, as in the case of Richard III, his voice remained without even an echo—or rather betrayed him to the enemy.

Two of the rifle brigade of the mice seized upon his wooden cloak; and at the same time the king of the mice cried with his seven mouths,

"On your heads, take him alive! Remember that I have my mother to avenge! This punishment must serve as an example to all future Nutcrackers!"

And, with these words, the king rushed upon the prisoner.

But Mary could no longer support that horrible spectacle.

"Oh! My poor Nutcracker!" she exclaimed: "I love you with all my heart, and cannot see you die thus!"

At the same moment, by a natural impulse, and without precisely knowing what she was doing, Mary took off one of her shoes, and threw it with all her force in the midst of the combatants. Her aim was so good that the shoe hit the king of the mice, and made him roll over in the dust. A moment afterwards, king and army—conquerors and conquered—all alike disappeared, as if by enchantment. Mary felt a more severe pain than before in her arm. She endeavoured to reach an armchair to sit down; but her strength failed her—and she fainted!

VI

THE ILLNESS

WHEN MARY AWOKE FROM HER deep sleep, she found herself lying in her little bed, and the sun penetrated radiant and brilliant through the windows. By her side was seated a gentleman whom she shortly perceived to be a surgeon named Vandelstern, and who said in a low voice, the moment she opened her eyes, "She is awake."

Then the judge's wife advanced towards the bed, and gazed upon her daughter for a long time with an anxious air.

"Ah! My dear mamma," exclaimed little Mary, upon seeing her mother; "are all those horrible mice gone? And is my poor Nutcracker saved?"

"For the love of heaven, my dear Mary, do not repeat all that nonsense," said the lady. "What have mice, I should like to know, to do with the Nutcracker? But you, naughty girl, have frightened us all sadly. And it is always so when children are obstinate and will not obey their parents. You played with your toys very late last night: you most likely fell asleep; and it is probable that a little mouse frightened you. At all events, in your alarm, you thrust your elbow through one of the panes of the cupboard, and cut your arm in such a manner that Mr. Vandlestern, who has just extracted the fragments of glass, declares that you ran a risk of cutting an artery and dying through loss of blood. Heaven be thanked that I awoke—I know not at what o'clock—and that, recollecting how I had left you in the room, I went down to look after you. Poor child! you were stretched upon the floor, near the cupboard; and all round you were strewed the dolls, the puppets, the punches, the leaden soldiers, pieces of the gingerbread men, and Fritz's hussars—all scattered about pell-mell—while in your arms you held the Nutcracker. But how was it that you had taken off one of your shoes, and that it was at some distance from you?"

"Ah! My dear mother," said Mary, shuddering as she thought of what had taken place; "all that you saw was caused by the great battle that took place between the puppets and the mice: but the reason of my terror was that I saw the victorious mice about to seize the poor Nutcracker, who commanded the puppets;—and it was then that I threw my shoe at the king of the mice. After that, I know not what happened."

The surgeon made a sign to the judge's lady, who said in a soft tone to Mary, "Do not think anymore of all that, my dear child. All the mice are gone, and the little Nutcracker is safe and comfortable in the glass cupboard."

The judge then entered the room, and conversed for a long time with the surgeon; but of all that they said Mary could only catch these words—"It is delirium."

Mary saw immediately that her story was not believed, but that it was looked upon as a fable; and she did not say anymore upon the subject, but allowed those around her to have their own way. For she was anxious to get up as soon as possible and pay a visit to the poor Nutcracker. She, however, knew that he had escaped safe and sound from the battle; and that was all she cared about for the present.

Nevertheless Mary was very restless. She could not play, on account of her wounded arm; and when she tried to read or look over her picture books, everything swam so before her eyes, that she was obliged to give up the task. The time hung very heavily upon her hands; and she looked forward with impatience to the evening, because her mamma would then come and sit by her, and tell her pleasant stories.

One evening, the judge's wife had just ended the pretty tale of "Prince Facardin," when the door opened, and Godfather Drosselmayer thrust in his head, saying, "I must see with my own eyes how the little invalid gets on."

But when Mary perceived Godfather Drosselmayer with his glass wig, his black patch, and his drab frock coat, the remembrance of the night when the Nutcracker lost the famous battle against the mice, returned so forcibly to her mind, that she could not prevent herself from crying out, "O Godpapa Drosselmayer, you were really very ugly! I saw you quite plainly, when you were astride upon the clock, and when you covered it with your wings to prevent it from striking, because it would have frightened away the mice. I heard you call the king with the seven heads. Why did you not come to the aid of my poor Nutcracker, naughty Godpapa were the cause of my bed."

The judge's wife listened to all this with a kind of stupor; for she thought that the poor little girl was relapsing into delirium. She therefore said, in a low tone of alarm, "What are you talking about, Mary? Are you taking leave of your senses?"

"Oh no!" answered Mary; "Godpapa Drosselmayer knows I am telling the truth."

But the godfather, without saying a word, made horrible faces, like a man who was sitting upon thorns; then all of a sudden he began to chaunt these lines in a gloomy and sing-song tone:

"Old Clock-bell, beat
Low, dull, and hoarse—
Advance, retreat,
Thou gallant force!

The bell's lone sound proclaims around
The hour of deep midnight;
And the piercing note from the screech-owl's throat
Puts the king himself to flight.

Old clock-bell, beat
Low, dull, and hoarse:—
Advance, retreat,
Thou gallant force!"

Mary contemplated Godfather Drosselmayer with increasing terror; for he now seemed to her more hideously ugly than usual. She would indeed have been dreadfully afraid of him, if her mother had not been present, and if Fritz had not at that moment entered the room with a loud shout of laughter.

"Do you know, Godpapa Drosselmayer," said Fritz, "that you are uncommonly amusing today: you seem to move about just like my punch that stands behind the store; and, as for the song, it is not common sense."

But the judge's wife looked severe.

"My dear doctor," she said, "your song is indeed very strange, and appears to me to be only calculated to make little Mary worse."

"Nonsense!" cried Godfather Drosselmayer: "Do you not recognise the old chant which I am in the habit of humming when I mend your clocks?"

At the same time he seated himself near Mary's bed, and said to her in a rapid tone, "Do not be angry with me, my dear child, because I did not tear out the fourteen eyes of the king of the mice with my own hands; but I knew what I was about—and now, as I am anxious to make it up with you, I will tell you a story."

"What story?" asked Mary.

"*The History of the Crackatook Nut and Princess Pirlipata*. Do you know it?"

"No, my dear godpapa," replied Mary, whom the offer of a story reconciled to the doctor that moment. "Go on."

"My dear doctor," said the judge's wife, "I hope that your story will not be so melancholy as your song?"

"Oh! No, my dear lady," returned Godfather Drosselmayer. "On the contrary, it is very amusing."

"Tell it to us, then!" cried both the children.

Godfather Drosselmayer accordingly began in the following manner.

The History of the Crackatook Nut and Princess Pirlipata (An Interlude)

Part I.
How Princess Pirlipata Was Born, and How the Event Produced the Greatest Joy to Her Parents

THERE WAS LATELY, IN THE neighbourhood of Nuremberg, a little kingdom, which was not Prussia, nor Poland, nor Bavaria, nor the Palatinate, and which was governed by a king.

This king's wife, who was consequently a queen, became the mother of a little girl, who was therefore a princess by birth, and received the sweet name of Pirlipata.

The king was instantly informed of the event, and he hastened out of breath to see the pretty infant in her cradle. The joy which he felt in being the father of so charming a child, carried him to such an extreme that, quite forgetting himself, he uttered loud cries of joy, and began to dance round the room, crying, "Oh! Who has ever seen anything so beautiful as my Pirlipatetta?"

Then, as the king had been followed into the room by his ministers, his generals, the great officers of state, the chief judges, the councillors, and the puisne judges, they all began dancing round the room after the king, singing:

> *"Great monarch, we ne'er*
> *In this world did see*
> *A child so fair*
> *As the one that there*
> *Has been given to thee!*
> *Oh! Ne'er, and Oh! Ne'er,*
> *Was there child so fair!"*

And, indeed—although I may surprise you by saying so—there was not a word of flattery in all this; for, since the creation of the world, a sweeter child than Princess Pirlipata never had been seen. Her little face appeared to be made of the softest silken tissue; like the white and rosy tints of the lily combined. Her eyes were of the purest and brightest blue; and nothing was more charming than to behold the golden thread of her hair, flowing in delicate curls over shoulders as white as alabaster. Moreover, Pirlipata, when born, was already provided with two complete rows of the most pearly teeth, with which—two hours after her birth she bit the finger of the lord chancellor so hard, when, being near sighted, he stooped down to look close at her, that, although he belonged to the sect of stoic philosophers, he cried out according to some, "Oh! The dickens!" whereas others affirm, to the honour of philosophy, that he only said, "Oh! Oh!" However, up to the present day opinions are divided upon this important subject, neither party being willing to yield to the other. Indeed, the only point on which the *Dickensonians* and the *Ohists* are agreed is, that the princess really did bite the finger of the lord high chancellor. The country thereby learnt that there was as much spirit as beauty belonging to the charming Pirlipata.

Everyone was therefore happy in a kingdom so blest by heaven, save the queen herself, who was anxious and uneasy, no person knew why. But what chiefly struck people with surprise, was the care with which the timid mother had the cradle of the infant watched. In fact, besides having all the doors guarded by sentinels, and in addition to the two regular nurses, the queen had six other nurses to sit round the cradle, and who were relieved by half a dozen others at night. But what caused the greatest interest, and which no one could understand, was that each of these six nurses was compelled to hold a cat upon her knees, and to tickle it all night so as to prevent it from sleeping, and keep it purring.

I am certain, my dear children, that you are as curious as the inhabitants of that little kingdom without a name, to know why these extra nurses were forced to hold cats upon their knees, and to tickle them in such a way that they should never cease purring; but, as you would vainly endeavour to find out the secret of that enigma, I shall explain it to you, in order to save you the headache which would not fail to be the result of all your guesswork.

It happened one day that half a dozen great kings took it into their heads to pay a visit to the future father of Princess Pirlipata, for at that time the princess was not born. They were accompanied by the royal princes, the hereditary grand dukes, and the heirs apparent, all most agreeable personages. This arrival was the signal for the king whom they visited, and who was a most hospitable monarch, to make a large drain upon his treasury, and give tournaments, feasts, and dramatic representations. But this was not all. He having learnt from the intendant of the royal kitchens, that the astronomer royal of the court had announced that the moment was favourable for killing pigs, and that the conjunction of the stars foretold that the year would be propitious for sausage making, the king commanded a tremendous slaughter of pigs to take place in the courtyard. Then, ordering his carriage, he went in person to call upon all the kings and princes staying in his capital, and invite them to dine with him; for he was resolved to surprise them by the splendid banquet which he intended to give them. On his return to the palace, he retired to the queen's apartment, and going up to her, said in a coaxing tone, with which he was always accustomed to make her do anything he wished, "My most particular and very dear love, you have not forgotten—have you—how doatingly fond I am of black puddings? You surely have not forgotten that?"

The queen understood by the first word what the king wanted of her. In fact she knew by his cunning address, that she must now proceed, as she had done many times before, to the very useful occupation of making, with her own royal hands, the greatest possible quantity of sausages, polonies, and black puddings. She therefore smiled at that proposal of her husband; for, although filling with dignity the high situation of queen, she was less proud of the compliments paid her upon the manner in which she bore the sceptre and the crown, than of those bestowed on her skill in making a black pudding, or any other dish. She therefore contented herself by curtseying gracefully to her husband, saying that she was quite ready to make him the puddings which he required.

The grand treasurer accordingly received orders to carry the immense enamelled cauldron and the large silver saucepans to the royal kitchens, so that the queen might make the black puddings, the polonies, and the sausages. An enormous fire was made with sandalwood; the queen put on her kitchen apron of white damask, and in a short time delicious odours steamed from the cauldron. Those sweet perfumes spread through the passages, penetrated into all the rooms, and reached the throne room where the king was holding a privy council. The king was very fond of good eating, and the smell made a profound impression upon him. Nevertheless, as he was a wise prince, and was famed for his habits of self-command, he resisted for a long time the feeling which attracted him towards the kitchens: but at last, in spite of the command which he exercised over himself, he was compelled to yield to the inclination that now ruled him.

"My lords and gentlemen," he accordingly said, rising from his throne, "with your permission I will retire for a few moments; pray wait for me."

Then this great king hastened through the passages and corridors to the kitchen, embraced his wife tenderly, stirred the contents of the cauldron with his golden sceptre, and tasted them with the tip of his tongue.

Having thus calmed his mind, he returned to the council, and resumed, though somewhat abstractedly, the subject of discussion. He had left the kitchen just at the important moment when the fat, cut up in small pieces, was about to be broiled upon the silver grid irons. The queen, encouraged by his praises, now commenced that important operation; and the first drops of grease had just dripped upon the live coals, when a squeaking voice was heard to chant the following lines:

> "Dear sister, pray give to the Queen of the Mice,
> A piece of that fat which is grilling so nice;
> To me a good dinner is something so rare,
> That I hope of the fat you will give me a share."

The queen immediately recognised the voice that thus spoke; it was the voice of Dame Mousey.

Dame Mousey had lived for many years in the palace. She declared herself to be a relation of the royal family, and was Queen of the kingdom of Mice. She therefore maintained a numerous court beneath the kitchen hearthstone.

The queen was a kind and good-natured woman; and although she would not publicly recognise Dame Mousey as a sister and a sovereign, she nevertheless showed her in private a thousand attentions. Her husband, more particular than herself, had often reproached her for thus lowering herself. But on the present occasion she could not find it in her heart to refuse the request of her little friend; and she accordingly said, "Come, Dame Mousey, without fear, and taste my pork fat as much as you like. I give you full leave so."

Dame Mousey accordingly leapt upon the hearth, quite gay and happy, and took with her little paws the pieces of fat which the queen gave her.

But, behold! The murmurs of joy which escaped the mouth of Dame Mousey, and the delicious smell of the morsels of fat on the grid iron, reached her seven sons, then her relations, and next her friends, all of whom were terribly addicted to gourmandising, and who now fell upon the fat with such fury, that the queen was obliged, hospitable as she was, to remind them that if they continued at that rate only five minutes more, there would not be enough fat left for the black puddings. But, in spite of the justice of this remonstrance, the seven sons of Dame Mousey took no heed of them; and setting a bad example to their relations and friends, rushed upon their aunt's fat, which would have entirely disappeared, had not the cries of the queen brought the man cook and the scullery boys, all armed with brushes and brooms, to drive the mice back again under the hearthstone.

But the victory, although complete, came somewhat too late; for there scarcely remained a quarter enough fat necessary for the polonies, the sausages, and the black puddings. The remnant, however, was scientifically divided by the royal mathematician, who was sent for in all possible haste, between the large cauldron containing the materials for the puddings, and the two saucepans in which the sausages and polonies were cooking.

Half an hour after this event, the cannon fired, the clarions and trumpets sounded, and then came the potentates, the royal princes, the hereditary dukes, and the heirs apparent to the thrones, all dressed in their most splendid clothes, and some riding on gallant chargers. The king received them on the threshold of the palace, in the most courteous manner possible; then, having conducted them to the banqueting room, he took his seat at the head of the table in his quality of sovereignhood, and having the crown upon his head and the sceptre in his hand. The guests all placed themselves at table according to their rank, as crowned kings, royal princes, hereditary dukes, or heirs apparent.

The board was covered with dainties, and everything went well during the soup and first course but when the polonies were placed on table, the king seemed to be agitated; when the sausages were served up, he grew very pale; and when the black puddings were brought in, he raised his eyes to heaven, sighs escaped his breast, and a terrible grief seemed to rend his soul. At length he fell back in his chair, and covered his face with his hands, sobbing and moaning in so lamentable a manner, that all the guests rose from their seats and surrounded him with great anxiety. At length the crisis seemed very serious; the court physician could not feel the beating of the pulse of the unfortunate monarch, who was thus overwhelmed with the weight of the most profound, the most frightful, and the most unheard of calamity. At length, upon the most violent remedies, such as burnt feathers, volatile salts, and cold keys thrust down the back, had been employed, the king seemed to return to himself. He opened his eyes, and said in a scarcely audible tone, "*not enough fat!*"

At these words, the queen grew pale in her turn, she threw herself at his feet, crying in a voice interrupted by sobs, "Oh! My unfortunate, unhappy, and royal husband, what grief have I not caused you, by refusing to listen to the advice which you have so often given me! But you behold the guilty one at your feet, and you can punish her as severely as you think fit."

"What is the matter?" demanded the king, "and what has happened that I know not of?"

"Alas! Alas!" answered the queen, to whom her husband had never spoken in so cross a tone; "Alas! Dame Mousey, her seven sons, her nephews, her cousins, and her friends, devoured the fat."

But the queen could not say anymore; her strength failed her, she fell back and fainted.

Then the king rose in a great rage, and cried in a terrible voice, "Let her ladyship the royal housekeeper explain what all this means! Come, speak!"

Then the royal namely, that being housekeeper related all that she knew; alarmed by the queen's cries, she ran and beheld her majesty beset by the entire family of Dame Mousey, and that, having summoned the cooks and scullery boys, the plunderers were compelled to retreat.

The king, perceiving that this was a case of high treason, resumed all his dignity and calmness, and commanded the privy council to meet that minute, the matter being of the utmost importance. The council assembled, the business was explained, and it was decided by a majority of voices, "That Dame Mousey, being accused of having eaten of the fat destined for the sausages, the polonies, and the black puddings of the king, should be tried for the same offence; and that if the said Dame Mousey was found guilty, she and all her race should be banished from the kingdom, and all her goods or possessions, namely, lands, castles, palaces, and royal residences should be confiscated."

Then the king observed to his councillors that while the trial lasted, Dame Mousey and her family would have sufficient time to devour all the fat in the royal kitchens, which would expose him to the same privation as that which he had just endured in the presence of six crowned heads, without reckoning royal princes, hereditary dukes, and heirs apparent. He therefore demanded a discretionary power in respect to Dame Mousey and her family.

The privy council divided, for the form of the thing, but the discretionary power was voted, as you may well suppose, by a large majority.

The king then sent one of his best carriages, preceded by a courier that greater speed might be used, to a very skilful mechanic who lived at Nuremberg, and whose name was Christian Elias Drosselmayer.

This mechanic was requested to proceed that moment to the palace upon urgent business. Christian Elias Drosselmayer immediately obeyed, for he felt convinced that the king required him to make some work of art. Stepping into the vehicle, he travelled day and night, until he arrived in the king's presence. Indeed, such was his haste, that he had not waited to change the drab-coloured coat which he usually wore. But, instead of being angry at that breach of etiquette, the king was much pleased with his haste; for if the famous mechanic had committed a fault, it was in his anxiety to obey the king's commands.

The king took Christian Elias Drosselmayer into his private chamber, and explained to him the position of affairs; namely, that it was decided upon to make a striking example of the race of mice throughout the kingdom; that, attracted by the fame of his skill, the king had fixed upon him to put the decree of justice into execution; and that the said king's only fear was lest the mechanic, skilful though he were, should perceive insurmountable difficulties in the way of appeasing the royal anger.

But Christian Elias Drosselmayer reassured the king, promising that in eight days there should not be a single mouse left in the kingdom.

In a word, that very same day he set to work to make several ingenious little oblong boxes, inside which he placed a morsel of fat at the end of a piece of wire. By seizing upon the fat, the plunderer, whoever he might be, caused the door to shut down behind him, and thus became a prisoner. In less than a week, a hundred of these boxes were made, and placed, not only beneath the hearthstone, but in all the garrets, lofts, and cellars of the palace. Dame Mousey was far too cunning and sagacious not to discover at the first glance the stratagem of Master Drosselmayer. She therefore assembled her seven sons, their nephews, and their cousins, to warn them of the snare that was laid for them. But, after having appeared to listen to her, in consequence of the respect which they had for her, and the veneration which her years commanded, they withdrew, laughing at her terrors; then, attracted by the smell of the fried pork fat, they resolved, in spite of the representations made to them, to profit by the charity that came they knew not whence.

At the expiration of twenty-four hours, the seven sons of Dame Mousey, eighteen of her nephews, fifty of her cousins, and two hundred and thirty-five of her other connexions, without reckoning thousands of her subjects, were caught in the mousetraps and ignominiously executed.

Then did Dame Mousey, with the remnant of her court and the rest of her subjects, resolve upon abandoning a place covered with the blood of her massacred relatives and friends. The tidings of that resolution became known, and reached the ears of the king. His majesty expressed his satisfaction, and the poets of the court composed sonnets upon his victory, while the courtiers compared him to Sesostris, Alexander, and Cæsar.

The queen was alone anxious and uneasy; she knew Dame Mousey well, and suspected that she would not leave unavenged the death of her relations and friends. And, in fact, at the very moment when the queen, by way of atoning for her previous fault, was preparing with her own hands a liver soup for the king, who doated upon that dish, Dame Mousey suddenly appeared and chanted the following lines:

> *"Thine husband, void of pity and of fear,*
> *Hath slain my cousins, sons, and nephews dear;*

But list, O Queen! To the decrees of fate:
The child which heaven will shortly give to thee,
And which the object of thy love will be,
Shall bear the rage of my vindictive hate.

Thine husband owneth castles, cannon, towers,
A council's wisdom, and an army's powers,
Mechanics, ministers, mousetraps, and snares:
None of all these, alas! To me belong;
But heaven hath given me teeth, sharp, firm, and strong,
That I may rend in pieces royal heirs."

Having sung these words she disappeared, and no one saw her afterwards. But the queen, who expected a little baby, was so overcome by the prophecy, that she upset the liver soup into the fire.

Thus, for the second time, was Dame Mousey the cause of depriving the king of one of his favourite dishes, where at he fell into a dreadful rage. He, however, rejoiced more than ever at the step he had taken to rid his country of the mice.

It is scarcely necessary to say that Christian Elias Drosselmayer was sent away well rewarded, and returned in triumph to Nuremberg.

Part II.

How, In Spite of the Precautions Taken By
the Queen, Dame Mousey Accomplishes Her
Threat in Regard to Princess Pirlipata

And now, my dear children, you know as well as I do, wherefore the queen had Princess Pirlipata watched with such wonderful care. She feared the vengeance of Dame Mousey; for, according to what Dame Mousey had said, there could be nothing less in store for the heiress of this little kingdom without a name, than the loss of her life, or at all events her beauty; which last affliction is considered by some people worse for one of her sex. What redoubled the fears of the queen was, that the machines invented by Master Drosselmayer were totally useless against the experience of Dame Mousey. The astronomer of the court, who was also grand prophet and grand astrologer, was fearful lest his office should be suppressed unless he gave his opinion at this important juncture: he accordingly declared that he read in the stars the great fact that the illustrious family of the cat Murr was alone capable of defending the cradle against the approach of Dame Mousey. It was for this reason that each of the six nurses was forced to hold a cat constantly upon her knees. Those cats might be considered as underofficers attached to the court; and the nurses sought to lighten the cares of the duty performed by the cats, by gently rubbing them with their fair hands.

You know, my dear children, that there are certain times when a person watches even while actually dozing; and so it was that, one evening, in spite of all the efforts which the six nurses made to the contrary, as they sate round the cradle of the princess with the cats upon their knees, they felt sleep rapidly gaining upon them.

Now, as each nurse kept her own ideas to herself, and was afraid of revealing them to their companions, hoping all the time that their drowsiness would not be perceived by the others, the result was, that, one after another, they closed their eyes—their hands stopped from stroking the cats—and the cats themselves, being no longer rubbed and scratched, profited by the circumstance to take a nap.

I cannot say how long this strange slumber had lasted, when, towards midnight, one of the nurses awoke with a start. All the others were in a state of profound lethargy: not a sound—not even their very breathing, was heard: the silence of death reigned around, broken only by the slight creak of the worm biting the wood. But how frightened was the nurse when she beheld a large and horrible mouse standing up near her on its hind legs, and, having plunged its head into the cradle, seemed very busy in biting the face of the princess! She rose with a cry of alarm; and at that exclamation, all the other nurses jumped up. But Dame Mousey—for she indeed it was—sprang towards one corner of the room. The cats leapt after her: alas! It was too late Dame Mousey had disappeared by a crevice in the floor.

At the same moment Princess Pirlipata, who was awoke by all that din, began to cry. Those sounds made the nurses leap with joy.

"Thank God!" they said; "Since Princess Pirlipata cries she is not dead."

They then all ran towards the cradle—but their despair was great indeed when they saw what had happened to that delicate and charming creature!

In fact, instead of that face of softly-blended white and red—that little head, with its golden hair—those mild blue eyes, azure as the sky itself—instead of all these charms the nurses beheld an enormous and misshapen head upon a deformed and ugly body. Her two sweet eyes had lost their heavenly hue, and became goggle, fixed, and haggard. Her little mouth had grown from ear to ear; and her chin was covered with a beard like grizzly cotton. All this would have suited old Punch; but seemed very horrible for a young princess.

At that moment the queen entered. The twelve nurses threw themselves with their faces against the ground; while the six cats walked about to discover if there were not some open window by which they might escape upon the tiles.

At the sight of her child the despair of the poor mother was something frightful to behold; and she was carried off in a fainting fit into the royal chamber. But it was chiefly the unhappy father whose sorrow was the most desperate and painful to witness. The courtiers were compelled to put padlocks upon the windows, for fear he should throw himself out; and they were also forced to line the walls with mattrasses, lest he should dash out his brains against them. His sword was of course taken away from him; and neither knife nor fork, nor any sharp or pointed instruments were left in his way. This was the more easily effected; inasmuch as he ate nothing for the two or three following days, crying without ceasing, "Oh! Miserable king that I am! Oh! Cruel destiny that thou art!"

Perhaps, instead of accusing destiny, the king should have remembered that, as is generally the case with mankind, he was the author of his own misfortunes; for had he known how to content himself with black puddings containing a little less fat than usual, and had he abandoned his ideas of vengeance, and left Dame Mousey and her family in peace beneath the hearthstone, the affliction which he deplored would not have happened. But we must confess that the ideas of the royal father of Princess Pirlipata did not tend at all in that direction.

On the contrary—believing, as all great men do, that they must necessarily attribute their misfortunes to others he threw all the blame upon the skilful mechanic Christian Elias Drosselmayer. Well convinced, moreover, that if he invited him back to court to be hung or beheaded, he would not accept the invitation, he desired him to come in order to receive a new order of knighthood which had just been created for men of letters, artists, and mechanics. Master Drosselmayer was not exempt from human pride: he thought that a star would look well upon the breast of his drab surtout coat; and accordingly set off for the king's court. But his joy was soon changed into fear; for on the frontiers of the kingdom, guards awaited him. They seized upon him, and conducted him from station to station, until they reached the capital.

The king, who was afraid of being won over to mercy, would not see Master Drosselmayer when the latter arrived at the palace; but he ordered him to be immediately conducted to the cradle of Pirlipata, with the assurance that if the princess were not restored by that day month to her former state of beauty, he would have the mechanic's head cut off.

Master Drosselmayer did not pretend to be bolder than his fellow-men, and had always hoped to die a natural death. He was therefore much frightened at this threat. Nevertheless, trusting, a great deal to his knowledge, which his own modesty had never prevented him from being aware of to its full extent, he acquired courage. Then he set to work to discover whether the evil would yield to any remedy, or whether it were really incurable, as he from the first believed it to be.

With this object in view, he skilfully took off the head of the Princess, and next all her limbs. He likewise dissected the hands and the feet, in order to examine, with more accuracy, not only the joints and the muscles, but also the internal formation. But, alas! the more he worked into the frame of Pirlipata, the more firmly did he become convinced that as the princess grew, the uglier she would become.

He therefore joined Pirlipata together again; and then, seating himself by the side of her cradle, which he was not to quit until she had resumed her former beauty, he gave way to his melancholy thoughts.

The fourth week had already commenced, and Wednesday made its appearance, when, according to custom, the king came in to see if any change had taken place in the exterior of the princess. But when he saw that it was just the same, he shook his sceptre at the mechanic, crying; "Christian Elias Drosselmayer, take care of yourself! You have only three days left to restore me my daughter just as she was wont to be; and if you remain obstinate in refusing to cure her, on Monday next you shall be beheaded."

Master Drosselmayer, who could not cure the princess, not through any obstinacy on his part, but through actual ignorance how to do it, began to weep bitterly, surveying, with tearful eyes, Princess Pirlipata, who was cracking nuts as comfortably as if she were the most beautiful child upon earth. Then, as he beheld that melting spectacle, the mechanic was struck for the first time by that particular taste for nuts which the princess had shown since her birth; and he remembered also the singular fact that she was born with teeth. In fact, immediately after her change from beauty to ugliness she had begun to cry bitterly, until she found a nut near her: she had then cracked it, eaten the kernel, and turned round to sleep quietly. From that moment the nurses had taken good care to fill their pockets with nuts, and give her one or more whenever she made a face.

"Oh! Instinct of nature! Eternal and mysterious sympathy of all created beings!" cried Christian Elias Drosselmayer, "Thou showest me the door which leads to the discovery of thy secrets! I will knock at it, and it will open!"

At these words, which surprised the king, the mechanic turned towards his majesty and requested the favour of being conducted into the presence of the astronomer of the court. The king consented, but on condition that it should be with a guard. Master Drosselmayer would perhaps have been better pleased to take that little walk all alone; but, as under the circumstances he could not help himself, he was obliged to submit to what he could not prevent, and proceed through the streets of the capital escorted like a felon.

On reaching the house of the astrologer, Master Drosselmayer threw himself into his arms; and they embraced each other a midst torrents of tears, for they were acquaintances of long standing, and were much attached to each other. They then retired to a private room, and examined a great number of books which treated upon likings and dislikings, and a host of other matters not a whit less profound. At length night came; and the astrologer ascending to his tower, and aided by Master Drosselmayer, who was himself very skilful in such matters, discovered, in spite of the difficulty of the heavenly circles which crossed each other in all directions, that in order to break the spell which rendered Princess Pirlipata hideous, and to restore her to her former beauty, she must eat the kernel of the Crackatook nut, the shell of which was so hard that the wheel of a forty-eight pounder might pass over it without breaking it. Moreover, it was necessary that this nut should be cracked in the presence of the princess, and by a young man who had never been shaved, and who had always worn boots. Lastly, it was requisite that he should present the nut to the princess with his eyes closed, and in the same way step seven paces backward without stumbling.

Such was the answer of the stars.

Drosselmayer and the astronomer had worked without ceasing for four days and four nights, to clear up this mysterious affair. It was on the Sunday evening,—the king had finished his dinner, and was just beginning on the dessert,—when the mechanic, who was to be beheaded next day, entered the royal dining room, full of joy, and announced that he had discovered the means of restoring Princess Pirlipata to her former beauty. At these news, the king caught him in his arms, with the most touching kindness, and asked him what those means were.

The mechanic thereupon explained to the king the result of his consultation with the astrologer.

"I knew perfectly well, Master Drosselmayer," said the king, "that all your delay was only through obstinacy. It is, however, settled at last; and after dinner we will set to work. Take care, then, dearest mechanic, to have the young man who has never been shaved, and who wears boots, in readiness in ten minutes, together with the nut Crackatook. Let him, moreover, abstain from drinking wine for the next hour, for fear he should stumble while walking backwards like a crab; but when once it is all over, is welcome to my whole cellar, and may chooses."

But, to the great astonishment of the king, Master Drosselmayer seemed quite frightened at these words; and, as he held his tongue, the king insisted upon knowing why he remained silent and motionless instead of hastening to execute the orders of his sovereign.

"Sire," replied the mechanician, throwing himself on his knees before the king, "it is perfectly true that we have found out the means of curing Princess Pilipata, and that those means consist of her eating a Crackatook nut when it shall have been cracked by a young man who has never been shaved, and who has always worn boots; but we have not as yet either the young man or the nut—we know not where to find them, and in all probability we shall have the greatest difficulty in discovering both the nut and the Nutcracker."

At these words, the king brandished his sceptre above the head of the mechanician, crying, "Then hasten to the scaffold!"

But the side of the queen, on her side, hastened to kneel by of Master Drosselmayer, and begged her august husband to remember that by cutting off the head of the mechanician he would be losing even that ray of hope which remained to them during his lifetime; that the chances were that he who had discovered the horoscope would also find the nut and the nutcracker; that they ought to believe the more firmly in the present prediction of the astronomer, inasmuch as nothing which he had hitherto prophesied had ever come to pass, but that it was evident his presages must be fulfilled someday or another, inasmuch as the king had named him his grand prophet; and that, as the princess was not yet of an age to marry (she being now only three months old), and would not even be marriageable until she was fifteen, there was consequently a period of fourteen years and nine months during which Master Drosselmayer and the astrologer might search after the Crackatook nut and the young man who was to break it. The queen therefore suggested that a reprieve might be awarded to Christian Elias Drosselmayer, at the expiration of which he should return to surrender himself into the king's power, whether he had found the means of curing the princess, or not; and either to be generously rewarded, or put to death without mercy.

The king, who was a very just man, and who on that day especially had dined splendidly upon his two favourite dishes—namely, liver soup and black puddings—lent a favourable ear to the prayer of his wise and courageous queen.

He therefore decided that the astrologer and the mechanician should that moment set out in search of the nut and the Nutcracker; for which purpose he granted fourteen years and nine months, with the condition that they should return, at the expiration of that reprieve, to place themselves in his power, so that, if they were empty-handed, he might deal with them according to his own royal pleasure.

If, on the contrary, they should make their reappearance with the Crackatook nut which was to restore the princess to all her former beauty, the astrologer would be rewarded with a yearly pension of six hundred pounds and a telescope of honour; and the mechanician would receive a sword set with diamonds, the Order of the Golden Spider (the grand order of the state), and a new frock coat.

As for the young man who was to crack the nut, the king had no doubt of being able to find one suitable for the purpose, by means of advertisements constantly inserted in the national and foreign newspapers.

Touched by this declaration on the part of the king, which relieved them from half the difficulty of their task, Christian Elias Drosselmayer pledged his honour that he would either find the Crackatook nut, or return, like another Regulus, to place himself in the hands of the king.

That same evening the astrologer and the mechanician departed from the capital of the kingdom to commence their researches.

Part III.

How the Mechanician and the Astrologer Wander
Over the Four Quarter of the World, and Discovered
a Fifth, Without Finding the Crackatook Nut

IT WAS NOW FOURTEEN YEARS and five months since the astrologer and the mechanician first set out on their wanderings through all parts, without discovering a vestige of what they sought. They had first of all travelled through Europe; then they visited America, next Africa, and afterwards Asia: they even discovered a fifth part of the world, which learned men have since called New Holland, because it was discovered by two Germans! But throughout that long series of travels, although they had seen many nuts of different shapes and sizes, they never fell in with the Crackatook nut.

They had, however, in, alas! A vain hope, passed several years at the court of the King of Dates and at that of the Prince of Almonds: they had uselessly consulted the celebrated Academy of Grau Monkeys and the famous Naturalist Society of Squirrels; until at length they arrived, sinking with fatigue, upon the borders of the great forest which touches the feet of the Himalayan Mountains. And now they dolefully said to each other that they had only a hundred and twenty-two days to find what they sought, after an useless search of fourteen years and five months.

If I were to tell you, my dear children, the strange adventures which happened to the two travellers during that long wandering, I should occupy you every evening for an entire month, and should then weary you in the long run. I will therefore only tell you that Christian Elias Drosselmayer, who was the most eager in search after the nut, since his head depended upon finding it, gave himself up to greater dangers than his companion, and lost all his hair by a stroke of the sun received in the tropics. He also lost his right eye by an arrow which a Caribbean Chief aimed at him. Moreover, his drab frock coat, which was not new when he left Germany, had literally fallen into rags and tatters His situation was therefore most deplorable and yet, so much do men cling to life, that, damaged as he was by the various accidents which had be fallen him, he beheld with increasing terror the approach of the moment when he must return to place himself in the power of the king.

Nevertheless, the mechanician was a man of honour: he would not break a promise so sacred as that which he had made. He accordingly resolved, whatever might happen, to set out the very next morning on his return to Germany. And indeed there was no time to lose; fourteen years and five months had passed away, and the two travellers had only a hundred and twenty-two days, as we have already said, to reach the capital of Princess Pirlipata's father.

Christian Elias Drosselmayer accordingly made known his noble intention to his friend the astrologer; and both decided that they would set out on their return next morning.

And, true to this intention, the travellers resumed their journey at daybreak, taking the direction of Bagdad. From Bagdad they proceeded to Alexandria, where they embarked for Venice. From Venice they passed through the Tyrol; and from the Tyrol they entered into the kingdom of Pirlipata's father, both sincerely hoping that he was either dead or in his dotage.

But, alas! It was no such thing! Upon reaching the capital, the unfortunate mechanician learnt that the worthy monarch not only had not lost his intellectual faculties, but was also in better health than ever. There was consequently no chance for him—unless Princess Pirlipata had become cured of her ugliness without any remedy at all, which was not possible; or, that the king's heart had softened, which was not probable—of escaping the dreadful fate which threatened him.

He did not however present himself the less boldly at the gate of the palace, for he was sustained by the idea that he was doing a heroic action; and he accordingly desired to speak to the king.

The king, who was easy of access, and who gave an audience to whomsoever he had business with, ordered the grand master of the ceremonies to bring the strangers into his presence.

The grand master of the ceremonies then stated that the strangers were of a most villainous appearance, and could not possibly be worse dressed. But the king answered that it was wrong to judge the heart by the countenance, and the gown did not make the parson.

Thereupon, the grand master of the ceremonies, having perceived the correctness of these observations, bowed respectfully and proceeded to fetch the mechanician and the astrologer.

The king was the same as ever, and they immediately recognised him; but the travellers were so changed, especially poor Elias Drosselmayer, that they were obliged to declare who they were.

Upon seeing the two travellers return of their own accord, the king gave a sign of joy, for he felt well convinced that they would not have come back if they had not found the Crackatook nut. But he was speedily undeceived; and the mechanician, throwing himself at his feet, confessed that, in spite of the most earnest and constant search, his friend and himself had returned empty-handed.

The king, as we have said, although of a passionate disposition, was an excellent man at bottom; he was touched by the punctuality with which Christian Elias Drosselmayer had kept his word; and he changed the sentence of death, long before pronounced against him, into imprisonment for life. As for the astrologer, he contented himself by banishing that great sage.

But as three days were still remaining of the period of fourteen years and nine months' delay, granted by the king, Master Drosselmayer, who was deeply attached to his country, implored the king's permission to profit by those three days to visit Nuremberg once more.

This request seemed so just to the king, that he granted it without any restriction.

Master Drosselmayer, having only three days left, resolved to profit by that time as much as possible; and, having fortunately found that two places in the mail were not taken, he secured them that moment.

Now, as the astrologer was himself condemned to banishment, and as it was all the same to him which way he went, he took his departure with the mechanician.

Next morning, at about ten o'clock, they were at Nuremberg. As Master Drosselmayer had only one relation in the world, namely, his brother, Christopher Zacharias Drosselmayer, who kept one of the principal toy shops in Nuremberg, it was at his house that he alighted.

Christopher Zacharias Drosselmayer was overjoyed to see his poor brother Christian Elias, whom he had believed to be dead. In the first instance he would not admit that the man with the bald head and the black patch upon the eye was in reality his brother; but the mechanician showed him his famous drab surtout coat, which, all tattered as it was, had retained in certain parts some traces of its original colour; and in support of that first proof he mentioned so many family secrets, unknown to all save to Zacharias and himself, that the toy merchant was compelled to yield to the evidence brought forward.

He then inquired of him what had kept him so long absent from his native city, and in what country he had left his hair, his eye, and the missing pieces of his coat.

Christian Elias Drosselmayer had no motive to keep secret from his brother the events which had occurred. He began by introducing his companion in misfortune; and, this formal usage having been performed, he related his adventures from A to Z, ending them by saying that he had only a few hours to stay with his brother, because, not having found the Crackatook nut, he was on the point of being shut up in a dungeon forever.

While Christian Elias was telling his story, Christopher Zacharias had more than once twiddled his finger and thumb, turned round upon one leg, and made a certain knowing noise with his tongue. Under any other circumstances, the mechanician would have demanded of him what those signs meant; but he was so full of thought, that he saw nothing; and it was only when his brother exclaimed, "Hem! Hem!" twice, and "Oh! Oh! Oh!" three times, that he asked the reason of those expressions.

"The reason is," said Christopher Zacharias, "that it would be strange indeed if—but, no—and yet—"

"What do you mean?" cried the mechanician.

"If" continued the toy merchant.

"If what?" again said Master Drosselmayer.

But instead of giving any answer, Christopher Zacharias, who, during those short questions and answers, had no doubt collected his thoughts, threw his wig up into the air, and began to caper about, crying, "Brother, you are saved! You shall not go to prison; for either I am much mistaken or I myself am in possession of the Crackatook nut."

And, without giving any further explanation to his astonished brother, Christopher Zacharias rushed out of the room, but returned in a moment with a box containing a large gilt filbert, which he presented to the mechanician.

The mechanician, who dared not believe in such good luck, took the nut with hesitation, and turned it round in all directions so as to examine it with the attention which it deserved. He then declared that he was of the same opinion as his brother, and that he should be much astonished if that filbert were not indeed the Crackatook nut. Thus saying, he handed it to the astrologer, and asked his opinion.

The astrologer examined it with as much attention as Master Drosselmayer had done; but shaking his head, he replied, "I should also be of the same opinion as yourself and brother, if the nut were not gilt; but I have not seen anything in the stars showing that the nut which we are in search of ought to be so ornamented. Besides, how came your brother by the Crackatook nut?"

"I will explain the whole thing to you," said Christopher, "and tell you how the nut fell into my hands, and how it came to have that gilding which prevents you from recognising it, and which indeed is not its own naturally."

Then—having made them sit down, for he very wisely thought that after travelling for fourteen years and nine months, they must be tired—he began as follows: —

"The very day on which the king sent for you under pretence of giving you an Order of Knighthood, a stranger arrived at Nuremberg, carrying with him a bag of nuts which he had to sell. But the nut-merchants of this town, being anxious to keep the monopoly to themselves, quarrelled with him just opposite my shop. The stranger, with a view to defend himself more easily, placed his bag of nuts upon the ground, and the fight continued, to the great delight of the little boys and the ticket-porters; when a waggon, heavily laden, passed over the bag of nuts. Upon seeing this accident, which they attributed to the justice of heaven, the merchants considered that they were sufficiently avenged, and left the stranger alone. He picked up his bag, and all his nuts were found to be cracked, save ONE—one only—which he handed to me with a strange kind of smile, requesting me to buy it for a new zwanziger of the year 1720, and declaring that the day would come when I should not repent the bargain, dear as it then might seem. I felt in my pocket, and was much surprised to find a zwanziger of the kind mentioned by this man. The coincidence seemed so strange, that I gave him my zwanziger; he handed me the nut, and took his departure.

"I placed the nut in my window for sale; and although I only asked two kreutzers more than the money I had given for it, it remained in the window for seven or eight years without finding a purchaser. I then had it gilt to increase its value; but for that purpose I uselessly spent two zwanzigers more; for the nut has been here ever since the day I bought it."

At that moment the astronomer, in whose hands the nut had remained, uttered a cry of joy. While Master Drosselmayer was listening to his brother's story, the astrologer had delicately scraped off some of the gilding of the nut; and on the shell he had found the word "CRACKATOOK" engraven in Chinese characters.

All doubts were now cleared up; and the three individuals danced for joy, the real Crackatook nut being actually in their possession.

Part IV.

How, After Having Found the Crackatook Nut, the Mechanician and the Astrologer Find the Young Man Who is to Crack It

CHRISTIAN ELIAS DROSSELMAYER WAS IN such a hurry to announce the good news to the king, that he was anxious to return by the mail that very moment; but Christian Zecharias begged him to stay at least until his son should come in. The mechanician yielded the more easily to this request, because he had not seen his nephew for fifteen years, and because, on recalling the ideas of the past, he remembered that at the time when he quitted Nuremberg, he had left the said nephew a fine fat romping fellow of only three and a half, but of whom he (the uncle) was doatingly fond.

While he was thinking of a handsome young man these things, of between eighteen and nineteen entered the shop of Christopher Zacharias, whom he saluted by the name of "Father."

Then Christopher Zacharias, having embraced him, presented him to Christian Elias, saying to the young man, "And now embrace your uncle."

The young man hesitated; for Uncle Drosselmayer, with his frock coat in rags, his bald head, and the plaster upon his eye, did not seem a very inviting person. But his father observed the hesitation, and as he was fearful that Christian Elias's feelings would be wounded, he pushed his son forward, and thrust him into the arms of the mechanician.

In the meantime the astrologer had kept his eyes fixed upon the young man with a steady attention which seemed so singular that the youth felt ill at his ease in being so stared at, and left the room.

The astrologer then put several questions to Christopher Zecharias concerning his son; and the father answered them with all the enthusiasm of a fond parent.

Young Drosselmayer was, as his appearance indicated, between seventeen and eighteen. From his earliest years he had been so funny and yet so tractable, that his mother had taken a delight in dressing him like some of the puppets which her husband sold: namely, sometimes as a student, sometimes as a postilion, sometimes as a Hungarian, but always in a garb that required boots; because, as he possessed the prettiest little foot in the world, but had a rather small calf, the boots showed off the little foot, and concealed the fault of the calf.

"And so," said the astrologer to Christopher Zecharias, your son has always worn boots?"

Christian Elias now stared in his turn.

"My son has never worn anything but boots," replied the toy man. "At the age of ten," he continued, "I sent him to the University of Tubingen, where he remained till he was eighteen, without contracting any of the bad habits of his companions, such as drinking swearing, and fighting. The only weakness of which I believe him to be guilty, is that he allows the four or five wretched hairs which he has upon his chin to grow, without permitting a barber to touch his countenance."

"And thus," said the astrologer, "your son has never been shaved?"

Christian Elias stared more and more.

"Never," answered Christopher Zecharias.

"And during the holidays," continued the astrologer, "how did he pass his time?"

"Why," replied the father, "he used to remain in the shop, in his becoming student's dress; and, through pure good-nature, he cracked nuts for all the young ladies who came to the shop to buy toys, and who, on that account, called him *Nutcracker*."

"Nutcracker!" cried the mechanician.

"Nutcracker!" repeated the astrologer in his turn.

And then they looked at each other while Christopher Zecharias looked at them both.

"My dear sir," said the astrologer to the toy man,"in my opinion your fortune is as good as made."

The toy man, who had not heard this prophecy without a feeling of pleasure, required an explanation, which the astrologer, however, put off until the next morning.

When the mechanician and the astrologer were shown to their apartment, and were alone together, the astrologer embraced his friend, crying, "It is he! We have him!"

"Do you think so?" demanded Christian Elias, in the tone of a man who had his doubts, but who only wished to be convinced.

"Can there be any uncertainty?" exclaimed the astrologer: "he has all the necessary qualifications!"

"Let us sum them up."

"He has never worn anything but boots."

"True!"

"He has never been shaved."

"True, again!"

"And through good nature, he has stood in his father's shop to crack nuts for young persons, who never called him by any other name than *Nutcracker*."

"All this is quite true."

"My dear friend," added the astrologer, "one stroke of good luck never comes alone. But if you still doubt, let us go and consult the stars."

They accordingly ascended to the roof of the house; and, having drawn the young man's horoscope, discovered that he was intended for great things.

This prophecy, which confirmed all the astrologer's hopes, forced the mechanician to adopt his opinion.

"And now," said the astrologer, in a triumphant tone, "there are only two things which we must not neglect."

"What are they?" demanded Christian Elias.

"The first is, that you must fit to the nape of your nephew's neck a large piece of wood, which must be so well connected with the lower jaw that it will increase its power by the fact of pressure."

"Nothing is more easy," answered Christian Elias; "it is the A, B, C of mechanics."

"The second thing," continued the astrologer, "is, that on arriving at the residence of the king, we must carefully conceal the fact that we have brought with us the young man who is destined to crack the Crackatook nut. For my opinion is that the more teeth there are broken, and the more jaws there are dislocated in trying to break the Crackatook nut, the more eager the king will be to offer a great reward to him who shall succeed where so many will have failed."

"My dear friend," answered the mechanician, "you are a man of sound sense. Let us go to bed."

And, with these words, having quitted the top of the house, they descended to their bedroom, where, having drawn their cotton night-caps over their ears, they slept more comfortably than they had done for fourteen years and nine months past.

On the following morning, at an early hour, the two friends went down to the apartment of Christopher Zecharias, and told him all the fine plans they had formed the evening before. Now, as the toy man was not wanting in ambition, and as, in his paternal fondness, he fancied that his son must certainly possess the strongest jaws in all Germany, he gladly assented to the arrangement, which was to take from his shop not only the nut but also the *Nutcracker*.

The young man himself was more difficult to persuade. The wooden counterbalance which it was proposed to fix to the back of his neck, instead of the pretty little tie which kept his hair in such neat folds, particularly vexed him. But his father, his uncle, and the astrologer made him such splendid promises, that he consented. Christian Elias Drosselmayer, therefore, went to work that moment; the wooden balance was soon made; and it was strongly fixed to the nape of the young man now so full of hope. Let me also state, to satisfy your curiosity, that the contrivance worked so well that on the very first the skilful mechanician received brilliant proofs of his success, for the young man was enabled to crack the hardest apricot stones, and the most obstinate peach stones.

These trials having been made, the astrologer, the mechanician, and young Drosselmayer set out immediately for the king's dwelling. Christopher Zecharias was anxious to go with them; but, as he was forced to take care of his shop, that excellent father resigned himself to necessity, and remained behind at Nuremberg.

Part V.
END OF THE HISTORY OF PRINCESS PIRLIPATA

THE MECHANICIAN AND THE ASTROLOGER, on reaching the capital, took good care to leave young Drosselmayer at the inn where they put up. They then proceeded to the palace to announce that having vainly sought the Crackatook nut all over the world, they had at length found it at Nuremberg: But of him who was to crack it, they said not a word, according to the arrangement made between them.

The joy at the palace was very great.

The king sent directly for the privy councillor who had the care of the public mind, and who acted as censor in respect to the newspapers; and this great man, by the king's command, drew up an article to be inserted in the *Royal Gazette*, and which all other newspapers were ordered to copy, to the effect that "*all persons who fancied they had teeth good enough to break the Crackatook nut, were to present themselves at the palace, and if they succeeded, would be liberally rewarded for their trouble.*"

This circumstance was well suited to show how rich the kingdom was in strong jaws. The candidates were so numerous, that the king was forced to form a jury, the foreman of whom was the crown dentist; and their duty was to examine all the competitors, to see if they had all their thirty-two teeth perfect, and whether any were decayed.

Three thousand five hundred candidates were admitted to this first trial, which lasted a week, and which produced only an immense number of broken teeth and jaws put out of place.

It was therefore necessary to make a second appeal; and all the national and foreign newspapers were crammed with advertisements to that purpose. The king offered the post of Perpetual Judge of the Academy, and the order of the Golden Spider to whomsoever should succeed in cracking the Crackatook nut. There was no necessity to have a degree of Doctor of Philosophy, or Master of Arts, to be competent to stand as a candidate.

This second trial produced five thousand candidates. All the learned societies of Europe sent deputies to this important assembly. Several members of the English Royal Society were present; and a great number of critics belonging to the leading London newspapers and literary journals; but they were not able to stand as candidates, because their teeth had all been broken long before in their frequent attempts to tear to pieces the works of their brother authors.

This second trial, which lasted a fortnight, was, alas! as fruitless as the first. The deputies of the learned societies disputed amongst themselves, for the honour of the associations to which they respectively belonged, as to who should break the nut; but they only left their best teeth behind them.

As for the nut itself, its shell did not even bear the marks of the attempts that had been made to crack it.

The king was in despair. He resolved, however, to strike one grand blow; and, as he had no male descendant, he declared, by means of a third article in the *Royal Gazette*, the national newspapers, and the foreign journals, that the hand of Princess Pirlipata and the inheritance of the throne should be given to him who might crack the Crackatook nut. There was one condition to this announcement; namely, that this time the candidates must be from sixteen to twenty-four years of age. The promise of such a reward excited all Germany.

All Competitors poured in from all parts of Europe; and they would even have come from Asia, Africa, and America, and that fifth quarter of the world which had been discovered by Christian Elias Drosselmayer and his friend the astrologer, if there had been sufficient time.

On this occasion the mechanician and the astrologer thought that the moment was now come to produce young Drosselmayer; for it was impossible for the king to offer a higher reward than that just announced. Only, certain of success as they were, and although this time a host of princes and royal and imperial jaws had presented themselves, the mechanician and the astronomer did not appear with their young friend at the register office until just as it was about to close; so that the name of NATHANIEL DROSSELMAYER was numbered the 11,375th, and stood last.

It was on this occasion as on the preceding ones.

The 11,374 rivals of young Drosselmayer were foiled; and on the nineteenth day of the trial, at twenty-five minutes to twelve o'clock, and just as the princess accomplished her fifteenth year, the name of Nathaniel Drosselmayer was called.

The young man presented himself, accompanied by his two guardians, the mechanician and the astrologer. It was the first time that these two illustrious persons had seen the princess since they had beheld her in her cradle; and since that period great changes had taken place in her. But I must inform you, with due candour, that those changes were not to her advantage. When a child, she was shockingly ugly: she was now frightfully so. Her form had lost, with its growth, none of its important features. It is therefore difficult to understand how those skinny legs, those flat hips, and that distorted body, could have supported such a monstrous head. And that head had the same grizzly hair—the same green eyes—the same enormous mouth—and the same cotton beard on the chin, as we have already described; only all these features were just fifteen years older.

Upon perceiving that monster of ugliness, poor Nathaniel shuddered and inquired of the mechanician and the astrologer if they were quite sure that the kernel of the Crackatook nut would restore the princess to her beauty: because, if she were to remain in that state, he was quite willing to make the trial in a matter where all the others had failed; but he should leave the honour of the marriage and the profit of the heir ship of the throne to anyone who might be inclined to accept them. It is hardly necessary to state that both the mechanician and the astrologer reassured their young friend, promising that, the nut once broken, and the kernel once eaten, Pirlipata would become that very moment the most beautiful princess on the face of the earth.

But if the sight of Princess Pirlipata had struck poor Nathaniel with dismay, I must tell you, in honour of the young man, that *his* presence had produced a very different effect upon the sensitive heart of the heiress of the crown; and she could not prevent herself from exclaiming, when she saw him, "Oh! How glad I should be if he were to break the nut!"

Thereupon the chief governess of the princess replied, "I think I have often observed to your highness, that it is not customary for a young and beautiful princess like yourself to express her opinion aloud relative to such matters."

Nathaniel was indeed calculated to turn the heads of all the princesses in the world. He wore a little military frock coat, of a violet colour, all braided, and with golden buttons, and which his uncle had had made for this solemn occasion.

His breeches were of the same stuff; and his boots were so well blacked, and sat in such an admirable manner, that they seemed as if they were painted. The only thing which somewhat spoilt his appearance was the ugly piece of wood fitted to the nape of his neck; but Uncle Drosselmayer had so contrived that it seemed like a little bag attached to his wig, and might at a stretch have passed as an eccentricity of the toilet, or else as a new fashion which Nathaniel's tailor was trying to push into vogue at the court.

Thus it was, that when this charming young man entered the great hall, what the princess had had the imprudence to say aloud, the other ladies present said to themselves; and there was not a person, not even excepting the king and the queen, who did not desire at the bottom of his heart that Nathaniel might prove triumphant in the adventure which he had undertaken.

On his side, young Drosselmayer approached with a confidence which encouraged the hopes that were placed in him. Having reached the steps leading to the throne, he bowed to the king and queen, then to Princess Pirlipata, and then to the spectators; after which he received the Crackatook nut from the grand master of the ceremonies, took it delicately between his forefinger and thumb, placed it in his mouth, and gave a violent pull at the wooden balance hanging behind him.

Crack! Crack!—And the shell was broken in several pieces.

He then skilfully detached the kernel from the fibres hanging to it, and presented it to the princess, bowing gracefully but respectfully at the same time; after which he closed his eyes, and began to walk backwards. At the same moment the princess swallowed the kernel; and, O! Wonder! Her horrible ugliness disappeared, and she became a young lady of angelic beauty. Her face seemed to have borrowed the hues of the rose and the lily: her eyes were of sparkling azure; and thick tresses, resembling masses of golden thread, flowed over her alabaster shoulders.

The trumpets and the cymbals sounded enough to make one deaf; and the shouts of the people responded to the noise of the instruments. The king, the ministers, the councillors of state, and the judges began to dance, as they had done at the birth of Pirlipata; and eau-de-cologne was obliged to be thrown in the face of the queen, who had fainted for joy.

This great tumult proved very annoying to young Nathaniel Drosselmayer, who, as you must remember, had yet to step seven paces backwards. He, however, behaved with a coolness which gave the highest hopes relative to the period when he should be called upon to reign in his turn; and he was just stretching out his leg to take the seventh step, when the queen of the mice suddenly appeared through a crevice in the floor. With horrible squeaks she ran between his legs; so that just at the very moment when the future Prince Royal placed his foot upon the ground, his heel came so fully on the body of the mouse that he stumbled in such a manner as nearly to fall.

O sorrow! At that same instant the handsome young man became as ugly as the princess was before him: his legs shrivelled up; his shrunken form could hardly support his enormous head; his eyes became green, haggard, and goggle; his mouth split from ear to ear; and his delicate little sprouting beard changed into a white and soft substance, which was afterwards found to be cotton.

But the cause of this event was punished at the same moment that she produced it. Dame Mousey was weltering in her own blood upon the floor. Her wickedness did not therefore go without its punishment. In fact, young Drosselmayer had trampled so hard upon her with his heel, that she was crushed beyond all hope of recovery. But, while still writhing on the floor, Dame Mousey squeaked forth the following words, with all the strength of her agonizing voice:

"Crackatook! Crackatook! Fatal nut that thou art,
Through thee has Death reached me, at length, with his dart!
Heigho! Heigho!

But the Queen of the Mice has thousands to back her,
And my son will yet punish that wretched Nutcracker,
I know! I know!

> *Sweet life, adieu!*
> *Too soon snatch'd away!*
> *And thou heaven of blue,*
> *And thou world so gay,*
> *Adieu! Adieu!"*

The verses of Dame Mousey might have been better; but one cannot be very correct, as you will all agree, when breathing the last sigh!

And when that last sigh was rendered, a great officer of the court took up Dame Mousey by the tail, and carried her away for the purpose of interring her remains in the hole where so many of her family had been buried fifteen years and some months beforehand.

As, in the middle of all this, no one had troubled themselves about Nathaniel Drosselmayer except the mechanician and the astrologer, the princess, who was unaware of the accident which had happened, ordered the young hero to be brought into her presence; for, in spite of the lesson read her by the governess, she was in haste to thank him. But scarcely had she perceived the unfortunate Nathaniel, than she hid her face in her hands; and, forgetting the service which he had rendered her, cried, "Turn out the horrible Nutcracker! Turn him out! Turn him out!"

The grand marshal of the palace accordingly took poor Nathaniel by the shoulders and pushed him downstairs.

The king, who was very angry at having a nutcracker proposed to him as his son-in-law, attacked the astrologer and the mechanician; and, instead of the income of six hundred pounds a year and the telescope of honour which he had promised the first,—instead, also, of the sword set with diamonds, the Order of the Golden Spider, and the drab frock coat, which he ought to have given to the latter,—he banished them both from his kingdom, granting them only twenty-four hours to cross the frontiers.

Obedience was necessary. The mechanician, the astrologer, and young Drosselmayer (now become a Nutcracker), left the capital and quitted the country. But when night came, the two learned men consulted the stars once more, and read in them that, all deformed though he were, Nathaniel would not the less become a prince and king, unless indeed he chose to remain a private individual, which was left to his own choice. This was to happen when his deformity should disappear; and that deformity would disappear when he should have commanded an army in battle,— when he should have killed the seven headed king of the mice, who was born after Dame Mousey's seven first sons had been put to death,— and, lastly, when a beautiful lady should fall in love with him.

But while awaiting these brilliant destinies, Nathaniel Drosselmayer, who had left the paternal shop as the only son and heir, now returned to it in the form of a nutcracker!

I need scarcely tell you that his father did not recognise him; and that, when Christopher Zacharias inquired of the mechanician and his friend the astrologer, what had become of his dearly beloved son, those two illustrious persons replied, with the seriousness of learned men, that the king and the queen would not allow the saviour of the princess to leave them, and that young Nathaniel remained at court covered with honour and glory.

As for the unfortunate nutcracker, who felt how deeply painful was his situation, he uttered not a word, but resolved to await patiently the change which must someday or another take place in him.

Nevertheless, I must candidly admit, that in spite of the good nature of his disposition, he was desperately vexed with Uncle Drosselmayer, who, coming at a moment he was so little expected, and having enticed him away by so many fine promises, was the sole and only cause of the frightful misfortune that had occurred to him.

Such, my dear children, is the History of the Crackatook, Nut, just as Godfather Drosselmayer told it to little Mary and Fritz; and you can now understand why people often say, when speaking of anything difficult to do, "That is a hard nut to crack."

The History of a Nutcracker (Resumed)

VII

The Uncle And The Nephew

IF ANYONE OF MY YOUNG friends now around me has ever cut himself with glass, which he has most likely done in the days of his disobedience, he must know by experience that it is a particularly disagreeable kind of cut, because it is so long in healing Mary was, therefore, forced to stay a whole week in bed; for she always felt giddy whenever she tried to get up. But at last she got well altogether, and was able to skip about the room as she was wont to do.

You would not do my little heroine the injustice to suppose that her first visit was to any other place than the glass cupboard, which now seemed quite charming to look at. A new pane had been put in; and all the windows had been so well cleaned by Miss Trudchen, that all the trees, houses, dolls, and other toys of the Christmas Eve seemed quite new, gay, and polished. But in the midst of all the treasures of her little kingdom, and before all other things, Mary perceived her Nutcracker smiling upon her from the second shelf where he was placed, and with his teeth all in as good order as ever they were. While thus joyfully examining her favourite, an idea which had more than once presented itself to the mind of Mary touched her to the quick. She was persuaded that all Godfather Drosselmayer had told her was not a mere fable, but the true history of the disagreement between the Nutcracker on one side, and the late queen of the mice and her son, the reigning king, on the other side. She, therefore, knew that the Nutcracker could be neither more nor less than Nathaniel Drosselmayer, of Nuremberg, the amiable but enchanted nephew of her godfather; for that the skilful mechanician who had figured at the court of Pirlipata's father, was Doctor Drosselmayer, she had never doubted from the moment when he introduced his drab frock coat into his tale. This belief was strengthened when she found him losing first his hair by a sunstroke, and then his eye by an arrow, events which had rendered necessary the invention of the ugly black patch, and of the ingenious glass wig, of which I have already spoken.

"But why did not your uncle help you, poor Nutcracker?" said Mary, as she stood at the glass cupboard, gazing up at her favourite; for she remembered that on the success of the battle depended the disenchantment of the poor little man and his elevation to the rank of king of the kingdom of toys. Then she thought that all the dolls, puppets, and little men must be well prepared to receive him as their king;—for did they not obey the Nutcracker as soldiers obey a general? That indifference on the part of Godfather Drosselmayer was so much the more annoying to little Mary, because she was certain that those dolls and puppets to which, in her imagination, she gave life and motion, really did live and move.

Nevertheless, there was now no appearance of either life or motion in the cupboard, where everything was still and quiet. But Mary, rather than give up her sincere belief, thought that all this was occasioned by the sorcery of the late queen of the mice and her son; and so firm was she in this belief, that, while she gazed up at the Nutcracker, she continued to say aloud what she had only begun to say to herself.

"And yet," she resumed, "although you are unable to move, and are prevented by enchantment from saying a single word to me, I am very sure, my dear Mr. Drosselmayer, that you understand me perfectly, and that you are well aware of my good intentions with regard to you. Reckon, then, upon my support when you require it; and in the meantime, do not vex yourself. I will go straight to your uncle, and beg him to assist you; and if he only loves you a little, he is so clever that I am sure he can help you."

In spite of the eloquence of this speech, the Nutcracker did not move an inch; but it seemed to Mary that a sigh came from behind the glass, the panes of which began to sound very low, but wonderfully soft and pleasing; while it appeared to Mary that a sweet voice, like a small silver bell, said, "Dear little Mary, thou art my guardian angel! I will be thine, and Mary shall be mine!" And at these words, so mysteriously heard, Mary felt a singular sensation of happiness, in spite of the shudder which passed through her entire frame.

Twilight had now arrived; and the judge returned home, accompanied by Doctor Drosselmayer. In a few moments Miss Trudchen got tea ready, and all the family were gathered round the table, talking gaily. As for Mary, she had been to fetch her little armchair, and had seated herself in silence at the feet of Godfather Drosselmayer. Taking advantage of a moment when no one was speaking, she raised her large blue eyes towards the doctor, and, looking earnestly at him, said, "I now know, dear godpapa, that my Nutcracker is your nephew, young Drosselmayer, of Nuremberg. He has become a prince, and also king of the kingdom of toys, as your friend the astrologer prophesied. But you know that he is at open war with the king of the mice. Come, dear godpapa, tell me why you did not help him when you were sitting astride upon the clock? and why do you now desert him?"

And, with these words, Mary again related, amidst the laughter of her father, her mother, and Miss Trudchen, the events of that famous battle which she had seen. Fritz and Godfather Drosselmayer alone did not enjoy the whole scene.

"Where," said the godfather, "does that little girl get all those foolish ideas which enter her head?"

"She has a very lively imagination," replied Mary's mother; "and, after all, these are only dreams and visions occasioned by fever."

"And I can prove *that*," shouted Fritz; "for she says that my red hussars took to flight, which cannot possibly be true—unless indeed they are abominable cowards, in which case they would not get the better of me, for I would flog them all soundly."

Then, with a singular smile, Godfather Drosselmayer took Mary upon his knees, and said with more kindness than before, "My dear child, you do not know what course you are pursuing in espousing so warmly the cause of your Nutcracker. You will have to suffer much if you persist in taking the part of one who is in disgrace; for the king of the mice, who considers him to be the murderer of his mother, will persecute him in all ways. But, in any case, remember that it is not I— but you alone—who can save him. Be firm and faithful—and all will go well."

Neither Mary nor anyone else understood the words of Godfather Drosselmayer: on the contrary, those words seemed so strange to the judge, that he took the doctor's hand, felt his pulse for some moments in silence, and then said, "My dear friend, you are very feverish, and I should advise you to go home to bed."

VIII

The Duel

DURING THE NIGHT WHICH FOLLOWED the scene just related, and while the moon, shining in all its splendour, cast its bright rays through the openings in the curtains, Mary, who now slept with her mother, was awakened by a noise that seemed to come from the corner of the room, and was mingled with sharp screeches and squeakings.

"Alas!" cried Mary, who remembered to have heard the same noise on the occasion of the famous battle; "Alas! The mice are coming again! Mamma, mamma, mamma!"

But her voice was stifled in her throat, in spite of all her efforts: she endeavoured to get up to run out of the room, but seemed to be nailed to her bed, unable to move her limbs. At length, turning her affrighted eyes towards the corner of the room, whence the noise came, she beheld the king of the mice scraping for himself a way through the wall, and thrusting in first one of his heads, then another, then a third, and so on until the whole seven, each with a crown, made their appearance. Having entered the room, he walked several times round it like a victor who takes possession of his conquest: he then leapt with one bound upon a table that was standing near the bed. Gazing upon her with his fourteen eyes, all as bright as carbuncles, and with a gnashing of his teeth and a horrible squeaking noise, he said, "Fe, fa, fum! You must give me all your sugar plums and your sweet cakes, little girl, and if not, I will eat up your friend the Nutcracker."

Then, having uttered this threat, he fled from the room by the same hole as he had entered by.

Mary was so frightened by this terrible apparition, that she awoke in the morning very pale and almost broken-hearted, the more so that she dared not mention what had taken place during the night, for fear of being laughed at. Twenty, times was she on the point of telling all, either to her mother, or to Fritz; but she stopped, still thinking that neither the one nor the other would believe her. It was, however, pretty clear that she must sacrifice her sugar plums and her sweet cakes to the safety of the poor Nutcracker. She accordingly placed them all on the ledge of the cupboard that very evening

Next morning, the judge's wife said, "I really do not know whence come all the mice that have suddenly invaded the house; but those naughty creatures have actually eaten up all my poor little Mary's sugar plums."

The lady was not quite right; the sugar plums and cakes were only *spoilt*, not *eaten up*; for the gluttonous king of the mice, not finding the sweet cakes as good as he had expected, messed them about so that they were forced to be thrown away.

But as it was not sugar plums that Mary liked best, she did not feel much regret at the sacrifice which the king of the mice had extorted from her; and, thinking that he would be contented with the first contribution with which he had taxed her, she was much pleased at the idea of having saved Nutcracker upon such good terms.

Unfortunately her satisfaction was not of long duration; for the following night she was again awoke: by hearing squeaking and whining close by her ears.

Alas! It was the king of the mice again, his eyes shining more horribly than on the preceding night; and, in a voice interrupted by frequent whines and squeaks, he said, "You must give me your little sugar dolls and figures made of biscuit, little girl; if not, I will eat up your friend the Nutcracker."

Thereupon the king of the mice went skipping away, and disappeared by the hole in the wall.

Next morning, Mary, now deeply afflicted, went straight to the glass cupboard, and threw a mournful look upon her figures of sugar and biscuit; and her grief was very natural, for never were such nice-looking sweet things seen before.

"Alas!" she said, as she turned towards the Nutcracker, "what would I not do for you, my dear Mr. Drosselmayer? But you must admit all the same that what I am required to do is very hard."

At these words the Nutcracker assumed so piteous an air, that Mary, who fancied that she was forever beholding the jaws of the king of the mice opening to devour him, resolved to make this second sacrifice to save the unfortunate young man. That very evening, therefore, she placed her sugar figures and her biscuits upon the ledge of the cupboard, where the night before she had put her sugar plums and sweet cakes. Kissing them, however, one after another, as a token of farewell, she yielded up her shepherds, her shepherdesses, and her sheep, concealing behind the flock at the same time a little sugar baby with fat round cheeks, and which she loved above all the other things.

"Now really this is too bad!" cried the judge's wife next morning: "It is very clear that these odious mice have taken up their dwelling in the glass cupboard; for all poor Mary's sugar figures are eaten up."

At these words large tears started from Mary's eyes; but she dried them up almost directly, and even smiled sweetly as she thought to herself, "What matter my shepherds, shepherdesses, and sheep, since the Nutcracker is saved!"

"Mamma," cried Fritz, who was present at the time, "I must remind you that our baker has an excellent grey cat, which we might send for, and which would soon put an end to all this by snapping up the mice one after another, and even Dame Mousey herself afterwards, as well as her son the king."

"Yes," replied the judge's wife; "but that same cat would jump upon the tables and shelves, and break my glasses and cups to pieces."

"Oh! there is no fear of *that*!" cried Fritz. "The baker's cat is too polite to do any such thing; and I wish I could walk along the pipes and the roofs of houses as skilfully as he can."

"No cats here, if you please!" cried the judge's wife, who could not bear those domestic animals.

"But, after all," said the judge, who overheard what was going on, "some good may follow from the remarks of Fritz: if you will not have a cat, get a mousetrap."

"Capital!" cried Fritz: "That idea is very happy, since Godpapa Drosselmayer invented mousetraps."

Everyone now laughed; and as, after a strict search, no such thing as a mousetrap was found in the house, the servant went to Godfather Drosselmayer, who sent back a famous one, which was baited with a bit of bacon, and placed in the spot where the mice had made such.

Mary went to bed with the hope that morning would find the king of the mice a prisoner in the box, to which his gluttony was almost certain to lead him. But o'clock, and while she was in her first sleep, by something cold and velvety that leapt arms and face; and, at the same moment, the whining and squeaking which she knew so well, rang in her ears. The horrible king of the mice was there seated on her pillow, with his eyes shooting red flames and his seven mouths wide open, as if he were about to eat poor Mary up.

"I laugh at the trap—I laugh at the trap," said the king of the mice: "I shall not go into the little house, and the bacon will not tempt me. I shall not be taken: I laugh at the trap! But you must give me your picture books and your little silk frock; if not, I will eat up your friend the Nutcracker."

You can very well understand that after such a demand as this, Mary awoke in the morning with her heart full of sorrow and her eyes full of tears. Her mother, moreover, told her nothing new when she said that the trap had remained empty, and that the king of the mice had suspected the snare. Then, as the judge's wife left the room to see after the breakfast, Mary entered her papa's room, and going up to the cupboard, said, "Alas, my dear good Mr. Drosselmayer, where will all this end? When I have given my picture books to the king of the mice to tear, and my pretty little silk frock, which my guardian angel sent me, to rend into pieces, he will not be content, but will every day be asking me for more. And when I have nothing else left to give him, he will perhaps eat me up in your place. Alas! What can a poor little girl like me do for you, dear good Mr. Drosselmayer? What can I do?"

While Mary was weeping and lamenting in this manner, she observed that the Nutcracker had a drop of blood upon his neck. From the day when she had discovered that her favourite was the son of the toy man and the nephew of the Doctor, she had left off carrying him in her arms, and had neither kissed nor caressed him. Indeed, so great was her timidity in this respect, that she had not even dared to touch him with the tip of her finger. But at this moment, seeing that he was hurt, and fearing lest his wound might be dangerous, she took him gently out of the cupboard, and began to wipe away with her handkerchief the drop of blood which was upon his neck. But how great was her astonishment, when she suddenly felt the Nutcracker moving about in her hands! She replaced him quickly upon the shelf: his lips quivered from ear to ear, which made his mouth seem larger still; and, by dint of trying to speak, he concluded by uttering the following words: "Ah, dear Miss Silberhaus—excellent friend—what do I not owe you? And how much gratitude have I to express to you? Do not sacrifice for me your picture books and your silk frock; but get me a sword—a good sword—and I will take care of the rest!"

The Nutcracker would have said more; but his words became unintelligible—his voice sank altogether—and his eyes, for a moment animated by an expression of the softest melancholy, grew motionless and vacant. Mary felt no alarm: on the contrary, she leapt for joy, for she was very happy at the idea of being able to save the Nutcracker, without being compelled to give up her picture books or her silk frock. One thing alone vexed her—and that was, where could she find the good sword that the little man required? Mary resolved to explain her difficulty to Fritz, who, in spite of his blustering manners, she knew to be a good-natured boy. She accordingly took him close up to the glass cupboard, told him all that had happened between Nutcracker and the king of the mice, and ended by explaining the nature of the service she required of him. The only thing which made a great impression upon Fritz was the idea that his hussars had really acted in a cowardly manner in the thickest of the battle: he therefore asked Mary if the accusation were really true; and as he knew that she never told a story, he believed her words.

Then, rushing up to the cupboard, he made a speech to his soldiers, who seemed quite ashamed of themselves. But this was not all: in order to punish the whole regiment in the person of its officers, he degraded them one after the other, and expressly ordered the band not to play the *Hussar's March* during parade.

The turning to Mary, he said, "As for the Nutcracker, to be a brave little fellow, I think I can manage his business; for, as I put a veteran major of horse guards upon half pay yesterday, he having finished his time in the service, I should think he cannot want his sword any longer. It is an excellent blade, I can assure you!"

It now remained to find the major. A search was commenced, and he was found living on his half pay in a little tavern which stood in a dark corner of the third shelf in the cupboard. As Fritz had imagined, he offered no objection to give up his sword, which had become useless to him, and which was that instant fastened to the Nutcracker's neck.

The fear which Mary now felt prevented her from sleeping all the next night; and she was so wide awake that she heard the clock strike twelve in the room where the cupboard was. Scarcely had the hum of the last stroke ceased, when strange noises came from the direction of the cupboard; and then there was a great clashing of swords, as if two enemies were fighting in mortal combat. Suddenly one of the duellists gave a squeak!

"The king of the mice!" cried Mary, full of joy and terror at the same time.

There was then a dead silence; but presently someone knocked gently—very gently at the door; and a pretty little voice said, "Dearest Miss Silberhaus, I have glorious news for you: open the door, I beseech you!"

Mary recognised the voice of young Drosselmayer. She hastily put on her little frock, and opened the door. The Nutcracker was there, holding the blood-stained sword in his right hand and a candle in his left. The moment he saw Mary he knelt down, and said,

"It is you alone, O dearest lady! Who have nerved me with the chivalrous courage which I have just shown, and who gave me strength to fight that insolent wretch who dared to threaten you. The vile king of the mice is bathed in his blood. Will you, O lady! Deign to accept the trophies of the victory—trophies that are offered by the hand of a knight who is devoted to you until death?"

With these words the Nutcracker drew from his left arm the seven golden crowns of the king of the mice, which he had placed there as if they were bracelets, and which he now offered to Mary, who received them with joy.

The Nutcracker, encouraged by this amiability on her part, then rose and spoke thus: "Oh! Dear Miss Silberhaus, now that I have conquered my enemy, what beautiful things can I show you, if you would have the condescension to go with me only a few places hence! Oh! Do not refuse me—do not refuse me, dear lady I implore you!"

Mary did not hesitate a moment to follow the Nutcracker, knowing how great were her claims upon his gratitude, and being quite certain that he had no evil intention towards her.

"I will follow you," she said, "my dear Mr. Drosselmayer; but you must not take me very far, nor keep me long away, because I have not yet slept a wink."

"I will choose the shortest, although the most difficult, path," said the Nutcracker; and, thus speaking, he led the way, Mary following him.

IX

THE KINGDOM OF TOYS

THEY BOTH REACHED, IN A short time, a large old cupboard standing in a passage near the door, and which was used as a clothes press. There the Nutcracker stopped; and Mary observed, to her great astonishment, that the folding doors of the cupboard, which were nearly always kept shut, were now wide open, so that she could see plainly her father's travelling cloak lined with fox-skin, which was hanging over the other clothes. The Nutcracker climbed very skilfully along the border of the cloak; and, clinging to the braiding, he reached the large cape, which, fastened by a piece of lace, fell over the back of the cloak. From beneath this

"Now, dear young lady," said the Nutcracker, "have the goodness to give me your hand and ascend with me."

Mary complied; and scarcely had she glanced up the sleeve, when a brilliant light burst upon her view, and she suddenly found herself transported into the midst of a fragrant meadow, which glittered as if it were strewed with precious stones!

"Oh! How charming!" cried Mary, dazzled by the sight. "Where are we?"

"We are in the Field of Sugar Candy, Miss; but we will not remain here, unless you wish to do so. Let us pass through this door."

Then Mary observed a beautiful gate through which they left the field. The gate seemed to be made of white marble, red marble, and blue marble; but when Mary drew near it she saw that it was made only of preserves, candied orange peel, burnt almonds, and sugared raisins. This was the reason, as she learnt from the Nutcracker, why that gate was called the Gate of Burnt Almonds.

The gate opened into a long gallery, the roof of which was supported by pillars of barley-sugar. In the gallery there were five monkeys, all dressed in red, and playing music, which, if it were not the most melodious in the world, was at least the most original. Mary made so much haste to see more, that she did not even perceive that she was walking upon a pavement of pistachio nuts and macaroons, which she took for marble. At length she reached the end of the gallery, and scarcely was she in the open air, when she found herself surrounded by the most delicious perfumes, which came from a charming little forest that opened before her. This forest, which would have been dark were it not for the quantity of lamps that it contained, was lighted up in so brilliant a manner that it was easy to distinguish the golden and silver fruits, which were suspended to branches ornamented with white ribands and nosegays, resembling marriage favours.

"Oh! My dear Mr. Drosselmayer," cried Mary, "what is the name of this charming place, I beseech you?"

"We are now in the Forest of Christmas, Miss," answered the Nutcracker; "and it is here that people come to fetch the trees to which the presents sent by the guardian angels are fastened."

"Oh!" continued Mary, "May I not remain here one moment? Everything is so nice here, and smells so sweet!"

The Nutcracker clapped his hands together; and several shepherds and shepherdesses, hunters and huntresses, came out of the forest, all so delicate and white that they seemed made of refined sugar. They carried on their shoulders an armchair, made of chocolate, incrusted with angelica, in which they placed a cushion of jujube, inviting Mary most politely to sit down. Scarcely had she done so when, as at operas, the shepherds and shepherdesses, the hunters and huntresses, took their places and began to dance a charming ballet to an accompaniment of horns and bugles, which the hunters blew with such good will that their faces became flushed just as if they were made of conserve of roses. Then, the dance being finished, they all disappeared in a grove.

"Pardon me, dear Miss Silberhaus," said the Nutcracker, holding out his hand towards Mary,—"pardon me for having exhibited to you so poor a ballet; but those simpletons can do nothing better than repeat, over and over again, the same step. As for the hunters, they blew their bugles as if they were afraid of them; and I can promise you that I shall not let it pass so quietly. But let us leave those creatures for the present, and continue our walk, if you please."

"I really found it all very delightful," said Mary, accepting the invitation of the Nutcracker; "and it seems to me, my dear Mr. Drosselmayer, that you are harsh towards the little dancers."

The Nutcracker made a face, as much as to say, "We shall see; but your plea in their favour shall be considered."

They then continued their journey, and reached a river which seemed to send forth all the sweet scents that perfumed the air.

"This," said the Nutcracker, without even waiting to be questioned by Mary, "is the River of Orange Juice. It is one of the smallest in the kingdom; for, save in respect to its sweet odour, it cannot be compared to the River of Lemonade, which falls into the southern sea, or the Sea of Punch. The Lake of Sweet Whey is also finer: it joins the northern sea, which is called the Sea of Milk of Almonds."

At a short distance was a little village, in which the houses, the church, and the parsonage were all brown; the roofs however were gilt, and the walls were resplendent with incrustations of red, blue, and white sugarplums.

"This is the Village of Sweet Cake," said the Nutcracker; "it is a pretty little place, as you perceive, and is situate on the Streamlet of Honey. The inhabitants are very agreeable to look upon; but they are always in a bad humour, because they are constantly troubled with the toothache. But, my dear Miss Silberhaus," continued the Nutcracker, "do not let us stop at all the villages and little towns of the kingdom. To the capital! To the capital!"

The Nutcracker advanced, still holding Mary's hand, but walking more confidently than he had hitherto done; for Mary, who was full of curiosity, kept by his side, light as a bird. At length, after the expiration of some minutes, the odour of roses was spread through the air, and everything around them now seemed to be of a rose tint. Mary remarked that this was the perfume and the reflection of a River of Essence of Roses, which flowed along, its waves rippling melodiously. Upon the sweet-scented waters, silver swans, with collars of gold round their necks, swam gently along, warbling the most delicious songs, so that this harmony, with which they were apparently much pleased, made the diamond fishes leap up around them.

"Ah!" cried Mary, "This is the pretty river which Godpapa Drosselmayer made me at Christmas; and I am the girl who played with the swans!"

X

THE JOURNEY

THE NUTCRACKER CLAPPED HIS HANDS together once more; and, at that moment, the River of Essence of Roses began to rise visibly;

and from its swelling waves came forth a chariot made of shells, and covered with precious stones that glittered in the sun. It was drawn by golden dolphins; and four charming little Moors, with caps made of the scales of goldfish and clothes of hummingbirds' feathers, leapt upon the bank. They first carried Mary, and then the Nutcracker, very gently down to the chariot, which instantly began to advance upon the stream.

You must confess that it was a ravishing spectacle, and one which might even be compared to the voyage of Cleopatra upon the Cydnus, which you read of in Roman History, to behold little Mary in the chariot of shells, surrounded by perfume, and floating on the waves of essence of roses. The golden dolphins that drew the chariot, tossed up their heads, and threw into the air the glittering jets of rosy crystal, which fell in variegated showers of all the colours of the rainbow. Moreover, that pleasure might penetrate every sense, a soft music began to echo round; and sweet silvery voices were heard singing in the following manner:

"Who art thou, thus floating where essence of rose
In a stream of sweet perfume deliciously flows?
Art thou the Fairies' Queen?

Say, dear little fishes that gleam in the tide;
Or answer, ye cygnets that gracefully glide
Upon that flood serene!"

And all this time the little Moors, who stood behind the seat on the chariot of shells, shook two parasols, hung with bells, in such a manner that those sounds formed an accompaniment to the vocal melody. And Mary, beneath the shade of the parasols, leant over the waters, each wave of which as it passed reflected her smiling countenance.

In this manner she traversed the River of Essence of Roses, and reached the bank on the opposite side. Then, when they were within an oar's length of the shore, the little Moors leapt, some into the water, others on the bank, the whole forming a chain so as to convey Mary and the Nutcracker ashore upon a carpet made of angelica, all covered with mint drops.

The Nutcracker now conducted Mary through a little grove, which was perhaps even prettier than the Christmas Forest, so brilliantly did each tree shine, and so sweetly did they all smell with their own peculiar essence. But what was most remarkable was the quantity of fruits hanging to the branches, those fruits being not only of singular colour and transparency—some yellow as the topaz, others red like the ruby—but also of a wondrous perfume.

"We are now in the Wood of Preserved Fruits," said the Nutcracker, "and beyond that boundary is the capital." And, as Mary thrust aside the last branches, she was stupified at beholding the extent, the magnificence, and the novel appearance of the city which rose before her upon a mound of flowers. Not only did the walls and steeples glitter with the most splendid colours, but, in respect to the shape of the buildings, it was impossible to see any so beautiful upon the earth. The fortifications and the gates were built of candied fruits, which shone in the sun with their own gay colours, all rendered more brilliant still by the crystallised sugar that covered them. At the principal gate, which was the one by which they entered, silver soldiers presented arms to them, and a little man, clad in a dressing gown of gold brocade, threw himself into the Nutcracker's arms, crying, "Oh! Dear prince, have you come at length? Welcome—welcome to the City of Candied Fruits!"

Mary was somewhat astonished at the great title given to the Nutcracker; but she was soon drawn from her surprise by the noise of an immense quantity of voices all chattering at the same time; so that she asked the Nutcracker if there were some disturbance or some festival in the Kingdom of Toys?

"There is nothing of all that, dear Miss Silberhaus," answered the Nutcracker; "but the City of Candied Fruits is so happy a place, and all its people are so joyful, that they are constantly talking and laughing. And this is always the same as you see it now. But come with me; let us proceed, I implore of you."

Mary, urged by her own curiosity and by the polite invitation of the Nutcracker, hastened her steps, and soon found herself in a large marketplace, which had the most magnificent aspects that could possibly be seen. All the houses around were of sugar, open with fretwork, and having balcony over balcony; and in the middle of the marketplace was an enormous cake, from the inside of which flowed four fountains, namely, lemonade, orangade, sweet milk, and goose berry syrup. The basins around were filled with whip syllabub, so delicious in appearance, that several well-dressed persons publicly ate of it by means of spoons. But the most agreeable and amusing part of the whole scene, was the crowd of little people who walked about, arm-in-arm, by thousands and tens of thousands, all laughing, singing, and chattering, at the tops of their voices, so that Mary could now account for the joyous din which she had heard. Besides the inhabitants of the capital, there were men of all countries—Armenians, Jews, Greeks, Tyrolese, officers, soldiers, clergymen, monks, shepherds, punches, and all kinds of funny people, such as one meets with in the world.

Presently the tumult redoubled at the entrance of a street looking upon the great square; and the people stood aside to allow the cavalcade to pass. It was the Great Mogul, who was carried upon a palanquin, attended by ninety-three lords of his kingdom and seven hundred slaves: but, at the same time, it happened that from the opposite street the Grand Sultan appeared on horseback, followed by three hundred janissaries. The two sovereigns had always been rivals, and therefore enemies; and this feeling made it impossible for their attendants to meet each other without quarrelling. It was even much worse, as you may well suppose, when those two powerful monarchs found themselves face to face: in the first place there was a great confusion, from the midst of which the citizens sought to save themselves; but cries of fury and despair were soon heard, for a gardener, in the act of running away, had knocked off the head of a Brahmin, greatly respected by his own class; and the Grand Sultan's horse had knocked down a frightened punch, who endeavoured to creep between the animal's legs to get away from the riot. The din was increasing, when the gentleman in the gold brocade dressing gown, who had saluted the Nutcracker by the title of Prince at the gate of the city, leapt to the top of the huge cake with a single bound; and having rung a silvery sweet-toned bell three times, cried out three times, "Confectioner! Confectioner! Confectioner!"

That instant did the tumult subside and the combatants separate. The Grand Sultan was brushed, for he was covered with dust; the Brahmin's head was fixed on, with the injunction that he must not sneeze for three days, for fear it should fall off again; and order was restored. The pleasant sports began again, and everyone hastened to quench his thirst with the lemonade, the orangeade, the sweet milk, or the gooseberry syrup, and to regale himself with the whip-syllabub.

"My dear Mr. Drosselmayer," said Mary," what is the cause of the influence exercised upon those little folks by the word *confectioner* repeated thrice?"

"I must tell you, Miss," said the Nutcracker, "that the people of the City of Candied Fruits believe, by experience, in the transmigration of souls, and are in the power of a superior principle, called *confectioner*, which principle can bestow on each individual what form he likes by merely baking him, for a shorter or longer period, as the case may be. Now, as everyone believes his own existing shape to be the best, he does not like to change it. Hence the magic influence of the word *confectioner* upon the people of the City of Candied Fruits, when pronounced by the chief magistrate. It is sufficient, as you perceive, to appease all that tumult; everyone, in an instant, forget earthly things, broken ribs, and bumps upon the head; and, restored to himself says, *'What is man? And what may he not become?'*"

While they were thus talking, they reached the entrance of the palace, which shed around a rosy lustre, and was surmounted by a hundred light and elegant towers. The walls were strewed with nosegays, of violets, narcissi, tulips, and jasmine, which set off with their various hues the rose-coloured ground from which they stood forth. The great dome in the centre was covered with thousands of gold and silver stars.

"O, heavens!" exclaimed Mary. "What is that wonderful building?"

"The Palace of Sweet Cake," answered the Nutcracker; "and it is one of the most famous monuments in the capital of the Kingdom of Toys."

Nevertheless, lost in wonder as she was, Mary could not help observing that the roof of one of the great towers was totally wanting, and that little gingerbread men, mounted on a scaffold of cinnamon, were occupied in repairing it. She was about to question the Nutcracker relative to this accident, when he said, "Alas! It is only a short time ago that this palace was threatened by a great disgrace, if not with absolute ruin. The giant Glutton ate up the top of that tower; and he was already on the point of biting the dome, when the people hastened to give him as a tribute the quarter of the city called Almond and Honeycake District, together with a large portion of the Forest of Angelica, in consideration of which he agreed to take himself off without making any worse ravages than those which you see."

At that moment a soft and delicious music was heard.

The gates of the palace opened by themselves, and twelve little pages came forth, carrying in their hands branches of aromatic herbs, lighted like torches. Their heads were made of pearl, six of them had bodies made of rubies, and the six others of emeralds, wherewith they trotted joyously along upon two little feet of gold, sculptured with all the taste and care of Benvenuto Cellini.

They were followed by four ladies, about the same size as Miss Clara, Mary's new doll; but all so splendidly dressed and so richly adorned, that

Mary was not at a loss to perceive in them the royal princesses of the City of Preserved Fruits. They all four, upon perceiving the Nutcracker, hastened to embrace him with the utmost tenderness, exclaiming at the same time, and as it were with one voice,

"Oh! Prince—dear prince! Dear—dear brother!" The Nutcracker seemed much moved; he wiped away the tears which flowed from his eyes, and, taking Mary by the hand, said, in a feeling tone, to the four princesses, "My dear sisters, this is Miss Silberhaus whom I now introduce to you: She is the daughter of Chief Justice Silberhaus, of Nuremberg, a gentleman of the highest respectability. It is this young lady who saved my life; for, if at the moment when I lost the battle she had not thrown her shoe at the king of the mice—and, again, if she had not afterwards lent me the sword of a major whom her brother had placed on the half-pay list—I should even now be sleeping in my tomb, or what is worse, be devoured by the king of the mice."

"Ah! My dear Miss Silberhaus," cried the Nutcracker, with an enthusiasm which he could not control, "Pirlipata, although the daughter of a king, was not worthy to unloose the latchet of your pretty little shoes."

"Oh! No—no; certainly not!" repeated the four princesses in chorus; and, throwing their arms round Mary's neck, they cried, "Oh! Noble liberatrix of our dear and much-loved prince and brother! Oh! Excellent Miss Silberhaus!"

And, with these exclamations, which their heartfelt joy cut short, the four princesses conducted the Nutcracker and Mary into the palace, made them sit down upon beautiful little sofas of cedarwood, covered with golden flowers, and then insisted upon preparing a banquet with their own hands. With this object, they hastened to fetch a number of little vases and bowls made of the finest Japan porcelain, and silver knives, forks, spoons, and other articles of the table. They then brought in the finest fruits and most delicious sugar plums that Mary had ever seen, and began to bustle about so nimbly that Mary was at no loss to perceive how well they understood everything connected with cooking. Now, as Mary herself was well acquainted with such matters, she wished inwardly to take a share in all that was going on; and, as if she understood Mary's wishes, the most beautiful of the Nutcracker's four sisters, handed her a little golden mortar, saying, "Dear liberatrix of my brother, pound me some sugar candy, if you please."

Mary hastened to do as she was asked; and while she was pounding the sugar candy in the mortar, whence a delicious music came forth, the

Nutcracker began to relate all his adventures: but, strange as it was, it seemed to Mary, during that recital, as if the words of young Drosselmayer and the noise of the pestle came gradually more and more indistinct to her ears. In a short time she seemed to be surrounded by a light vapour; then the vapour turned into a silvery mist, which spread more and more densely around her, so that it presently concealed the Nutcracker and the princesses from her sight. Strange songs, which reminded her of those she had heard on the River of Essence of Roses, met her ears, commingled with the increasing murmur of waters; and then Mary thought that the waves flowed beneath her, raising her up with their swell. She felt as if she were rising high up—higher—and higher; when, suddenly, down she fell from a precipice that she could not measure.

CONCLUSION

ONE DOES NOT FALL SEVERAL thousand feet without awaking: thus was it that Mary awoke; and, on awaking, she found herself in her little bed. It was broad daylight, and her mother, who was standing by her, said, "Is it possible to be so lazy as you are? Come, get up, and dress yourself, dear little Mary, for breakfast is waiting."

"Oh! My dear mamma," said Mary, opening her eyes wide with astonishment, "whither did young Mr. Drosselmayer take me last night? and what splendid things did he show me?"

Then Mary related all that I have just told you; and when she had done her mother said, "You have had a very long and charming dream, dear little Mary; but now that you are awake, you must forget it all, and come and have your breakfast."

But Mary, while she dressed herself, persisted in maintaining that she had really seen all she spoke of. Her mother accordingly went to the cupboard and took out the Nutcracker, who, according to custom, was upon the third shelf.

Bringing it to her daughter, she said, "How can you suppose, silly child, that this puppet, which is made of wood and cloth, can be alive, or move, or think?"

"But, my dear mamma," said Mary, perpetually, "I am well aware that the Nutcracker is none other than young

At that moment Mary heard a loud shout of laughter behind her.

It was the judge, Fritz, and Miss Trudchen, who made themselves merry at her expense.

"Ah!" cried Mary, "How can you laugh at me, dear papa, and at my poor Nutcracker? He spoke very respectfully of you, nevertheless, when we went into the Palace of Sweet Cake, and he introduced me to his sisters."

The shouts of laughter redoubled to such an extent that Mary began to see the necessity of giving some proof of the truth of what she said, for fear of being treated as a simpleton. She therefore went into the adjoining room and brought back a little box in which she had carefully placed the seven crowns of the king of the mice.

"Here, mamma," she said, "are the seven heads of the king of the mice, which the Nutcracker gave me last night as a proof of his victory."

The judge's wife, full of surprise, took the seven little crowns, which were made of an unknown but very brilliant metal, and were carved with a delicacy of which human hands were incapable. The judge himself could not take his eyes off them, and considered them to be so precious, that, in spite of the prayers of Fritz, he would not let him touch one of them. The judge and his wife then pressed Mary to tell them whence came those little crowns; but she could only persist in what she had said already: and when her father, annoyed at what he heard and at what he considered obstinacy on her part, called her a little "storyteller," she burst into tears, exclaiming, "Alas! Unfortunate child that I am! What would you have me tell you?"

At that moment the door opened, and the doctor made his appearance.

"What is the matter?" he said, "And what have they done to my little goddaughter, that she cries and sobs like this? What is it? What is it all?"

The judge acquainted Doctor Drosselmayer with all that had occurred; and, when the story was ended, he showed him the seven crowns. But scarcely had the doctor seen them, when he burst out laughing, and said, "Well! Really this is too good! These are the seven crowns that I used to wear to my watch-chain some years ago, and which I gave to my goddaughter on the occasion of her second birthday. Do you not remember, my dear friend?"

But the judge and his wife could not recollect anything about the present stated to have been given. Nevertheless, believing what the godfather said, their countenances became more calm. Mary, upon seeing this, ran up to Doctor Drosselmayer, saying, "But you know all, godpapa! confess that the Nutcracker is your nephew, and that it was he who gave me the seven crowns."

But Godfather Drosselmayer did not at all seem to like these words; and his face became so gloomy, that the judge called little Mary to him, and taking her upon his knees, said, "Listen to me, my dear child, for I wish to speak to you very seriously. Do me the pleasure, once for all, to put an end to these silly ideas; because, if you should again assert that this ugly and deformed Nutcracker is the nephew of our friend the doctor, I give you due warning that I will throw, not only the Nutcracker, but all the other toys, Miss Clara amongst them, out of the window."

Poor Mary was therefore unable to speak anymore of all the fine things with which her imagination was filled; but you can well understand that when a person has once travelled in such a fine place as the Kingdom of Toys, and seen such a delicious town as the City of Preserved Fruits, were it only for an hour, it is not easy to forget such sights.

Mary therefore endeavoured to speak to her brother of the whole business; but she had lost all his confidence since the moment when she had said that his hussars had taken to flight. Convinced, therefore, that Mary was a storyteller, as her father had said so, he restored his officers to the rank from which he had reduced them, and allowed the band to play as usual the *Hussar's March*—a step which did not prevent Mary from entertaining her own opinion relative to their courage.

Mary dared not therefore speak further of her adventures. Nevertheless, the remembrance of the Kingdom of Toys followed her without ceasing; and when she thought of all that, she looked upon it as if she were still in the Christmas Forest, or on the River of Essence of Roses, or in the City of Preserved Fruits; so that, instead of playing with her toys as she had been wont to do, she remained silent and pensive, occupied only with her own thoughts, while everyone called her "the little dreamer."

But one day, when the doctor, with his wig laid upon the ground, his tongue thrust into one corner of his mouth, and the sleeves of his yellow coat turned up, was mending a clock by the aid of a long pointed instrument, it happened that Mary, who was seated near the glass cupboard contemplating the Nutcracker, and buried in her own thoughts, suddenly said, quite forgetful that both the doctor and her mamma were close by, "Ah! My dear Mr. Drosselmayer, if you were not a little man made of wood, as my papa declares, and, if you really were alive, I would not do as Princess Pirlipata did, and desert you because, in serving me, you had ceased to be a handsome young man; for I love you sincerely!"

But scarcely had she uttered these words, when there was such a noise in the room, that Mary fell off her chair in a fainting fit.

When she came to herself, she found that she was in the arms of her mother, who said, "How is it possible that a great little girl like you, is so foolish as to fall ask off can your chair—and just at the moment, too, when young Mr. Drosselmayer, who has finished his travels, arrives at Nuremberg? Come, wipe your eyes, and be a good girl."

Indeed, as Mary wiped her Godpapa Drosselmayer, with his hat under his arm, and back, entered the room. He eyes, the door opened, and his glass wig upon his head, his drab frock coat upon his wore a smiling countenance, and held by the hand a young man, who, although very little, was very handsome. This young man wore a superb frock coat of red velvet embroidered with gold, white silk stockings, and shoes brilliantly polished.

He had a charming nosegay on the bosom of his shirt, and was very dandified with his curls and hair-powder; moreover, long tresses, neatly braided, hung behind his back. The little sword that he wore by his side was brilliant with precious stones; and the hat which he carried under his arm was of the finest silk.

The amiable manners of this young man showed who he was directly; for scarcely had he entered the room, when he placed at Mary's feet a quantity of magnificent toys and nice confectionery—chiefly sweet cake and sugar plum, the finest she had ever tasted, save in the Kingdom of Toys. As for Fritz, the doctor's nephew seemed to have guessed his martial taste, for he brought him a sword with a blade of the finest Damascus steel. At table, and when the dessert was placed upon it, the amiable youth cracked nuts for all the company: the hardest could not resist his teeth for a moment. He placed them in his mouth with his right hand; with the left he pulled his hair behind; and, crack! the shell was broken.

Mary had become very red when she first saw that pretty little gentleman; but she blushed deeper still, when, after the dessert, he invited her to go with him into the room where the glass cupboard was.

"Yes, go, my dear children, and amuse yourselves together," said Godpapa Drosselmayer: "I do not want that room anymore today, since all the clocks of my friend the judge now go well."

The two young people proceeded to the room; but scarcely was young Drosselmayer alone with Mary, when he fell upon one knee, and spoke thus:

"My dear Miss Silberhaus, you see at your feet the happy Nathaniel Drosselmayer, whose life you saved on this very spot. You also said that you would not have repulsed me, as Princess Pirlipata did, if, in serving *you*, I had become hideous. Now, as the spell which the queen of the mice threw upon me was destined to lose all its power on that day when, in spite of my ugly face, I should be beloved by a young and beautiful girl, I at that moment ceased to be a vile Nutcracker and resumed my proper shape, which is not disagreeable, as you may see. Therefore, my dear young lady, if you still possess the same sentiments in respect to myself, do me the favour to bestow your much-loved hand upon me, share my throne and my crown, and reign with me over the Kingdom of Toys, of which I have ere now become the king."

Then Mary raised young Drosselmayer gently, and said, "You are an amiable and a good king, sir; and as you have moreover a charming kingdom, adorned with magnificent palaces, and possessing a very happy people, I receive you as my future husband, provided my parents give their consent."

Thereupon, as the door of the room had opened very gently without the two young folks having heard it, so occupied were they with their own sentiments, the judge, his wife, and Godpapa Drosselmayer came forward, crying "Bravo!" with all their might; which made Mary as red as a cherry. But the young man was not abashed; and, advancing towards the judge and his wife, he bowed gracefully to them, paid them a handsome compliment, and ended by soliciting the hand of Mary in marriage. The request was immediately granted.

That same day Mary was engaged to Nathaniel Drosselmayer, on condition that the marriage should not take place for a year.

At the expiration of the year, the bridegroom came to fetch the bride in a little carriage of mother of pearl in crusted with gold and silver, and drawn by ponies of the size of sheep, but which were of countless worth, because there were none others like them in the world. The young king took his bride to the Palace of Sweet Cake, where they were married by the chaplain. Twenty-two thousand little people, all covered with pearls, diamonds, and brilliant stones, danced at the bridal.

Even at the present day, Mary is still queen of that beautiful country, where may be seen brilliant forests of Christmas; rivers of orangade, sweet milk, and essence of roses; transparent palaces of sugar whiter than snow and clearer than ice; in a word, all kinds of wonderful and extraordinary things may there be seen by those who have eyes sharp enough to discover them.

BABES IN TOYLAND

I

AT UNCLE BARNABY'S HOUSE

"ALAN, DO YOU HEAR ME? Stop scraping your plate!" cried Uncle Barnaby from the head of the table.

"But I'm so hungry," answered Alan, pushing the very last grain of gruel upon the edge of his spoon.

"I'm hungry, too!" sighed Jane, as she held the milk jug upside down above her cup, hoping that another spoonful might drip from it.

"Hungry, eh," snapped Uncle Barnaby, "after you've eaten everything on the table! You ought to be ashamed of yourselves. You'll eat me into the poorhouse yet. And listen, Master Alan: good pewter plates cost a shilling apiece, and I won't allow you to scrape holes in mine!"

Alan ate the last grain in silence. Jane made sure that the milk jug was empty, and sadly put it down.

Uncle Barnaby shook his crooked finger at them, and for the hundredth time told them what a care they had been and how much they had cost him since their mother died and left Jane and Alan in his charge. His words did not frighten or hurt them, for a scolding went with every meal at Uncle Barnaby's, and all meals there were alike— three pieces of dry bread on a cracked plate and a fourpenny bowl of yellow clay, which, when it was not filled with very thin soup, held three little portions of watery gruel. The portions had been smaller than ever that evening, and to Jane and Alan it seemed they had never been quite so hungry.

"Might we have some jam?" asked Jane.

Uncle Barnaby could hardly believe his ears. Jam! Never had such a thing been asked for in his house, and never had a jar of it stood upon the always empty shelves of his kitchen pantry.

"Do you know," added Alan, "the children have jam every night at the Widow Piper's."

"That isn't so!" snorted Uncle Barnaby. "Jam for fourteen once a day! A banker's widow couldn't afford it, and Mrs. Piper is only the widow of a carpenter. Those naughty young Pipers have been telling you stories again. Such children—if I were their father I'd teach them!"

It was said in the Village without a Name—for that is where the people of this story lived—that had it not been for the little Pipers Uncle Barnaby would have married Mrs. Piper soon after her good husband left her a widow.

Of her children you have surely heard, for they are famous, and rhymes and songs about them are sung by other children all over the world. She lived with them in a fine old house, with a big garden in front of it, and in this garden Contrary Mary, who was the Widow Piper's eldest daughter, grew silver bells and cockle shells, and when her sisters walked through it they were the pretty maids all in a row. There were fourteen of the Piper boys and girls, all good and jolly and kind-hearted, but Uncle Barnaby had found a cause to dislike each of them, and his hatred was as deep as Jane and Alan's love for them.

"If they were mine," he repeated, "I'd teach them!"

Then he thumped the table so fiercely that the empty bread-plate danced a jig with the still emptier gruel bowl.

"They've been ever so kind to us," Jane began.

Alan joined in her praise of the Pipers, and together they spoke up bravely for their friends, until Uncle Barnaby stopped them by another blow on the table which made the gruel bowl skip so high it cracked itself when it came down again.

"I'll tell you why I don't like them," the old man continued. "There's Bo Peep, to begin with. She let her sheep eat up all the clover in my best pasture. Jack and Jill use my spring whenever they're sent for a pail of water and never ask me if they may. Red Riding Hood and Sallie Waters and Curly Locks sent back the toys I gave them last Christmas. Miss Muffett told Simple Simon I frightened her more than spiders, and Simon told everybody at the fair. Peter never thinks of anything but eating. Boy Blue's cows stray all over my land, and Bobby Shaftoe makes boats out of my fence rails. When Tom Tom meets me he always forgets his manners, and Contrary Mary, she—she hasn't any!"

With this Uncle Barnaby arose and lit two candles; for the night had come and lights were already shining from the windows of the Piper house across the road.

"Now, my loving niece and nephew," he sneered, "you may go to bed—to the nice soft beds under the roof that I'm keeping over you. Goodnight, my dears, and before you go to sleep give a thought to all the poor orphans in this world who haven't a dear uncle to watch over them!"

Up the garret stairs went Alan and Jane, up to the two hard cots in the cubby-hole under the eaves that they called their room, and there, sad at heart and lonely, they went to bed in the dark. It was so hot and stuffy in the garret that they could not sleep at first, but after a while the night wind drew a veil of cloud over the moon and stars, and a summer rain began to fall. Softly and steadily it pattered upon the tiles above them until Jane and Alan began to fancy that all the drummers of Fairyland were beating a march outside, and then—they were thousands and thousands of miles away, in one of those beautiful countries that only good children find in dreams.

Uncle Barnaby, left alone downstairs, was delighted to get rid of the children. The dreary, dusty old home, which would have frightened anyone else, had no terrors for Uncle Barnaby, who indeed was rather a terrifying object himself. The light from the two candles cast his shadow on the wall like a queer black ogre.

With a stealthy step he went about the house, bolting the doors and windows and seeing that there was no danger from thieves. To be sure you would not have thought there was anything in that bare house which a thief would wish to steal, but Uncle Barnaby was very careful. When everything was fast for the night, he went to a big iron chest which stood in a dark corner, unlocked it, and raised the lid. Then he rubbed his hands together, gloating, for the chest was filled with bags of gold. He began to count them under his breath, and stroked them as if he loved them; for Uncle Barnaby was a miser, and gold was dearer to him than anything in the world.

The biggest bag of all had sewn on it a paper that bore the names of Alan and Jane. Uncle Barnaby seemed to have a particular affection for that bag, and he took it up many times, and held it, and weighed it, and smiled at it. In the bag was a great fortune in pieces of gold, and this fortune belonged to Alan and Jane. When their mother died, years before, she had left all this money in the care of her brother Barnaby, and he was to keep it for the children until they grew up. He was the children's guardian, and their only living relative. Being a miser, of course he wanted to keep the fortune always, and he might do so,—*if Alan and Jane should never grow up!*

As Uncle Barnaby bent over the chest there came the sound of a knock. He dropped the iron lid, and taking a candle went to the door. Though the rain was falling hard and the hour was late, it was clear that he was not surprised to receive visitors. When he opened the creaking door and peered out he saw that two men were waiting.

"Your names?" he asked, in a hoarse whisper.

"Gonzorgo and Roderigo," came the answer.

"Come in," said Uncle Barnaby.

The door was closed again. A few moments later, the three were sitting in the room where the iron chest stood, looking at each other by the dim candlelight. The two callers were sailors, as could be easily seen by their clothes and the way they walked.

"You have brought the boat?" asked Uncle Barnaby.

"Yes," said Gonzorgo, "the leakiest old tub we could find."

"Where is it?"

"At anchor, just off the shore."

Uncle Barnaby rubbed his hands with satisfaction. "Now," he said, "you are sure that you understand? You are to take my nephew and niece for a sail,—a pleasant holiday sail," he smiled in a horrid way, "and—"

"And," put in Gonzorgo, "we're to see that boat, nephew, and niece never come back. Is that right?"

Uncle Barnaby nodded and smiled and rubbed his hands. He could not resist a happy glance toward the iron chest.

"Be here at ten o'clock tomorrow morning," he said; "and remember, if you fail you get no money!"

"Trust us!" said Gonzorgo. "We'll do the thing properly, never fear. Goodnight, we'll be here at ten sharp."

And the two sailor men went off with their rolling walk.

Uncle Barnaby bolted the door again, and went back to his iron chest. He took out the big bag marked with the children's names, emptied the gold pieces on the table, and, sitting down beside his treasure, clinked the pieces together, two by two, to be sure that not one was bad or counterfeit. The candles burned down to two little hills of tallow, but he still sat there. Then he swept all the money into one big pile and buried his hands in it, letting the coins run through his fingers as though he were washing his hands in gold.

"Tomorrow night," chuckled Uncle Barnaby, "I shall be without a niece and nephew, —but this shall be mine!"

II

The Wreck of the Galleon

"I've a pleasant surprise for you," said Uncle Barnaby to Jane and Alan the next morning.

A pleasant surprise! They could hardly believe their ears. The old miser was smiling and cheerful and seemed almost affectionate. He allowed them an extra share of gruel each, and called them "my dear" several times.

He told them that he was going to send them off on a sailboat for the afternoon, with two seafaring friends of his, and he hoped they would have a nice time.

The children were delighted, for they both loved the water and had always longed to go sailing. And for a whole afternoon! They put on their best clothes, and waited in wild excitement for ten o'clock. And sure enough, just on the stroke of ten, the two sailors appeared.

Uncle Barnaby said goodbye to Alan and Jane most kindly, and quite beamed upon them as they went merrily off with Gonzorgo and Roderigo.

"After all," said Alan, as they scampered along to the shore, "it *was* nice of Uncle Barnaby to plan this sail for us."

"Yes," said Jane, looking a little puzzled, "it was *very* nice. Do you suppose he—he is getting to *like* us, Alan?"

"No," said Alan, "I don't think he can be. He doesn't look as though he liked us."

"Just the same, it *is* kind in him to send us out on the water," said Jane.

"Come along, young uns," called one of the seamen,—he seemed to be the leader, and he was dreadful to look at—"you must hurry up."

They had reached the beach by this time, and soon they were all seated in a little boat, which was rowed out to the galleon lying at anchor just off the shore. Alan did not know much about ships, but the seamen said it was a galleon, so he supposed it must be, and felt as though he were reading a storybook.

"Oh," cried Jane, as the little boat danced on the fresh, blue waves, "*dear* Uncle Barnaby!"

You see they were such simple, loving, kindly, little souls that they did not even hate Uncle Barnaby,—though they were somewhat afraid of him,—and it never crossed their minds that he could really want any harm to come to them.

As they were being rowed out to the galleon the children chattered and askedquestions all the time: What were their companions' names? And were they sailors? And was it very wonderful to be a sailor? And they would have loved to ask them how they happened to know Uncle Barnaby, and things of that sort, only they knew that that would not be polite nor well-mannered, and though they were often naughty they were never rude. They found out soon that the biggest and blackest and wickedest-looking ruffian was Gonzorgo, and that the long, thin, pale one, whose eyes were red and weepy, and who seemed much afraid of his comrade, was Roderigo. Alan felt certain that they must have been Pirates at some time in their lives, and sailed under a black flag!

The truth was that Gonzorgo was a hardened villain, and while he thought of Uncle Barnaby's gold pieces, he did not mind making away with the children in the least.

But Roderigo was a weak-minded person, with no great talent for being wicked, and he felt very unhappy. Jane's round pink and white face, and yellow curls, and Alan's slender figure and frank, merry eyes, went to his heart, and once in a while he snivelled, just because he was so sorry for them. They were very nice-looking children, and they were wearing spick and span clean sailor suits; and not only did they suspect nothing, but they seemed to be having a very good time. When he looked at them, Roderigo did not like to think of the holes in the bottom of the galleon. So he wept a little now and then. But whenever he wept Gonzorgo managed to kick him hard, while the children were not looking.

The village, with Uncle Barnaby, and the Piper family, and Contrary Mary's garden, seemed far away when the little boat reached the galleon. Either the rising waves had made their progress very slow, or the seamen had rowed very feebly, for it was nearly dark when they climbed on board. Storm clouds were gathering, too, and the air was full of the rumbles and flashes of a growing tempest.

The children began to be frightened. The darkness, the coming storm, the galleon tossing on the waves, their two strange guardians,—all these things made little shivers run up and down their spines. Jane trembled all over, but Alan, with his arm around Jane, held himself very straight, as befitted the oldest, and a man!

But if they were frightened then, imagine how they felt when they found that they were to be left alone on the galleon! No sooner were the children on board than Gonzorgo and Roderigo, crying that they had forgotten something for the rigging of the boat, pushed off, and began to row quickly toward the shore. As they went, Gonzorgo called back some strange words that are used on ships, to confuse the children so that they would not suspect anything.

"We can't get out of the harbor without tacking, with the wind in this quarter!" shouted the sailor through his hands.

"What did he say? And where have they gone?" wailed Jane, clinging to Alan.

"They—they said something about tacking," said Alan, doubtfully. "It's—I think it's something to do with sailing, Jane."

"I didn't know you sailed a boat with tacks," said Jane, watching the departing ruffians.

Alan was going to say "Neither did I!" but remembered that it is never wise to confess ignorance on any point to a girl, so he was silent. The next moment the waves near them were flattened and darkened by a big squall of wind, and the storm broke.

I do not know how to describe to you that terrible tempest: the waves that dashed the leaky and clumsy galleon finally on a rocky reef, the rain that beat on it, the wind that shook it, the awful sheets of lightning that covered sky and sea, the rumble of the thunder on every hand!

Alan and Jane clung to each other and to a mast, while the deck rocked under them and the spray drenched them over and over again. Sometimes a wave would go completely over the boat, almost washing the poor children away, but still they clung there, dizzy and frightened, and longing for the black, stormy night to end.

The good sea-spirits must have had them in their keeping, for otherwise it would have been impossible for them to escape death in the storm. But they did escape, and at last the morning broke and the tempest died down. The galleon (the bottom of which had been riddled with holes) was only a wreck, but still clinging to the broken mast were Alan and Jane. They were tired and frightened but still safe. The sea grew calmer and calmer, and the sun came up in the east like a good friend.

Then in the early morning sunlight that followed in the wake of that great storm, fishing boats began to push out from the various fishing villages along the coast.

"Jane," whispered Alan, "there's a boat!" There, sure enough, quite close to them, was a small craft, with a sail swelling out brightly in the early morning air, and standing up in it was something that looked like a man.

"Do you suppose Uncle Barnaby has sent it out to rescue us?" asked Jane.

"Perhaps," said the boy, but as the boat came nearer they could see that the man was a stranger, and was very roughly dressed.

"Ship ahoy!" he shouted. "What's the trouble?"

Alan jumped up,—he and Jane had been huddled together to keep warm,—;and waved his arms. He could not work them very well, for he was stiff with cold, but he managed to move them up and down a few times, and sang out:

"Can't you help us?"

"We're shipwrecked," cried Jane in a very weak voice.

The fisherman had come nearer by this time, and caught the word. "Shipwrecked?" he replied. "Well, you look it!"

His boat was soon alongside, and the children climbed down into it. The fisherman was a rough fellow, but seemed kind. He would have been glad to help Alan and Jane to get home, he said, but he had his own affairs to look after, so all he could do was to put them ashore, wish them luck, and sail off once more.

Alan and Jane found themselves at the edge of a wood, and when they were rested they plunged into it. They had not gone far when they heard voices singing, and this is what they sang:

> *"Hey, good comrades, come along!*
> *Sing with us the marching song!*
> *In the field, and through the grove,*
> *Free and happy do we rove!*
> *Empty purse and ragged cloak;—*
> *Come and join the Gypsy folk!"*

The children looked at each other with a thrill of excitement. "Gypsies!" they cried, with one voice.

III

THE GYPSY BAND

JOINING HANDS, ALAN AND JANE ran on until they came to the forest clearing from which the sound of singing came. They had always wanted to see real Gypsies.

There indeed was the Gypsy band, in ragged but bright coloured garments, and carrying their bundles on rough, wooden sticks. Some were old, some young, but all looked happy and healthy, brown and kind. The children told them their story, and the woodpeople were much interested and invited Alan and Jane to travel with them. They promised to see them safely to the Village without a Name. And as the children's sailor suits were not fit to wear they offered them some of their own clothes. But there were no little girls or big boys in the whole band, and finally they had to manage in quite a funny way. Jane put on the clothes of a little boy, and Alan dressed in the holiday finery of a pretty Gypsy girl who called herself Floretta, the Fawn of the Forest.

At last one of the older Gypsies cried:

"Brothers and sisters, the sun is high! We must be on our way."

With this the Gypsies all picked up their sticks and bundles, and soon the band started out. So Alan and Jane began their homeward journey.

They were now quite content. They had forgotten the dangers and sufferings of the wreck, and they were on their way home to Mary and Tom-Tom, and the rest of their playfellows. What did the past matter? Besides, they had always longed for adventures, and were they not having adventures in plenty now? They looked upon their journey with the Gypsy band as a delightful joke, and the strolling wood-people, on their side, were charmed with their small charges, and treated them with great kindness.

Alan had great fun with his Gypsy dress. He journeyed along, dancing and jingling the tambourine, and insisting that he was Floretta, the Fawn of the Forest, until Jane shriekedwith laughter, and all the Gypsies showed their teeth with amusement. He told the fortunes of all the country people they passed, and shocked the good housewives living along the road by romping about in a manner which would have been quite proper in Alan, but was highly undignified in Floretta, the Fawn of the Forest.

The real Floretta enjoyed the joke, and she and another Gypsy called Nino became very fond of Alan and Jane. Indeed, all the Gypsies were sorry to think of the day when they should have to say goodbye to the two children they had taken in charge.

The journey was very interesting to Alan and Jane. They slept out of doors, around a big, red campfire, with the dark trees overhead, and when they woke in the night they could hear owls and other queer birds calling to each other through the woods.

They learned any number of new things: the legends of the forest, and many other bits of out-of-door knowledge, though not everything, as they were to discover later, all of which only the real wood-people know, and the animals.

They heard also strange and terrible stories of the Spider's Forest, —a wooded region, which lay on the other side of their own village,—a region which no Gypsy would ever enter, and which even wood-cutters avoided. The Gypsies whispered the very name with fear: The Spider's Forest! The terror of the country for hundreds of miles around! The haunt of evil beasts and strange spirits! The place of Goblins, it was said, and all kinds of magic! The home of bears and wolves, and every kind of dangerous beast you could imagine! But worst of all the terrors of the black wood was the thing which gave it its name, the Giant Spider. It was said to be as big as a man, twice as strong, and was avoided by all who valued their lives. It lived in the very centre of the Forest.

One evening, as the band sat about the fire, waiting for the pot of stew to be ready for their supper, Jane asked timidly what the true history of the Giant Spider might be. An old, old Gypsy crone, with a dark, wrinkled face, and long, tangled, white hair like a witch, was the only one who could answer her question, so, as they all sat or lay around the fire, she told the story:

"Once upon a time the King of All the Fairies lived in a Silver Palace in the middle of the Forest. He was a good King, and friendly to everything alive, whether elf, beast, or man, and he was such a great King that he ruled over the whole world. In those days the fairies were the ruling people, and men didn't amount to much. They were just allowed to breathe the air, and grow grain to live on, through the kindness of the King of All the Fairies. He, of course, looked upon men as very weak things indeed, but he was very generous and good to them just the same.

"Well, the King of All the Fairies had a Prime Minister who was as mean and wicked as the King was great and kind. He wanted to rule the world, too, and he hated the King, and made up his mind to kill him and steal his Magic Power.

"The King kept his Magic Power in a gold bottle, which he always wore on a chain around his neck. One night the Prime Minister took a little file, which the Wicked Gnomes had made for him, and carefully filed the chain in two. Then he seized the gold bottle and pulled it off the chain. But as he did so the stopper came out, and the Magic Power was spilled.

"Then the King woke up, and saw what had happened, and cried out in a great fright. And the Prime Minister, knowing that the King had no Magic Power anymore, drew his dagger and stabbed him. But one drop of Magic Power had fallen on the King's finger, and he touched the Prime Minister with that finger, and said: 'In punishment for this crime you shall become a creature hated and feared by every living thing!'"

"Then the King of All the Fairies died, and the Silver Palace fell in little pieces, and everything in the world was different. The Magic Power trickled away, and sank into the ground, and was drunk up by the roots of some flowers. The fairies picked the flowers and used them for wands, so we have a little Magic Power left in the world, but not much, and it's growing less every day. And the fairies, instead of being the rulers of the world, hardly ever dare to appear nowadays.

"As for the wicked Prime Minister, when the Silver Palace fell in little pieces, he was crawling about among the ruins in the shape of a Giant Spider. And though it all happened thousands of years ago, he's crawling about still!"

The old crone stopped.

"Is that all?" asked Alan and Jane in one breath.

"That's all," said the old crone. "And the pot has begun to boil."

"And he's still alive?" asked Jane, her eyes growing big.

"The Giant Spider? Altogether too much so!"

"And is he just as wicked as ever? "asked Alan.

"I'm told he's wickeder," returned the crone.

"Oh, dear!" said Jane with a shiver.

"I'm glad *this* isn't the Spider's Forest!"

As the children listened to all this how little they guessed that the day would come when they would find themselves in the Spider's Forest itself, at the mercy of the Giant Spider and all the other dreadful creatures that lived there!

Meanwhile, day by day, the band was drawing slowly near the Village without a Name. And now, as they have almost reached the end of their journey, we will leave them for a short time and see what has been happening in Uncle Barnaby's house and Contrary Mary's garden while they have been away.

IV

CONTRARY MARY'S GARDEN

THERE MUST, OF COURSE, HAVE been days when the sun did not shine in Contrary Mary's garden; when the rain fell and made mud puddles among the rose bushes, and the sky looked frowningly down on the rows of gaily colored poppies nodding their heads, and silver-white lilies ringing their bells in the wind. But that it was pleasant weather in the garden, generally, seems certain, because Contrary Mary always wore dainty little shoes, and they were never muddy! And her gowns were like the pictures in the Nursery books, crisp, and clean, and pretty, and she never seemed to get them wet!

Contrary Mary, thoughshe was the oldest of the Widow Piper's fourteen children, was still very far from being grown up. She loved to play with Alan and Jane, and her brother Tom-Tom, as well as to water and weed her garden.

The garden, by the way, was the talk of the village. All the boys and girls in town lovedto come and look at it and inquire how it was getting on, which suggested to Mother Goose the first two lines of her song:

> *"Mary, Mary, quite contrary,*
> *How does your garden grow?"*

She *was* contrary, was Mary Piper, and sometimes even a bit naughty and disobedient too; but she was kind and sweet, and a faithful friend to Alan and Jane. As for her brother Tom-Tom, who was a year younger than Mary, he was the jolliest boy in the world, and as devoted as he could be to the two children next door. But for all that he was a dreamy fellow, too, always building air-castles of faraway places which he wanted to explore, and getting restless at home. He had a great longing for adventure,—like most boys. While he was still very little, his father had told him so many stories of the wonderful countries he had visited that Tom-Tom felt he must go travelling himself.

This is how it came about that when Jane and Alan disappeared, and Old Barnaby reported far and wide that they were dead, Tom-Tom declared his intention of going off to hunt for them.

"Old Barnaby may have had them kidnapped, or hidden, or something," he said. "But I don't believe they're dead."

So he packed some clothes in a bundle, which he meant to carry on a stick, as he had seen Gypsies do. Mary felt strongly tempted to go with him, for she was not only as anxious about Jane and Alan as he was, but she was very unhappy at home. The Widow Piper was often bad-tempered and unjust, and to make matters worse, she was beginning to be great friends with old Uncle Barnaby, so that, altogether, Mary thought the very best thing she could do would be to run away herself. But she said nothing about her plan to anyone this time—not even to Tom-Tom.

Meanwhile, Uncle Barnaby seemed almost happy. The great bag of money, according to law, would be his in a very short time, if Alan and Jane did not appear to claim it; and to judge by his satisfied look he really believed they never could claim it, and that they were actually drowned somewhere at the bottom of the old sea.

Yet, though this thought pleased him much, it was plain that he had still something to worry about. All his life he had been making enemies; now he began to want friends. He believed—poor man! That his great fortune could buy them, and he made up his mind to win the hearts of the villagers by being generous to them. The trouble was that he did not know what real generosity was. He would give a beautiful party, but on the same day, maybe, would turn some poor family out of their cottage because the unlucky father couldn't pay the rent. Of course the people of the Village without a Name could not be expected to like that sort of a man, just because he happened to be rich!

One day, in their hope of making people like them, Uncle Barnaby and the Widow Piper together gave a most wonderful Garden Party for all the children of the village, in the garden in front of the Widow Piper's house—Contrary Mary's garden, if you please. The invitations were sent out in fine style and made quite an excitement all over town. All the children in town were scrubbed and tubbed and all their best clothes patched up. But the little Pipers, who hated Old Barnaby, got no pleasure out of these preparations, and made up their minds to keep as far away as possible on the day of the party.

The day arrived and the village children came, all dressed in the prettiest frocks and suits they had. There were little girls in white, and little girls in blue, and little girls in pink, and yellow, and green and red,—just like so many extra flowers and butterflies in the garden. And the little boys were just as nicely dressed as the little girls. The "refreshments," as Uncle Barnaby called them, consisted of lemonade and sponge cake, and ice cream, and candy, and popcorn balls, and bread and jam, and strawberries and cream, and cut-up peaches, and sandwiches! It was really a lovely Garden Party, and everybody had a good time. Even the Piper children, hiding behind the garden wall, began to smell the cakes and strawberries, and felt sorry they hated Uncle Barnaby so much that they had refused to go to his party! The worst of it was, so far as they could see, the entertainment was getting along finely without them, though they were the children who rightfully belonged in the garden. So all the time, at least some of the village children, Tom-Tom packing his things upstairs, and the little Pipers, hiding and peeking, were not really enjoying the party so much. To make things still worse they could not help thinking it a great pity that Alan and Jane could not be there. Alan and Jane's right place, of course, was to be receiving the guests and saying "How d'ye do?" and "We are so glad you could come," or something else very polite, in a grown up way.

Instead, Old Barnaby was going round everywhere, in his musty, brown suit, and skull cap, tapping-tapping with his cane as he walked. Every now and then he would twist his wrinkles into a smile for the children, and say in the sweetest tones he could coax into his rasping old voice:

"My dears, I hope you are enjoying yourselves?"

Strangely enough, whenever Barnaby came up to a group of children this way, a sudden silence fell upon them. The girls giggled and looked at their shoes, and the boys grew red. No one seemed to think of an answer to make to Uncle Barnaby. The children all had an idea that Mrs. Piper was giving the party, and not the greatly disliked old miser. The pauses began to be very embarrassing, when one boy whispered to another:

"Did you know that Master Barnaby was giving this party? I just heard it!"

The news spread fast among Old Barnaby's guests, who began to feel very miserable, and to wish they had never come. Master Barnaby! Why, Master Barnaby, did not like boys and girls at all. He didn't like anything! He shook his stick at them all, over his front fence, and never had a kind look for anything,—not even for the cunningest babies and kittens! Why was he giving a party?

The uncomfortableness began to spread all through the company. Finally a little girl spoke up and said, quite distinctly:

"He turned poor old Mother Hubbard and her dog out of her house this very morning!"

A murmur passed round at this, for everybody remembered. Uncle Barnaby squirmed.

"What for?" exclaimed several children.

They all loved Mother Hubbard, who was as good as she was needy; and her poor dog, who was always begging for a bone, though her cupboard was always empty, was a village pet.

"Because she couldn't pay her rent, my father told me," said another girl.

"How awful!" exclaimed everyone, and one boy, quite red with anger, said:

"He ought to be ducked under the town pump!"

All the other boys, and some quite big ones, looked as though they would have liked to do this at once, and Barnaby grew very nervous. He was wondering what in the world he had better do, when, all of a sudden, Tom-Tom came out of the house, with his stick and his bundle. So eagerly had the boy been preparing for his adventure, that the merry voices in the garden had not disturbed him in the least, and he tumbled into the midst of the company now with a rush, all ready for his journey.

Old Barnaby made a dash at him.

"Tom-Tom!" he cried, trembling with rage. "These are ill-mannered little brats! They—"

The children broke out into a shrill chorus of explanations.

"We didn't know it was his party!"

"We would'nt have come!"

"It hasn't been a very nice party, anyway."

"Well," said Tom-Tom, "you've had a pretty good time, and you needn't be cross. You'd better go home, now, if you don't mind."

"But we didn't know—" began several children again. "Oh, well, you mustn't be disagreeable," said Tom-Tom. "After all," he added,—for he was very honest and also polite,—"it was his party, you know."

So the young guests began to get ready to go home. Some of them kept their little boxes of cake and snapdragons and tissue paper caps, and did them up carefully. Others, though quite sorry to do so, left them behind, as a matter of principle, because they hated Old Barnaby. One by one they filed through the garden gate and disappeared.

When the last little petticoat and knickerbocker had fluttered down the street and round the turn in the road by Mother Hubbard's house, the garden was empty of everybody except Tom-Tom. The garden gate was open, still swinging, and clicking a little on its hinges. Tom-Tom stood a while. He was not sorry to go. He just wanted to stop and get a good taste of the fun of running away.

But he was not to get off just yet. Suddenly the gate clicked again and in flew little Bo Peep in tears.

"I've lost my sheep!" she wailed.

"Oh, pshaw!" said Tom-Tom. Then he added, so as not to be unkind, "Don't you know where to find them?"

"No!" wailed Bo Peep again. "I've lost my sheep!"

"And I've lost Alan and Jane," said Tom-Tom, "and I'm going to try to find *them* and bring them back again."

With this he shouldered his bundle and made off. Sturdily along the dusty road he trudged, and when he turned for one last look at the Village without a Name he could only see the golden weathervane upon the Widow Piper's barn.

If Tom-Tom had known how many days would pass, how many strange things would happen, before his, return,—but he did not, nor must you know, until we come to them.

V

Uncle Barnaby Has A Shock

B o Peep meanwhile was still very much worried about her lost sheep, and her brothers and sisters, who all ran into the garden in a flock to see if the party was over, promised to help to find them.

So they all went off to look for the sheep. Scarcely had they disappeared when Hilda came hurrying out of the house crying: "Oh, Master Tom-Tom! Where *have* you gone?" She had discovered that some of his clothes were missing, and she couldn't find him, so she was sure he had run away. You see Tom-Tom had always threatened to run away since he was old enough to talk at all!

"Oh, dear," sighed Hilda to herself, "now we shall never see him anymore. He will be lost forever, like poor Master Alan and Miss Jane!"

But just at that moment who should come running into the garden but a small person dressed in a rough brown suit, with a cap and heavy boots, a shock of yellow curls, a giggle, a dimple, and a general look of mischief.

Hilda gasped and flung up both hands. The small person, still giggling, threw herself into the good woman's arms and hugged her excitedly.

"Mercy on us!" cried Hilda, looking as though she had seen a ghost. "Mercy, mercy on us all!"

For it was Jane!

"And where is Master Alan?" asked Hilda as soon as she could speak.

"Alan," said Jane, with a chuckle, "is mending a tear in his skirt!"

"His skirt!" exclaimed Hilda. "Really they are the most surprising children!" she said to herself. Jane explained, and just then Alan appeared, jingling his tambourine, and crying:

"I am Floretta, the Fawn of the Forest! Won't you let the Fawn of the Forest tell your fortunes?"

Hilda of course had not an idea what this meant, but she was delighted to see both children safe and sound, for she had been very unhappy since she had heard the rumours of their death. She took them into her nice, cosy kitchen, with the beautifully scoured pots and pans shining on the wall, and made them sit down and tell her all the adventures they had met with since they left home. There was such a delicious smell of baking cake in the room that they could not help sniffing it, and she gave them each a piece fresh from the oven, and a glass of milk, and made herself a cup of tea. In return they told her all about everything. Hilda was very much interested.

When they came to the part about their being left on the galleon in the storm, she shook her head and sighed heavily, and thought to herself: "Poor innocent lambs! At the mercy of such a hard-hearted, cruel man!"

But out loud she encouraged them to tell her the rest of their story. When they had finished she said:

"Well, dear Miss Jane and Master Alan, I think both the good angels and good fairies must have had you in their keeping. Now you are safe home again, you'll stay always, I hope, for I think you've had enough adventures."

"Uncle Barnaby will be so glad to see that we are not drowned!" cried Jane, jumping up. "We must go home and see him, and get some clothes."

"Wait a bit, Miss Jane," begged Hilda, who had her own opinion of Uncle Barnaby. "I think a suit of Master Tom-Tom's might fit you, Master Alan, he's so tall for his age; and I'm sure that Miss Bo Peep is just Miss Jane's size."

"But why not get our own clothes?" said Jane.

Hilda did not want to tell them that she was not at all sure Uncle Barnaby would be glad to see them, so she only said:

"Just to please me, Miss Jane; come upstairs the back way, and let me get you into Miss Bo Peep's dress and find out what my little master has left."

"Left!" exclaimed Alan. "Tom-Tom hasn't gone away, has he?"

"Yes, indeed," said Hilda, looking ready to cry, "he went off this very day."

"Oh, how dreadful!" cried both the children.

At that moment the kitchen door opened and the Widow Piper came in. She saw the two little Gypsies, but did not recognise them, and began to scold Hilda angrily for feeding beggars.

Just for a joke Alan ran up to her, keeping his face hidden under the shadow of the big hat, and asked if she would not like Floretta, the Fawn of the Forest, to read the future for her.

"That," said the Widow Piper, "depends on what you read."

"You have a neighbour who has just lost two members of his family," began Alan, meaning to lead up to telling who he and Jane really were. "Poor man! He misses them very much, but he will soon have a pleasant sur—" He was going to say "surprise," when the widow interrupted him.

"He certainly has lost two members of his family," she said, "but he doesn't miss them, or oughtn't to! It's a very good thing for him, for he gets their money."

Alan walked thoughtfully over to the window and stood beside Jane until the widow had left the kitchen.

"It's no use, Jane," he whispered, "Uncle Barnaby *does* hate us, and will be sorry to have us back."

"Come, dears," said Hilda, when her mistress had gone, "come and change your clothes."

So they all three climbed the stairs to one of the many nurseries. Fourteen children took up a great deal of room, even when they used trundle beds, as the Pipers did. Then Hilda helped Alan and Jane to dress. They looked very nice and neat, and were glad to be Alan and Jane again instead of two Gypsies.

"But where's Mary?" asked Alan, when they were dressed.

"Miss Mary!" called Hilda, going to Mary's door.

There was no answer. When, presently, she opened the door and peered in she found the room greatly upset, and some of Mary's clothes missing, just as Tom-Tom's had been.

"Deary me! Deary me!" wailed Hilda, coming out in tears, "Mary's run away too!"

This was too much for Alan and Jane. Their two best friends gone, and their uncle glad of their own disappearance! They both began to cry, and Hilda cried with them. Then Alan remembering once more that he was the oldest and a man stopped suddenly.

"I—I'll tell you, Jane," he burst out, "we'll run away!"

"Master Alan!" exclaimed Hilda.

But Jane cried eagerly:

"All right! Where shall we run away to?"

"Let's go and find Mary," said Alan.

"And Tom-Tom," added Jane.

"But we don't know where they've gone," said Alan.

"No," agreed Jane, sadly.

"That's lucky," said Hilda to herself; but Alan declared cheerfully:

"Then, we'll just leave it to the good fairies, and start out in any direction that we like."

"Oh, mercy me!" sighed Hilda.

"We'll get a map," said Jane, delightedly.

"And we'll get a pin," said Alan.

"Here's the pin," said Jane, pulling one out of her dress.

"And we'll stick it in the map, just anywhere," continued Alan, "and the place where it sticks we'll go to."

"So!" said Jane, excitedly, and pinched Alan so hard that he jumped.

"Hold on, Jane, I'm not the map!" he said. "But I'll tell you what we must do; we must have money, if we're going to travel."

"Let's ask Uncle Barnaby," suggested Jane.

"Yes," said her brother, "we'll ask Uncle Barnaby for our money. He ought to be glad to give it to us, for then we'll go away and he'll never be bothered with us anymore."

"There's Uncle Barnaby now," cried Jane, who could see through the window from where she stood.

"Let's go and ask him," exclaimed Alan, and, taking each other's hands they rushed downstairs and out of the house, frightening a big tortoise-shell cat that was asleep in the hall, almost out of her wits.

Into Contrary Mary's garden, his stick tapping, tapping, on the nicely rolled path, came Uncle Barnaby. Out of the Widow Piper's house rushed his nephew and niece, crying:

"Hello, Uncle Barnaby! Here we are, Uncle Barnaby."

Uncle Barnaby retreated a few steps and leaned against the high brick garden wall.

"Ghosts!" he whispered, with dry lips. "Ghosts, of course. They can't be alive."

For he thought Alan and Jane were dead at the bottom of the sea, you know.

But Alan hurried forward in the least ghost-like manner possible.

"We're all right, Uncle," he said cheerfully, "and we want to ask you to please let us have—"

Turning from them, Uncle Barnaby fled out of the garden, shaking and gasping, with the two children after him.

At that very moment, Mary, with all her twelve brothers and sisters looking on, was climbing over the back garden wall. When they had got home after finding the sheep, she met them with the announcement that she, like Tom-Tom, was going to run away.

"Perhaps I shall catch up with him," she said. "What road did he take, Bo Peep?"

"I don't know," said Bo Peep.

"He would surely never dare to go through the wood," said Miss Muffet.

"Then," said Mary, "he went by the highway, probably, that leads to Toyland."

"Where's that?" asked Curly Locks.

"I don't know, but father went there once, and he used to tell Tom-Tom and me about it," said Mary. "Goodbye, boys and girls. If I never come back Curly Locks, you may have all my sofa pillows—you like cushions—and you, Bo Peep, may have my tortoise-shell cat. Be sure that the guinea pigs are fed; and oh, *please*, see that my dear garden is weeded and watered every day! Goodbye!"

When she had dropped safely to the ground on the outer side of the wall, she could just see the children's heads over the top. They handed down her bundle, her bag, her birdcage, and everything which she had made up her mind to take with her, and shouted a chorus of shrill goodbyes. She could make out little Red Riding Hood's hood among the others till she could not see them or the old wall anymore.

Bo Peep, meantime, who felt much more cheerful now that her sheep had been found, looked after her sister.

"Tom-Tom and Mary both gone in one day," she remarked. "Mother will be pleased!" Then they all went off to the house for their supper.

When Uncle Barnaby grasped the fact that Jane and Alan were not ghosts, and had never been drowned at all, he lost no time in planning another scheme for getting rid of them, something more certain than a mere wreck at sea.

He told them that he had bought a beautiful new house in which he wanted them to live, with him, and said that he would send them there that evening with the same trusty friends who had taken them to the galleon, and that he himself would follow in the morning. The children had never believed that Gonzorgo and Roderigo had meant to harm or desert them, so they agreed willingly enough, and were rather pleased by the thought of going to a brand new house in a brand new place.

"But Uncle," said Alan, "we do want our money, please, right away. We want to travel!"

"We'll talk of that tomorrow, my dear," said Uncle Barnaby, sweetly. "You'll see me, you know, in the morning."

But to himself he murmured: "They'll never see me, and they'll never see the morning!"

The two villainous seamen had been hastily sent for once more, this time their orders were whispered into their ears with a fierceness which made even Gonzorgo shiver. They were to lead the children into the thickest, darkest, and most dangerous parts of the Spider's Forest, and there lose them!

No wonder Gonzorgo and Roderigo trembled at the thought of so terrible a deed. The dangers of the stormy ocean were nothing in comparison with the horrors of the dreadful Spider's Forest. But there was good gold to be had for the work, so they tried to keep up their courage, and obey the wicked old Miser's commands.

Uncle Barnaby said goodbye to his nephew and niece with a great show of affection, and once more the two children and the two ruffians started off together.

So fresh adventures began for Alan and Jane.

In Contrary Mary's garden the "silver bells" of the lilies, and the "cockle shells" of the poppies blew in the evening breeze, and the "pretty maids all in a row" passed along the village street, and peered over the garden gate, singing the little rhymes that Mother Goose had made out of their ceaseless questions:

> "Mary, Mary, quite Contrary,
> How does your garden grow?
> With silver bells, and cockle shells,
> And pretty maids all in a row!"

The Widow Piper's twelve remaining children quarrelled over their bread and milk and peaches, and over the feeding of Mary's guinea pigs, and wondered what had become of Tom-Tom and Mary.

And Alan and Jane were trudging along the woodpath, with their two false guides, going always deeper and deeper into the Spider's Forest.

THE SPIDER'S FOREST

NOW YOU MUST IMAGINE YOURSELF in the Spider's Forest!
It is very dark, for not only is it already night, but the trees grow so thickly that they shut out what little starlight there may be. So dark is it that the tree trunks cast no shadows, and the mouth of the Bear's Den is only a little blacker than the rock wall into which it reaches. Little shivering winds go stealing through the woods, rustling the leaves, and making strange noises in the underbrush. Tumbled-down trees lie here and there; vine-creepers twine overhead in thick masses; big boulders are all about. SSh-h-h!! Walk very carefully, for this is the Spider's Forest.

The Bear's Den is one of the Giant Spider's favourite haunts, for the Giant Spider has no real home of his own, but crawls and squirms and wriggles everywhere, on his many legs, turning honest beasts out of their dwellings, and spinning his evil webs across their front doors. One and all, they are fearfully afraid of the Giant Spider.

Just inside the Bear's Den the Giant Spider has spun a small, strong web, to hold a victim that he has long wished to devour, a very important victim, as you will see later. If you look closely you will notice something white struggling in the web; something—but wait till Alan and Jane see it too.

Of course, the Giant Spider has no right to use Mother Bear's house as a prison for his captives, but he does not care for that!

Now look closely: the moon must have risen, somewhere outside the Spider's Forest, for a little, faint, white light is flickering down between the branches into the clearing in front of the Bear's Den. Can you see those little green creatures hopping about? They are the Frogs, from the neighbouring pool, and they are having their Night Dance. Did you never hear of the Frog's Night Dance? They never miss a night, and they dance until morning. At least, they do in the Spider's Forest.

But see! They are all frightened; they are hopping away in wild confusion. And no wonder; for here comes the Giant Spider himself!

He is big and green, and terrible to see, and his wicked legs wiggle and wave, and cling to things in a frightful way! Up he goes over the crooked tree trunks, seeking fresh prey, and finally disappears among the black branches overhead.

And now comes a heavy, lumbering step, followed by a lighter, shuffling one. Bears inside the Den!

Just think of poor Alan and Jane coming, step by step, nearer this dreadful place, so full of strange and dangerous beasts!

Mother Bear and Baby Bear come out of the Den together. Perhaps they are going to market, for Mother Bear carries a basket. The Giant Spider has frightened Baby Bear, and Baby Bear is crying. Mother Bear tries to quiet him; she rolls over and over and over to amuse him. Then she wipes his eyes with a large white handkerchief, but still he refuses to be comforted. At last she gives him a bottle of milk, after which he stops crying and jogs along behind her, much cheered. You see small Bears are very like small Boys, after all. Nothing on earth is quite so comforting to them both as supper!

When the Bears had disappeared, another couple, less innocent by far, come creeping through the crackling underbrush,—Gonzorgo and Roderigo, who have deserted the children in the depths of the forest and are on their way home by a short cut. They lose no time in leaving the neighbourhood of the Bear's Den, for they know well the dangers of the place, and, shaking with fear, they make their way backthrough the woods, and report to Uncle Barnaby.

Then, after a few minutes, as silent as the grave, four very tired little feet come carrying two very tired little bodies over the logs and —undergrowth at the edge of the clearing, and Alan and Jane stand trembling together, at the very mouth of the Bear's Den!

They left Uncle Barnaby with light hearts not long before the darkness fell. In the woods they had grown frightened. The bigness and blackness of the forest made them afraid they never, never, could get out of it. They began to wonder how far it was to Uncle Barnaby's beautiful new house, and, at the bottom of their hearts, they began to doubt if there were any such house at all. Every minute they expected to see goblins or wild animals glaring at them from the bushes, and once in a while they did fancy that they saw and heard things which were not quite usual in an ordinary forest. Then the next thing they knew, in the very darkest part of the woods, their guides had disappeared. Alan and Jane did not stop to wonder whether or not they had been deserted on purpose. Whatever was the matter, they were quite alone now, as they had been on the galleon that awful night during the storm. They struggled along as bravely as they could, Alan supporting Jane and biting his lips to keep back unmanly tears, and Jane growing more and more tired and frightened and miserable.

So they came to the Bear's Den, the spot so greatly beloved by the Giant Spider.

"I can't go any farther," said Jane, with a sob, "I'm too tired."

"Then rest a while," suggested Alan, as comfortingly as he could, "and try to sleep a bit."

"I—I can't!" wept Jane. "I'm too frightened!"

"Why in the world should you be frightened?" said Alan, stoutly. At the same moment a twig cracked in the wind, and he jumped. But he recovered himself, and added, looking big, "You mustn't be frightened, Jane; *I* am with you!"

He hoped that Jane did not feel him shaking with fear.

"What was that? "cried Jane, with a gasp, as a night-bird flew by.

"N-nothing, nothing at all, Jane!" declared Alan, holding her tight, and blinking away the tears. "Go to sleep, dear, and dream of Tom-Tom and Mary, and forget all about this horrid wood." A tear fell just then, but Jane did not see it, so it made no difference.

"There," he continued, pointing toward the Bear's Den, "there's a nice place to lie down, away from the dampness. Let's go in."

"Oh, look!" exclaimed Jane, peering into the Den. "There's a big Spider's web, and a poor little white moth caught there, tangled up in that web. Like you and me in this awful wood," she added gloomily.

There indeed was the Spider's latest victim, struggling feebly among the strong, fine threads that the creature had spun.

"Perhaps," went on Jane, softly, "it's the Moth Queen."

"The Moth Queen?" repeated Alan, puzzled. Boylike, he had never paid as much attention to the legends of the Spider's Forest as Jane had.

"Why, yes!" exclaimed Jane. "I heard the Gypsies speak of it. They say that she often goes about in the shape of a little white moth to watch over her friends and spy upon her enemies. Oh, do set it free, poor little thing! See how it struggle and flutters!"

Alan quickly disentangled the delicate white wings, and the moth flew quickly away into the darkness.

"There it goes, flying for dear life," he said. "And now let us try to go to sleep, Jane. We really must, you know."

Already, for some strange reason, they felt less frightened. It seemed suddenly as though they were surrounded by friends and protectors. Was it imagination, or did they really hear soft voices singing about them?

No, luckily for Alan and Jane, it was not all their fancy. But they were only mortals, so they could not see the Wood-Spirits drawing near to guard them through the night,—the Spirit of the Oak, and the Spirit of the Maple, and the Spirit of the Pine, and the Spirit of the

Willow,—quietly waving their leafy wands toward them, and singing so softly that their voices seemed like the murmur of the night wind in the swaying trees.

So the children lay down quite peacefully, just within the Bear's Den, and soon were sleeping soundly—so soundly that they did not hear the cracking of twigs and rustling of dead leaves as a dreadful Something came toward them through the darkness.

VII

The White Moth

WRIGGLING AND CRAWLING ALONG, WHAT should it be but the wicked Giant Spider!

When he squirmed and scampered his way into the Den, he found two, new, human victims in place of the white moth. He was angry at losing the moth, for he had his own private plans for getting rid of it, but still the prospect of so delightful a meal as two mortal children charmed his wicked soul. For fear of waking them he would not bind them with threads, as was his custom. Instead, he spun a very beautiful, strong, thick web across the mouth of the Den, to keep his captives quite safely imprisoned until he should feel hungry.

How little did Alan and Jane know their danger! They were still fast asleep, dreaming, probably, of Contrary Mary's garden.

Then, just as the Giant Spider had finished spinning his web, who should come lumbering home from market but Mother Bear and Baby Bear.

The Giant Spider had long planned to eat up the Baby Bear, so he smiled,—as much as a Spider could smile,—and crawled along to meet them.

Now Mother Bear had endured the Spider's wickedness as long as she could. She had been patient while he made himself at home in her Den and used her front hall as a prison for his moths and frogs; but to be driven out of her own house, and to have her child's life threatened, was simply more than she could stand. So she ordered Baby Bear away, who ran back into the woods, and then she threw aside her marketing basket, lowered her big, brown head, and charged at the Giant Spider herself.

The birds, and beetles, and frogs, and rabbits, and bats, and fairies, and goblins, and gnomes that saw that fight talked about it for the rest of their lives. They called in all their friends to look, and though a human eye could not have seen a sign of life anywhere about, there really was a large and excited audience hidden among the leaves and grass blades.

Everyone believed that the Giant Spider would win, for the forest-folk had come to believe that nothing could ever harm him. But perhaps the Wood-Spirits helped Mother Bear, for, after a long and terrible struggle, the Giant Spider, the terror of the woodlands, and the enemy of all good beasts, lay dead.

Mother Bear wasted no time in undue pride, but called Baby Bear, took his paw, and prepared to tear aside the Spider's web and enter the Den.

Alan and Jane were once more in danger you see.

But, suddenly and swiftly as a shadow, a misty figure crossed the clearing, a figure leaf-crowned and beautiful, holding a delicate branch in its outstretched hand. It was one of the Wood-Spirits, she, in fact, who dwells in the heart of the great and noble oak tree,—and she had come to protect the children.

"Go back," she said to Mother Bear, in her soft whispering voice. "I have friends to guard and to lead safely from this place. Go back into the forest, and come not to your home till the dawn be here. Obey me: I am the Spirit of the Oak!"

Of course Mother Bear was quite willing to obey the Wood-Spirits, who are the rightful rulers over all wild creatures, so she and Baby Bear trotted off once more and stayed away until morning. When they came back the web was torn away from the front door and the children were gone.

When Alan and Jane awoke they seemed to be imprisoned in mist as thick and hard to see through as a heavy, grey veil. A dim light came through it, but when they put out their hands they met a silky surface as soft as a cloud, but as impossible to get through as a stone wall.

It was the Spider's web, you know, which he had spun across the door of the Den.

More frightened than ever, they wandered about the dim cave, and pressed hopelessly against the grey wall which shut them in. What sort of a prison was this?

Surely one of the mysterious spells common to the Spider's Forest was binding them! They clung to each other, fearing that by some terrible chance they would become separated and would never be able to find each other in this strange and dreadful place.

Suddenly Alan saw something move on the ground at his feet. He bent to look closer, and then sprang back, amazed and almost terrified, for even as he looked two shining globes of light appeared there, with a pair of softly moving wings for shades,—the eyes of a moth.

"Jane, Jane, see!" he cried.

Catching each others hands tight, they watched, with a breathless feeling that something was going to happen.

Suddenly, with a whir of wings, a great Moth rose from the ground. Light seemed to gleam from its eyes and from its wings, which trembled like poplar leaves.

And then… a strange thing happened. Perhaps the children were confused or still dreaming, for it seemed that the Moth was no longer a moth, but a beautiful lady, with two glittering round lights in her hair, and white wings with a thousand changing colours.

She smiled at the children, a beautiful, protecting smile, and all fear left them instantly. They went quickly up to her, their eyes fixed on her wonderful radiant face and wings.

At that she turned with the whirling, darting motion of a butterfly, and, while her wings fluttered and flashed like bubbles in the sun, led them through the cobweb wall.

The wall seemed no stronger than mist now, and the mist continued for a long, long time. The children walked on and on. They were on solid ground, but they seemed to move more quickly than ever before, and with less trouble. Their guide was always just in front of them, and as they went on they began to see other butterflies too, of a hundred different colours, floating along in a silent group. When Alan and Jane looked closely at them, they saw that they were like their guide, only less brilliant, and of them, too, they could not be sure whether they were butterflies or women.

And then the mist cleared swiftly, and a great cloud of perfume met them, perfume stronger and sweeter than anything they had ever dreamed of. Before them was the big red moon just setting over what looked like a bank of flowers, and in front of them, and on every side, were shadowy wings fluttering, fluttering, fluttering, in air that was as sweet as flowers, and making a soft rushing sound in the darkness.

Then suddenly the moon was gone. And a golden light that was not moonlight, nor starlight, nor sunlight, poured down on them. They were standing close beside their beautiful guide. Her great wings were outspread, floating like silver. She was dressed all in white that sparkled as though it were covered with diamonds.

On every side were other shining beings, with broad, quivering wings, green, and gold, and purple, and crimson and blue. And everywhere were flowers, flowers as big as the butterfly ladies themselves: great irises, and tulips, and orchids, and asters, and poppies, and lilies, and roses, all with a wonderful fragrance coming from them.

Alan and Jane, bewildered but not at all frightened now, drew nearer to their beautiful white friend. She smiled at them, and her wings seemed to flutter toward them as though she would protect them beneath their shining whiteness.

Then she spoke, in a voice so soft that it sounded like the whir of tiny wings at dusk, when the moths come to visit the flowers in the garden.

"Look at me, my children," she said. "I am the Moth Queen, whose life you saved. And this is my Palace of Flowers."

VIII

THE PALACE OF FLOWERS

ALL THE TIME THEY WERE in the Palace of Flowers, Alan and Jane seemed to be in a beautiful dream. They ate honey and pollen and drank dew, just as the butterflies did, and when the heavy perfume sent them into long, deep slumbers, they curled up on banks of violets or beds of moss. The golden light almost dazzled their eyes, and they passed their days in a state of wondering happiness with the Moth Queen and her radiant subjects.

All their lives the children remembered the beautiful white Butterfly-Lady, and the many bright creatures in the Palace. of Flowers. Years afterward, when the Spider's Forest was nothing but a dreamy n:iemory, they spoke of the dainty winged people who had been their friends, and, in those later days, when a little grey night moth fluttered softly by at twilight, Jane would whisper:—"One of the Moth Queen's messengers."

And you will do well to remember this, too. If ever you see a little, fragile thing beating its wings against a lamp, rescue it as tenderly as may be, for who knows? It may be one of the Moth Queen's court ladies! And if it is, why—when you set it free, and it flies away through the darkness, you may be sure that it has gone to tell the Moth Queen, and that they will soon be saying pretty things about you in the Palace of Flowers.

After they had recovered from their first shyness, Alan and Jane asked so many eager questions that at last the Moth Queen said that she would tell them her history, and all about how she became a Moth Queen. Then they could see for themselves just what and who she was, and what was the beginning of the war between herself and the Giant Spider.

Her subjects stood around in a rainbow semicircle, while she sat on her flower throne with Alan and Jane at her feet. When nothing much was happening in her story the butterflies stood still; when it became exciting they moved their wings or fluttered so violently that the children were reminded of a great number of little flags flapping in the wind.

"Once upon a time, when the King of All the Fairies was alive," began the Moth Queen, "I was a great Princess, and I lived in a Castle of Frosted Glass. I had many suitors, the Duke of the Goblins, the Lord of the Dragons, the Baron of the Mermen, the Count of the Sun-Spirits, the Marquis of the Fire-Fairies, and the Prince of the Gnomes. But I was a very proud Princess, and would have nothing to do with any of them. I had an old nurse who was a Witch, one of the very few good Witches that ever lived.

"She loved me, and she used to spin me wonderful white robes, more fine and delicate than any other royal garments in the world. She spun them out of snowflakes and white violets, and her distaff was made of glass, so fragile that only a Witch could use it without breaking it.

"Whenever a suitor presented himself, I would tell my Witch-Nurse to go down to the door of the Frosted Glass Castle and send him off. She had a different way of getting rid of each of them. She used to think them up and chuckle over them, while she was spinning with her glass distaff. When the Baron of the Mermen came, all dressed in green seaweed, and dripping salt water, with his attendant courtiers loaded down with pearls and coral branches and wonderful shells as offerings to me, my Witch-Nurse put out her hand toward the South and whispered a spell. At her command a great hot wind came suddenly, full of desert sand, and it blew upon the Baron of the Mermen till he cried: 'I'm drying up! I'm drying up!' and he ran away with all his followers, and that was the last we saw of him.

"The Marquis of the Fire-Fairies came with tongues of flame leaping out from his red robes, and was followed by a train of little demon attendants, bearing great lumps of gold dug from the hearts of volcanic mountains. For him my Witch-Nurse ordered out a big storm cloud, and it came and poured rain down upon him, till he ran away puffing little clouds of steam and crying: 'I'm being put out! I'm being put out!' For of course he was made of fire, and the rain would have put him out if he'd stayed any longer.

"For the Count of the Sun-Spirits, who brought me rare draperies woven of rainbows and sunset clouds, my Witch-Nurse had great masses of darkness and mist, which frightened him away. And for the Prince of the Gnomes, whose ebony chariot was filled with glowing gems, she had blinding rays of sunlight which he could not bear for a moment. For every suitor she had a weapon fitted especially to repulse him, and him alone. So, one by one, she got rid of them all, while I sat at my window in the Castle of Frosted Glass, dressed in my dainty robes that were spun from snowflakes and white violets, and laughed at my would-be lovers as they ran away.

"And then one day came one who was unlike the others. He came with no retinue, he brought no gifts. He looked up at the Castle of Frosted Glass and laughed, and cried:

"'Oh, beautiful Princess of the Snowflakes and White Violets! You who will not smile upon any of the Princes of the Fairy World, come out!'

"I looked from my window and saw that he seemed to be a handsome shepherd. I felt curious to speak further with him, so I went down my glass stairway. My Witch-Nurse was angry and called out storm, and fire, and darkness, and wind, to put him to flight. But still the new suitor stood outside the Castle of Frosted Glass and laughed at her efforts, and cried:

"'Come out, beautiful White Princess!'

"So I went out and my Witch-Nurse hobbled off, and, in a helpless rage, broke her glass distaff in tiny pieces.

"'Princess,' said the stranger, 'you are the fairest and sweetest Princess in the Fairy World. Will you marry me?'

"I said 'Yes!' for of course I was already very much in love with him!

"He knelt at my feet and said:

"'Greeting, Oh Queen of All the Fairies!'

"'What can you mean?' I asked.

"Then he told me that he was the King of All the Fairies.

"'But,' I said, 'you come dressed as a shepherd.'

"'The Princes and Barons and little Lords must let everyone see their rank,' he answered. 'It is only the King who has no need for a retinue nor for gorgeous robes when he goes a-wooing!'

"Naturally, I felt very happy over the honour which had been done me, and promised to become Queen of the Fairies the following day. So he went away, laughing as he had come, and I wondered, as I watched him, that I had not known at once that he was the King.

"My old Witch-Nurse was so sad and so angry at the thought of losing me that she hobbled away into the woods as fast as ever she could. I never heard of her again.

"And that very night what do you suppose happened? The King of All the Fairies was killed!"

"By his wicked Prime Minister!" cried Alan and Jane, for they remembered the story told them by the Gypsy crone.

"Yes," said the Moth Queen, who seemed surprised that they knew this, "yes, that is quite true. So I never became Queen of All the Fairies after all!"

She sighed, and all the butterflies drooped their wings in sympathy. After a moment she continued:

"The news was brought me by a kindly bat, who happened to be flying past my Castle. Of course I felt very sad, and just a little frightened, for now that my Witch-Nurse had also left me I was quite alone. I decided that I would go to the Silver Palace, in the centre of the Forest, where the King of All the Fairies had lived since the beginning of things, and see for myself if the report were really true.

"So I ran out of my Castle of Frosted Glass in such a hurry that I did not give a single look behind me. I never entered it again.

"There was the most dreadful confusion everywhere. The news of the King's death had been a great shock to his subjects, and all sorts and kinds of Elves flew wildly in different directions, crying:

"'The King! The King! The Prime Minister has killed the King! Who will rule us now? And what has become of the Magic Power? The King! The King!'

"No one paid any attention to me, and I ran safely and quickly to the centre of the Forest to hunt for the Silver Palace. But the Silver Palace was gone! All that seemed to be left of it were some shining splinters of silver lying on the moss. There was an enormous Spider wriggling about among them, as though he were looking for something, and wheezing: 'What has become of the Magic Power? Where is the Magic Power?'

"'Where is the King?' I cried.

"'Dead!' answered the Spider, with a squeal of pleasure. 'But I've spilt the Magic Power!'

"Then I knew that he was the wicked Prime Minister himself. And I seized one of the silver splinters and chased him away with it. As he wriggled off he cried out:

"'Just wait, you pretty, proud Princess, with your airs and graces, and your Castle of Frosted Glass! I'll be revenged upon you yet! Someday you'll be sorry you were so rude to me!'

"Then he vanished into the Forest, and I was left alone. I was very miserable and frightened, and I wished that I had my Witch-Nurse back again. The Witches have always had a certain amount of Magic Power of their own, you know.

"As I still held the silver splinter in my hand, I saw that it was wet with some liquid that stung my fingers a little, and had a fragrance like honeysuckles and lilacs mixed together. A sudden thought came to me. Suppose that some of the Magic Power were on that silver splinter!

"At that moment a great cloud of Winged Goblins flew by, fighting, and I grew terrified, and wanted to hide myself. I saw a little Moth fluttering about near me, and it looked so insignificant and safe that I whispered, holding the silver splinter up before me, and looking at it:

"'Oh, dear Magic Power! If there's any of you left on this silver splinter, will you please turn me into a Moth?'

"Then, for a moment, I felt very, very dizzy. Then I felt very light and free. Then I felt as though I were rising softly from the ground. And, indeed, I *was* rising,—rising on two pretty white wings! I was a Moth!

"The silver splinters of the King's palace lay far beneath, and as I flew along I could see, down below, the Spider Minister smashing my Castle of Frosted Glass into pieces, while his wicked eyes blazed with rage.

"The little Moth that I had noticed while I was still a Princess flew up to me, and I made friends with her. She brought me here, and the Butterfly people, who were in need of a ruler, crowned me Queen. So here I have lived and reigned over the Kingdom of Moths for hundreds of years.

"Yesterday the Giant Spider caught me, and tied me up in his web, but you rescued me, so all is well again. Now one of my messengers brings the news that Mother Bear has killed the wicked beast at last, and hereafter the forest-folk may go abroad in peace.

"That, dear children, is the story of the White Moth Queen."

Alan and Jane thanked her and said it had been very interesting.

There were several questions they wanted to ask, but they were too polite, for they were sure the Moth Queen must be tired, she had talked so long.

Then she called out from the circle of winged listeners two cream-coloured Moth Millers, and ordered them to bring refreshments. The Moth Millers hurried away, and were soon back with pollen bread and essence of violets, served on poppy petals. It tasted very good, and while they were eating and drinking, six pretty, pale pink butterflies fanned them with their wings. "But, how," asked the Queen, suddenly, "did you ever hear anything about the death of the King of All the Fairies? It has never been known by any mortal before."

"An old woman told us," answered Alan.

"An old Gypsy woman," added Jane.

"Did she look at all like a Witch?" cried the Queen excitedly.

"Why yes, I think she did!" exclaimed Alan and Jane together.

The Queen almost wept.

"She must be my Witch-Nurse herself!" she cried. "I have not seen her for hundreds and hundreds of years. How glad I am to have news of her again! You are doubly welcome in the Palace of Flowers, since, besides saving my life, you bring me news of my dear old Witch-Nurse." The Moth Queen would have liked to keep Alan and Jane with her for a long time, but they were eager to get home again. So after a day or two more they told the Moth Queen that they wanted to find their way out of the forest.

"But you might get lost," said the Moth Queen. "Oh, no! That will never do at all. I shall send for Fuzzy to guide you and take care of you."

The children wondered who "Fuzzy "might be, but they did not ask questions. The Moth Queen sent out a messenger, who soon returned saying that Fuzzy was quite delighted to take the two human children safely out of the wood. Fuzzy, the messenger added, was waiting outside the Palace of Flowers.

Alan and Jane said goodbye to their kind friend, the Moth Queen, and her court. The Moths waved their many-coloured wings to them, as they left the palace, and the flowers sent out great clouds of their very strongest and delicious fragrance, which accompanied them far on their way, like a sort of magical incense.

The children were very curious to see Fuzzy, their new guide. They could not imagine who or what he might be. Would he be a fairy, or a goblin, or some kind of elfin moth?

When they came out of the palace they found themselves face to face with a fat, brown, furry little creature, sitting on his haunches, and looking at them out of a pair of small, twinkling eyes.

"Fuzzy" was a little brown bear!

IX

Three Children in the Woods

THE TWO HUMAN CHILDREN STARED at the animal child, and the animal child stared at them.

"So you are the Moth Queen's friends?" said the little bear.

"And you are Fuzzy," said Alan and Jane.

"Yes, indeed, I am certainly Fuzzy," said the bear. "And I'm to take you through the forest and show you the way to the nearest mortal town."

They lost no time in starting off upon their journey, and soon left the region of the Moths far behind them. The three children soon became great friends. Fuzzy was the jolliest sort of comrade, and Alan and Jane thought him one of the nicest playmates they had ever had.

Before long they found themselves travelling through a wild country where there were wooded hills to climb, ravines to struggle through, rushing streams to cross, and great rocks over which they stumbled constantly. Here Alan and Jane found difficulty in walking, so rough was the way, and so thick the undergrowth. They were very tired and hungry too, and they began to look upon Fuzzy with more and more respect, because he did not seem at all affected by the hardships of the journey. As for Fuzzy, he regarded them with with deep pity.

"What is the matter with your faces?" he asked, "and your paws—I mean your hands?"

"They are scratched by these horrid thorns and branches," replied Jane, making a face as a blackberry vine caught in her stocking and pricked her ankle sharply.

"Dear me!" exclaimed Fuzzy. "Now I wear a coat that the thorns can't get through."

"And gloves too," said Alan, putting a torn finger into his mouth, and looking enviously at the bear's furry paws.

"Oh, dear!" sighed Jane, "I'm so hungry!"

"Hungry?" repeated Fuzzy. "Why, here are plenty of nuts."

There were indeed quantities of nice big walnuts lying about, which the bear-child cracked easily with his strong, sharp teeth. But when Alan and Jane tried to bite into them, they found that they could not even dent the hard shell. Again Fuzzy looked at them pityingly.

"How in the world do you get along?" he demanded, as they all sat under a big tree, resting. "Your shins are thin and soft and white, and are always getting scratched by the branches. You can't crack nuts. You can't even move about quietly, on account of the queer things you wear on your feet. While as for me,"—he stretched out a softly padded foot,—"I can go wherever I please, and no one can hear me."

"But we don't have to go about without being heard," said Alan.

Fuzzy seemed to open his twinkling eyes a little wider.

"But then," he exclaimed, "how do you hunt?" He shook his head, and looked quite sorry for them both. "Then, besides," he went on, "you have no claws! And without claws how can you fish and defend yourselves?"

He spread out his big soft paws and showed them the beautiful, long, sharp claws with which he could hunt, fish, climb trees, and fight. He showed them, too, how he sharpened the claws upon a tree trunk when they grew dull. Jane and Alan were much impressed.

"You can do *ever* so many more things than we can!" said Jane. "What fun it would be to be a Bear!"

"Yes," said Fuzzy, "it's nice to be a Bear, a child Bear especially. It's such a comfort in winter."

"Why?" asked both children.

"Because," Fuzzy explained, "we're the only animals who don't suffer from cold, or have any bother getting food."

"What do you do?" asked Alan.

"We sleep! As soon as winter starts in, my mother and I go away into the Den, out of reach of the wind and the snow, and curl up with our noses between our paws, and go fast asleep. And we don't even open an eye till it's spring!"

This was a delightful idea to the children, who felt as if they should like to begin a winter sleep then and there.

"Oh!" exclaimed Fuzzy, "I see something over there that I think even you can eat!"

He then showed them the partridge berries glowing like little red beads among the dead leaves. A big brown bird, which had been pecking at them, flattened itself out presently and lay still, so still that they could hardly tell the bird's feathers from the leaves about it.

"A partridge," Fuzzy told them; "he is trying to hide from us. He thinks we want to hunt him."

"Why, what an idea!" exclaimed Jane, and she called: "May we have some of your berries, please, Mr. Partridge?"

But the partridge was not of a trustful nature, and would neither answer nor move.

The children ate some of the red berries, which tasted like winter-green candy that was not quite sweet enough, and then Fuzzy hurried them on. Suddenly the Bear stopped short, his head on one side, his pointed nose lifted up, sniffing the air.

"What's the matter?" asked the other two, who, being merely human, could smell nothing.

"Smoke!" returned Fuzzy. "Stay here while I see where it comes from."

He trotted off among the trees. In a little while he appeared again, calling to them to follow him.

"It's a woodchopper's fire," he explained, "deserted and almost out. Come along!"

They soon came to the clearing where the wood-choppers had made their camp. Alan added some dry sticks to the embers of the fire, and it was soon crackling again quite cheerily.

"I wish we could cook something!" said Jane. "Oh, Fuzzy! What can we find to cook?"

"The wood is full of things to cook, if you like cooked things," responded Fuzzy. "Let's see. I know—we'll go fishing!"

Off they all three ran to the edge of the lake, by a way which Fuzzy seemed to know quite well. He led them to a rocky bit of shore, and they knelt on the stones and peered over into the clear water. Below the surface, on the mossy bottom, they could see a circle of snowy white sand, and in the circle a big fish.

"That's the nest of a Mother Black Bass," said Fuzzy.

"How did she make it so clean and neat and pretty?" asked Jane.

"She swept the moss and dead leaves away with her fins," said Fuzzy. "She is sitting on her eggs now,—hundreds of them!"

"Hundreds!" cried Alan. And Jane exclaimed: "They must be *very* little eggs!"

"They are," said Fuzzy, "and when they hatch out there will be hundreds of very little Bass babies!"

"Oh, what is that?" cried Alan, pointing upward.

High, high up,—almost a pin-point in the blue sky,—hung a bird, seemingly motionless, just above the spot where they were.

"The Fish-Hawk!" replied Fuzzy. "He is waiting to catch Mother Bass, but he has to be patient, for she watches him as closely as he watches her. Poor thing, she has a good deal of trouble, keeping the other fish and frogs away from her nest. Her worst enemy is that Fish-Hawk. But," he added, suddenly, "we came here to fish! Now I must see if I can catch Mother Bass!"

Evidently Mother Bass heard him, for she came swimming up to the surface, poked her nose out of the water, and said:

"Now, Fuzzy Bear! Go home to your Mother and leave me in peace with my eggs!"

She spoke so severely that Fuzzy looked quite ashamed of himself, and hung his head. "Who are your friends, Fuzzy Bear?" asked Mother Bass, giving her tail a wiggle so as to keep on the surface.

Fuzzy explained, and she became very polite and amiable at once. The four talked together in the most friendly manner possible, and quite forgot that anyone had ever thought of fishing.

Suddenly something dropped out of the sky and hit the water with a splash that spattered all three of them. Alan and Jane could not see on account of the water in their eyes, but at last, winking and blinking, they made out the Fish-Hawk, all wet and dripping, flapping away toward the woods. Mother Bass watched him go, wiggling her fins proudly.

"Every day, just so, he tries to catch me," she remarked, cheerfully, "but he never will! Not he! I'm too quick for him."

At that moment a big bumble bee went lumbering by, on outstretched, buzzing wings, carrying his bag of honey. Fuzzy gave chase and galloped clumsily off, followed by the children. They chased him until they found his hive, which was in a hollow tree, and Fuzzy began to pull out the honeycombs.

"Run away!" he called to the children. "You might get stung."

"Oh, Fuzzy, be careful!" cried Jane anxiously, as she and Alan retreated to a safe distance.

The bees fell upon Fuzzy in clouds, and though his thick coat protected him a good deal from their stings, he finally found them too much for him, and rushing into the lake, he let himself sink slowly, till only the tip of his nose showed above the water. The bees hummed and buzzed angrily, but they could not get at him. Fuzzy growled with delight, and his growls made little air bubbles that kept coming to the top of the water.

Meanwhile Alan and Jane seized the honeycombs and ran back to the woodchopper's camp as fast as their legs could carry them. There Fuzzy joined them after a while when the bees had got tired of waiting for him to come out of the lake. He was very wet, but as cheerful as ever, and began to shake himself dry, scattering water like a watering-cart, while the children ran laughing and screaming away from the shower. Next he rolled over and over on the ground, and finally sat up, with lots of dry leaves and broken twigs clinging to his wet fur. Alan and Jane helped him brush these off, and then the three children dined contentedly and merrily upon their honey.

When they had eaten it all up Fuzzy clambered to his feet, gave himself a final shake, and said: "It's growing late, and we must hurry out."

So off they started on their journey once more. They met wood creatures of all kinds, and each and all had a friendly word for them. At dusk they could faintly see little green gnomes sitting under toadstools, blinking merrily at them. A little green snake hissed "good luck" as they passed, and a red squirrel offered them nuts to eat if they grew hungry again. They found it great fun to be going through woods with a bear.

They went on and on through woods and plains, past ponds and lakes and across rivers.

After a time they met with an army of Black Ants.

"Where are you going?" asked Fuzzy.

"To war with the Red Ants," answered the Ant Leader. "Greet the people in our village for us when you come to it."

And they went marching along in precise military order. Alan and Jane and Fuzzy came by and by to the ant village to which the army belonged. Everything was going on as peacefully and methodically as though such a thing as war had never been heard of. Fuzzy gave the ant leader's message to a citizen whom he saw, but the ant citizen merely said: "We have other things to think of besides the war with the red ants," and went about his business.

"Dear me!" said Alan. "They're very different from us. If we had a war we shouldn't be thinking of anything else at all!"

"Come, come!" cried Fuzzy, "We must not lose any more time!"

They went on now faster than ever, and after a while they noticed that the underbrush began to be thinner and the trees farther apart. They could see open country ahead of them, too, and the way was smoother under foot.

At last they came out on a hillside, on which the warm afternoon sun was shining, and Fuzzy, sitting down on his haunches to rest, announced:

"There are the roofs and chimneys of a mortal town in that valley. Our journey is nearly over."

X

THE MEAN PEOPLE OF MEAN TOWN

WHEN THEY HAD ALL RESTED for a few moments they plunged down the hillside in the direction of the town, which, as Fuzzy had said, could plainly be seen in the valley. Their path led out presently on the high road, and Alan and Jane could not help feeling a tiny bit glad to be walking on a road again. Fuzzy, on the other hand, did not like it at all, but of course he would not think of leaving them till he had led them safely into the town. As they trudged along, a ray of sunlight fell upon something shiny, lying in the dust before them.

"Oh, look!" exclaimed Alan. "What is that?"

He stooped, picked up the object, and looked at it.

"A ring!" cried Alan.

"A ruby ring!" declared Jane.

Indeed the ring was large and heavy, and the ruby was a splendid one. "I wonder whose it is?" said Alan. "Nevermind; we'll find out, perhaps, when we come to the town."

Poor Alan! He certainly did find out when he came to the town.

He put the ring in his pocket for safe keeping, and they went on, their eyes fixed hopefully upon the town walls ahead of them. Fuzzy, by the way, had a very small opinion of the ruby ring. He sniffed at it, and tasted it with the tip of his tongue, and remarked, disgustedly, that he could not see what it was good for!

Before long they came to the gate of the town, and there at the gate was the warder, a stern looking man, with a long stick and bushy whiskers.

"What is the name of this place?" asked Alan.

"Mean Town," said the Warder. "I hope you've plenty of money. You'll need it here."

The children looked at each other in dismay.

"We haven't any!" cried Jane; "and how—"

"Hush!" whispered Fuzzy. "I have an idea. You'll certainly need money if this is Mean Town, and here is a way to get it. I'll pretend to be a trained bear,—the kind they have in circuses,—and I'll do tricks! You, Alan, can be my keeper, and Jane can pass the hat!"

"What a lovely plan!" cried Jane, clapping her hands. "But, oh, Fuzzy! Shall you like being a trained bear?"

"Oh, I think it will be great fun!"declared Fuzzy, stoutly. He really did not like the idea at all, but he was a friendly little soul, and having grown fond of Alan and Jane he wanted to get them out of their troubles if possible.

"Well?" growled the Warder of Mean Town, "Are you coming in,—you and your Bear? By the way, I hope he's tame?"

"Oh, dear, yes!" cried Alan and Jane in one breath. "He's a trained Bear and does tricks."

"Oh, in that case, come along. But don't let the Mayor see him. The Mayor doesn't approve of amusement."

The three children hurried through the gate and found themselves among some of the more deserted streets of Mean Town. Jane pulled a ribbon from her dress and tied it around Fuzzy's neck. Then Alan found an empty barrel, and they all picked from a tree near the town walls as many apples as Jane's skirt and Alan's pocket would hold. With these preparations they were ready to amuse Mean Town.

After a little practising, Fuzzy succeeded in walking unsteadily upon an overturned barrel, rolling it along under him. He also stood upon his hind legs, threw apples up in the air and caught them in his mouth. So they went on their way. They met people now and then, but all of them looked at the three little wanderers crossly and passed on. At last they reached the Market Place, where there were a good many townspeople, and Alan whispered eagerly:

"Now, Fuzzy, begin!"

Fuzzy climbed up on the barrel promptly, and rolled it along, sticking his tongue out of the side of his mouth in his excitement, and casting a proud glance about him now and then, as much as to say: "What's wrong with this?"

But no one seemed especially interested in Fuzzy, and, after passing Alan's hat for fifteen minutes without result, Jane stamped her foot and exclaimed, with tears in her eyes: "Mean, horrid things!"

"Of course we are Mean," cheerfully declared a citizen, who had overheard her. "This is Mean Town!"

Jane was so angry that she turned her back, and the citizen chuckled.

"Fuzzy," said Alan, sadly,—"Try the apples!"

Fuzzy was tired and out of breath, but he jumped off the barrel and juggled with the apples until his paws ached. But all that happened was that a cross-looking child took an apple which Fuzzy dropped, and went off with it. There was no question about it. Mean Town deserved its name.

All the townspeople looked ill-humoured, and seemed to have only one wish: to save money. The beggars did not even beg, but sat around the Market Place looking so hopeless that Fuzzy ended by dividing the remaining apples among them. Fuzzy really was a nice bear! The beggars, however, were so overcome by being given anything in Mean Town that they forgot to thank him.

Just then who should come marching along with his guard but the Lord Mayor of the Town. Of all the mean persons inside its gates the Lord Mayor was the meanest, and he was unkind besides. He and his guard were richly dressed, and looked very impressive walking through the Market Place, but nobody cheered, for the Lord Mayor's face was so hard and cruel that people ran away when they saw it,—if they could. Unfortunately the children had no time to run away, and the Lord Mayor, catching sight of the trio, stopped short and pointed his long forefinger at them.

"What are these?" he demanded.

The citizen who had offended Jane stepped forward.

"Some travelling player folk, I think, my lord," he said. "The animal there seems to be a trick bear. It balances itself on barrels in a very silly way, and throws apples up, and does not catch them when they come down."

"What a story!" exclaimed Fuzzy, indignantly, for he thought that he had juggled beautifully. However, he managed to smother his own words with a growl of protest. "We have yet to find out," ended the citizen, "what it does things for."

"Let the creature be taken to the Public Gardens," commanded the Lord Mayor. "The Gardens have long needed some wild animals in cages. But wild animals, unless captured, like this one, are expensive. Put it in a cage, and the people may look at it on Sundays, by paying three pence a piece!" Fuzzy growled louder than ever, but two officers seized him, and began to drag him off in spite of his struggles.

"The others," continued the Lord Mayor, pointing to Alan and Jane, "may be put into prison for the present. Tomorrow morning let them be brought before me as vagabonds! That is all." And he marched on with his guard.

Alan and Jane were taken prisoners by two more officers, and were led away to the town jail. They caught up with and passed Fuzzy, on the way.

"Oh Fuzzy, dear!" called Jane, tearfully, as they were hurried by. "I do so hope you'll get away!"

"I shall get away!" howled Fuzzy, finally. "I won't be put in a cage for the people to stare at for three pence a piece on Sundays!"

"No, I don't believe he will!" murmured Alan in Jane's ear. "Just look at him, Jane!"

And indeed it looked as though no one could possibly wish to keep him long! As they turned a corner, still looking back, they could see their small bear friend kicking, scratching, biting, cuffing, and making himself so unpleasant in so many ways that his captors were almost ready to let him go.

The children were put into a prison cell which fronted on the Public Square. As they mournfully looked out between the bars, Alan gave a sudden cry:

"Jane, Jane,—look over there,—in the middle of that crowd of people!"

"Why, it's the Gypsy Crone,—the one who told us about the Giant Spider!" exclaimed Jane.

"And who the Moth Queen said was her Witch-Nurse," added Alan. "What can she be doing in Mean Town?"

Their old friend the crone appeared to be very angry.

They could see that she was saying something very decidedly to the people around her, and raising her hand with a threatening gesture. Then she hobbled off through the Town Gate, frowning and muttering as she went.

"Oh, Gypsy Crone! Dear Gypsy Crone!" cried Jane, through the bars. "Come back and help us! Don't go away!"

But the Gypsy Crone did not hear, and was soon out of sight.

"I wish we could have heard what she said," said Alan. "She seemed ever so much in earnest about it."

As a matter of fact it was just what she said which got them both into a fine lot of trouble a little later—as you will see in the next chapter.

XI

THE SPELL OF THE GYPSY CRONE

NOW THE GYPSY CRONE HAD come to town to earn a few pennies by telling fortunes. But the mean people of Mean Town did not like giving pennies for anything nor to anyone, and from everyone she approached she heard but, one word—"No." She left the town in a rage,— as the children had seen,—but before she went she cast a spell upon the place: *For twenty-four hours nobody within its walls should be able to say "No!"*

And the very first victims of the spell were Alan and Jane.

When morning came the two children were taken before the Lord Mayor in the Mean Town Court, and charged with being vagabonds.

"Probably they are thieves as well!" declared the Lord Mayor.

"Officers, search the vagrants, and let us see whether or not they have any stolen goods upon their persons."

And of course the officers began by finding the ruby ring which Alan had found and put in his pocket the day before! When the Lord Mayor saw it, he cried:

"My ring, which was stolen from me yesterday! I should say they were thieves!"

As a matter of fact, the Lord Mayor had lost the ring as he was riding out to hunt, but he insisted on believing that it had been stolen.

"Boy!" continued the Lord Mayor in a stern voice,—"Did you not steal this ring?"

Alan was very indignant and opened his lips to reply, "No, indeed!" But to his horror the word "No" would not come. Neither he nor Jane could utter a word of denial, and they stood speechless before the court.

"Ah! They confess,—they confess!" exclaimed the Lord Mayor. "And have you stolen other things besides the ring?"

Again they could not say "No!"

"Ah! They have stolen other things!" shouted the Lord Mayor. "You are thieves and vagrants. What else are you? You have broken all of our laws, I'm sure!"

The children stammered, and struggled to explain, but they could not say "No" to anything.

"Send them to prison for the rest of their lives!" roared the Lord Mayor. "They admit everything! I shall have more to say to them later, but for the present put them in prison. Vagrants! Thieves!" The Lord Mayor positively choked with indignation.

"May it please your lordship," spoke up a court officer, "The Keepers of the Public Gardens have brought the Bear to court."

"The trained Bear?" asked the Lord Mayor.

"If he's a trained Bear," said a weary voice near the door,—"he's been trained to do very queer things!"

Three of the Keepers of the Public Gardens entered, leading Fuzzy, who seemed as quiet and sweet-tempered as possible, just at present, except for a strange gleam in his eye.

"This bear, your lordship," said the Head Keeper, in the same weary voice, "gives us no peace. If we go near him he attacks us. See!" He showed the rents in his nice uniform. "And when he's left to himself he runs about and howls in an awful way. And he takes the food we give him and throws it at us through the bars."

"Let him be killed at once!" ordered the Lord Mayor.

"Oh, dear, dear Fuzzy!" sobbed Jane. "How dreadful!"

But Fuzzy winked at her when no one was looking, and he did not seem at all worried.

The three prisoners were marched out of the court. Fuzzy was still the picture of gentleness and meekness, and the tired keepers loosened their hold a little as they came to the street. No sooner were they out of the door than there was a little scuffle, and the next moment Fuzzy was scampering away,—a mere ball of fur in the distance,—and the three keepers were running wildly after him.

"They might as well save their strength," said one of the officers who were with Alan and Jane. "They'll never get that bear again. And if I were they I shouldn't want to."

Alan and Jane were delighted that their comrade had escaped, but they felt very sad over their own fate. They were taken to their cell again, and then left by the officers. The gaoler locked them in, explaining th.at he would bring them some bread and water for their midday meal a little later.

Meanwhile the spell of the Gypsy Crone was having a startling effect upon the town. The townspeople had gone through life saying "no" to every request, and, unable to use that important word, they got themselves into all sorts of strange scrapes.

On his way home from the Court the Lord Mayor was stopped by a beggar who had not lived very long in Mean Town, perhaps, and did not know the people very well.

"Oh, your worship, won't you give a poor starving man a penny?"

The Mayor wanted to say "No," but he could not, and, to his own rage, found himself handing the beggar a coin. The man became bolder.

"More money, your worship,—more money!"—he begged.

Groaning, the Lord Mayor emptied his pockets. The beggar thought himself dreaming, but decided to make the most of the chance before he could wake up.

"Now the chain, noble sir!" he cried. "Your handsome, thick gold chain of office!" The chain was his.

"Now your hat with its fine, long plume! Your velvet and ermine cloak! Your sword with the jewelled hilt!"

Gasping with helpless rage, and choking with his effort to refuse, the Lord Mayor was forced to give the beggar what he asked. The beggar put on cloak and hat, sword and chain; then looked at the Mayor and laughed aloud.

"I leave you the rest, your worship," he cried. "Many thanks for your charity, my Lord Mayor of Mean Town!"

And off he went with the velvet and ermine cloak floating from his shoulders.

The poor Lord Mayor went home with almost nothing on to shelter him from the cool winds.

Other queer things happened in the town that day. Ten good little boys were taken to a big candy shop by their sailor uncle who had just come home from sea. Eager to give them a treat to be remembered, the sailor uncle offered them one thing after another. The ten good little boys were not able to say "No" to anything of course, and they ate ice cream, cake, and candy, until they were red in the face and could not walk. In a very short time ten doctors were called to take care of ten good little boys who could not say "No!"

Promises were broken, punishments were stayed, beggars became rich, and rich people grew poor—all in one day, and all because of the spell of the Gypsy Crone.

Alan and Jane felt that there was no chance of ever escaping from Mean Town and getting back to their own village.

"Whatever they said we've done, we don't seem to be able to say 'No!'" said Alan, gloomily. "No wonder they lock us up!" The children could not understand things at all, and felt quite hopeless. But, as it happened, the very spell which had plunged them into so much trouble was to get them out of it at last.

After a time the gaoler appeared, with their bread and water. The gaoler was a gruff person of few words. As he did not say anything really cross, Jane thought that he must be more tender-hearted than the other townspeople, and, while they were eating the bread he brought, she murmured to Alan, "Don't you think he looks kind?"

"Kinder than the Lord Mayor," Alan admitted.

"Oh, Alan," whispered Jane, with innocent excitement, "let's ask him to let us go!"

Alan laughed at the idea, but Jane exclaimed: "I'm going to try anyway!"

And aloud she said pleadingly, "Oh, Mr. Gaoler! Won't you let us go, please?" To Alan's amazement (and to Jane's, too, for that matter), the gaoler could not say "No!" He struggled to refuse, but in vain. He opened the door of the cell, and the children, gasping breathless thanks, fled from the prison. Out across the Public Square they rushed,—it happened to be empty, for everyone was at dinner,—and off toward the great Western Gate at the side of the town opposite to where they had first entered. Another warder was standing guard there.

"Oh, will you please let us go through?" cried Alan. The warder knew who they were, and had heard of their trial and imprisonment, but he could not say "No!" The great gate swung open and then banged heavily after they had gone through. The walls of Mean Town lay behind; in front rose a chain of mountains looking very high and grand.

Alan and Jane, to their own great surprise, were free.

XII

THE TIN RAILWAY

"COME, JANE!" SAID ALAN, as soon as he could catch his breath. "We must hurry on; for they may try to catch us!"

"But where shall we go?" said Jane.

"Anywhere;—up among the mountains first, I guess. Hurry up!"

They ran to the woodlands that covered the lower part of the mountain slopes. After they had hurried along for several minutes in breathless silence they were startled by a voice:

"So you are all right? I *am* glad!"

It was their friend Fuzzy.

The children were overjoyed to see him again, and he trotted on with them for some minutes as they told him of their escape.

"I waited around to try to get some news of you before leaving for home," he explained, when they were through. "But now that you are safe out of that awful place I shall have to turn back, for I have to travel around the town, outside, to get back to my forest, you know!"

"Oh, Fuzzy, can't you come with us?" pleaded Jane.

"No, my mother will be getting anxious as it is, and I don't dare to go farther. I wish I might, but I've always promised her that, whatever I did, I'd never try to climb these big hills."

"What are they called?" asked Alan.

"The Impassable Mountains," replied Fuzzy. "No one has ever climbed to the top, and no one knows what lies beyond them."

The children shivered a little as they looked up at the high, rocky summits.

"But at least," added Fuzzy, "you will be safe from the mean people of Mean Town for they would never dare to come here to look for you. Now,"—he concluded, coming to a standstill, "I must go back. But I shall get my mother to hunt in this region soon, and I shall have news of you from the animals that live about here. Now goodbye, Alan and Jane,—don't forget me!" Alan and Jane hugged him tearfully, and he looked so sad that they thought he was going to cry too. But he did not do anything so foolish or so unbear-like. Instead, he hugged them both in return, rubbed his furry head against their cheeks, said "good luck" in a cheerful voice, and went off down the mountainside at a quick trot.

Alan and Jane watched him out of sight, and then once more set out upon their journey,—alone.

The hill up which they were climbing grew steeper and steeper. From a clearing where they paused to rest they could look down upon the roofs of Mean Town, and glad they were to be safe outside its walls;— even though they were up among the Impassable Mountains.

Suddenly Alan exclaimed: "Gracious! What's that?"

Just in front of them was a red and white railway signal.

"A railway" continued Alan. "A railway here in the Impassable Mountains!"

"It can't be!" declared Jane.

They hurried up to look closer. Yes,—there were a real track, and rails; it *was* a railway. It ran along the side of the mountains, and the children determined to follow it and see where it led them.

"How funny to find a rai—" began Jane.

But just then Alan gasped: "Jane, do you see what it is?"

"What?" cried Jane.

"It's tin!" said Alan, solemnly. "It's a toy railway?"

"But it's so big—" said Jane.

"I don't care," returned her brother, getting down on his hands and knees to examine the rails more carefully. "It *is* a toy railway. The kind Tom-Tom got for a present last Christmas."

"And look!" cried Jane, pointing. "There's a train."

Alan jumped to his feet, and they stared up the toy track. There in front of them stood an engine. When they ran up to look they saw that it too was made of tin, and was as new and shiny as a toy could be. Attached to it was a string of tin cars.

"I wonder," began Alan, "If there's a tin engineer anywhere about? You remember, Jane, Tom-Tom's had a—"

"At your service!" said a high, squeaky voice. The children stared but could see nothing. They rubbed their eyes as the voice continued: "I am the Tin Engineer. I am cut out of tin. You do not see me because I am a profile man. When I face you, I vanish. You can't see me unless I turn sideways. Allow me!—"

They found themselves looking upon the queerly shaped outline of a man. He was very stiff and thin, and his profile was made up chiefly of a ceaseless smile. A nice red suit had been painted upon him once, but most of it had rubbed off.

Now visible, now invisible, he showed Alan and Jane what the trouble was with his train. The clockwork of the engine had gone wrong somehow, and the main-spring would not wind up properly. "I can't turn the key alone," he explained.

"Oh, we'll help you," exclaimed the children.

"Thanks," said the Tin Engineer, becoming invisible as he faced them, and bowed politely. "I shall be most grateful to you. Is there anything I can do for you in return?"

"Oh, won't you help us to get home?" cried Jane.

"Or at least tell us the way to the nearest mortal town?" asked Alan.

"I'm not good at geography," answered the Tin Engineer, appearing again, as he turned away to ponder. "I am merely part of the Toy Railway, and I only know the two places between which I run."

"What are they?" asked Jane.

The Tin Engineer waved his arm impressively. "This train, young strangers," he announced, "is filled with goods for Santa Claus! And it comes from the place where all the toys in the world are made."

"Really?" exclaimed Alan and Jane, much interested. "And where is that?"

"It lies behind the Impassable Mountains," said the Tin Engineer, "and in order to connect with it, this railway runs through a Secret Tunnel a little distance below the summit of this mountain. But,—" he exclaimed suddenly, "I have no more time! If you will help me to turn the key, I will be off at once to the Country of Santa Claus."

"Oh, please take us with you!" pleaded Jane.

"Impossible!" declared the Tin Engineer. "No mortals are allowed in the Country of Santa Claus! Come! Get into the engine, and help me wind up the machinery."

They all three climbed into the cab of the engine, where, instead of levers and throttles and the other things which they have in real engines, there was nothing to be seen but a large keyhole and a key.

Alan and Jane helped the engineer to turn this. It sounded just like a big clock being wound up, and the more they turned, the harder it was. Suddenly the works inside the engine began to whir and rattle, and the cab shook until the children could hardly stand upright.

"It's going to start!" exclaimed Alan, excitedly.

The next moment the Tin Engineer gave a wild, shrill, tinny cry: "We've wound it up the wrong way!"

For the toy *train* had started—backward!"

That was a wonderful ride! No journeys that Alan and Jane ever took in later years seemed to them to be one quarter so exciting as that trip on the Toy Railway with the Tin Engineer.

They seemed to go faster and faster every moment, and the buzzing noise in the machinery grew louder and louder. Trees whizzed past; mountain cascades and great rock-walls appeared and vanished; the valley seemed farther and farther below. Up-up-up-they went. On-and-on up the steep grade of the mountainside. The children clung together in the engine-cab; the Tin Engineer rattled about, hitting every side of the cab, and giving out a constant noise of jangling tin. And on they went, always backward,—whirling up that amazing road at a speed which was terrific.

Suddenly blackness fell upon everything, and the noise from the clockwork grew louder. In front of them, growing smaller and farther away every second, was a circle of light. They were in the Secret Tunnel.

"Isn't it fun?" gasped Alan, holding on to his hat and Jane.

"Y-y-yes!" returned Jane, breathlessly. "But I'm f-frightened, too!" Buzz-whir-clatter,—whiz,—rattle,—bang,—shake,—jar!—through the Secret Tunnel backed the toy train! And suddenly they came out into the sunshine again. The train seemed to be moving more slowly; the noise was growing less; the clockwork was running down!

Peering out from the cab of the engine, the children saw what seemed to be a city of dolls' houses.

"This," said the Toy Engineer, "is Toyland."

XIII

THE NOAH'S ARK HOUSE

"I F YOU WISH TO TAKE lodgings during your stay in Toyland," said the Tin Engineer when he bade Jane and Alan goodbye at the railway station, "you had better apply at the Noah's Ark House."

"How shall we find it?" asked Alan.

"Look for a cottage with two india-rubber cats on the doorstep, and a purple hobby horse grazing on the lawn."

They left the Tin Engineer oiling the clockwork of his engine, and marched boldly down the alley that led from the station.

Suddenly they came to a sharp turning, and found themselves on a neat, bright street, with trim, gaily painted houses on either side. The alley had been dim and dark like most alleys, and they had noticed nothing unusual about it; but this,—this was *most* unusual!

"Jane," gasped Alan, "did you *ever* see such a street?"

"Never!" said Jane, simply. She was so surprised that, for once, she could not say anything more.

The street was paved in slates, all set close together,—the wooden frames and dark squares giving a curious effect,—like queerly shaped cobblestones turned inside out. Some of the houses were built of brightly painted wood; some of those funny terra-cotta blocks which everyone has played with, and which fit into each other nicely, if one knows how to put them together.

In front of the houses were prim, bright-green trees on wooden stands, and gay paper flowers, in pink and blue China pots. Wooden dogs kept guard at the stiff, little, front gates, and here and there a group of beautifully coloured tin hens dotted the green, velveteen lawns. Occasionally they saw an enormous woolly lamb on a huge wooden stand and rollers,—but they looked in vain for india-rubber cats and a purple rocking horse.

No people were anywhere to be seen, and, wondering more and more, Alan and Jane walked along on the slate pavement, past the gay, trim houses, the stiff, green trees and flowers, and the big, toy animals.

"Nothing but toys anywhere!" said Alan, in a whisper. "Oh, Jane, these people *must* be toys,—or else crazy, to keep rubber cats and dogs and tin hens!"

"They look like the playthings the littlest Pipers had," said Jane, "only bigger."

"Yes," agreed Alan, "*much* bigger! Really, they're *awfully* big!"

Suddenly Jane stopped short, listening.

"Alan!" she exclaimed, "If I didn't know that it *couldn't* be so, I'd believe I heard Uncle Barnaby's cane!" They stood motionless for a moment, and they could certainly hear a tapping, tapping sound going down a side street. The sound faded away, and they looked at each other much puzzled.

At the opening of this side street there was a painted sign that said: "To the Master Toymaker's Workshop."

"Shall we go that way?" asked Alan. "If it *was* Uncle Barnaby,—though of course it couldn't have been,—we ought to follow him."

But at that moment Jane's attention was distracted by something else.

"Oh, Alan!" she exclaimed, with a relief that was almost tearful, "there's a *live* little boy!"

And the little boy was riding a purple rocking horse before a house which looked like an overgrown Noah's Ark. Some wooden ark animals stood, or lay overturned, in front of it, as well as those queer, cone-shaped trees they knew so well. The house was painted bright yellow, with blue trimmings, and looked as fresh and new and neat and gay as all the houses in Toyland.

The boy upon the rocking horse was beating it with a heavy stick.

"What are you doing that for?" called Alan.

The boy stopped, glanced at them, then began beating again, harder than ever.

"He won't go," he answered, between blows. "And the Master Toymaker promised that he should."

The painted coat flew off its wooden sides in great pieces, but the horse did not move.

"It's lucky they *do* have nothing but toy animals here!" whispered Jane. "If it were a live horse, wouldn't it be awful?"

"Aren't you afraid you'll break it?" asked Alan of the small boy.

"Don't care if I do," was the answer. "The Master Toymaker'll give me another."

"Dear, dear!" said a voice from the doorway of the Noah's Ark House. "Do behave better! Press the spring under the mane, and stop spoiling your nice, new toy."

A round, cheerful woman, very gaily dressed, was standing at the open door. The children thought that she looked something like a middle-aged doll, she was so smiling as to face, and so gorgeous as to costume.

The small boy found the spring, and pressed it. In a minute the big toy was whizzing around in circles before the house, and he, sitting on it, was filling the air with his shouts of delight.

The children spoke to the woman, who was still standing smiling in the doorway of the Noah's Ark House, and she greeted them most politely. She invited them to come in and sit down, and they succeeded in dashing across the make-believe lawn and into the big Ark, in between the whizzing rushes of that marvellous mechanical horse.

"It's rather different from our world, isn't it?" whispered Jane.

"Yes," said Alan, "There our lives were in danger from mean Lord Mayors, and Giant Spiders and things, but here it's giant toys!"

The mistress of the Noah's Ark House offered them some real food,— not paper nor painted wood. And after they had eaten it and thanked her, they told her some of their adventures. She was much interested, and when they had finished she said: "Dear, dear! How funnily things come about, to be sure. I've another young Master and Miss staying here, and by their clothes they must come from the same part of the world as yourselves. They came quite suddenly, not very long ago, and took rooms, and I'm as fond of them as fond can be. It's a pity they're out now."

If Alan and Jane had only known the names of the two children of whom she spoke they would have been much excited, but, as it was, they were more interested in finding out about Toyland. Their kind hostess was quite willing to tell them whatever they wished to know.

"You see," she explained in answer to their question, "The Master Toymaker has made us such wonderful toys that we no longer take the trouble to have real things. Our painted trees give just as good shade as growing ones, and our rubber cats will mew when they are pinched, just like live cats. Why should we not be content?" And she smiled like a child.

"Does the Master Toymaker rule over you?" asked Alan.

"Well," she answered. "We have a Government, and a Court Royal to decide bothersome questions, but the Master Toymaker is the one whom we really love and serve. He has done so much for everyone here that the Government has built him a Castle outside the city gates, and he is a very great person in Toyland. But he goes to his work every day as simply, and with as few airs, as though he were one of his own 'prentices, instead of the head Toymaker of the whole world."

All the time she had been talking the sound of whirring machinery outside the house told of the continued activity of the toy horse. This noise now suddenly ceased. The toy had run down. The small boy dismounted and went off to wind up the tin hens so that he might chase them.

"Dear, dear!" sighed his mother. "He never will give his poor toys any peace."

Going to the open door she called.

"Why don't you go and see Grumio, and ask him to take you to the Christmas Fair?"

"Don't want to, and won't!" was the small boy's only reply.

"Well" said the small boy's mother "Grumio's pretty busy today, anyway. Perhaps it's as well."

"Who is Grumio?" asked Alan.

"The Master Toymaker's head 'prentice," she answered, "and a good lad though careless. The Master spoils him as he spoils everyone. Today they're all busy,—the people from the workshop. You know, the Toy Regiment parades today for the first time."

"The Toy Regiment?" asked Alan. "Yes, the Master Toymaker has made us a regiment which he says is one just as good as a real regiment."

"Do they walk?" exclaimed Jane.

"Dear me, yes!" said the Noah's Ark Woman. "They go by clockwork,— the Master Toymaker's own specially invented clockwork; and they march and do everything soldiers ought to do."

"Fight?" asked Alan.

The Noah's Ark Woman looked doubtful.

"I don't know," she said, "I never heard anything about that. But anyway, the parade is going to be a fine one."

"When is it to be?"

"After the Christmas Fair is over that's going on now. The regiment is to march out over the big bridge, and down past the grove."

"Then come on, Jane," exclaimed Alan, "We must hurry up!"

Just at that moment Jane gave a little cry of surprise.

"Look!" she said, pointing to a chair. On the chair was a dainty sun-bonnet.

"It belongs to the little girl who has a room here," said the woman.

"It belongs to Mary Piper!" said Jane. "Oh, let me look inside, please. Hilda always put the different names on everything the children had."

She turned the bonnet over, and there inside, sure enough, was a finely embroidered "Mary!"

The children were more puzzled than ever.

"Are you *sure*, Jane?" asked Alan, doubtfully.

"Well," said Jane, "I should be sure, if I could think how Mary could possibly be here."

"Hurry up," said the mistress of the Noah's Ark House. "You must have time to see the Christmas Tree Grove before the parade begins!"

XIV

TRAVELLERS

NOW WE MUST GO BACK a little way.

When the absence of Contrary Mary and Tom-Tom was discovered by the Widow Piper there was wild excitement and much anger. The children were all questioned, and were scolded and even punished for helping their brother and sister to escape. Many, many were the tears that were shed by the twelve little Pipers.

Worst of all, in the general excitement, Tommy Tucker,—who was always a good deal of a goose, and easily frightened, blurted out the fact that Mary had said something about Toyland!

Simon and Peter boxed his ears, afterward, for having told Mary's secret, and Bo Peep said he was a "tell-pie tit," and Red Riding Hood wouldn't play with him for a week, but the deed was done.

The Widow Piper lost no time in sending for her friend and adviser next door,—dear old Master Barnaby! So, the next morning, over he came to call, his stick tapping, tapping as usual.

Gongorzo and Roderigo had returned late the night before and told him how they had left the children in the blackest portion of the Spider's Forest.

Master Barnaby had paid them their promised reward with a light heart and a willing hand. Now, at last, his hated nephew and niece were safely out of the way and their fortune would soon be his. According to a law in that land, if Alan and Jane were absent for a certain number of weeks all of their money would go to their uncle. So he felt quite cheerful about *that*.

When he passed through the garden, the twelve Pipers cast hateful glances at him from the various distant corners where they had run to be out of his way. Barnaby shook his stick at them one by one.

"Little fiends!" he growled, "How I'd like to punish them for hating me so!"

"Horrid old wretch!" said the children to each other, in low tones.

"Goodmorning, darlings!" said Barnaby trying to smile instead of snarl. The twelve Pipers turned their backs. "Little angels!" he murmured, shaking with rage, as he entered the house.

He and the Widow Piper had a long talk, while the children wandered about the garden with a feeling that something was going to happen. The result of the long talk was that the Widow Piper called her family together, ordered Hilda to pack everything up, put on an old flowered costume which she never wore except for travelling, and, accompanied by her twelve children, the faithful maid, and Uncle Barnaby, set upon a journey. They were going to Toyland to hunt for Contrary Mary and Tom-Tom.

"*Now* I hope you're satisfied!" whispered Bo Peep, as she pinched Tommy Tucker.

"D-don't!" he whimpered. "I didn't mean any harm, Bo Peep!"

"Bo Peep, stop teasing your poor brother!" snapped the Widow Piper, boxing Bo Peep's ears. "You all do nothing but torment Tommy!"

"Crybaby!" breathed Bo Peep into Tommy's ear. "Tell-pie-tit *and* crybaby! I should think you'd be ashamed!"

You see Bo Peep was a *very* naughty little girl. Indeed, I don't think any of the Pipers were very good children.

So the garden was left, deserted and uncared for, and the weeds sprang up among the "silver bells and cockle shells," and the village maids might wander in and out at will, and pick as many flowers as ever they liked. And there was no more reason for anyone to stop at the garden and sing:

> *"Mary, Mary, quite contrary,*
> *How does your garden grow?"*

To Toyland they went, and the Pipers took lodgings in a pretty, cardboard cottage, with a stout vine made all of nicely carved wood, and of green india-rubber, fastened firmly to the outside. Uncle Barnaby soon found out through the Toyland police, several facts which convinced them all that Mary and Tom-Tom were indeed in the town, and it seemed only a matter of time before they would both be brought back to the Widow Piper.

Meanwhile, the children frisked about the place, and drove their mother and Hilda frantic by getting lost all day and every day. They bounced about on rocking horses, and made pets of paper chickens, rubber puppies, and mechanical canaries, and caught tin goldfish in the pond. They thoroughly enjoyed themselves,—all, that is, except Jill. *She* was rather bored. There wasn't enough to do, and she missed the stable at home, the live guinea pigs, and kittens and chickens,—and the hundred and one real things that made up her life.

Then, too, the Widow Piper's temper was growing worse every day, and, as Jill was the one who usually annoyed her mother most sorely (both by her untidiness and her mischievous pranks), she had a rather unhappy time. Indeed, she began to make plans for going away to hunt for Mary on her own account before long.

The chief excitements of the Piper family at present were their visits to that most interesting and wonderful person,—the Master Toymaker. The children adored him, and thought it was a splendid thing to call on anyone clever enough to have designed all the marvellous mechanical dolls and lifelike animals of Toyland, alone, to say nothing of being the originator of all the toys of the world! The entire family had gone to see him in his big, gloomy castle just outside the city gates, where the volcano just above, though it had not made itself disagreeable for many years, gave visitorsquite acreepy feeling. But thoughthe youthful Pipers had been duly impressed by the grandeur of the dwelling which the Government had given him, they greatly preferred the workshop.

This workshop, down on one of the side streets of Toyland, was a delightful place, and the children went to see it and him whenever they were allowed, and very often when they were not. He gave them beautiful toys,—"to remind them of him," he said, and petted them most affectionately.

"This little girl is always talking about her sheep at home," he said, smiling at Bo Peep,—"Here is a lamb to make her miss her flock less keenly!"

The lamb was white as to wool, and squeaky as to baa, and Bo Peep seized it.

"Oh, thank you!" she exclaimed. "But perhaps mother won't like me to keep it! Perhaps you'd better take it back!" As she spoke she hugged the lamb tighter than ever, and the Master Toymaker could not help laughing outright. He knew very well that nothing would induce Bo Peep to give up that lamb. He gave them all just the things they liked best, and they were all grateful. When I say "all" I must and will except Jill. She politely refused all his lovely presents and clung to her own beloved old doll,—a creature made entirely of rags with no face at all to speak of! I think Jill was in a pretty fair way to lose her sunny temper in those days. Perhaps travelling did not agree with her; it doesn't with some people.

"And can you make toys that talk?" Bo Peep asked the Master Toymaker, with much curiosity.

"Yes," said he. "Toys that talk, and toys that walk, and toys that do everything but think. I can give them everything but a soul. And sometimes," —he paused, and then added, slowly and dreamily, as though forgetting the children,—"I think I may be able to give them even that."

The children drew away with a little, creepy feeling.

They dimly felt that there was something very strange about the Master Toymaker. They could not say just what it was, and it did not interfere with their fondness for him, but in his deep eyes and his absent-minded smile, there was something a little bit queer.

They, however, like everyone else, loved the good Master, who proved himself a kindly and genuine, if rather a serious, Santa Claus.

Of course Uncle Barnaby made friends with him and ordered great quantities of beautiful toys. His reason was to win popularity, and indeed he tried very hard. He gave toys to every child he saw, and in spite of his deep dislike of the Piper youngsters would have loaded them with presents. The Pipers, however, never would accept anything at all from him in spite of their mother's commands.

At last, one day, there was great excitement in the Pipers' cardboard cottage: Tom-Tom had been found I In an hour after his capture he was shut up in an upstairs room in the cottage. He gave everyone fair warning that he would run away again the first chance he got. Master Barnaby's interference made him as angry as it made the others, and his mother's unkind welcome of him did not make him wish to stay.

"I *must* get away!" he sighed to himself. "And I *must* warn Mary!"

From this you will see that he and Mary had been together all along! On the very day of his capture, after he had been locked in his room to think over his misdeeds, a head appeared at the window.

"Hello, Tom-Tom!" said his brother Simon's voice, cheerfully. "Open the window a bit wider, and let us all in."

Tom-Tom obeyed quickly enough, and the whole twelve crawled into the room, one after the other. They had climbed up the wood-and-rubber vine outside, and had come, they said, to pay him a call, though it was against the Widow Piper's orders.

Tom-Tom hugged them all.

"But why have you come?" he asked.

"You know you'll only get whipped all around,—or scolded at least."

"Nonsense!" said Peter,—"Who cares, anyway? We've come to help you get away, only first do tell us two things. Have you and Mary been together?"

"Oh, dear me, yes," said Tom-Tom. "She even wrote me the very first day, and we have not been separated at all until now."

"And now," said Peter, "Do please tell us where Mary is."

"No, don't!" said Bo Peep, "Tommy Tucker might tell again!"

Poor Tommy Tucker looked ready to cry, as the others told the story of his faithlessness. "Nevermind, Tommy Tucker," said Tom-Tom, soothingly. "Mary will forgive you. And I'm sure you'll not tell anything else."

"Never! Never! Never!" wailed Tommy Tucker.

"Well, then," said Simon, impatiently. "Go ahead. Where is Mary? In Toyland of course?"

"Yes," answered Tom-Tom, "and she's a doll's dressmaker!"

"Oh, what fun!" cried Bo Peep, and Sallie Waters, and Red Riding Hood, and Curly Locks, and Miss Muffet, all together.

"She calls herself 'Ma'amselle Eliselte,'" went on Tom-Tom, "and she likes it awfully!"

"And what have you been doing yourself?" asked Boy Blue.

"I've been a page in the Court Royal of Toyland," answered Tom-Tom. "And if I could get away, I'd go back and be one again."

"Well, go ahead," said Simon. "Who's stopping you? Didn't you ever notice that nice, thick, rubber vine outside? Where we came up you can go down. Good luck to you!"

Tom-Tom rushed to the window and looked. "How stupid I've been!" he exclaimed. "I'll not lose another moment! Goodbye, boys and girls!"

He climbed over the window-sill and was down like a shot.

"Wait a minute!" shouted a shrill voice behind him, and Jill went flying down after him. She only went down half the way on the vine. The rest she fell! But, as usual, she landed without any broken bones, and, scrambling up, rushed off with her brother, waving her hand, now and then, to the eleven heads that were all trying to lean out of the window at once. Temptation had been too much for tomboy Jill, and,—without even waiting for her twin, Jack,—she, too, had run away!

When the Widow Piper unlocked Tom-Tom's room, to scold him a little more, and to ask him a few more questions as to Mary's whereabouts, he was not to be found. Instead of her eldest son she saw eleven of her naughty children standing solemnly in a row.

And Simple Simon, acting as spokesman greeted her as follows:

"Tom-Tom has gone away, Mother. We helped him off,—all of us. And—And it's no use asking Tommy Tucker about it, please, for if he tells anything more we'll thrash him!"

XV

THE CHRISTMAS TREE GROVE

ALAN AND JANE HAD NO trouble in finding their way to the Christmas Tree Grove. Indeed, they could hardly have missed it, for while they were still some distance away they could see the glow of the lighted candles.

To enter the grove they passed under an imposing bridge. This ran from one high point of land to another, and formed an arch, which was the entrance to the Christmas Tree Grove. When they stood, finally, in the grove itself, they could do nothing save stare about them, and say "Oh!" and "Ah!" in the silliest way possible,—so beautiful was the sight before them.

There were dozens and dozens of huge Christmas trees, brilliantly lighted, and covered with the shining, tinselly, fuzzy stuff that always *is* on Christmas trees. Hanging on the green branches were, also, brightly coloured glass balls, and ropes of popcorn, and big, glistening ornaments of gold and silver thread, and stars, and half-moons, and wreaths of red and blue and green and yellow and purple paper, and little, wee horns and drums, and great big French dolls with gorgeous hair, and soldiers, and popguns, and a thousand kinds of lovely toys, and silver paper bags of candy, and peppermint canes, and things that jingled, and things that glittered, and—oh, dear! I simply couldn't begin to tell you all the wonderful things that were on those trees, in the Christmas Tree Grove!

No other trees were to be seen anywhere, and all stood in nice, neat, round tubs, painted bright green.

Alan and Jane could not help wondering whether anything had *ever* grown in Toyland, before the Master Toymaker spoiled the inhabitants for real things, with his marvellous toys.

"It's perfectly mag-nif-i-cent!" declared Jane. "Alan, see the bridge!"

In passing under the bridge, they had not noticed how remarkable it was. Now they could look back, and up, at it, and they both decided that it was quite the queerest thing which they had seen in Toyland—so far.

It was entirely built of big, square blocks, made of wood, and covered with coloured paper. There were big, bright letters on them, and they looked exactly like the ordinary alphabet blocks in every nursery. The effect was almost startling.

While Alan and Jane were standing looking up at the bridge, they heard voices, evidently those of men, talking nearby. As they turned their eyes in the direction from which the voices came, Alan and Jane noticed what they had been too interested to see before,—a great castle, rather sombre and gloomy in appearance, on a rocky hillside.

"The Master Toymaker's Castle!" said Alan.

"And look above it!" added Jane.

A high, dark mountain rose above and beyond the castle, its summit capped by a faint curl of smoke, which seemed to ooze lazily out of the top and drifted away into the blue.

"A volcano!" the two children whispered, and ran behind a Christmas tree rather frightened. They had read about volcanoes in their geography, but to see one—! Really, there seemed no end to their adventures!

At that moment two men came into sight, walking toward them, and talking interestedly. They did not notice the children, who caught each other's hands, as one sentence echoed clearly through the grove:

"Yes, they are both dead, now."

The voice was Uncle Barnaby's!

The two men had paused, here, and were standing just where a big, sparkling tree hid them from view.

"Your nephew and niece, you say?" said a second voice,—a stranger's.

"Yes, two little friends,—a boy and a girl,—left in my charge by my sister who died. But they were lost in a forest in my country, and were never found! And now their fortune will be mine in another week, according to law!"

"Unless they come to claim it," said the second voice.

"Oh, but that they cannot do!" chuckled Uncle Barnaby. "You can see that I shall soon have more money than ever, and I can pay you well for all the toys I have ordered you to make for me."

"Do you love children, Master Barnaby?"

"I loathe them! But I wish to make them love me. I want to be liked, admired, welcomed. *You* are that. That is why I have tried to make friends with you. That is why I came to Toyland. —Because I knew that I could buy toys here which would buy *me* love!"

"Oh, Master Barnaby, I fear love is only bought with love. If you hate children, they will hate you. By the way, those are charming little ones whom I see with you."

"The Piper children! They make fun of me! I should like to be even with them. You—you wouldn't care to make me some *dangerous* toys for them, would you?" with a fiendish giggle.

"Master Barnaby, Master Barnaby! Do not say such things to me, the Toymaker of the World!"

The voice sounded shocked.

"Oh, well, I was only joking," said Uncle Barnaby. "That's merely what I'd *like*, you know. You've a fine display here."

"Toylanders seem never to grow tired of their toys," said the stranger's voice, with an indulgent tone in it. "These playthings are but small matters. Wait until you see my regiment march today,—all wood and tin, but brave soldiers,—with a wooden captain at their head, who will surprise you!"

The children could hear the stranger's kindly laugh.

Then Uncle Barnaby replied:

"Like enough,—like enough! Now, come! We must go on, and join our friends."

The two men passed on. So close were they to the children that, with hardly an extra step, they might have touched them. But, thanks to the green tubs, which stood so close together that the branches of the different trees touched here and there, Alan and Jane were not seen.

As though waking from a dream, Alan whispered reproachfully:

"Oh, Jane! We *listened*!"

"I know, but we couldn't help it," breathed Jane, whose sense of honour was feminine. "And I don't care, anyway."

"Shh! They've passed. Let's peek!" said Alan.

They tiptoed out, in time to see the two men before they disappeared through the arch of the Block Bridge.

There was no question about one of them being Uncle Barnaby. He was better dressed than he had been when they saw him last. A respectable hat had taken the place of the old skull-cap, and his coat was quite grand to behold, but he *was* Uncle Barnaby,—crabbed, spider-like Uncle Barnaby,—and he always would be, no matter what he might wear.

His companion was a tall, grave-looking man, with eyes which seemed to see more than most people's. He was dressed in dark, but very rich clothes, and his hair was grey and rather long.

Even in their excitement over what they had just heard, Alan and

Jane felt a little extra thrill of interest as they gazed after him. It really was quite an experience to be looking at the Master Toymaker of the World.

XVI

A Friend at Last

"ALAN!" CRIED JANE, WHEN THE two men had disappeared under the arch of the Wooden Block Bridge, —"What *can* Uncle Barnaby be doing in Toyland?"

"I can't imagine," said Alan, "unless he is looking for *Mary*!"

"That was Mary's sun-bonnet in the Noah's Ark House!" added Jane. "It's very queer."

"Yes," assented Alan, "It is,—and then, besides, they talked about the Pipers, didn't they, Uncle Barnaby and the Toymaker?"

"You don't suppose," began Jane,—"that Uncle Barnaby—"

"The worst of it all," interrupted Alan, "is what Uncle Barnaby said about *us*. Did you hear, Jane?"

"About—about the money being his, if we were not back in a week?"

"Yes, it's very hard to know what to do." Alan was thinking deeply.

"Alan," cried Jane, indignantly, "He must have had us lost on *purpose*! The Spider's Forest—"

"And the galleon, before—! Oh, Jane, I'm afraid Uncle Barnaby must have *tried* to have us killed!"

Both children were horrified by this thought,—more at the idea of Uncle Barnaby's wickedness, than their own narrow escape.

"And we should have been, probably," went on Alan.

"If we hadn't happened to save the Moth Queen," cried Jane. "But Alan!—*Now* what are we to do?"

"Go home, of course," replied Alan. "We simply must get home in time to claim our money, and—"

"Listen!" exclaimed Jane, catching hold of his arm. A sound of laughter and of merry singing burst suddenly upon the air. It came nearer and nearer, until a crowd of boys and girls ran under the Block Bridge, and into the Christmas Tree Grove. They were gaily dressed, as though for a Carnival or Masquerade, and they all seemed in the wildest of good spirits. Some were dressed like the Kings, Queens, and Knaves in a pack of cards. Some wore costumes marked like chessboards, checkerboards, and backgammon boards, with chessmen caps on their heads, or crowns made of dice. Some looked like the tinselly ornaments on the Christmas trees; some were clowns jingling their bells, or doll-like circus riders carrying paper hoops;—but one and all seemed to have copied their quaint array from picture books, and from the ever-present toys of Toyland.

When they saw Alan and Jane, they rushed up to them, reaching out curious hands to touch their clothes, and laughing, not only loudly but rudely.

"What queer looking things!" cried one.

"Where can they have come from?" exclaimed another.

"What clothes!" laughed a third.

"Where *do* you suppose they wear clothes like that?" shouted a fourth, pointing with scorn.

Poor Alan and Jane looked down at their simple and commonplace things with much embarrassment.

"They must have fallen from the moon!" declared one very pretty girl, turning to the others and laughing gleefully.

They all shouted with merry mockery, and closed around the children, with a chorus of loud questions:

"Where did you come from?"

"How did you get here?"

"Who are you?"

"Where is your home?"

"What race of creature are you?"

—and a dozen other queries.

Jane was crying by this time, her little heart much hurt by the thoughtlessness and unkindness of the gay young Toylanders. Alan put his arm around her, and faced their tormentors defiantly, trying, at the same time, to answer them with dignity:

"We were lost in a forest at home," he said. "After ever so many strange adventures, a toy train of cars brought us here, and,"—he looked around him, resentfully—"we don't care how soon another train takes us away."

The boys and girls of Toyland burst out into renewed peals of laughter, shriller and sharper than before. The children saw that one of them was the little boy in the bright, pink suit, who had been chasing the tin hens in front of the Noah's Ark House, when they last saw him.

At last a pretty girl, who had been the one who suggested that the children must have fallen from the moon, turned carelessly away, shaking her tinsel-crowned head till it glittered.

"Come on, boys and girls," she said. "Nevermind these queer little things any longer. Let's go to the Christmas Fair. It's getting late, and we must be back here in time to see the parade of the toy regiment that the Toymaker is giving the town today. Hurry up!"

"To the Christmas Fair!" they all shouted. "To the Christmas Fair!"

Forgetting all about Alan and Jane, they turned, and rushed off between the Christmas trees, as fast as their feet could carry them. Their merry voices and hasty footsteps died away, and the two children were again alone in the Christmas Tree Grove.

"*They're* not toys, either,—horrid, unkind things!" sobbed Jane. "Oh, Alan, *let's* go away from Toyland!"

"We *must* go away from Toyland," said Alan, firmly.

He was anxious, but he had not lost heart. "But first of all, Jane, we must get some other clothes."

"Yes," agreed Jane, "Uncle Barnaby would be sure to find us, in these. Nobody in Toyland ever dressed like *this*!"

"I wish we knew *someone* in Toyland," said Alan. "Someone, I mean, besides Uncle Barnaby. Now if that really *was* Mary's sun-bonnet—!"

He scowled, as he thought. Suddenly Jane sighed.

"Alan," she said, softly, "Did you realise it was Christmas already? How long we must have been away!"

"Jane, you're homesick" said Alan, sternly.

"So are you!" said Jane, defiantly, wiping her eyes on the skirt of her gown,—she couldn't find her handkerchief at the moment. "Oh, Alan, *wouldn't* you like to see one of the children this minute?"

"I—I think I should like,—rather,—to be at home again," admitted her brother, slowly. Indeed they both felt lonely and friendless, and Contrary Mary's garden seemed a million miles away.

Suddenly a voice uplifted itself behind them, in tones of delight:

"It isn't—It can't be! Is it?—It *is*! Oh, Jane! Oh, Alan! Where *did* you come from? We all thought you were dead!"

They both turned, at the joyful shout. A very untidy and bedraggled little girl was hurrying toward them, a little girl who was dragging a yard of torn ruffle as she came, and whose eager face was topped by two, bright red pigtails that stood wildly erect.

"Alan!" cried Jane, with a sort of shriek of delight.

"It's Jill;—it's dear Jill Piper!"

The untidy little girl fell first into Jane's arms and then Alan's.

"You dear things!" she laughed, between hugs. "Yes, it's Jill,—and a runaway, too,—just like you!"

She drew back to regard them, her red pigtails bobbing with the energy of her affectionate nods.

"*Who,*" she said breathlessly, "would ever have thought that we'd meet in Toyland? Oh, dear me! How glad I am that you're alive after all!"

XVII

GRUMIO, THE PRENTICE

GRUMIO, THE 'PRENTICE, HAD A shock of sandy hair, a large, fat, smiling face, a snub nose, and small, good-tempered eyes. He was never seen with a coat on. His gay red waistcoat was usually unbuttoned, too, and his white shirt-sleeves were rolled up high on his fat arms. He always sang as he worked, and tried little dance steps as he walked, and he was constantly falling down, or upsetting things, or getting in his own and everyone else's way.

Everyone in Toyland liked Grumio, but everyone wondered how the Master Toymaker could keep Grumio as his head apprentice. As a matter of fact, the boy was quick in his work, and a help in the workshop. Besides, his fat, genial smile would have disarmed the Master Toymaker if he had ever thought seriously of sending him away.

After Jill had gone with her brother, Tom-Tom, she managed, very soon, to get herself completely lost. Tom-Tom gave up hunting for her at last, and went back to the Noah's Ark House to see, or leave a message for Contrary Mary, that she might know all that had been happening since the morning.

Meanwhile, Jill met Uncle Barnaby! Of course he tried to drag her home, and of course she screamed, and kicked, and struggled. In fact, she made herself just as horrid as she knew how to be, which was very horrid indeed.

At that moment Grumio appeared upon the scene. A little girl, struggling with a furious old gentleman, and crying loudly, was a sight to arouse even the mild-mannered apprentice, and he stopped singing and taking dance steps, and rushed forward to the rescue.

He fell down several times on the way, but at last he reached the excited pair, and pulled Jill out of old Barnaby's angry grasp.

"Really, sir!" he gasped, trying to be respectful, in spite of his indignation. "You—you really shouldn't, sir! You know very well, sir, that you shouldn't!"

Jill was still shrieking in a way that made Uncle Barnaby want to put his fingers in his ears. Though he would have dearly loved to beat her with his stick, he contented himself with promising her all sorts of punishments later. He then departed, shaking with rage, and tapping away with his stick faster than usual.

Jill stopped screaming promptly, and thanked Grumio, and then and there they became friends.

The 'prentice thought Jill a very fine little lady indeed, for Jill at once put on her very best behaviour. She held herself very straight, and acted much less like a tomboy than usual,—so that "the nice, fat boy" might continue to see that she was what he called her: "One of the real quality!"

When he heard that she had run away he was eager to help her. He showed her the way to the back workroom in the Toymaker's workshop, and told her that he was quite sure that she could be engaged to dress dolls and glue toys together, as soon as she learned how to do it neatly. He showed her how to fasten the flaxen wigs on the pretty French dolls, and how to stick the Noah's Ark trees on their wooden stands. Jill loved the work, and her eyes grew big as she saw how fine and lifelike many of the toys in that workroom seemed. They looked a good deal more remarkable there than they did out of doors.

The front room in the workshop was where the Master Toymaker himself worked, and where all the very fine toys were finished, but the back room was where the rougher and simpler work was done, and there Jill settled herself, quite content. It was a big place, and dolls and animals in all stages of manufacture were lying on big tables, or hanging on the wall, and in a dim light it was rather uncanny. Jill peered, once, into the front workroom and thought it looked like Fairyland by contrast. Of course she had visited it before with her brothers and sisters, but now she took a personal interest in the entire workshop.

She knew that if she visited there long enough, she would be sure to see Mary, if Mary was a doll's dressmaker, and she wanted to see her very much. But, meanwhile, she was determined not to miss the Toy Parade, so after a while she ran out of the workroom and off to the Christmas Tree Grove. And there, as we have seen, she met Alan and Jane.

It took some minutes for her to tell our two children all that we have been finding out in the last chapter. When she had finished her story, and they had explained that it would take them "simply ages" to tell theirs, Jane asked her anxiously for her advice.

"We must get away," she declared, and her brother added:

"And we must have different clothes,—something which will disguise us."

"What *can* we do, Jill?" asked Jane.

"Why," said Jill, "that ought to be very easy in Toyland. Everyone seems to wear such queer things here."

"Did they laugh at you too?" asked the children.

"Oh, yes," said Jill, "we didn't care! Let me see—Let me see—I have it!" she cried suddenly. "Lots of the Dutch dolls in the workshop are as big as you, Jane, and now, that they know me in the back workroom, they will let me come and go as I like. I can easily get you one of the dresses!"

"Goody! Goody!" cried Jane, clapping her hands, "A doll's dress: what fun!"

"But how about me?" asked Alan, anxiously.

"That's going to be harder," replied Jill. She grasped a red pigtail in each hand, and tugged savagely. "There must be some way!"

Then she began to chuckle.

"What is it?" cried both the children eagerly. "Have you an idea?"

Jill chuckled more and more, and rocked herself back and forth, as though with delight.

"Oh, it's such a *lovely* idea!" she gasped, wiping her eyes on the torn ruffle which was dangling from her dress. "It's rather naughty to do it, but it's *lovely*,—if we only *can*! Just wait a moment!"

"Well?" they demanded, after a long minute in which she thought it over.

"Well,—we can do it!" said Jill briskly. "Come along! Come along! You've got to hurry more than you ever hurried in all your lives before!"

She led the way out of the Christmas Tree Grove, on a run, and Alan and Jane followed her as fast as they possibly could.

About twenty-five minutes later, Grumio stumbled into the grove, so dazed and frantic that he talked stammeringly to himself and to the object which he held—a large, wooden head.

"O-oh!" he gasped, "What shall I do? What shall I say to the Master? O-o-oh!"

At that moment Jill came dancing along under the Wooden Block Bridge.

"What's the matter, Grumio?" she called, her little face twinkling with laughter, and her whole, small, untidy body in the highest spirits possible. Grumio held out the wooden head.

"Look at it!" he groaned. "It's the head of the Wooden Captain who was to have led the toy regiment today. He was all nicely dressed up,—so he was! Waiting to be wound up, so he was! And now just look at him!"

Grumio almost wept.

"Someone,"—he ended, explosively, "has stolen his clothes, knocked off his head, and mussed up his main springs! O-oh! Just let me find the one who did it! Just let me!"

He shook his fist.

"Here she is!" chuckled Jill. "I did it, Grumio! I did it!"

"You!"

Grumio paused, speechless.

"Yes,—I! I'm sorry if I've gotten you into trouble, but it *is* a joke, you know! And anyway I had to do it."

"Wh-wh-why?" stuttered Grumio.

"There!" said Jill, turning, and pointing. "That's why. Look!"

Grumio looked. What he saw was the vision of Alan and Jane, approaching hand in hand, and clothed in garments most wonderful to behold. Jane was dressed as a Dutch doll, a stiff, flaxen wig covering her own pretty curls, and a pair of white kid mittens over her hands to hide their human skin. And Alan—Alan in every detail of costume, was the Wooden Captain who was to have led the Toy Parade that day.

Jill had taken the uniform for him, and it fitted him fairly well. He, too, had put on a wig, and on top of the wig was a queer kind of military hat, held on by a strap under his chin.

He and Jane were both giggling, and Jill clapped her hands as she looked at them.

"There, Grumio!" she said, after she had explained the situation to the poor 'prentice. "You'll *have* to say that they make perfectly splendid dolls! And *isn't* he a fine Captain?"

Grumio looked at Alan in silence for some seconds. "Well, I'll tell you," he burst out finally. "There's one thing I've got to say: As long as he's turned himself into the Wooden Captain,—" he paused, and looked from one to the other,—"*he's got to lead that parade!*"

XVIII

THE WOODEN CAPTAIN

WHEN GRUMIO, THE 'PRENTICE, MADE this extraordinary suggestion, the other children thought,—at first, at least,—that he had gone crazy. Alan stared at him, speechless; and Jane said, "Why, what *do* you mean?"

Jill recovered first, and her bright eyes grew big with delight.

"Grumio, you're simply splendid!" she exclaimed. "That's *just* what he's got to do."

"And there's no time to be lost, either," added Grumio, excitedly. "The parade has got to come off in about two minutes. You can see the people beginning to gather already."

In truth, the high points of land at both ends of the Wooden Block Bridge were becoming crowded with people, gaily dressed, and moving about restlessly.

"The Grove will fill up, too, in another second," Grumio said. "Go ahead, and play your part!"

Alan felt his knees shake under him. When Jill had robbed the big Wooden Captain of his beautiful new uniform, he had seen the ranks on ranks of tin and wooden soldiers, all as big as he was, waiting to be wound up. And even standing still they were a pretty imposing sight. When he thought of what they would be like wound up and marching along behind him, he felt chilly all over. Besides, how could he look like a wooden captain? How could he walk in the way that soldiers with machinery, instead of insides, would be likely to walk?

"I say, you know," he blurted out, "I—I don't see how I can do it;—*really*, I don't!"

"Do it? Nonsense!" said Jill, shortly. "Course you can do it. And you will, too."

"You—just—simply—*must!*" said Grumio.

"But how—" began Alan.

Jane, who was growing enthusiastic herself, interrupted him:

"Oh, it won't be so hard, Alan," she said, comfortingly. "You just be yourself. That's all you have to do!"

The others laughed at that, but poor Alan said, a little crossly:

"I don't think that's so awfully funny, Jane!"

But, as he thought of Grumio's plan, he began to like the idea. Moreover, Grumio himself might prove of real service, afterward. He seemed a good soul, and he knew this strange city and its ways.

"Oh," exclaimed Alan, turning to the 'prentice, "I wonder if *you* could help us to get out of Toyland?"

"Sure!" returned Grumio. "Come to the Toymaster's Workshop right after the parade."

"So, if I lead the toy soldiers, you'll help us off?" said Alan.

"That's about the way it is," answered Grumio.

Alan hesitated no longer. It would be rather a lark, on the whole; and, anyway, it seemed to be the best, if not the only, thing to do.

"All right," he said, flushing as he faced them, "I'll do it. I'll march."

"And I'll march with you!" cried Jane, in great excitement. "I may, mayn't I, Grumio, *please*?"

"Why yes," answered the apprentice, doubtfully. "I don't see why you shouldn't—"

"You can be a *viv-viv andiere*," said Alan. "Those girls that go with regiments."

"I'll have to make up some story about it for the Master," said Grumio.

"Say you fixed up the Dutch doll with marching machinery and things, as a surprise for him, and to show what good dolls you can make yourself," suggested Jill. Then she added, with a chuckle, as she looked at Jane, "Oh, you know, she is a fine doll, and no mistake!"

Grumio considered her suggestion.

"That'll do," he said, "And, anyway, there's a band of Dutch dolls going to march, and dance afterward in the Dolls' Quadrille. She can lead them. I'll fix it up easily—And now," he added, with a grin, as he saluted Alan in military fashion, "You've got your marching orders, Captain! Come along!"

"All right,—here goes!" cried the new officer. "Forward march!"

And he jammed his hat tighter upon his head, and ran off. Jane started to follow him, but Jill, who was in the highest spirits possible, seized her hand, and,—with Grumio joining in at intervals, they sang:

> *"Oh, we've come to see Miss Jennie O'Jones,*
> *Miss Jennie O'Jones, Miss Jennie O'Jones,*
> *We've come to see Miss Jennie O'Jones,*
> *And how is she this morning?"*

Then the two little girls said solemnly:
"She's—dead!"

After which they all three danced about in a circle crying:

> *"We 're very glad to hear it, to hear it, to hear it,—"*

and rushed off, screaming with laughter.

Jane took her place among the Dutch dolls, Grumio got out his big key to wind up the whole troop, and Jill stationed herself where she could see everything.

All the people of Toyland seemed to have come to see the Master Toymaker's wonderful regiment and magnificent Wooden Captain. Jill could see that her mother, her brothers and sisters, and Uncle Barnaby were all there. The Master Toymaker went about smiling kindly, and seeing more interested in what was to come than anyone.

"Oh, I hope they'll do well!" thought Jill. "Now I'd love to lead a toy army, but I'm not at all sure that I could!" Meanwhile, the toy regiment was preparing for the Parade.

"Steady all!" whispered Grumio, in the ear of his Wooden Captain, as the latter stood motionless and stiff at the head of the lined-up regiment.

"When you march," continued the 'prentice, "You go straight along, between the lines of people, across the Block Bridge, and down the sloping path at the other end. Then you enter the Christmas Tree Grove and mark time while the troops line up. Then you march halfway back again to meet the Dutch dolls, and scarecrows, and Santas, and things. And be sure you don't forget all that, because it's what the toys will do,—they're drilled for it, made for it, in fact, and if you stop somewhere that you oughtn't to they're liable to walk on over you. Understand?"

The Wooden Captain did not dare to nod, but he murmured "I-I guess so!" rather faintly, and Grumio passed on. He went along the ranks of toy soldiers, and with his big key wound up each. The toys had been so cleverly constructed that even after being wound up the front rank did not begin to march until Grumio had taken the key from the very last soldier.

Alan, standing at the head of this mass of mechanical warriors, could hear their machinery buzzing away behind him;—and the buzzing grew in sound with the winding up of every fresh one. He felt a little thrill of excitement. It was fun to be an officer, even of a toy army. Besides these were not ordinary toys at all. He waited, breathless.

Then the toy trumpeters blew a sharp blast, and the Toylanders, ranged up to watch the sight, began to cheer loudly. Alan heard a faint squeak of machinery, and then one queer clicking step close behind him. At the same moment, Grumio called in a low, clear voice:

"March, Captain, march for your life. They're off!"

Alan drew a long breath, raised his left foot as jerkily as he knew how and started forward.

The Toy Parade had begun!

XIX

The March of the Toy Soldiers

The people of Toyland agreed, afterwards, that never, in any land, at any time, or under any circumstances, could there have been such a parade.

As for Alan, he seemed to be in a dream, and really was conscious of hardly any effort, as he jerked his legs forward in true toy fashion, and stared ahead almost as glassily as he thought a doll would stare. It seemed as though the toys behind him had some queer physical effect upon him. At times he felt as though he really must be a toy himself! Jane had the same feeling. Indeed, when they talked it over later, they found that the Toy Parade had affected both of them in the same way.

Alan led the entire procession. Then came the trumpeters and drummers, and then the soldiers,—the wonderful make-believe warriors designed by the Master Toymaker of the world.

Some wore red coats, and white trousers, and high black hats or caps such as real Majors wear. Some had blue uniforms, some green, some scarlet. Some were made of lead, some were of wood, and some were of shiny tin. Some carried shapeless, wooden rifles, some spindly bayonets.One andall werecleverlyfittedoutwith machinery that carried them through the long drill without a slip; one and all marched stiffly and regularly, and not once did any one get out of step. They made a gay picture, and it is no wonder that the Toylanders cheered them loudly, and then cheered the great and good Master Toymaker more loudly still.

Left, right,—left, right,—went the funny, ungainly feet; click, clack, click, clack! And now and then there was a faint creak, when a toy turned suddenly on its new and unused joints.

And all the time the toy drummers drummed with fine spirit, and the toy trumpeters tooted, and everything was as martial as possible.

Jane headed the Dutch dolls. There were quite a number of them, half dressed as boys and half as girls. They had flat faces and straight hair, and their machinery was less steady and smooth than that of the soldiers. The girls wore green and red Dutch dresses, and white baby-caps tied under their chins; the boys, green and red suits, with full, baggy knickerbockers, and black hats. Both boys and girls clattered along on big, wooden shoes. Every five or six steps the Dutch Dolls stopped, to bow politely though stiffly, with outstretched, wooden arms; and, of course, Jane had to bow too. Altogether it looked very queer indeed.

Then there were mechanical Santa Clauses carrying little Christmas trees, instead of rifles, and there were big, white scarecrows carrying brooms, and there were a number of very little dolls all made of square, coloured pieces of jointed wood, and having short sticks held stiffly at their sides. Oh, there were no end of remarkable things walking in that Toy Parade!

The toys marched with strange, halting steps, but in perfect time. When they stood still their machinery whirred so that you could easily hear it, and their arms and legs moved shakily up and down as though, in their queer, toy way, they were trying to mark time. The drill was perfect. So admirably had the Master Toymaker put his soldiers together that there was not a hitch, and altogether it was a very splendid parade.

"Oh, it's great! It's glorious!" chuckled Grumio, in delight, to Jill whom he had joined when the parade started. "Those friends of yours are fine!"

Jill clapped her little hands and cried "Splendid!" under her breath, every other minute.

Somehow, Alan and Jane did do very well. After the first few moments they found that it was great fun to lead a toy regiment, and entering into it heart and soul, they marched proudly along with stiff arms and jerky steps, while the Toylanders cheered them excitedly.

As they passed each other during the drill in the Christmas Tree Grove,—Alan leading his soldiers, and Jane her dolls,—the former murmured, between half-shut lips.

"How are you getting on, Jane? You look queer."

"Queer!" answered Jane, staring straight before her as she jerked herself past her brother. "I should think that I might look queer! Don't you see that Uncle Barnaby is looking at us?"

Alan felt his knees shake as he saw that she was right. Uncle Barnaby *was* looking at them! They had decided very suddenly upon leading this parade, and had not had time to think it over properly, and they had quite forgotten that Uncle Barnaby would be sure to be among the spectators! Indeed, it was a very foolish and dangerous thing to have done. Still, their disguises were very good, and Uncle Barnaby's eyes were not, and they might have passed unrecognised if Tommy Tucker, who was standing near the old miser, had not suddenly cried out:

"Doesn't that Wooden Captain look like Alan?" Tommy was *always* stupid! Then Uncle Barnaby began to stare very hard, and it was then that Jane caught his eyes and whispered the news of his presence to Alan. Both the children knew that Uncle Barnaby would lose no time in laying fresh plots. As soon as the parade should be over, they must run as hard and fast as they could to the workshop, and beg Grumio to hide them somewhere.

Uncle Barnaby was glaring at them by this time, and looked very white and savage. To himself he was saying:

"Is it merely my own fancy, or are those dolls really my detestable nephew and niece come back a second time to make me wretched?"

After the Parade there was a wonderful Doll's Quadrille. Oh, it was a splendid sight. The Master Toymaker had done his best, and the result was perfection. There were beautiful French Dolls, with yellow curls, and lovely, wax faces, and fluffy pink dresses, and pink hats and pink shoes and pink stockings. And they danced with Punches,—white satin Punches, very marvellous to see, who hopped about as though they must be alive.

The dance music was played on toy violins, and the Dolls looked as though they enjoyed it. The Dutch Dolls danced a clog dance, and of course Jane had to lead them all, and to take care that she danced better than any of them!

"Really," said the Widow Piper to the Master Toymaker, "this is a wonderful sight!"

"They do very well, very well, indeed," admitted the Master Toymaker. He spoke in the proud tone that a father might use in speaking of his children. "I think that the Parade is quite a success. And I am glad to see that my people are pleased." And he smiled at the crowds of Toylanders benevolently.

At last the soldiers stopped marking time and whirring, and the dolls stopped dancing. The trumpeters stopped trumpeting, and the drummers stopped drumming. All the toys stood stock-still, staring straight ahead, and looking as though they had never even played at being alive. The crowd began to break up. The Toy Parade was over. Soon all the people had left the Christmas Tree Grove, and with the rest had gone Uncle Barnaby, looking wickeder than ever, as though he were planning fresh villainy already.

Jill remained in hiding in the grove, and as soon as everyone else had gone, she ran out, crying: "Hurry up! Come just as fast as you can!" Jane and Alan stretched their stiff, aching legs and arms, and caught each other's hands. And the three children began to run, as fast as they possibly could, in the direction of the Master Toymaker's Workshop.

In the Master Toymaker's Workshop

A BIG, RED ROOM, WITH A soft light; a low ceiling, and walls hung with bright and fantastic toys; a room full of the rarest and loveliest toys in Toyland, just being completed and prepared to go out into the world; a room that bewildered the eyes, with its gay colours and its many pretty things—this was the Master Toymaker's Workshop.

Here he planned the wonderful machinery which made his dolls so nearly alive; here he put the finishing touches on his pet toys with his own hands; here he directed his skilled apprentices; here he lived, and worked, and smiled, and dreamed,—the dear, wonderful, mysterious, kindly Master Toymaker!

Back of this room was the workroom, which Jill knew, and above it was an attic full of the materials used for making toys,—wood and wax, china and tin, sawdust and paint, wire and cotton-wool, and ever so many other things. It was in this attic that Grumio had made up his mind to hide Alan and Jane.

When the three children arrived at the workshop they found that Grumio was already there. He sent Jill into the back workroom, for she was such a wild, noisy little thing that he thought they could now manage better without her.

Before they went up to the attic, the 'prentice showed Alan and Jane both the workrooms.

"That barn of a place back there," he said, with a shrug, "isn't anything much. But this, now,—this room where the Master works,—this is a place worth looking at. Queer, too. Sometimes *I* think it's *haunted!*"

Alan looked up at the walls. Half-made dolls, and grotesque masks were hanging there, and all sorts of beasts, dragons, guinea pigs, and wonderful roosters were all about the floor.

"They look almost alive," he said. "Wouldn't it be funny if they were?"

"Funny!" snorted Grumio. "No, I don't think it would be a bit funny! I think it would be very nasty.—Oh, look out! Here comes the Master! Run!"

He hurried them up the attic stairs, and they heard the door downstairs open and close. The Master Toymaker had come in.

Grumio gave the children a big bag of candy,—that being the only food he could find at the time,—and left them, promising to come back for them as soon as he had found a way for them to escape.

They settled themselves on the floor in the dimly lighted place, and, with the help of the candy, passed the time quite cheerfully. Nothing ever worried these two for a very long time, and in spite of all their troubles, they were soon laughing merrily over their queer adventures in Toyland. There was a small window at one end of the attic, and once in a while they ventured to peer out, just for a second, though they knew that this was very foolish, and that they were in danger of being seen.

It was while they were at the window that Alan pinched Jane, and whispered, "Look!"

There was Uncle Barnaby, coming toward the workshop, and walking very fast indeed,—so fast that his stick seemed to be fairly dancing along.

"Do you suppose he's coming for us?" breathed Jane, looking very frightened.

Alan shook his head doubtfully.

"N-no, I really don't. Not yet. But I do think it's rather horrid, having him come here like this. Wonder what he *has* come about!"

They kept a sharp lookout after that, so that they might be sure to know when he went away.

Meanwhile, Uncle Barnaby made a call upon the Master Toymaker. He found the good Master sitting at a table in the big front room of his workshop. On this table, strange to say, were a number of bottles and boxes, and in the very centre was a large glass flask. When Master Barn aby entered the Toymaker was bending over this flask, and watching it intently, as he poured a rose-coloured liquid into it from a tiny bottle.

"No use!" he muttered, shaking his head, "I cannot find the spell!"

Then he looked up, and, seeing Barnaby, rose to welcome him, saying most politely, that he was glad to see him.

"But," he added, kindly,—"you look disturbed."

"I-I am," returned the miser, who was panting and trembling. "That is why I have come. I am afraid that my nephew and niece are alive and in Toyland!"

"Afraid!" repeated the Master Toymaker.

"Yes," snarled Barnaby, "*Afraid!* That's what I said. And there's something else I'm afraid of—I'm afraid *you've* got something to do with it!"

"I!" exclaimed the Toymaker. "Master Barnaby! What could I have to do with your nephew and niece? Why should you think I knew anything about them?"

"Because," said Uncle Barnaby, "either I'm blinder than I think, or—that Wooden Captain who led your tomfoolery parade this afternoon was *my nephew Alan!*"

Of course the Master Toymaker thought that Uncle Barnaby was crazy. He drew himself up, looking at the old miser quite sternly.

"I made that Wooden Captain myself," he said, "and I am sorry that you found our parade so foolish!"

He said this with marked displeasure, for he was justly proud of his work, and Uncle Barnaby had been very rude.

"You made him yourself!" gasped Uncle Barnaby. Oddly enough, he really did believe that the Master Toymaker was telling him the truth. For that matter, so did the Master Toymaker! Then a sudden thought came to the old miser. "And the girl,—the Dutch Doll?" he asked, "Did you make that too?"

The Toymaker seemed disturbed.

"Why, no," he answered, "I did not. And I do not remember having given any orders for the Dutch dolls to have any leader at all. But Grumio has told me that he had fitted up that doll with machinery as a surprise for me."

"Then you may be sure that it is this Grumio who is at the bottom of it all," said Uncle Barnaby. "Well, what I want to do *now* is to search this place, and see if the fellow has hidden them here."

"Them?" questioned the Master Toymaker.

"Well, *her*, if you insist that the Captain is not Alan."

"I most certainly do!" declared the Master Toymaker.

"And as for searching my shop, Master Barnaby, I shall not let you do anything of the sort."

"Indeed!" said Uncle Barnaby, choking with anger. "Then I'll get a warrant from the Toyland Police, and you'll *have* to!"

At that moment the door opened, and a little girl ran in, carrying a tiny bandbox. When she saw Uncle Barnaby she gave a cry and rushed past him into the workroom at the back of the house.

"Who was that? Who was that?" exclaimed Uncle Barnaby, sharply.

"Ma'amselle Elisette, one of our dolls' dressmakers," answered the Master Toymaker, "and a very sweet child."

"She looked—" muttered Uncle Barnaby,— "She looked like Mary Piper! And *she's* not a sweet child!"

"Well, sir?" said the Master Toymaker, coldly. "Do you mean to bring the Toyland Police to search my workshop?"

"I do!" growled Uncle Barnaby. "Good afternoon!"

"Good afternoon," returned the Master Toymaker, politely, and the old miser went on his wicked way. He did not know that Alan and Jane were watching him from the attic window! The Master Toymaker looked after him. "A strange man!" he said to himself. "And one to be pitied! He loves neither toys nor children.—Poor soul! Poor soul!"

"If you please, Master," said Grumio, respectfully, appearing at the door between the two workrooms. "Could you come in here for a bit? That big, new dog's tail won't wag, and we're afraid to fool with the spring, for fear we'll get it more out of order than it is."

The Master Toymaker looked as though he did not like to leave his table, with its bottles and boxes, but he went at once into the back room. Grumio closed the door behind him with a sigh of relief.

"That tail'll keep him busy for twenty minutes," he remarked to himself. After which, he rushed to another door, and shouted:

"Bring in two crates right away!"

Four apprentices dragged in two enormous pine boxes. "That's all," said Grumio, and the other apprentices departed.

Then Grumio went to the foot of the attic-stairs and called softly:

"Alan! Jane! Come down!—But don't make any noise."

The children hurried down as quietly as they could.

"Well?" they asked eagerly. "What are you going to do with us?"

Grumio pointed calmly to the two crates and said: "They are your only chance."

"Grumio, what *are* you talking about?" cried Alan.

"Those boxes," explained Grumio, "are made to carry toys out of Toyland. There's a big pile of boxes already packed down on the shore now. In one of these I'm going to put a Dutch doll, and in the other a Wooden Captain. *Now* do you see what I mean?"

The two children stared at him as though they could not believe their ears. Then they stared at each other.

They,—Alan and Jane,—were going to be sent out of Toyland *in crates!*

XXI

"Right Side Up with Care"

"Now then," said Grumio, impatiently, "get into your boxes. I'm sorry, but it's the only way, and there's no time to be lost."

"All right," said Alan. "But you've got to mark them '*Right side up with care!*'"

"Of course," said Grumio.

"And 'Use *no* hooks!'" added Alan, laughing.

"I'm all ready!" cried Jane, and jumped into the smaller box. As usual, she looked on this fresh adventure in the light of a joke.

Grumio said: "Good for you!" and nodded approvingly. Then he dropped the wooden lid and nailed it on tightly, and finally he took a piece of black crayon and wrote: "Right Side Up with Care—Very Perishable—Use No Hooks!" on the top.

"Now, my young sir, get into yours!" he said to Alan.

But just at that instant the door opened. "Grumio!" called a clear, little voice, a voice which made Alan jump.

"Stiffen up!" commanded the 'prentice. Alan obeyed, becoming once more the wooden soldier. He was standing beside the big box, and Grumio tried to take him up bodily and pack him into it. But he only succeeded in getting him in (head first) up to his waist, and thus he remained,—his legs sticking up in the air.

"Oh, Grumio," continued the clear voice, "please go out and buy me some more pale pink silk. There are so many new dolls for me to dress!"

"Certainly, Ma'amselle Elisette," said Grumio, nervously. "Just wait a moment—" He pushed Alan a little further into the box, and jammed the lid down upon him hard. Poor Alan's legs still stuck out from under the lid in a stiff, queer way, but Grumio hoped that Ma'amselle would not notice them one way or another.

She, meanwhile, looked quite cross.

"Grumio, I'm in a dreadful hurry," she said. "And *really* I think you might—"

"I'll go, Ma'amselle, right away!" exclaimed Grumio, hastily. "I was just packing that doll. It's all right now. I'll be back as soon as I can, Ma'amselle," and he hurried off.

"Stupid boy!" remarked Ma'amselle Elisette. "He ought to be discharged!"

You know she had always been unreasonable and quick tempered. Before coming to Toyland, she had given her friends a good deal of trouble under the name of Contrary Mary!

It was at that moment that the legs sticking out from under the lid of the pine box began to kick convulsively. Elisette,—or, as we shall still call her, Contrary Mary,—jumped with surprise.

"Gracious! What's the matter with it?" she gasped.

The legs kicked harder. Poor Alan felt very uncomfortable, and had decided that he must get out of that box at any cost. Mary rushed to the crate and raised the lid. "What a way to pack a doll!" she exclaimed. "That boy shall be discharged!"

She stood Alan up beside the box, and there he stayed, just as she had placed him, with stiff arms and glassily staring eyes. Mary started back.

"I wonder if she knows me, in spite of the disguise?" thought Alan.

"Only a wooden doll, with no senses and no brains," exclaimed Mary. "And yet how he reminds me of Alan!"

Alan did not think it was very kind in her to put it in *just* that way, but he still looked glassily in front of him, and continued to be a wooden doll.

Mary looked again at the Wooden Captain, and, being a very busy, young person, and fond of doing useful things, it occurred to her that it would be nice to nail a bright, new medal on this toy officer's chest. So she took a ribbon with a pretty, gilt medal glued on it, and with a small hammer in her hand, she went up to Alan, to decorate him.

But this was more than he cared to endure, and, as he had only played his part to Mary as a joke, he dropped his stiffness and woodenness, and cried gaily:

"Oh, come now, Mary! You wouldn't be so horrid to me as that!"

Mary smothered a scream, and looked at Alan speechlessly for a moment. Then she gasped:

"Something must be *very* wrong with its machinery!"

"Machinery!" repeated Alan, with scorn.

"Mary, I don't think you're much of a friend, not to know me! Don't you see it's Alan?"

"Oh, Alan, Alan!" cried Mary, joyfully. "How simply splendid! And how glad I am to see you! But I can hardly believe my own eyes, even now! Do tell me what you are doing here."

She sat down on the smaller, wooden box and listened breathlessly, while Alan explained his presence in the workshop, and his toy clothes.

"But," she asked, "in that case, where's Jane?"

"In that case!" laughed Alan, pointing to the crate on which she was sitting. Mary jumped again, with another scream.

At the same time the Master Toymaker came in from the back workroom.

"The tail will wag now, quite properly," he called back, and then closed the door.

Alan was standing as straight as a wooden soldier ever stood, and Mary tried to hide her excitement.

"Packing the dolls, Ma'amselle?" asked the Master Toymaker. "That should be Grumio's work."

"I was only looking at the-the Wooden Captain," said Mary, nervously. "Is he to be sent away, too?"

"Yes," said the Master Toymaker. "A special order came today and has to be filled. I can make a better captain than he is to lead our regiment. What is in that closed crate?"

"Jane," answered Mary. "I-I mean—a Dutch doll."

"Boys," called the Master Toymaker. Four apprentices appeared.

"Paste this label on that crate," he said, "and take it down to the shore at once." And the four apprentices lifted Jane's prison and carried it off.

"Goodbye, Jane!" said Alan, as they passed him.

"What was that?" asked the Master Toymaker, sharply.

"His-his machinery, I think!" faltered Contrary Mary.

The next moment there was a loud noise, the noise of a large box or trunk being put into a wagon.

"What was that?" cried Mary.

"The crate," said the Toymaker.

"Jane!" sighed Alan.

Mary managed to pass near enough to whisper: "I'm going down to the shore myself, to see that nothing really dreadful happens to her!"

She patted his arm and hurried out. The Master Toymaker drew a deep breath of relief. He was alone at last,—alone with the Wooden Captain and his beloved crystal flask. He seated himself at the table, his face alight with eagerness.

"At last!" he murmured,—"I may once more set to work upon my search for the missing charm."

XXII

"The Light within the Flask"

Now is the time for me to explain part of the mystery of the Master Toymaker. The magicians of old, you know, believed that they could make wonderful charms, by mixing certain chemicals together,—charms which would give them power over the Spirit World. And the Master Toymaker had carefully studied this mysterious art.

It was secret work, and day by day he laboured over it,—all for one purpose—he wanted to give his dolls souls! He knew that he could never make souls himself, so he toiled and studied, trying to find the spell which would call up the Spirits of the Underworld that they might inhabit his toys and make them live. This was what he was always doing at his table of bottles and boxes, and that was why he was so glad to be left alone (as he thought) to mix his liquids afresh and search for the charm. He always hoped that the next moment, would show him a crimson liquid within the flask; for this would be his sign of success. This would be the signal which would inform him that the Spirits of the Underworld were at his command.

It was beginning to grow dark in the Workshop, for, by this time, it was very late in the afternoon. The Master Toymaker sat at his table, and the Wooden Captain stood motionless by the pine crate.

"No light!" sighed the Master Toymaker,—"No light within the flask! Whatever I do, I cannot find the element which would make the charm complete!"

He poured some silvery liquid into the flask, then shook his head.

"Ah!" he cried, "Spirits of the Underworld,—I call you,—call you again and again! Come up to me, out of the depths of the earth, that I may give you forms like human beings!"

Alan felt much excited, and just a little creepy. He wished with all his heart that Jane were back again. He decided that he did not like having adventures by himself.

The Master Toymaker leaned over the crystal flask and dropped some powder into it from a tiny box. The powder was bright turquoise blue, and had fine particles of gold through it.

"Why can I never find the right mixture?" he groaned. Then he gave a quick start, as though waking from a dream, and rose. "I am wasting time!" he exclaimed. "While I am hunting for my poor dolls' souls, I must not neglect their bodies."

He took a candle from a shelf, lighted it, and went toward the back workroom. As he passed Alan, he paused.

"Sometimes," he said, musingly, "You seem to me to be almost alive already."

For a moment Alan felt tempted to throw aside his absurd disguise, and to tell the strange, kindly, old magician all about his situation, but he hesitated, and, the next instant the Master Toymaker had left the room, and taken the candle with him.

Then, some little distance up the street, rose the sound of an angry voice, and measured steps on the pavement. Alan ran to the window.

Uncle Barnaby, and four of the Toyland policemen were approaching. Alan drew back from the window. What should he do? Instinct told him they had come to look for him and that they would search the house: There was no use in hiding in the attic again. They were coming nearer. Alan could hear the *tap, tap* of Uncle Barnaby's stick now. He looked around desperately. Should he appeal to the Master Toymaker? No, he was Uncle Barnaby's friend,—and besides he could do nothing. Then an idea came to him, an idea which made him dizzy for a moment, —a thought without form, a hope without reason.

He groped his way through the deepening shadows to the Magician's table. He could feel the big crystal flask, and the numbers of little bottles and boxes. He caught up a tiny phial, at random, and emptied it into the flask.

"Oh, if I could only get the mixture that makes the charm!" he gasped.

He seized a little box and shook the powder from it into the flask. Uncle Barnaby's voice came clearly to his ears,— "Come on, come on!"

There was a tall, slender bottle on the table.

"There's luck in three trials," Alan said to himself. He did not uncork it—that would take too much time,—but broke the neck of it on the edge of the table. The splintered glass fell to the floor, and Alan plunged the broken bottle into the flask.

There was a bubbling, hissing noise,—and then,—Alan stumbled back from the table, with a sob.

"The light!" he whispered,—"The light!"

XXIII

The Rising of the Toys

A CRIMSON GLOW HAD APPEARED IN the crystal flask. The whole workshop was lighted by it, and, catching the ruby brightness like little clouds at sunset, were faint wings and faces, transparent forms and delicate hands,—crowding softly, silently into the room,—who could know how or whence?

Alan trembled. He could hear hands fumbling at the door; the police had come.

Then a clear, spirit voice said: "Who has sent for us? What is your will with us, Finder of the Charm?"

The knob turned; the door opened.

"Enter the toys," whispered Alan, breathlessly. "Protect me against these people!"

Spirits move swiftly. When Uncle Barnaby and the four policemen entered the workshop, the glimmering wings and faces had vanished. The glow, too, had faded into darkness, and they peered about by the light of the lanterns they carried. They were Japanese lanterns, and cast queer flickering colours about the workshop.

Alan was standing quietly near the table, and as his Uncle approached he went to meet him, saying, quite simply: "How do you do, Uncle Barnaby?"

Uncle Barnaby shook his fist at him, and snarled with rage.

"So he was lying!" he cried. "The old Toymaker said that you were only a wooden soldier."

"He thought I was," returned Alan. "He was not lying, Uncle Barnaby."

The door between the two rooms opened.

"What is this?" exclaimed the Master Toymaker.

"I've come to arrest this boy!" said Barnaby.

"Boy!" gasped the Toymaker. He put his candle down on the table, and stood, trembling. "Where is my Wooden Captain?"

"I can explain, sir, later," said Alan, respectfully. "First I want to ask Uncle Barnaby why he is going to arrest me?"

"The charge—" began one of the policemen.

They never knew what charge Uncle Barnaby had invented on which to imprison his nephew and niece, for at that moment—something happened.

The toys began to move! Dolls, soldiers, masks, animals, birds, punches, they all descended from the walls and the shelves, came out from cabinets and dark corners, poured in through the empty door of the other workroom, and ranged themselves behind Alan. This time they did not merely walk along mechanically and stiffly, like the toy regiment. They moved, breathed, turned their heads as they chose; their eyes looked threateningly at Master Barnaby; *they were alive!*

"The toys!" gasped the policemen.

"The toys!" shouted Barnaby.

"The toys!" cried the Master Toymaker, with shining eyes. He bent over the crystal flask eagerly. "Red!" he muttered. "I left the mixture purple." Then he turned to Alan. "Boy, whoever you are," he cried, "you have happened on the charm for which I have struggled all these years!"

The living toys made a pretty terrifying sight, you may be sure.

But, frightened though he was, Uncle Barnaby would not give up the matter so easily. He came forward, boldly, seized Alan's arm, and cried: "Pooh! This is all some trick! Come, officers, arrest this boy as you promised me that you would. Who cares for a parcel of toys?"

No sooner had he spoken than he was surrounded by the very toys of which he had spoken so lightly. They dragged him away from Alan, they beat him with his own stick, they tore his coat, and pulled his hair, until he shrieked for mercy.

"Come, come!" shouted Alan. "You must not hurt him! It is quite enough to frighten him."

The toys, however, were really enjoying themselves, and Alan had to repeat his command twice before they let Uncle Barnaby alone. Finally, they retreated, and gathered around Alan, waiting for fresh orders.

Uncle Barnaby rose, gasping and groaning, and said to the police in a whimpering tone:

"Will you stand by and see me so outrageously treated?—And by toys, too!"

Alan declared later that two toys actually smiled when he said that.

The police had been standing rigid with surprise, staring at Alan and his mysterious followers. But just at that moment all the toys took one step toward them. With cries of terror they turned and, followed by Uncle Barnaby himself, fled from the workshop.

"Now come!" said Alan.

And he and his toys marched out into the street and through the City of Toyland. The police ran wildly ahead, warning inhabitants with their terrified cry:

"The toys have risen! The toys have risen! The toys have become alive!"

As for Uncle Barnaby, he had disappeared.

People rushed to windows and ran out of houses, with lanterns and candles, all talking at once, shouting, asking questions, and repeating over and over again: "The toys have risen!" Toyland was in an uproar.

"To the shore first," commanded Alan, and they went on past the Christmas Tree Grove, and the Block Bridge, down the Street of Toys, until they reached the wharf, and the sea.

Several crates were lying on the wharf, and Alan and the toys set to work opening them. At last they came to the one that held Jane, and Alan felt ready to cry with relief. When they found her she was sound asleep, curled up in her packing box like a kitten.

Then Mary and Jill came running up. They had met in the workroom, and when Mary had come down to the shore to keep guard over Jane's crate, Jill had followed her. Together they all went up through the streets once more. This time they were bound for the Court Royal of Toyland, for Alan wanted to ask for the protection of the Government for himself and Jane.

When they reached the Court Royal they found Tom-Tom, who, as we know, was one of the pages there. He led them to one of the Royal Justices, who heard their story and promised that they should have no further trouble in Toyland. And when that was all settled, Alan thanked the Spirits of the Underworld, and told them to take the toys back to the workshop, and then to leave them there and return to their own country.

Meanwhile, the five runaways laughed and cried and all talked at once, and said, "How *glad* I am to see you again!" over and over again. Finally Jill said: "And where shall we go now?"

I think she said it rather wistfully, for she was tired and homesick, poor, bad, little Jill!

The others looked at each other for a moment in silence. And then Mary,—wilful, naughty, wayward. Contrary Mary,—surprised them all by saying, with a little choke in her voice: "L-let's go back to mother and the rest of the children."

And so the runaways went home.

XXIV

Goodbye to Toyland

THE WIDOW PIPER HAD HAD so much anxiety over her truant children that she forgot to be severe when the runaways came to her. She forgave them all, and, on their side, they had had quite enough adventures, and all promised that they never would run away again. When the Widow heard the whole story, she insisted that Alan and Jane should live with her and the fourteen children until they were old enough to go where they pleased. And of course they were only too glad to agree with her kind suggestion.

Uncle Barnaby left Toyland at daybreak. No one knew where he went, and no one cared very much, not even the Widow Piper.

As they were all together now they decided to go home to the Village Without a Name at once. But first the sixteen children went to the workshop to say goodbye to the Master Toymaker and Grumio. The old Magician was sitting, dreaming over his table. When he saw his little guests he roused himself, and said with a smile: "Old habits, you see! I must break myself of them. I shall have all my bottles and boxes,—liquids and powders,—thrown away. And I will make pretty toys all the rest of my life."

"You aren't going to try anymore to give them souls?" asked Alan.

He shook his head.

"No," he answered. "Toys are toys and very good things in their way. I shall leave them as they are!" He looked about him at the toys which, the night before, had lived for one short hour, but now hung there lifeless for the rest of their days.

The children said goodbye to him, affectionately, and left him among his toys,—smiling his wise smile, and dreaming those mysterious daydreams that a Magician and the Master Toymaker of the world should dream.

It did not take long to say goodbye to the Noah's Ark Woman and to Grumio, and that afternoon they said goodbye to Toyland.

Grumio was heartily sorry to see them go.

"You'll come back again someday, won't you?" he said.

"Oh, yes,—someday," answered the children. But as a matter of fact they never saw Toyland again.

They left Toyland by way of the Toy Railway, and Alan and Jane were quite pleased to meet their friend the Tin Engineer again. He was extremely polite to them, and this time the tin train ran beautifully and carried them all safely through the tunnel and down the mountain side.

"Oh, look!" cried Contrary Mary, as they rattled along,—"What is that over there?"

"A bear!" exclaimed Tom-Tom.

"Where? Where?" cried Alan and Jane, rushing to a window to look. A small brown bear was sitting on his haunches waving his paw to them.

"Fuzzy!" cried our two children—"Oh, if we could only stop and speak to him." But the train had left him far behind. They passed Mean Town and the Forest was far behind them, when at last the Tin Engineer stopped the train, and let them alight, pointing out to them the best way for them to get home. "I'm off to Santa Claus's country, now," he said—"I hope that you will all run smoothly for the rest of your lives, and that your springs will never stick or rust."

Which was the best sort of a blessing he knew how to give.

So they all came back to Contrary Mary's Garden. They found it overgrown with weeds, and they all worked for a long time making it look like its old dear self. And Alan and Jane told the story of their wonderful adventures, while the others listened breathlessly. At the end of the story they all had comments to make.

"You didn't get a single piece of pumpkin pie while you were gone, did you?" said Peter.

"Nor any strawberries and cream!" said Curly Locks.

"I should have missed my sheep!" said Bo Peep.

"And I my cows," said Boy Blue.

"But Fuzzy must have been a jolly little chap,—better than cows or sheep!" said Simon.

"Of course the woods were lovely," said Riding Hood.

"But it must have been awfully dark and scary!" said Sallie Waters.

"That awful spider!" said Miss Muffet.

"It's too bad you didn't have any adventures by sea," said Bobby Shafter.

"What a dreadful place Mean Town was!" said Tommy Tucker.

"Well, anyway, you're back now!" said Contrary Mary. "And you're going to *stay*, this time!"

"And now," said Tom-Tom, "after all your adventures, tell us which you really think was the nicest."

"Finding you all," said Alan, promptly.

"And what's nicer than any adventure in the whole world," added Jane, happily, "is getting back to Contrary Mary's Garden."

Over the garden wall floated the voices of some passing villagers. And once more they were singing:

> *"Mary, Mary, quite contrary,*
> *How does your garden grow?*
> *With silver bells, and cockle shells,*
> *And pretty maids all in a row!"*

THE CHRISTMAS REINDEER

I

Tuktu and Aklak

Tuktu was a little Eskimo girl. Tuktu means caribou. She had been given this name, because only a few days before her birth, a relative named Tuktu had died; and as is the custom, this name had been given to the baby. She was well named, for caribou were to have much to do with her life. On the very day that she was born, Kutok, her father, had killed a caribou when food was greatly needed. That year, for some unknown reason, caribou had moved from their usual feeding grounds, and Kutok and his family had had to depend almost wholly on seal and polar bear, and these had been none too plentiful. So this caribou had brought great joy to the home of Kutok. In the days following, he found the caribou back in their old feeding grounds. Later, Kutok was to become a herder of reindeer, and the reindeer, you know, are first cousins of the caribou. So it was that Tuktu was well named.

Aklak, her brother, bore the name of the great Brown Bear. Aklak was two years older than Tuktu and gave promise of being like his father—a mighty hunter. Already he had killed his seal and none knew better than he how to snare the ptarmigan. In the summer he and Tuktu gathered eggs when the waterfowl came north in untold thousands for the nesting. Whatever Aklak did, Tuktu tried to do.

While the children were still small, their father had become a herder of reindeer, and the little folk spent much of their time with the deer. They helped herd them. They did their part at the annual round up. In the spring they hunted for stray calves that had lost their mothers. Both learned to drive deer to a sled.

During the long winter nights, the herders often gathered in Kutok's house, and there they told stories while the children listened. There were stories of hunting, stories of adventure, stories of many strange things. But the story that Tuktu and Aklak liked the best of all was that of the chosen deer of the Valley of the Good Spirit. This was especially true of Tuktu. She used to dream of that wonderful valley. And whenever she saw the Northern Lights, the Aurora, shooting up high overhead, she would wonder what would happen to anyone who might stray into that valley, for it was said that it was from this valley that those lights came.

At last there came a time when she and Aklak actually were to live for a week or two almost on the border of that valley. Do you wonder that she tingled clear to the tips of her fingers and toes with little thrills of anticipation, excitement, and perhaps just a wee bit of fear? It was the fulfilment of a promise that their father had made them, that, when the deer moved over from their summer feeding grounds to the Valley of the Good Spirit, they should go with him to keep watch from a distance.

Even Aklak was excited, though he did his utmost not to appear so, and trudged along behind his father as if visiting the Valley of the Good Spirit were an everyday affair. All day they traveled. That is, they traveled what would have been all day where you and I live. It wasn't all day there, for you know way up in the North there is no real night in summer.

At last they reached the hut in which they were to live while the deer grazed on the hills of the Valley of the Good Spirit. This hut was a very rude affair, built partly in the ground and partly on the ground. It was of wood and stone with a skin roof and a long entrance passage. While not as big and comfortable as the house at home, it was the sort of thing these children were used to and it was quite good enough.

That night after the evening meal, Tuktu begged her father to once more tell the story of the Valley of the Good Spirit and of the chosen reindeer. "Why is it called the Valley of the Good Spirit?" she asked.

"Because," replied Kutok, "a wonderful and good spirit lives and moves there."

"Has anyone ever seen him?" Aklak asked.

"No," replied Kutok, "none but the deer people, and of these only the chosen ones ever go down into that valley. But we know that a good spirit lives there, for always the deer that graze on the hills about the valley are safe from the wolf, the bear, and all other enemies. They do not need to be watched. There need be no herder here, were it not that it is well to know when the herd moves out, for then the summer grazing is over. It is a good spirit, for is it not true that every year eight deer are chosen and the next year returned to us the finest sled-deer in all the North? The Good Spirit dwells there and with him live many lesser spirits, who do his bidding."

Thus it was that Kutok told the children of what you and I know as fairies, and elves, and gnomes, and trolls. Eskimo children know nothing about these little unseen people. To them, all are spirits.

"Have you ever looked down into the valley?" asked Aklak.

"No," replied Kutok. "It is not well to be curious. I am content to stay here and wait for the deer to move. So must you be."

"What would happen if one should venture down into the valley?" asked Aklak.

"That no man knows, for no man has ever been so bold as even to think of doing such a thing," replied his father. "My son, be wise with the wisdom of your elders, and be satisfied. None but the deer folk ever enter that valley and these, only the chosen ones. We will stay here and from a distance watch the herd."

"If it is such a good spirit," thought Tuktu, although she didn't venture to express her thought aloud, "why should anyone fear to go down into the valley?"

And she was still wondering as she fell asleep.

II

KRINGLE VALLEY

FOR THE GREATER PART OF the short Arctic summer, the great herd of reindeer had grazed within sound of the waters of the Arctic Ocean lapping on the beach. More than two thousand deer were in that herd. They were not all Kutok's, although all were in his charge, for he was chief herder. Only about two hundred of the deer were his, as shown by the earmarks. It was in deer that Kutok was paid for his services in looking after the great herd, which was owned by white men. With the approach of the long winter, the deer would move inland to winter range, and Kutok and his family would return to their permanent home.

For several days before the opening of this story the deer had been uneasy. They had done more or less milling. This means that they had gathered in a great body, the outer members traveling in a large circle and trotting tirelessly most of the time. Kutok knew the sign. "They will soon seek the Valley of the Good Spirit," said he to the other herders who assisted him. That very afternoon, the herd, as if at a signal from some wise old leader, began to move inland. In a short time, all the deer but the trained pack animals, which had been fastened, had disappeared.

It was then that Kutok had taken Tuktu and Aklak to the hut not far from the entrance to the Valley of the Good Spirit. It was the greatest event in the lives of these two little Eskimo folk, for always they had heard this valley spoken of with awe that was almost reverence. Now perhaps they might be permitted to see the wondrous colored mists that were said to rise from it.

Kringle Valley was the name by which it was known to the white men, none of whom believed in it, for none had ever seen it. But to the Eskimos, it was, as I have already stated, the Valley of the Good Spirit. Did they not know that on its gentle slopes wild grasses grew in such abundance and such richness as could be found nowhere else in all the North? Were not the hillsides carpeted with wildflowers until they glowed in patches of brilliant color? You see, even the Arctic has its summer. It is a short summer, but a wonderful summer. Up there above the Arctic Circle there are days when the sun does not set at all and the number of days during which the sun does not set increases as one goes North, until at the North Pole there are six months and five days of continuous daylight. When the sun does set for a few hours, the twilight is so brilliant that it is difficult to think of the day as having ended when the sun disappears.

Kringle Valley is a valley of mystery. No man as yet has been privileged to enter it. No man has even looked down into it, save from a distance. It is said to be filled with a soft many-colored mist, which is neither of dampness nor of smoke. The Eskimos believe it to be the birthplace of the ever-changing, many-colored lights of the Aurora. Only the herders of the reindeer, which yearly seek pasturage on the hills about the valley, have ever ventured near enough to see even from a distance the curtain of many-colored mist.

Around the winter firepots the story is told to the children of how every year just before the great herd leaves the valley, the deer gather at the upper end, and, there for a time, mill.

There is no fear among these milling deer. As they trot tirelessly in a huge circle, there is a constant shifting, until in turn each of the bucks has made at least one circuit in the outer ring. Thus each has a chance to show his full strength and beauty. From time to time as at a signal, one of these trotting deer leaves the circle and stands motionless just without the curtain of colored mist. When eight have been thus chosen, they disappear in single file in the mist of the valley, while the leaders of the great herd at once start the southern migration, and the herders know that no longer will the deer feed in Kringle Valley until toward the end of another summer.

And the herders know, too, that when the winter round up in the corrals is made for the yearly count, the eight best sled-deer in all the herds will be missing. They will be the ones which vanished in the shimmering mists of Kringle Valley. And the herders whose deer have so disappeared will rejoice greatly. They will be counted as being blessed above their fellows. They know that their deer are not lost. They know that when once again the great herd moves to Kringle Valley, they will find there the eight deer—fat, sleek, well-cared for. They know that these deer thereafter will never mingle with the herd, but will be for as long as they live the finest sled-deer in all the world. So it is considered good fortune if, after the herd leaves Kringle Valley, one's deer be found missing.

III

TUKTU'S SOFT HEART

T HESE WERE HAPPY DAYS FOR Tuktu and Aklak. Tuktu's only duties were to cook meals for her father and brother. An Eskimo girl learns these things very young and Tuktu had been well taught. Aklak spent most of his time hunting. Their father did little but sit for long hours smoking and watching the distant hillsides where the reindeer grazed above the Valley of the Good Spirit. These were lazy, happy days and Kutok was making the most of them, for the summer was nearly at an end and he knew that when the herd moved there would be little time for lazing.

Tuktu roamed about picking the flowers that grew in such profusion, and also hunting for the flocks of young ptarmigan, for she dearly loved to watch these pretty "Chickens of the North." Not for the world would Tuktu have harmed one of them. Not for the world would she have told her brother Aklak how she felt when he brought in ptarmigan and other birds for the cooking pot. But despite the fact that she ate them and enjoyed the eating, there was all the time in her heart a wee feeling of sadness, for Tuktu's heart was the loving heart.

Aklak was a good herder and had a way with the deer which some of the older herders might well have envied; but there was no one among all the herders or their families who could go among the deer as freely and unnoticed as could Tuktu. It was as if she held some strange power over the deer people; as if they had accepted her as one of their own number. She could approach the most timid and nervous among the wilder members of the big herds. As for the sled-deer, they might balk and strike at others, but never at Tuktu when she harnessed them. She loved them, every one, and seemingly they knew it.

So it was that Tuktu found her playmates among the wild people, who were not wild with her. Many a time had she stroked a ptarmigan on the nest. Many a time had the Arctic Hare fed from her fingers. The sea fowl paid no attention to her. Love has a strange way of making itself felt among the wild folk, and the soft heart of Tuktu was soft because of love.

So it was that when she found the home of a Blue Fox, about the entrance to which four half-grown little foxes were playing, she did not tell her brother. Each day she would steal away and sit by the entrance to the den, taking with her bits of meat for the little foxes. How she loved to see them roll and tumble about her feet. Sometimes two of them would get hold of the same piece of meat and then there would be a tug of war. Tuktu's eyes would dance and she would laugh softly. And then, when one little fox had succeeded in pulling the meat from the other, she would give the loser the extra piece which she always had for that purpose. And a short distance away sat Mother Fox, grinning happily.

While she picked the flowers and played with the foxes, and now and then mothered a young ptarmigan that had been lost from the flock, she dreamed of the Valley of the Good Spirit. It seemed such a little distance to the brow of the nearest hill overlooking that valley that she couldn't help but wonder what she would see if she should climb up there. But not once did the thought of really doing it enter her head. It was enough for Tuktu that it was forbidden. It was not that she was afraid. She knew that her father was afraid. She knew that Aklak was afraid. She knew that they regarded the Good Spirit and the valley where he lived with reverence and awe. But Tuktu was not afraid. It was enough for her that the Valley of the Good Spirit was sacred and not to be approached by other than the deer people. So, no matter how great her longing to look down from that hilltop, the thought of actually trying to do such a thing never entered her wildest dreams.

She would sit for hours looking over toward the valley and wondering what the deer folk saw therein. Now and again she could see the deer moving on the upper hills. Once as she was watching them, she said softly—for she had a way of talking to herself: "I wish I were really a Tuktu—a caribou."

"Why?" asked Aklak, who had stolen softly up behind her, just in time to hear what she said.

"Because then I might go into the Valley of the Good Spirit and I might even be chosen by the Good Spirit. Who knows?"

Aklak laughed, but it was a good-natured laugh. "It is the reindeer, not the caribou, who go down into the valley," said he.

"But the caribou go too," replied Tuktu quickly, "for only this morning I saw a band of them heading that way; and after all the reindeer are but tame caribou."

"You saw a band this morning!" exclaimed Aklak excitedly, for all that morning he had been hunting for caribou and had not seen one.

Tuktu nodded. "Yes," said she. "And Aklak, I'm glad you didn't see them. I am glad they have gone where you cannot follow, for I would not like to have a caribou killed here so near to the Valley of the Good Spirit."

Aklak opened his mouth for a quick retort, then thought better of it. Perhaps after all Tuktu was right. Perhaps it were better that there should be no killing of the deer folk so near the Valley of the Good Spirit. He remembered that not even the wolves, nor the great Brown Bear for whom he was named, ever killed there.

IV

WHITEFOOT GOES ASTRAY

THE TWO PACK-DEER WITH WHICH Kutok had moved up near the Valley of the Good Spirit had been kept fastened, each with a long rawhide line. But Kutok well knew that should they be allowed to go free, they would be likely to join the herds over on the hills above the valley. So they were kept tethered by long lines, and each day were moved to a new grazing ground. Sometimes Kutok attended to this; sometimes Aklak.

It happened one day that both Kutok and Aklak had gone hunting. Tuktu was not at all lonely, for loneliness is something that Eskimo folk know little about. Had she not the two deer for company, to say nothing of the little foxes with whom she played daily? It was nothing new for her to be left alone while her father and brother went hunting. It was Aklak who had moved the deer to new grazing ground just before starting that morning. Two or three times Tuktu wandered over to pat them and pet them, as was her habit. When she became sleepy, she lay down for a nap. It was when she awoke from this that she discovered one of the deer had pulled the peg by which he had been fastened, and had wandered away.

"It must be that Aklak was in too much of a hurry when he drove that peg," thought Tuktu. "I must find Whitefoot and bring him back, or father will be very angry. He will blame Aklak, and it will be very unpleasant to have only one deer when it is time to move. Yes, I must find Whitefoot and bring him back." Whitefoot was the deer's name, for his off forefoot was white.

Having often helped in the rounding up of strays from the herd, Tuktu was skilled in reading signs. Almost at once she found traces of the wandering Whitefoot. He was grazing as he moved along, taking a bit now on this side and now on that side. Once she found a little bush in which the dragging peg had become entangled. Whitefoot had broken the branches of the bush in tearing himself free. Tuktu hurried on, for she saw that the course was leading toward the hills above the Valley of the Good Spirit.

"I must catch him before he gets much farther," thought Tuktu as she hurried on. "Father was right. Whitefoot is doing just what father said the deer would do if they should be free; he is going to join the great herd. I must get him before he gets there, or we shall see no more of him until the herd moves out from the valley."

It was warm work, for in summer it becomes unpleasantly hot, even way up there in the Northland. Tuktu was panting and perspiring, and she was growing tired. But not for an instant did she delay.

"I must get him. I must get him," she kept saying over and over. "I must get Whitefoot."

At last, from a little rise of ground, she saw the wanderer just going up a little hill. "Whitefoot!" she called, "Whitefoot! Stop, Whitefoot!"

At the sound of her voice, Whitefoot lifted his head and looked back. "Whitefoot! Whitefoot!" she called, hurrying forward. Whitefoot hesitated. He looked back in the direction in which he had been traveling. Somewhere ahead of him was the great herd. The scent of it was borne to him on the wind. The longing to join it was almost irresistible. Behind him rang the commands of the little mistress he had learned to love and obey. "Stop, Whitefoot! Stop!" His nose demanded obedience to the call of the herd. His ears demanded obedience to the command of his little mistress. Which should he obey? No wonder Whitefoot hesitated.

It was not for nothing that Tuktu was known among her companions as "Little Fleetfoot." She was out of breath, she was tired and she was— oh, so hot! But despite all this, she ran now as if she were running a race. Just as Whitefoot decided that the call of the herd must be heeded, Tuktu threw herself forward on the dragging peg at the end of the long line which trailed behind Whitefoot. The decision was no longer his. Tuktu had won.

Holding fast to the line, Tuktu seated herself in the grass and slowly drew the reluctant Whitefoot toward her. All the time she talked to him, chiding him for wandering away; telling him how necessary he was; calling him names of endearment in one breath and scolding him in the next. Whitefoot stamped once or twice impatiently. Then, as if having made up his mind that he might as well make the best of the matter, he fell to grazing.

For a long time Tuktu sat there, for as I have said, she was tired. At last she arose. "Whitefoot," she said severely, "you have made me run a long way. Now you will have to carry me back."

As you know, Whitefoot was a pack animal. He had been trained to carry loads on his back. Tuktu had ridden him many times. So it was nothing new for him to feel his little mistress on his back. She turned his head toward camp and then she saw the white, thick mist of the Arctic fog rolling in from the coast. Already it had almost reached them.

V

LOST IN THE FOG

IN FROM THE DISTANT SEA rolled the Arctic fog. It was as if one of those great, white fleecy clouds you have seen sailing high in the sky had come to earth and was being pushed forward to bury everything in its fleecy depths. Tuktu urged Whitefoot forward in the swinging trot the reindeer know. Would he be able to get her to camp before that swiftly moving fogbank would cut off all sight in any direction? She knew all about the fogs of the Far Northland. Had she been at home, she would not have minded it. But to be caught far from the camp was another matter.

"But I can trust Whitefoot," thought Tuktu. "The deer folk can find their way even though they cannot see. So long as I am safe on the back of Whitefoot, I need not worry. Whitefoot is headed in the right direction and he will take me safely back."

The soft mist swirled about them and Tuktu could see nothing. She could see nothing and she could hear nothing but the clicking of Whitefoot's feet. There was no other sound. It was as if she and Whitefoot were alone in a white, wet world of silence. Click, click,

click, click sounded Whitefoot's feet—a click with every step. It was comforting to hear that much, for each click meant a forward step, and each forward step meant so much nearer to the camp. At least, that is what Tuktu encouraged herself by thinking.

"I wonder where Father and Aklak are," she thought. "This fog must have caught them first, for they were hunting in the direction of the seacoast. They must have seen it coming and probably made camp. They will stay there until the fog lifts. If only I were back at the camp, I would not mind a bit. Trot, Whitefoot! Trot! Remember that Tuktu is on your back and she wants to get home."

Whitefoot did trot. He trotted steadily, despite the fact that he could see nothing. His head was carried forward and his nose out and his nostrils were extended. With every breath he was testing the damp air. By the motion, Tuktu could tell when he was going up a hill and when he started down again. She was enjoying the ride.

But there came a time when Tuktu began to wonder. "We should be there by this time," she thought. "Yes, indeed, we should be there by this time. Whitefoot has been traveling so fast that I am sure we should have been home long ago. If he did not trot along so steadily, I should think he were lost and wandering about But he seems to know just where he is going. Oh dear, I wish I could see just a little way. Whitefoot, what is that?"

Whitefoot stopped abruptly. Through the mist at one side a dim form moved. Tuktu gave a little sigh of thankfulness and was about to drop to the ground, for she was sure that this was the other pack-deer that had been left grazing near the camp. But she didn't drop, for she became aware that another dim form was on the other side of her. And then she heard the muffled click, click, click of many feet—a sound that could be heard only where many deer were near. Too often had she listened to it not to know that she was now in the midst of a herd. She heard the click in front, behind, and on both sides, and as she strained her eyes could see dim shapes appear and disappear on all sides.

"Whitefoot!" she whispered, "Whitefoot, where have you taken me?"

She wondered if by chance some other herd of reindeer had moved in from the seacoast on its way to the Valley of the Good Spirit. She wondered if it might be that she was in the midst of a band of caribou. She decided that this must be it. Probably Whitefoot had smelled, or perchance heard them, so had joined them.

She was not afraid. Did she not know that the reindeer are the most gentle of animals? Had she not lived with them and loved them from babyhood? She would remain on Whitefoot's back and hope that the fog would lift soon. If it did not, she would stop Whitefoot and push the peg into the ground to fasten him. Then they would remain there together until such time as the fog should disappear. There was only one thing that worried Tuktu. If she had to remain there long, what should she eat? But even this did not greatly worry her, for she was sure that the fog would last but a little while and she knew they could not be far from camp.

Whitefoot no longer was trotting, nor were any of the other deer folk. All seemed to be grazing, moving along slowly as they grazed. Tuktu became drowsy. Once or twice she nodded and the wonder was that she didn't slip from Whitefoot's back. And all about her there was the gentle click, click, click, click of moving feet, and now and then the soft intake of breath and gentle sniff of grazing deer.

<h1 style="text-align:center">VI</h1>

THE AWAKENING OF TUKTU

UNAFRAID, TUKTU RODE IN THE midst of the great herd. How long it was before she had a chance to slip from Whitefoot's back, she had no idea. But presently from sundry sounds, dull but unmistakable, which reached her through the fog, she knew that the deer were bedding down. They were lying down to chew the cud, as you have so often seen cattle do. Whitefoot stopped. Tuktu slipped from his back. A moment later Whitefoot lay down. Tuktu snuggled up against his back. Despite the dampness of the fog, she was conscious of a pleasant warmth. In a few minutes she was asleep.

Tuktu was awakened by the sound of a bell. She knew it was a bell, because she had once heard a bell on a ship which had come in close to the shore when they were camped there. But this bell was sweeter far than had been that bell on the ship, though that had seemed the most wonderful sound that she and Aklak had ever heard. Slowly she opened her eyes. Abruptly she sat upright and rubbed both eyes with her knuckles. Her first thought was that she was still in the fog. But when she looked up, she saw there was neither fog nor cloud. It was only when she looked below that she saw a fog, and this fog was not like any fog she ever had known. It was a mist of many colors, that shimmered and blended and parted and flashed, as she had so often seen the northern lights, or Aurora, do in the winter. And somewhere, hidden by that wondrous colored mist, was that silver bell. Do you wonder that Tuktu rubbed her eyes?

She was on the slope of a great hill. All about her, contentedly chewing their cuds, were the deer people. As far as she could see in either direction, and across on the sides of the opposite hill, the deer lay. She knew that not only was Kutok's herd here, but also many other herds. Never had she seen such rich pasture. Never had she seen such flowers. And there were great masses of reindeer moss, lichens, showing the season's growth. No wonder the deer people sought the hillsides of this wondrous Valley. She caught her breath. It had come to her where she was! She knew that she was with the herd on one of the slopes of the Valley of the Good Spirit. It was just as she had heard it described around the winter firepots, only far more beautiful.

Tuktu rubbed her eyes and rubbed her eyes. Perhaps this was only a dream. She put out her hand. There was Whitefoot contentedly chewing his cud, and Whitefoot was no dream. He was real, for even as she touched him, he bent his head and gently scratched one of his antlers with the point of a hind hoof.

Again she heard the soft, clear, silvery notes of that hidden bell. Then clearly, though faintly, she heard many other sounds. There was the blowing of trumpets, the beating of drums, fairy music coming from the heart of that wonderful mist below her, and the mist itself—never had she seen anything so beautiful! All the colors of the rainbow, all the wondrous colors of the sunset, all the shooting, flashing fires of the Aurora, seemed mingled there.

Tuktu knew that she ought to be afraid. Had not her father said that only from a distance had any man looked into that wondrous valley? Had she not seen fear in his eyes at the mere mention of the Valley of the Good Spirit?—he, who was not afraid to meet Nanuk, the polar bear, single-handed. Had she not heard the herders speak in whispers when they told of the Valley of the Good Spirit? Of a certainty, she should be afraid. But somehow she wasn't. She knew she ought to be, for she knew that she was where not even the boldest man in all the great Northland would dare to put his foot. Yet she was not afraid.

"It must be that the Good Spirit means no harm to little children," thought Tuktu. "It must be that the Good Spirit who loves the deer folk loves also little children, or he would not have allowed Whitefoot to bring me here. I wonder what is going on below that wonderful mist. I wonder!

Oh, how I wonder. But if it were meant that I should know, or that anyone should know, that mist would not be there. I guess it is all right to wonder, but it would be all wrong to try to find out. The deer people are satisfied to stay on these hills, so I will be satisfied. But there must be something very wonderful and very beautiful down there. I wish Aklak were here. He will not believe me when I tell him that I have looked into the Valley of the Good Spirit. My father will not believe me. No one will believe me. Only the deer folk will know. I, Tuktu, am looking down in the Valley of the Good Spirit and no harm has come to me. I think it must be because the Spirit of Love is here. The deer are rising. I wonder what that means. I must hold fast to Whitefoot, for he must take me home."

Whitefoot already had scrambled to his feet. Once more Tuktu climbed on his back. Then Whitefoot began to move toward the upper end of the Valley and Tuktu saw that all the other deer on both sides were moving in the same direction.

VII

THE GREAT MILL

NEVER HAD TUKTU SEEN so many deer together. Behind her, on both sides, in front of her, all along that hillside, the deer were moving forward. On the farther hillside countless numbers also were moving toward the head of the valley. They were moving slowly, but steadily, as with a purpose. As they drew near the upper end of the valley, Tuktu saw that there was a level plain surrounded by the hills. Out into the middle of this plain moved the great herd of deer. Then it was that Tuktu discovered that young deer and the mothers with the fawns were gradually being pushed to the center. She knew what it meant. She knew that presently that great herd would be milling on that plain.

Many times had Tuktu watched the deer mill. She had seen them mill in the great corrals into which they were driven for the yearly counting and earmarking. She had seen them mill when they were grazing. But never had she seen such a mill as this one. Presently, Whitefoot began to trot. He had joined the ring of deer circling the outer edge of the great herd. There was a constant shifting and Tuktu saw that gradually the biggest and finest of the bucks were working to the outer edge of the herd. From Whitefoot's back she looked over what was like a forest of dead tree branches, all clashing and tossing as if in a wind. They were the newly-grown antlers of the deer not yet wholly out of the velvet, strips of the brown skin fluttering from them like pennants. Only the fawns were without antlers, for the does among the reindeer have antlers just as do the bucks. It is only in the caribou tribe that this happens in the deer family.

Faster and faster trotted that outside ring. More and more quiet became the great mass within the ring. Presently, all were still and only the outer deer were moving. Whitefoot was a splendid animal. That is why he had been chosen for a pack-deer. So he continued to trot in the outer circle. Click, click, click, click, click, sounded the feet of the trotting deer. There is no sound like it in all the animal world. It comes from within the foot as the deer steps, sometimes it is when the weight is put on the foot and sometimes when it is lifted from the foot. It is not made by the snapping together of the two parts of the hoof, as long was supposed, even by the herders themselves. The sound comes from within the foot, and just its purpose no one knows. Click, click, click, click, click—never had Tuktu seen the deer trot in a mill as they were now trotting. It seemed as if each was trying to show his best pace and each was trying to look his best. They had had plenty of food and their new coats for the coming winter had grown. All the old hair had fallen, giving way to the new hair.

Suddenly the deer stopped. They stopped and stood motionless. A moment later they started trotting again. Tuktu had been on the far side at the upper end of the plain, farthest from the curtain of beautiful mist. Now, when she came around, she saw that standing just outside the edge of that many-colored curtain was a magnificent reindeer. He stood motionless, his head held proudly to show to best advantage his widespreading antlers with many points.

Once more the herd began to mill. Presently, it stopped as abruptly as before. This time, when Whitefoot brought Tuktu around where she could see, there were two deer standing motionless, one behind the other, at the edge of the beautiful mist.

So it went on, until seven deer were standing there. Tuktu knew what it meant. She knew that she was looking at the chosen deer of the Good Spirit. She knew that one more was to be chosen. So far, she had not seen the choosing. Each time she had been on the far side of the herd when it had so abruptly stopped.

Perhaps you can guess how her heart was beating with excitement, as once more the outer ring of deer took up that fast, clicking trot. Would the eighth and last deer be chosen while she was on the far side and could not see?

Round and round the deer trotted. Once more Tuktu was coming in sight of the seven chosen deer. It seemed to Tuktu as if from that colored mist there shot out a flash of light. The deer stopped. Motionless they stood, as if frozen in their tracks. Tuktu held her breath. She saw that the head of every deer was turned toward that shining curtain of colored mist. A ray of light shot out from it. It touched a splendid deer two places ahead of Whitefoot. At its touch he stepped out from the circle and slowly took his place with the seven standing deer. It was Speedfoot, the finest deer in Kutok's herd.

The sound of a silver whistle was heard and the eight deer began to move forward. Slowly, proudly they walked. The leader disappeared in the wonderful mist. The second followed; and so on until the last one had vanished. Then once more the outer deer of the great herd began to mill. Tuktu saw that no longer were the does and fawns standing motionless within that milling circle. They were all headed in one direction and that was toward a low place in the hills leading out of the valley—a pass out to the great wide prairie. The time had come for the herd to leave the Valley of the Good Spirit.

Would Whitefoot insist on going with them? Or, when they had left the valley, would he take her back to the camp?

He was once more bringing her around to the point nearest the cloud of mist, wherein the eight chosen deer had disappeared. Tuktu looked eagerly to see if by any chance she might get one more glimpse of them. And even as she looked, that ray of light shot out once more, and this time it touched Whitefoot. Whitefoot stepped out from the herd and stood motionless.

VIII

The Good Spirit

MOTIONLESS, FACING THE CURTAIN OF glorious mist, Whitefoot stood. On his back, as motionless, sat Tuktu. Once more the clicking of many feet had begun. The great herd was moving. Tuktu did not turn to look. She was not exactly frightened, but she was filled with a great awe. She felt as if she could not take her eyes from that curtain of mist, even if she would. The clicking back of her grew fainter. Then it ceased altogether. Still Whitefoot stood motionless.

Directly in front of Tuktu the mist began to glow, first faintly pink, then a beautiful rose, and finally a rich, warm red. Tuktu drew a long breath and closed her eyes.

When she opened them again, there stood before her one such as she had never seen before.

He was short and jolly and round and fat, with a fur-trimmed coat and a fur-trimmed hat.

He was dressed all in red. His hair was white and he wore a long, white beard. Never had Tuktu seen such a beard before. Eskimos have beards that are straggly and black. His eyes twinkled, like the twinkling of the stars on a frosty night. Around them were many fine wrinkles. They were laugh wrinkles. He was laughing now.

> He laughed "Ha! Ha!" and he laughed "Ho! Ho!"
> "Hello, little girl," he cried, "Hello!
> What are you doing alone up here?
> Have you come in search of your straying deer?"

Poor Tuktu! She couldn't find her tongue. She knew who this must be. She knew that this must be the Good Spirit—the Good Spirit whom no one had ever seen. She felt that she ought to slip from Whitefoot's back and bow herself at the Good Spirit's feet. But she couldn't move. No, sir, she couldn't move. When at last she could find her tongue, all she could do was to whisper, "Are you the Good Spirit?"

Those eyes looking at her in such a kindly way, twinkled more than ever, and all the little laugh wrinkles around them grew deeper. He began to shake all over. He shook and shook. And he laughed so merrily that presently Tuktu herself began to laugh. She couldn't help it. It was catching. Yes, sir, it was catching.

> "Ho! Ho!" said he, "My dear Tuktu,
> It may be I am that to you.
> I hope I am. It seems to me
> That nothing could much nicer be.

> "But elsewhere all the great world 'round,
> Wherever there are children found,

I'm known as Santa Clause, my dear;
Or else, perchance, of me you hear
As Old Saint Nick, who once a year
With pack and sleigh and wondrous deer
To little folk who have been good,
And done those things that children should,
Brings Christmas Day the books and toys
That always gladden girls and boys.
But when the Christmas season ends
I hasten here to where my friends
The Fairies, Elves, and busy Gnomes
For countless years have made their homes.
Ho! Ho! Ho! You are, my dear,
The first whoever ventured here."

It was such a jolly voice, and those eyes twinkled so, and he shook all over so when he laughed, that Tuktu no longer had the slightest fear. "If you please, Good Santa," said she, "I have never heard of Christmas. What is Christmas?"

Santa's face sobered. No longer was the twinkle in his eyes, nor the laugh in the wrinkles around them. All the lines softened from his face and it became very beautiful. Simply, so that Tuktu could fully understand, he explained that Christmas is the season of loving thought. It is the season when self is forgotten and the desire of each is to make others happy.

It was a wonderful story he told her, a wonderful story of how all through the long years he had carried Christmas joy to the boys and girls of all the great world. He told her how all the year through the Fairies and Elves and Trolls and Gnomes were busy down in this valley, hidden by the wondrous many-colored mist, making the things which he was to take on his yearly journey to make glad the hearts of little children. He explained how it grieved him when sometimes he could leave nothing, because a little girl or a little boy had not been good. He told her how the Spirit of Love was abroad throughout all the Great World in the Christmas season, and how those who do for and give to others are the ones in whom the Christmas spirit lives all the year through, and who thus find the greatest happiness.

"It is not in receiving, my dear," said he,
"But in giving in love you will find to be
That fullness of joy, and that sweet content
For the beautiful Christmas season meant."

"And does no one give to you, kind Santa?" Tuktu asked a little breathlessly.

You should have heard Santa Claus laugh then. Indeed, you should have heard him laugh! You should have seen his eyes twinkle. "Every year I receive the greatest gift in all the Great World," said he.

"And what is that?" whispered Tuktu.

"The love of little children," replied Santa Claus. "Not in all the Great World is there any gift to compare with the love of little children. And it is mine—all mine—every Christmas."

IX

THE CHOSEN DEER

TUKTU STILL SAT ON THE back of Whitefoot. As Santa Claus talked, he came over to Whitefoot and gently stroked his face. Whitefoot stood without motion. It was the more surprising, because Whitefoot had always been rather unruly. He never had been one to willingly acknowledge a master. Only Tuktu had been able to handle him without trouble. Santa looked up straight into the eyes of Tuktu. "Tell me, my dear," said he, "how you came to venture into this valley. Did you not know that only the deer folk come here?"

"Yes, I knew," replied Tuktu in a low voice. "I knew, Good Santa, and I would not have thought of coming myself. It was Whitefoot who brought me here. He brought me here, and I didn't know where he was bringing me."

Then she told how she had been lost in the fog, and how when she had awakened from her nap in the midst of the great herd, she had discovered where she was. She told how she would have left, even then, but could not. And her lips trembled a little as she talked, for she was fearful that the Good Spirit might think that she had done wrong.

"And why do you think that the deer folk come here every year?" inquired Santa Claus.

"That the blessed eight may be chosen," said Tuktu.

"And what, my dear, do you mean by the blessed eight?" Santa Claus inquired.

Then Tuktu told him of the tales she had heard around the winter firepots, and how it had been long known that every year eight deer were chosen from the great herd in the Valley of the Good Spirit; and how the following year these deer always returned to their owners, and were the finest sled-deer in all the North, so that the owner of one of these was considered blessed above his fellows.

Santa Claus sighed. "They ought to be good sled-deer," said he. "I spend enough time in training them. For what purpose, my dear, do you think these deer are chosen each year?"

Tuktu shook her head. "That," said she, "no one knows. All that is known is that each year the eight deer are chosen, and the following year they are returned to bless their owners. That is enough. The Good Spirit has some wise purpose, or the deer would not be taken and returned."

"Do you know," said Santa, "that the reindeer are among the oldest of all the peoples of the earth? It is so. It has been said that man was created to look after the reindeer, and the reindeer were created to look after man. Almost since man was, the reindeer have furnished him with food and clothing, and have carried him or drawn him wherever he wished to go. Have you driven deer to the sled? Have you ever sat behind a running reindeer and felt the rush of the cutting wind? And felt now and then the sting of the snow thrown from his flying feet?"

Tuktu's eyes shone and she clapped her hands softly. "Don't you love it?" she cried.

Santa Claus nodded, and he chuckled. "That is why the eight deer are chosen each year," said he. "When I made my first Christmas journey, it was a reindeer who drew my sled. My pack was small and my journey was short, and a single deer was all I needed. But as the Christmas spirit swept farther and farther throughout the Great World, and more and more children looked for my coming, my pack became larger and I had to travel much faster. So then I used two deer; and then three, four, five, until now eight are needed. Eight of the finest deer to be found in all the herds.

"They must have speed and strength, for they must take me fast and carry me far. They must have beauty, with antlers of many points. They must be stout of heart and full of courage. They must be gentle. So it is that each year I must get a new team, and so each year the reindeer, the finest in all the great Northland, feed for a while in Kringle Valley. Then when the time comes, as it came today, they pass before me at their best, that I may choose those for my next Christmas journey into the Great World. Those you saw vanish in the colored mist are the eight who will take me next Christmas to carry joy to little folk. In all that great herd you saw, there is none other the equal of those chosen. And all the deer folk know it. Just once will they make that wonderful journey, for only for that one time will they be at their very best. At the next Christmas there will be eight others to take their places. But always the eight bear the same names. Would you like to hear them, Tuktu?"

Shyly Tuktu nodded. "If you please," she said.

My, how the eyes of old Santa Claus twinkled! "They are Donder and Blitzen, Dancer and Prancer, Dasher and Vixen, Comet and Cupid" said he. "I couldn't drive deer by any other names. They are magic names. And those deer will become magic deer when they start on their Christmas journey. Now, my dear, Whitefoot will take you straight back to the place from which he brought you. You have seen that which you may never see again—the choosing of the deer. But always you will remember that in the Valley of the Good Spirit, love dwells, and that love may be carried throughout the world, the blessed reindeer are chosen each year."

X

TUKTU'S HAPPY THOUGHT

"DONDER AND BLITZEN, DASHER AND Vixen, Dancer and Prancer, Comet and Cupid," repeated Tuktu to herself, and her eyes were like stars. "Do the children out in the Great World love them?"

You should have seen Santa's eyes twinkle then. And you should have seen all the laugh wrinkles around his eyes. "I suspect they do," said he. "I suspect they do, for they love me and they must love the ones who bring me to them each year. But they have never seen my reindeer, so I really don't know."

And then you should have seen Tuktu's eyes open. "Do you mean," she asked, "that they never, never have seen your deer?"

Santa Claus nodded. "That's what I mean," said he. "You see, the night before Christmas when I make that magic trip, I must go so far and I must go so fast that there is no time, not even one wee minute, to waste. And so, no one sees me then. Sometimes little boys and girls hide and watch for me and for my deer. But they never see us. And those little boys and girls do not always find all the things they hoped I would bring them."

A dreamy look had come into Tuktu's eyes, a very faraway look. "Do they have as fine deer out there in the Great World as we have here?" she asked.

The laugh wrinkles wrinkled up more than ever, and Santa Claus laughed right out. "They have no deer at all, Little One," said he. "That is, they have no reindeer. Most of them would not know a reindeer if they saw one."

"No reindeer!" cried Tuktu, and such a look of astonishment as spread over her face. "How can they live without the wonderful deer? Oh, I am so sorry for those children. I wish—" Tuktu paused.

"What do you wish, Child?" Santa Claus asked in his kindly voice. "Tell me what you wish, for you know it is my business to make the wishes of children come true."

Tuktu hesitated. She dropped her eyes shyly. "I wish," she said very softly, "that I could send them some reindeer."

Santa Claus looked at her sharply. He could read her thoughts and there was not one single little thought of self there. She was thinking of the children who had never seen the reindeer and how wonderful it would be if only they could see the blessed eight. When she looked up and saw Santa's kindly eyes studying her, she spoke impulsively.

"Kind Santa Claus," said she, speaking hurriedly, so hurriedly that the words tripped over each other, "couldn't you go down early some year with your blessed deer so that the children of the Great World might see them? I know they would love them, just as I do."

Santa Claus sighed. "I am afraid," said he, "there isn't time. You know it takes time to train deer, and there are no deer in all the Great Northland so well trained as those which take me out into the Great World every Christmas. You saw the eight chosen today. It will take me most of my time from now until Christmas to get them properly trained for that magic journey. If the deer were better trained when I got them, I might be able to do it. You know I do not even have to have reins, they are so perfectly trained. That is why when I am through with them, they are the finest sled-deer in all the world. They are no longer magic deer, but they are wonderful sled-deer. So you think the children of the Great World would like to see the deer? Perhaps they would! Perhaps they would! I shall have to think it over, my dear. I certainly shall have to think it over."

"Oh, if you only would!" cried Tuktu, her dark eyes shining with excitement "I-I-I wish I could help. I am so sorry for children who have never seen the beautiful deer."

Down somewhere in the midst of the wonderful mist a silver bell rang. It was so clear, so sweet, that Tuktu turned her head to listen. When she looked back—Santa Claus had disappeared. The bell rang again and from out the curtain of mist came Santa's voice once more.

"Goodbye, little girl," said he. "The great herd moves, and you must leave the valley. But remember this, my dear, that whenever you think of others, others will think of you. And to those who love is love given in return. That is why Christmas is. Remember that, my dear, and always your Christmas will be merry. Better than that, it will be happy."

Abruptly, Whitefoot turned and began to move away.

XI

TUKTU TELLS HER STORY

WITH HIS LONG, SWINGING TROT, Whitefoot rapidly made his way out of the Valley of the Good Spirit. Once only did Tuktu look back at the cloud of shimmering, many-colored mist. At one point it glowed a rich deep red, and as she looked, this turned to rose and finally to a faint pink and then vanished. Nowhere was the Good Spirit to be seen.

Out of the valley, over the hill, climbed Whitefoot, and Tuktu turned him in the direction of the camp. There presently she fastened him where Aklak had put him to graze. Her father and brother had not returned. As in a dream, she looked back to the hills around the Valley of the Good Spirit. Could it be that she had been there? Was it not all a dream? But if it were a dream, it had been a wonderful dream—the most beautiful of all dreams. She knew that Kutok and Aklak would not believe the story she had to tell. They would say that she had been asleep and the dream spirits had visited her. She looked across to the distant hills above the valley, and with a suddenness that startled her, she realized that not a deer was to be seen. Of course not. Had she not seen them move out of the upper end of the valley? There was the proof.

With the realization of this, all thought of anything else was driven from the mind of Tuktu—even the wonderful experience she had been through. The great herd was moving and there were no herders! She must get word back to the herders on the coast. She would take the other pack deer, for Whitefoot must be tired. Perhaps she would meet her father and brother on the way. She had just prepared to start when in the distance she saw Kutok and Aklak approaching. When they reached her, they were in high spirits. They had had good hunting and they brought with them plenty to eat.

"They have moved!" cried Tuktu. "The deer have left the Valley of the Good Spirit." Kutok threw down his load and hurried to the rise of ground from which he had been accustomed to watch the deer on the distant hills. Long he looked, searching every bit of ground within range of his eyes. Not a deer was to be seen.

"It is so, Little Tuktu," said he on his return. "The herd has started for the winter grazing grounds. It is time that we also should move. Aklak shall go back to carry word to the herders, while you and I will follow the deer. They will move slowly, so there is no hurry. But it is well that we should catch up with them soon, lest the wolves attack, finding them unguarded."

So Aklak started back to the summer camp to send up the herders and to help break the camp and move toward the winter home. Tuktu and her father, with a small skin iglu or tent wherein to sleep, and food enough for their immediate needs, started at once to catch up with the great herd. Through years of experience, Kutok knew in what direction the deer would travel and the shortest way to reach them.

They traveled too fast for much talking. Tuktu longed to tell her father what she had seen in the Valley of the Good Spirit, but somehow she couldn't. "He will laugh at me," she thought. "He will not believe, and he will laugh at me; and I do not want to be laughed at." So she said nothing. But all the time there was a song in her heart.

It was not until Aklak had rejoined them that she told of her adventure in the Valley of the Good Spirit. At first Aklak laughed, as she had known he would. "It was a dream, Tuktu," he cried. "It was a dream. You must have slept through that fog while Father and I were hunting, and the dream spirits took you with them. No one ever has seen the Good Spirit, and no one ever will."

But Tuktu stubbornly insisted that it was not a dream, until at last even Aklak began to believe that it might be so. You would have laughed to hear him ply her with questions, all the time pretending that he didn't believe a word of it. But Tuktu caught him looking at her with a respect in his black eyes which was new in her experience. And she noticed, too, that he no longer teased her, and that now he was never selfish. The biggest share of anything was always hers. Never had he been so gentle and thoughtful. Yet never once could she get him to say that he believed her story of the Valley of the Good Spirit.

Now there was one thing that Tuktu did not tell Aklak. It was that the last deer chosen was from their father's own herd. Never had Kutok had a deer chosen by the Good Spirit from his herd until now. Tuktu had known that it was her father's deer, because she had been near enough to see the earmark. Besides, there was no other deer in the herd to compare with it. Sometimes when Aklak insisted that it was all a dream, she would be almost persuaded that he was right. Then she would remember that it was her father's finest deer Speedfoot, which had been chosen.

"If," she would say to herself, "we cannot find Speedfoot in the round up, I shall know for a certainty that I did not dream. It will be the proof."

Thereafter she spent many hours wandering in and out through the great herd looking for this particular deer and rejoicing that she could not find it.

XII

THE DEER PEOPLE

WINTER HAD COME. THE DEER were on their winter feeding grounds. Could you have been there, you would, until you had watched them awhile, have wondered where they could find anything to eat. As far as could be seen, and far, far beyond that, there was nothing but snow.

But the deer people minded this not at all. They knew that the snow was but a blanket to protect and keep in splendid condition the food they loved best, the reindeer moss as it is called, which carpeted the ground, the lichens which nature had provided specially for the reindeer and caribou.

Tuktu liked to go out and watch them paw down through the snow. "See, Aklak," she cried, "they know just where they will find the best food. Do you suppose they never make mistakes?"

"The deer are wise with a wisdom not given us," replied Aklak. "Perhaps they make mistakes sometimes, but it is not often. I heard such a queer thing the other day. It makes me laugh every time I think of it."

"Tell me, for I want to laugh too," cried Tuktu. "What was it, Aklak?"

Aklak chuckled. "You remember the visitors that came in great ships last summer," said he. Tuktu nodded. "Well, one of them who never had seen reindeer before, asked if the deer used their horns to shovel away the snow in winter. He said that he had been told this, and that many people believed it to be so. It is a lucky thing it isn't so, or those big, old bucks would go hungry now that they have dropped their horns. But just look at the way they are pawing up that moss over there. I guess it is a good thing they haven't their horns, or they would be so greedy and selfish that they would get all the best of the food. See, Tuktu! See that young spikehorn over there driving away the old buck from that moss he has uncovered!"

Sure enough, a youngster with only two sharp spikes for horns was butting a big old buck who had just pawed away the snow from a bed of reindeer moss. Those spikes were sharp and they made the old buck grunt. Having no horns himself, he could not fight back except by striking with his forefeet, and these the youngster took care to avoid. So finally the old fellow gave up and went to look for a new supply of food while the youngster ate undisturbed.

"I have wondered a great many times," said Tuktu, "why it is that the old bucks drop their wonderful antlers so long before the mother deer and the young spikehorns do. But I guess I know now. It is because they are the strongest, and so they are made to look after the weaker ones, whether they want to or not."

Aklak nodded. "That's it I guess," said he. "By and by those little spikes will drop. Then the only ones to have horns will be the mothers. Theirs will not drop until after the fawns are born. Do you know why the reindeer always face the wind when they are feeding?"

"So that the wind may bring them the scent of any enemies that may be ahead of them," replied Tuktu promptly.

Aklak nodded. "That is one reason, but it isn't the only reason," said he. "The wind keeps their eyes clear of drifting snow. So they always face the wind, no matter how bitter it may be. They are a wise people, the deer people. They know how to take care of themselves. They cannot see as well as some other animals, but they can smell and hear better than most. Their wild cousins, the caribou, are the same way. When we are hunting them we have to take the greatest care that they neither hear nor smell us."

The children were standing on the outer edge of the herd. As always, Tuktu was watching for a glimpse of Speedfoot, the splendid deer she felt sure the Good Spirit had chosen. Now, for the first time she mentioned it to Aklak. He knew the deer she meant. He had hoped that some day he might have it for his own. So now when Tuktu told him that she was sure it had been chosen by the Good Spirit, and that she had been unable to find it anywhere in the herd, he straightway began keeping watch himself.

Together they passed back and forth through the grazing herd. They are a gentle people, these reindeer folk. The children could quite safely go about among them as freely as they pleased. There was nothing to fear.

Long they searched, but in the end Aklak had to admit that Speedfoot was missing. "It may be that Amarok, the wolf, has gotten him," said he. "Or it may be that he has strayed into one of the other herds. We cannot know until the deer are driven into the corrals and counted."

Tuktu merely smiled. "I know," said she. "Amarok has never set tooth in him, and he has not strayed to another herd. He is one of the chosen of the Good Spirit. You shall see, Aklak, that I am right when the count comes."

"But not even the count will tell us if Amarok has killed him," said he.

There was a faraway look in Tuktu's eyes and a half-smile hovering around her lips. "You will find him next summer when we move over near the Valley of the Good Spirit," said she. "Then will you know that I speak truly. He is of the chosen eight, the blessed deer of the Good Spirit."

XIII

THE WILFUL YOUNG DEER

OF ALL THE YOUNG DEER in the great herd,—and there were many,— Little Spot was the most wilful. He was called Little Spot because he was marked exactly like his mother, who was known as Big Spot. Each had a white spot between the eyes. Now, Big Spot was one of the wisest leaders among all the reindeer people. She was wise in the ways of the wolf and the bear, and she was wise in the ways of men. Under her leadership the herd thrived and increased and was seldom troubled.

But with all her wisdom, Big Spot was a poor mother. You see, she was just like a great many other mothers—she spoiled her children. So Little Spot, who was so like his mother, had never been taught to mind.

Almost from the day of his birth, which had been in the spring before the snow had melted, he had been headstrong and wilful. He had been a handsome baby, as reindeer babies go, and his mother had been very proud of him. Perhaps that is why she spoiled him. Anyway, he went where he pleased and did what he pleased and was forever in trouble of some sort. When he got his first horns, two sharp spikes, he made such a nuisance of himself that he soon became known as the worst young deer in the whole herd. Other young deer would have nothing to do with him, because he was so overbearing. He was a little bigger and a little stronger than any others of his own age, and this, together with the fact that he had been allowed to have his own way, had quite spoiled him.

"My son," said his mother, when she found him with a small band of caribou which he had run away to join, "follow me to the top of yonder hill. I want to talk to you."

"I don't want to be talked to," said Little Spot, with an angry toss of his head. "I know what you want. You want me to go back with the herd. I'm not going. I'm going to stay with my wild cousins, the caribou. I don't want to go back to the herd. I won't go back to the herd." He stamped his feet in the naughtiest way.

"Very well," said his mother. "You may stay with your cousins, the caribou. But remember that if you need me, you will find me on the top of that hill over there."

Little Spot tossed his head. He sniffed. You see, he didn't like it at all that his mother should think that he had any need of her. Had he not horns already? He felt quite equal to taking care of himself. So he tossed his head and sniffed, then went over to join some of the young caribou about his own age.

His mother said nothing more, but slowly walked away in the direction of the hill. When she reached the top, she stood motionless for a long time. Looking up, Little Spot could see her against the sky and, he, being a foolish young deer, became very angry. He felt that she was keeping watch over him. So he pretended not to see her, and, when presently the small band of caribou started to move away briskly, he trotted along with them. They were glad to have him; at least they made no objections. The farther he got from that hill where his mother still stood, the bigger and more important he felt. He was out in the Great World now. He was master of his own movements. There was no one to make him do this or do that. He held his head high and he stepped high. You see, he was trying to look as important as he felt.

Without warning, four great gray wolves swept out from behind some willow trees to cut off the young caribou from the remainder of the band. Such terror as there was then! Each young caribou started in a different direction. It was well for Little Spot that he was swifter of foot than any of the others. At the first glimpse of the dreaded wolves, he had whirled about and started back for that hill where his mother was. They were the first wolves he had ever seen, but he knew what they were. Not once did he look behind to see what was happening to the young caribou. Forgotten was all his pride. He wanted his mother, and he wanted her as he had never wanted her before. Was she not the wisest of all the mothers of the big herd? She would know what to do. She would know how to care for him.

He looked over to the top of that little hill. For a moment it seemed as if his heart stopped beating. He could not see Big Spot anywhere. Had she left him after all? Had she started off on that long swift trot of hers to get back to the herd? The mere thought that he might never see her again gave added speed to Little Spot. Never had he run as he was running now. But it was not good running. It was unwise running, for it was taking his wind and his strength. He was panting hard when he came over the top of the hill. There, in a little hollow just beyond, stood his mother.

"What is it, my son?" said she, as little Spot crowded against her, panting as if he could never get his breath again. "What is it, my son? I thought you wanted to go out into the Great World."

"Wolves!" panted Little Spot, "Wolves! We must run!"

His mother merely walked up to the brow of the hill and looked back. "Truly, my son, they are wolves," said she, and returned to him as if wolves were the most commonplace things in the world.

XIV

WHEN THE WORLD WAS YOUNG

LITTLE SPOT, THE WILFUL YOUNG reindeer, trembled as he crowded up to his mother. He couldn't get close enough to her. He no longer wanted to be out in the Great World by himself. He wondered that his mother did not run. Every moment or two he looked back to see if those wolves were coming up over the hill. But Big Spot seemed in no hurry at all. You see, she was wise with the wisdom of experience. She didn't want Little Spot to get over his fright so soon that he would forget the lesson he had learned. Then, too, she wanted him to get rested a little and get his wind back.

At last, she quieted Little Spot's fears. "Those wolves did not chase you, my son," said she. "They chased the young caribou, and it is very fortunate for you that they did."

"I'm sure I could run faster than those wolves," said Little Spot boastfully.

"Yes, you could," replied his mother. "You could run faster than they could for a while, but you do not know the patience of wolves, my dear. You would have run so hard and so fast that presently you would have tired yourself out so that the wolves would have had no trouble in catching you. Ever since you were a little fawn I have told you about the wolves, and that they are our worst enemies; but I don't think you ever have believed it. Now you have seen them and you know what they are like. The wolves are very smart people. They watch for a deer to stray away. Then they get between the herd and that deer. When this happens, that deer will not live long."

"Have the deer always been afraid of the wolves?" asked Little Spot.

"Ever since the days when the world was young," replied his mother.

"Tell me about the days when the world was young," begged Little Spot.

For a few moments his mother said nothing. Gradually, into her big, dark eyes there crept a faraway look. "Once upon a time," she began at last, "the world was mostly water, like the salt water that you saw in the summer."

"But where did the deer live then?" interrupted Little Spot.

"There were no deer then," said his mother. "There were no deer and there were no wolves and there were none of those two-legged creatures called men. You see, Old Mother Nature had not made them yet, for there was no land for them to live on. But by and by there was land and then for a very long time Old Mother Nature was very, very busy making the different kinds of people to live on the land. Some of these people she made to live where it was summer all the year round."

You should have seen Little Spot's big ears prick up at that. "Is there such a place?" he cried.

His mother nodded. "Yes," said she, "I am told there is a land where it is summer all the time. How do you think you would like that?"

Little Spot thought it over for a moment. "I shouldn't like it," he decided. "Why, if it is summer all the time, there can be no snow! What a queer land it must be without the beautiful snow. I shouldn't like it."

His mother again nodded her head approvingly. "Neither should I, my son," said she. "But it seems that in those days when the world was young, all the people, big and little, wanted to live where it was summer. So after awhile it became difficult for all the people to get food enough. It was then that the hard times began, and some of the big people began to hunt the little people for food.

"Now, it happened that Mr. and Mrs. Caribou, the first of all the caribou, had wandered beyond the land where it was summer all the time. They had come to the land where it was summer for half the year and winter for the other half. When the winter came, they moved back, because you see they were not fitted to make their living when snow covered the ground, and they were not clothed warmly enough to stand the bitter winds. But they always stayed as long as they could before moving south, for they loved the Northland. Then, too, they felt safer there, for there were fewer to hunt them.

"It was on the edge of the Northland that Old Mother Nature found Mr. and Mrs. Caribou looking longingly at the land they must leave because of the coming of the snow and ice. 'How would you like to live in the Northland all of the time?' asked Old Mother Nature.

"Mr. Caribou looked at Mrs. Caribou, and Mrs. Caribou looked at Mr. Caribou, and then both looked at Old Mother Nature. Mr. Caribou spoke rather hesitatingly. 'We could not eat when all the ground is covered with snow,' said he.

"'There is always plenty of food beneath the snow,' replied Old Mother Nature. 'You could dig away the snow with your feet and find plenty.'

"'But we should freeze,' protested Mrs. Caribou, and shivered; for in those days the coats of the caribou were thin.

"'But supposing I gave you warm coats and fitted you to live in the Northland; would you do it?' Old Mother Nature asked.

"Again Mr. Caribou looked at Mrs. Caribou and Mrs. Caribou looked at Mr. Caribou, then both nodded.

"So Mother Nature gave them warm coats. She gave them each a thick mantle of long hair on the neck, so that it hung down and the wind could not get through it. She fashioned their feet so that they were different from the feet of any other of the deer family, and they could walk in snow and on soft ground, where others could not go. Then she sent them into the Northland, and there the caribou have been ever since."

"But what about the reindeer?" cried Little Spot.

"I am coming to that," replied his mother.

XV

THE FIRST REINDEER

M R. AND MRS. CARIBOU WERE the first of all the caribou to make their home in the Far North, and they loved it. Old Mother Nature had told them truly that they would find plenty of food. So they and their children and their children's children took possession of all the great land where the snow lay most of the year. "They found the moss, which you like so well, my son," said his mother. "They found the moss, and they found that it was best in winter. It isn't true moss you know, but is called reindeer moss by everybody. In the summer they lived on grass and other plants, just as we do. So in time there became very many caribou, and they lived in peace, for it was long before others came to live in the Land of Snow.

"But there came a time when these two-legged creatures called men appeared. They were hunters, and they hunted the caribou. They needed the meat for food and the skins for clothing and to make their tents. So the caribou became necessary to men. Then one day the hunters surrounded a band of caribou and captured alive all the fawns and young caribou. These they kept watch over and protected from the wolves and the bears, which had by this time come to live in the Northland. And because there were no wise old deer to protect these young deer, the young deer did not try to run away. They were content to graze near the homes of the hunters. In time, they grew and had fawns of their own, and these grew, and the herd increased. And these, my son, were the first reindeer. They were necessary to man if he would live in the Far North, and they found that man was necessary to them.

"They furnished man with food and clothing. From their antlers he made tools. Man furnished them protection and found the best feeding grounds for them, so that they lived better and more contentedly than their cousins, the wild caribou, for the latter had always by day and night to be on the watch for enemies.

"Then one day a boy fastened a halter to a pet deer and fastened him so that he could not stray away. In time that deer became used to the halter and to being fastened. Then the boy built a sled. It wasn't such a nice sled as the sleds of today, because you know this was the first sled of its kind. Then he fastened the deer to the sled and, with a long line fastened to the halter on each side of the deer's head, so that he might guide him, the boy climbed on the sled. Of course, that deer was frightened and he ran. By and by the sled upset. But the boy still held the reins. That was the first reindeer to be driven by man. The boy's father had seen all that happened. He built a better sled, and he and the boy trained that deer and other deer. Then with these deer they made long journeys. So it was that the reindeer became of still more use to man."

"But I don't want to be harnessed and driven and have to drag a sled," said Little Spot.

"That shows your lack of wisdom, my son," replied his mother. "The deer who best draw the sleds are the deer that are cared for best, and will live longest. Other deer are killed for food and for their skins, but not the deer who draw the sleds. Those are the deer that are thought most of, and it is my hope that you will one day be the finest sled-deer in all the herd. Who knows? Perhaps you may be chosen in the Valley of the Good Spirit to be one of the eight deer who once in the early winter of each year carry the Good Spirit on a wonderful journey out into the Great World, that he may spread Love and Happiness. Do you remember, my son, how on the day we left the Valley of the Good Spirit, all we mother deer and all you youngsters stood while the finest bucks in all the herd milled around us? And how every once in a while they stopped?"

Little Spot bobbed his head. "I remember," said he.

"Each time they stopped," replied his mother, "the Good Spirit chose one of their number to be added to his team for that wonderful journey out into the Great World. They become magic deer just for a little while, at a time that men folk call Christmas. They become magic deer, and all the children of the Great World love them, though they never have seen them. So, my son, be wise in the wisdom of the deer folk. Be not unruly, should it be that you are chosen to draw the sled of a man, for it is only the best sled-deer that are chosen by the Good Spirit and become the Christmas deer for that magic journey into the Great World. Now, we must be getting back to the herd, or those wolves may get upon our trail."

Little Spot trotted beside his mother, Big Spot, over the snow-covered prairie, and as he trotted he thought deeply of all his mother had told him. And as he thought, his eyes were opened, so that by the time they reached the big herd, Little Spot was no longer a wilful young deer. He no longer thought that he knew all there was to know, but he did his very best to try to learn all there was for a wise deer to know. And you know when one tries to learn, it is surprisingly easy.

So, from being the most wilful and unruly of all the young deer, Little Spot became the most obedient and the best-mannered.

XVI

LITTLE SPOT AND TUKTU DREAM

D O YOU EVER HAVE DAYDREAMS? If you do, you know that they are made up partly of wishes, partly of plans and partly of the same sort of stuff that sleep dreams are made of. Tuktu was very busy these winter days. She was very busy indeed, as were all the Eskimo girls and their mothers. What do you think she was doing? You never would guess. She was chewing. Yes, sir, she was chewing. And it wasn't gum that she was chewing, either, although she dearly loved to chew gum when she got the chance. She was chewing skins.

What's that? You think I am fooling? I'm not. Tuktu was chewing skins. Tuktu was making boots for her brother and her father. They were made of skin, and Tuktu was chewing this in order to soften it and make it workable.

But as she chewed, and later as she sewed, making the skin clothing for herself and for her brother and father, she did a great deal of dreaming. Perhaps you can guess what she dreamed of. It was Santa Claus. She didn't call him Santa Claus even to herself. She still called him the Good Spirit. I think myself that is rather a beautiful name for Santa Claus.

And it wasn't of things that she wanted Santa Claus to bring her that Tuktu dreamed. It was of helping Santa Claus. It seemed to her that nothing in all the Great World would be so good, or make her so happy, as to help the Good Spirit spread the message of love and good cheer and happiness to all the little children less fortunate than she. Now, this is going to surprise you. Tuktu actually thought that she lived in the finest part of all the Great World, and she was sorry for little boys and girls who lived where there were no reindeer and where snow and ice were seldom found. She was sorry for boys and girls who had never ridden behind a fast-trotting deer. Yes, Tuktu thought that she lived in the very best part of all the Great

World, and she loved it. And she wished somehow that she could help Santa—the Good Spirit—when he carried happiness and joy to all the Great World. Sometimes when she dreamed, she would forget to chew the skin that she was at work on, and her mother would gently remind her that the boots were needed.

She wondered if she could make a pair of boots for the Good Spirit, and then her face grew warm with shame at her boldness. How could anyone even think of doing anything for the Good Spirit? For could not the Good Spirit have all things he desired? And then she remembered something. She remembered that the Good Spirit had said that those chosen deer ought to be good sled-deer because of the time he spent training them. Supposing she and Aklak could get the deer trained so well beforehand that the Good Spirit would not have to spend time in training them. Perhaps then he could start earlier. Then she sighed, for how could she be sure the Good Spirit would choose the deer she and Aklak trained?

And while Tuktu dreamed her daydreams as she worked, Little Spot, the finest young deer in all the herd, was dreaming daydreams. And the queer part of it is, his dreams were very like the dreams of Tuktu. He dreamed of being a magic deer. He dreamed of being one of that team of magic deer with which the Good Spirit made his wonderful journey out into the Great World each Christmas. And because he remembered what his mother had said, he tried very hard to be what a young deer should be, for he hoped that in time he would be chosen for a sled-deer. Perchance if he were chosen for a sled-deer and became the best sled-deer in all the great herd, he might some day be chosen in the Valley of the Good Spirit. So he did his best to grow strong and handsome, and to be the swiftest-footed, for he had discovered that it was the strongest, handsomest and swiftest deer that were chosen to draw the sleds of the herders.

But there was one big difference in the dreaming of these two young dreamers. Tuktu had no thought of self, whereas Little Spot was thinking chiefly of his own glory. He had no thought of others, but only great ambition for himself. There are many people like Little Spot in this Great World.

Now, I don't want you to think that Tuktu spent all her time chewing and sewing skins. That was work which could be done when the great storms and the bitter cold kept her indoors. She had her play time, as well as her working time, and there were many happy hours spent with Aklak, helping him herd the deer, for she dearly loved the deer people and they loved her. Even the wildest of them and the most unruly would allow Tuktu to approach and even to pet them. Aklak was growing to be a very fine herder. His father, Kutok, said that Aklak would one day be the best herder in all the Northland. But not even Aklak understood the deer as did Tuktu.

XVII

TUKTU AND AKLAK HAVE A SECRET

IT WAS WHILE TUKTU WAS watching Aklak training a young deer to the sled, the great idea came to her. It just happened that the young deer was none other than Little Spot. And because he wanted to be a sled-deer, and because he was very proud over having been chosen, Little Spot was making no trouble at all. He was not yet old enough to be a real sled-deer, and Aklak had started to train him just for fun. He was looking forward to the day when Little Spot should be fully grown. He wanted to see if he would be a better sled-deer for having begun his training early.

"Aklak," cried Tuktu. "I know you don't really believe that I saw the Good Spirit, but you know that the deer visit the Valley of the Good Spirit every year; and you know that every year some are chosen and do not return with the herd; but are found the next year."

Aklak nodded. "Yes," said he, "I know all that."

"Then listen to me, Aklak," said Tuktu. "Those deer are chosen because they are the finest in all the great herd. They are chosen to be the sled-deer of the Good Spirit when he makes his great journey to carry the message of love and happiness to the children of the Great World. Why couldn't we train those deer for the Good Spirit, that he may not have to do it himself?"

Boylike, Aklak laughed. "How," he demanded, "can we train the deer when we do not know which deer the Good Spirit will choose? You say that this year he has chosen one from our own herd, but it is the first time it has happened even if it be true. The other deer were chosen from other herds. So how can we know what deer the Good Spirit may choose?"

"We cannot know," replied Tuktu. "That is, we cannot know for a certainty. But we can do this, Aklak: we can pick out the finest and the handsomest, the swiftest and the strongest of the deer in our herd, and we can train them—I mean, you can train them, Aklak, and perhaps I can help a little. Then, perhaps, when the herd visits the Valley of the Good Spirit next summer, he will discover that these deer are already trained. I just know that he will *know*. Just think, Aklak, how wonderful it would be to help Santa, the Good Spirit."

Now, Tuktu's thought was all of helping the Good Spirit, but Aklak, though he thought of this, was more selfish in his thoughts, though he said nothing to Tuktu. To himself he thought, "If Tuktu should be right and the Good Spirit should choose the deer I have trained, it would be the first time that all the magic deer have been chosen from one herd. If the owner of one or two chosen by the Good Spirit is blessed, how much greater would the blessing be if the eight deer should be chosen from one herd."

The more Aklak thought over Tuktu's plan, the better it seemed to him. So, a few days later when they were out together, he promised to try it.

"But we must keep the secret," said he. "No one must know what we are doing, for the herders would laugh at us and make fun of us. They will see me training the deer, but they will not suspect that they are being trained for a special purpose. Let us go out now and pick out those to be trained."

Now, Aklak was a splendid judge of deer. He knew all the fine points, for he had been well taught by his father. So it was that often when Tuktu would point out what seemed to her a particularly fine animal, Aklak would shake his head and would point out to her that it was not as fine as it seemed. There would be some little blemish. Now and then he would find a deer that suited him. Sometimes the deer would be wild and difficult to approach. Then Tuktu would help. Sometimes the deer would struggle after it had been roped, and every time that Aklak came near would strike with its forefeet, as only a reindeer can. Then Tuktu would pet it and soothe it, until in a few days it would be gentle and easy to handle.

At first, Aklak would look only among his father's deer. He wanted those eight deer to be from his father's herd. And so he would not look at some of the finest deer of the great herd, which his father did not own, but of which he had charge. That was the selfishness in Aklak. But when Tuktu refused to have anything to do with these deer, because there were finer ones in the great herd, he admitted after a while that she was right. He didn't want to admit it, but he was honest. He knew that Tuktu was right. He knew that the Good Spirit would not choose less than the best.

All that winter Aklak worked with his eight deer. Everyday he drove one or another of them. The other herders began to take notice, and some of them became envious. But he was the son of Kutok, the chief herder, and there was nothing they could do about it. As for Kutok, he became very proud. "Said I not that Aklak would one day become a great herder?" he would demand, as he watched the boy driving a deer as none of the other herders could drive it.

And all that winter Tuktu and Aklak kept their secret.

XVIII

THE ROUND UP

SPRING CAME, AND BEFORE THE snow was gone, the fawns were born. It was a cold, cold world that those baby deer came into, but they did not seem to mind it. Those were busy days for Tuktu and Aklak, for they spent much time looking up the mother deer to see that their babies were properly taken care of. Now and then they would find a fawn that had lost its mother and then would begin a search for the mother. Little by little the snow disappeared and the big herd began to move toward the sea. It was heading toward the summer range.

Tuktu and Aklak looked forward eagerly to the summer visit to the coast—Aklak for the hunting and fishing, and Tuktu for the delight of watching the sea fowl and hunting for their eggs. Then there was the great round up. That was always exciting. Tuktu took no part in it, but Aklak was big enough now to help. The round up would occur soon after the herd reached the coast. Some of the herders had already gone ahead to prepare the great corral. This was simply a huge pen of brush and sticks with wings to it, so that as the grazing herd came on, it got between these wings without knowing it at first, and then kept on going until the whole herd was in the great pen, called the corral. The herders would follow and shut them in.

The families of the herders who had gone ahead were taken with them, so that the camp was made and everything ready before the arrival of the deer. The latter had not been driven, but had been allowed to take their own time, grazing as they went. But they too were eager to get to the shore, and so they had moved forward quite rapidly.

One morning Aklak came hurrying in with word that the great herd was approaching. Everybody went out to see the round up and to help by seeing that none of the deer were allowed to get outside of the wings of the corral. The leaders of the big herd unsuspiciously came up over the brow of a little hill. It was beyond this hill that the great corral had been built, so that the deer would not see it until they were over the hill. At first, the herd was widely spread, but as they came within the wings of the great corral, the fences forced them nearer together, until as they entered the corral they were closely packed. Once inside, they began to mill, which is, as you know, to go around and around. It was a wonderful sight. It would have been still more wonderful had they had their antlers, but these had been shed and the new ones had but just started. On the farther side of the corral was a gateway opening into a very narrow passage, which grew narrower and narrower until it was just wide enough for one deer to pass through. Into this the herders turned the milling animals as fast as they could be handled. As the deer came through this narrow passage, they were counted and the earmarks were noted. Of course, there were the earmarks of several owners in that great herd and each kept a record of the deer bearing his earmark, as they came through this narrow passage called the "chute." The fawns going through with their mothers were roped as they came out of the chute and earmarked, each one being given the earmark of its mother. It was very exciting.

Now, could you have sat on the corral fence and seen that great herd of animals milling within the corral, I am sure you would have held tight to your seat. You would have been quite sure that no one could go down inside without being trampled to death. But the deer people are a gentle people. More than once Tuktu or Aklak, wishing to be on the other side of the corral, walked right through the herd, the deer making way for them as they walked.

Perhaps you can guess how eagerly Tuktu watched to see if Speedfoot, that deer of her father's, which she was sure the Good Spirit had chosen, would appear in the herd. She was sure he wouldn't, but there would be no convincing Aklak until the last deer had passed through the chute. Aklak was so busy helping in the marking of the unmarked deer, that he could not watch all the deer that passed through, but you may be sure he kept as good a watch as he could.

At last, the round up was over. All the fawns had been earmarked. Each owner had counted his deer and knew just how much his herd had increased. As soon as there was a chance, Tuktu whispered in Aklak's ear, "I told you that Speedfoot was not in the herd. Wait now until the herd moves up to the Valley of the Good Spirit, and you will find him there."

Of course Kutok had been watching for that particular deer. It had been the pride of his heart the year before, and its disappearance had worried him. He had thought that somehow it might have been overlooked on the winter grazing grounds, but when the round up was over, he knew that the animal was not in the herd. Then he was torn between fear and hope. His fear was that the animal had strayed from the herd and been killed by wolves. His hope was—I do not have to tell you what his hope was. It was that this summer they would find Speedfoot bearing the earmarks of the Good Spirit. To Kutok and to Aklak it was merely a hope, but to Tuktu it was a certainty. She hadn't the least shadow of doubt, and her heart sang for joy.

XIX

The Christmas Story

THAT WAS A NEVER TO be forgotten summer to Tuktu and Aklak. A ship came in the harbor near which they were camped, and they had a chance to see how the white men lived on the ship and all the wonders that the ship contained. One of the white men spent much time at their camp asking through one of the herders, who could speak his language, all sorts of questions, questions that made Tuktu and Aklak think that he knew very little. But then when they in their turn began asking questions, he told them such wonderful things that they began to think that they knew very little.

One day, as he sat watching Tuktu and her mother, Navaluk, making a coat—with a hood attached, trimmed with a fringe of wolverine fur around the edge—he told them stories, and the story that he told of Christmas was the story that Tuktu liked best of all. She told it to Aklak.

"What do you think, Aklak?" she said. "The children outside of our beautiful Northland have no reindeer. Most of them have never seen a reindeer."

"What drags their sleds then, dogs?" demanded the practical Aklak.

"No," replied Tuktu, "they have other animals called horses. But they cannot be beautiful like our deer, for they have no antlers. But all those children have heard of our reindeer, Aklak, and there is a certain time in the winter called Christmas when in the night after every one is asleep, there comes the children's saint and visits each home. And, Aklak, he comes with reindeer!"

Aklak looked up quickly. "The Good Spirit?" he cried.

Tuktu's eyes were shining as she nodded. "It must be," she said, "for who else would have reindeer? And, listen, Aklak: he is short and round and shakes when he laughs; and he has a white beard and a fur-trimmed coat and a fur-trimmed hat; and his reindeer take him right up on the roofs of the houses; and then he takes a pack on his back and goes right down the chimney; and he leaves gifts for little children while they are asleep. And if any little boy or little girl lies awake and peeps and tries to see him, he doesn't leave any presents for that little girl or that little boy and they never do see him. When he has made his visit, he goes right up the chimney again and jumps in his sleigh and calls to his reindeer and away he goes to the next stopping place. And he makes all those visits in one night. No wonder he wants reindeer. No wonder he wants the very best reindeer."

"But if no one ever sees him, how do they know what he looks like?" demanded practical Aklak.

"Oh," replied Tuktu, "it is only on the night before Christmas that he never is seen. I mean he is never seen coming down the chimney and putting the gifts for the children where they will find them. But he is seen often going about before Christmas, for he has to find out who have been good, that they may receive presents. And the children give him letters and tell him what they want, and if they have been good, he tries to give them what they want. So he leaves the Northland early, some time before Christmas, and goes out into the Great World. Then he returns for the gifts and the night before Christmas makes that wonderful flying trip with the deer. He loves reindeer."

"Of course he loves the reindeer!" Aklak interrupted. "How could he help loving the reindeer? Aren't they the most important animals in all the Great World?"

"That is what I said, but the man said that horses are more important down there. I asked him if they ate the meat of the horses and he said no. And I asked him if they made clothing from the skins of the horses and he said no. He said they were important because they worked for men."

Aklak shrugged his shoulders. "The reindeer work for men also. They carry us where we want to go. We do not have to carry food for them, for they find it for themselves. They furnish us with food and clothing and our tents. I would not for the world live down there where there are no reindeer. Did the man tell you anything else?"

Tuktu's eyes were like stars. "Yes," said she. "He said that all over that land at Christmas time they have beautiful green trees covered with lights at night and many shining things. And sometimes these trees are hung with presents for the boys and girls; and sometimes the Good

Saint appears at one of these trees and with his own hands gives the gifts to the children. But the very day after Christmas he disappears and he is seen no more until the Christmas season comes again; and no one knows where he is. All the children wonder and wonder where he is all through the year, but they have never been able to find out."

"Did you tell the man that we know?" Aklak asked.

Tuktu shook her head. "He wouldn't believe," said she. "But we do know, Aklak, for that children's saint is the Good Spirit who lives in the Valley of the Good Spirit. Oh, Aklak, wouldn't it be too wonderful if he would choose our deer for that marvelous Christmas journey?"

XX

THE GREAT TEMPTATION

Tuktu and Aklak loved the summer by the shore. Yet both were impatient for the coming of the time when the herds would move up to the Valley of the Good Spirit. The eight deer Aklak had so carefully trained had been grazing with the herd all summer. The two children had kept their secret well, but, oh, how eager they were to see if the Good Spirit would choose any of their deer!

At last the big herd moved and as before Kutok took the two children with him to watch that the deer should not leave the valley without knowledge of the herders. When they got there, they found grazing near the camp Speedfoot, the missing deer, which Tuktu had seen chosen in the Valley of the Good Spirit. Looking at the ears, they found Kutok's mark, but also a new mark, the mark of the Good Spirit, for it was unlike any other mark in all that region. This splendid deer and seven others were grazing near the hut, and Kutok and Aklak promptly fastened them, that they might not go back with the herd. For were not these the blessed deer?

But the herd moved on. Looking over toward the hills around the valley, the children could see the grazing deer in the distance, but they were too far away to tell one deer from another.

This year Aklak spent less time hunting than he had the previous year. He could think of nothing but those eight deer. "If the Good Spirit chooses all of them, how wonderful it would be! I do hope he will," said he.

Tuktu hoped so, too, but she didn't say so. She merely reminded Aklak that only one of his father's deer had been chosen the year before.

As the days slipped by, Aklak was less and less certain that his deer would be chosen. Finally, he confessed to Tuktu that if the Good Spirit would just take one, he would be satisfied.

"He will. I know he will," replied Tuktu.

One morning when their father was off hunting, Aklak proposed that they take the two pack-deer and go over to the edge of the Valley of the Good Spirit, where they could look down into it. Tuktu shook her head and there was a startled look in her big eyes. "Oh, no, Aklak," she cried, "we mustn't do that!"

"Why not?" demanded Aklak. "You went down into the valley last year. Why should you be afraid to do it again?"

"But I didn't go of my own will," cried Tuktu. "I was taken there without knowing I was going, and that is very different. I think the Good Spirit knew and meant for me to come."

"Well, anyway," said Aklak, "let's go up on the hills where we can look down on the curtain of beautiful mist. That will do no harm. Besides, I want to see if those deer I trained are all right."

But Tuktu would not be moved. "Do you remember the story the white man told, and that I told you?" she demanded.

Aklak nodded. "What of it?" said he.

"Do you not remember that the children who peek, not only never see the good saint when he visits them at Christmas, but get no gifts?"

Aklak hung his head. "Yes," he admitted, "I remember. But this is different."

"No," said Tuktu, "it is not different. Have we not always been told that the deer people only may visit the Valley of the Good Spirit? If we should anger the Good Spirit, our deer would not be chosen."

"Perhaps they won't be anyway," declared Aklak.

"Perhaps they won't," agreed Tuktu, "but I know the Good Spirit will know that we trained them for him. And even if he does not choose them for his Christmas journey, I think he will be pleased. Aklak, we mustn't do anything so dreadful as even to seem to be spying on the Good Spirit. If he wants us to visit him, I am sure he will let us know in some way."

Aklak looked over toward the specks dotting the distant hillside, the deer feeding above Kringle Valley. He sighed. "Of course you are right, Tuktu," said he, "but, oh dear, I should so like to look down in that valley." His face brightened suddenly. "Perhaps we will have a fog," he exclaimed. "If we have a fog, we will just get on the two pack-deer and perhaps they'll take us in there. I'll ride Whitefoot, because he has been there before."

"We won't do anything of the kind," replied Tuktu decidedly. "That would be just as bad as going right up in there ourselves. Aklak, I feel it in my bones that the Good Spirit is going to choose some of our deer. So, let's forget all about wanting to see into that valley."

XXI

ATTACKED BY WOLVES

SUMMER THIS YEAR WAS SHORTER than usual. As if they knew that the winter would come early and be long and hard, the deer left the Valley of the Good Spirit earlier than ever before, and began the slow journey back toward the winter grazing grounds. At the first movement of the herds, Aklak and Tuktu had been sent back to the main camp to help break camp and move to their winter home. So it was not until the deer were back on the home pastures that they had an opportunity to look for the deer Aklak had so carefully trained.

An unusually bold family of wolves had attacked the herd on the way. There are no more cunning people in all the great world than the wolves. For days they had followed the deer without once being discovered by either the deer or the herders. Perhaps the latter had grown careless. Perhaps they had allowed the deer to scatter too widely. Anyway, the attack came when there were no herders near enough to interfere.

A wary, clever old mother was the leader of those wolves. She knew deer as not even the herders knew them. She knew just how to cut out a small band of animals from the main herd and drive them into the hills to be killed at leisure. She knew how to do it without stampeding the rest of the herd, and she and her well-grown children did it. It wasn't until one of the herders found their tracks in newly-fallen snow that the presence of the wolves was suspected. Then it didn't take long to discover what had happened.

Two of the herders, who were also noted hunters, set out on the trail of the wolves to make sure that the band was not still hanging around. They also hoped that they might find some of the missing deer.

But those deer had been run hard and fast and all the hunters found were the cleanly picked bones of several. The others had been so scattered that it was useless to try to round them up.

There was no way of knowing whose deer the wolves had killed until the winter round up. Then when the count was made, it would be discovered whose deer were missing. But it was a long time to wait for that winter round up, so Tuktu and Aklak spent much time going about in the herd looking for those trained deer. And they were not the only ones who were looking. Kutok, their father, had been very proud of those deer, and as soon as the herd was back on the home pastures, he asked Aklak where they were. Of course Aklak had to tell him that he hadn't seen them.

Now trained sled-deer are valuable animals, and Kutok at once called the other herders to him and told them to watch out for these particular deer. He remembered the attack of the wolves and he feared greatly that the eight sled-deer might have been the victims. This was the same fear that was tugging at the hearts of Aklak and Tuktu. There was no way for them to know whether the Good Spirit had chosen those deer, or whether the wolves had killed them. There could be no way of knowing until the return of the herds to the seashore in the early summer. Meanwhile, Aklak was busy training more deer, and one of these was Little Spot. He was still young for sled work, but he was such a splendid young deer, so big and so strong and so willing, that everybody who saw him said that in time he would make the finest sled-deer in all the Northland.

Of course, Tuktu and Aklak said nothing to their father of their hope that the Good Spirit had chosen those deer. They suspected that should they tell, they would be laughed at. Also, they were afraid their father would not like it that they should have dared to think that they could train deer for the Good Spirit. So, when the round up came and none of the deer were found, but it was discovered that several others of Kutok's deer were also missing, they pretended to think as did all the other folk, that Kutok had been unfortunate and that the wolves had gotten his deer. This was what every one believed and it was repeated so often that Tuktu and Aklak found it difficult at times not to believe that it was true. "Had it not been for those wolves, we should know," Tuktu kept saying over and over. "I hate those wolves! I do so!"

Kutok also hated the wolves. He hated them for the same reason that Tuktu did, and he hated them because he knew that if those deer were not safe in the Valley of the Good Spirit, they most certainly had been eaten by this time and all his hard work had gone for nothing. So it was that the wolves brought worry to the home of Kutok.

XXII

The Christmas Invitation

IT HAD BEEN KNOWN TO the village since the forming of new ice that the ship which they had visited in summer had not left for the faraway country from which it had come, but was now frozen in the ice and would spend the winter in the Far Northland. So there was no surprise when one day there arrived two white men and an Eskimo guide, who had journeyed overland by dog sledge. One of these men was the one who had told Tuktu the story of Christmas. As Kutok's house was the largest and the best house in the village, the visitors were entertained there.

They remained two or three days and when they left to return to their ship, all the village turned out to see them go. They had brought things to trade and in return for deer meat and warm clothing of deerskin had left things which were of equal value to the Eskimos. And they had left the feeling of goodwill, for in all their trading they had taken the greatest care to be fair. When they left they had taken with them a promise that those of the men who could be spared from their duties in watching the deer, together with some of the women and children from the village, would visit the ship at a certain time, which the white men called Christmas. There would be much feasting and merrymaking and strange things to see on the ship.

The white man who had made friends with Tuktu had made Kutok promise that Tuktu should come. And this her father had been the more willing to grant, because he had been given a knife he had long wanted. So it was arranged that unless the weather should be too bad, so there could be no traveling, Ikok, Navaluk, and the two children, and perhaps some others of the village, should pay a Christmas visit to the ship.

Tuktu and Aklak could think of and talk about little else. Aklak saw to it that the sled-deer were in the best possible condition. It would take them at least two days and one sleep. That sleep would be at the herder's hut near Kringle Valley. At least, that is the way that Kutok planned to go. There was a longer way around by way of another village and this would be the way that others from the village would go.

Kutok and Aklak went to work on the sleds. They must be put in the best condition for such a long journey. They would take six, one for each of them and two extra to carry provisions and things for trade. It would not be necessary to have extra drivers, for often one driver handles at least three sleds. He rides on the first one, the deer drawing the second one is attached to the rear of his sled, and to the rear of that sled is attached the third deer. So, it would be a simple matter to look out for the extra sleds on this journey. Kutok was to drive Speedfoot; Tuktu would drive Big Spot; Aklak would drive Little Spot; and Navaluk would drive Whitefoot.

While her father and brother were busy going over the sleds and seeing to it that they were in perfect order, Tuktu and her mother were equally busy. They had promised two pairs of boots and two new suits, for which they had taken the measurements when their visitors were with them, and there would be none too much time to get them ready. As she worked, Tuktu kept thinking of all that she had heard from the white man about Christmas. This would be her first Christmas and she wondered if she would see the wonderful Santa Claus. Then she remembered that he would be on his journey around the great world. Besides, had not she been told that those who peeked never saw him? But, despite this, right down in her heart, she couldn't help hoping that she might get just a glimpse of him. She did want to see if this Santa of the white man was in very truth the Good Spirit whom she had seen in Kringle Valley.

The cold grew stronger. The Northern Lights flashed, and the stars seemed so close that one could almost pick them from the sky. It was a world of white, but the snow was not so deep but that the deer could easily paw down through it and get their food. It was just right for good sledding and as the time for the start approached, Tuktu and Aklak watched anxiously lest a fierce northern blizzard should sweep down and delay their journey.

But the blizzard did not come, and at last they were ready to start. Each wore two suits. The inner one was worn with the fur turned in and the outer one with the fur out. The inner hood was trimmed with wolverine fur, because frost does not cling to this fur. With any other fur, the moisture from the breath would freeze and soon make a ring of ice around the face.

The outer hood was trimmed with wolfskin, the long hair of which would protect the face from the bitter wind. With their bearskin trousers and their double boots, they had nothing to fear from the cold. So with Kutok leading, with a deer and one of the luggage sleds following, Aklak next with the second extra deer and sled behind him,

Navaluk next, and Tuktu at the end, the little procession started for their Christmas outing.

XXIII

The Christmas Vision

I t was late when Kutok and his family reached the camp near the Valley of the Good Spirit. It had been a wonderful journey. The snow had been just right and the reindeer had traveled steadily and fast, for they were in splendid condition. Now they were fastened out, each tied by a long line to a hummock under the snow. There was plenty of food here and the deer at once began to paw down to get it. It is one of the advantages in traveling with reindeer that their food does not have to be carried for them. They will get their own food at the end of the day's trip.

Kutok and Navaluk had no thought for anything but rest after the evening meal. But not so the two children. They could not forget that they were in sight of the hills around the Valley of the Good Spirit and that it might be that over there in that Valley were the eight missing deer. So, when their father and mother were asleep, they slipped out from the hut for a look over toward the wonderful valley, for was it not from that valley that the marvelous Northern Lights flashed up through the sky?

There was no wind. The cold was intense. But Tuktu and Aklak were dressed for it and they minded it not at all. It seemed as if the stars were so close that they could be reached. It was not moonlight, for this was the period when the moon was not visible. But the starlight almost made up for it.

And then as they stood there, looking over toward the Valley of the Good Spirit, a long streamer of light suddenly flashed out, and up, up, up, until it was quite overhead. It quivered, almost died down, then shot up again! Then came another and another and another. The Northern Lights—the Merry Dancers of the Sky—dimmed the stars and made the night almost as light as day. At first, these Northern Lights were simply white; and then they were shot with yellow and red.

All their lives Tuktu and Aklak had been familiar with these fires of the sky, but never had they seen them as they now saw them. They caught their breath and held to each other with a little bit of fear. Those fires were no longer mere flashing white, shimmering, dancing streamers of light. They were yellow and red in many shades, and they appeared, as if in very truth they were fires leaping high up in the sky. And as they had so often heard it said, those dancing, leaping lights were coming out of the Valley of the Good Spirit. Certainly, they were flashing from directly behind the hills that shut away that valley, so of course they must be coming from the valley.

The lights died down. For a few moments there was no light save from the stars. Then from directly over the Valley of the Good Spirit a long streamer of white flickering light crept up and up, and as it crept, it broadened until it was like a broad path across the sky toward the south. There was the tinkle of silver bells. Tuktu touched Aklak. "See, Aklak! See the deer!" she whispered.

But Aklak had already seen them. On that broad shining path a pair of reindeer had appeared. He knew them instantly. They were two of the deer he had trained, and which had disappeared. Out of the shimmering light behind them moved two more. And these he recognized. There could be no doubt. He would have known them among ten thousand deer. They were harnessed two and two, and as they moved forward, another pair appeared, and then another.

Clinging together, breathless, round-eyed, Aklak and Tuktu stared. Eight deer they counted—eight deer harnessed two and two. Would there be more? The curtain of light low above the hilltop seemed to burst in a glory of color such as made what they had seen before seem as nothing. And out of the midst of that glory, drawn by the eight deer, came a sled. On it Tuktu recognized instantly Santa Claus, the Good Spirit, whom she had seen in the Valley.

> *He was short and jolly and round and fat,*
> *With a fur-trimmed coat and a fur-trimmed hat.*
> *He laughed "Ha! Ha!" and he laughed "Ho! Ho!"*
> *"Hello, Little Folk," he cried, "Hello!*
> *The boys and girls of the world this year*
> *Will see for themselves my splendid deer;*
> *Will see and love them and surely know*
> *That the reindeer come, though there be no snow.*
> *For they're magic deer for my magic sleigh,*
> *And we circle the world in a single day.*
> *There is naught so faithful and naught so quick*
> *To carry the message of Old St. Nick.*
> *By training my steeds you have saved for me*

Some weeks of labor; and so you see
It happens I'm able to start this year
In time for the children to see the deer.
And all who see them I tell you true
A Christmas greeting will send to you.

"As you will have given joy to all the little folk of the Great World this year, in like degree will your own Christmas be merry, and will happiness fill your hearts. And now, my dears, I must away."

Santa waved a mittened hand to them, then turned to his deer and cried:

"Now, Dasher! Now, Dancer! Now Prancer and Vixen!
On, Comet! On, Cupid! On, Donder and Blitzen!"

Down a shining path of light, across the sky toward the south, the eight deer dashed, until in a breath they were mere specks. Up from the valley the orange and red lights streamed higher and higher, until all the sky was a blaze of beautiful light. When they died down, only the stars were to be seen, twinkling so close that it seemed as if they might be picked from the sky.

With shining eyes Tuktu and Aklak returned to the hut. "No one will believe us if we tell it," whispered Tuktu. "They'll say we dreamed it. We'll wait, Aklak, until the blessed deer are returned to us by the Good Spirit next summer, and we can show his earmark. Then all will know that we speak truly."

Thus it was that it was made possible for the boys and girls of the Great World to really see Santa Claus and his blessed reindeer. And thus it was that Tuktu and Aklak found happiness and great content, and the real joy of the blessed Christmas Spirit.

A NOTE ABOUT THE BOOK

This collection features the work of a dozen storytellers spanning over a hundred years. Among the most acclaimed are: Washington Irving, who was among the first American writers to earn acclaim in Europe; Alexandre Dumas, one of the most universally read French authors; John Kendrick Bangs, who influenced the creation and recognition of the Bangsian fantasy genre; and Zona Gale who was the first woman to win the Pulitzer Prize for Drama in 1921.

A NOTE FROM THE PUBLISHER

Spanning many genres, from non-fiction essays to literature classics to children's books and lyric poetry, Mint Edition books showcase the master works of our time in a modern new package. The text is freshly typeset, is clean and easy to read, and features a new note about the author in each volume. Many books also include exclusive new introductory material. Every book boasts a striking new cover, which makes it as appropriate for collecting as it is for gift giving. Mint Edition books are only printed when a reader orders them, so natural resources are not wasted. We're proud that our books are never manufactured in excess and exist only in the exact quantity they need to be read and enjoyed. To learn more and view our library, go to minteditionbooks.com

bookfinity & MINT EDITIONS

Enjoy more of your favorite classics with Bookfinity,
a new search and discovery experience for readers.
With Bookfinity, you can discover more vintage
literature for your collection, find your Reader Type,
track books you've read or want to read,
and add reviews to your favorite books.
Visit www.bookfinity.com, and click on
Take the Quiz to get started.

Don't forget to follow us
@bookfinityofficial and @mint_editions

CPSIA information can be obtained
at www.ICGtesting.com
Printed in the USA
JSHW021853270922
31064JS00003B/3

9 781513 201238